UNTIL THERE WAS YOU MY SWEET HEART

UNTIL THERE WAS YOU MY SWEET HEART

Christina Ragozzino

Copyright © 2010 by Christina Ragozzino.

Library of Congress Control Number:	2009912572
ISBN:	Hardcover	978-1-4500-0511-1
	Softcover	978-1-4500-0510-4
	Ebook	978-1-4500-0234-9

All rights reserved. No part of this book may be reproduced or transmitted in any form or by any means, electronic or mechanical, including photocopying, recording, or by any information storage and retrieval system, without permission in writing from the copyright owner.

This book was printed in the United States of America.

To order additional copies of this book, contact:
Xlibris Corporation
1-888-795-4274
www.Xlibris.com
Orders@Xlibris.com
69497

CONTENTS

CHAPTER 1	THE HOUSE ON WEST 58TH.	7
CHAPTER 2	THE WAR ON DISASTERS.	20
CHAPTER 3	THE HONEY PIT.	25
CHAPTER 4	ZANNY AND NANNY THE BABYSITTERS.	35
CHAPTER 5	THE TURTH ABOUT WHAT HAPPENED TO 58TH ST.	39
CHAPTER 6	THE ADVENTURE OF THE TWINS.	47
CHAPTER 7	THE DEVONSHIRE MEWS.	60
CHAPTER 8	THE TWERPS.	68
CHAPTER 9	A BIG GATHERING OF SHADOWS.	76
CHAPTER 10	THE MAN WITH THE LISP AT THE TOWER OF LONDON.	85
CHAPTER 11	THE STRETCH LIMO BIRTHDAY BLAST!	92
CHAPTER 12	A ELECTRICAL STORM TO REMEMBER.	102
CHAPTER 13	THE CRACK IN THE WALL AT THE EAVES.	108
CHAPTER 14	THE FEELING OF A SHADOW PRESENCE	114
CHAPTER 15	THE BOW STREET RUNNERS.	122
CHAPTER 16	THE BIG OLD HOUSE UP ON DEVOSHIRE PLACE.	128
CHAPTER 17	THE STRATFORD FRUSTRATION.	132
CHAPTER 18	THE NIGHT OF THE CHARGED PARTICLES.	134
CHAPTER 19	THE HIDDEN DOOR.	138
CHAPTER 20	THE RETURN OF THE VANISHING TWIN.	141
CHAPTER 21	THE WORLD ACCORDING TO SHADRACH.	151
CHAPTER 22	THE COURT.	163
CHAPTER 23	THE SWAN SOLICITOR.	168
CHAPTER 24	BACK INTO THE HONEY PIT.	173
CHAPTER 25	THE BLUE CARBUNCLES.	176
CHAPTER 26	THE BIG SOLUTION.	181
CHAPTER 27	JUST PLAIN OLD ME!	185
CHAPTER 28	BORN ON THE FOURTH OF JULY	192

CHAPTER 29	SHADRACH RETURNS WITH THE LAST MISSION.	195
CHAPTER 30	MY FIRST VERY OWN APARTMENT.	200
CHAPTER 31	THREE STRUCTURES OF WORLD WAR TWO.	219
CHAPTER 32	JORDAN'S HOMEWORK.	238
CHAPTER 33	BEING EARLY	259
CHAPTER 34	THE SECRET LIFE OF THE UNDERGROUND PATH.	275
CHAPTER 35	WORKING FOR THE MAN KNOWN AS THE REVEREND	294
CHAPTER 36	RICKIE'S IN LOVE WITH THE REVEREND.	313
CHAPTER 37	IT'S A MAN'S WORLD	330
CHAPTER 38	THE PLANE CRASH	349
CHAPTER 39	MAN ON THE RUN.	365
CHAPTER 40	WORST CASE SCENARIO	386
CHAPTER 41	THE INDIAN COLONY.	401
CHAPTER 42	THE PERFECT MIX.	420
CHAPTER 43	LOTS OF THINGS TO DO.	438
CHAPTER 44	THE MORNING AFTER THE BIG NEWS FORM DEBORAH.	454

CHAPTER 1

THE HOUSE ON WEST 58TH.

TINA RAGOZZINO LEANED OUT OF HER BEDROOM WINDOW AND THE THIRD-FLOOR ROOM WAS ROUND LIKE A CASTLE TURRET AND IT ALSO HAD A BIG OLD TREE GROWING IN THE FRONT YARD WITCH IT WAS SHADING HALF OF THE HOUSE. TINA LOOKED OUT THROUGH THE WINDOW AND THE TREE HAD REE'S INKY GREEN LEAVES AT THE PEACEFUL MORNING OF THE DAWN AND SHE HEARD THE CREAK OF THE PORCH SWING PUSH THE WHISPERED WIND AND THAT WHISPER DID IT ECHO DEEP IN YOUR MIND? THEN TINA RAN HER HANDS THOUGH HER LONG HAIR.

SHE HAD BEEN AWAKE SINCE SUNRISE AND IT FELT AS IF A VOICE IN HER DREAM HAD BEEN SPEAKING DIRECTLY INSIDE HER BRAIN BUT IT WASN'T A LOUD VOICE IT WAS JUST A WHISPER BUT SHE COULDN'T REMEMBER THE DREAM AND NOW EVEN THE WHISPER SEEMED TO HAVE VANISHED. ONLY A DIM MEMORY LIKE AN ECHO WAS LEFT SO SHE LISTENED AGAIN BUT THIS TIME SHE LISTENED MORE ATTENTIVELY TO THE WIND PUSHING THE SWING.

ALL THE OTHER HOUSES ON TINA'S BLOCK WERE MAD OF BRICK AND HAD SHARP CORNERS BUT ALL THE OTHER BIG TREE'S ON THE BLOCK WERE TULIP TREES AND MAPLES TREES BUT THE RAGOZZINO'S HOUSE HAD TWO HUGE IDENTICAL TURRETS ONE CUPOLA AND VERY FEW SHARP CORNERS. THE TREE THAT GREW OUTSIDE OF TINA RAGOZZINO'S CURVED WINDOW WAS NOT A TULIP TREE BUT AN ELM TREE ONE OF THE LAST IN THE ENTIRE COUNTY AFTER THE DEADLY ELM EPIDEMIC DECADES BEFORE AND

FINALLY THE RAGOZZINO'S HOUSE WAS SHINGLE NOT BRICK BUT DESPITE THE BIG HUGE DIFFERENCES TINA THOUGHT THAT HER HOME WAS PROBABLY SEEMED AS PEACEFUL AS THE NEXT.

GIVEN YOUR AVERAGE MARTIAN, "AVERAGE MARTIAN!" JR. BURST THROUGH THE CONNECTING DOOR TO HIS TWIN SISTER'S ROOM. "WHAT IS AN AVERAGE MARTIAN TINA?" TINA STARED AT HER BROTHER WITH HIS BLACK HAIR SLASHED ACROSS HIS BROW AT THE SAME STEEP ANGLE AS HER OWN EXCEPT HIS SLASHED RIGHT AND HERS SLASHED LEFT. THIS MORNING HIS GRAY EYES WERE STILL FOGGY WITH SLEEP WHILE HERS WERE CLEAR AND ALERT BECAUSE HAD BEEN UP FOR HALF AN HOUR.

JR. WAS SHORT FOR JOHN RAGOZZINO AND LOT OF PEOPLE CALLED HIM BY HIS INITIALS. A SELECT FEW CALLED HIM JELLY BEAN BECAUSE OF HOW HE WAS SHAPED. THE TWINS HAD BEEN BORN WITHIN FIVE MINUTES OF EACH OTHER DURING THE FIRST HOUR AFTER MIDNIGHT IN MARCH SO THAT'S WHY THEIR PARENTS NAMED THEM TINA & JOHN. "MARTIANS SHOULD NOT BE YOUR CONCERN THIS MORNING TINA JR. SAID. "YOU MEAN DAD SHOULD?" SAID TINA. "I'M TIRED OF DAD BEING OUR MAJOR CONCERN IT'S GETTING BORING THEN SHE PAUSED FOR A MINUTE AS HER EYES WORRIED AND THEN SHE SAID IT"S ALSO SCARY."

TINA KNEW WHAT HER BROTHER MEANT IT WAS SCARY. THINGS WEREN'T NORMAL ANYMORE AND AT FIRST IT WAS FUN HAVING DAD AT HOME WHEN WE GOT HOME FROM SCHOOL IN THE AFTERNOON AND GOING TO THE GROCERY STORE AND HELPING US WITH ARE HOMEWORK BUT THEN IT STARTED TO GET FRUSTRATING. THEIR FATHER HAD BEEN OUT OF WORK FOR A WEEK WHEN HE FIRST SAT DOWN AT THE DINING ROOM TABLE WHERE THEY ALWAYS DID THEIR HOMEWORK AND ANNOUNCED HE HAD SOME HOMEWORK OF HIS OWN BUT HE HAD CALLED IT WORLD-WORK. THAT WAS WHEN HE HAD

STARTED CLIPPING THINGS FROM THE NEWSPAPER ABOUT ENVIRONMENTAL PROBLEMS. THERE HAD BEEN A LOT THAT WEEK ABOUT THE OZONE LAYER AND WITHIN TWO DAYS THEIR FATHER KNEW ALL ABOUT IT SO MUCH THAT BOTH TWINS DECIDED TO DO A REPORT ON IT FOR THEIR CURRENT EVENT CLASS IN SCHOOL. THEY HAD A FIGHT ABOUT THAT HOWEVER WHEN THEY REALIZED THEY BOTH COULDN'T DO THE SAME THING SO THEIR FATHER OBLIGINGLY FOUND THEM A SECOND ENVIRONMENT PROBLEM CALLED: "ACID RAIN" AND HE BEGAN CLIPPING ARTICLES LIKE CRAZY FOR THAT ONE.

TINA INSTEAD DECIDED TO DO HER OWN REPORT ON THE LATEST FINDINGS ON TWINS THAT HAD BEEN SEPARATED AT BIRTH BUT YET PAIRS HAD GROWN UP APART YET WOUND UP DRINKING THE SAME BRAND OF BEER, LIKING THE SAME KINDS OF BOOKS AND LIKES WEARING THE SAME KINDS OF STUFF MEANING CLOTHES. SOMETIMES WHEN THEY MARRIED THEY EVEN GAVE THEIR CHILDREN THE SAME NAMES WITHOUT EVER KNOWING IT. TINA HAD ALWAYS BEEN VERY INTERESTED IN THE SCIENCE OF TWINS THE BIOLOGY OF TWINS AND THE PSYCHOLOGY OF TWINS EVEN THE MYTHOLOGY OF TWINS ALSO. TWINOLOGY AS SHE CALLED IT WAS ONE OF HER FAVORITE AREAS OF RESEARCH.

IT WAS GOOD TO HAVE THEIR DAD HELPING THEM OUT WITH THEIR OWN REPORTS AND DOING ALL THE RESEARCH BUT IT WAS UNSETTLING TOO. IT WAS HARD TO EXPLAIN FRIENDS WHEN THEY CAME IN AND SAW HIM AT HOME. THERE HE WOULD BE SITTING AT THE TABLE WITH THEM WHILE THE TWINS WERE DOING THEIR HOMEWORK AND THEIR FATHER WAS CLIPPING AT THE NEWSPAPERS DOING HIS WORLD WORK AS HE CALLS IT. HOW COULD THEY EXPLAIN A FATHER WHO DID WOLD WORK? EVERYBODY ELSE ON THE SAME STREET HAD A FATHER WHO LEFT THE HOUSE TO GO TO WORK AND MOST OF THEM HAD A MOTHER WHO LEFT FOR WORK TOO.

"HE DOESN'T EXACTLY SEEMED WORRIED ENOUGH DOES HE?" JR. "HE DOESN'T SEEM WORRIED AT ALL TINA REPLIED." "MOM SEEMS OK.

"YEA SORT OF TINA SAID." "HE SEEMS SO HAPPY ABOUT BEING OUT OF WORK." "WELL HE'S GOING TO DRIVE US NUTS WITH ALL HIS NEW IDEAS." IF I HEAR HIM USE THE WORD 'EXPLORE' ONE MORE TIME I'M GOING TO BARF UP MY BREAKFAST SO TINA PAUSED AND BIT HER LIP LIGHTLY. "SO WHAT ABOUT THAT LONDON JOB?" SHE ASKED HER FATHER.

"IT'S LIKE TO GOOD TO HOPE FOR." "WHAT DO YOU MEAN HOPE?" IT'S JUST AN OFFER HER FATHER SAID. "IT'S TOO COMPLICATED WITH MOM NOT BEING ABLE TO GO EXCEPT ONCE A MONTH SAID TINA." NO WAY SHE CAN RUN THE FACTORY FROM THREE THOUSAND MILES AWAY.

THEIR MOTHER MARYJO VIOLA WAS THE LARGEST MANUFACTURER OF BALLET TUTUS IN THE UNITED STATES BUT SHE MADE MORE THAN TUTUS. SHE SPECIALIZED IN RECITAL WEAR. THIS MEANT EVERYTHING FROM LEOTARDS AND TUTUS TO SPLASHY SEQUIN NUMBERS WITH ALL THE ACCESSORIES BUT THERE WERE MORE THEN FIVE THOUSAND BALLET SCHOOLS IN NORTH AND SOUTH AMERICA AND MARYJO VIOLA HAD A DEFINITE CORNER ON THE BIG MARKET. A LARGE PERCENTAGE OF THOSE FIVE THOUSAND SCHOOLS BOUGHT ESSENTIALLY CHOREOGRAPHED THESE RECITALS EACH YEAR BUT THROUGH HER CLEVERLY DESIGNED COSTUMES. IF HER SUPPLIERS WERE LONG ON DOTTED SPANDEX AND TULLE MARYJO THOUGHT "GUMDROPS!" AND THAT JUNE ACROSS THE COUNTRY THOUSANDS OF FORTY-YEAR-OLDS WADDLED OUT ON STAGES FROM TRENTON TO TACOMA TO DO THE BIG GUMDROP DANCE IN THEIR DOTTED COSTUMES.

JR. WAS RIGHT IT WAS A BUSINESS THAT COULD NOT SIMPLY BE LEFT THREE THOUSAND MILES BEHIND SOME

SO MARYJO VIOLA COULD FOLLOW HER HUSBAND TO LONDON WHERE HE HAD BEEN OFFERED THE POST OF UNDER SECRETARY TO THE AMBASSADOR TO THE COURT OF ST. JAMES AND EVEN IF SHE WERE ABLE TO GO WHO WOULD TAKE CARE OF THE FOUR VIOLA CHILDREN? TINA AND JR. HAD TWO YOUNGER SISTERS NAMED CHARLY AND MOLLY WHO WERE ALSO IDENTICAL FIVE-YEAR OLD TWIN GIRLS. IN THE TWIN BUSINESS CHARLY AND MOLLY WERE WHAT WAS KNOWN AS A MIRROR-IMAGE IDENTICAL TWINS. THIS MEANT THAT WHILE ONE TWIN WAS LEFT-HANDED THE OTHER WAS RIGHT-HANDED AND THEY ALSO HAD THE SAME SPIKY RED HAIR WHICH STUCK OUT ALL OVER THEIR HEADS MOST OF THE TIME BUT CHARLY'S BRADES SWIRLED CLOCKWISE WHILE MOLLY'S LONG BRADED HAIR WENT COUNTERCLOCKWISE. MOLLY HAD A TINY LITTLE RED STRAWBERRY MARK ON HER RIGHT EARLOBE AND CHARLY HAD THE SAME STRAWBERRY MARK BUT IT WAS ON HER LEFT EARLOBE AND IT WAS AS IF THEY WERE REFLECTIONS OF ONE ANOTHER-MIRROR IMAGES.

MIRROR-IMAGE TWINS HAPPEN ONLY ONCE FOR EVERY THREE HUNDRED FIFTY SETS OF IDENTICAL TWINS BORN. ALTHOUGH THEY WEREN'T MIRROR—IMAGE TWINS TINA AND J.R. WERE ABOUT IDENTICAL AS TWIN BROTHER AND SISTER COULD GET BECAUSE THEY HAD THE SAME HAIR EXCEPT TINA WORE HERS IN A PONYTAIL AND J.R.'S FELL SHAGGY AROUND HIS EARS THEY ALSO HAD THE SAME BRAND OF FRECKLES ACROSS THEIR NOISES AND THE SAME LUMINOUS GRAY EYES FRINGED WITH DARK LASHES AND THEY EVEN HAVE THE SAME DIMPLE THAT FLASHED WHEN THEY SPOKE.

BROTHER AND SISTER TWINS WERE RARELY AS PHYSICALLY INDENTICAL AS TINA AND J.R. AND FOR ONE FAMILY TO HAVE TWO SETS OF TWINS ONE PAIR MIRROR-IMAGE AND THE OTHER SET OF TWINS PAIR ALMOST THE SAME MIRROR-IMAGE WAS AGAINST ALL ODDS. SO IF ONE WERE TO ADD IN THE ELM TREE AND THE

SHINGLED HOUSE THE RAGOZZINO'S WERE A BIG HUGE STATISTICALLY RARE FAMILY. ONE MIGHT SAY A SINGULAR FAMILY IF IT WEREN'T FOR TWO PAIRS OF TWINS BUT WHAT MAD IT UNCOMFORTABLY SINGULAR THIS MORNING WAS THAT THIS WAS THE ONLY HOUSE ON THE BLOCK WHERE THE FATHER WAS OUT OF WORK.

"WELL SAID TINA, "I HOPE LONDON ISN'T TOO MUCH TO WISH FOR." "ME TOO" SAID MOLLY AND THE OTHER TWO TWINS. J.R. WENT BACK TO HIS OWN ROOM IN THE SECOND TURRET AND IT WAS CONNECTED TO TINA'S ROOM BY A SMALL HALLWAY AND ON THE WAY THERE HE LOOKED AT THE SCULPTED BRONZE BUST OF SHERLOCK HOMES THAT OCCUPIED AT A TABLE OPPOSITE OF HIS DOOR AND AS SUNLIGHT STREAMED DOWN THROUGH THE CURVED WINDOW THE HEAD WAS CROSSHATCHED WITH GLINTS AND BIG GLEAMS AND THE DARK EYES TOOK ON A STRANGE INTENSITY THAT NO ONE HAD SEEN BUT J.R. AND HIS BREATH HAD LOCKED IN HIS THROAT. HE STEPPED CLOSER TO THE HEAD AND LOOKED AGAIN. NO THE EYES HAD NOT FLICKERED BUT THE FEATURES SUDDENLY APPEARED MORE EXPRESSIVE AND THE ENTIRE FACE SEEMED TO POSSESS SOMETHING NO ORDINARY ARTIST COULD HAVE SCULPTURED AND J.B.'S MOTHER HAD BOUGHT THE BUST AT A RODESIDE SOUVENIR SHOP FOR TEN DOLLARS. IT WASN'T EVEN REAL BRONZE AND THERE HAD BEEN AT LEAST TWENTY OTHERS IDENTICAL TO THIS ONE. J.R. BACKED AWAY AND THE SHADOWS SEEMED TO GATHER AROUND THE EYES AGAIN AND THE HEAD LOOKED QUITE NORMAL ONCE MORE BUT UNDOUBTEDLY HIS IMAGINATION HAD BEEN WORKING A LITTLE BIT OF OVERTIME BUT STILL HE WAS LEFT WITH A SLIGHTLY UNCOMFORTABLE FEELING.

THOSE GLINTS AND GLEAMS HAD REMEMINDED HIM OF SOMETHING ELSE BUT WHAT WAS IT? SO HE THOUGHT FOR A MOMENT AND THEN HE SAID IF TINA HAD STILL BEEN UPSTAIRS IT MIGHT HAVE DRWNED ON HIM QUICKER BUT

YES OF COURSE THAT'S WHAT IT WAS! IT HAD TO DO WITH THE MIND TELEPATHY HE AND HIS SISTER SHARED.

THE TWINS ALL FOUR OF THEM HAD ALWAYS BEEN ABLE TO COMMUNICATE TELEPATHICALLY AND THE CURRENT WAS STRONGEST ON THE TWO-WAY CIRCUIT WITHIN EACH SET OF TWINS BUT IT WAS BY NO MEANS A CLOSED CIRCUIT AND SOMETIMES ALL FOUR OF THEM COMMUNICATED WITH ONE ANOTHER EVEN THOUGH THERE WAS USUALLY A BIT OF STATIC BUT NOW SOMETHING HAD CHANGED A BIT BECAUSE IT WASN'T AS IF THE QUALITY OF THE TELEPATHY WAS WORSE IN ANY WAY BUT IF ANYTHING IT SEEMED TO BE BETTER IN FACT IT WAS SO MUCH BETTER THAT TINA AND MOLLY HAD SEEMED TO BE PICKING UP OTHER SIGNALS NOT REALLY COMPLETE BUT HALF MESSAGES OR EVEN FRAGMENTS OF MESSAGES BUT RATHER DIM ECHOES BUT FROM WHERE? THE ECHOES IF INDEED THAT'S WHAT THEY WERE BUT WERE ECHOES OF FAMILIAR SOUNDS BUT SHADOWS OF SOMETHING STRANGE AND UNKNOWN.

J.R. KNEW TINA HAD SENSED THESE ECHOES TOO BUT HE COULD JUST TELL BY THE BREAKS IN HER OWN TELEPATHIC THOUGHT BUT THESE BREAKS WERE COMPLETELY IN SYNC WITH HIS OWN WHEN THEY HAPPENED IT WAS AS IF SOMETHING ELSE WAS TRYING TO PUSH INTO MY MIND. ANOTHER CONSCIOUSNESS? NO IT'S MORE LIKE AN ECHO AND THEY WERE BOTH STRAINING TO HEAR IT TOGETHER. YET THEY NEVER SPOKE ABOUT IT EITHER TELEPATHICALLY OR VAGUELY DISTURBING INVASIVE ABOUT IT.

J.R. TRIED NOT TO WORRY ABOUT IT AND WITH DAD ACTING SO WEIRD LATELY HE MORE IMMEDIATE THINGS TO THINK ABOUT AND BESIDES SO LITTLE WAS KNOWN ABOUT TELEPATHY MAYBE THIS WAS PERFECTLY NORMAL BUT THINGS CHANGED J.R. KNEW SOMETHING WAS UP. THIS CHANGE IN THEIR TELEPATHIC COMMUNICATION COULD BE A SIGN OF PUBERTY RIGHT? IF THE BODY

COULD CHANGE WHY COULDN'T THIS SEEMED PERFECTLY REASONABLE.

    HE WENT OVER TO THE MIRROR ABOVE HIS DRESSER AND LEANED CLOSE AND THEN HE SEARCHED HIS UPER LIP. DAM! LAST WEEK HE COULD HAVE SWORN HE SAW A SHADOW THERE. WAS IT JUST DIRT? IT WASN'T A HAIRRY MUSTACHE? HE GRABBED THE MAGNIFYING GLASS HE KEPT ON THE OLD WINDOWCELL AND HELD IT BETWEEN HIS UPPER LIP AND THE MIRROR. HE STUDIED THE SKIN ABOVE HIS LIP MINUTELY. HE COULD ALMOST FEEL THE SCULPTED HEAD OF SHERLOCK HOMES LOOKING AT HIM OVER HIS OWN SHOULDER. IT'S BLANK EYES WERE CLOACKED IN SHADOWS BUT WERE THEY LAUGHING AT HIM?

    NOT A HAIR! OH WELL WHAT DID HE CARE. HE WAS MUCH TO YOUNG TO BE SPROUTING FACIAL HAIR. THERE WERE ONLY A FEW GIRLS HE LIKED TO GO OUT WITH ANYWAY AND YOU DIDN'T HAVE A MUSTACHE TO LIKE A GIRL. OH MAN! THIS WAS A STUPID CONVERSATION HE WAS HAVING WITH HIMSELF. HE WAS GLAD TINA WAS DOWNSTAIRS OUT OF RANGE.

    J.R.'S OWN DEERSTALKER CAP HAD FALLEN OFF THE TOP OF THE SCULPTED HEAD WHERE HE KEPT IT SO AFTER IT FELL OFF HE PICKED IT UP AND TOSSED IT BACK ON THE SCULPTED HEAD. BOTH TINA AND J.R. LOVED SHERLOCK HOMES AND TO THINK THEY WERE SO CLOSE TO MOVING TO LONDON THE SETTING FOR SO MANY OF THE GREAT DETECTIVE'S ADVENTURES BUT THE CITY WHERE THE ARTHOR OF SHERLOCK HOMES TALES SIR ARTHUR CONAN DOYLE HAD LIVED! J.R. GRABBED A BASEBALL CAP FROM HIS BEDPOST AND HEADED OUT OF HIS ROOM AND DOWNSTAIRS TO EAT BREAKFAST. ON THE SECOND FLOOR HE PASSED CHARLY AND MOLLY'S ROOM AND THEY WERE DAWDLING A BLANK LOOK ON THERE FACES. CHARLY AND MOLLY WERE OLYMPIC DAWDLERS AND THEY COULD find more things to do in the course of getting dressed in the morning than most people can found to do in a whole day. Charly was lying on the floor twirling her sock over her face and she was rolling a marble through one of the tunnels of the toilet roll kingdom a city they had built for their toilet roll people. He sighed as he looked in then went down the stairs. What world problem would Dad be trying to solve this morning? Yesterday it had been bacon and ozone layer over lightly with cheerios and bananas and "White Band Disease!" The words rolled ominously over the top edge of the Washington Post newspaper but from behind the newspaper a hand reached for a mug of coffee. The paper lowered a bit and the top of a bald head shone then two intelligent but sober eyes appeared from behind half-spectacles. "Here that J.R.?" "Hear what Dad?" "White Band Disease." Danny Viola paused for a few darmatically minutes. It's not a rock group and it's something you should know about. "What is it?" Did you have to ask? He felt Tina teleaflash the question. "A plague and it's attacking the elkhorn coral of the Caribbean. It has actually struck from Colombia to Venezuela and as far north as Florida Dad said but don't they do anything to promte environmental awareness and education in your school? He looked sharply at J.R. when he said that out loud.

"Well you know they teach a little bit about the normal stuff but not about White Band Disease? What about the fluorcabons?" Dad leaned forward to hear what Tina had to say. "Well what about them?" Tina asked. "Is there any sort of active campaign to be educateing students and their families about the dangers of the aerosol cans to the ozone layer?

"UH NOT THAT I KNOW OF" TINA SAID. "HMMM" DAD SAID AS HE LEANED BACK IN HIS CHAIR AND PICKED UP HIS COFFEE CUP. HIS EYES SEEMED DISTANT AS IF HE WAS CONTEMPLATING SOMETHING FAR AWAY. TINA AND JULY BOTH GOT A FUNNY SINKING FEELING. "OH DEAR!" MARYJO VIOLA WAS WEARING RUNNING SHOES AND RUNNING SHORTS AND SHE WAS JOGGING THROUGH THE KITCHEN WITH A FRIED EGG IN A SMALL SKILLET AND A BAGEL. SHE DIDN'T JOG FOR PLEASURE OR FOR EXERCISE SHE ONLY RAN IN HER KITCHEN AND THAT WAS BECAUSE IN THE MORNING SHE WAS ALWAYS IN A RUSH AND WHEN THE CHILDREN LEFT FOR SCHOOL SHE WOULD SLIP INTO THE LAUNDRY ROOM AND GET DRESSED FOR WORK AND SHE ALSO WORE HER RUNNING SHOES TO WORK TOO BUT SHE ALWAYS KEPT A PAIR OF DRESS-UP SHOES AT HER OFFICE FOR IMPORTANT MEETINGS WHEN SHE HAD TO LOOK TALL, TOUGH AND FASHIONABLE OTHERWISE SHE LOOKED SIMPLY SHORT AND SENSIBLE.

"NOW AS I UNDERSTAND IT MARYJO SAID AS SHE DELIVER THE EGG AND BAGEL TO HER HUSBADN. HE THEN SAID TO HIS WIFE "YOU MY DEAR ARE RESPONSIBLE FOR DINNER TONIGHT RIGHT." SO WHAT TIME DID YOU HONEY FOR? "HONEY!" TINA AND J.R. SAID. "MOM IS AUNT HONEY COMING FOR DINNER?" TINA SAID OUT LOUD. "YES DEAR BUT DON'T WHINE SHE TRIES TO BE NICE TO US SOMETIMES J.R. MUTTERED." "WELL HAVE TO BREAK THE NEWS TO HER ABOUT DAD SAID TINA." "SHE DOSEN'T KNOW ABOUT DAD YET?" WHERE HAS SHE BEEN FOR THE LAST PAST THREE WEEKS? "OUT OF THE COUNTRY ON VACATION" THEIR MOTHER REPLIED.

"MOM WHAT DO YOU MEAN BREAK THE NEWS?" DAD SNAPPED HIS NEWSPAPER SHUT AND FOLDED IT IN TWO QUICK MOVEMENTS. "I WAS FIRED AND MY RESIGNATION WAS NOT ASKED FOR AND THERE IS NOTHING SHAMEFUL ABOUT QUITTING A JOB BECAUSE OF PRINCIPLES. "DO I

HAVE TO REMIND YOU?" THE CHILDREN KNEW EXACTLY WHAT WAS COMING UP NEXT... "SUI VERITAS PRIMO!" DAD SAID THE WORDS SOLEMNLY. IT WAS THE RAGOZZINO'S FAMILY MOTTO AND IT HAD TRANSLATED DOWN THROUGH GENERATIONS ON A COAT OF ARMS. IT HAD BEEN INVENTED IN LATIN BY DANNY RAGOZZINO MOM'S EX-HUSBAND.

"I DON'T MEAN TO SOUND HIGH-MINDED ABOUT THIS DAD COUNTINUED BUT MORE PEOPLE IN THIS TOWN SHOULD THINK ABOUT THEIR PRINCIPLES BECAUSE IF THEY DID WE WOULDN'T NEED SO MANY GRAND JURY INVESTIGATIONS AND SPECIAL CONEGRESSIONAL COMMITTEES ON THE ETHICS AND NOT TO MENTION THOSE WHITE-COLLAR PRISONS WERE THE GOVERNMENT EMPLOYEES CAUGHT DOING DIRTY TRICKS TO GO PLAY GOLF FOR THEIR PRISON TERMS." "MOM SAID OF COURSE DEAR AS SHE RAN HER FINGERS ACROSS HER HEAD. IF THERE HAD BEEN HAIR THERE IT PROBABLY WOULD HAVE LOOKED LIKE A MORE SOOTHING GESTURE BUT THERE WASN'T BECAUSE DAD WAS BALD SHINY BALD ON TOP OF HIS HEAD AND HE DID NOT SEEM SOOTHED BY HIS WIFE'S STROKING ON HIS HEAD.

TINA AND JULY LOOKED NERVOUSLY AT EACH OTHER BUT WOULD THIS LEAD TO AN ARGUMENT? "I REALLY RESENT THIS ATTITUDE ON THE PART OF MY FAMILY. I'M LOOKING AT THIS AS A TIME OF GREAT EXPLORATION GROWTH AND ANY NEW DISCOVERIES."

TINA LOOKED OVER HER CEREAL BOWL STRAIGHT AT HER DAD AND SAID VASCO DA GAMA MEANING HE'S NOT THOUGHT BUT OF COURSE DEER BUT ABOUT DINNER TONIGHT DAD CONTINUED "I SHALL MAKE THE DINNER AND IT SHOULD ALL BE READY BY 6:00 PM." HE SMILED STIFFLY AND ALMOST MECHANICALY CRIED. J.R. CAUGHT A GLIMPSE OF IT OUT OF THE CORNER OF HIS EYE AND LOOKED DEEPER INTO HIS CHEERIOS.

"REMEMBER NO MEAT NOT ONE SINGLE CHOP DAD SAID." TINA'S EYES FLEW OPEN WHEN HER DAD SAID THAT. CHOP OF WHAT? JULY HAD ASKED HER DAD. MY THOUGHTS PRECISELY SHE REPLIED. YOU SAID IT DON'T YOU KNOW? I KNOW I SAID IT I MEAN I GUESS I DID. ARE YOU TRYING TO SAY YOU DON'T KNOW WHAT YOU'RE TALKING ABOUT? NO OF COURSE NOT I SAID IT BUT I JUST DON'T KNOW WHY. "CHOP" WAS SIMPLY NOT A WORD IN TINA'S VOCABULARY AT LEAST NOT IN THE WAY SHE HAD JUST SAID IT BUT HAD SHE ACTUALLY SAID IT? SHE THOUGHT AGAIN OF THAT WHISPER OF THE WIND THAT PUSHED THE FRONT-PORCH SWING AND THOSE DIM ECHOES THAT HAD PRESSED HER FROM SLEEP SO EARLY.

"HOW COULD I FORGET?" DAD SAID. "YOUR SISTER HAS BEEN A VEGETARIAN FOREVER." JULY CONTINUED TO REPEAT THE WORD CHOP IN HER MIND. IT HAD A RING TO IT AND AN ECHO. YES OF COURSE!!!!! OF COURSE WHAT? TINA ASKED. THINK ABOUT THE WAY THE ENGLISH PEOPLE TALK LIKE SHERLOCK HOMES FOR EXAMPLE. THEY NEVER SAY "A SLICE OF ROAST BEEF" OR "A HAMBURGER PATTY." THEY DIDN'T HAVE HAMBURGER PATTIES THEN TINA SAID TO HER DAD BUT YET SHE FELT A SLIVER CRAWL UP HER SPINE. THAT'S NOT THE POINT SAID TINA'S DAD BECAUSE THEY ALWAYS TALK ABOUT CHOPS. THERE'S THAT RESTAURANT THAT MOM AND DAD GO TO CALLED "THE LONDON CHOP HOUSE."

TINA DIDN'T WANT TO HEAR ANYTHING ABOUT IT ANYMORE SO SHE HAD TURNED HER ATTENTION BACK TO WHAT HER MOTHER WAS SAYING. "BEING A VEGETARIAN IS A MATTER OF PRINCIPLE ON MY SISTER'S PART TINA SAID POINTEDLY AND SMILED AT HER DAD."

TINA AND J.R. LOOKED AT EACH OTHER AGAIN BECAUSE THEIR PARENTS WEREN'T YELLING EXACTLY BUT THIS WAS JUST AS BAD AS POKING EACH OTHER WITH LITTLE TOOTHPICK SOWRDS AND BOTH TWINS WERE TOYING

AROUND WITH THEIR SOGGY BOWL OF CHEERIOS WHEN TINA FELT A SMALL TWINGE IN HER STOMACH. SHE FELT CAUGHT IN A CROSSFIRE BETWEEN THE RAZOR-SHARP VOICES OF HER PARENTS BICKERING AND THOSE DIM ECHO VOICES I HEAR IN MY MIND. WHERE WERE THEY COMING FROM? TINA SAID TO HERSELF.

"NO MEAT" DAD SAID OUT LOUD AGAIN. "NO MEAT!" CHARLY HAD SCREAMED OUT LOUD AS SHE CAME RUNNING INTO THE KITCHEN AND MOLLY FOLLOWED YAWNING AND ASKED "IS AUNT HONEY COMING FOR DINNER?" "YOU GUESSED IT" J.R. SAID. "MERCY, MERCY, MERCY!" MOLLY SAID OUT LOUD. THEIR MOTHER HAD BEEN READING THEM "LITTLE HOUSE ON THE PRAIRIE" AND ONE OF MOM'S FAVORITE BOOKS AND EXPRESSIONS.

"WHY DOSEN'T AUNT HONEY LIKE MEAT?" CHARLY ASKED. "BECAUSE SHE THINKS IT MAKES YOU AGGRESSIVE, VIOLENT AND GENERALLY DISGUSTING TINA SAID." "SHE IS DISGUSTING" ALL FOUR TWINS THOUGHT TOGETHER BUT HOW DID CHARLY AND MOLLY KNOW NOT TO SAY IT OUT LOUD? THEIR BROTHER J.R. WONDERED. WHO KNOWS? AND WHO CARES? THEY DIDN'T THAT'S WHAT COUNTS TINA REPLIED IN A SLIENT TELAFLASH. I THINK I'M GETTING INDIGESTION-WHITE BAND DISEASE OR SOMETHING ELSE AUNT HONEY. CHEERIOS! IT'S ALL TO MUCH ON AN EMPTY STOMACH AND DON'T FORGET THE SNOT WHEN WILL CHARLY AND MOLLY LEARN TO WIPE THEIR LITTLE NOSES WITH KLEENEX? SHUT UP AUNT HONEY! BOTH THE LITTLE TWINS TELAFLASHED TO EACH OTHER. CHARLY BEGAN TO RAISED HER RIGHT ARM AS MOLLY RAISED HER LEFT ARM AND THEN AUNT HONEY SAID "NO NOT ON YOUR SLEEVES GIRLS" SO THEN AUNT HONEY RAN OVER TO THEM WITH A BOX OF KLEENEX AND TWO BOWLS OF CHEERIOS.

CHAPTER 2

THE WAR ON DISASTERS.

For the life of him J.R. couldn't remember the exact shapes of the Great Lakes because he just had too much other stuff on his mind and this is one of the qusetions on his geography test.

He hated it when his parents bickered and that scowl his mom had given his dad made him feel like he had eaten something sour and then there was this London thing too. Why did it have to be so darn complicated? Stop with the London thing he said out loud to everyone. It's the grate lakes you have to think about right now but if he couldn't get the shapes right he'd have a heck of a time getting all those states around them. He was in trouble and he knew it. He couldn't afford to have a low grad on this test.

Suddenly there was a glint and a twinkling outline flickered in his mind's eyes. Tina was telaflashing him an image or a shape of some sort. You've got Lake Huron all wrong! It's got a thumb that sticks out on the southwest side-Saginaw Bay and then there is this blob looking thing on the northeast side-Georgian Bay his sister telaflashed. Thanks a million Tina! Now that you've got that straight kindly tells me what is the capital of Minnesota?

Tina! I can't believe it I got it—"The Twin Cities" what a stupid idiot I am. The message telaflashed

DIAGONALLY ACROSS THE ROOM FROM J.R. WHO WAS SITTING WAY IN THE BACK OF THE CLASSROOM TO TINA WHO WAS SITTING IN THE FRONT OF THE CLASSROOM. NO INTERFERENCE FROM CHELSEA COHEN'S NEWLY PERMED HAIR WHICH STUCK OUT A FEW LIGHT YEARS FROM HER HEAD. WHICH ONE STUPID? THAT'S NOT MY PROBLEM HE SAID. ST. PAUL OR MINNEAPOLIS? THIS IS DRIVING ME NUTS AND I CAN'T TAKE IT ANY MORE!!!!!! MENTAL TELEPATH WAS PARTICULARLY USEFUL IN SCHOOL DURING TESTS BUT THE TWINS DIDN'T CONSIDER IT CHEATING. IT WAS JUST A PART OF THE WAY THEIR MINDS WORKED? TINA WAS BETTER AT SEEING WHOLE PICTURES AND LARGE CONGIFURATIONS AND PATTERNS AND J.R. WAS BETTER AT UNDERSTANDING THE SMALL PARTS WITHIN A PATTERN OR A PICTURE. TOGETHER THE TWINS MAKE A GOOD TEAM BUT AS SKILLFUL AS HE WAS WITH SMALL PARTS J.R. STILL WORRIED ABOUT CERTAIN SMALL THINGS LIKE THE SCOWL ON HIS MOTHER'S FACE AND THE POINTED WAY HIS DAD HAD SAID "BUT OF COURSE DEER" WHEN AGREED TO MAKE DINNER FOR AUNT HONEY.

CAN YOU BELIEVE THIS! IT WAS FIFTH PERIOD ALREADY AND WEDNESDAYS FIFTH PERIOD WAS ALWAYS A SCHOOL ASSEMBLY. THE GEOGRAPHY TEST HAD BEEN OVER FOR MORE THEN AN HOUR. TINA AND MOLLY COULD NEVER HAVE ANTICIPATED WHAT WOULD FOLLOW AFTER MR. JOHNSON THE PRINCIPAL MADE HIS ANNOUNCEMENT OVER THE PA SYSTEM. AT THE ASSEMBLY THAT MORNING THERE WOULD BE A GUEST WHO WOULD TALK TO THE STUDENTS ABOUT A VERY SPECIAL AND EXCITING PROJECT. I DON'T BELIEVE #3 ON THIS TESTS J.R. DO YOU SEE WHAT I SEE? MOLLY AND TINA WERE SITTING ROWS APART IN THE AUDITROIUM AND THE QUALITY OF THEIR VERY WIRED TELEPATHY POWERS WAS FAIRLY JAGGED WITH LOTS STATIC BECAUSE OF THEIR HIGH ANXIETY LEVEL AND THE ACUTE EMBARRASSMENT THEY WERE SUFFERING AND FOR DANNY RAGOZZINO WAS WALKING ON THE STAGE THE MR. JOHNSON THE PRINCIPAL.

WHY HADN'T THEIR DAD WARNED THEM? OR HAD HE IN HIS OWN WAY? THE CEASELESS ABOUT THE OZONE LAYER OR THE RISING TEMPERATURES OF THE WORLD AND THE CORAL DISEASE IN THE CARBBEAN HIS QUESTIONS ABOUT THEIR SCHOOLING IN ENVIRONMENTAL ISSUES BUT SHOULD ALL THIS EVIDENCE HAVE TIPPED THEM OFF?

"BOYS AND GIRLS" MR. JOHNSON BEGAN "OUR FEATURED SPEAKER COULD NOT MAKE IT TODAY. SO WE'RE LUCKY THAT ONE OF OUR LOCAL RESIDENTS WAS ABLE TO MAKE SOME LAST MINUTE PLANS TO COME TO TALK TO US ABOUT A VERY IMPORTANT SUBJECT. AS YOU GUYS MIGHT KNOW ONE OF THE GREAT ENVIRONMENTAL HAZARDS ARE AFFLICATING OUR PLANET TODAY IS OUR DAMAGED OZONE LAYER.

"IT'S MY GREAT PRIVILEGE" MR. JOHNSON CONTINUED "TO INTRODUCE TO YOU OUR GUEST SPEAKER FOR TODAY" MR. DANNY RAGOZZINO. "I JUST WANT TO SAY HELLOW CHILDREN MR. RAGOZZINO WAS SAYING" BUT TINA AND J.R. WERE SLUMPED DOWN IN THERE SEATS BECAUSE IT WAS TO EMBARRASSING TO HAVE THERE DAD UP CALLING THREE HUNDRED-FIFTY KIDS WHO KNEW THEM AS "CHILDREN." I MEAN HAS THIS MAN BEEN A KID IN THE LAST THOUSAND YEARS? TINA'S MEASSAGE GOT THROUGH CLEARLY THIS TIME. "I'M ASKING YOU" DAD WENT ON "TO JOIN ME IN WHAT I AM CALLING THE WAR ON FLUORCARBONS." HE WAS HOLDING ALOFT AN AEROSOL CAN OF DEODRANT.

DID HE HAVE TO USE THE DEODRANT CAN? WHY NOT AT LEAST HAIRSPRAY OR LYSOL? TINA HAD NEVER EXPERIENCED SUCH AGONY. "I AM ASKING YOU IN THE NEXT WEEKS TO COLLECT ALL THE CANS YOU CAN FIND AND JOIN ME IN THE MARCH. TWO WEEKS FROM THIS SATURDAY ON JUNE SECOND WE SHALL PROCEED DOWN PENNSYLVANIA AVENUE PAST THE WHITE HOUSE THEN GOES UP TO THE CAPITOL. ONE THE STEPS OF THE CAPITOL WE SHALL DEPOSIT OUR COLLECTION OF AEROSOL CANS

AND REMEMBER CHILDREN OUR SLOGAN: "SOME CANS ARE RETURNABLE BUT OUR PLANET IS NOT!" OH DRAT HE MUST HAVE BEEN UP ALL NIGHT THINKING UP THAT ONE! JEEZ-LOUISE! IS THIS CHILD ABUSE OR WHAT? HOW CAN HE BE DOING THIS TO US? I DON'T KNOW AND I DON'T CARE. WE HAVE TO GET HIM TO TAKE THAT JOB IN LONDON NO MATTER WHAT.

IT LASTED LONGER THAN A SHOT AT THE DOCTOR'S OFFICE AND NO ONE TINA AND MOLLY THEY WERE BRAVE AFTERWARDS EVEN THOUGH THEY DIDN'T CRY BUT THEY DID CONSIDER EXILE AND THE LITTLE SCENARIOS RAN THROUGH THEIR HEADS MOVING IN WITH THEIR FAVORITE BABYSISTER ZANNY DUGGAN. RUNNING AWAY TO LONDON WITHOUT THEIR PARENTS. AT RECESS AT SCHOOL BOTH TINA AND MOLLY RACED TO THE OFFICE PHONE. "THIS IS AN EMERGENCY IRIS. IF MOM IS IN A MEETING GET HER OUT!" TINA NEARLY SHOUTED AT IRIS WETZEL THEIR MOTHER'S SECRETARY AND THIS IS ALSO SO HUMILIATING TINA SAID TO HER TWIN SISTER. "THIS IS WORSE THAN THAT TIME WE HAD TO GO ICE-SKATING WITH AUNT HONEY AND SHE WAS WHIRLING AROUND ON THE ICE IN A DUMB OUTFIT WITH HER BIG FAT BUT HANGING OUT! "HELLO MOM IT'S US." WHAT'S THE BIG HUGE EMERGENCY? IS SOME ONE DEAD? "NO NOBODY'S DEAD!" TINA YELLED INTO THE PHONE FROM BEHIND MOLLY. "DO YOU KNOW WHAT DAD DID TODAY?" TINA QUICKLY EXPLAINED TO MOM. "NO!" TINA I DON'T KNOW WHAT YOUR DAD DID TODAY? TINA WAS SO OUT OF BREATH TALKING SO FAST. "OH DEAR!" I KNEW MR. JOHNSON CALLED THIS MORNING BUT I HAD NO IDEA WHY BUT I DIDN'T THINK IT SOUNDED IMPORTANT. OH DEAR WELL OKAY NOW DON'T YOU WORRY I'M GOING TO SET MY MIND TO THIS BUT DAD JUST NEEDS TO GET INVOLVED IN SOMETHING BUT I UNDERSTAND HE DOESN'T HAVE TO INVOLVE YOU. MOLLY GRABBED THE PHONE AND SAID "I MEAN MOM IT'S NOT THAT TINA AND I ARE FOR FLUOROCARBONS AND AGAINST THE OZONE LAYER BUT I MEAN DOSE DAD HAVE TO BRING HIS WAR,

MARCH OR WHATEVER HE CALLS IT RIGHT INTO OUR OWN LITTLE SCHOOL?" TINA GRABBED THE RECEIVER BACK FROM HER TWIN SISTER AND SAID "MOM I GOT GOOD NEWS FOR YOU MOM WE'RE GOING TO DIE, DIE, FROM TERMINAL EMBARRASSMENT AND IT'S GOING TO GET US BEFORE THE OZONE LAYER DOSE. DAD'S GOT TO TAKE THAT JOB HE LOVES SO MUCH IN LONDON NO MATTER WHAT!"

CHAPTER 3

THE HONEY PIT.

"I DO THINK THAT THIS LONDON OFFER IS A WONDERFUL OPPORTUNITY" BUT DARLING WE'D HARDLY GET TO SEE EACH OTHER SO IT WOULD BE LIKE HAVING A COMPUTER MARRIAGE."

"I KNOW IT WOULD REQUIRE SACRIFICE AND I THINK IT'S BEST THAT THAT THE KIDS GO WITH YOU BECAUSE I'M JUST TOO BUSY AT THE FACTORY THIS TIME OF THE YEAR TO BE ABLE TO TAKE CARE OF THEM HERE IF YOU'LL BE GONE. IT WOULD BE GOOD FOR THEM TOO TO SEE WHAT LIFE IS LIKE IN A NOTHER COUNTRY AND I KNOW THERE'S A WAY WE COULD FIGURE OUT THE CHILD CARE. THERE HAS TO BE SOMEBODY THAT WOULD WATCH THE KIDS WHILE YOU AT WORK."

TINA AND J.R. EXCHANGED A RELIEVED GLANCE AS THEY WENT UP ON TO THEIR FRONT PORCH LANDING. "SO THE KIDS WERE REALLY UP-SET ABOUT ME COMING TO THEIR SCHOOL?" DAD ASKED. "MOM SAID WELL YES A LITTLE BIT." A BIT J.R. CRACKED A SLIGHT SMILE AND SAID "THAT THE BIGEST UNDERSTATEMENT OF THE MILLENIUM!"

COOL IT SHE'S JUST TRYING TO PLAY HER CARDS RIGHT AND THE POINT OF ALL OF THIS IS TO GET TO LONDON. YOU'RE RIGHT SHE SAID AND AT THAT MOMENT BOTH TWINS GLANCED TOWARD J.R.'S BEDROOM AND SAW THAT HE HAD LEFT HIS LIGHT ON AGAIN AND THE ON THE FLOOR WAS A BIG TALL SHADOW OF SHERLOCK HOMES'S SCULPTED HEAD STRETCHED OUT OVER THE CARPETING OF J.R.'S BEDROOM FLOOR. THE DEERSTALKER'S HAT HAD

SEEMED THREE FEET TALL AND THE PIPE CLENCHED BETWEEN SHERLOCK'S TEETH LOOKED AT LEAST ONE FOOT LONG.

IT STARTED TO RAIN OUTSIDE AGAIN AND BIG DROPS SPLASHED AGAINST THE WINDOWPANES BUT THERE WAS SOMETHING BEATING IN TINA'S HEAD SO SHE SQUEEZED HER EYES SHUT TO GET RID OF THE BEATING SOUND OUT OF HER HEAD. YOU'RE HEARING IT AREN'T YOU? J.R. TELEAFLASH BACK TO TINA AND SHE SHUT HER EYES TIGHTER SO SHE WOULDN'T HEAR THE ECHOES. YES, YES, SHE FINALLY ACKNOWLEDGED IT'S LIKE THE RAINDROPS ON THE WINDOWPANES AND THAT'S HOW THE ECHOES BEAT INSIDE YOUR HEAD TINA? YOU CAN HEAR THEM TOO? I CAN'T BELIEVE IT. THEN SUDDENLY A DOOR OPENED IT WAS THE FRONT DOOR DOWNSTAIRS. "HELLO!" A VOICE CALLED OUT "IT'S ME AUNT HONEY AND its ABSOLUTELY SOBBING WET OUTSIDE AND THEN THE RAIN JUST STOPPED INSTANTLY." "HONEY!" YOUR FINALLY HEAR!" AUNT HONEY GLIDED ACROSS THE LIVINGROOM FLOOR TO EMBRACE HER TWO TWIN SISTER. NO SET OF TWINS HAD EVER HAIR AS BRIGHT AS BRASS AND BIG SHINEY EYES MADE BIGGER BY THICK GLOBS OF MASCARA. TINA HAD BLACK HAIR FLICKED WITH GRAY AND BROWN EYES UNADORNED BY MASCARA ALSO BUT SHE WAS THREE INCHES SHORTER AND SEVEN MINUTES YOUNGER THAN HONEY. ALTHOUGH HONEY HAD RETIRED FROM THE ICE CAPADES ALMOST FIVE YEARS BEFORE SHE STILL SEEMED TO HAVE HER SKATES ON BUT SHE ALWAYS APPEARED TO GLIDE AND THERE WAS ALWAYS THAT PHONY LITTLE MEGAWATT SMILE ON HER FACE AND WHATEVER HAD BEEN BEATING ON HER WINDOWPANES OF THEIR BRAINS HAD RECOILED COMPLETELY WITH THE ARRIVAL OF AUNT HONEY.

"CHILDREN!" THEIR MOTHER CALLED UPSTAIRS "YOUR AUNT HONEY IS HERE DOWN IN THE LIVINGROOM." BRACE YOURSELF TINA TELAFLASHED TO HER SISTER "AUNT HONEY IS HERE." MAYBE YOU SHOULD PUT ON YOUR SKATES BECAUSE ONE NEVER KNOWS HOW TO PLAY IT WITH

AUNT HONEY J.R. HAD TELAFLASHED BACK TO HIS TWIN LOOK ALIKE SISTER TINA HE ALSO HAD TELAFLASHED HER THAT CHARLY AND MOLLY WERE ALREADY DOWNSTAIRS AS TINA AND J.R. HIT THE LAST STEP AUNT HONY HAD SPUN AROUND AND SMILED BORADLY. "AREN'T WE GETTING TO BE A BIG GIRL NOW AND SOON WE'LL BE DEVELOPING INTO A YOUNG LADY SAID AUNT HONEY."

THIS WAS BEYOND BELIEF THIS JERK-AUNT-ICE-BUNNY! TINA BEGAN TO HAVE THE MOST VIOLENT THOUGHTS AND J.R. TINA'S BROTHER HAD HID HIS SMILE WHEN HIS SISTER TINA TELAFLASHED THAT TO HIM BUT MOLLY QUICKLY DEFLECTED THE CONVERSATION. "HONEY WE HAVE A LITTLE ANOUNCEMENT TO MAKE" AS HER SISTER BLANCHED VISIBLY UNDER ALL THE MAKE-UP.

"OH NO TINA! YOU CAN'T BE PREGNANT AGAIN BECAUSE ANOTHER SET OF TWINS WOULD KILL YOU AND YOU KNOW THAT. HOW DO YOU LIKE THOSE GUYS? J.R. SAID TELRPATHICALLY. AUNT HONEY THINKS MOM IS PREGNANT WITH ANOTHER SET OF TWINS. WE'RE TWO SETS OF TWINS? HOW IS THAT POSSIBLE? WE'RE INTERCHANGEABLE, INDISTINGUISHABLE AND ALL PARTS INCLUDED, VERY LITTLE ASSEMBLY REQUIRED AND WE'RE KILLERS! MOLLY ALMOST WAILED OUT LOUD BUT MANAGED BY GREAT CONTROL TO HER DISTRESS WITHIN THE TELEAPATHIC CHANNELS.

"NO MORE CIA" FOR DAD TINA SAID AS SHE SMILED BRIGHTLY. DAD HAS LEFT THE CIA" "DAD DID WHAT?" AUNT HONEY WAS STUNNED. "TELL ME WHAT I'M HEARING ISN'T SO!" "IT IS AND WE ARE VERY PLEASED." "HE ACTUALLY LEFT THE CENTRAL-INTELLIGENCE AGENCY?" AUNT HONNY SAID OUT LOUD "THAT'S THE MOST REDICULOUS THING I'VE EVER HEARD." WHY! WHY! WHY IN HEAVEN'S NAME DID YOU LEAVE?"

SO THERE FAT-FACE! CHARLY TELEPAPATHICALLY SAID AS SHE GROWLED WHILE GIVING THE SWEETEST LITTLE

DIMPLED SMILE TO HER AUNT. THIS WAS NOT A LOST ON AUNT HONEY BUT ON HER INSTEAD. SHE REACHED OVER AND GAVE CHARLY'S CHUBBY FRECKLED CHEEK A DISTRANCTED PINCH.

"IS THAT A FACE?" SHE COOED. NO AUNT HONEY IT'S A FOOT ! J.R. HAD SAID. THEN CHARLY GIGGLED OUT LOUD AND TELEAPATHICALLY AT THE SAME TIME WHICH MADE THE AIR BETWEEN THE FOUR CHILDREN SIZZLE.

WOULD YOU ALL SHUT UP! TINA TELAFLSHED A WARNING. I'M TRYING TO CONCENTRATE ON DAD'S RESPONSE TO THIS AND I CAN'T WITH ALL OF YOU'RE CRACKLING. IT'S LIKE BEING IN THE MIDDLE OF AN ELECTRICAL STORM. THEIR FATHER TOOK A DEEP BREATH AND SAID "I QUIT FOR A VERY SIMPLE REASON AUNT HONEYS MY PRINCIPLES."

"YOU'RE PRINCIPLES!" AUNT HONEY SHRIEKED. "WHAT DOES THAT HAVE TO DO WITH ANYTHING? WHAT COULD THE CIA EVER HAVE ASKED YOU TO DOSE THAT HURT YOUR PRINCIPLES? "THEY ASKED HIM TO DO THE UNTHINKABLE" TINA SAID SOFTLY. "MURDER!" AUNT HONEY'S VOICE SEEMED ALMOST BRIGHT WITH EXPERCTATION. "OH FOR HEAVEN SHAKE!" DAD SCOFFED. "WELL WHAT DID THEY ASK YOU TO DO THAT GOT YOU TO GIVE UP A PERFECTLY DECENT JOB?" "THEY ASKED ME TO WHAT TINA SO APTLY DESCRIBED AS THE "UNTHINKABLE" TO SUBVERT MY IDENTITY." TINA AND J.R. COULD TELL THEIR FATHER WAS GETTING STEAMED NOW JUST THE WAY HE HAD BEEN WHEN HE HAD COME HOME FROM THE OFFICE THREE WEEKS BEFORE.

"THEY WANTED HIM TO WEAR A WIG AND USE A VOICE CHANGER" TINA SAID WEARILY. "YOU WOULDN'T DO THAT?" AUNT HONEY WAS AGHAST BY THIS NEWS. "WHAT'S THE BIG DEAL?" DAD SAID. "TO HIDE WHAT YOU IS A BIG DEAL IN MY BOOK AUNT HONEY." TINA SAID. SUI VERITAS

PRIMO IT MEANS "TRUTH TO YOURSELF" AND THAT IS ARE FAMILY MOTTO. I HAVE WORKED AT THE AGENCY FOR AT LEAST TEN YEARS AND I THOUGHT WE HAD UNDERSTOOD THE REQUIREMENTS FOR WORKING THERE. THEY KNOW I AM EXTREMELY UNCOMFORTABLE WITH THE CLOAK-AND DAGGER ASPECTS OF THE AGENCY BUT THEY ORIGINALLY ASKED ME TO DO WHAT I DO BEST BE A MEDIATOR IN THE DEPARTMENT AND A LIAISON WITH THE HOUSE OF CONGRESS AND THAT IS WHAT I HAVE DONE UNTIL NOW."

"WELL I DON'T UNDERSTAND WHAT'S SO TERRIBLE ABOUT ALL THIS. WHY DID THEY WANT YOU TO WEAR A WIG AND USE A VOICE CHANGER?" "YOU KNOW I CAN'T DIVULGE THAT INFORMATION AUNT HONEY." "I THINK WE SHOULD MOVE INTO THE DININGROOM" TINA SAID. "DINNER IS READY ISN'T IT DAD?" "YES IT IS." DAD SAID. LET GO EAT DINNER NOW TINA SAID. TINA AND J.R. HAD JUST BROUGHT IN THE LAST OF THE PLATES AND WERE SITTING DOWN. THEN THE MAIN COURSE WAS SPAGHETTI COVERED WITH A BUTTERY SAUCE AND ALL SORTS OF BRIGHT VEGETABLES. CHARLY'S AND MOLLY'S PLATES LOOKED A LITTLE DIFFERENT THEN THE OTHERS. THEY DIDN'T LIKED FOOD THAT "TOUCHED" SO THEY EACH HAD A MOUNT OF PLAIN SPAGHETTI IN THE MIDDLE AND SEPARTE LITTLE PILES OF VEGETABLES HEAPED AROUND THE EDGES OF THEIR PLATES LIKE COLORFUL SATELLITES.

"IT'S THAT CERISE TUTU WITH THE OSTRICH FEATHERS I TESTSKATED FOR YOU STILL YOUR NUMBER-ONE SELLER?" AUNT HONEY ASKED. "WELL YES WITH CERTAIN SCHOOLS OF COURSE THE ICE SHOWS STILL ORDER IT YEARLY." "IT WAS RATHER INGENIOUS THAT IDEA OF KNITTING IN THE FEATHERS IF I DO SAY SO MYSELF." "WELL AUNT HONEY I'VE ALWAYS SAID IF IT HOLDS UP ON ICE IT WILL HOLD UP ANYPLACE." "AH YES SHE SMILED. SHE ALWAYS TAKING CREDIT FOR MOM'S BUSINESS BECAUSE SHE'S JEALOUS OF MOM AND SHE CAN'T STAND

IT THAT MOM HAS MADE ALL THAT MONEY ON HER OWN AND SHE'S ONLY MADE IT FROM MARRYING RICH GUYS J.R. HAD ANSWERED.

"DELISH! TINA!" EXCLAIMED AUNT HONEY AS SHE TOOK A BITE. WHY CAN'T SHE JUST SAY THE WHOLE WORD? TINA WONDERED. "DON'T PAY ATTENTION TO HER." HOW CAN I IGNORE HER? "I DIDN'T MAKE IT TINA WAS SAYING AND THIS IS ALL DAD'S DOING."

"WHEN DOES DAD HAVE THE TIME?" "WHY DOES SHE THINK MOM HAS MORE TIME THEN DAD WHEN MOM HAS TO WORK ALL DAY AND HAS TO DRIVE ALL THE WAY TO CHEVY CHASE AND DAD ONLY HAS A TEN MINUTE COMMUTE TO HIS OFFICE?"

I TOLD YOU SHE'S JEALOUS OF MOM. ELEMENTARY MY DEAR TINA AS SHERLOCKHOMES WOULD SAY. AT THAT MOMENT THEY BOTH THOUGHT OF THE SHADOW CAST UPSTAIRS AND BARELY HEARD THE SOUND OF AUNT HONEY'S LAUGHTER.

"I FORGOT YOU'RE UNEMPLOYED NOW AND YOU HAVE PLANTY OF TIME TO COOK." AUNT HONEY PICKED UP HER WATER GLASS AND SIGHED HAD WEARILY. "OH DEAR I HOPE THIS ISN'T A MISTAKE ON YOUR PART BECAUSE THAT WAS A WONDERFUL JOB SAID AUNT HONEY." YOU'D BEEN THERE FOREVER AND YOU WERE A SENIOR MAN ALSO. I WAS SO PROUD OF YOU OF HAVING A BROTHER-IN-LAW WORKING IN THIS SACRED BRANCH OF OUR UNITED STATES GOVERNMENT.

SACRED! TINA SLIENTLY EXCLAIMED. SEPARATION OF A CHURCH AND A STATE THAT WAS OUR FIRST CIVICS LESSION. WHERE WAS AUNT HONEY FOR FIFTH-GRADE CIVICS? J.R. WONDERED. DOING DOUBLE AXLE SPINS WITH THE THREE STOOGES. THEY BOTH GIGGLED AT THEIR SLINT TELEAPATHIC JOKES.

SUDDENLY TINA AND J.R. FELT A SILVERY SHIMMER IN THEIR HEADS AND A DIM ECHO ALMOST LIKE A CASCADE OF THIN COINS RAINING DOWN IN A TINKLY PATTER OR WAS IT ALMOST LAUGHTER? YOU HEARD IT TOO? TINA TELAFLASHED TO J.R.

WAS SOMEONE ELSE LAUGHING? I MEAN IT WAS FUNNY BUT NOT THAT FUNNY. WHAT DO YOU MEAN NOT THAT FUNNY? TINA ASKED. SHE KNEW J.R. WAS NOT BEING CRITICAL. I'M NOT SURE HE ANSWERD HONESTLY. I THINK I MEANT THAT IT WAS NOT SO FUNNY THAT HE GROPED FOR SOME KIND OF MEANING.

THAT SOMEBODY OUTSIDE OF THE FAMILY WOULD GET IT LET A LONE HEAR IT TINA SAID AS SHE FINISHED HER THOUGHT BUT YOU HEARD IT IN YOUR HEAD DIDN'T YOU? I'M NOT SURE IT'S LIKE I'M NOT SURE WHETHER I HEARD IT OR FELT IT I JUST KEEP THINKING OF THE RAINDROPS OUTSIDE BEATING INSIDE MY HEAD. "THEY'RE DOING IT AGAINA" AUNT HONEY SNAPPED GLARING AT TINA AND J.R. "DOING WHAT?" DAD ASKED. "THAT MENTAL STUFF OF THEIRS" SHE GROWLED. SOUNDS LIKE A MEAT EATER TO ME! J.R. TELAFLASHED TO HIS SISTER TINA. THEY BOTH STIFLED ANOTHER GIGGLE BY LOADING FORKFULS OF SPAGHETTI INTO THEIR MOUTHS.

"YOU MEAN TELEPATHY?" TINA ASKED MILDLY. "PRECISELY IT'S VERY UNSOCIABLE AND I KNOW THEY DO IT ABOUT ME AND THE LITTLE ONES DO IT TOO."

TINA HATED IT WHEN PEOPLE REFERRED TO HER CHILDREN AS SETS BUT SHE IGNORED IT. "THIS SPAGHETTI SMELLS A GOOD AS IT TASTES AND I JUST LOVE THAT GARLIC BREAD TOO SHE SAID AS SHE BENT OVER HER PLATE AND INHAILED DEEPLY AND TRIED NOT TO THINK THAT AUNT HONEY WAS RIGHT. THE "LITTLE SET" WAS TALKING ABOUT HER AND THEY ALSO LIKED HER THICK ORANGE LIPSTICK TOO. THEY DIDN'T LIKE MUCH ELSE ABOUT HER THOUGH.

I DON'T SMELL JUST THE GARLIC BREAD I SMELL . . . . LIPSTICK! MOLLY SAID AS SHE FINISHED CHARLY'S THOUGHT. LOOK AT THOSE BIG HUGE SMOOCH MARKS AUNT HONEY'S LIPSTICK LEAVES ON THE WATER GLASS BOTH TWINS TELAFLASHED TO EACH OTHER.

"OH DEAR ARE YOU COMING DOWN WITH COLDS?" "NO!" THEY BOTH BLURTED OUT LOUD. "JUST SMELLING THE GARLIC BREAD" CHARLY SAID QUICKLY. WHAT A DIPLOMAT! TINA CHIMED IN A TELAPATHIC WAY.

NEITHER TINA OR J.R. COULD PICK UP WORD FOR WORD TRANSLATION OF THE TELEPATHIC EXCHANGE BETWEEN MOLLY AND CHARLY BUT THEY KNEW IT HAD SOMETHING TO DO WITH ORANGE LICKSTICK AND HOW IT SMELLED. PERSONALLY I PERFER THE GARLIC J.R. TELAFLASHED. THE LIPSTICK IS TOTALLY YUCKY.

IT IS NOT THEY BOTH SILENTLY BLURTED OUT. THE CHANNELS WERE NOW MORE FULLY OPENED BETWEEN THE OLDER TWINS AND THE YOUNGER TWINS EACH WORD WAS COMING IN CLEARLY. IT USUALLY TOOK ONLY A MATTER OF SECONDS FOR ALL TWINS TO BEABLE TO CROSS-COMMUNICATE VERY CLEARLY. THERE WAS JUST A BIT OF TIME LAG LIKE THE SIGNAL DELAY IN SATELLITE COMMNUICATIONS THEIR WORDS CAME THOUGH CLEARLY BUT JUST A SPLIT SECOND LATE WHEN ALL FOUR OF THEM WERE TELAFLASHING TOGETHER.

SHE PUTS IT ON SO THICK MOLLY WAS SAYING THAT YOU CAN SMELL IT EVEN THOUGH THE GARLIC KIND OF SWEET AND CREAMY. I THINK IT'S A BIT SOAPY AND LOOK SOME IS STUCK TO THAT PIECE OF SPAGHETTI THAT SHE'S SLURPING UP NOW.

YUCK! TINA AND MOLLY BOTH TEAFLASHED TO EACH OTHER. "HONEY I DON'T THINK WE'VE TOLD YOU ABOUT THE WONDERFUL JOB OFFER DAD IS SERIOUSLY

CONSIDERING TINA SAID." WONDERFUL JOB OFFER! THE AIR BECAME STATIC WITH TELAFLASHED EXCITEMENT. THOSE WORDS SERIOUSLY AND CONSIDERING WERE MUSIC TO THEIR EARS AND IF MOM WAS MENTIONING IT TO HONEY IT MUST BE SERIOUS.

SHE'S NOT JUST SAYING THIS TO PLEASE ME AUNT HONEY IS SHE? SHE CAN'T BE J.R. REPLIED. TINA AND DAD PROCEEDED TO EXPLAIN THE JOB OFFER TO AUNT HONEY.

"YES UNDER SECRETARY TO THE AMBASSADOR IN LONDON COURT OF ST. JAMES MY FOCUS WOULD ACTUALLY BE PLEASING." "IT'S REALLY LIKE BEING AN UNDER AMBASSADOR TINA ADDED PROUDLY.

THE CHILDREN ALL FOUR OF THEM WERE CONCENTRATING SO HARD THEY BARELY HEARD THE WORDS. THEY HAD TO CONVINCE THEIR FATHER THAT HE COULD DO IT AND THAT THE PROBLEMS WERE MINOR. THEY WANTED THIS TO HAPPEN MORE THEN ANYTHING ALL FOUR OF THEM BUT ALL FIVE OF THEM IF YOU INCLUDED TINA AND ALL SIX OF THEM IF YOU INCLUDE THE BIG SHADOW UPSTAIRS.

OH LET IT HAPPEN! THEY ALL TELAFLASHED IN UNISON FOR EVEN CHARLY AND MOLLY SOMEHOW SENSED THIS WAS VITALLY IMPORTANT. "DAD! HOW MARVELOUS! WHY HAVEN'T YOU SAID YES IMMEDIATELY?"

OH SAY YES! LIKE A SILENT CHANT THE CHILDREN'S TELEPATHIC SIGNALS SEIZED THE AIR. SAY YES DADDY AND MAKE IT BECOME TRUE! "WELL DEAR THERE ARE PROBLEMS WITH MOVING AN ENTIRE FAMILY TO LONDON. FOR ONE THING TINA OBVIOUSLY COULD NOT COME EXCEPT OCCASIONALLY AND WE'VE DECIDED IT WOULD BE BEST IF THE CHILDREN WERE TO COME WITH ME IT WOULD BE A GREAT EXPERIENCE FOR THEM BUT THIS MEANS THEY WOULD BE WITHOUT THEIR MOTHER AND EVEN IF WE

COULD ARRANGE FOR CHILD CARE WHO WOULD WANT THAT JOB?"

"LOOK" AUNT HONEY SAID "I THINK THIS JOB OFFER IN LONDON SOUNDS WONDERFUL AND I DON'T THINK YOU SHOULD DISMISS IT JUST BECAUSE OF THE CHILD-CARE PROBLEMS BUT IT IS SUMMER NOW SO THAT IS A BIT HARD IN TERMS OF WHAT TO DO WITH THEM."

SHE MAKES US SOUND LIKE WE'RE THE CLASSROOM GERBILS OR SOMETHING THAT HAS TO BE TAKEN CARE OF OVER THE SCHOOL VACATION TINA TELAFLASHED TO HER OLDER SISTER MOLLY.

WE'RE NOT GERBILS! TINA AND MOLLY SILENTLY BLURTED OUT LOUD BUT AUNT HONEY CONTINUED "I DON'T SEE WHY I COULDN'T COME AND HELP YOU OUT FOR A FEW WEEKS UNTIL YOU'VE FOUND SOMETHING OVER THERE YOU KNOW. I MEAN ENGLAND OF ALL PLACES THEY HAD INVENTED NANNIES. THEY HAVE NANNY SCHOOLS AND I CAN TAKE CARE OF THE CHILDREN FOR A FEW WEEKS AND HELP INTERVIEW NANNIES.

THE TWINS WERE HORRIFIED TO IMAGINE WHO AUNT HONEY WOULD PICK AS A NANNY IF INDEED THEY EVEN SURVIVED HER BUT THEIR PARENTS WERE LOOKING ACROSS THE TABLE AT ONE ANOTHER AS IF THEY THOUGHT THIS WAS A PERFECTLY REASONABLE IDEA. THE TWINS SUDDENLY REALIZED THEY WERE IN REAL DANGER. THE UNTHINKABLE WAS ACTUALLY HAPPENING! SECONDS BEFORE THE AIR HAD BEEN CRACKLING WITH THE ELECTRICITY OF THEIR TELEPATHIC COMMUNICATIONS BUT NOW IT WAS STILL AND AS THE REALIZATION SUNK IN A SICKENING FEELING OF POWERLESSNESS OVERWHELMED EACH CHILD. THEY FELT INDEED AS IF THEY WERE FALLING INTO A BOTTOMLESS PIT A BIG HONEY PIT TO BE EXCAT! THER WAS NOTHING ABSOULUTELY THEY COULD DO TO REVERSE THE FALL.

CHAPTER 4

ZANNY AND NANNY THE BABYSITTERS.

ZANNY DUGGAN HAD PARKED A BLOCK AWAY AND BEGUN TO STROLL TOWARD DAKOTA STREET ON THIS FINE SATURDAY MORNING. THE BALMY AND THE SMELL OF THINGS YOUNG AND GREEN FILLED THE BREEZE. IT WAS HARD TO RUCH EVEN THOUGH THE MESSAGE ON HER ANSWERING MACHINE FROM HER FRIENDS JULY AND LIBERTY HAD SOUNDED RATHER DESPERATE. "IT'S NOT A FATE WORSE THEN DEATH BUT PERTTY CLOSE SOUND JULY'S VOICE HAD SQUEAKED WITH ANXIETY." "JUST IMAGINE AUNT HONEY BABYSITTING US FOR THREE WEEKS!." THEN LIBERTY'S VOICE HAD CAME ON IN A SECOND MESSAGE.

"WOULDN'T YOU LIKE NEVER TO HAVE TO DEAL WITH THAT LITTLE MISERABLE PRINCIPAL OF SPRINGDALE SCHOOL AGAIN? WOULDN'T YOU LIKE NEVE TO HAVE TO TEACH ANOTHER CHILD OF THE KENDALL FAMILY? ADMIT IT ZANNY YOU SAID YOU HAD NEVER MET A CHILD YOU DIDN'T LIKE AND THEN YOU KNOW WE OVERHEARD YOU TELL YOUR MOM THAT THEY WERE THE MOST DISGUSTING CHILDREN. EVERY TEACHER IN YOUR ENTIRE SCHOOL DREADS GETTING THEM AND THERE'S A VERY GOOD CHANCE YOU COULD GET RANDY KENDALL NEXT YEAR."

LIBERTY HAD EXCEEDED THE MESSAGE TIME ON THE TAPE AT THIS POINT SHE HAD CALLED HER BACK. "WOULD YOU NOT INSTEAD AS OPPOSED TO THOSE DISGUSTING CHILDREN PREFER THE LOVELY ENGAGING AND THE

ABSOLUTELY TERRIFIC RAGOZZINO CHILDREN KNOWN FOR THEIR WIT CHARM ELEGANT MANNERS AND ALL THIS IN AN EXOTIC SETTING LONDON?"

JULY'S AND LIBERTY'S WORDS STREAMED THOUGH ZANNY'S MIND ALONG WITH THOUGHTS OF SPRING AND THE END OF THE SCHOOL YEAR. THE TWINS COULDN'T HAVE KNOWN THAT SHE WAS THINKING OF TELLING HER PRINCIPAL SHE WOULDN'T BE BACK IN THE FALL. OR COULD THEY SAID OUT LOUD? BECAUSE THEY KNOW SOMEHOW THEY OFTEN SEEMED TO KNOW THINGS. SHE HAD ROUNDED THE CORNER ONTO DAKOTA STREET AND HAD HEARED THE METALLIC CLANK OF A STATION WAGON AND IT'S WHEELS COMING DOWN A SHORT DEAD-END STREET THAT DIPPED FROM A VERY HIGH HILL. SUDDENLY A RED BLUR HURTLED TOWARD HER AND IN THE FRONT SEAT OF THE WAGON A DOG BARKED FURIOUSLY.

"CHARLY! "MOLLY!" ZANNY DUGGAN LOWERED HERSELF SLIGHTLY HUNCHED OVER SPREAD HER ARMS AND ASSUMED THE POSTURE OF A HOCKEY PLAYER GUARDING THE GOAL. THE RED WAGON AND THE LITTLE TWINS WILD-EYED AND HAIR STIFFED WITH MOUSSE CRASHED RIGHT INTO SHE AND THEY ALL CRUMPLED INTO A HEAPPING PILE. YAPPING AROUND THE TANGLE OF LEGS AND UPTURNED WAGON WHEELS WAS A DOG THAT APPEARED TO BE MAD BUT YET THE DOG'S WAS A WELSH TERRIER AND WAS NOT FOAMING FROM THE MOUTH INSTEAD IT WAS FOAMING ON THE TOP OF IT'S WIRY AND STRANGELY COPPED HEAD.

"WHAT IN THE WORLD!" ZANNY SPUTTERED AND GOT UP SHAKING OUT HER SKIRT. "WOULD YOU PIPE DOWN?" SHE SNAPPED AT THE DOG THEN BENT OVER AND PATTED HIM TO CALM HIM DOWN. "OH NO" SHE SIGHED AS SHE LOOKED AT THE TWINS. A SIGN WAS TAPED TO THEIR WAGON AND IT SAID: BU-TEE-ON-WHEELS. THEN SHE SHW A FLASH OF THE DOG'S BIG BRIGHTLY PAINTED TOENAILS

AND SAW THE HAIR CURLERS IN IT'S TAIL. IT WAS ALL COMING TOGETHER NOW.

"YOU DIDN'T SHE SAID LOOKING UP AT THE TWINS." THEY NODDED VERY SOLEMNLY. "YOU DON'T UNDERSTAND ZANNY." "NO I GUESS I DON'T SHE SAID WITH PATIENCE." ZANNY DUGGAN HAD INFINITE PATIENCE AND THAT IS WHAT MADE HER SUCH A GOOD FOURTH-GRADE TEACHER? SHE WAS THE DAUGTHER OF ROSEMARIE DUGGAN THE PRODUCTION MANAGER OF THE RAGOZZINO RECITAL WEAR AND SHE HAD BABYSAT ALL THE RAGOZZINO CHILDREN OVER THE YEARS AND ALL THE KIDS LOVED HER AND SHE LOVED THEM AS WELL.

"SO TELL ME ABOUT THIS GIRLS" SHE SAID SCRATCHING GENTLY AT THE DOG'S THROAT. "WELL WE TRIED TO GET A GIRL TO DO OUR BEAUTY ON BUT OUR FRIEND HEATHER FARNHAM SAID NO SO SHE TOLD US WE COULD DO IT ON HER DOG INSTEAD SAID CHARLY.

"OH DEAR!" ZANNY SIGHED WITH RELIEF AND ROLLED HER EYES UPWARDS TOWARDS HEAVEN AND WAS THANKFUL THAT HEATHER FARNHAM WAS SPARED THE BEAUTY.

"DO YOU KNOW THAT IF DAD TAKES THE JOB IN LONDON AUNT HONEY IS GOING TO TAKE CARE OF US?" MOLLY ASKED. "YES I HEARD THAT SO CALLED RUMOR." "WELL DO YOU WANT THAT TO HAPPEN?" CHARLY SAID AS SHE SHOVED HER FACE AND HER RUNNY NOISE RIGHT UP TO ZANNY'S FACE. HER LITTLE COWLICKS STUCK OUT RIGID WITH MOUSSE AND HER BRIGHT BLUE EYES WERE WIDE AND UNBLINKING. "WELL OF COURSE NOT BUT I CAN'T SEE A PROBLEM." "THERE'S NO PROBLEM IF WE DON'T GO TO LONDON AND IF WE CAN MAKE MONEY THEN DAD WON'T HAVE TO GO TO WORK." SAID CHARLY.

"OH NO!" ZANNY SPOKE SOFTLY BUT SLAPPED HER OWN CHEEK IN VERY DISBELIEF. SHE DID LOVE FIVE-YEAR

OLDS EVEN LITTLE SAMMY KENDALL WHO HAD BEEN OK WHEN HE WAS FIVE BUT NOW THEY HAD JUST DECIDED TO HOLD HIM BACK A YEAR WHICH MEANT HE WOULD HAVE TO REPEAT THE FOURTH-GRADE AND JANE GERSTEIN THE FOURTH-GRADE TEACHER WASN'T UP TO HIM AGAIN SO THAT COULD MEAN BOTH SAMMY AND RANDY INTO HER CLASSROOM AND OH GOSH LONDON DID SOUND VERY GOOD RIGHT ABOUT NOW!

THAT EVENING THE LIGHT OF AN ALMOST FULL SPRING MOON STREAMED THROUGH BOTH THE CURVED WINDOWS IN THE TWIN TURRETS OF THE OLDER CHILDREN'S BEEDROOMS BUT IN J.R.'S BEDROOM ILLUMINATED BY THE BIG MOON'S LIGHT THE HEAD OF SHERLOCK HOLMES CAST A LARGE JAGGED SHADOW AND IT HAD STRETCHED RIGHT UP THE WALLS AND COVERED THE CEILING ABOVE THE BED WHERE J.R. HAD SLEPT AND IN CHARLY'S ROOM ALTHOUGH THERE WAS NO SHADOW OF SHERLOCK DEEP WITHIN HER DARK SLEEP SOMETHING SILVERY SPLASHED AGAINST HER DREAM AND IT WAS A DISTANT ECHO FROM ANOTHER WORLD AND ANOTHER TIME.

CHAPTER 5

THE TURTH ABOUT WHAT HAPPENED TO 58TH ST.

THEY HAVE ONLY BEEN IN LONDON A DAY BUT ZANNY HAD PROMISED TO TAKE THEM TO 58TH STREET AS SOON AS POSSIBLE SO THEY COULD TRY AND FIND NUMBER # 221B WHERE SHERLOCK AND DR. WATSON HIS SO CALLED PARTNER IN SOLVING CRIMES HAD LIVED. NOW LIBERTY AND JULY WHO LIVE IN LONDON AND ARE FRIENDS OF MOLLY AND CHARLY FELT A QUEASY FEELING WAY DOWN DEEP IN THEIR STOMACHS.

IT WAS LIKE A BAD DREAM AS THEY CAME UP THE ESCALATOR FROM THE SUBWAY OR THE UNDERGROUND AS LONDONERS CALLED IT THE TILED BIG WALLS OF THE WEST 58TH STREET STOP SEEMED TO EXPLODE WITH CRAGGY SILHOUETTES OF SHERLOCK HOLMES AND EACH TILE WAS BORE THE VERY FAMOUS PROFILE COMPLETE WITH THE DEERSTALKER CAP AND THE BIG MEERSCHAUM PIPE JAMMED IN BETWEEN HIS TEETH. IT WASN'T LIKE SEEING DOUBLE IT WAS LIKE SEEING MULTIPLES SQUARED. EVERYWHERE THE PROFILE UNTILL THEY FINALLY EMERGED INTO THE GLARING OF THE LIGHTS ON WEST 58TH STREET.

THERE WAS A PUB CALLED MORIARTY'S AFTER THE EVIL GENIUS WHO WAS HOLMES'S ARCHENEMY AND THERE WAS ALSO A SHERLOCK HOLMES BIG HOTEL ALL MODERN AND UGLY MADE OF GLASS AND CHROME. THE BIG HOTEL BOASTED A WATSON ROOM AND ALMOST NEXT DOOR WAS AN ITALIAN RISTORANTE MORIARTY AND JUST ABOUT

EVERY CORNER BOASTED A SOUVENIR SHOP HAWKING KEY CHAINS, MUGS, PLACEMATS, SOAP, PENS, POSTCARDS, PENCILS CASES, NAPKINS, T-SHIRTS AND EVEN SO CALLED PICTURES OF SHERLOCK HOLMES AND IT WAS ALL FOR SALE. IT WAS

IMPOSSIBLE TO ESCAPE THE PROFILE FOR IT HAD BEEN EMBLAZONED ON THE SURFACE WHERE ONE WALKED OR LOOKED ON EVERY ITEM ONE MIGHT BUY BUT QUOTES FROM THE TALES HAD BEEN INSCRIBED OVER DOORWAYS OF PUBS, RESTAURANTS, AND GIFT SHOPS.

IT'S ALMOST LIKE GRAFFITI LIBERTY TELAFLASHED AS SHE SPOTTED YET ANOTHER PROFILE OF SHERLOCK HOLMES. THIS ONE WAS ABOVE THE DOOR ENTRANCE TO A CHEMIST'S SHOP. "IT IS?" JULY TELAFLASHED BACK. WELL AFTER ALL HE'S JUST A CHARACTER IN A NOVEL. "WHAT DO YOU MEAN JUST A CHARACTER IN A NOVEL? THAT NOT GRAFFITI!

JULY FOUND LIBERTY'S ATTITUDE ANNOYING. LIBERTY HERSELF KENW IN A MICROFLASH THAT WHAT SHE HAD SAID WASN'T TRUE AT ALL AND SHE HAD REGRETTED IT ALMOST IMMEDIATELY. SHERLOCK HOLMES WAS A GOOD CHARACTER AND IN MANY WAYS HE WAS MORE FAMOUS THAN HIS BIG BROTHER WHO WAS A CERATOR OF WRITING FAMOUS BOOKS. SHE WASN'T SURE WHAT IT MEANT BUT SHE KNEW IT DIDN'T MEAN THIS KIND OF CHEAP PLASTIC EXPLOITATION.

"WELL KIDS" ZANNY SAID WITH A LOW VOICE "LET'S FIND NUMBER #221B ON WEST 58TH STREET." SHE SENSED THEIR DISAPPOINTMENT BUT ALL THE BIG BUILDINGS IN LONDON ON 58TH STREET APPEARED DECIDEDLY MODERN WITH THEIR GLASS AND CONCRETE EXTERIORS HARDLY THE DARK OLD VICTORIAN LONDON IN THE BOOKS. THEY STOOD BEFORE A DRYCLEANING STORE WITH A SIGN THAT SAID: "SHERLOCK HOLMES WOULD HAVE USED OUR SERVICES."

"NUMBER #221B" JULY SAID THAT IS THE EXACT ADDRESS RIGHT?" BUT THIS GUIDEBOOK HERE SAYS THAT THERE NEVER WAS ANY 221B AND THE ACTUAL ADDRESS IS PROBABLY THE PRESENT DAY NUMBER 31." "WELL HERE WE ARE AT NUMBER #50 SO WE MUST BE NEAR IT ZANNY SAID."

THEY CROSSED THE STREET TO A BLOCK OF RATHER UGLY MODERN CONCRETE BUILDINGS AND IN FACT A SMALL OVAL PLAQUE BEARING THE PROFILE OF SHERLOCK HOLMES WAS ON THE FRONT OF THE BUILDING. IT STATED THAT THIS WAS WHERE THE FICTIONAL DETECTIVE'S ROOM WOULD HAVE BEEN IF HE HAD ACTUALLY EVER LIVED AT THE ADDRESS #221B IN VICTORIAN LONDON.

JULY AND LIBERTY WHO ARE FRIENDS WITH MOLLY AND CHARLY TRIED TO IMAGINE A NARROW OLD BUILDING WITH A TALL BRICK CHIMNEY. THEY ENVISIONED THE ROOMS THAT SHERLOCK HOLMS AND DR. WATSON HAD RENTED THE ROOMS IN WHICH THEY SAT AND FIGURED OUT THE SOLUTIONS TO THE GREAT CRIMES OF THE CENTURY. THEY TRIED TO IMAGINE HOLMES'S STUDY, THE TICK OF THE CLOCK, THE GLOWING EMBERS IN THE GREAT BIG FIREPLACE, THE SOLITARY POOL OF LIGHT FROM HIS READING LAMP, THE SMOKE CURLING FROM HIS PIPE AS SHERLOCK THE GREAT DETECTIVE EVER CONTEMPLATED A CASE. THEY HAD KNOWN IT WAS FICTION BUT THAT ISN'T REALLY TRUE BUT DID IT HAVE TO BE THIS FALSE AND THIS PLASTIC?

CHARLY'S LITTLE VOICE PIPED UP AND SAID: "THIS IS WHERE THAT GUY HAD LIVED? THIS IS SO BORING CHARLY SAID AND I THINK DINSEY WORLD COULD DOES IT BETTER?" "HUSH CHARLY! SAID ZANNY BUT JULY AND LIBERTY DIDN'T EVEN CARE BECAUSE THEY KNEW CHARLY WAS RIGHT ANYWAY AND THAT DISNEY WORLD WOULD HAVE DONE IT BETTER."

THE RAGOZZINO'S HAD FOUND A SMALL HOTEL IN MARYLEBONE THAT WAS FAVORED AS A WAY STATION FOR NEWLY ARRIVED EMBASSY FAMILIES LOOKING FOR MORE PERMANENT RESIDENCES. IT WAS IDEAL AS FAR THE CHILDREN WERE CONCERNED. REGENT'S PARK A WONDERFUL PLACE WAS TWO BLOCKS AWAY AND 58TH STREET WAS TWO BLOCKS IN THE OPPOSITE DIRECTION. MADAME TUSSAUD'S THE FAMOUS WAX-WORKS WAS A MERE TEN-MINUTE WALK FROM THE HOTEL. THERE WERE ALL KINDS OF NEAR BY RESTAURANTS AND MOVIE THEATERS AND EVEN A MCDONAL'S THANK GOODNESS WE'RE NEAR BY BECAUSE I'M HUNGR! LET'S GO EAT. NONE OF THE TWINS WAS PARTICULARLY EXCITED BY ENGLISH CUISINE.

"BANGERS!" MUTTERED CHARLY STARING AT A FAT GRILLED SAUSAGE ON HER PLATE. AFTER THE DISAPPOINTMENT OF 58TH STREET THE CHILDREN HAD BEEN SO HUNGRY THEY STOPPED FOR LUNCH IN A PUB.

"SHEPHERD'S PIE! I THOUGHT IT WOULD BE QUICHE" LIBERTY WHISPERED OUT LOUD. "THIS LOOKS LIKE MYSTERY MEAT AND WHAT IS THAT ON THE SIDE ZANNY?" "POTATOES" ZANNY SAID. "THEY'RE SO GRAY LOOKING" JULY SAID OUT LOUD. "THEY LOOK MORE LIKE OATMEAL THEN POTATOES." "DUST PUPPIES!" MOLLY SAID. "THEY LOOK JUST LIKE THOSE DUST PUPPIES MOM SLURPS UP WITH THE HAND VACUUM BEHIND THE COUCH." "OH GROSS!" SAID ALL THE TWINS. "HUSH!" ALL OF YOU. THIS IS NOT THE LEAST BIT POLITE AND HOW CAN YOU BE SO NARROW MINDED?" ZANNY LOOKED AT THEM SHARPLY. "WE CAN GO TO MCDONAL'S IN WASHINGTON BUT WE'RE IN LONDON NOW. IT'S TIME WE BROADENED OUR HORIZONS NOT TO MENTION OUR TASTES. WE ARE HERE TO LEARN ABOUT A NEW CULTURE SHE SAID AS SHE LOOKED CAREFULLY AT ALL FOUR CHILDREN. ZANNY HAD CURLY BUT YET REDDDISH-BLONDE HAIR THE COLOR OF AN APRICOT AND A FACE OF COPPER FRECKLES. HER EYES WERE A BRIGHT CORNFLOWER BLUE. THEN CHARLY THE

OLDER TWIN SAID TO ZANNY: "REMEMBER OUR DEAL?" CHARLY SAID TO ZANNY "NO SCHOOL RIGHT?" CHARLY SAID AS SHE POINTED HER FINGER AT ZANNY WHEN SHE SAID THAT. "NOT IF WE CAN HELP IT." ZANNY SAID TO THE TWINS AS SHE SMILED.

THE CHILDREN AND ZANNY HAD HATCHED A PLAN TO AVOID SCHOOL FOR THE WHOLE YEAR. "WHY GO TO AN AMERICAN SCHOOL IN LONDON? JULY HAD ASKED ON THE PLANE TRIP OVER." IF MOM THINKS LIVING IN THIS LONDON WOULD BE SUCH A WONDERFUL LEARNING EXPERIENCE WHY NOT ALSO GO TO AN ENGLISH SCHOOL?

IT TURNED OUT THAT ENROLLING ANY OF THE CHILDREN IN A BIG HUGE CONVENIETLY LOCATED ENGLISH SCHOOL WOULD BE VERY DIFFICULT BUT THEN ZANNY WHO BASICALLY AGREED WITH JULY HAD COME UP WITH THE NOTION THAT SHE COULD BE THE CHILDREN'S TEACHER BECAUSE AFTER ALL SHE HAD JUST QUIT HER JOB TEACHING IN A CHEVY CHASE ELEMENTARY SCHOOL. SHE HAD DECIDED TO TAKE A BREAK BUT MAYBE SHE WOULD GO BACK TO GRAD SCHOOL OR MAYBE SHE WOULD TEACH AGAN IN A YEAR OR TWO BUT FOR NOW WHY NOT HAVE A HOME SCHOOL WITH THE GREAT RAGOZZINO CHILDREN? THE ONLY DIFFERENCE WOULD BE THAT THE HUGE CURRICULUM WOULD BE THE CITY OF LONDON AND ENGLISH HISTORY.

DAD THOUGHT IT SOUNDED APPEARLING. MADELINE THE TWINS MOTHER WAS LESS CERTAIN BUT THEY WOULD MULL IT OVER DURING THE SUMMER BREAK.

THE KIDS THOUGHT IT SOUNDED FANTASTIC AND THAT'S WHY THE TWINS LOVE ZANNY. THEY KENW THEY COULD ALWAYS TRUST HER AND THAT ZANNY DIDN'T ALWAYS FOLLOW PARENTAL RULES. HOWEVER THAT NIGHT JULY AND LIBERTY WOULD BREAK A RULE THAT THEY KNEW WOULD STRETCH ZANNY'S UNDERSTANDING BUT

IT WAS TOO TEMPTING AND THOSE STRANGE ECHOES KEPT THURUMMING IN THEIR HEADS THE ECHOES OF A VOICE THAT PERHAPS KNEW NO RULES AND THAT GAVE THEM COURAGE.

    IN THE HOTEL LIBERTY SHARED A ROOM WITH ZANNY BUT JULY WAS IN A CONNECTING ROOM AND THEY ALL BEEN SOUND ASLEEP FOR HOURS BUT JUST THEN SOMETHING HAD STIRRED LIBERTY'S SLEEP LONG BEFORE DAWN SO SHE TURNED OVER AND PULLED THE COVERS UP AROUND HER NECK. AT FIRST SHE THOUGHT SHE WAS HAVING A DREAM ABOUT SAND FOR THERE WAS A DRY WHISPERY SOUND BUT THEN THE SOUND OF THE SAND TURNED TO THAT SILVERY RAIN THEN SAND AGAIN. NO PERHAPS A FINE DRIZZLE OR SOMETHING ELSE LIKE RAIN, WIND, A STORM OF TINY PARTICLES THAT HAD BOMBARDED HER DREMLESS SLEEP AND AT THE EYE OF THE STORM WERE THREE MORE THAN THE WHISPERED WEATHERY SOUNDS? WERE THERE LOTS OF SMEARED WORDS WITH MUFFLED VOICES? "THIS IS NOT A DREAM!" SO LIBERTY SAT BOLT UPRIGHT AND SCREAMED OUT LOUD. THIS WAS NOT A BIG MYSTERY ABOUT THAT VOICE. SHE KNEW IMMEDIATELY HER OWN VOICE HAD SPOKEN THOSE FIVE WORDS AND THE WORDS HAD COME STRIGHT OUT OF HER MOUTH NOT HER MIND, NOT TELAFLASHED TO OR FROM HER LITTLE BROTHER. GOOD GRIEF SHE COULD HAVE WAKENED UP ZANNY.

    SHE LOOKED OVER AT THE OTHER BED AND SAW ZANNY WAS STILL SLEPT ON UNDISTURBED BY LIBERTY'S OUTBURSTS. SHE LOOKS PRETTY WHEN SHE SLEEPS LIBERTY THOUGHT. HER HAIR WAS ALL FRIZZY AND GOLDEN RED AROUND HER FACE. LIBERTY YAWNED AND SHE HAD A FEELING THAT SHE LOOKED DUMB WHEN SHE SLEPT BECAUSE HER MOUTH PROBABY HUNG A LITTLE OPEN AND SHE SUSPECTED THAT SHE HAD DROOLED TOO BECAUSE SOMETIMES THERE WAS A SMALL DAMP SPOT ON HER PILLOW.

LIBERTY TURNED AND LOOKED OUT THE WINDOW AND SAID HOW ODD SHE THOUGHT IT WAS SO LIGHT OUTSIDE, TOO LIGHT FOR THE TIME: 2:00 O'CLOCK IN MORNING AND YET SHE COULDN'T SEE THE BUILDINGS ACROSS THE STREET FROM THE HOTEL. SHE CLIMBED OUT OF BED AND WENT OVER TO THE WINDOW. "IT'S FOG!" SHE WHISPERED TO HERSELF AND IT WAS THE THICKEST FOG SHE HAD EVER SEEN AND IT WAS BEAUTIFUL TOO. THE BIG STREETLIGHTS WRAPPED IN THE THICK VAPOR LOOKED LIKE HUGE LUSTROUS PEARLS.

LIBERTY WAS ENCHANTED BY THE MAGICAL FOG IN THE NIGHT. SHERLOCK HOLMES WOULD WALK WITH WATSON TROUGH A FOG LIKE THIS WHEN THEY WERE TRYING TO SOLVE CRIMES. SUDDENLY LIBERTY'S IMAGINATION FILLED WITH IMAGES OF DARK WATER, MISTY WHARVES AND SWIRLING FOG SHROUDING STEALTHY FIGURES THAT SLICED THROUGH A LONDON NIGHT.

AT THAT VERY MOMENT JULY APPEARED IN THE DOORWAY RUMPLED AND SCRATCHING HER HEAD. "HOLMES USED TO UP HIS DOG TOBY ON PINCHIN LANE RIGHT DOWN BY THE RIVER SHE SAID AS SHE COVERED HER MOUTH TO YAWNE."

LIBERTY USALLY DIDN'T ACTUALLY WAKE JULY UP WITH HER THOUGHTS BUT THIS TIME THE IMAGES IN HER MIND HAD BEEN SO VIVID, BEAUTIFUL AND POWERFUL PAINTINGS ONLY IF HER PAINT HAD SPILLED OFF HER CAVANS ONTO ANOTHER MEANING HER BROTHER'S BUT THAT WAS ONLY PART OF IT THERE WAS MORE. SHE REMEMBERED THOSE WHISPERS FROM BEFORE WHEN SHE HAD A WOKE THE ECHOING DREAMS. NOT HER DREAMS PERHAPS BUT OTHER DREAMS. THERE WAS SOME OTHER VOICE TRYING TO BREAK INTO HER MIND BUT FROM WHERE AND WHY? SHE BET JULY'S SLEEP HAD BEEN LACED BY THE SAME DIM ECHOES. THERE WAS SOMETHING ODDLY WRONG AND

DISTURBING AND YES INVASIVE ABOUT IT AND JULY WOULD HAVE UNDERSTAND IT.

THEN THE THOUGHT SEIZED THEM BOTH AT THE SAME TIME AS IF THE IDEA HAD BEEN SWEPT IN BY THE WHISPERING WIND BEHIND THE SWIRLING FOG OUTSIDE BUT IT WAS SO BOLD, TANTALIZING, AND OUTRAGEOUS AND NOT TO MENTION IN VIOLATION OF EVERY RULE OF COMMON SENSE AND THE SAFETY THAT THEY KNEW NOT TO SAY IT OUT LOUD.

I THINK WE SHOULD GO FOR A WALK THROUGH THE CITY. OF COURSE SAID JULY. WHERE DO YOU WANT TO START? CHARLY SAID. HOW ABOUT THE RIVER AND PINCHIN LANE? SAID JULY. THAT'S A GREAT IDEA CHARLY SAID. WHERE ELSE DID YOU WANT TO GO AFTER GOING TO THE RIVER AND PINCHIN LANE? I DON'T KNOW YET, LET'S JUST GO TO PINCHIN LANE AND THE RIVER FRIST JULY SAID AND THEN WE WILL TAK IT ONE STEP AT A TIME FROM THERE OK. THAT SOUNDS GOOD TO ME CHARLY SAID. OK THEN LET'S GO!" SO JULY AND CHARLY HEADED OUT THE FRONT OF THE HOTEL DOOR AND HEADED OFF TO THE RIVER AND PINCHIN LANE.

IT WOULD BE DANGEROUS AND THEY KNEW THAT FROM THE START. TWO KIDS ALONE MAKING THEIR WAY THROUGH A STRANGE CITY IN DENSE FOG IT WAS PREPOSTEROUS THE TWINS THOUGHT. ZANNY WOULD RESIGN OR GET FIRED IF SHE DISCOVERED THEY WERE DOING IT AND DIDN'T STOP THEM AND THEIR PARENTS WOULD DIE IF THEY FOUND OUT ABOUT THIS LITTLE CITY TRIP BUT THIS DIDN'T STOP THEM AS J.R. SLIPPED A MAP INTO HIS POCKET LIBERTY BEGAN TO HAVE THE STRANGEST FEELING THAT SOMETHING POWERFUL AND SOMETHING MOMENTOUS WAS ABOUT TO HAPPEN AN ADVENTURE WORTHY OF THE GREAT MASTER OF DETECTION HIMSELF SHERLOCK HOLMES!

CHAPTER 6

THE ADVENTURE OF THE TWINS

THEY STEPPED OUT INTO THE CHILLY MIDNIGHT AIR AND THE STREETLIGHTS REALLY DID HANG LIKE PEARLS HUGE BEAUTIFUL SOFT LUMINOUS PEARLS SWIRLED IN VEILS OF FOG. SHAPES MELTED INTO THE MILKY NIGHT AND THE BREATH OF THE FOG TOGETHER WITH A FAINT WIND SEEMED TO STIR THINGS AND CHANGE ORDINARY OBJECTS LIKE STREET SIGNS, HANGING PLANTS, STOPLIGHTS INTO SOMETHING SLIGHTLY STRANGE AND VERY EXTRAORINARY. IT WAS NOT A NIGHT TO TRUST THE APPEARANCE OF THINGS, THE FAMILIAR, THE NORMAL OR THE KNOWN. IT WAS RATHER A NIGHT THAT SUGGESTED THE POSSIBILITY OF GREAT TRANSFORMATIONS.

THE TWINS STOOD BRIEFLY ON THE CORNER OF THE INTERSECTION OF MARYLEBONE HIGH STREET AND NOTTINGGRAM AND THE MIST SWIRLED AROUND THEM. THE UNDERGROUND HAD STOPPED BUT IT DIDN'T MATTER BECAUSE THEY WANTED TO WALK THE REST OF THE WAY AND ENJOY THE MISTY FOG THAT WAS SOROUNDING THEM. SO THEN THEY SET OFF DOWN MARYLEBONE IN THE PEARLY LIGHT FOG.

NORMALLY BUSY DURING THE DAY THE STREET WAS NOW ALMOST VERY DESERTED SO THEY HEADED FOR THE THAMES RIVER TOWARD PINCHIN LANE HOME OF SHERLOCK HOLMES DOG TOBY. TOBY HAD BEEN HALF SPANIEL, HALF LURCHER AND SHERLOCK HOLMES USED

HIM TO TRAIL SUSPECTS. ON AND ON THE TWINS WALKED TOWARD THE RIVER.

THEY HAD J.R.'S MAP AND WHEN THE FOG OCCASIONALLY THINNED TO A POINT WHERE THEY COULD READ THE NAMES ON THE MAP. "THIS MUST BE CARLOS PLACE" LIBERTY SAID AS SHE PASSED A VERY FANCY HOTEL WHERE A DOORMAN TIPPED HIS TOP HAT AND SAID: "LOVELY EVENING FOR A STROLL."

IT WAS FUNNY HE DOESN'T THINK IT'S WEIRD TWO KIDS OUT ALL BY THEMSELVES J.R. TELAFLASHED TO HIS SISTER AS THE DOORMAN HAD REPLACED HIS TOP HAT. YES THAT IS WEIRD BUT . . . . BUT WHAT? J.R. SAID TO HIS SISTER. I'M NOT SURE BUT THERE WAS SOMETHING IN THAT NICE DOORMAN'S VOICE KIND OF LIKE . . . . KIND OF LIKE WHAT? J.R. ASKED HIS SISTER. KIND OF LIKE THE ECHOES WE HAVE IN ARE MINDS I GUESS. WHO KNEW LIBERTY THOUGHT. THE EVENING SEEMED SO MAGICAL. IF THE STREETLIGHTS LOOKED LIKE PEARLS MAYBE J.R. AND JULY LOOKED LIKE GROWN-UPS IN THE THICK FOG.

CARLOS PLACE LED TO MOUNT STREET AND TWO RIGHT TURNS BROUGHT THEM TO CURZON STREET AND THEN OUT OF THE FOGGY MIST CAME TWO CATS WITH THEIR YELLOW EYES BLAZING LIKE GOLDEN NUGGETS. SO THEN AFTER THE CHILDREN PASSED THE CATS THEY WENT DOWN HALFMOON STREET TO SEE IF THEY SEE THE RIVER YET BUT THEY COULDN'T SEE A THING SO THEN THEY CROSSED THE STREET OVER TO PICCADILLY STREET. "THIS MUST BE THE PARK" LIBERTY SAID. "WHICH ONE?" J.R. ASKED LIBERTY. "LET' LOOK" LIBERTY SAID AS SHE UNFOLDED THE MAP. "IT'S GREEN PARK" SAID LIBERTY.

"WISHED I'D HAD BROUGHT MY SKATEBOARD" J.R. MUTTERED AS THEY TROTTED ALONG A NARROW FOOTPATH. "WHAT'S THAT?" LIBERTY SAID AS SHE STOPPED

DEAD IN HER TRACKS. A HEAD IN THE FOG LOOMED AN IMMENSE SHAPE AND THE STRANGE SWIRLING MISTS SEEMED TO OBLITERATE THE EDGES OF THINGS AND CONTOURS AS WELL AS BOUNDARIES. WHEN LIBERTY LOOKE UP SHE FELT THE CRUSHING PRESENCE OF A SHAPE THAT MIGHT TUMBLE DOWN ON HER.

"OH" SHE SAID WITH A SIGH OF RELIEF AS THEY WALKED RIGHT UP TO THE BASE OF THE PEDESTAL. "IT IS QUEEN VICTORIA" SAID LIBERTY. IN ORDER TO READ THE LETTERS J.R. HAD TO PRACTICALLY PUT HIS NOISE AGAINST THE BRONZE PLAQUE.

"IT'S GOT TO BE AT LEAST EIGHTY FEET TALL" LIBERTY SAID OUT LOUD. "I READ THIS IN A GUIDE AND HOW I REMENBER THAT IF SHE'S HERE THEN ST. JAMES'S PARK MUST BE RIGHT OVER THERE" SAID LIBERTY AS SHE POINTED HER FINGER INTO THE FOG. J.R. LOOKED AND SHOOK HIS HEAD AS HE POINTED THE TIP OF HIS FINGERI INTO THE DISSLVEING MISTY FOG AND SAID: "THIS WOULD BE THE MOST DIRECT WAY TO THE RIVER." YOU SAY PINCHIN LANE IS RIGHT NEAR WESTMINSTER BRIDGE? ASKED J.R. "YES HE SAID THIS IS THE OLDEST OF THE ROYAL PARKS IN LONDON." "YOU GOT THAT FROM THE GUIDE TOO?" "NO THAT WAS ZANNY PART OF ARE ENGLISH CURRICULUM THE ONE THAT'S GOING TO SAVE US FROM GOING TO A BIG REGULAR SCHOOL. YOU'VE GOT TO TAKE IT MORE SERIOUSLY JULY. IF WE REALLY PAY ATTENTION TO ZANNY BELIEVE ME MOM AND DAD WILL FORGET ABOUT OUR GOING TO THAT SCHOOL THEY CALLED UP." "IF WE REALLY PAID ATTENTION TO ZANNY WE WOULDN'T BE DOING THIS RIGHT NOW!"

THE TRUTH OF J.R.'S REMARK WAS SO OVERWHELMINGLY APPARENT THAT THERE WAS NOTHING ELSE FOR MINUTES AS THEY WALKED. ARE WE REALLY FOOLISH? YEAH SAID J.R. BUT . . . . BUT WHAT? SAID JULY. WE'RE OUT HERE ALL ALONE IN THIS FOG. ARE YOU SCARED? NO NOT REALLY.

There could be criminals lurking around here! Liberty thought of all the books she had been reading that talked about the big thieves, pickpockets and muderers of old London. In those days children were not just kidnapped but brought and sold like a big bag of goods and worked untill they were worn out and wrose of all they could still be captured and mutilated and then set out to beg. Minus a finger or an eye they would appear so pathetic that no selfrespecting Englishman could walk by without tossing them a farthing. London has been known as one of the most vicious capitals in the western Europe in the century. There was a staggering crime rate and the streets of Gin Lanes teemed with professional criminals, gangs of burglars, and highwaymen are carzy. "Yikes!" What are we doing out here! It was really your idea Liberty. Don't go chicken on me now, look in this fog they can't even see us and we can't see them! J.R. said to Liberty. If the criminals that might be lurking in the fog-shrouded night could not see them July and Liberty were certainly not going to let them hear them neither. So in silent agreement the twins dicided not to talk out loud untill they were back safe in their hotel rooms. They continued walking to St. James's Park following the path around a house statue that reared with it's rider into the fog.

Henry the eighth built this park Liberty telaflashed trying to change the subject. Was that before or after he chopped off his wife's head? Thanks, thanks a bunch J.R.! Well I was just wondering that's all. I mean just imagine he came up with this nice little idea for a pretty park on the same day he cut off his wife" s head. It should be named Anne Boleyn.

SUDDENLY A POWERFUL SWEET FRAGRANCE ENVELOPED THEM. A WIND HAD COME UP AND PUSHED THE SCENT OF ROSES THROUGH THE HEAVY THICKENING OF THE FOG. WHERE'S IS IT COMING FROM? J.R. ASKED. IT WAS ABSOLUTELY IMPOSSIBLE TO SEE ANYTHING NOW. THE FEW LIGHTS IN THE PARK WERE JUST DIM SMEARS IN THE NIGHT. LET'S FOLLOW THE SCENT AND SEE IF WE CAN FIND THE ROSES. WE WOULD BE ROSE HOUNDS INSTEAD OF BLOOD HOUNDS J.R. SAID. LOOK RIGHT HERE! WE FOUND THEM. A BIG GUST OF WIND HAD JUST MADE A SUDDEN CLEARING IN THE FOG JUST WHERE JULY WAS STANDING. I CAN SMELL THEM I THINK THEIR JUST FEW FEET AHEAD OF LIBERTY J.R. SAID AS HE HAD FOUND HIMSELF IN THE MIDDLE OF TWO FACING CRESCENTS OF ROSES. THE ROSES APPEARED TO BE PINK, GOLDEN AND PEACHY. THEIR PETALS WER EMBROIDERED WITH TINY BEADS OF MIST THAT GAVE THEM A SILVERY SHEEN. THE FRAGRANCE WAS VERY OVERPOWERING AND INTOXICATING. I FEEL LIKE WE'RE BREATHING MAGIC LIBERTY TELAFLASHED. SHE CLOSED HER EYES JUST FOR A MINUTE THEN SHE HEARD AN ECHO IN HER HEAD. LIBERTY! YOU LOOK ALL SILVERY AND BRIGHT AND SO DO YOU LIBERTY SAID TO HER BROTHER J.R. THEY LOOKED AT EACH OTHER IN AMAZEMENT. IT WAS AS IF THEY HAD SUDDENLY GROWN OLDER. THEIR JET BLACK HAIR WAS AS SILVER AS THEIR GRANDMA'S OUT IN KANSAS BUT THEIR FACES WERE STILL THE YOUNG AND FRECKLED AND THEIR EYES WERE BRIGHT.

LIBERTY NOTICED A FUNNY EXPRESSION ON JULY'S FACE BECAUSE SHE HAD SEEN THAT SMILE BEFORE SOMEWHERE. IT WAS SO FAMILIAR THE MOUTH SLIGHTLY PARTED IN A DARING HALF SMILE OF ANTICIPATION. SHE HAD SEEN IT IN HISTORY BOOKS IN THE PORTRAITS OF EXPLORERS AND YES IN THE PICTURES OF SHERLOCK HOLMES HIMSELF.

YOU'RE SMILING LIBERTY; YOU MUST BE STARTING TO ENJOY YOURSELF. I'M SMILING? LIBERTY SAID OUT LOUD TO HERSLEF. SUDDENLY SHE FELT AS IF SHE HAD BEEN

ADMITTED TO THE MOST EXCLUSIVE CLUB IN THE WORLD. IS SHE REALLY LOOKING AT HER MIRROR IMAGE? WAS SHE A TRUE, TRUE ADVENTURER ONE WHO COULD ALMOST SMILE AND BE AFRAID AT THE SAME TIME? YOU ARE AND YOU KNOW IT.

    THE TWO LITTLE WORDS BOKE LOOSE IN HER HEAD BUT IT WAS NOT J.R. SPEAKING, IT WAS THE ECHO. SHE KNEW THERE WAS NO TURNING BACK NOW THAT THEY HAD LEFT THE HOTEL. THEY WENT LEFT ON THE BRIDCAGE—WALK WHICH BORDERED THE SOUTH SIDE OF THE PARK. THEY HAD GONE A LITTLE MORE THEN A BLOCK WHEN THEY HEARD CHIMES. ONE . . . TWO . . . THREE TIMES THEY SOUNDED. SUDDENLY THE TWINS FELT AS IF THEIR OWN BODIES HAD GROWN HOLLOW AND THE GONGS OF THE CHIMES WERE FILLING THEIR BEINGS. THERE SEEMED TO BE NO SEPARATION BETWEEN THEM AND THE CHIMES BUT WHEN THE RINGING STOPPED AND THE LAST ECHOES HAD FADED FROM THEIR BRAINS THE FEELING LEFT. THEIR BODIES BECAME THEIR OWN AGAIN AND THEY WALKED STRAIGHT TO WESTMINSTER BRIDGE. IN THE MIDDLE THEY STOPPED TO WATCH THE FOG HOVERING OVER THE RIVER AND A FEW FAINTLY PULSING OF GREEN AND RED LIGHTS ON THE RIVERBOATS MAKING THEIR WAY UP OR DOWN THE RIVER.

    CHRISTMAS TREES! FLOATING THROUGH CLOUDS THE TWINS SAID AS THAT THOUGHT HAD FILLD BOTH THE TWINS MINDS AT ONCE. WHEN THEY HAD REACHED THE OTHER SIDE OF WESTMINSTER BRIDGE THEY STOOD UNDER A VERY DIM STREETLIGHT SO J.R. GOT OUT HIS SHERLOCK HOLMES MYSTERY MAP OF LONDON TO SEE IF THEY WERE GOING IN THE RIGHT DIRECTION. IT WAS A GOING AWAY PRESENT FROM ZANNY'S MOTHER. HE THEN TOOK OUT OF HIS BACK POCKET THE NEW EDITION OF SIR. ARTHUR CONAN DOYLE'S THE SIGN OF FOUR. HE POINTED TO THE MAP AND SAID IF WE ARE HERE AT WESTMINSTER BRIDGE THEN HOW DO WE GET DOWN TO THE RIVER? J.R. HAD SAID TO

LIBERTY. WHAT? LIBERTY SAID. IT WAS UNBELIEVABLE! THE TWINS COMMUNICATION WAS BREAKING UP. THIS RARELY HAPPENED AND HAD NEVER IN THESE CIRCUMSTANCES. THEY HAD EXPERIENCED STATIC BEFORE LIKE WHEN THEIR FATHER HAD MADE THE VISIT TO THEIR SCHOOL FOR THE WAR ON FLUOROCARBONS OR ONCE WHEN THEY WERE ON A CAR TRIP AND DRIVEN ALONG A STRETCH OF HIGHWAY WHERE THERE WERE MASSIVE ELECTRICAL TRANSFORMERS BUT THAT WASN'T THE CASE HERE AT ALL. THEY HAD JUST CROSSED THE THAMES AND WERE STANDING ON WHAT LOOKED LIKE A VERY SMALL QUIET STREET. LIBERTY HAD TRIED AGAIN BUT IT WAS IMPOSSIBLE TO GET THROUGH TO HER BROTHER J.R. THEIR TELEPATHIC CHANNELS HAD CAME AS AN ECHOE AND IT CAME GENTLY WITH A SOFT WIND-WHISPERY SONG. THIS WAS PURE SCRATCHY STATIC LIKE THE SOUND OF FINGERNAILS ON A BLACKBOARD AND IT MADE THEM SHIVER.

"IT'S AWFUL" LIBERTY BLURTED OUT LOUD. "HUSH! IF WE HAVE TO TALK OUT LOUD WE CAN AT LEAST WHISPER." JULY TOOK OUT THE MAP AND SAID "LOOK WE NEED TO GO AROUND HERE SOMEPLACE." "WHAT DO YOU CALL THAT?" LIBERTY SAID POINTING TO A LARGE RED AND WHITE BUILDING THAT IS DIRECTLY IN FRONT OF THEM. "DO YOU THINK THAT'S A HOSPITAL?" J.R. ASKED. "WELL SAID LIBERTY IT'S CERTAINLY TOO BIG FOR A HOUSE." SO THEY WALKED CLOSER AND SAW THE EMERGENCY SIGN BEFORE THEY SAW THE ONE THAT SAID ST. THOMAS'S HOSPITAL.

"OKAY AHA!" EXCLAIMED J.R. "THE GAME IS A FOOT!." JULY SEEMED TO HAVE FORGOTTEN COMPLETELY THAT THEIR ABILITY TO TELECOMMUNICATE HAD BEEN TOTALLY INTERRUPTED. DOESN'T HE CARE? LIBERTY HAD SAID TO HERSELF. SHE HERSELF FELT AS IF HER ARM OR LEG HAD BEEN AMPUTATED.

"SHOOT! I SHOULD HAVE RECEMBERED TO WEAR MY SHERLOCK HOLMES HAT! CAN YOU BELIEVE IT? NO SHE

COULDN'T BELIEVE IT? HERE SHE IS WORRIED MORTALLY WORRIED ABOUT HIS STUPID DEERSTALKER HAT! HE WAS FUMING.

"I'M FINALLY OUT OF WASHINGTON D.C. AND NOW I'M IN LONDON ENGLAND AND ACTUALLY RETRACING DR. WATSON'S STEPS IN THE SIGN OF FOUR AND I FORGET TO WEAR MY HAT." "JULY HOW CAN YOU BE SO WORRIED ABOUT YOUR HAT? DON'T YOU REALIZE WHAT HAS HAPPEN TO US? LIBERTY WAS SPEAKING IN A WHISPER THAT QUICKLY BECAME A RASP OF DESPERATION.

"WHAT ARE YOU TALKING ABOUT?" HE LOOKED UP HIS GRAY EYES A BLANK. THERE WAS NO RECOGNIZABLE GLIMMER IN THOSE EYES. IT HAD BEEN A NIGHT OF STRANGE TRANSFORMATIONS ALREADY BUT THIS WAS THE MOST TERRIFYING OF ANY IMAGINABLE. WAS HER OWN TWIN BROTHER BECOMING A STRANGER? "J.R. DON'T YOU CARE?" "CARE ABOUT WHAT?" J.R. SAID. THE STATIC AND ARE TELEPATHY SIGNALS ARE GETTING WORSER SO WE BETTER STICK TOGETHER SO WE DON'T GET LOST LIBERTY SAID. "WHAT WILL WE DO WITHOUT IT?" "YOU ARE GOING TO HAVE TO LEARN TO ADAPT IT." "ADAPT TO WHAT?" LIBERTY SAID. THIS WAS UNBELIEVABLE THAT SOMETHING WAS TAKING OVER J.R. BUT HE LOOKED THE SAME AND YET J.R. SAID HE CAN'T BELIEVE IT NEITHER. WE'VE ALWAYS BEEN TELEPATHIC BOTH OF THE TWINS SAID OUT LOUD TOGETHER.

"IT'S NOT GOING TO KILL US TO TALK OUT LOUD." LIBERTY WAS BEYON DISMAY AND WHO KNEW IT JUST MIGHT KILL THEM. HADN'T THEY AGREED IN THE PARK TO TALK SILENTLY BECAUSE OF ALL THE CRIMINALS?

"JULY IS A PART OF US AND HOW WOULD YOU FEEL IF SOMEBODY CAME UP AND SAID: "WELL JUST AMPUTATE YOUR LITTLE TOE HERE IT WON'T KILL YOU?" "LITTLE TOE J.R. SAID AS HE LOOKED UP VACANTLY FROM THE MAP AND

THEN HE LOOKED DOWN AT THE MAP AGAIN. "OKAY" J.R. SAID GIVING THE MAP A SNAP AS HE CONTINUE I CAN DEDUCT THAT IF THIS BUILDING HERE IS ST. THOMAS'S HOSPITAL THEN IF WE TURN RIGHT WE ENTER A SECTION CALLED LAMBETH AND IF WE FOLLOW DOYLE'S DIRECTIONS THAT I GOT MARKED HERE THEN WE SHOULD BE AT THE RIVER SOON SAID J.R."

IT WAS UNLESS MAYBE THIS CHANGE IN JULY AND THE INTERRUPTION OF THE TELEPATHIC CHANNELS WAS TEMPORARY I HOPE J.R. SAID. SHE'D BETTER JUST GO ALONG WITH HIM AND "READ DOYLE'S DIRECTIONS" HER TWIN SISTER LIBERTY SIAD IN A WEARY VOICE.

"JUST A MINUTE" SAID J.R. AS HE TURNED THE PAGES RAPIDLY IN THE BOOK. "OKAY HERE WE GO" SAID J.R. AS HE BEGAN TO READ FROM THE STORYBOOK THAT WAS ATATCHED TO THE MAP: "PINCHIN LANE A ROW OF SHABBY TWO-STORIED BRICK HOUSES IN THE LOWER QUARTER OF LAMBETH AND I HAD TO KNOCK FOR SOME TIME AT NUMBER#3 BEFORE I COULD AN IMPRESSION BUT AT LEAST HOWEVER THERE WAS A GLINT OF A CANDLE BEHIND THE BLIND AND A FACE LOOKED OUT OF THE UPPER WINDOW AND SAID: "GO ON YOU DRUNKEN VAGABOND AND IF YOU KICK UP ANY MORE ROWS I'LL OPEN THE KENNELS AND LET OUT ALL FORTY-THREE DOGS UPON YOU NOW GET OUT OF MY YARD."

JULY STOPPED READING BUT NOW OVER HERE ON THE NEXT PAGE IT SAYS THAT TOBY SHERLOCK HOLMES'S DOG LIVES AT NUMBER#7 ON THE LEFT HERE. HE MOVED SLOWLY FORWARD WITH HIS CANDLE AMONG THE QUEER ANIMAL FAMILY WHICH HE HAD GATHERED AROUND HIM. REMEMBER THAT PART? LIBERTY SAID TO J.R. I ALWAYS THOUGHT IT WAS SO SPOOKY SAID LIBERTY.

"YOU MEAN THE GUY WHO KEEPS HOLMS'S DOGS?" LIBERTY FELT A BIG GLIMMER OF HOPE BECAUSE JULY FELT

A LITTLE BIT MORE LIKE HERSELF AND I THINK IT WAS BECAUSE SHE KEPT J.R. TALKING. NOW MAYBE THINGS CAN GET BACK TO NORMAL."

"YEAH THAT GUY DOSE SPOOKE ME A LITTLE J.R. SAID. REMEMBER HE HAD A SORT OF KENNEL BUT NOT JUST DOGS. LISTEN TO THIS J.R. SAID. SO JULY HUNCHED OVER THE BOOK THAT J.R. WAS READING: IN THE BIG HUGE UNCERTAIN A SHADOWY LIGHT I COULD SEE DIMLY THAT THERE WAS WERE GLANCING GILMMERING EYES PEEPING DOWN AT US FROM EVERY LITTLE CRANNY AND CORNER. EVEN THE RAFTERS ABOVE US WERE LINED BY SOLEMN FOWLS WHO LAZILY SHIFTED THEIR WEIGHT FROM ONE LEG TO THE OTHER AS ARE VOICES DISTURBED THEIR SLUMBERS."

"OOOH CREEPY!" LIBERTY SAID. "I HOPE WE DON'T SEE ANY ANIMALS SAID LIBERTY BECAUSE I'M REALLY NOT THAT BIG ON ANIMALS SHE SAID ESPECIALLY SMALL CREEPY VICIOUS ONES." "COME ON!" J.R. URGED. "WE HAVE TO GET TO THE LOWER QUARTER OF LAMBETH."

THEY TURNED DOWN AN ALLEY BEHIND ONE OF HOSPITAL BUILDINGS THAT SEEMED TO LEAD IN THE DIRECTION OF LOWER LAMBETH. ONE DUMPSTER WARNED OF TOXIC WASTE MATERIALS. SOMETHING SCURRIED UNDER A FENCE AND BANGED AGAINEST AN EMPTY METAL DRUM. DARK SQUARISH SHAPES LOOMED OUT OF THE FOG AND CONTAINERS FOR THE DISPOSABLES THE TRASH OF A HOSPITAL. IT WAS NOT PLEASANT TO THINK ABOUT THE TRASH OF A HOSPITAL AND WHAT IT MIGHT BE IN THOSE CONTAINERS. SO SUDDENLY A BRIGHT LIGHT MELTED THE FOG AROUND THEM.

"QUICK AGAINST THE WALL!" JULY HISSED AND GRABBED J.R.'S HAND. "I DON'T THINK WE SHOULD BE HERE." EVEN HIS HAND FELT A LITTLE DIFFERENT NOW. WAS THIS REALLY HER TWIN? A STRANGE UNKNOWABLE FEELING HAD SEEMED

TO INVADE HER BODY. FOR THE FIRST TIME SHE FELT VERY SEPARATE AND DISCONNECTED AND SINGLE. IT WAS SUCH AN ODD FEELING THAT SHE ALMOST REELED FROM IT LOSING GRAVITY WOULD NOT HAVE FELT ANY STRANGER AND WOULD HAVE PROBABLY BEEN A LOT MORE FUN. THIS WAS AWFUL AND SCARRY TOO. IT WAS PROFOUNDLY SAD TO HAVE THIS BAD FEELING OF SEPARATENESS WHEN THE THAT HELD HERS WAS GENETICALLY DOWN TO THE LAST MOLECULE AND THE CLOSEST IDENTICAL TO HER OWN IN THE ENTIRE UNIVERSE. IN THAT ONE SPLIT SECOND LIBERTY REALIZED SHE WAS FEELING AN EMOTION SHE HAD NEVER EXPERIENCED IN HER LIFE LONG LONELINESS. SHE FELT AS IF SHE WERE STANDING ON THE RIM OF THE BLACKEST OF THE DEEP ABYSS. THIS MIGHT BE WORSE THEN DEATH SHE HAD THOUGHT.

WHERE HAVE YOU GONE J.R.? MY OLD JELLY BEAN WHERE HAVE GONE? THERE WAS ONLY SILENCE FROM JULY AND ALTHOUGH THERE WAS NO BIG STATIC INTERFERANCE LIBERTY COULD SENSE THAT HER OWN FLASHES HAD GROWN DIM LIKE THE EMBERS OF A DYING FIRE.

A VERY LONG CAR SWUNG INTO THE ALLY AND AFTER IT HAD STOPPED TWO ATTENDANTS JUMPED OUT TO OPEN THE REAR DOOR. "HELLO MATE!" A VOICE CALLED OUT CHEERFULLY. "GOT ONE HERE FOR YOU FROM THE HEATHROW AIRPORT AND WAS BOUNDED FOR SUNNY SPAIN. THIS IS A SIX A.M. FLIGHT. NOT THE WAY I'D WANT TO GO MIND YOU BUT I'D THOUGHT ME AND MY WIFE AND I COULD SAVE SOME PENNIES FOR A TRIP."

TWO WHITE COATED PEOPLE COME OUT A GARAGE DOOR CARRYING A STRETCHER. ON THE STRETCHER WAS A LUMPY FORM AND IT WAS DRAPED WITH A SHEET ON TOP AND THE SHEET BLEW SLIGHTLY IN THE WIND AND LIBERTY HAD TO SQUEEZE HER EYES SHUT. WHAT IF THE WIND HAD BLEW IT SO HARD THAT SHE SAW A HAND A DEAD MAN'S HAND?

WHEN THE HEARSE PULLED AWAY WITH IT'S CARGO THEY CAME OUT FROM THE NIGHT SHADOWS AND CREPT DOWN THE ALLEY. HERE THE ALLEYWAYS NEVER SEEMED TO RUN STRAIGHT FOR MORE THEN A FEW YARDS AT A TIME BECAUSE THEY TWISTED AND TURNED AND BECAME AS CROOKED AS A BIG DOG'S HIND LEGS. THERE WERE NO LONGER SIMPLE ROWS OF SHABBY TWO STORIED BRICK HOUSES. A FEW WERE LEFT BUT MOST HAD BEEN TORN DORN TO DUST.

IT APPEARED THAT THE SPRAWLING HOSPITAL COMPLEX HAD GOBBLED UP MUCH OF THE EREA. MANY OF THE ALLEYS AND LANES REMAINED UNDER MARKED SO IT WAS POSSIBLE THAT PINCHIN LANE MIGHT HAVE LOST IT'S STREET SIGN. AFTER ALL DOYLE HAD WRITTEN THE SIGN OF FOUR NEARLY A HUNDRED YEARS AGO AND THE STREETS AND NEIGHBORHOODS EVEN THE STREETS OF LONDON COULD CHANGE OVER THE COURSE OF A CENTURY J.R. SAID. JUST THEIR LUCK TO FIND A MCDONALD'S OR WORSE YET SUPPOSE THE LANE WAS STILL THERE AND SOMEONE HAD OPENED UP A SOUVENIR SHOP WITH TOBY KEY CHAINS, TOBY T-SHIRTS, CHOCOLATE BARS AND TOBY DOGGIE TREATS. OH DEAR HE THOUGHT AS HE HOPED IT WOULD NOT TURN OUT BE LIKE WEST 58TH STREET.

LIBERTY'S THOUGHTS WERE FOLLOWING A DIFFERENT PATH ALTOGETHER. SHE COULDN'T GET THE DEAD BODY OUT OF HER MIND AT ALL BECAUSE OF ALL THE LUMPY HEAPS AND THERE WERE SEVERAL PEOPLE WERE THEY DEAD AND GOING TO MORGUE TOO? ON THE CREEPINESS SCALE THIS WAS A BIG SOILD TEN SAID LIBERTY BUT WORSE THEN THAT SHE COULD NOT GET USED TO THIS STRANGE NEW FEELING OF SEPARATENESS OF BEING A SINGLETON. IT JUST HAD TO BE TEMPORARY.

"THIS IS IT!" JULY SAID SOFTLY. "WHAT?" LIBERTY ASKED. "THIS MUST BE PINCHIN LANE!" JULAY SAID NOT CONCEALING THE DELIGHT IN HER SOFT VOICE. IT WAS

A NARROW LITTLE LANE LIBERTY SAID AS THEY STOOD IN FRONT OF AN IRON GATE AND PEERED THOUGH. NO DUSTBINS WERE VISIBLE BUT IN THE FOG IT APPEARED THAT THERE WERE SEVERAL SMALL BUILDINGS THAT COULD HAVE BEEN HOUSES OR MAYBE EVEN LITTLE ROW HOUSES. PERHAPS JULY WAS THINKING THINGS HAD NOT CHANGED THAT MUCH FROM THE TIME WHEN SR. ARTHUR CONAN DOYLE HAD WRITTEN THE SIGN OF FOUR. THEN SUDDENLY FROM BEHIND THEY HEARD A LOW GROWL COMING OUT FROM SOMEWHERE BUT THEY DIDN'T KNOW WHERE. A VERY HORRIBLE BARK RENT THE FOG BLOODCURDLING FULL OF FEAR AND RAGE AND THAT'S WHEN THE TWINS SCREAMED OUT LOUD AHHHH! THE ECHOES THAT HAD BEEN HAUNTING THEM FROM WASHINGTON TO LONDON PRESSED IN EVEN CLOSER AND GROWING TO A DULL ROAR. INSTANTLY THE CURRENT OF THOUGHT BETWEEN JULY AND LIBERTY BECAME CHANGED SIZZLING WITH A BARRGE OF STRANGE INCOMPREHENSIBLE SIGNALS AS THEY DASHED ACROSS THE STREET. "IT BIT ME! SCREAMED LIBERTY. "MY CHEEK MY CHEEK IT BIT MY CHEEK!" IT'S OK THERE'S NO BLOOD LIBERTY. WHAT ARE YOU BACK JULY? I'VE ALWAYS BEEN RIGHT HERE HAVEN'T I? JULY ASKED LIBERTY. OH JULY I'M GLAD YOUR BACK TO NORMAL NOW.

CHAPTER 7

THE DEVONSHIRE MEWS.

There was only a scrawl of thin white foam across Liberty's cheek and across the alley an immense Dobermanpinscher dog thrashed madly against it's chain as it tried to leap right through the fence. It's head hung between the bars and the dogs mouth was still frothing with foam and it's eyes were narrow green slits in the night.

Above the mad dog barking a voice called out "Get out! "Get out!." "I got worse than that Dobermanpinscher up here I also have a wiper in this bag and I'll drop it on your head if you guys don't get out of my yard.

Too frightened to scream the twins took off running down the street. July remembered the strange speech defect of the kennel keeper's voice in the sign of the four. Liberty then said that voice sounds firmiler I think we heard it a couple of blocks ago Liberty felt her heart pounding rapidly as they ran down the street. As they ran down the street Liberty felt scrawl of dog spittle flatten against her cheek. A horrible crackle mixed with the baying of the Dorbermanpinscher Liberty was so scared and her heart was beating so hard she wondered if it could burst but it wasn't just fear she was happy wildly happy about something. Her mouth parted slightly in that daring half smile of the adventurer and she felt the damp mist on

HER LIPS. SHE WAS NO LONGER A SINGLETON AND THE AIR BETWEEN LIBERTY AND HER TWIN CRACKLED. TAKE A LEFT HERE! NOW TAKE A RIGHT. IS THAT RIGHT? SAID LIBERTY. THAT'S CORRECT! SAID JULY. THE TWINS RAN BACK THREADING THEIR WAY THOUGH A MAZE OF ALLEYS AND HOSPITALS UNTILL THEY PASSED THE PLACE WHERE THE HEARSE HAD CAME TO MEET THE DEAD PERSON BOUND FOR SPAIN. THEY SPRINTED ACROSS WESTMINSTER BRIDGE BUT THEY DIDN'T EVEN NOTICE THAT THE FOG HAD BEGAN TO LIFT AND THE TRACERY OF THE OLD CLOCK NOW SHONE THROUGH THIN SCUDDING WHITE CLOUDS. JULY WAS THE FIRST ONE TO FALTER AS HE CLUTCHED HIS RIBS.

I'VE GOT A TERRIBLE STITCH IN MY SIDE JULY SAID, I HAVE TO STOP. THEY HAD STOPPED ON THE FAR SIDE OF THE BRIDGE JUST UNDER THE BIG BEN. THE OLD CLOCK BEGAN PEAL THE HOUR THRRRINNG . . . THRRINNG . . . THRRRINNG . . . AND THRINNNGGG. AGAIN THE TWINS FELT THEMSELVES FILLED WITH THE CHIMES OF THE DAWNS BRIGHT SUNLIGHT RISEING UP THROUGH THE WHITE CLOUDS. THE CACKLE AND BARKS FADED AWAY BECOMING AS DIM AS FOOTPRINTS ON A SANDY BEACH WHEN TIDE ROLLS IN.

LIBERTY GASPED TRYING TO CATCH HER BREATH. WHAT HAPPEN TO TOBY THE NICE HALF-SPANIEL? HE SEEMS TO HAVE TURNED INTO THE HOUND OF THE BASKERVILLES. THE COLOR IN HER CHEEKS WAS HIGH AS SHE BEGAN TO LAUGH. I DON'T KNOW! BOY CAN YOU IMAGINE WHAT MOM, DAD AND ZANNY WOULD DO IF THEY FOUND OUT ABOUT ALL THIS!

FORGET IT! LIBERTY FLASHED AS SHE TOUCHED HER FACE WHERE THE DOG'S SPITTLE HAD BEEN. SHE WAS WONDERING IF JULY WAS AWARE OF WHAT HAD HAPPENED? SHE SEEMED TO HAVE FORGOTTEN ALL ABOUT THE INVASION OF THEIR TELEPATHIC CHANNELS.

WHAT'S THAT LIBERTY? YOU DON'T REMEMBER DO YOU? REMEMBER WHAT? HOW ARE TELEPATHIC CHANNELS BROKE UP BEFORE WE GOT TO PINCHIN LANE. WHAT BROKE UP? OUR TELEPATHIC COMMUNICATION. I DON'T BELIEVE YOU YOU'RE KIDDING RIGHT? NO I'M NOT SAID JULY BUT WE AGREED TO ONLY TELEFLASH. THAT'S ALL WE'VE BEEN DOING RIGHT? WRONG ARE TELEPATHIC CHANNELS WERE INVADED. IT WAS ALL STATIC AND THEN NOTHING SAID LIBERTY. NOTHING? SAID JULY AS HER EYES WIDENED WITH HORROR. YOU DIDN'T FEEL ALONE? ASKED LIBERTY. WHAT DO YOU MEAN LIBERTY? ALL SEPARETED. SEPARETED? YOU MEAN LIKE A SINGLTON? OH GOSH GEE! YOU MEAN YOU FELT THAT WAY?

LIBERTY NODDED SOLEMNLY AS A TEAR BEGAN TO ROLL DOWN HER LITTLE CHEEK. J.R. REACHED OUT HIS HAND AND SAID "YOU CROSSED OVER." IT WAS A STATEMENT NOT A QUESTION. LIBERTY KNEW WHAT JULY MEANT. SHE HAD BRIEFLY INHABITED THIS WORLD ALONE TOTALLY ALONE AS NO TWO TWINS HAVE EVER DONE. FOR ALTHOUGH TWINS CAN BE IN TWO DIFFERENT PHYSICAL PLACES AT ONCE SINCE THERE IS NEVER A SENSE OF SEPARATION BETWEEN TWINS. "CROSSED OVER" WAS A GOOD AND BAD WAY TO PUT IT LIBERTY HAD SAID TO HER TWIN SISTER JULY. SHE HAD AFTER ALL NOT WILLFULLY CROSSED OVER BUT IT WAS MORE AS IF SHE HAD BEEN ABANDONED, LEFT BEHIND AND TO HER MORE PRESSING QUESTION WAS THIS: "WHERE HAD JULY GONE WHEN SHE HAD LEFT HER BEHIND? SHE NOW ACTED AS IF SHE HAD AMNESIA. SHE SIMPLY DIDN'T RECALL THE INVASION OF THEIR TELEPATHIC CHANNELS AT ALL.

WHAT WAS IT THE ECHOES AGAIN? IS THAT WHAT CAUSED THE BREAKUP? OH NO THE ECHOES AREN'T SO BAD. THIS WAS DIFFERENT SAID JULY. LIKE I SAID BEFORE ALL STATIC AND THEN NOTHING, NO ECHOES, NO WHISPERS JUST NOTHING SAID JULY.

J.R. BIT HIS LIP LIGHTLY IN CONCENTRATION. DO YOU REMEMBER WHAT THE PERSON YELLED OUT THE WINDOW? OF COURSE I REMEMBER LIBERTY SAID. IT WAS ABOUT THE "WIPER" AND HOW SHE WAS GOING TO DROP IT ON ARE HEADS IF WE DIDN'T LEAVE HER YARD. LIBERTY HAD REMEMBERED IT TOO WELL. J.R. HAD LOOKED AT LIBERTY WITH LUMINOUS FEAR IN HIS GRAY EYES OF HIS. SOMETHING REALLY WEIRD IS HAPPENING J.R. SAID TO LIBERTY BUT I JUST DON'T KNOW WHAT YET J.R. SAID. I MEAN WHEN YOU TELL ME FIRST OF ALL THAT OUR TELEPATHIC CHANNELS WERE INVADED . . . ." YEAH LIBERTY SAID BUT WHAT DOSE THAT HAVE TO DO WITH WHAT THE MAN YELLED OUT THE WINDOW? LIBERTY ASKED J.R. LIBERTY THOSE ARE THE SAME EXACT WORDS THAT THE MAN IN THE STORYBOOK YELLED OUT THE WINDOW TO WATSON WHEN HE WENT TO GET THE DOG. THEY ARE ALL RIGHT THERE IN THE STORYBOOK J.R. SAID TO LIBERTY. NO! SAID LIBERTY AS SHE TELAFLASHED IN DISBELIEF.

I'LL SHOW YOU WHAT I MEAN J.R. SAID TO LIBERTY. JULY PULLED THE PAPERBACK OUT OF HIS JACKET POCKET. I JUST HADN'T READ IT TO YOU BEFORE BECAUSE I KENW IT WOULD SCARE YOU BECAUSE I KNOW YOU DON'T LIKE SNAKES TO MUCH. HE TURNED QUICKLY TO THE PAGE AND UNDER A STREETLIGHT AT NORTH END OF WESTMINSTER BRIDGE THE TWINS READ THE PASSAGE. THE WORDS WERE IDENTICAL TO THE ONES THAT HAD CRACKLED THROUGH THE NIGHT ON PINCHIN LANE. AFTER THE TWINS READ THAT PASSAGE OUT OF THE STORYBOOK THEY LOOKED UP AT ONE ANOTHER.

WHAT IN THE WROLD IS GOING ON? THIS CAN'T JUST BE CHANCE J.R. SAID TO LIBERTY. NO WAY! SAID LIBERTY THE ODDS WERE IMPROBABLE MORE THEN IMPROBABLE VIRTUALLY IMPOSSIBLE! J.R. SAID. THOSE FEW WORDS OUT OF ALL THE BILLIONS, TRILLIONS OF WORDS IN THE ENGLISH LANGUAGE ARE THE VERY SAME WORDS AS IN THE

STORYBOOK AND IN EXACT SAME ORDER AND WITH THE SAME EXACT SPEECH DEFECT. "THE IDENTICAL WORDS TUMBLING OUT OF A WINDOW ON THE EXACT SAME LANE ONE STORYBOOK THAT WAS MADE HUNDRE YEARS LATER! HOW COULD THAT BE? J.R. SAID. THE SIGN OF THE FOUR HAD BEEN A MADE-UP STORY AND THIS WAS REAL LIFE. WHAT COULD BE MORE REAL THAN LIBERTY AND JULY RAGOZZINO STANDING ON THE PAVEMENT IN THE THINNING MIST OF A CHILLY LONDON DAWN?

SO WHAT COULD HAVE HAPPENED? WHAT COULD THIS ALL MEAN? J.R. HAD WONDERED. WAS THERE SOME SHERLOCK SCHOLAR TUCKED AWAY ON PINICHIN LANE LIVING OUT THE LIFE OF THE KENNEL KEEPER? AND WHAT ABOUT TOBY? HAD HE INDEED BEEN TRANSFORMED INTO THAT BIG BALEFUL DOBERMANPINSCHER?

THEY WALKED THE REST OF THE WAY BACK QUIETLY FOLLOWING THE PATH ONCE MORE AROUND ST. JAMES'S PARK. THE GILT-TRIPPED BLACK GATES OF BUCKINGHAM PALACE GLEAMED IN THE PINK-GRAY MORNING LIGHT AND ABOVE THE ROOF OF THE ROYAL STANDARD FLEW INDICATING THE QUEEN WAS IN RESIDENCE AND JUST INSIDE THE COURTYARD THEY COULD SEE THE GUARDS IN FRONT OF THE GUARDHOUSES IN THEIR TOWERING NICE SMOOTH BARESKIN HATS AND SCARLET TUNICS GLISTENING WITH BRIGHT BIG BUTTONS AND BADGES.

THEY THEN TOOK A SLANTING PATH ACROSS GREEN PARK TO PICCADILLY PARK AND SAW THAT THE TOWN OF PICCADILLY WAS JUST WAKING UP AND IN MAYFAIR A FEW HOUSEMAIDS AND MANSERVANTS WERE OUT WASHING DOWN THE WHITE MARBLE STEPS THAT LED UP TO CREAM-COLORED HOUSES AND POOLS. SOON THE TWINS CROSSED OXFORD STREET AND LINGERED IN FRONT OF A DISPLAY WINDOW OF A DEPARTMENT STROE THAT SHOWED A LOT OF DISCO WEAR.

AS A CITY WAKES EACH SOUND COMES SEPARATELY AND DISTINCTLY AND EVEN THE MOST COMMON SOUND ACQUIRES A CERTAIN GRACE OF IT'S OWN AT THAT EARLY HOUR. THE CREAKING OF A LORRY OR TRUCK AS IT ROUNDS THE CORNER OR OF THE BUS EXHALING IT'S FUMES, THE CRANK OF AN AWNING LOWERED BY A SHOPKEEPER, THE SOUND OF KEYS IN A DOORWAY OR THE THWAP OF A NEWSPAPER TOSSED ON A STEP ALL OF THESE SOUNDS HAD A COZY DISTINCTION BUT WHITHIN AN HOUR THEY WOULD BLUR INTO THE WHITE NOISE OF A CITY FULLY AWAKE.

THE TWINS HAD THOUGHT THEY HAD ENTERED MARYLEBONE THROUGH THE SAME ROUTE THEY HAD FOLLOWED HOURS EARLIER BUT INDEED THEY HAD CROSSED OXFORD STREET ONE BLOCK TO THE EAST AND HAD SOMEHOW GONE TO FAR AND BEFORE THEY KNEW IT THEY FOUND THEMSELVES ON WIMPOLE STREET. FOR SOME REASON J.R. AND LIBERTY FELT ALMOST UNCONSCIOUSLY DRAWN TO THAT STREET. IT WAS KINDA CHARMING, NARROW, ELEGANT AND IMMACULATELY CLEAN BUT YET THE HOUSES WERE BUILT OUT OF VARIETY OF MATERIALS, SOME WERE BRICK, SOME WERE A DEEP RUBY PINK SANDSTONE, SOME A DARK CHARCOAL GRAY AND EACH ENTRYWAY WAS UNIQUE AND SPECIAL IN SOME SMALL WAY. ONE HOUSE HAD AN ELABORATELY CARVED DARK WOODEN DOOR OILED AND POLISHED TO A DEEP LUSTER, ANOTHER HOUSE HAD A BIG LONG GLEAMING BLACK DOOR AND IT'S FRONT STEPS WERE A BLACK AND WHITE CHECKERBOARD PATTERN OF MARBLE AND AT THE TOP OF THE STREET WAS DEVONSHIRE PLACE. INEXPLICABLY THE TWO CHILDREN WITHOUT SAYING A WORD THEY TURNED RIGHT AND THEN RIGHT AGAN AND THEN THEY HAD FOLLOWED A CROOKED LITTLE ALLEY BUT THIS ONE WAS NOT DARK NOR FILLED WITH DUSTBINS AND IT WIDENED INTO A BROADER COURTYARD.

I THINK THIS IS WHAT THEY CALL A MEWS LIBERTY TELEAFLASHED. WHAT'S A MEWS? J.R. ASKED LIBERTY. IT'S KIND OF A SMALL HIDEAWAY STREET BEHIND A BIGGER STREET WHERE THEY'VE TURNED THE OLD HORSE STABLES INTO HOUSES SAID LIBERTY. STABLES? J.R. SAID. YEAH YOU KNOW FROM THE OLDEN TIMES LIBERTY SAID. AREN'T THEY CUTE? LIBERTY SAID. JULY HAD TO AGREE WITH LIBERTY ON THAT ONE. THEY LOOK LIKE SMALL PAINTED DOLLHOUSES AND EACH ONE WAS PAINTED A DIFFERENT ICE-CREAM COLOR, ONE WAS PALE PINK, ANOTHER WAS SOFT GREEN WITH BRIGHT YELLOW FLOWERS CASCADING GAILY DOWN FROM THE WINDOW BOXES, ANOTHER WAS PEACH WITH DAZZLING SPRAY OF MORNING GLORIES JUST OPENING AGAINST IT'S FRESHLY WHITEWASHED WALLS BUT IT WAS THE PLAIN ONE AT THE END WITH UNPAINTED CHARCOAL GRAY BRICK AND VARNISHED WOODEN DOORS THAT DREW THE TWINS ATTENTION.

IT ALMOST BECKONED THEM WITH AN INVISIBLE FINGER AND THERE WAS ALSO A BIG COPPER TUB BRIGHTLY POLISHED WITH SPARKLING BRASS WORK OF THE FRONT DOORKNOB THAT IT GLRAMED IN THE MORNING SUNLIGHT. A RIOT OF ORANGE AND YELLOW NASTURTIUMS EXPLOADED SOFTLY OVER IT'S EDGES. THERE WAS A RENTAL SIGN IN THE WINDOW WITH A PHONE NUMBER ON IT. WELL WE SHOULD LIVE HERE LIBERTY TELAFLASHED. OF COURSE! OF COURSE! WHY NOT. I'M NOT SURE WHY. LIBERTY SAID. ME NEITHER J.R. SAID BUT THIS PLACE IS FOR US CAN'T YOU JUST TELL? YES. WHO SAID THAT? LIBERTY TELAFLASHED. WHO SAID WHAT? ASKED JULY. WHO SAID YES? SAID LIBERTY. I THOUGHT IT WAS YOU JULY. IT WASN'T ME SAID JULY BUT YOU HEARD IT TOO? YES SAID LIBERTY. YES! THERE IT IS AGAIN! BOTH TWINS TELAFLASHED AS THEIR WORDS SEEMING COLLIDE IN MID-AIR.

IT'S LIKE THE WORD "CHOP" BACK IN WASHINGTON THAT DAY AUNT HONEY CAME OVER FOR DINNER AND THAT WORD JUST POPPED UP. I MEAN IT POPPED UP IN MY

HEAD BUT IT WASN'T LIKE AN ECHO SAID J.R. BUT IT'S LIKE THIS OTHER VOICE IS ALWAYS TRYING TO BREAK INTO ARE MINDS AND IS LISTENING TO OUR THOUGHTS. WE SHOULD REMEMBER THIS PHONE NUMBER ON THE SIGN AND GIVE IT TO MOM AND DAD SO THEY CAN CALL AND MAKE AN OFFER ON THIS HOUSE. THEY MIGHT WANT TO LOOK AT THIS PLACE BECAUSE IT MIGHT JUST BE THE NICEST PLACE TO LIVE. THEY BOTH CONCENTRATED ON MEMORIZING THE PHONE NUMBER.

JULY AND LIBERTY'S EYES OPENED WIDE AS THEY EACH REPEATED THE NUMBER ONCE. THEY HAD BOTH HEARD IT AGAIN AND IT WAS QUITE AN ECHO BECAUSE IF IT HAD BEEN AN ECHO OF THEIR TELEPATHIC CHANNELS THERE HAD BEEN TWO ECHOES ONE FOR EACH VOICE. THEY TURNED THEIR HEADS AS IF THEY WERE LOOKING FOR SOMEONE LIKE ANOTHER PERSON OR SOMETHING. THIS TIME THEY KNEW IT WAS NO ECHO. A CLEAR SOFT VOICE HAD JUST SPOKEN, A VOICE THAT ONLY THE TWINS COULD HEAR.

CHAPTER 8

THE TWERPS.

CHARLY AND MOLLY WEREN'T TAKING TO THE ENGLISH CURRICULM WITH QUITE THE ZEST ZANNY HAD HOPED THEY WOULD. AT THIS VERY MOMENT IN FACT THEY WERE PLAYING THEIR FAVORITE GAME CALLED RANCH. RANCH WAS A DISTINCTLY AMERICAN GAME. BASICALLY THEY FOUND SOMETHING THEY COULD STRADDLE . . . A FOOTSTOOL OR A STURDY CARTON AND PRETENDED THEY WERE RIDING THEIR HORSES AROUND THE RANCH WEARING OF COURSE THEIR DAVY CROCKETT COONSKIN CAPS WHICH TO THEM WERE FINE SUBSTITUTES FOR THE COWBOY HATS THEIR AUNT HONEY HAD BROUGHT THEM. THEY LOVED THE COONSKIN CAPS MORE THEN ANYTHING AND HAD SCREAMED BLOODY MURDER WHEN THEIR FATHER HAD SUGGESTED THEY SHOULD LEAVE THEM BACK IN THE UNITED STATES.

LIBERTY AND JULY HATED TO HEAR THEM PLAY RANCH ESPECIALLY NOW WHEN WERE SO TIRED. THEY HAD CREPT BACK INTO THE HOTEL APARTMENT JUST IN TIME FOR BREAKFAST. JULY HAD GONE BACK DOWN TO GET THE NEWSPAPER AS SHE DID EVERY MORNING BUT TODAY HOWEVER THE TWINS HAD TURNED TO THE REALESTATE SECTION AND THERE WAS THE HOUSE IN THE MEWS WITH THE SAME NUMBER LISTED THAT THEY HAD MEMORIZED! THEY PLACED THE NEWSPAPER FOLDED OPEN TO THIS SPOT AT THEIR FATHER'S PLACE WHERE HE SITS IN THE MORNING FOR BREAKFAST. THERE WAS NO WAY DAD COULD MISS THIS AD AND HE SAID IT LOOKED PROMISING. HE LEFT IMMEDIATELY AFTER BREAKFAST TO LOOK AT THAT HOUSE.

AS TIRED AS LIBERTY AND JULY WERE SLEEP PROVED IMPOSSIBLE WITH THE RANCH RACKET GOING ON. NOT ONLY WERE THE YOUNGER TWINS NOISY WHEN THEY PLAYED THE RANCH GAME BUT THEY YELLED AT THEIR MAKE-BELIEVE HORSES IN VERY SERVERE VOICES. THEY WERE INTO "HORSEY DISCIPLINE" AS MOLLY CALLED IT BUT THEIR MOTHER DISMISSED IT AS AN UNDERSTANDABLE PART OF BEING THE YOUNGEST FAMILY MEMBERS AND NEEDING TO BOSS SOMEONE EVEN AN IMAGINARY HORSE. THEY ACTUALLY HAD THREE HORSES AND THEY WERE NAMED RANCHER, FRED, AND CHERRY GARCIA. THE THIRD HORSE WAS FOR THEIR FATHER'S FAVORITE ICE-CREAM FLAVOR. ZANNY NOW STOOD SCOWLING IN THE DOORWAY OF THE LIVINGROOM SUITE WHERE MOLLY AND CHARLY WERE STRADDLING TWO LARGE SUITCASES AND A THIRD SUITCASE WAS TIED WITH A CURTAIN CORD TO A NEARBY END TABLE.

"YOU'RE A VERY NAUGHTY HORSE CHERRY!" MOLLY SAID AS SHE SLAPPED AND KICKED THE SUITCASE. "COME ON STOP EATING IT'S TIME TO CATCH THOSE COWS." "OH RANCHER'S A GOOD BOY!" SAID MOLLY BUT CHARLY'S HORSE FRED WAS BAD! COME ON RANCHER LET'S RIDE OVER THERE. FRED YOU'RE GOING TO HAVE TO BE PUNISHED."

"OH GEE THIS IS SICK!" JULY SAID. HE WAS TIRED FROM HIS NIGHT'S JAUNT THROUGH THE FOG AND DIDN'T HAVE THE PATIENCE TO HEAR IMAGINARY HORSES BEING SCOLDED BY HIS TWERPY LITTLE SISTERS AT THE TOP OF THEIR LUNGS.

"YOU'RE WRECKING THE SUITCASES WHEN YOU KICK THEM LIKE THAT SAID ZANNY. "NOT TO MENTION THOSE YUCKY RUNNY NOSES THAT ARE STARTING TO DRIP ON THEM" LIBERTY YAWNED.

"COME ON CHILDREN IT'S TIME FOR LUNCH SAID ZANNY." NOT ME I'M NOT HUNGRY RIGHT NOW I'LL

GET SOMETHING LATER SAID MOLLY. "DO YOU WANT ME TO READ YOU PETER RABBIT?" ASKED ZANNY. "YOU SAID YOU WOULD MAKE US PETER BUNNY COSTUMES" INTERRUPTED CHARLY. NOT ME J.R. SAID. "I DON'T WANT TO BE SOME DUMB RABBIT" J.R. SAID. "I'D RATHER BE JEMIMA PUDDLE-DUCK J.R. SAID. SHE GETS TO WEAR A PRETTY DRESS AND A HAT SAID MOLLY. "NOT A DRESS EXACTLY, A SCARF AND BONNET "SAID CHARLY. "A SHAWL" LIBERTY SAID. "YEAH" MOLLY SAID AS SHE NODDED HEAD SOLEMNLY. "A SHAWL AND A BONNET I WANT ONE, ME TOO SAID CHARLY." ZANNY SIGHED AND OF COURSE SEEING SHE WAS SO TIRED THEY STRUCK.

"WE WANT SHAWLS! "WE WANT BONNETS!" THEY CHANTED KICKING THEIR IMAGINARY STEEDS. "I DON'T BELIEVE THIS!" JULY GROAMED. "YOU ARE ACTING LIKE TOTAL CREEPS" LIBERTY SAID OUT LOUD ABOVE THE OTHERS.

"TWERPS TWIN TWERPS HAVING TANTRUMS!" JULY SAID. "YOU'RE BEING VERY IMMATURE GIRLS" ZANNY SAID OUT LOUD EVENLY THROUGH HER CLENCHED TEETH.

"IMMATURE!" J.R. EXCLAIMED. "THEY ARE BEING PREMATURE PRENATAL NUCKLEHEADS!" THE TWINS BEGAN TO DANCE MADLY AROUND THEIR OLDER BROTHER. THERE WERE AS WILD AS BANSHEES CHANTING AND FLAILING THEIR ARMS ABOUT THEIR RED HAIR SPARKING UP LIKE LICKS OF FLAME. THEY STUCK OUT THEIR TONGUES AND MADE FACES AT THEIR LITTLE BROTHER.

"SHUT UP YOU LITTLE SUN-RIPENED PIG DROPPINGS!" HE YELLED. "SHUT UP YOURSELF YOU SON OF A MOTHERLESS GOAT!" "SON OF A MOTHERLESS GOAT!" "SON OF A MOTHERLESS GOAT!" THEY NOW BEGAN CHANTING.

ZANNY CLAPPED HER HANDS TOGETHER LOUDLY. "IF ALL OF YOU DON'T SETTLE DOWN THIS INSTANT I WILL

NOT ONLY TELL YOU THE SURPRISE AND IF YOU DON'T IMPROVE YOU BEHAVIOR IMMEDIATELY YOU WILL NOT GET TO BE PART OF THE SURPRISE NEIGHTER SAID ZANNY."

THE TWINS FROZE STILL AND SAID "YOU MEAN WE'LL BE LEFT OUT?" CHARLY GASPED. "PRECISELY" SAID ZANNY. "LEFT OUT." SHE SAID THE WORDS SLOWLY AND DISTINCTLY BUT THEN AGAIN IF YOU DON'T KNOW WHAT THE SURPRISE IS THEN YOU WON'T KNOW WHAT YOU'RE MISSING SO IT WON'T MATTER AT ALL NOW WILL IT SAID ZANNY." "YES IT WILL!" MOLLY SAID AS SHE WIPED HER RUNNY NOSE ON HER SLEEVE. "ME AND CHARLY ARE ALWAYS GETTING LEFT OUT OF THINGS WE DON'T KNOW ABOUT." "YEAH" SAID CHARLY AND BY THE WAY WE DON'T LIKE IT ONE BIT."

"IF YOU DON'T ABOUT IT HOW DO YOU KNOW YOU'RE BEING LEFT OUT?" LIBERTY ASKED ZANNY. SUCH REASONING WAS LOST ON MOLLY AND HER SISTER CHARLY. "WE DON'T KNOW WE JUST DO." CHARLY DIRECTED A WITHERING LOOK TOWARD LIBERTY. "SO WHAT'S THE SURPRISE?" SHE HAD ASKED AS SHE TURNED BACK TOWARDS ZANNY.

"IT'S ABOUT JULY AND LIBERTY'S BIRTHDAY" ZANNY SAID. THE LITTLE TWINS SETTLED DOWN IMMEDIATELY. THEY LOVED ANYTHING TO DO WITH BIRTHDAYS. "WHAT ABOUT THEIR BIRTHDAYS?" MOLLY ASKED. "YOU'RE DAD WAS ABLE TO GET ONE OF THE STRETCH LIMOS FROM THE EMBASSY FOR THE WHOLE DAY TO DRIVE THROUGH THE COUNTRYSIDE OR ANYWHERE WE WANT TO GO." "YOU MEAN ONE OF THOSE FANCY ONES?" "YES COMPLETE WITH SNACKS, TELEVISION, TELEPHONE AND SHE WAS SAVING THE BEST FOR LAST BECAUSE SHE KNEW THE LITTLE TWINS WOULD LOVE THIS, "LIGHT MAKE-UP MIRRORS WITH LITTLE COUNTERS AND BUILT-IN SHELVES."

"OH MY GOODNESS!" EXCLAIMED MOLLY. BOTH TWINS WERE IN AN ABSOLUTE LATHER OF EXCITEMENT. CHARLY AND MOLLY LOVED PLAYING WITH MAKE-UP EVEN MORE

THEN LOVED PLAYING THE RANCH GAME. THEY HAD BROUGHT MAKE-UP KITS TO ENGLAND FILLED WITH SAMPLES OF STUFF AUNT HONEY GOT IN THE MALL OR PICKED UP FREE IN DEPARTMENT STORES AS WELL AS THEIR FAVORITE GIFT PRESS-ON-NAILS. LIBERTY FIGURED THAT BETWEEN THEM THE LITTLE TWINS HAD ENOUGH PRESS-ON-NAILS FOR TWO THOUSAND FINGERS OR A SMALL TOWN. "I'M GOING TO BE LOATH TO TAKE SUCH IMMATURE LITTLE GIRLS ZANNY SAID LOOKING AT THEM VERY STERNLY."

"OH GOODIE!" MOLLY AND CHARLY SQUEALED. ZANNY LOOKED LIKE SHE WAS SLIGHTLY CONFUSED AS CHARLY AND MOLLY BEGAN LEAPING ABOUT WITH A NEW CHANT "WE'RE GOING TO THE COUNTRY IN A STRETCH LIMO!" "I SAID 'LOATH' TO TAKE YOU NOT 'LOVE' TO TAKE YOU." THE GIRLS STOPPED DANCING AND IT WAS THEIR TURN TO LOOK CONFUSED. "WHAT DO YOU MEAN LOATH?" MOLLY ASKED. THE WORD MEANS ZANNY SPOKE DISTINCTLY IT MEANS "I DON'T WANT TO TAK YOU IF YOU ARE ACTING LIKE LITTLE IMMATURE GIRLS SAID ZANNY." "OH!" MOLLY AND CHARLY SAID WITH A NEW SOBERNESS IN THEIR VOICES.

JUST THEN MOM AND DAD CAME THROUGH THE DOOR OF THE HOTEL SUITE AND THEY WERE SMILING BROADLY. "GREAT NEWS!" DAD SAID. "YOU GOT THE HOUSE IN THE MEWS!" LIBERTY EXCLAIMED. "WE MOST CERTAINLY DID!" SAID MOM. "I'M GOING TO FEEL MUCH BETTER NOW ABOUT YOU BEING HERE. I REALLY DON'T WANT TO FLY BACK TO WASINGTON UNTILL WE GOT YOU GIRLS SETTLED."

I KNEW IT! JULY TELAFLASHED. ISN'T IT A LITTLE STRANGE BUT GOOD?

LIBERTY TELAFLASHED BACK. BOTH OLDER TWINS WERE JUMPING UP AND DOWN WHEN THE HEARD THE GOOD NEWS ABOUT THE HOUSE IN THE MEWS AND SO JULY

ASKED "WHEN DO WE MOVE IN?" DAD THEN SAID "THE DAY AFTER TOMORROW." "THEY'RE HAVING A CREW CLEAN UP AND WE CAN MOVE IN THE NEXT DAY SAID DAD."

IT WAS A FESTIVE EVENING AND THEY WERE ALL THRILLED ABOUT THE UNPAINTED HOUSE IN THE MEWS, TRIM AND PLAIN AS A QUAKER LADY WITH IT'S VARNISHED DOORS AND BRIGHT COPPER TUB SPILLING OUT ORANGE AND YELLOW NASTURTIUMS.

IT HAD BEEN A LONG DAY BUT FOR LIBERTY AND JULY IT HAD BEGUN JUST AFTER MIDNIGHT. AS J.R. WALKED PASSED CHARLY AND MOLLY'S ROOM HE SAW THE LITTLE TWINS CROUCHED UP ON THE FLOOR. "DARE YOU!" MOLLY SLAPPED SHUT A VERY SMALL BOOK. "I CAN LOOK AT IT SAID CHARLY AS SHE GLARED FIERCELY AT HER SISTER. "IT DOSEN'T SCARE ME CHARLY SAID TO MOLLY." "WHAT ARE YOU TWO DOING IN THERE?" SAID J.R. AS HE HAD STOPPED IN FRONT OF THEIR DOOR. "SHE'S SCARED TO LOOK AT THE PICTURE SAID MOLLY." "WHAT PICTURE?" J.R. ASKED. "THE PICTURE IN ROLY POLY PUDDING" MOLLY SAID. "IT'S A PICTURE OF TOM KITTEN BEING ROLLED UP IN A PIECE OF DOUGH." CHARLY'S BOTTOM LIP STARTED TO TREMBLE. J.R. WALKED OVER TO WHERE THE TWINS WERE AND SAID "LET'S SEE IT" J.R. SAID AND SO MOLLY OPENED THE SMALL BOOK AND SHOWED J.R. THE PICTURE. A LITTLE KITTEN RIGID WITH FEAR HIS EYES STARING WILDLY NOT BELIEVING WHAT WAS ACTUALLY HAPPENING TO HIM HAD INDEED BEEN WRAPPED UP IN DOUGH AND ROLLED INTO A SAUSAGE SHAPE. TWO RATS WERE ROLLING THIS LITTLE BUNDLE UNDER THEIR ROLLING PIN. THERE WAS SOMETHING VERY GROTESQUE ABOUT THIS PICTURE. J.R. COULD SEE WHY CHARLY WAS VERY SCARED OF THIS PICTURE. HE FELT A QUEASINESS SWIM UP IN THE BACK OF HIS THROAT. "THEY'RE GOING TO BAKE THIS CAT INTO PUDDING?" "YEP" SAID CHARLY. "THEY'RE MAKING HIM INTO A DUMPLING FIRST. "HOW DO THEY DO THAT?" CHARLY ASKED. "WELL FIRST THEY CHATCH HIM FIRST

AND TIE HIM UP THEN SMEARED HIM WITH BUTTER" SAID MOLLY. "YUCK THAT'S REALLY DISGUSTING" SAID CHARLY. MOLLY WA CLEARLY SATISFIED SHE HAD MADE AN IMPRESSION ON HER BIG BROTHER SO THAT WAS ENOUGH FOR HER AND SHE FORGOT ABOUT DARING CHARLY ANY MORE.

J.R. WALKED BACK TO HIS OWN ROOM BUT THERE HAD BEEN A TIME JUST A FEW YEARS BEFORE WHEN J.R. HAD TO DARE HIMSELF TO LOOK AT A BAD PICTURE LIKE THAT. IT WAS AN ILLUSTRATION FROM THE HOUND OF THE BASKERVILLS AND IT SHOWED A MAD DOG LOPING THROUGH THE NIGHT WITH HIS EYES ROLLED BACK SO MOSTLY THE WHITE OF THE EYEBALLS WAS SHOWING AND HIS FANGS GLISTENING IN THE MOONLIGHT AND NOW HE REMEMBERED THE DARK LANE OF HOURS BEFORE THE FOGGY NIGHT AIR TORN BY THE BLOODCURDLING BARK OF THE DOG AND THEN THE WORDS THE EXACT SAME WORDS THAT WATSON HAD HEARD WHEN HE HAD GONE DOWN TO PINCHIN LANE IN SEARCH OF TOBY THE HALF-SPANIEL. THERE'S SOMETHING DEEP WITHIN HIM SHUDDERED AND J.R. FELT HAIR ON THE OF HIS NECK STAND UP. THERE HAD BEEN A MURDER . . . OF COURSE! HOW COULD HAVE FORGOTTEN THAT? IN THE SIGN OF THE FOUR A TWIN HAD BEEN MURDERED AND IT WAS "BARTHOLOMEW SHOLTO" THE TWIN BROTHER OF THADDEUS SHOLTO. J.R. TURNED ABRUPTLY AND WENT BACK TO LIBERTY AND ZANNY'S ROOM. ZANNY WAS NOT IN BED YET BUT TALKING IN THE LIVINGROOM WITH MOM AND DAD. LIBERTY WAS SITTING UP IN BED WITH A PEN AND PAPER WRITING A LETTER TO HER OLD FRIEND MURIEL BRAVERMA WHO LIVED BACK IN WASHINGTON DC. "IT WAS REAL" SHE SAID BEFORE J.R.COULD EVEN ASK THE QUESTION. "I THOUGHT I GUESS I KINDA OF HOPED IT MIGHT HAVE BEEN A DREAM." "NO" SAID LIBERTY IT'S NOT A DREAM WE WERE THERE ON PINCHIN LANE." THE LANE WAS REAL, THE DOG WAS REAL AND THE WORDS I LOOKED THEM UP IN THE SIGN OF FOUR AND THEY WERE EXACTLY

THE SAME. "YOU KNOW" J.R. SAID, "THE MAN FROM THE BIG WINDOW SAID "WIPER FOR VIPER" JUST LIKE IN THE STORYBOOK J.R. SAID. "YES" WHISPERED LIBERTY AND SHE TOUCHED HER FACE LIGHTLY WHERE THE SCRAWL OF THE DOG'S SPITTLE HAD MARKED HER CHEEK.

CHAPTER 9

A BIG GATHERING OF SHADOWS.

IT SEEMS AS IF THERE IS A SHADOW J.R. TELAFLASHED. LIKE THE ELM LEAVES BACK IN WASHINGTON COOL AND NICE LIBERTY REPLIED. YES BUT THERE'S NO ELM TREE OR ANY TREE IN SIGHT. HOW DO YOU EXPLAIN IT? I DON'T KNOW IT'S A FEELING AND YOU CAN ALWAYS EXPLAIN FEELINGS. I WONDER IF WE'LL FEEL IT TONIGHT WHEN IT GETS VERY DARK?

IT WAS MOVING DAY AND THERE WAS LUGGAGE AND BOXES AND RECENTLY BOUGHT FURNITURE WERE BEING CARRIED INTO THE NEW HOUSE UP IN DEVONSHIRE MEWS. J.R. AND LIBERTY WERE COMMNUICATING TELEPATHICALLY BECAUSE THE MOVERS WERE ALL OVER THE PLACE AND THE REALTOR FROM THE COMPANY THAT RENTED THE HOUSE TO THEM WAS THERE AS WELL AND SO THERE WAS NO WAY THE TWINS COULD SPEAK OUT LOUD ABOUT THE STRANGE SENSATIONS THEY BEEN EXPERIENCING EVER SINCE THEY HAD ENTERED THE HOUSE THAT MORNING.

"ODD PLACE FOR A BELL ROPE" SAID ONE OF THE MOVERS A BURLY MAN ALMOST BOLD HAD PAUSED TO LOOK AT THE THICK ROPE THAT HUNG DOWN ONE WALL OF THE GARDEN ROOM WHERE THEY WERE NOW STANDING.

"OH I BELIEVE ACTUALLY" SAID MR. MOONPENNY THE MAN FROM THE REAL ESTATE OFFICE "THAT THE KITCHEN IN FORMER TIMES WAS UPSTAIRS AND WERE WE NOW

STANDING WAS THE TERRACE GARDEN BEFORE THEY ENCLOSED IT THAT IS. IF THEY TOOK TEA OUT HERE IT WOULD MAKE SENSE TO HAVE A BELL ROPE TO SUMMON THE MAID SERVANTS." "PERFECT SENSE" SAID THE BURLY MOVER. BOTH MEN LOOKED AT J.R. AND LIBERTY WHO ALSO NODDED AUTOMATICALLY JUST TO BE POLITE. PERFECT SENSE J.R. TELAFLASHED. YES OF COURSE I SUMMON MY MAID SERVANTS WHEN I'M IN THE GARDEN TAKING TEA SAID LIBERTY AS SHE SMILED. "YES OF COURSE" THE THREE WORDS HAD ECHOED AND LIBERTY AND J.R.'S EYES FEW OPEN. NEITHER ONE OF THE OLDER TWINS TELAFLASHED THOSE LAST THERE WORDS. THE OTHER VOICE TELAFLASHED IN UNISON J.R. SAID.

"HOW ARE THE PLANTS?" MOM ASKED J.R. COMING INTO THE GARDEN ROOM. "SHOW ME WHAT YOU PICKED OUT." MOM HAD GIVEN THE TWINS THE FUN JOB OF BUYING PLANTS AND NOW EMPTY THE GARDEN ROOM APPEARED TO BE BUILT ALMOST ENTIRELY OF SUNLIGHT, GLASS AND PALE ROSY BRICK. IT WAS A LOVELY BRIGHT SPACE MOM SAID. IN SUCH A SPACE J.R. AND LIBERTY FELT EXCEEDINGLY ODD THINKING OF SHADOWS BUT DESPITE FRESHLY PAINTED WALLS AND ABUNDANT OF SUNLIGHT THE SHADOWS TRAILED THEM THROUGHOUT THIS HOUSE IN THE MEWS. YET LIBERTY AND J.R. WERE THE ONLY ONES WHO COULD SEE OR FEEL THEM. THERE WAS NOTHING SCARY, HEAVY OR DEPRESSING ABOUT THESE SHADOWS BUT NEVERTHELESS THE OLDER TWINS FELT A TINGE OF SADNESS ABOUT THE PLACE.

THEY WERE NOT SORRY THEY HAD CAME HOWEVER, LIBERTY AND J.R. FELT ABSOUTELY AT HOME IN THIS HOUSE THAT WAS AT THE TOP OF DEVONSHIRE MEWS. IT FELT PERFECTLY RIGHT AND THE SHADOWS DISPITE THE TINGE OF SADNESS REMINDED THEM OF THE COOL SHADE OF THE ELM TREE BACK ON 58TH STREET. PERHAPS IF THE SHADOWS COULD HAVE BEEN EXPLAINED THEIR OWN FEELINGS WOULD BECOME CLEARER. BOTH SENSED THAT

THEY HAD BEEN BROUGHT HERE TO THIS HOUSE FOR SOME REASON. THE GARDEN ROOM WAS PARTICULARLY NICE SAID MOLLY. AMONG THE PLANTS THE TWINS HAVE CHOSEN WAS A WHITE JASMAINE GUARANTEED ACCORDING TO THE LADY AT THE FLOWER SHOP TO CLIMB A WALL, SPRAWL AND SPREAD IT'S WONDERFUL SWEET FRAGRANCE THROUGHOUT A ROOM. IT ALREADY HAD SEVERAL RUNNERS TWO OR THREE FEET LONG AND THE TWINS PLANNED TO THREAD IT THROUGH THE PALE GREEN LATTICE TRELLISES THAT ARCHED AGAINST THE NORTH SIDE OF WALL IN THE GARDEN ROOM. THEY IMAGINED A WALL OF WHITE BLOSSOMS HANGING FROM THE TRELLIS.

ON THE OPPOSITE SIDE OF THE TRELLIS AT THE OTHER END OF THE GARDEN ROOM THE WALL CURVED INTO AN ACLOVE AND THE FLOOR IN THE ALCOVE DROPPED AWAY TO A SMALL TILED POOL. CHARLY AND MOLLY WERE BUSILY SCRUBBING IT OUT BECAUSE THEY PLANNED TO FILL IT WITH WATER BECAUSE ZANNY HAD PROMISED TO TAKE THEM TO BUY FISH AND PERHAPS EVEN A WATER LILY OR TWO BECAUSE THE LADY AT THE FLOWER SHOP HAD SAID SHE COULD GET SOME. THE LOVELIEST PART OF THE GARDEN ROOM WAS THE CEILING. ALL AROUND THE EDGES OF THE CEILING SOMEONE HAD PAINTED GARLANDS OF CLIMBING ROSES AND IVY ON IT.

MOM CAME THROUGH THE GARDEN ROOM AGAIN BUT THIS TIME SHE WAS FOLLOWED BY DAD'S SECRETARY MRS. RHODES FROM THE EMBASSY. THEY WERE CARRYING WICKER FURNITURE. "LOOK WHAT WE FOUND AT THE DISCOUNT DEPARTMENT STORE AT THE MALL SAID J.R.'S MOM." NOW WHAT DO YOU CALL THAT AGAIN? SAID J.R.'S MOM. "LUCILLE" SAID MRS. RHODES DAD'S SECRETARY AS SHE TURNED TOWARD THE WOMEN. "A JUNK SALE" SAID MOLLY AND CHARLY. "YES A JUNK SALE" IT'S THE SAME AS A BIG RUMMAGE SALE J.R. SAID. THEY'RE HAVING ONE DOWN AT THE CHURCH DOWN ON THE CORNER AND WE FOUND

THESE TWO WICKER ROCKERS AND A LOVELY TABLE TO MATCH BUT THE TABLE ISN'T IN AS GOOD SHAPE BUT WE'LL PUT A TABLECLOTH ON TOP OF IT WITH A LONG SKIRT AND THE HANDYMAN AT THE EMBASSY CAN CUT US A PIECE OF GLASS FOR THE TOP J.R.'S MOTHER SAID. MADELINE J.R.'S MOTHER PUT DOWN THE CHAIR THAT SHE WAS CARRING AND TURNED AROUND. "OOOH LOOK! BLEEDING HEARTS" J.R.'S MOTHER SAID SPYING THREE SMALL POTS THAT WERE ON THE LONG WINDOWCELL.

THE PINK HEART-SHAPED BLOSSOMS HAD DARK RED CENTERS THAT SEEMED TO DRIP LIKE BLOOD AND DISPITE THE SIMILARITY TO A WONDERFUL HEART THEY WERE RATHER HAPPY LOOKING FLOWERS. "THEY WILL LOOK SO NICE ON THE TABLE ESPECIALLY WITH A PINK TABLECLOTH! OH THIS ROOM IS GOING TO BE JUST LOVELY." MADELINE J.R.'S MOTHER CLASPED HER SOFT HANDS TOGETHER AND SMILED AS SHE SAID "WARM ALL WINTER WITH THE SOUTHERN EXPOSURE AND THE HEAT FROM THE KITCHEN AND I'LL BET YOU'LL BE ABLE TO EAT OUT HERE." CHARLY AND MOLLY YOU'RE DOING SUCH A GOOD JOB ON THE FISH POND THAT IT WILL BE A VISION OF SUNLIGHT WITH GOLDFISH AND BLEEDING HEARTS SHOOTING THROUGH WITH THE SENT OF JASMINE FLOWERS AND LILYS TO MAKE THE GARDEN ROOM SMELLS NICE.

DON'T FORGET ABOUT THE SHADOWS! SAID J.R. AND LIBERTY. THE TWO WORDS WERE NOT SPOKEN BUT THEY TELAFLASHED DARKLY THROUGH THE SUNLIT ROOM. THAT EVENING SHADOWS BEGAN TO GATHER AND HAD DARKEN AT DINNER TIME AND BY BED TIME THEY WERE INDEED A PRESENCE BUT ONLY TO J.R. AND LIBERTY. NO ONE ELSE SEEMED AWARE BUT STILL THEY WERE NOT THREATENING OR FRIGHTENING IN ANY WAY AND ALTHOUGH THEY WERE THICK AND DEEP THEY WERE NEVER OPPRESSIVE.

LIBERTY AND J.R. SLEPT IN THE ATTIC BECAUSE IT WAS REALLY ONE BIG ROOM PARTIALLY DIVIDED BY STORAGE

UNIT WITH DRAWERS AND LITTLE SHELVES FOR THEM TO PUT THEIR STUFF ON. THE UNIT CAME OUT HALF WAY ACROSS THE FLOOR FROM ONE WALL AND THEIR WAS A BED ON EITHER SIDE OF THIS PARTITION UNIT. THE CHILDREN COULD SEE OVER THE UNIT AND BOTH SIDES OF THE SHELVES AND THE DRAWERS COULD BE OPENED FROM EITHER LIBERTY'S OR J.R.'S SIDE OF THE BEDROOM. COMING OUT FROM THE WALL OPPOSITE OF THE UNIT WAS A TALL BOOKCASE BUT IN THE MIDDLE OF THE BOOKCASE SOME SHELVES HAD BEEN REPLACED BY A BIG LARGE DESKTOP. THIS DESKTOP COULD BE SHARED BY SIMPLY DRAWING UP A CHAIR FROM EITHER SIDE OF THE BEDROOM.

IT WAS A WONDERFUL ROOM AND NOW J.R. AND LIBERTY WERE FINISHING OFF THEIR QUARTERS DOING THE ONE THING THAT THE ARCHITECTS HAD NOT DONE WHICH WAS TO DIVIDE THE DESK SO THAT TWO PEOPLE'S MESSES WOULDN'T GET MIXED-UP. J.R. PUT A PIECE OF MASKING TAPE DOWN THE CENTER OF THE DESK THEN THEY SAT FACING EACH OTHER ACROSS THE MASKING-TAPE LINE. BOTH TWINS COULD FEEL THE SHADOWS IN THE UPPER CORNERS OF THE ATTIC. LIBERTY STARED AT THE MASKING TAPE LINE AND IT LOOKED DULL AGAINST THE LIGHT WOOD OF THE DESK. "I'VE GOT AN IDEA" LIBERTY SAID SUDDENLY. SO SHE WENT TO A CARTON FILLED WITH HER JUNK AND SAID "I KNOW I PUT THEM HERE SOMEPLACE I JUST KNOW IT." "WHAT?" "AH HA! HERE THEY ARE SHE SAID." SHE DREW OUT A BAG OF M&M'S AND BROUGHT THEM BACK TO THE DESK AND THEN SHE TORE OPEN THE BAG OF M&M'S AND SAID "WE NEED A LITTLE COLOR HERE." SO SHE BEGAN LINING UP THE M&M'S ALONG THE MASKING TAPE LINE. "GOOD IDEA" SAID J.R. AS HE STARTED TO HELP HER. LIBERTY SAID TO J.R. THESE ARE A NEW KIND OF SPECKLED BRAND OF M&M'S.

THE THOUGHT SLITHERED THROUGH THE AIR OF THE ATTIC ROOM WITH ALL THE SERPENTINE GRACE OF THE DEADLY SWAMP ADDER IN "THE ADVENTURE OF

THE SPECKLED BAND." BOTH TWINS NOW RECALL THE FRIGHTENING SHERLOCK HOLMES STORY IN WHICH A WRATHFUL MAN KILLED ONE OF HIS STEPDAUGHTERS BY TRAINING A DEADLY SNAKE TO CRAWL THROUGH A VENTILATOR AND DOWN A BELL ROPE THAT HUNG OVER HER BED. THE GIRL HAD DIED A HORRIBLE DEATH WHILE CRYING OUT WITH HER LAST BREATH "IT WAS THE BAND! THE SPECKLED BAND!" NO ONE HAD KNOWN WHAT SHE HAD MEANT UNTILL OF COURSE SHERLOCK HOLMES HAD ARRIVED AND HAD DISCOVERED THAT THE SPECKLED BAND WAS A VENOMOUS SNAKE.

DO YOU REMEMBER THAT BELL ROPE DOWNSTAIRS IN THE GARDEN ROOM THE ONE THE MAN SAID WAS IN AN ODD PLACE FOR A BELL ROPE? LIBERTY HAD TELAFLASHED TO HER BROTHER J.R.

"YEAH BUT J.R.'S THOUGHTS DWINDLED OFF BUT IT SEEMED WEIRD NOW THAT THEY HAD JUST HOURS BEFORE MADE JOKES ABOUT THAT ROPE. AT THE TIME HE HADN'T EVEN THOUGHT OF "THE ADVENTURE OF THE SPECKLED BAND." ARE YOU SCARED? NO NOT REALLY SCARED LIBERTY SAID AS SHE PUT A BIG YELLOW M&M ON THE MASKING TAPE. IT'S NOTHING LIKE THE WAY I FELT WHEN WE WERE ON PINCHIN LANE BUT THERE IS SOMETHING HAPPENING HERE SAID LIBERTY. DON'T YOU FEEL WE'RE CLOSE TO THE CENTER OF IT? THOSE FUNNY ECHOES AND THAT OTHER VOICE BUT I'M NOT REALLY HEARING IT RIGHT NOW. MAYBE WE'RE TOO CLOSE LIBERTY SAID TO J.R. "WHAT DO YOU MEAN TOO CLOSE?" J.R. SAID. MAYBE WE'RE AT THE THE VERY SOURCE OF THE ECHOE AND WHERE IT COMES FROM. SO MAYBE IT'S NOT JUST AN ECHO NOW, MAYBE THIS IS IT AND WE'LL HEAR THE FIRST ORIGINAL SOUND IF WE LISTEN CAREFULLY SAID LIBERTY. LIBERTY PAUSED FOR A MOMENT IN HER THOUGHTS. DON'T YOU WONDER WHY WE WERE BROUGHT HERE? YES I SAID BROUGHT J.R. SAID LIBERTY. WE WERE BROUGHT WEREN'T WE? IT WASN'T LIKE WE JUST CAME HERE.

NO NOT AT ALL WE WERE SUMMONED JUST LIKE THE SERVANTS WERE WITH THE BELL ROPE BUT THEY WERE EITHER CALLED, CONVENED, SINGNALED. A FLOCK OF SYNONYMS BESAT ON SILENT WINGS THROUGH THE AIR AND CONFIRMING ONE SIMPLE THING. THE CHILDREN WERE NOT HERE BY ACCIDENT BUT BY DESIGN. THIS VERY ROOM SEEMED IN SOME PECULIAR WAY TO BE AT THE CENTER OF MYSTERIOUS EVENTS THAT REACHED FURTHER BACK THAN JUST PINCHIN LANE BUT PERHAPS TO WHEN THEY HAD FIRST BEGUN TO HEAR THOSE STRANGE ECHOES BOUNCING THROUGH THEIR TELEPATHIC CHANNELS ALL THE WAY BACK IN WASHINGTON. NOTHING APPEARED TO BE AN ACCIDENT OR A COINCIDENCE NOW EVERYTHING HAPPENED ON PURPOSE. WHAT WAS THE EXACT PURPOSE OR DESIGN WAS THERE THEY COULD NOT BE SURE BUT THAT WAS THEIR DESTINY TO FIND AND DISCOVER IT'S MEANING AND TO LIGHTEN THE SHADOWS AND OF THIS THEY HAD NO DOUBT.

OUTSIDE THE TWO DORMER WINDOWS IN THE GABLES OF THE ATTIC THE SOFT GLOW OF THE STREETLIGHT BURNISHED THE COPPER TUB AND THE NASTURTIUMS DANCED IN THE WIND LIKE LICKS OF FLAMS CASTING QUICK SHADOWS ON THE PAVING STONES. REAL SHADOWS MIXED WITH LOTS OF PHANTOM UNTILL THEY BECAME INDISTINGUISHABLE FROM ONE ANOTHER AND OVER FILLED THE COPPER TUB. ALL OF THESE SHADOWS GATHERED ABOUT LIBERTY AND J.R. AS THEY CLIMBED INTO THEIR BEDS THAT NIGHT. A SLIVER OF A NEW MOON HUNG IN ONE OF THE WINDOWPANES. THEY WERE GLAD TO HAVE REAL WALLS BETWEEN THEM AND THEIR ENDS OF THE ATTIC ROOM. THE SHADOWS AS WELL AS THE MOONLIGHT AND STARLIGHT COULD BE SHARED AND COULD FLOW BETWEEN THEM FROM ONE END OF THE ATTIC TO THE OTHER. J.R. AND LIBERTY COULD EACH BE ALONE AND YET THIS CORD OF SILVER LIGHT AND DANCING SHADOWS CONNECTED THEM WHENEVER THEY WANTED.

THEY WERE BOTH GROWING SLEEPY EACH TWIN WITH SEPARATE THOUGHTS NOW. LIBERTY WAS THINKING OF WHY THE DARKNESS DIDN'T SCARE HER AND THE OPPOSITE OF LIGHT WASN'T AFTER ALL DARKNESS. WEREN'T THEY IN ONE SENSE BOTH PART OF SOMETHING ELSE AND BOTH PART OF THE VERY SAME THING? NOT JUST THE EARTH AND THE FACT THAT WHEN IT WASN'T NIGHT IN ONE PLACE BUT DAY IN ANOTHER. WASN'T THERE MORE TO IT THAN THAT? DIDN'T IT GO BEYOND JUST THE EARTH? DAY AND NIGHT LIGHTNESS AND DARKNESS WASN'T IT ALL LIKE KIND OF SKIN OF THE BIG UNIVERSE? IT WAS ONE SKIN. THAT WAS IT BUT COULD THERE BE OTHER UNIVERSES? LIBERTY YAWNED AS SHE FINALLY FELL ASLEEP.

J.R.'S BRAIN MEANWHILE HAD BEEN SWIRLING WITH WORDS, FRAGMENTS OF SENTENCES AND PARAGRAPHS FROM SHERLOCK HOLMES STORIES THAT HE HAD READ. THE TERRIBLE VOICE ON PINCHIN LANE HAD DISSOLVED INTO THE NIGHT BUT OTHER PARTS OF THE STORIES LOOMED IN HIS MIND LIKE SHADES OF BRIGHT LIGHT THESE STORY FRAGMENTS WOULD FIERCELY BLAST THROUGH AND THEN BE SWALLOWED BY THE DARKNESS BUT ONE STORY IN PARTICULAR THREADED IT'S WORDS THROUGH THE ATTIC AT NIGHT AND IT WAS "THE SPECKLED BAND." J.R. COULD HEAR HOLMES'S VOICE NOW AND THE WORDS HE MUTTERED IN THE STORY: "WHERE DOES THAT RINGING BELL COMMUNICATE WITH? SHERLOCK WAS SPEAKING ABOUT THE BELL ROPE THAT HUNG BY THE VENTILATOR IN THE CHAMBER OF THE MURDERED YOUNG WOMAN. HE HAD CONTINUED "WHAT A FOOL A BUILDER MUST BE TO OPEN A VENTILATOR INTO ANOTHER ROOM WHEN WITH THE SAME TROUBLE HE MIGHT HAVE COMMUNICATED WITH THE OUTSIDE AIR ! "DUMMY BELL-ROPES AND VENTILATORS WHICH DO NOT VENTILATE HOLMES WONDERED TO HIMSELF OUT LOUD." WHOLE PIECES OF CONVERSATION FROM THE STORY CAME BACK TO J.R. NOW LIKE A DISTANT ECHO BUT AS CLEARLY AS IF THE BOOK WAS RIGHT HERE IN FRONT OF HIS EYES.

"I HAVE ALWAYS HEARD A LOW CLEAR WHISTEL IN THE MORNING." THESE WERE THE WORDS OF JULIA STONER THE MURDERED SISTER A FEW NIGHTS BEFORE HER DEATH. "I CAN'T TELL WHERE IT CAME FROM PERHAPS THE NEXT ROOM MAYBE." "I COULDN'T SLEEP THAT NIGHT BECAUSE "HELEN STONER JULIA'S SISTER HAD TOLD SHERLOCK HOLMES A VAGUE FEELING OF IMPENDING MISFORTUNE IMPRESSED ME." THEN A SCREAM TORE J.R.'S SLEEP AND HE WOKE STARTLED BUT HE HAD BEEN THE ONLY ONE TO HEAR IT LIKE THE LOW CLEAR WHISTLE THAT ONLY THE MURDERED SISTER HAD HEARD FOR SEVERAL NIGHTS BEFORE HER DEATH? ON THE SIDE OF THE PARTITION LIBERTY SLEPT ON AND DREAMING OF THE SKIN OF THE NIGHT AND IMAGINING OTHER UNIVERSES BUT THERE HAD BEEN A SCREAM SILENT BUT NEVERTHELESS A SCREAM AND IT STILL HUNG IN THE AIR.

CHAPTER 10

THE MAN WITH THE LISP AT THE TOWER OF LONDON.

"I REALLY DO FIND THE SILVER SHARKS KIND OF SCARY" ZANNY SAID. THEY WERE IN A PET STORE AND MADELINE J.R. AND LIBERTY'S MOTHER HAD LEFT THAT MORNING ON A FLIGHT BACK TO WASHINGTON D.C. AND ZANNY HAD PLANNED A DAY FULL OF FUN THINGS TO CHEER THE KIDS UP SINCE THEY WOULDN'T BE SEEING THEIR MOTHER FOR SEVERAL WEEKS UNTILL SHE GETS BACK FROM HER TRIP. THE FIRST STOP OF THE DAY WAS THE PET STORE ON WIGMORE STREET THAT SPECIALIZED IN EXOTIC FISH.

THE SPOTTED FISH AND STRIPERS DON'T REALLY GET ALONG WITH EACH OTHER SAID HEATHER THE LADY WHO OWNED THE PET STORE. YES MADAM SIAD ZANNY I'LL KEEP THAT IN MIND THANKS. "DID YOU HEAR THAT MOLLY AND CHARLY?" ZANNY ASKED THE TWINS. THEY WERE MESMERIZED BY THE MINIATURE PREDATORS SLICING THEIR WAY THROUGH THE WATER IN THE TANK.

"GUPPIES ARE ALWAYS GOOD" LIBERTY OFFERED. "AH BUT DIDN'T YOU SAY YOU HAD A RATHER LARGE POOND IN YOUR GARDEN ROOM?" THE LADY ASKED. "YES" REPLIED ZANNY. "I THINK IT'S ABOUT THIS WIDE AND THIS DEEP ZANNY SAID AS SHE SHOWED THE LADY WITH HER HANDS. THE LADY SAID "WELL THEN THESE FISH THE SPOTTED GOLDS AND THE STRIPERS FISH WOULD SPLENDIDLY."

LIBERTY LOVED THE WAY THE ENGLISH USED THE WORD "SPLENDID." IT WAS SUCH A TRULY GLITTERING WORD AND FIT CERTAIN THINGS SO NICELY LIKE THESE BRIGHT GOLD FISH FOR EXAMPLE. "YES" THE LADY CONTINUED, "I SHOULD THINK THESE FISH MIGHT GROW TO QUITE AN IMPRESSIVE SIZE GIVEN THE DIMENSIONS OF YOUR POOL."

CHARLY LOOKED UP FROM UNDER HER COONSKIN CAP AND SAID "LOOKS JUST LIKE JAWS?" CHARLY SAID AS SHE SMILED. "OH DEAR I SHOULD HOPE NOT!" THE PET STORE OWNER SAID. "NOW WHERE DID YOU TWO GET THOSE INTERESTING HATS? AND "WHAT DO YOU CALL THEM?" WE GOT THEM FROM ARE FATHER AND THEIR CALLED "DAVY CROCKETT CAPS." "DAVY CROCKETT?" "HE WAS A FRONTIER GUY" MOLLY SAID AND "HE DIED AT THE ALAMO" HER BROTHER J.R. ADDED. "OH SAID THE HEATHER THE OWNER OF THE PET STORE AND THEN SHE CHANGED THE SUBJECT. "SO WILL IT BE THE SPOTTED GOLDS AND THE STRIPERS?" ASKED THE OWNER OF THE PET STORE. "YES TWO OF EACH PLEASE SIAD ZANNY AND THE TWINS HAD AGREED WITH HER." SO THE OWNER OF THE PET SHOP PUT THE FOUR FISH IN A CLEAR BAG AND GAVE IT TO ZANNY TO HOLD. THEY THEN TOOK THEM BACK TO THE HOUSE IN THE MEWS AND ON THEIR WAY THEY CHECKED IN WITH THE LADY AT THE FLORISTS BECAUSE SHE HAD SET ASIDE TWO BEAUTIFUL PALE PINK WATER LILIES FOR THEM SO SHE SCOOPED THEM UP ROOTS AND ALL AND PUT THEM IN A BAG OF WATER.

THE WATER IN THE POOL WAS JUST THE RIGHT TEMPERATURE AND THEY PUT THE FISH AND LILIES IN AS SOON AS THEY GOT HOME. THERE WERE GREAT ARGUMENTS ABOUT WHAT TO NAME THE FISH BUT NAMES WERE FINALLY SETTLED ON. THEY WERE CHARLY'S AND MOLLY'S CHOICES AND SO THEY NAMED THE FOUR FISH, DAVY, MADELINE, BARBIE AND KEN.

"I THINK IT'S WEIRD NAMING A FISH AFTER MOM" LIBERTY SAID BUT SHE WASN'T PREPARED TO ARGUE ABOUT it because they were eager to get to the next stop of the day which was the Tower of London and parts of Britain. "Many places in Britain seem to attract ghosts of all sizes and shapes but the greatest number of spooks undoubtedly reside in the Tower of London Zanny said as she was reading form a guidebook as the children were standing on a ramp that was going down towards the Tower of London and so the ran down the ram as Zanny was still reading from the guidebook "There's no telling what you might find in the dark passageways and silent rooms of the Tower but it's said that you might run into anyone or anything from regiments of long-dead soldiers to Anne Boyleyn herself." The Tower was not to the children'd surprise a single simple tower but a fortress. So Zanny had given them a list illustrated with small drawings of heads that she had traced of all the famous people who had been held prisoner and had been beheaded in the Tower of London. A special tour had been arranged for them through the American Embassy and not two minutes after they had given their names at the gate a man approached them.

He was wearing a broad-brimmed black hat full with a bunch of embroidery and puff-ball shoulders and he also had a scarlet jacket that was a deep crown color with red decorations. The britches he wore stopped at the knees and were met by hose or tights. Clanking with swords and medallions he cut a striking figure as a Yeoman Warder or a Beefeater as the guards of the Tower were more popularly known.

"The Ragozzino party!" he exclaimed heartily. Never was there a man who could talk more cheerfully and crack more jokes about the

BEHEADINGS AND THE GRIM DOINGS THAT HAD OCCURRED IN A PREVIOUS AGE AT THE TOWER OF LONDON. YEOMAN JACK BEGAN THE TOUR BY LEADING THEM UP TO A DISPLAY OF WEAPONRY AND THE TORTURE EQUIPMENT IN ONE OF THE TOWER'S GALLERIES. THEY THEN POCEEDED TO TOWER GREEN. CHEERFULLY HE TICKED OFF THE NAMES OF THE MOST FAMOUS VICTIMS TO LOSE THEIR HEAD THERE ON TOWER GREEN. OF COURSE FAMOUS ONES ONLY ANNE BOLEYN WAS EXECUTED WITH A SWORD BUT THE REST HAD BEEN KILLED WITH AN AX. THE TWINS SCRUNCHED UP THEIR SHOULDERS AS THEY IMAGINED BIG BEHEADINGS.

GRUESOME THOUGHTS CRACKLED BETWEEN THEM AS THEY WONDERED ABOUT HAVING THEIR HEADS CHOPPED OFF. WHICH WOULD FEEL BETTER AN SWORD OR AN AX? AN AX WOULD BE HEAVIER BUT MAYBE IT WOULD MAKE IT QUICKER. HOW ABOUT A BUTTER KNIFE? MOLLY TELAFLASHED TO HER SISTER CHARLY. NEARBY ANOTHER BEEFEATERS HAD NOW THEY REACHED THE PART OF THE STORY WHERE THEY WERE TELLING ABOUT THE BEHEADING OF MARY QUEEN OF SCOTS. JACK SIAD "AND THE SCOTTISH QUEEN WENT COMPOSED AND WELL DREESS TO HER DEATH. SHE WORE HER LOVELY AUBURN HAIR PILED HIGH IN THE STYLE OF THE DAY BUT WOULD YOU BLEIEVE IT AFTER THE AX FELL THE HEAD OF THE QUEEN OF SCOTS HAD ROLLED AND THE EXECUTIONER WENT TO PICK IT UP" BUT HE PAUSED VERY DRAMATICALLY AND HELD HIS HAND IN THE AIR AS IF HOLDING AN

IMAGINARY HEAD. THEN HE CONTINUED "WELL MY GOODNESS! THE HAIR CAME OFF IN HIS HANDS. FOR THE QUEEN WAS NEARLY BALD EXCEPT FOR A FEW STRANDS OF DULL GRAY HAIR ON HER RATHER SMALL HEAD." THE CHILDREN AND ZANNY ALL GASPED WHEN THEY SAW THAT.

THE OTHER BEEFEATER WAS JUST ABOUT AT THE SAME POINT IN THE STORY BECAUSE HE HAD A SLIGHT LISP AND

TO J.R. AND LIBERTY THE VOICE HAD A VAGUELY FAMILIAR QUALITY AND VEN THE OTHE BEEFEATER CONTINUED "THE EXECUTIONER WENT TO PICK UP THE HEAD AND A CHILL RAN THROUGH

BOTH THE TWINS BUT BY SURPRISE IT WAS A WIG!" THEIR BLOOD WENT COLD AND THE AIR FILLED WITH STATIC. LIBERTY WAS LOSING HIM AGAIN AND SHE KNEW IT. SHE HAD BEEN CONCENTRATING SO HARD ON J.R. THAT SHE HAD NOT NOTICED THAT THE LISPING BEEFEATER WAS APPROACHING THE TWO OLDER TWINS MOLLY AND CHARLY. LIBERTY STOOD TRANSFIXED BECAUSE SHE COULD HEAR TINY CRACKLINGS. THE LITTLE TWINS WERE TRYING COMMUNICATION BUT IT WAS BREAKING UP TOO AND IT WAS DWINDLING OFF INTO THE DIMMEST FLICKERINGS AND ALL SHE COULD THINK OF WAS DYING FIREFLIES ON A SUMMER NIGHT JUST LIKE THE ONES MOLLY AND CHARLY ALWAYS KEPT IN THEIR JARS TOO LONG BUT EXCEPT NOW IT WAS THEIR TURN TO FLICKER OUT.

AS IF IN SLOW MOTION THE BEEFEATER PLUCKED CHARLY'S AND MOLLY'S COONSKIN CAPS OFF THEIR HEADS AND SAID "THE QUEEN OF SCOTS'S HAIR WAS RED AND THESE TWO LITTLE DARLINGS!" SAID THE BEEFEATER WERE WEARING COONSKIN CAPS.!" THE WORDS CURDLED IN THE AIR AND EVERYTHING WAS STATIC. LIBERTY FELT HERSELF HELPLESSLY BEING DRAWN TO THE EDGE OF THAT DREADFUL ABYSS AGAIN. SHE COULDN'T BEAR THAT FEELING OF ONCOMING SEPARATENESS THAT SHE COULDN'T CROSS OVER AGAIN. SHE GASSPED WEAKLY AND FAINTED.

YEOMAN JACK CLEARED THE AREA QUICKLY AND SAID "STAND BACK PLEASE KINDLY STAND BACK!" GIVE THE GIRL A LITTLE ROOM. MOVE YOUR GROUP ALONG SIR HE SAID TO THE OTHER BEEFEATER. THE MAN AND HIS LITTLE GROUP SEEMED TO VANISH IN A FLASH. "WHO THE DEVIL IS THAT BLOKE?" YEOMAN JACK MUTTERED TO HIMSELF. ZANNY

AND THE OTHER CHILDREN WERE ALL ON THEIR KNEES CLUSTERED AROUND LIBERTY. "IS SHE DEAD?" WAILED MOLLY. "OF COURSE I'M NOT DEAD" LIBERTY SAID AS HER EYES FLEW OPEN. "JUST A LITTLE . . . . SHE PAUSED AND SAID AGAIN "A LITTLE . . . BUT SHE COULDN'T FIND THE WORDS TO SAY WHAT SHE WANTED TO SAY SO JACK HELPED HER TO HER FEET.

"I'M NOT SURE WHAT HAPPENED." SHE BLINKED AT MOLLY AND CHARLY AND THEN AFTER A LITTLE BIT THEIR COONSKIN CAPS WERE FIRMLY PLANTED ON THEIR HEADS. THEY LOOK FINE SHE SAID AS SHE LOOKED AROUND FOR THE OTHER BEEFEATER BUT HE WAS NO WEAR TO BE IN SIGHT SO SHE THEN LOOKED AT J.R.

I FELT THIS TIME LIBERTY AND IT WAS TERRIBLE. THERE WAS THE STATIC AND THEN THERE WAS NOTHING. WORSE THEN NOTHING THEY WEREN'T JUST INVADING THE CHANNELS IT WAS ME! I FELT LOCKED AND I HAD TO FIGHT SO HARD YOU DON'T KNOW HOW HARD BUT I FELT MYSELF SLIPPING AWAY AND I FELT YOUR FEER. I ALSO FELT YOU STANDING THERE AT THE ABYSS AND ME NOT BEING ABLE TO HELP YOU.

J.R. DIDN'T LOOK GOOD BUT LIBERTY DOUBTED IF SHE LOOKED MUCH BETTER BECAUSE HIS SKIN WAS DEATHLY PALE AND HIS FRECKLES STOOD OUT LIKE A TERRIBLE RASH AND HIS CLEAR GRAY EYES WERE CERTAINLY NOT VACANT THIS TIME BUT FULL OF A FEAR SHE COULDN'T RECOGNIZE.

YOU MUST HAVE DONE SOMETHING J.R. BECAUSE LOOK THE CHANNELS ARE CLEAR NOW. YEAH BUT LOOK AT YOU, YOU FAINTED. YEAH BUT BUT LOOK AT YOU; YOU DON'T LOOK SO HOT YOURSELF J.R. SAID. ZANNY ACTYALLY LOOKED WORSE THEN ANY OF THEM DESPITE THE FACT THAT SHE KEPT HER VOICE EVEN IN A SMOOTH FLOW OF REASSURING WORDS.

"IT'S ALL RIGHT KIDS I'M SURE IT'S JUST A LITTLE TUMMY UPSET." PLAY IT AS A TUMMY UPSET LIBERTY. I GUESS YOU'RE RIGHT BUT I STILL THINK SHE MIGHT BE SUSPICIOUS. I MEAN THAT GUY WAS WEIRD AND SHE NOTICED IT TOO I'M SURE OF IT. "YEAH THIS ENGLISH FOOD ZANNY IT'S STARTING TO GET TO ME. DO WE REALLY HAVE TO INCLUDE IT IN THE BIG ENGLISH CURRICULUM?"

"YOU MEAN YOU'D ENJOY A MINOR LAPSE?" "YEAH RIGHT INTO MCDONALD'S. I THINK A COKE AND SOME FRIES WOULD SET ME UP JUST FINE." "OKAY BUT ARE YOU SURE YOU'RE ALRIGHT?" "YES I'M ALRIGHT IT WAS JUST LIKE YOU SAID A TUMMY UPSET." THE WORDS SOUNDED HOLLOW JACK INSISTED THEY COME BACK WITH HIM TO THE YEOMAN'S QUARTERS SO LIBERTY COULD HAVE "A BIT OF TEA."

EVERYONE WAS VERY KIND AND CONCERNED SO THEY BROUGHT THE CHILDREN SOME POP AND BISCUITS WITCH AS THE ENGLISH WOULD CALL THEM COOKIES AND BROUGHT TEA FOR ZANNY. THE TWINS FELT RATHER SMALL AND INSIGNIFICANT IN A ROOM WITH LARGE MEN DECKED OUT IN SCARLET AND EACH ON CLANKING WITH METAL AND CARRYING AT LEAST A POUND OF GOLD EMBROIDERY.

"I SAY" JACK SAID TO ONE OF THE BEEFEATER, "DO WE HAVE A NEW MAN TODAY?" BECAUSE I SAW ONE I DIDN'T RECOGNIZE." "NEW MAN?" SAID THE OTHER BEEFEATER. "LET ME THINK... AH YES I BELIEVE THERE IS A NEW BLOKE ON THIS MORNING HE'S FILLING IN FOR HARRY WHO HAS BEEN SICK THIS LAST FEW DAYS." CAN'T SAY I CARE FOR HIM ALL THAT MUCH. HE DOES LOOK A BIT DIFFERENT AND HE HAS AN ODD TWIST TO HIS SPEECH. I THINK HE CAME OVER FROM LAMBETH ROAD AREA YOU KNOW BY ST. THOMAS'S HOSPITAL I THINK. IT CAN'T BE! J.R. TELAFLASHED. THEN LIBERTY SAID IT "ST. THOMAS'S HOSPITAL?" "YES" SAID THE MAN. "DO YOU KNOW IT?" "NOT REALLY" SHE SAID AS SHE TOOK ANOTHER SWALLOW OF HER COKE."

CHAPTER 11

THE STRETCH LIMO BIRTHDAY BLAST!

WHAT IF THE CHAUFFEUR IS THE MAN FROM PINCHIN LANE THE BEEFEATER? FOR ONE SPLIT SECOND THE MOST DREADFUL THOUGHT PASSED THROUGH BOTH J.R.'S LIBERTY'S HEADS. THE CHILDREN WERE STANDING ON THE CORNER OF WIMPOLE AND DEVONSHIRE AWAITING THE BIRTHDAY LIMO. FOR INDEED THE CAR WAS TOO STRETCHED TO MAKE THEM TURN INTO THE MEWS. THEY WERE BOTH BESIDE THEMSELVES WITH EXCITEMENT.

"I SEE IT!" MOLLY SAID OUT LOUD. "IT'S COMING!" CHARLY SAID AS SHE JUMPED UP AND DOWN SHOUTING AND THAT WAS WHEN THE TERRIBLE THOUGHTS FLASHED THROUGH THE OLDER TWIN'S MIND. THE DAYS HAD SLIPPED BY RATHER QUICKLY AND THE MEMORY OF THE INCIDENT AT THE TOWER OF LONDON SEEMED TO RECEDE AS THEIR EXCITEMENT ABOUT J.R. AND LIBERTY'S UPCOMING BIRTHDAY GREW BUT NOW THE DREADFUL THOUGHT SEEM TO LASH OUT IN THE AIR AROUND THEM AS THE LONG SILVER LIMO TURNED RIGHT FROM NEW CAVENDISH STREET ONTO WIMPOLE. LIBERTY AND J.R. NEARLY COLLAPSED WITH RELIEF WHEN A LONG WOMEN WITH GLASSES AND SHORT-CROPPED BROWN HAIR JUMPED OUT. THE TWO FLAG HOLDERS ON EITHER SIDE OF THE HOOD OF THE LIMO PROUDLY FEW RED AND BLUE BALLOONS.

"J.R. BURTON RAGOZZINO AND "LIBERTY RAGOZINO THE NICE LADY SAID. "YES THAT'S US SAID LIBERTY AND

J.R." WELL HAPPY BIRTHDAYS! "I'M YOUR CHAUFFEUR KATE." SHE HELD OUT HAND AND SHOOK HANDS FIRST WITH J.R. "I UNDERSTAND THAT YOU BEAT YOUR SISTER INTO THIS WORLD BY FOUR MINUTES." SHE THEN TURNED TO LIBERTY AND SHOOK HER HAND TOO AND SAID "STEP THIS WAY PLEASE." KATE OPENED UP THE BACK REAR CURBSIDE DOOR J.R. STEPPED IN FOLLOWED BY HIS SISTER LIBERTY.

"OH WOW!" LIBERTY EXCLAIMED. THE INTERIOR OF THE LIMO HAD BEEN DECORATED WITH STREAMERS AND BALLOONS AND THERE WAS A HAPPY BIRTHDAY SIGN TOO.

"COOL." "COOL" "COOL." "COOL." THE WORD WAS UTTTERED AT LEAST TWENTY TIMES IN THE FIRST MINUTE AND HALF.

"WHERE'S THE MAKE-UP COUNTER?" CHARLY AND MOLLY IMMEDIATELY WANTED TO KNOW. THEY HAD DECIDED TO BRING THE MAKE-UP KITS AUNT HONEY HAD GIVEN THEM FOR CHRISTMAS. THE IDEA OF PUTTING ON THE LIPSTICK AND PERFUME WHILE IN A MOVING CAR WAS AN EXCITING ONE AND THAT WAS ALL THEY SEEMED TO THINK ABOUT.

LIBERTY AND J.R. DID NOT HAVE MAKE-UP ON THEIR MINDS. THEY HAD BEEN CONCERNED WITH PLANNING THE PICNIC. NOW WITH ZANNY'S HELP THEY STASHED THE FOOD IN TWO BUILT-IN REFRIGERATORS. THERE WERE SANDWICHES, COLD DRINKS, PLENTY OF JUNK FOOD SNACKS AND OF COURSE THE BIRTHDAY CAKES. THAT WAS RULE NUMBER ONE OF TWINDOM WHICH MEANS THE TWINS SHOULD NEVER HAVE TO SHARE A BIRTHDAY CAKE. MADELINE HAD READ ABOUT THIS EARLY ON WHEN SHE HAD FIRST BECOME THE MOTHR OF TWINS IN THE MAGAZINE CALLED THE TWINSEY REPORT. IF SHE HADN'T READ IT SHE MIGHT HAVE REMEMBERED FROM HER OWN

CHILDHOOD AND FAILING THAT THE TWINS WORLD HAD TOLD HER IMMEDIATELY.

THERE WASN'T ROOM IN THE LIMO'S FREEZER FOR THE ICE CREAM SO THEY DECIDED TO STOP AND GET IT IF THEY REALLY NEEDED IT. AFTER ALL IT WAS J.R. AND LIBERTY'S BIRTHDAY AND AS THE RAGOZZINO FAMILY BIRTHDAY SAYING WENT "BIRTHDAY IS BOSS DAY." THEY HAD NEVER BOTHERED TO TRANSLATE THIS FAMILY MOTTO INTO LATIN. THE LIMO TRIP WOULD WIND UP AT THE AMBASSADOR'S RESIDENCE FOR A FOURTH OF JULY PARTY AND IT WAS COMPLATE WITH FIREWORKS. "WHERE TO?" KATE ASKED FROM THE FRONT OF THE CAR AS HER VOICE CAME THROUGH OVER THE INTERCOM INTO THE BACK SEAT OF THE LIMO. THE FIRST STOP WAS THE BRITISH MUSEUM TO TAKE IN A FEW MUMMIES AND THE FAMOUS ELGIN MARBLES THAT ZANNY HAD TOLD THEM THE ENGLISH HAD STOLEN FROM THE PARTHENON OF ANCIENT GREECE. THE CREEKS HAD NEVER FORGIVEN THE ENGLISH FOR THIS THEFT.

AFTER THE MUSEUM AND BACK INTO THE LIMO THE CHILDREN BROKE OUT AN EARLY MORNING SNACK OF NOCHOS WITH SALSA AND CHEESE ON THEIR WAY TO GREENWICH THE VERY SPOT NOT FAR FROM THE CITY OF LONDON FROM WHICH ALL TIME IS MEASURED AND WHERE STANDARD TIME IS SET. "YOU'D THINK THAT THE QUEEN WOULD BE EMBARRASSED ABOUT THIS" LIBERTY SAID AS SHE WAS MUNCHING ON SOME NOCHOS.

"EMBARRASSED ABOUT WHAT?" ASKED ZANNY. "HER PEOPLE RIPPING OFF THE GREEKS." I MEAN SHE'S SO PROPER AND EVERYTHING WITH HER CROWN AND SHE'S ALWAYS WEARING THOES WHITE GLOVES IN EVERY SINGLE PICTURE OF HER." "YEAH" J.R. SAID. "YOU DON'T THINK OF HER AS BAD CRIMINAL?" "WELL INTERJECTED KATE FROM THE FRONT SEAT "YOU KNOW SHE'S REALLY JUST A

FIGUREHEAD YOU KNOW WITH NO REAL POWER AND IT HAPPENED LONG BEFORE HER REIGN."

"WHAT'S A FIGUREHEAD?" MOLLY ASKED. "YEAH AND WHAT IS AN HARBORING?" ASKED CHARLY. IT TOOK THE REST OF THE CAR TRIP TO GREENWICH TO EXPLAIN FIGUREHEAD AND HARBORING CRIMINALS TO CHARLY AND MOLLY.

FROM GREENWICH THEY WENT ON TO FOUR ANCIENT CASTLES INCLUDING ONE WITH A MAZE. A SOFT RAIN BEGAN TO FALL JUST WHEN THEY PULLED UP TO A MEADOW WHERE THEY THOUGHT THEY WOULD HAVE THEIR PICNIC BUT INSTEAD THEY FLICKED ON THE TELEVISION. THEY WATCHED ONLY FIVE MINUTES OF "GILLIGANS ISLAND" THEN IT WAS "THE BRADY BUNCH SHOW" BUT SOMEHOW THE BRADY BUNCH LOOKED REALLY STUPID SINGING AWAY WITH THEIR LITTLE FRECKLED CHEERFUL FACES AS THE CREDITS ROLLED BY. THE PROGRAM WAS STILL ON WHEN THEY FINISHED THEIR SANDWICHES AND KATE STARTED THE LIMO. "THIS WILL CLEAR OFF SOON I GUARANTEE IT" SHE SAID. "IT WILL BE FINE BY THE TIME YOU'RE READY TO EAT YOUR BIRTHDAY CAKES AND KEEP A SHARP LOOKOUT FOR THE RIGHT PLACE."

"OKAY" LIBERTY AND J.R. REPLIED. THEY SETTLED BACK IN THE VERY COMFORTABLY UPHOLSTERED SEATS AND WATCHED THE REST OF "THE BRADY BUNCH SHOW."

HOW WOULD WE LOOK IF THERE WAS A TELEVISION PROGRAM CALLED "THE RAGOZZINO BUNCH?" LIBERTY WONDERED. PEOPLE WOULD JUST THINK THEIR TV'S WERE BROKEN AND THEY WERE GETTING DOUBLE IMAGES J.R. TELAFLASHED.

CHARLY AND MOLLY HAD FOLDED OUT THE HIDEAWAY VANITY. THERE WERE COMPARTMENTS THAT SLIDED

OPEN WITH COMBS AND TISSUES AND FANCY LOTIONS. THEY FLIPPED UP A DOUBLE-SIDED MIRROR AND CHOSE THE MAGNIFIED SIDE. TAKING OUT THEIR MAKE-UP KIT'S THE TWINS BEGAN TO PUT ON LIPSTICK AND BLUSHING POWDER. THEIR HUGE TWIN IMAGES CROWDED INTO THE FRAME.

"MOVE OVER MOLLY" CHARLY SAID. "I CAN'T FIT MY EYE IN. I WANT TO PUT ON SOME OF THIS EYESHADOW." SHE WAS HOLDING A LITTLE POT OF CHARTREUSE POWDER AND WAS TRYING TO DAB SOME ON HER EYELID. SHE MISSED LEAVING A YELLOW-GREEN SMUDGE BY HER EAR INSTEAD.

"GIRLS I DON'T DO MAKE-UP WHILE WE'RE MOVING. I'M AFRAID YOU MIGHT POKE YOUR EYES OUT" ZANNY SAID. "OH ZANNY!" CHARLY SAID. "I KNOW "SAID ZANNY. "I'M INCREDIBLY BORING AND NO FUN AT ALL. SO PLEASE WAIT WITH THE EYE MAKE-UP UNTILL WE'RE STOPPED OKAY.

"HOW ABOUT PRESS-ON-NAILS?" MOLLY ASKED. THEY ALL EXCEPT FOR MOLLY AND CHARLY GROANED AT THE MENTION OF THIS. PRESS-ON FINGERNAILS HAD BEEN A SUBJECT OF MUCH CONTROVERSY SINCE BEFORE THEY EVEN LEFT FOR ENGLAND. EVERYONE EXCEPT FOR CHARLY AND HER SISTER MOLLY HATED THE NOTION OF THESE LITTLE TYKES GOING AROUND WITH FAKE FINGERNAILS THAT LOOKED LIKE MINIATURE DAGGERS. THE PRESS-ON NAILS HAD BEEN AT THE TOP OF THEIR CHRISTMAS LISTS AND BIRTHDAY LISTS SINCE THEY WERE FOUR YEARS OLD AND AUNT HONEY HAD ALWAYS OBLIGED THEM. BOTH J.R. AND LIBERTY HAD TRIED THERE BEST TO HUMILIATE THE LITTLE TWINS BY SAYING THAT MARY AND LAURA INGALLS IN "LITTLE HOSUE ON THE PRAIRIE" WOULD HAVE NEVER WORN PRESS-ON NAILS BUT THE TWINS DID AN END RUN AROUND THAT BIG ARGUMENT. "THEY WEREN'T INVENTED THEN AND IF THEY HAD BEEN THEY WOULD HAVE WANTED

THEM!" IT WAS DIFFICULT TO ARGUE WITH THAT LIBERTY AND J.R. SAID.

"OHAYA" SIGHED ZANNY. "YOU CAN PUT THEM ON BUT REMEMBER TO TAKE THEM OFF BEFORE WE GO TO THE PARTY THIS EVENING AT THE AMBASSADOR'S HOUSE."

WHAT DOES THE AMBASSADOR KNOW ABOUT MARY AND LAURA ANYHOW? MOLLY TELAFLASHED. YEAH I BET MR. AND MRS AMBASSADOR WOULD LIKE PRESS-ON.... UH! OH CHARLY AGAIN TRIED TELAFLASH THE WORD "PRESS-ON NAILS" BUT THE STRANGE STATIC WAS HAPPENING AGAIN AND THE TINY CRACKLINGS LIKE THE ONES THAT HAD FILLED THE AIR JUST BEFORE LIBERTY HAD FAINTED AT THE TOWER OF LONDON. THE LITTLE TWINS WEREN'T DISTURBED BY THE STATIC BECAUSE THEY THOUGHT OF IT AS A TEMPORARY INTERRUPTION RATHER THEN AN INVASION OF THEIR TELEPATHIC CHANNELS AND SINCE THEY KNEW NOTHING OF THE EVENTS IN PINCHIN LANE THEY GAVE IT NO THOUGHT BUT INSTEAD THEY QUICKLY BECAME ABSORBED IN THE BUSINESS OF PUTTING ON THEIR PRESS-ON NAILS.

NEITHER JULY NOR LIBERTY SEEMED AWARE OF ANY PROBLEMS. THEY WERE LOOKING OUT THE WINDOW OF THE LIMO AT THE PASSIING OF THE COUNTRYSIDE AS THE SUN HAD JUST STARTED TO BREAK THROUGH WHEN THE ROAD DROPPED DORN INTO A LITTLE GULLY. THERE WAS A SMALL LITTLE STONE BRIDGE AHEAD AND THE DARK WATER OF THE RIVER RAN SMOOTH AS A BLACK SATIN RIBBON AROUND A DEEP BENDS. THE WOODS HAD TREES THAT LOOKED OLDER THEN TIME AND IN THE VERY SAME INSTANT J.R. AND LIBERTY BOTH BLURTED OUT "THAT'S THE PLACE!" "THE CAKE PLACE YOU MEAN?" KATE'S VOICE SAID AS IT CAME THROUGH THE INTERCOM. "YES!" BOTH LIBERTY AND J.R. SHOUTED OUT LOUD. 'LOOKS PERFECT TO ME" SAID KATE SO SHE SLOWED DOWN THE LIMO IMMEDIATELY.

"WHY KIDS IT MORE THEN PERFECT" ZANNY SAID LOOKING AT HER LITTLE GUIDEBOOK. "WHAT DO YOU MEAN?" J.R. AND LIBERTY ASKED. "WE'RE IN SUSSEX RIGHT?" "RIGHT" SAID KATE. "HADN'T YOU KIDS MENTIONED THAT CONAN DOYLE'S HOME IN HIS LATER YEARS WAS HERE?" "YES" SAID J.R. "IF YOU LOOK AHEAD" ZANNY NODDED TOWARD THE FRONT OF THE LIMO. ON THE OTHER SIDE OF THE ROAD WHERE THE LAND OPENED UP BEYOND THE WOODS FIVE GABLES SCRATCHED AT THE NOW BLUE SKY.

"IT'S WINDLESHAM!" J.R. EXCLAIMED. "YES I DO BELIEVE YOU'RE RIGHT" KATE SAID LOOKING AT THE MAP SHE HAD IN HER HAND. "I THINK CONAN DOYLE WAS BURIED HERE TOO." ARE YOU SCARED LIBERTY? "NO DON'T BE STUPID LIBERTY SAID I'M FINE." "DO YOU FEEL THE ECHOS?" "YES BUT IT'S KIND OF WEIRD BECAUSE THEY AREN'T AS LOUD AS THEY WERE BACK AT THE HOUSE."

I KNOW I WAS THINKING THE SAME THING. YOU KNOW WHAT THESE WOODS ARE CALLED? J.R. ASKED. NO WHAT ARE THEY CALLED? LIBERTY WAS ALMOST AFRAID TO KNOW. "SLAUGHTER GLEN." J.R. SAID. J.R. ARE YOU TRYING TO SCARE ME?" NO NOT REALLY J.R. SAID. DO YOU HEAR A FUNNY CRACKLING SOUND NOT REALLY LIKE STATIC? I'M RECEIVING YOU LOUD AND CLEAR. IT MUST BE THE LITTLE TWINS THEY MIGHT BE BREAKING UP A LITTLE.

OH NO! DON'T WORRY BUT J.R. COULD SENSE THAT LIBERTY WAS STILL WORRIED ABOUT THE LITTLE TWINS. WAS THERE PERHAPS MORE TO THE CRACKLING AND BREAKING UP IN THEIR TELEPATHY THEN MET THE EYE? J.R. SAID. FUNNY THINGS AND SCARY THINGS HAPPENED TO TWINS BEFORE IN THE SHERLOCK HOLMES STORIES. A CHILL WENT DOWN HIS SPINE AS HE HAD REMEMBERED BARTHOLOMEW SHOLTO'S DEATH BY POISON DARTS AND WASN'T THERE ANOTHER SET OF TWINS IN ANOTHER STORY? NEXT TO HIM LIBERTY FIDGETED AND BIT NERVOUSLY ON HER INDEX FINGER. J.R. STOPPED HIS

THOUGHTS BEFORE HIS SISTER LIBERTY COULD TUNE IN. YOU KNOW HOW THEY GET WHEN IT'S NOT THEIR BIRTHDAY. PROBABLY JUST THE STRAIN OF NOT BEING THE CENTER OF ATTENTION FOR DAY A YEAR BUT ANYHOW AS I WAS SAYING I READ SOMETHING IN A BOOK ABOUT HOW DOYLE'S STUDY LOOKED RIGHT OUT ON THIS CLUMP OF TREES AND HE WOULD TELL PEOPLE ABOUT THE TIMES LONG BEFORE WHEN SMUGGLERS, HIGHWAYMEN AND GYPSIES USED TO HIDE OUT IN THESE WOODS AND STEAL BIRTHDAY CAKES AND ALSO PREY ON INNOCENT KIDS.

NO I'M NOT SCARED AT ALL AND I THINK THIS WOULD BE THE PERFECT PLACE FOR OUR PARTY. SO IT WAS DECIDED AND BOTH OF THE BIRTHDAY CAKES LIBERTY DECORATED WITH STARS AND STRIPES AND J.R.'S WITH EXPLODING FIRECRACKERS THAT WER BROUGHT OUT. THEY SPREAD THE TABLECLOTH AND PUT OUT THE PAPER PLATES. KATE BROUGHT MATCHES FROM HER CAR AND LITE ONE SET OF CANDLES WHILE ZANNY LITE THE OTHER SET OF CANDLES. THE CANDLES HELD STEADY IN THE LIGHT WIND AS ZANNY, KATE, CHARLY AND MOLLY SANG "HAPPY BIRTHDAY" TO J.R. AND LIBERTY. SUNLIGHT STREAMED THROUGH THE GNARLED BRANCHES OF THE OLD TREES AND JUST AS THEY WERE SINGING THE VERY END OF THE LAST VERSE LIBERTY THOUGHT SHE SAW MOLLY'S EYES FOCUSED ON SOMETHING BEYOND THEM JUST OFF IN THE TREES BUT SHE WAS CONCENTRATING ON GATHERING HER BREATH TO BLOW OUT THE CANDLES AND DIDN'T TURN TO LOOK.

"HAPPY BIRTHDAY J.R. AND LIBERTY!" J.R. AND LIBERTY WERE CROUCHED ON THEIR KNEES ABOUT TO BLOW OUT THE CANDLES WHEN A SUDDEN WIND BLEW UP. THE WIND WILL HELP YOU BLOW OUT YOUR CANDLES J.R. LIBERTY TELAFLASHED. DO I SEEM THAT OLD? J.R. BEGAN BUT THEN SOMETHING HAPPENED. A BIG TERRIBLE LAUGH FILLED THE VERY CENTER OF THE WIND AND LIBERTY SAW CHARLY'S AND MOLLY'S FACES FREEZE INTO MASKS

OF TERROR AND THE WIND LIBERTY THOUGHT AS SHE EXHALED MIGHTILY DIDN'T SEEM TO HELP AT ALL. ONE CANDLE'S FLAME WAS STILL WAVERING ON HER CAKE AND SO WAS ONE ON J.R.'S CAKE AND THEN SHE HEARD ZANNY SCREAM.

IT ALL HAPPENED SO FAST IT WAS HARD TO KNOW THE PRECISE ORDER BUT ZANNY SEEMED TO GRAB ONE CAKE AND BOTH SMALL TWINS AT THE SAME TIME AND KATE GRABBED THE OTHER CAKE. OUT OF THE DEPTHS OF TREES CALL SLAUGHTER GLEN A FIGURE OF A MAN HAD APPEARED AND HE WAS HOLDING A STICK AND ON THAT STICK WAS A SNAKE A LIVE SPECKLED SNAKE. "JUST A VEE WIPER!" THE SNAKE WRITHED ON THE END OF THE STICK AND IT'S DIAMOND SHAPED HEAD SWAYING THE FORKED TONGUE STRKING OUT AND THE NECK PUFFED IN FURY.

HOW SHE GOT ALL THE CHILDREN AND THE CAKES INTO THE CAR ZANNY WOULD NEVER KNOW. SHE SANK BACK AGAINST THE UPHOLSTERED SEAT. "I CAN'T BELIEVE IT!" KATE EXCLAIMED THROUGH THE INTERCOM. "I MEAN I DON'T SCARE EASILY BUT THAT BLOKE WAS TERRIBLE AND UP TO NO GOOD AND WANTS TO CAUSE TROUBLE." THEY WERE ROARING ALONG THE ROAD AND J.R. AND LIBERTY STILL PEERED IN STUNNED DISBELIEF OUT THE REAR WINDOW.

IT CAN'T BE TRUE. ARE YOU SURE? COUNT THE CANDLES J.R. YOU SAW IT AS WELL AS I DID AND YOU SAW HIM STANDING THERE. THEY DIDN'T WANT TO SAY IT OUT LOUD AND THEY DIDN'T EVEN WANT TO TELAFLASH IT OR EVEN THINK ABOUT IT. ALTHOUGH YOU CAN STOP WORDS SPOKEN OUT LOUD BOTH TWINS KNEW IT WAS ALMOST IMPOSSIBLE BANISH TELEPATHIC IMAGES AND NOW ONE WAS CRACKLING IN THEIR BRAINS. ONLY THEY HAD SEEN THE MAN AND IT WAS THE SAME MAN WHO HAD BEEN A BEEFEATER AT THE TOWER WITH THE SAME VOICE AS THE MAN ON PINCHIN LANE AND HE HAD WALKED OVER TO

THE VERY SPOT WHERE THEY HAD BEEN BLOWING OUT THE CANDLES. AS THE CAR DROVE OFF THE TWINS HAD WATCHED HIM AS HE SLOWLY BENT OVER AND BLEW OUT THE TWO CANDLES THAT WERE BURNING ON THE GROUND AND THEY WERE THE SAME TWO CANDLES J.R. AND LIBERTY HAD FAILED TO BLOW OUT WHEN THE WIND HAD COME UP. THE MAN HAD PICKED THEM UP HELD THEM AND SIMPLY STARED AT THE CHILDREN WITH A TRACE OF THE MOST AWFUL GRIN ON HIS FACE. THAT WAS THEIR LAST VIEW OF HIM FROM THE LIMO AS KATE SPED AWAY.

SLOWLY J.R. TURNED AROUND IN HIS SEAT AND SANK BACK. THE LIMO WAS A MESS WITH CRUMBS AND FROSTING ALL OVER AND THE CANDLES J.R. COUNTED SLOWLY. LIBERTY WAS RIGHT THERE WERE TWENTY-FOUR CANDLES ONE FOR EACH OF THEIR TWELVE YEARS. YET TWO CANDLES WERE MISSING THE TWO TO GROW ON.

CHAPTER 12

A ELECTRICAL STORM TO REMEMBER.

J.R. AND LIBERTY COULDN'T GET THAT AWFUL SCENE OUT OF THEIR HEADS BECAUSE THE TWO SMALL FLAMES OF THOSE BIRTHDAY CANDLES HAD FICKERED WITH A TERRIBLE BRILLIANCE. THE FIREWORKS NOW AT THE AMBASSADOR'S HOUSE WAS DOING LITTLE TO ERASE THE IMAGE. THEY WERE BEING PURSUED THAT WAS FOR SURE BUT WHY AND FOR WHAT AND BY WHOM? WHAT HAD THEY DONE TO DESERVE THIS?

APPARENTLY IT DIDN'T BOTHER ZANNY BUT THIS DID WORRY BOTH J.R AND LIBERTY. SHE SEEMED TO DOUBT WHAT SHE HAD JUST SEEN.

"ZANNY" LIBERTY BLURTED OUT "THERE WAS A MAN STANDING THERE IN BROAD DAYLIGHT HOLDING A SNAKE ON A STICK." "HE COULD HAVE JUST BEEN A NATURALIST SNAKE COLLECTOR OUT FOR AN AFTERNOON STROLL."

UNBELIEVABLE! ABSOLUTELY UNBELIEVABLE J.R. TELAFLASHED. "I THINK SHE WAS BEWITCHED!" SHE WAS AS SCARED AS WE WERE AND NOW TRYING TO PASSTHIS GUY OFF AS A NATURALIST OR SOME BIRD-WATCHER TYPE!

"YOU HAVE TO REALIZE CHILDREN . . ." WHENE SHE CALLS US CHILDREN YOU KNOW SHE'S HEADING OFF IN THE WRONG DIRECTION. SHE'S TRYING TO BE MRS. SUPER ADULT LIBERTY TELAFLASHED TO HER BROTHER J.R. I KNOW CAN YOU BELIEVE IT? SHE'S READY TO BLOW THIS

WHOLE THING OFF AND IN ANOTHER TEN SECONDS SHE'S GOING TO BE GETTING INTO PSYCHOLOGY AND ALL THAT STUFF J.R. TELAFLASHED.

IT TOOK ZANNY ABOUT EIGHT SECONDS TO GET TO THE PSYCHOLOGY PART. "YOU HAVE TO REALIZE WE HAVE BEEN IN A HEIGHTENED STATE OF ANXIETY SINCE WE'VE COME TO A FOREIGN COUNTRY. IT MAKES MORE OF US PSYCHOLOGICALLY SUSCEPTIBLE AND MORE INCLINED TO TWIST THINGS IN OUR MINDS. WELL NOT TWIST THINGS BUT WE GET A LITTLE PARANOID AND MIGHT THINK WE'RE SEEING ONE THING WHILE IT MIGHT BE ENTIRELY DIFFERENT."

"WAIT A MINUTE HOLD ON RIGHT THERE" LIBERTY SAID. "DO YOU AGREE THAT YOU SAW A MAN COMING OUT OF THE WOODS HOLDING A SNAKE?" "WELL YES BUT IT WAS A DELUSION ON YOUR PART THAT HE WAS ACTUALLY THREATENING YOU IN ANY WAY." DELUSION SHE CALLS IT! J.R. SAID. IT'S DELUSIONS MY FOOT SAID LIBERTY. DELUSION MY BRAIN J.R. SAID BACK TO LIBERTY. SEE I TOLD YOU IT WOULD TAKE HER ABOUT TEN SECONDS TO GET TO THE PSYCHOLOGY PART BUT I THINK IT WAS LESS J.R. SAID TO HIS SISTER LIBERTY.

ZANNY WAS TURNING INTO YOUR STANDARD GROWN-UP. THIS WAS WHAT ALWAYS HAPPENED TO GROWN-UPS EVEN THE BEST ONES LIKE ZANNY WHO MOST OF THE TIME DIDN'T ACT LIKE GROWN-UPS. THEY CAME HOME AND TOOK A SHOWER LIKE ZANNY HAD TO GET RELAXED AND DECIDE THE KIDS ARE NUTS AND HAD TO BE TAUGHT A LESSION TWO SOONER OR LATER.

"IT WASN'T A DELUSION" LIBERTY SAID. I SAW THE LOOK ON YOUR FACE ZANNY. YOU ARE SCARED TOO JUST LIKE ME SAID LIBERTY. "OKAY I ADMIT I WAS FRIGHTENED JUST LIKE YOU WERE BUT IT WAS BECAUSE THE GUY WAS WEIRD. MAYBE HE WASN'T A NATURALIST SAID ZANNY. I THINK HE

WAS.... ZANNY HASITATED FOR A MINUTE "YOU KNOW YOUR RUN OF THE MILL PERVERT WHO JUMPS OUT OF THE WOODS AND SCARES PEOPLE AND YOU KNOW LIKE THOSE PEOPLE WHO ENJOY MAKING DIRTY PHONE CALLS."

ZANNY COULD TELL THE TWINS WEREN'T BUYING THIS. LOOKING BACK AT IT NOW IT SEEMED VERY CHILDISH TO THINK SHE HAD BECOME SO VERY FRIGHTENED AND ALMOST PANICKED THE MOMENT THE STRANGE MAN CAME OUT THE WOODS. SHE HAD TO REALIZE THE RAGOZZINO CHILDREN WERE NOT ORDINARY IN THE LEAST AND THEY ARE VERY HIGHLY ARTICULATE AND IMAGINATIVE. IT WAS EASY TO GET DRAWN INTO THEIR WORLD AND TO CROSS SOME IMAGINARY LINE BETWEEN THE ADULT WORLD OF LOGIC AND ORDER INTO THEIR FANCIFUL WORLD.

SO ACCORDING TO ZANNY WE'VE JUST GOT A RUN-OF THE-MILL PERVERT HERE J.R. SAID. YEAH LIKE THOSE GUYS WHO MAKE DIRTY PHONE CALLS AND IT MIGHT NOT JUST BE ONE. IT COULD BE THREE DIFFERENT PERVERTS LIBERTY ASNWERED. JEEZ HOW LUCKY CAN YOU GET? J.R. SIGHED. THE SIGH WAS LIKE A LITTLE GLIMMER IN THE AIR BETWEEN THEM. WELL LIBERTY TELAFLASHED BACK WHEN YOU'RE TWO SETS OF TWINS I GUESS CALL IT NOT EXACTLY BUT "DOUBLE TROUBLE SQUARED."

LIBERTY RECALLED THAT CONVERSATION NOW AS FIREWORKS EXPLODED ABOVE HER ON THE AMBASSADOR'S LAWN BUT SHE FOUND IT SO VERY HARD AND DISHEARTENING. SHE THOUGHT THAT THREE MIGHT HAVE BEEN A POSSIBILITY OF LETTING ZANNY IN ON ALL OF THIS BUT APPARENTLY THAT WAS NOT TO BE FOR IT WAS NOW UP TO J.R. AND LIBERTY. THAT WAS A LITTLE BIT SCARY SAID MOLLY AND CHARLEY.

SHE FOCUSED ON CHARLY AND MOLLY WHO WERE SITTING ON THE GRASS IN FRONT OF HER. CHARLY HAD JUST LICKED HER RUNNY NOSE WITH HER TONGUE A

TALENT BOTH LITTLE TWINS SHARED. THEY COULD STICK THEIR TONGES STRAIGHT UP AND WIPE THE SPACE BETWEEN THEIR UPPER LIPS AND THE BOTTOM OF THEIR NOSES. THEIR TONGES WERE JUST LIKE LITTLE WINDSHIELD WIPERS. IT WAS EXCEEDINGLY CUTE BUT GROSS. WHY THEN DID THE LITTLE TWINS SEEM SO SUDDENLY PRECIOUS TO HER? HOW COLD THEY BE SO DEAR AND GROSS AT THE SAME TIME THESE LITTLE SNOT NOSED TWERPS. THEY LICKED THEIR UPPER LIPS AGAIN. LIBERTY HOPED THE AMBASSADOR'S WIFE WASN'T WATCHING THEM BECAUSE MRS. WHITMORE WAS VERY PROPER.

THEY LOOKED LIKE LITTLE DOGGIES! THE LITTLE TWINS WERE SILENTLY DISCUSSING THE AMBSSADOR'S FAMILY SPECIFICALLY HIS WIFE. LIBERTY KNEW WHAT THEY SAYING IN A GENERAL WAY NOT WORD FOR WORD BUT SOMETIMES SHE COULD ONLY GET GLIMMERINGS. RIGHT NOW THE GLIMMERINGS SEEMED TO MATCH UP WITH LIBERTY'S OWN THINKING AND AMBASSADOR WHITMORE AND HIS WIFE AND TWO DAUGTHERS ALL HAD LOOKED LIKE DOGS. MRS. WHITMORE LOOKED EXACTLY LIKE POOKIE AUNT HONEY'S PEKINGESE. SHE HAD THICK SILKY DARK BLOND HAIR THAT IS EASY TO BUSH OUT AROUND HER HEAD. HER FACE WAS SMUSHED UP TOWARD HER FOREHEAD AND THE LIPS WERE CURLED TOWARDS THE NOSE AND NOSE POINTED STRAIGHT UP JUST LIKE A PENKINGESE. SHE WOULD HAVE NO TROUBLE LICKING A RUNNY NOSE WITH HER TONGUE IF SHE HAD THAT GROSS BUT SHE WASN'T.

AMBASSADOR WHITMORE WAS LARGE WITH COAL BLACK HAIR AND HEAVY BLACK EYEBROWS. HIS CHEEKS SEEMED TO COLLAPSE INTO PUDDLES OF FLESH AROUND HIS MOUTH AND IF THE AMBASSADOR WASN'T HUMAN VERSION OF BLACK LABADORS THEN LIBERTY DIDN'T KNOW WHO WAS. THE TWO TEENAGE DAUGTHERS ISABELLA AND FIFI WERE ANOTHER BREED ENTIRELY. THEY WERE PUNK VERSIONS OF CHIHUAHUAS. SMALL AND PAINFULLY SKINNY AND THEY BOTH WORE THEIR HAIR EXTREAMELY

SHORT AND LIKE CHIHUAHUAS THEY HAD SLIGHTLY POINTY EARS AND BULGY EYES. THEY HAD LOTS OF EYE MAKE-UP ON AND WORE TEENY TINY MINI-SKIRTS WITH STARS AND STRIPED STOCKINGS. THEY WERE VERY NICE TO THE CHILDREN THOUGH AND THEY GAVE THEM LITTLE COLORED STARS TO STICK ON THEIR FACES. LIBERTY JUST HOPED CHARLY AND MOLLY WOULDN'T SAY ANYTHING ABOUT HOW MUCH THE WHITMORES LOOKED LIKE DOGS AND OF CORSE SHE HOPED THEY WOULDN'T LICK THEIR SNOTTY NOSES IN FRONT OF THE AMBASSADOR AND HIS WIFE MRS. WHITMORE.

LIBERTY HEARD MRS. WHITMORE APOLOGIZING FOR HOW ISABELLA AND FIFI WERE DRESSED WHICH DIDN'T MAKE HER THINK MUCH OF HER AS A MOTHER. AMBASSADOR AND HIS WIFE MRS. WHITMORE SLOBBERED A LOT ALL OVER THE LITTLE TWINS AND NOBODY SEEMED TO NOTICE THEY HAD NEGLECTED TO TAKE OFF THEIR PRESS-ON—NAILS.

"REMARKABILE! REMARKABLE!" AMBASSADOR WHITMORE KEPT SAYING OUT LOUD. "TO THINK OF TWO SETS IN ONE FAMILY." A HANDSOME LOT YOU'VE GOT THERE PUTMAN! I'LL BE! GRACIOUS SNAKES MUST KEEP YOUR WIFE BUSY. OH THAT'S RIGHT I FORGOT SHE'S TENDING THE STORE HAR DEE HAR HAR THE AMBASSADOR SAID. YOU KNOW ABOUT MADELINE RAGOZZINO AND LULU? REAL DYNAMO THAT WOMEN!" AMBASSADOR WHITMORE WAS FULL OF MEANINGLESS HEARTY PHASES.

"YES I'VE HEARD OF HER SAID PUTMAN. I WAS TELLING LADY ABERDEEN ABOUT HER JUST THE OTHER DAY. YOU KNOW MRS. LADY ABERDEEN MR RAGOZZINO? SHE'S A LADY IN WAITING THE QUEEN AND LULU WAS DROPPING ROYAL NAMES RIGHT AND LEFT. LIBERTY COULD SEE FIFI AND ISABELLA FOUND THEIR MOTHER AS EMBARRASSING AS THEIR MOTHER FOUND THEIR CLOTHING.

"LADY LULU'S AT IT AGAIN!" SHE HEARD ISABEELA WHISPER TO FIFI. "BET SHE WISHES SHE HAD MORE THEN THESE SECOND-STRING ROYALS HERE TONIGHT?" "HARDLY!" SAID FIFI STICKING A STAR STICKER BACK ON HER LITTLE CHEECK. "THESE ARE JUST SUB-ROYALS" SHE SAID LOOKING AROUND THE COURTYARD. "A FEW TITLES BUT NONE WITH REALLY GOOD COURT CONNECTIONS AND NO ONE FROM KENSINGTON PALACE."

A RUMBLE OF THUNDER WAS FOLLOWED BY A ROLL OF GROANS. "LETS HOPE THE REST OF THESE FIREWORKS BEAT THE RAIN OR ELSE IT'S GOING TO PING-PONG IN DOORS!" THE AMBASSADOR'S VOICE BOOMED OUT LOUD FOR EVERYONE TO HEAR AND JUST AT THAT MOMENT LULU CALLED TO HIM.

WHAT A WIT! LIBERTY TELAFLASHED. HE'S NOT PAID TO BE A WIT HE'S PAID TO CORDIAL THAT'S ALL. DAD DOSE MOST OF THE THINKING FOR HIM AND RUNS THE AMBASSY. THE AMBASSADOR'S VERY DIPLOMATIC BECAUSE THAT'S HIS JOB. YOU'RE TOO HARD ON HIM LIBERTY. THE FIREWORKS BEAT OUT THE RAIN BY TWENTY MINUTES AND BY THE TIME THEY ARRIVED BACK AT THE DEVONSHIRE HOUSE UP ON THE HILL IN THE MEWS IT WAS POURING BUCKETS OF RAIN OUTSIDE.

CHAPTER 13

THE CRACK IN THE WALL AT THE EAVES.

THE HOUSE IN THE MEWS FELT COZY AND WELCOMING WHEN THEY HAD RETURNED. THE CORNERS WERE STEEPED IN SHADOWS WHICH DESPITE THE LIGHTS PUTMAN HAD TURNED ON SEEMED THICKER THEN EVER.

BOTH J.R. AND LIBERTY HAD A FUNNY FELLING THEY WERE AT SOME KIND OF A TURNING POINT AND NOT SIMPLY BECAUSE THEY HAD TURNED TWELVE THAT DAY. SOMETHING MORE WAS BEGINNING TO HAPPEN WITHIN THE HOUSE SO THEY CLIMBED THE STEPS TO THE ATTIC BEDROOM TO SEE WHAT WAS GOING ON UP THERE.

THE RAIN HAD COME DOWN HARDER SO J.R. HAD TURNED ON HIS LITTLE RAIDO HE HAD RECEIVED FOR HIS BIRTHDAY. AS THEY GOT READY FOR BED THEY HAD THE BBC WEATHERMAN READ THE MARTIME REPORT WITH THE CLIPPED SPEECH AND EVEN TONE HE WAS LIKE THE CALM EYE AT THE CENTER OF THE STORM. "THERE ARE WARNINGS OF GALES IN THE SOLENT, SHANNON, FASTNET, IRISH SEA, THE HUBRIDES, THE BISCAY, PORTLAND, PLYMOUTH, AND STRAIT OF DOVER. GOOD SAILING." SAID THE WEATHERMAN.

"MY GOODNESS ISN'T HE CHEERFUL SAID LIBERTY. THE NERVE OF HIM TELLING THESE PEOPLE GOOD SAILING." PUTMAN HAD COME UP TO THE ATTIC TO WISH THEM HAPPY BIRTHDAY AND KISS THEM GOOD NIGHT. SO

THERE HE SITS IN HIS COZY LITTLE STUDIO WARNING OF GALES IN EVERY LITTLE QUADRANT THE BBC COVERS AND HE WISHES THE SAILORS GOOD SAILING TOO! IT'S A MESSY NIGHT SAID PUTMAN LOOKING OUT THE DORMER WINDOWS AS RAGGED OILY LOOKING CLOUDS TORE ACROSS THE MOON STREAKED NIGHT AND THE SKY HAD LOOKED LIKE ASHES.

AGAIN PUTMAN WISHED THEM A HAPPY BIRTHDAY, HUGGED THEM AND TOLD THEM TO GET TO SLEEP. LIBERTY DID THIS PROMPTLY BUT AS TIRED AS SHE WAS SHE COULDN'T FALL ASLEEP. SUPPOSING HE THOUGHT THAT THE MAN FROM SLAUGHTER GLEN FOUND THEM. J.R. HEARD LIBERTY TURN OVER IN HER BED BECAUSE OF THIS DISTURBEING DREAM SHE HAD.

J.R.'S MIND RAN ON TO DIFFERENT PLACES WHILE HE WAS A SLEEP AND LIBERTY WAS STILL TURNING IN HER BED. SUPPOSE THAT THE LIGHT OF THE TWO BIRTHDAY CANDLES LED THE MAN RIGHT TO THIS HOUSE AND UP INTO THE ATTIC J.R. SAID TO LIBERTY AND THAT GAVE J.R. A CHILL DOWN HIS SPINE. LIBERTY MOANED A LITTLE IN HER SLEEP I GUESS SHE WAS HAVING ANOTHER BAD NIGHTMEAR J.R. SAID. J.R. SUDDENLY FELT HUNGRY SO HE WENT DOWNSTAIRS TO GET SOMETHING TO EAT FROM THE REFRIGERATOR AND THEN HE WENT BACK UPSTAIRS TO BED BUT BEFORE HE GOT BACK INTO BED HE WENT OVER TO LIBERTY'S BED TO SEE HOW SHE WAS DOING.

THE SPECKLED BAND OF M&M'S DIVIDING THE TERRITORY HAD BEEN EATEN UP THE WEEK BEFORE AND SO NOW THERE WAS A LINE OF JELLY BEANS ALONG THE TAPE LINE. AFTER GETTING BACK INTO BED J.R. WAS STILL HUNGRY SO HE TOOK ONE JELLY BEAN OFF THE TAPE LINE AND ATE IT BEFORE HIS SISTER LIBERTY SAW HIM. AFTER ALL THE JUNK FOOD HE HAD EATEN TODAY HIS MOTHER WOULD CALLED THIS AN OUTRAGEOUS ASSAULT ON HIS GUTS.

JUST AS J.R. WAS ABOUT TO TURN TO GO TO BED HE HAD FROZE BECAUSE SOMETHING WAS WRONG SO HE PEERED MORE CLOSELY AT THE SPECKLED BAND OF M&M'S. THEY HAD JUST FILLED IT FOR THE EVENING BEFORE BUT SEVERAL M&M'S WERE MISSING FROM THE TAPE LINE. THEY COULDN'T HAVE EATEN THAT MANY ESPECIALLY WHEN THEY HAD BEEN GONE ALL DAY. THIS WAS J.R.'S FIRST SINCE THEY HAD FILLED THEM IN LAST NIGHT. WHEN THEY HAD GOTTEN UP THIS MORNING THE LINE WAS COMPLETE. HE REMEMBERED NO GAPS AND HADN'T NOTICED LIBERTY EAT ANY BEFORE SHE WENT BACK TO BED. CHARLY AND MOLLY HARDLY EVER COME UP TO THE ATTIC. THEY HAD FALLEN ASLEEP COMING HOME IN THE CAR FROM THE AMBASSADOR'S HOUSE. DAD AND ZANNY HAD CARRIED THEM IN SO IT WASN'T THEM. DO YOU THINK IT COULD HAVE BEEN A MOUSE?

J.R. LOOKED DOWN AT THE TAP AGAIN AND IN THE GAPS WHERE THE JELLY BEANS HAD BEEN HE COULD SEE DIM LITTLE BEAN SHAPED BLOTCHES LIKE COLORED SHADOWS. THEY WERE VERY PALE, SOME WERE PINK, SOME WERE, ORANGE AND SOME WERE GREEN THE COLORS OF JELLY BEANS. IT WAS VERY ODDLY THAT THEY HAD DISSOLVED INTO THIN AIR LEAVING ONLY A GHOSTLY TRACE BEHIND? AS HE RUBBED HIS FOREHEAD, WAS HE SEEING THINGS?

J.R. FELT RESTLESS, TIRED AND YET HE KNEW HE COULDN'T SLEEP SO HE PUT ON HIS BATHROBE AND WALKED OVER TO THE WINDOW. THE RAIN THRUMMED AGAINST THE WINDOW PANES SO HARD THAT THE DROPS WERE SQUASHED FLAT INTO A BLACK GLAZE OF WATER. THE NIGHT AND THE RAIN MADE A MIRROR OF THE GLASS AND J.R. LOOKED AT HIS FACE IN IT. HIS FACE APPEARED SLIGHTLY BLURRED LIKE A WATER COLOR THAT WAS STILL WET. HE DIDN'T LOOK VERY REAL EITHER HE THOUGHT.

THEN THE RHYTHM OF THE RAIN CHANGED AND SO DID THE WIND. IT LESSENED AND EVERYTHING SEEMED

TO SLOWLY EASED UP. THE WATER MADE RUNNELS DOWN THE PANE AND WATCHED THE IMAGE OF HIS FACE BREAK INTO PIECES LIKE THOSE OF A JIGSAW PUZZLE.

THERE WAS A PUZZLE ABOUT THIS HOUSE IN THE MEWS BUT IT WASN'T HIM. HE TURNED TO GO TO BED BUT IN THAT SLIVER OF AN INSTANT OUT OF THE CORNER OF HIS EYE HE CAUGHT A SMALL FLICKERING IN ONE OF THE WINDOW PANES. A TWIN FLICKERING ACTUALLY AS FROM TWO LITTLE FLAMES.

HIS BLOOD FROZE AND HIS FEET SIMPLY WOULDN'T MOVE. HE WAS TOO AFRAID TO TURN AROUND AND FACE THE WINDOW BUT TOO CURIOUS TO RUN TO BED. FINALLY VERY SLOWLY HE RAISED THE POLISHED SURFACE OF HIS DIGITAL WATCH TO CATCH THE REFLECTION OF THE LIGHT. ON THE SCRATCHED AND DISTORTED WATCH FACE HE CAUGHT THE TWO FLICKERING LICKS OF A FLAME AND THE REFLECTION OF TWO BIRTHDAY CANDLES! HE CRIED OUT AND WHEELED AROUND BUT THE WINDOWPANE WAS PERFECTLY BLACK WITH BEATING RAIN.

HE STARED IN DISBELIEF BECAUSE HE KNEW HE HAD SEEN THE TWIN IMAGES OF THOSE FLICKERING BIRTHDAY CANDLES BUT NOW THEY WERE GONE. LIBERTY HADN'T EVEN AWAKENED WHEN HE SCREAMED. HE HAD MADE HIS WAY STRAIGHT TO BED AND CLIMBED IN DRAWING THE BIG THICK COMFORTER RIGHT UP TO HIS EARS. HE THEN WATCHED THE SHADOWS GATHER AROUND HIM AND HE HAD NEVER FELT SO ALONE IN HIS LIFE.

J.R. DIDN'T KNOW HOW LONG HE HAD BEEN ASLEEP BUT SOMETHING HAD WOKE HIM UP. HE WASN'T SURE WHETHER IT WAS THUNDER OR A BOLT OF LIGHTNING BUT THE NIGHT HAD TURNED WILD. A FULL GALE TORE AT THE HOUSE AND THE AIR OUTSIDE HAD AN EERIE LUMINESCENCE AS LIGHTNING FRACTURED THE SKY. THE PROFILES OF ROOFTOPS AND CHIMNEY POTS WERE LIMNED in harsh light of the storm's fierce electrical display. The chimney behind Liberty's bed gulped great downward drafts of air and seemed to alternately moan, hiccup and gasp. Liberty could sleep through anything J.R. had thought. Then the most ferocious bolt of thunder exploded directly over head.

A flash filled the room with a sickly unnatural light. Within that flash J.R. caught sight of an almost imperceptible crack in the corner of the attic across from his bed. It was there on the windowless side of the room where the ceiling of the attic had dropped down beneath the eaves of the house. What was it? It seemed too regular to be the kind of random crack one might find in an old ceiling of an old house. Ventilators and long bell ropes! The words from the Sherlock Holmes story came back to his mind. The bell rpoe was there "as a bridge for something passing through the hole and coming to the bed" and a bridge for a swamp adder or that snake on the stick from that late afternoon in the woods where you guys had the birthday party for Liberty and J.R.!

J.R. was rigid with fear so he buried his head under the covers. He heard Liberty moan softly in her sleepand turn over again and he was too scared to call to her but he knew that somewhere deep whitin her dreams she was feeling his fear and anxiety. Oh for this night to be over would be great! J.R. thought of the Dr. Watson's description of the sound he and Sherlock had heard "a very gentle soothing sound like that of a small jet of stream escaping continually from a kettle." That was how he had described the noise the snake had made as it descended the bell rope to strike it's victims but as frightened as J.R. was it became difficult

TO HOLD HIS EYES OPEN. HIS EYELIDS FLUTTERED AND SAGGED DOWN. THIS DAY AND THIS NIGHT HAD BEEN TOO MUCH FOR LIBERTY'S LITTLE BROTHER JR. HIS IS EYES FELT SO HEAVY THAT HE COULD HARDLY KEEP THEM OPEN. HE TRIED TO KEEP THEM OPEN BUT HE COULDN'T SO HE THEN THOUGHT OF THE AWNINGS SHOPKEEPERS UNROLLED EVERY SUNNY MORNING ON MARYLEBONE HIGH STREET. IT WAS AS IF SOME SHOPKEEPER A SHOPKEEPER OF SLEEP WAS UNROLLING HIS EYELIDS AND LETTING THEM ROLL DOWN. WHAT A SILLY THOUGHT J.R. SAID. AS HE STARTED TO YAWN HIS EYES OPENED SLIGHTLY AGAIN AND THEN DROPPED AGAIN. DID HE HEAR A SOFT CLEAR WHISTLING IN THE NIGHT? OH GEE HADN'T THE BIG HORRIBLE MAN CALLED BACK THE SWAMP ADDER BY WHISTLING? NO THAT WAS JUST THE WIND IN THE CHIMNEY. WAS HE REALLY TO TIRED NOW EVEN TO BE FRIGHTENED? I GUESS THE SHOPKEEPER WON.

CHAPTER 14

THE FEELING OF A SHADOW PRESENCE

"THERE'S THE SCARLET THREAD OF MURDER RUNNING THROUGH THE COLOURLESS SKEIN OF LIFE AND ARE DUTY IS TO UNRAVEL IT, ISOLATE IT AND EXPOSE EVERY INCH OF IT." THE WORDS THAT NOW RAN THROUGH J.R.'S MIND WERE FROM THE SHERLOCK HOLMES STORY A BIG STUDY IN SCARLET BUT OF COURSE J.R. WASN'T LOOKING AT THE SCARLET THREAD BUT A VERY FADED SPECKLED BAND AND HE WAS NOT FEELING SMART.

IT WAS THE FOLLOWING EVENING BUT THAT MORNING J.R. HAD TOLD LIBERTY ABOUT HIS SLEEPLESS NIGHT STARTING WITH THE MISSING JELLY BEANS AND MOVING ON TO THE FLICKERING OF IMAGE OF THE LOST BIRTHDAY CANDLES. FOR SOME REASON HE HADN'T TOLD HER ABOUT THE CRACK IN THE CEILING. SUPPOSED HE HAD HELD BACK BECAUSE RELATED THE CRACK TO THE BELL ROPE AND THE SNAKE. HE KNEW HOW FEARFUL HIS SISTER LIBERTY WAS ON SNAKES AND HE ALSO KNEW THAT LIBERTY WAS AWARE THAT HE WAS HOLDING SOMETHING BACK FROM HER. SHE COULD SENSE THESE THINGS BUT TODAY SHE DIDN'T WANT TO PUSH THE SUBJECT RIGHT NOW.

"WHOEVER HAS BEEN EATING THESE DOESN'T LIKE THE YELLOW ONES" J.R. SAID SCRATCHING HIS HEAD. HE LOOKED OVER AT LIBERTY BUT SHE WAS TOTALLY ABSORBED IN HER READING RESEARCH SHE SAID BUT FOR THE LIFE OF HIM HE COULDN'T FIGURE OUT HOW READING A BOOK

ON THE DEVELOPMENT AND PERSONALITIES OF TWINS WOULD HELP HER WITH THIS PROBLEM. HE TURNED OFF THE DESK LIGHT AND WAS ABOUT TO GET UP AND GO TO BED WHEN NOTICED A DIM GLOW THAT SEEMED TO RADIATE FROM THE TAPE.

"GOOD GRIEF!" J.R. EXCLAIMED. "LIBERTY COME OVER HERE." "WHAT IS IT?" LIBERTY SAID AS SHE LOOKED UP FROM HER BED. "THE JELLY BEANS SPOTS THEY'RE GLOWING IN THE DARK!" J.R. SAID. LIBERTY LEAPED OFF HER BED AND RAN OVER TO THE DESK WHERE J.R. WAS STANDING. "INCREDIBLE!" LIBERTY SAID AS SHE STARED DOWN AT THE SOFTLY GLOWING POOLS OF COLORS.

"I WONDER WHAT THEY'RE DOING TO OUR GUTS IF THEY DOING THAT TO THE TAPE? YUCK THEY BOTH THOUGHT AS THEY IMAGINED A SPECKLED BAND OF DAY-GLOW JELLY BEANS COILED IN THEIR INTESTINES. THEY WERE BOTH LOOKED IN SLIENCE BUT THE AIR CRACKLED WITH THEIR TELEPATHIC COMMUNICATIONS.

THIS IS VERY CURIOUS LIBERTY SAID. IT'S LIKE A KIND OF AFTER IMAGE J.R. TELAFLASHED. AFTER IMAGE? J.R. SAID WITH A PUZZLEING LOOK ON HIS FACE. YOU REMEMBER IN SCIENCE CLASS LIBERTY SAID WHEN WE WERE STUDYING THE HUMAN EYE? AFTER THE IMAGE IS FORMED ON THE RETINA IT'S ONLY THERE FOR A FRACTION OF A SECOND BEFORE IT FADES TO FROM THE NEXT IMAGE. REMEMBER THE EXPERIMENTS WE DID WHEN WE LOOKED AT SWITCHED ON LIGHT BULB AND THEN CLOSED OUR EYES AND WE COULD STILL SEE IT? THAT'S THE AFTER IMAGE. MAYBE THAT WOULD EXPLAIN THE REFLECTIONS OF THE BIRTHDAY CANDLES I SAW RIGHT HERE IN THE WINDOW OR RATHER MY WATCH FACE.

YEAH I GUESS SO. IT'S HOW THEY DO ANIMATED CARTOONS IN THE BIG MOVIES. RIGHT YOU THINK IT'S ALL ONE SMOOTH MOVING PICTURE BUT IT'S TWENTY-FOUR

DIFFERENT ONES IN ONE SECOND. THE AFTER IMAGES IN YOUR BRAIN IS WHAT SMOOTHS IT ALL OUT. THEY CALL IT PERSISTENCE OF VISION.

WHAT DO THESE JELLY BEANS SPOTS HAVE TO DO WITH ALL THAT? LIBERTY TELAFLASHED BACK TO J.R. I DON'T KNOW J.R. SAID. "WE HAVE GOT TO START DEDUCTING AND DETECTING JUST LIKE SHERLOCK HOLMES WOULD" LIBERTY SAID AS SHE KEPT ON SPEAKING OUT LOUD.

SHE WAS RIGHT UP UNTILL NOW THEY HAD JUST BEEN LETTING THE DIM SHADOWS GATHER AROUND THEM AND CONFOUNDING THEM AND ALSO GONFUSING THEM AS WELL. IT'S TIME TO START THINKING ABOUT WHAT TO DO ABOUT THESE SHADOWS SAID LIBERTY. "YOU'RE RIGHT LIBERTY" J.R. HAD SAID TO HIS SISTER. "CRIME IS COMMON BUT LOGIC IS RARE SO THEREFORE IT IS UPON LOGIC RATHER THEN CRIME THAT YOU SHOULD DWELL."

OH BRAVO BRAVO! THE WORDS FLASHED THROUGH THE AIR J.R. SAID AS LIBERTY'S EYES OPENED WIDE. "NOT ME!" J.R. MOUTHED THE WORDS. "THE OLDER VOICE" LIBERTY WHISPERED TO HER BROTHER. SUDDENLY THE AIR SEEMED TO FILL WITH STATIC AND LOTS OF DIFFERENT TRANSMITTERS BUT IT WAS AS IF THERE WAS A BIG HUGE ELECTRICAL STORM IN THE TWINS HEADS BUT THEIR WASN'T. THEN IS SUBSIDED AS SUDDENLY AS IT HAD BEGUN.

LIBERTY SHUT HER EYES TIGHT FOR A MOMENT AND SHOOK HER HEAD VIGOROUSLY TRYING TO CLEAR OUT THE LAST REMNANTS OF STATCI. "LET'S GEET BACK TO LOGIC OKAY? LIBERTY SAID. "WHAT'S WITH THE CRACK YOU REFUSE TO TALK ABOUT?"

SO SHE HAD GUESSED IT DESPITE HIS EFFORTS TO KEEP THE CRACK A SECRET. "YOU WERE KEEPING ME AWAKE ALL NIGHT WITH YOUR DAM DREAMS!" "YOU WERE NOT AWAKE

LIBERTY BELIEVE ME YOU SLEEP LIKE A LOG" SAID JR. "WELL START THERE ANYWAYS" SAID LIBERTY.

J.R. EXPLAINED WHAT HE THOUGHT HE HAD SEEN ILLUMINATED IN THE FLASH OF LIGHTNING DURING THE ELECTRICAL STORM. TEN MINUTES LATER LIBERTY WAS STANDING ON A STOOL EXAMINING THE CEILING BENEATH THE EAVES BUT NOTHING SEEMED UNUSUAL TO HER. WHERE HE THOUGHT HE HAD SEEN THE CRACK THERE WAS A KIND OF PAINTED OVER SEAM. THEN AGAIN THE SEAMS SPREAD AT REGULAR INTERVALS ALL OVER THE ATTIC ROOM WHERE SHERLOCK HOLMES HAD LIVED BUT A WALL COVERING USED INSTEAD OF PLASTER HAD BEEN INSTALLED. YET WHEN LIBERTY LOOKED DOWN AT J.R. HER FACE WAS QUITE PALE.

"THERE'S A PRESENCE HERE" LIBERTY WHISPERED. "I FEEL IT LIBERTY SAID. I'M NOT HEARING IT OR ANYTHING BUT I DO FEEL IT BREATHING ALMOST AND I KNOW WE ARE VERY NEAR TO IT." "GET DOWN!" J.R. SAID. "LET ME GET UP THERE." SO LIBERTY GOT DOWN OFF THE STOOL AND J.R. WENT UP. SHE WAS RIGHT SOMETHING WAS THERE. THE AIR SEEMED TO ALMOST TINGLE AND YET TO THE EYE IT APPEARED NO DIFFERENT FROM ANY OTHER WALL OR CEILING SURFACE IN THE ROOM.

WHETHER IT WAS INTUITION OR JUST A STAB IN THE DARK NEITHER ONE WOULD EVER KNOW. SUDDENLY LIBERTY WANTED TO CONSULT HER TWIN RESEARCH ILTERATURE AGAIN. MEANWHILE J.R. GOT OUT HIS BIG HUGE MAGNIFYING GLASS AND BEGAN TO EXAMINE THE EREA BENEATH THE EAVES. AT THIS TIME OF THE NIGHT THE LIGHT WAS DIM. HIS FLASHLIGHT WAS OUT OF BATTERIES AND HE COULD ONLY DRAG A FLOOR LAMP SO FAR. SO INSTEAD HE SETTLED ON EXAMINING THE COLORED SPOTS LEFT FROM THE VANISHED JELLY BEANS.

J.R. TRIED TO APPLY SOME SIMPLE DEDUCTION TO THE PRINTS. STAINS HAD BEEN LEFT BY THE JELLY BEANS

AND FURTHERMORE THEY GLOW IN THE DARK. HE TRIED TO INDUCT TO MAKE A COMPARISON OF THESE FACTS TO SOMETHING SIMILAR TO GO FROM PARTICULAR TO THE GENERAL AND FROM THERE GO TO THE BIGGER PICTURE. YET IF HE COULD DO THE DEDUCTING AND FIGURE OUT THE SMALLER BITS AND LIBERTY COULD DO THE INDUCTING AND FIGURE OUT THE LARGER PARTS EVENTUALLY THEIR THOUGHTS MIGHT COME TOGETHER LIKE PIECES OF PATCHWORK QUILT.

J.R. KEPT THINKING ABOUT THE COMPARISON OF THE STAINS TO THE AFTER IMAGE LEFT ON THE RETINA. THE VISUAL IMPRESSION LINGERED AFTER THE OBJECT MEANING THE STIMULUS WAS GONE. HE THOUGHT OF A THE WAY ANIMATED FILM WORKED. HE THOUGHT AND THOUGHT AND THOUGHT SOMEMORE BUT HIS HEAD STARTED TO HURT SO HE STOPPED THINKING FOR AWHILE. IT WAS LIBERTY'S TURN TO THINK NOW. SO SHE THOUGHT TO HERSELF "IN WHAT WAY WERE THESE STAINS LIKE AN AFTER IMAGE?" LIBERTY WONDERED.

SHE KNEW HER BROTHER J.R. HAD BEEN THINKING ABOUT THE AFTER IMAGE STUFF AND SHE TOO WAS THINKING ABOUT IT. SHE STAYED UP ALL NIGHT READING. THE NOTION OF AN AFTER IMAGE HAD REMINDED HER OF SOMETHING SHE HAD CAME ACROSSED IN THE TWINS RESEARCH FOR HER SCHOOL REPORT. WHEN J.R. WOKE UP THE NEXT MORNING LIBERTY WAS SITTING UP IN BED LOOKING ALERT. A PILE OF BOOKS AND PAPERS HAD SURROUNDED LIBERTY.

"FINALLY!" SHE SAID OUT LOUD. "GADS TALKING ABOUT ME SLEEPING LIKE A LOG." "HAVE YOU BEEN UP ALL NIGHT?" J.R. ASKED RUBBING HIS EYES. "NO I TOOK A COUPLE OF CATNAPS THE LAST ONE WAS JUST BEFORE DAWN" J.R. SAID. SHE LOOKED AT HIM WITH A HARD SERIOUS LOOK ON HER FACE. "NOW LISTEN TO THIS" LIBERTY SAID. "HAVE YOU COME UP WITH SOMETHING?" J.R. ASKED. "WELL

SORT OF SAID LIBERTY. IT'S NOT EXACTLY NEW BUT IT WAS SOMETHING I WAS JUST LED TO. I'M NOT SURE WHY BUT I THINK IT CONNECTS SOMEHOW WITH THE AFTER IMAGE STUFF."

IT'S THAT DISGUSTING THING ISN'T IT? THAT THING YOU READ ME BEFORE WHEN YOU WERE DOING YOUR REPORT? IT'S NOT DISGUSTING LIBERTY SAID IT'S SCIENCE. NOW DON'T GO SQUISHY ON ME BUT J.R. WAS ALREADY FEELING SLIGHTLY NAUSEATED AND ALL THIS WAS HAPPENING BEFORE BREAKFAST SO IT WAS BETTER THAT IT WAS ON AN EMPTY STOMACH BEFORE BREAKFAST.

IT'S THE VANISHING TWIN THEORY LIBERTY FINISHED SAYING THE WORDS AND THE THOUGHTS OUT LOUD. THERE WAS NO PUSSYFOOTING AROUND ABOUT THIS THING. SHE OPENED HER FAVORITE BOOK ON TWINS AND IT WAS ILLUSTRATED WITH PHOTOGRAPHS AND WRITTEN BY TWO WOMEN WHO WERE TWINS. "LISTEN TO THIS SAID LIBERTY AS SHE BEGAN READING OUT OF THE BOOK.

"THE BOND BETWEEN TWINS IS OFTEN SO STRONG THAT IT REMAINS EVEN WHEN ON TWIN DIES BEFORE OR SOON AFTER BIRTH. IN ONE CASE A DOCTOR WHO HAD GROWN UP AS A SINGLE CHILD HAD AWAYS FELT A SPECIAL AFFINITY TO TWINS EVEN TO THE POINT OF DREAMING HE WAS A TWIN. WHEN HE MENTIONED THESE FEELINGS TO HIS MOTHER J.R. STARTED TO SCRUNCH UP HIS FACE. HE KNEW HIS PART BUT LIBERTY HAD TO READ THIS TO HIM BEFORE. IT MADE HIM SHUDDER TO THINK ABOUT HOW THE MAN FOUND OUT THAT HE HAD A TWIN WHO HAD BEEN BORN AT THE SAME TIME EXCEPT IT HAD BEEN A STILLBORN.

"OKAY LIBERTY SAID QUICKLY "YOU KNOW THAT PART SO I'LL SKIP THOSE DETAILS BUT LISTEN TO THIS IT'S DEFINITELY WEIRD." SHE PICKED UP A PHOTOCOPY OF A MAGAZINE ARTICLE. "IT'S LIKELY THAT MANY PEOPLE

MAY HAVE HAD A TWIN BEFORE THEY WERE BORN WHICH COULD EXPLAIN IN BIOLOGICAL TERMS THE LOGING SOME SINGLETION CHILDREN HAVE FOR AN IMAGINED LONG-LAST TWIN." SHE PAUSED FOR A MINUTE AND THEN SAID "NOW HERE'S THE BIOLOGICAL BASIS."

"IT'S IT YUCKY?" J.R. ASKED. "NO! NO!" LIBERTY SAID AND RESUMED READING THE ARTICLE. "IT'S JUST MISCARRIAGE AND ONLY ONE TWIN MISCARRIES AND THE OTHER GOES ON TO BE BORN." "THAT'S ALL I WANT TO KNOW ABOUT THAT." J.R. SAID. "NOW WHY ARE YOU TELLING ME ALL THIS?" J.R. ASKED. "WHAT DOES THIS VANISHING TWIN BUSINESS HAVE TO DO WITH ANYTHING." J.R. SAID.

LIBERTY'S FACE SUDDENLY WENT BLANK. INDEED SHE DID NOT KNOW WHY SHE HAD TOLD HIM THIS BUT ON THE OTHER HAND FACE IN IT'S BLANKNESS WAS LIKE A SCREEN ABOUT TO RECEIVE AN IMAGE.

"HELEN STONER" SHE SPOKE SOFTLY "IN THE ADVENTURE OF THE SPECKLED BAND SHE WAS A TWIN WASN'T SHE?" HER SISTER WHO WAS MURDERED BY THE SWAMP ADDER WAS HER TWIN SISTER WASN'T SHE? "YES J.R. WHISPERED OUT LOUD. HE HAD FELT IT COMING ON ALL AT THE TIME HE HAD BEEN THINKING ABOUT THE JELLY BEANS SPOTS ON THE TAPE AND THE SPECKLED BAND AND HE KENW THERE HAD BEEN SOMETHING IN THE STORY HE HAD AVOIDED THINKING ABOUT. ON THEIR BIRTHDAY WHEN LIBEERTY HAD BEEN SO WRRIED ABOUT CHARLY AND MOLLY HADN'T HE ALMOST THOUGHT OF THE STONER SISTERS THEN? SO HE PUSHED IT OUT FROM HIS MIND. HELEN AND HER MURDERED SISTER JULIA STONER HAD BEEN TWINS.

NOW SIMULTANEOUSLY BOTH J.R.'S AND LIBERTY'S ATTENTION WAS DRAWN BACK TO THE SEAM IN THE EAVES. THEY COULD FEEL THE TINGLING FROM WHERE THEY SAT. THERE WAS A PRESENCE AND THE PRESENCE AT

THIS MOMENT TO BE FILLING THE ENTIRE ROOM. THEY COULD STAND IT NO LONGER AND BOTH CHILDREN GOT UP AND BOLTED FOR THE DOOR. DON'T LEAVE ME! THE VOIVE CRIED OUT.

CHAPTER 15

THE BOW STREET RUNNERS.

WHEN THE CHILDREN FLED THE ROOM IT WASN'T SO MUCH BECAUSE THEY WERE FRIGHTENED BUT IT WAS BECAUSE FOR A BRIEF INSTANT THERE WASN'T ENOUGH ROOM FOR ALL OF THEM. J.R., LIBERTY AND WHOEVER THE THIRD PERSON THIS PRESENCE WAS. THERE DIDN'T SEEM TO BE ENOUGH AIR. J.R. AND LIBERTY HAD HEADED OFF IN DIFFERENT DIRECTIONS OUT OF MEWS. LIBERTY WENT TO A NEARBY PARK WHERE ZANNY HAD TAKEN CHARLY AND MOLLY TO PLAY. AS SOON AS J.R. LEFT THE THE MEWS HE HAD BEGUN TO WALK AIMLESSLY DOWN THE STREET.

HE JUST TURNED THE CORNER ONTO DEVONSHIRE WHEN HE HEARD A SCOLDING VOICE CURL OUT INTO THE FRESH MORNING AIR. IT WAS COMING FROM A HOUSE A RATHER GRAND HOUSE ON DEVONSHIRE PLACE THAT BACKED RIGHT UP TO THE RAGOZZINO'S HOUSE IN THE MEWS. INDEED THEIR HOUSE HAD MOST LIKELY BEEN THE STABLES FOR THE GRAND HOUSE IN A PREVIOUS ERA BEFORE SHERLOCK HOLMS HAD DIED AND WENT TO A BETTER PLACE.

"NOW THIS IS THE LAST TIME I WANT TO CATCH YE'ROUND HERE BECAUSE NEXT TIME I'LL CALL THE POLICE." YOU AND YOUR TRICKS THE VOICE HAD SCOLDED. THEN J.R. SAW A TINY FIGURE LIKE A SOOTY SMUDGE STREAK DOWN THE BLOCK.

THE FIGURE STOPPED AND LOOKED DIRECTLY AT J.R. AND ALTHOUGH HE DIDN'T BECKON HIM J.R. FOLLOWED

THE FIGURE FOR SEVERAL BLOCKS THROUGH THE ALLEYWAYS TURNING LEFT AND RIGHT THEN LEFT AND LEFT AGAIN. AT ONE POINT THE FIGURE LET HIM CATCH UP A LITTLE. THERE WAS SOMETHING EERIE ABOUT THE CHILD, HE WAS DIRTY AND UNKEMPT. HIS ILLFITTING CLOTHES DIDN'T LOOK ANYTHING LIKE THE CLOTHES CHILDREN WORE TODAY. HIS PANTS STOPPED AT THE KNEES LIKE NICKERS AND HE WORE A FUNNY LITTLE TORN DOUBLE BREASTED JACKET AND ON HIS HEAD HE WORE AN OLD CAP WITH A RIDICULOUSLY SHORT BILL THAT STUCK OUT NO MORE THAN AN INCH, HIS SHOES WERE OLD FASHIONED HIGH CUT BOOTS THAT WERE SO RAGGED THAT THE TOES OF HIS LEFT FOOT STUCK OUT. HE DIDN'T LOOK OLD BUT YOU WOULD NEVER CALL HIM YOUNG DESPITE HIS SIZE BUT THOUGH HIS FACE DIDN'T LOOK SAD IT HAD CERTAINLY SEEN TOO MUCH TO LOOK JOYFUL.

J.R. REALIZED THE STRANGE LITTLE FIGURE HAD LED HIM TO BAKER STREET AND HE WAS GOING DOWN THE STEPS MARKING THE ENTRANCE TO THE UNDERGROUND. J.R. STARTED TO DIG IN HIS POCKET FOR A FIFTY CENT PIECE COIN FOR HIS FARE. THE BOY HOWEVER WINKED AND WENT RIGHT PAST THE MANCHINE WHERE PEOPLE BOUGHT THEIR TICKETS BUT NEVER THE LESS J.R. WENT UP TO A MANCHINE WHERE THERE WERE NO LINES AND QUICKLY PUT IN HIS MONEY.

THE TICKET CAME OUT AND J.R. WAS SOON RIDING THE LONG ESCALATOR DOWN TO THE TRACKS. THE BOY WAS STILL AHEAD OF HIM BUT IN SIGHT. JR FOLLOWED HIM THROUGH THE PASSAGEWAYS TO THE JUBILEE LINE AND THEY BOARDED THE SAME CAR BUT ONCE J.R. WAS IN THE CAR THE BOY HAD VANISHED INTO THIN AIR. HOW COULD J.R. LOSE HIM AFTER ALL THAT?

THERE WAS NO PASSING THROUGH THE CARS TO SEARCH FOR HIM BUT AT GREEN PARK THE SECOND STOP

He saw the boy exit on to the train's platform. J.R. was up and out of the car like a flash and he had followed the boy to the Piccadilly Line track just as a train had pulled in. This time he saw the boy get into another car. He had definitely didn't seem to want to ride in the same car as JR. Okay have it your way J.R. thought.

He was alert though and this time he stood near the door to see where the boy would get off next. They passed through the Piccadilly Circus and Leicester Square but still the boy stayed on the train. Finally at Covent Garden J.R. saw him get off the train and so J.R. got off the train too and followed the boy up the long flat plated stairs.

When they came up out of the underground the boy was almost a block away. They had crossed Bow Street and went half a block to an alley and just under a sign was a black gilt lettering where the boy had vanished into thin air again. The sign read "The Bow Street Runners." Underneath were the words specialists in detective literature. The entrance to the shop was just around the corner in the alleyway that passed between Bow Street and Drury Lane.

J.R. went in but as he went in the light was dim and yellowish as if filtered through old parchment paper. Everything had been covered with a layer of dust including the man behind the long counter who was speaking in a low creaky voice to a couple of adults. There was no sign of the boy but for a brief moment J.R. hoped that the boy was the couple's son. It was an idiotic thought J.R. said to himself. The couple was American and dressed in contemporary clothes. The woman wore Reebocks and the man had a little polo

PLAYER ON HIS STRIPED SHIRT. THERE WAS NO WAY THAT THE DIRTY SMUDGY KID WITH HIS TORN JACKET AND HIGH CUT BOOTS BELONGED TO THESE MODERN PEOPLE.

"SO YOU SEE" THE CLERK WITH THE CREAKY VOICE WAS SAYING "THE BOBBIES OUR POLICEMEN ARE A RELATIVELY NEW ORGANIZATION. THEY WERE ONLY ESTABLISHED ABOUT ONE HUNDRED AND FIFTY YEARS AGO. SO IN THE TIME BEFORE THE BOBBIES OR EVEN SCOTLAND YARD IN THE LATE EIGHTEENTH AND EARLY NINETEETH CENTURIES A DIFFERENT KIND OF POLICE ORGANIZATION EXISTED IN LONDON. IT WAS THE BOW STREET MAGISTRACY AND THE BOW STREET RUNNERS WERE THE CONSTABLES ATTCHED TO THE COURT. THIS SHOP IS NAMED AFTER THEM. THEY DID THE FINEST DETECTIVE WORK IN TOWN AND THEY WERE ALSO BRILLIANT IN THEIR PERFORMANCE AND THIS OF COURSE RIGHT HERE WAS THE CENTER OF IT ALL. LONDON AT THE TIME OF THE FOUNDING OF THE BOW STREET RUNNERS WAS A TERRIBLE DISEASE RIDDEN SQUALID PLACE FILLED WITH GIN PARLORS OVER TURNED BY CRIMINALS. THE BOW STREET RUNNERS BEGAN TO SOLVE SOME OF THE MOST NOTORIOUS CRIMES THAT PLAGUED THE CITY LIKE SWINDLES AND BIG TIME MURDERS, ASSAULTS AND KIDNAPPINGS. THE OLD POLICE STATION WAS LOCATED JUST DOWN THE BLOCK. IF YOU ARE A SHERLOCK HOLMES FAN YOU MIGHT REMEMBER MENTION OF WATSON AND SHERLOCK HOLMES COMING TO THE OLD STATION IN THE STORY "THE MAN WITH THE TWISTED LIPS."

J.R.'S EARS PIRKED UP AND A SHIVER RAN STRAIGHT HIS SPINE. HE HAD THOUGHT THE OLD BOARDS OF THE SHOP WOULD QUAKE UNDER HIM. THE CLERK WORE A STIFF WINGED COLLAR YELLOWED WITH AGE AND IT HAD MATCHED THE SALLOWNESS OF HIS SKIN WHICH WAS THE COLOR OF OLD AN OLD NWESPAPER. HE TOOK OFF HIS WIRE RIMMED SPECTACLES AND JR SWORE A SMALL CLOUD OF DUST FELL AS THE MAN BEGAN RUBBING WITH A WHITE HANDKERCHIEF. THE CLERK SQUINTED HIS EYES

AND LOOKED OVER TOWARD J.R.'S WAY AND ASKED HIM "ARE YOU INTERESTED IN SHERLOCK HOLMES LAD?"

"YES I GUESS I AM" J.R. SAID. "WELL YOU NEED NOT GUESS HERE" THE CLERK SAID CHEERFULLY. "WE HAVE THE LARGEST COLLECTION SHERLOCK HOLMES MATERIALS IN THE WORLD. HERE'S A NEW BOOK RIGHT HERE BY A WORLD EXPERT ON SHERLOCK HOLMES AND SIR ARTHUR CONAN DOYLE AND THIS ONE COVERS HIS EARLY YEARS IN LONDON WHEN HE LIVED IN THE MARYLEBONE UP ON THE TOP OF WIMPOLE STREET WHICH WAS DOWN BY THE DEVONSHIRE HOUSE TO BE EXACT."

"HE DID?" J.R.'S EYES WIDENED. "HE DID INDEED AND I WAS JUST THESE NICE FOLKS ABOUT THE BOW STREET RUNNERS FOR WHOM THIS SHOP IS NAMED AFTER. NOW THESE WERE CRACK DETECTIVES BUT IT IS THOUGHT THAT THEY EMPLOYED SMALL RUFFIAN BOYS TO DO MUCH OF THE LEGWORK BUT YOU KNOW A SMALL BOY IN DIRTY OLD LONDON BANK THEN COULD APPEAR LIKE ANOTHER SMUDGE ON THE SCENE AND SLIP INTO PLACES A FULL GROWN MAN COULDN'T GO WITHOUT BEING NOTICED."

THE IMAGE OF THE SMALL BOY LIKE A DIRTY STREAK ON THE SURFACE OF A NEW MORNING EXPLODED IN J.R.'S BRAIN. WHAT IN THE WORLD WAS HAPPENING? FIRST THE MAN ON PINCHIN LANE AND NOW THIS.

THE CLERK CONTINUED "AND YOU SEE IT IS THOUGHT THAT PERHAPS DOYLE USED THE SMALL BOYS WHO HELP THE BOW STREET RUNNERS AS HIS MODELS OR PROTOTYPES FOR THE BAKER STREET IRREGULAS. THOSE ARE THE YOUNGSTERS HOLMES REFERRED TO THEM AS THE "STREET ARABS" THE BOYS HE EMPLOYED TO PICK UP THE VITAL INFORMATION."

OF COURSE THAT WAS IT! THAT WAS WHY THE BOYS HAD AN EERIE FAMILIARITY TO HIM AND YET LOOKED

LIKE SOMETHING FROM ANOTHER CENTURY. HE HAD TO BE FROM ANOTHER CENTURY BECAUSE IT WAS THE FACE J.R. ALWAYS IMAGINED WHEN DOYLE WROTE OF THE BAKER STREET IRREGULAS THE WAIFS SHERLOCK HOLMES HAD HIRED TO HELP HIM. HADN'T HE ALWAYS IMAGINED SOME CHILD JUST ABOUT THAT SIZE AND JUST ABOUT THAT DIRTY? THAT CHILD IN FACT HAD LED HIM HERE TO THIS BOOKSHOP FOR A PURPOSE. J.R. THOUGHT IT MIGHT HAVE SOMETHING TO DO WITH THE BOOK THE MAN JUST MENTIONED. "HOW MUCH IS THAT BOOK YOU WERE JUST TALKING ABOUT?" J.R. ASKED THE CLERK. "LET'S SEE HERE, THREE POUNDS WILL BE JUST ENOUGH." J.R. HAD JUST ENOUGH LEFT OVER FROM HIS BIRTHDAY MONEY TO MAKE THE PURCHASE.

CHAPTER 16

THE BIG OLD HOUSE UP ON DEVOSHIRE PLACE.

"DOYLE'S NEXT HOME WAS IN A QUIET NEIGHBORHOOD IN MARYLEBONE WHERE THE YOUNG WRITER FIRST BEGAN HIS WORK ON THE SHERLOCK HOLMES STORIES. THE HOUSE WAS AN IDEAL PLACE TO SET UP HIS WORK PRACTICE AS WELL SITUATED ON DEVONSHIRE PLACE AT THE END OF WIMPOLE STREET. J.R. LOOKED UP FROM THE BOOK HE WAS READING TO HIS SISTER LIBERTY AND SAID "WIMPOLE STREET?" DEVONSHIRE PLACE?" LIBERTY THAT'S THIS HOUSE! AND THE MEWS IS THE STABLE FOR DOYLE'S HOUSE!" J.R. SAID OUT LOUD.

ELEMENTARY! THE WORD HUNG IN THE AIR BETWEEN THEM. THEY BOTH TURNED TOWARD THE CORNER WHERE THE CEILING DROPPED DOWN BELOW THE EAVES. THE VOICE WAS BACK! BUT THEY WEREN'T SPOOKING EACH TIME NOW. SOLWLY LIBERTY AND J.R. HAD BEGUN TO ADJUST TO THESE INTERRUPTIONS THAT SOUNDED LIKE DIM ECHOES FROM LONG AGO. "THAT HOUSE ON DEVONSHIRE PLACE IS TALLER THAN OURS" ISN'T IT? LIBERTY ASKED.

"YES BUT WE BACKED RIGHT UP TO IT" J.R. SAID STILL LOOKING AT THE CORNER. "IN OTHER WORDS" LIBERTY SAID "WE SHARE A WALL." J.R. NODDED HIS HEAD. LIBERTY CONTINUED SAYING "THEN ARE ATTIC MUST COME OUT JUST ABOUT AT THEIR SECOND FLOOR. THIS WAS PROBABY NOT REALLY AN ATTIC AT ALL BUT A HAYLOFT FOR HORSES."

"YES!" J.R. SAID SUDDENLY AS HIS STARTED SCANNING A PAGE IN THE BOOK. "LISTEN TO THIS J.R. SAID: "DOYLE TURNED HIS CONSULTING ROOM ON THE SECOND FLOOR INTO A WRITING ROOM. EVERY DAY HE WOULD SHUT HIMSELF IN THAT ROOM AND FOCUS UPON HIS WORK AND WRITING THROUGH THE GREATER PART OF THE AFTERNOON."

THE TWINS HEADS TURNED TOWARD THE SHARED WALL. "I'VE GOT TO GO OUTSIDE AND SEE WHAT THE ROOF LINE OF THIS HOUSE IS LIKE" J.R.'S SISTER LIBERTY ANNOUNCED. SHE WAS TAKING NO CHANCES AND SHE WANTED TO GET A PICTURE IN HER HEAD OF HOW THIS HOUSE CAME TOGETHER.

BOTH TWINS KNEW THEY WOULD HAVE TO RE-EXAMINE INCH BY INCH THAT CORNER OF THE ATTIC OR THE HAYLOFT AS LIBERTY NOW PREFERRED TO CALL IT. INDEED THERE WAS SO MUCH TO KEEP IN THEIR HEADS LIKE THE HOUSE DESIGNS, THEORIES OF VANISHING TWINS, GOLW IN THE DARK JELLY BEANS STAINS, THE BEEFEATER, THE TWO BIRTHDAY CANDLES THAT THE OLD MAN TOOK WHEN WE AT THE PARK FOR ARE BIRTHDAYS AND THAT STRANGE LITTLE BOY THREADING HIS WAY THROUGH THE BIG STREETS AND THE UNDERGROUND OF LONDON. SO MUCH TO THINK ABOUT AND SO LITTLE TIME. LESS THEN THEY REALIZED FOR EVERYTHING SEEMED TO COME BETWEEN THEM AND THEIR INTENDED INVESTIGATION.

"I CAN'T BELIEVE YOU COULD HAVE FORGOTTEN THAT YOUR MOTHER IS COMING THIS AFTERNOON!" ZANNY STOOD FLABBERGASTED IN THE GARDEN ROOM AS SHE WATCHED MOLLY AND CHARLY FINISH FEEDING THE FISH.

IF THE ATTIC HAD BECOME A WORLD TO LIBERTY AND J.R. THEN THE GARDEN ROOM HAD BEEN ONE FOR MOLLY AND CHARLY. THEY HAD DISCOVERED THAT THE LEAVES

OF THE WATER LILIES WERE SO STRONG THEY COULD ACTUALLY HOLD THINGS UP. SO THEY HAD GONE TO THE A SHOP ON MARYLEBONE STREET AND BOUGHT TINY CHINA ANIMALS THAT WEIGHED LESS THEN AN OUNCE EACH TO PUT ON THE BROAD GREEN LEAVES OF THE FLOATING PLANTS THAT WERE IN THE WATER. THEIR FIRST PURCHASE HAD BEEN A SMALL BRIGHT GREEN FROG, THEN A LITTLE KITTEN AND THEN AFTER THAT ZANNY BROUGH THEM A VERY SPECIAL TREAT AND IT WAS A CHINA THATCHED COTTAGE. THEIR DAD HAD FOUND ANOTHER LITTLE HOUSE AND A FIGURE OF AN ELF. THE GARDEN POOL WAS BEGINNING TO LOOK LIKE A SMALL FLOTTING VILLAGE.

THE SMALLER TWINS NOW CROUCHED BY THE POOL ON THEIR KNEES WATCHING THE FISH SWIM UNDER AND AROUND THIS FLOATING WORLD BUT AFTER AWHILE THEIR KNEES STARTED TO HURT SO THEY GOT UP. THEY SPENT LOTS OF HOURS PLAYING HERE BECAUSE IT'S SO NICE. IT HAS BECOME A KIND OF WATER DOLLHOUSE TO THEM. THE MANAGED IT ALL JUST LIKE REAL HOUSE. THEY FILLED IT WITH CHARACTERS AND SCENERY AND THEN GRANDMA STELLA DIRECTED THE ACTION EXCEPT FOR THE FISH OF COURSE. IT WAS THEIR WORLD AND THEY WERE THE BOSSES AND THEY WERE ALSO TRYING TO SAVE SOME MORE MONEY UP SO THEY COULD EXPAND THEIR FLOATING VILLAGE. THEY HAD SEEN A LITTLE CHINA CASTLE AND A FAIRY PRINCESS WITH WINGS.

"WE DIDN'T REALLY FORGET EXACTLY" LIBERTY WAS SAYING RATHER LAMELY. "IT'S JUST THAT SHE WILL BE HERE IN LESS THAN TWO HOURS AND IT'S HERE BIRTHDAY." "OH GEE!" BOTH LIBERTY'S AND J.R.'S MOUTHS DROPPED OPEN. THERE WAS NO DENYING THAT THEY HAD FORGOTTEN THAT THEIR MOTHER WAS ARRIVING ON HER BIRTHDAY. DON'T YOU REMEMBER? WE'RE GOING TO STRATFORD UPON AVON SHAKESPEARE'S BIRTHPLACE BECAUSE THAT'S WHAT YOUR MOM WANTED TO DO FOR HER BIRTHDAY AND YOU GUYS ARE GOING TO THE BIG HUGE PRODUCTION OF

THE SHAKESPEARE PLAY WHICH WILL BE TOO LONG FOR CHARLY AND MOLLY BUT YOU'LL FIND IT INTERESTING. WE'RE STTAYING AT A CHARMING OLD INN CALLED THE "ROSE CROWN." IT'S VERY HARD TO GET INTO AND YOUR DAD MADE RESERVATIONS WEEKS AGO.

"YOU MEAN WE'RE NOT GOING TO BE HERE TONIGHT?" J.R. ASKED DUMBFOUNDEDLY. "NO THAT'S WHAT I JUST SAID." "WELL WHAT ABOUT TOMORROW NIGHT?" LIBERTY ASKED FEARFULLY. "NO BECAUSE YOUR MOTHER HAS RESERVATIONS TWO NIGHTS BECAUSE SHE REALLY WANTS TO SEE "A MIDSUMMER NIGHT'S DREAM AND RICHARD THE THIRD." "WHAT ARE THOSE?" LIBERTY ASKED. "SHAKESPEARE PLAYS!" FOR GOODNESS SAKES YOU HAVE HEARD OF WILLIAM SHAKESPEARE HAVEN'T YOU?" SIAD ZANNY. ZANNY COULDN'T IMAGINE WHAT WAS WRONG WITH THE OLDER TWINS BECAUSE THEY HAVE BEEN ACTING KIND OF ODD LATELY.

CHAPTER 17

THE STRATFORD FRUSTRATION.

ALL OUR PLANTS SQUASHED! THE TELEPATHIC IMAGES WERE SPRINTING ACROSS LIBERTY'S BRAIN. YOU SEE ONE OF THESE OLD INNS YOU'VE SEEN THEM ALL J.R. TELAFLASHED.

CAN YOU BELIEVE HOW BORING THAT PLAY WAS? I MEAN IF A MIDSUMMER NIGHT'S IS WHAT THEY CALLED FUNNY FOUR HUNDRED YEARS AGO YOU KIND OF WONDER HOW THEY GOT FROM THAT TO MONTY PYTHON. LIBERTY SAID.

YEAH COME TO THINK OF IT WHY CAN'T WE AT LEAST BE AT A MONTY PYTHON FESTIVAL INSTEAD OF THAT DUMB BORING SHAKESPEARE FESTIVAL SAID LIBERTY.

ZANNY GAVE THEM A SEVERE LOOK AFTER THEY SAID THAT ABOUT THE SHAKESPEARE PLAY. SHE HAD A FEELING THAT THE B-WORD AS IN B-FOR BORING WAS HOVERING IN THE AIR. THEY WERE SITTING IN THE PUB ROOM OF A SIXTEENTH CENTURY INN HAVING A PLOWMAN'S LUNCH WHICH CONSISTED OF BREAD, CHEESE AND SOMETHING THAT LOOKED LIKE LIVERWURST. THE CHILDREN ALL HATED THIS LUNCH BUT IT WAS BETTER THAN ANYTHING ELSE ON THE MENU.

"THEY SHOULD LEARN HOW TO MAKE SQUISHY WHITE BREAD IN THIS COUNTRY" CHARLY SAID. "I'LL EAT THIS BECAUSE I KNOW IT'S HEALTHY FOR ME AND WILL HELP

ME GROW UP STRONG AND I'LL EVEN EAT THE PATTY." "YES MOLLY SAID BUT ZANNY HAD CORRECTED CHARLY. "IT'S CALLED PATE REFERRING TO THE SLICE OF LIVER PATE ON THEIR PLATES AS SHE SAID THAT WITH A BIG SMILE ON HER FACE." "YES WHILE YOU'RE LIVING IN A FOREIGN COUNTRY IT IS NICE TO TRY AND BROADEN YOUR TASTES." YES SAID CHARLY AS SHE NODDED HER HEAD AND SAID "THAT'S WHAT WE'RE DOING BROADENING ARE TASTES." COULD YOU THROW UP OR WHAT? LIBERTY TELAFLASHED. MISS GODDY TWO SHOES MOLLY SAID TO LIBERTY. SO THEN THAT MAKES MISS GODDY FOUR SHOES THEN LIBERTY SAID BACK TO MOLLY.

CHARLY AND MOLLY WERE LAYING IT ON THICK BECAUSE THEY HAD SENSED THAT SOMETHING WAS MAKING THEIR OLDER BROTHER AND SISTER DISTANT AND DIFFICULT AND THEY ALSO KENW ZANNY WAS SLIGHTLY ANNOYED WITH J.R. AND LIBERTY. AS SO MUCH OFTEN HAPPENS IN A BIG FAMILY WHEN ONE CHILD IS BEING STUBBORN OR DIFFICULT THE OTHER BECOMES EXTRA GOOD.

ZANNY LOOKED AT THE LITTLE TWINS NOW AS THEY SO SWEETLY SPOKE OF HEALTH AND BROADENING THEIR TASTES. SHE KNEW EXACTLY WHAT THEY WERE DOING AND SHE DIDN'T TRUST THE SITUATION AT ALL. AS FAR AS SHE WAS CONCERNED THERE WERE FOUR CHILDREN THAT WAS IN CHARGE OF WHEN THE PARENTS WERE NOT AROUND AND SOMETHING WAS UP! SHE WASN'T SURE WHAT IT WAS BUT IT COULD MEAN TROUBLE BECAUSE TWO PAIRS OF TWINS EACH PAIR NOT ONLY DIFFERENT BUT EACH INDIVIDUAL CHILD IS VERY DIFFERENT SO THEREFORE IT WAS NOT MERELY TWO PAIR OF TWINS ADDING UP TO FOUR KIDS IT WAS INSTEAD THE SQUARE OF THE SUM OF THE PAIRS. THE SQUARE OF A NUMBER IS THAT NUMBER TIMES ITSELF SO IT WAS FOUR TIMES FOUR. IT WAS IN SHORT AS LIBERTY LIKED TO SAY "DOUBLE TROUBLE SQUARED."

CHAPTER 18

THE NIGHT OF THE CHARGED PARTICLES.

THEY COULDN'T HAVE RETURNED TO THE DEVONSHIRE MEWS FAST ENOUGH FOR LIBERTY'S AND J.R.'S TASTE. IT WAS RAINY LATE IN THE EVENING AND PASSED EVERYONE'S BEDTIME AND EVERYBODY WAS TIRED AND THEY GROGGILY MADE THEIR WAY TO BED WITHOUT BRUSHING THEIR THEETH OR EVEN WASHING THEIR FACES. EVERYONE WAS ASLEEP WHITHIN A HALF HOUR AFTER THEIR RETURN. EVERYONE THAT IS EXCEPT FOR J.R. AND LIBERTY RAGOZZINO WHO WERE NOT SLEEPY AT ALL. THEIR MOOD WAS WILD AS THE WEATHER. THE SOFT DRIZZLE THEY DRIVEN HOME IN HAD ESCALATED INTO A POUNDING RAIN AND A HUGE SMOKY THUNDERHEAD BLOTTED OUT THE MOON. SOON THE LONDON SKY OUTSIDE THEIR ATTIC WINDOW WAS VEINED WITH THE CRACKLE OF LIGHTNING. THEY HAD PRETENDED TO GO TO SLEEP AND LIBERTY HAD CREPT DOWNSTAIRS TO CHECK WORRIED PERHAPS THE THUNDERSTORM MIGHT KEEP THE FAMILY AWAKE BUT SHE COULD TELL THAT THE HOUSE SLEPT. SHE KNEW HER FAMILY WELL AND SHE HAD A SENSE OF THESE THINGS. HER EAR WAS AS FINELY ATTUNED TO THE NICE OF SLEEP AT LEAST THE SLEEP OF HER OWN FAMILY AS A BIG HUGE CONDUCTOR'S TO THE INSTRUMENTS OF HIS ORCHESTRA. SHE HAD PICKED OUT THE MUSIC OF TRUE DEEP SLEEP IN EACH MEMBER OF HER FAMILY IN THE SAME WAY A CONDUCTOR CAN HEAR THE BIG DIFFERENT PARTS BUILD A CHORD. NOW AS LIBERTY MOUNTED THE ATTIC STAIRS ONCE MORE SHE KNEW THAT HER FAMILY SLEPT VERY DEEPLY. WHEN SHE ENTERED THE

ROOM J.R. WAS STANDING BAREFOOT IN HIS PAJAMAS BY THE DESK. THE NEW JELLY BEANS THEY HAD SET OUT BEFORE THEY HAD LEFT FOR STRATFORD UPON AVON WEREN'T THERE ANY MORE BECAUSE THEY WERE GONE. THE SPECKLED BAND OF TAPE WAS MORE MOTTLED WITH COLOR THAN EVER. LIGHTNING NOW FLASHED IN THE ROOM ILLUMINATING IT WITH THE FRENZIED PULSATING LIGHT OF A DISCO BALL BUT THERE WERE NO DANCES JUST TWO FRAGILE LOOKING CHILDREN IN THEIR NIGHT CLOTHES WITH THEIR LARGE LUMINOUS GRAY EYES, THEIR PALE FRECKLED FACES AND SOMBER BROWS SLASHED WITH JET BLACK BANGS.

LONG ZIGZAGS OF WHITE BLAZED IN THE SKY AND THE MASSIVE CLOUDS HEAVY AND DARK AT THEIR BASES HAD SPREAD AND WERE FLATTENED ON TOP BY THE WIND WHICH HAD GROWN STRONGER BUT THE LONG SHARKISH CLOUDS STREAKED THROUGH THE TURBULENT SKY AND J.R. WAS MESMERIZED BY THE DISPLAY. HE KNEW HOW TO JUDGE THE DISTANCE OF THE STORM CENTER BY COUNTING THE SECONDS BETWEEN THE FLASH AND LIGHTNING AND THE BOOM OF THUNDER. A FIVE SECOND GAP EQUALED A MILE BUT NOW THE GAPS WERE TWO AND THREE SECONDS APART AND LIBERTY'S ATTENTION WASN'T ON THE BIG ELECTRICAL STORM OUTSIDE THEIR WINDOW BUT ON THE STORM SHE HAD HEARD IN HER HEAD AS SHE WATCHED THE CORNER OF THE ROOM THAT SHARED A WALL WITH THE HOUSE THAT HAD ONCE BEEN DOYLE'S. SHE STARED AT THE EAVES AND WAS IMAGINING THAT SHE WAS VISUALIZING THE PRESENCE THAT NIGHT.

J.R. KEPT WATCHING THE CLOUDS THAT WERE CIRCLING, SCHOOLING LIKE PREDATORY FISH NOW AND DISCHARGING THEIR ENORMOUS BIG ELECTRICAL BURDEN THAT SHATTERED THE SKY. THE TIME BETWEEN THE FLASH AND THE THUNDER WAS GROWING SHORTER WHICH MEANT THE CENTER OF THE STORM WAS COMING CLOSER. THERE WERE NO MORE SECONDS TO COUNT ONLY SLIVERS OF SECONDS

BETWEEN THE FLASH OF LIGHTNING AND THE BOOM OF THE THUNDER. HE KNEW ALL ABOUT THE THUNDERHEADS AND STORM CLOUDS AND HE ALSO KNEW HOW THE TOP LAYER ATTRACTS THE STRONG POSITIVE ELECTRICAL CHARGE WHILE THE MIDDLE AND BOTTOM LAYERS BEGIN WITH MOSTLY NEGATIVE CHARGES BUT HE ALSO KNOWS HOW HARD A PROCESS CALL INDUCTION IS AND HOW HARD DEDUCTION IS BECAUSE HE DEDUCTED THE GROUND BELOW AND THE CLOUDS BECAME VERY STRONG CHARGED AND SOMETIMES EVEN CAUSING PEOPLE'S HAIR TO STAND ON END. HE KNEW HOW ICE CRYSTALS COULD FORM IN ELECTRICAL STROMS EVEN IN THE SUMMERTIME AND UPON COLLISION BECOME POSITIVELY CHARGED. THESE CRYSTALS WOULD THEN DROP AND MELT AS NEGATIVELY CHARGED RAIN AND HE KNEW THAT WITH EACH SECOND ALL AROUND THEM THE AIR WAS HEAVY WITH ZILLIONS AND ZILLIONS OF COLLISIONS FROM CHARGED PARTICLES. SOMETHING WAS GOING TO HAPPEN J.R. SAID.

THERE'S MORE THEN JUST SEAMS THERE BECAUSE ALL OF THE WALLS AND THE CEILING HAVE THE SAME SPACE BETWEEN THE SEAMS WHERE THE WALL COVERING WAS TAPED BUT THERE IS ANOTHER LINE STARTING AT THE BASE WHERE THE WALL MEETS THE FLOOR. WE WEREN'T ALWAYS LOOKING AT THE CEILING BEFORE.

CEILING.... WHAT TAPE? I CAN'T READ YOU. TOO MANY PARTICLES AND THE AIR IS TOO CHARGED LIBERTY SAID TO JR. THE TWINS TELEPATHIC COMMUNICATION BETWEEN THEM WAS BREAKING UP AND BECAME TOO RACKED WITH STATIC FOR GOOD TRANSMISSION. THEY HAD JUST BEGUN TO TALK OUT LOUD WHEN SUDDENLY THERE WAS A HUGE CLAP OF THUNDER AND THE SKY FLASHED AT THE SAME TIME. A WHITE ENERGY SEARED INTO THE ATTIC. THE SPECKLED BAND GLOWED LIKE A GEMSTONE SERPENT.

"I SEE IT!" LIBERTY WAILED OUT LOUD TO JR. J.R. SPUN AROUND AS HIS HEART SKIPED A BEAT AND THEN FROM

THE CORNER THERE WAS A TERRIBLE SOUND OF A SOFT HISSING LIKE A JET OF STEAM EXCAPING AND IT WAS THE SAME KIND OF SOFT HISSING THAT JULIA STONER MUSH HAVE HEARD BEFORE THE DEADLY SWAMP ADDER STRUCK.

CHAPTER 19

THE HIDDEN DOOR.

It wasn't the hiss of the swamp adder that J.R. heard. It was the sound of tape being peeled off the wall by his sister. "We're so stupid" Liberty was saying. "We were always looking up toward the ceiling and not down." She was on hew knees crouched in the corner under the eaves. "When that last flash of lightning lit up the room I just happened to be looking down. They got a little sloppy here and I could see the bulge." J.R. was now down on his knees beside her. Within ten minutes they had untaped a three foot square area on the wall just beneath the eaves. They removed two pieces of plasterboard and were now looking at what had appeared to be very old thin narrow laths of wood that were joined together to make a support structure for the long big plasterboard.

"Look they're damp" J.R. said. "Rain must be getting in here."

"Of course!" Liberty said. A picture of the rooflines flashed in her mind. She remembered their distinctive profile from when she had gone out to the sidewalk a few days before to look at the houses like the mews and the big house on Devonshire Place.

The roofs join at a funny angle Liberty said. The water must pool where they come together.

"YOU WOULD HAVE THOUGHT THEY WOULD HAVE DONE BETTER JOB OF REFINISHING."

"QUICK AND DIRTY AND PROBABLY DIDN'T HAVE TIME TO REPLACE ALL THESE LITTLE WOOD PIECES." J.R. PULLED OUT PIECES OF THE LATHS BECAUSE THEY CAME OUT EASILY. "LOOK THEY PUT IN A LITTLE BIT OF INSULATION BACK HERE BUT IT'S GETTING ROTTEN TOO FROM ALL THE THE DAMPNESS." HE THEN PULLED OUT SOME WADDED STUFFING THAT LOOKED LIKE HEAVY COURSE OF COTTON.

"WHAT'S BEHIND IT THERE?" LIBERTY ASKED. "WHAT DO YOU MEAN?"

J.R. ASKED LIBERTY. "LOOK SHE SAID AS SHE PULLED OUT MORE OF THAT INSULATION MATERIAL. THERE WAS A PANEL OF DARK WOOD THAT WAS IN MUCH BETTER SHAPE THAN THE LATHS BECAUSE THEIR WAS ONLY A CRACK OR TWO IN THE WOOD. "WELL THE INSULATION MUST HAVE DONE SOME GOOD HERE" J.R. WAS SAYING. "LOOK JR! THOSE AREN'T CRACKS SAID LIBERTY. THEY'RE TOO EVEN TO BE LITTLE CRACKS LIBERTY HAD SAID OUT LOUD TO HER BROTHER JR. THIS IS A VERY SMALL DOOR" LIBERTY SAID.

"OH MY GOSH! YOU'RE RIGHT AND LOOK THERE ARE MORE OF THE JELLY BEAN STAINS." INDEED J.R. SAID. AROUND ONE OF THE CACKS THERE WAS A CLUSTER OF DAY GLOW BEAN SHAPED SPOTS. WHAT IN THE WORLD COULD IT BE? J.R. ASKED LIBERTY. HOW HAD THE JELLY BEAN STAINS GOTTEN TO THIS POINT FROM THE TAPE ON THE DESK?

BOTH TWINS HANDS WERE ON THE SMALL PANEL DOOR WHEN IT MOVED SLIGHTLY UNDER THEIR TOUCH. THEY LOOKED INTO ONE ANOTHER'S EYES SEARCHINGLY. THE LIGHTNING AND THUNDER HAD LET UP AND THEIR TELEPATHIC CHANNELS WERE CLEARING.

SHOULD WE PUSH IT OPEN ALL THE WAY? I DON'T KNOW. DO YOU THINK THERE'S A SNAKE IN THERE? I HAVEN'T HEARD ANY HISSING SOUNDS. IT'S CREEPY SAID JR. I KNOW SAID LIBERTY. MAYBE IF WE PUSH IT A LITTLE BIT TOGETHER. THEY PUT THEIR HANDS TOGETHER OVER LAPPING ONE ON TOP OF THE OTHER AND PUSHED ON THE LITTLE DOOR THAT WAS ON TOP OF THE ROOF. AFTER AWILE OF PUSHING ON THE LITTLE DOOR IT SWUNG OPEN. THE LIGHT WAS DIM BUT PEERING RIGHT THROUGH A SPACE NO BIGGER THAN A SMALL CLOSET AND SMALLER THAN A LARGE CUPBOARD. IT WAS DUSTY WITH COBWEBS BUT IN THE DIM LIGHT THEY COULD SEE ANOTHER SMALL DOOR OPPOISITE OF THE DOOR THEY JUST OPENED.

INSIDE BETWEEN THE TWO DOORS WAS A PACKAGE WRAPPED IN HEAVY CLOTH. THEIR HANDS WERE DRAWN TO THE PACKAGE LIKE IRON FILINGS TO A MAGNET. THEY DIDN'T EVEN PAUSE TO ASK SHOULD WE OR COULD WE FOR THEY KNEW THAT IT WAS FOR THIS PACKAGE THAT THEY HAD BEEN BROUGHT HERE OR SUMMONED ON SOME BIG CONVENED SIGNALE TO THESE MEWS. IT WASN'T BY ACCIDENT THAT HAD FOUND THEIR WAY TO THE DEVONSHIRE MEWS BUT INDEED BY A DESIGN AND THE DESIGN WAS ABOUT TO BE UNVEILED AND THE SKEIN OF THE MYSTERY UNVEILED THE SHADOWS LIGHTENED AND THE BIG MEANING REVEALED.

THE TWINE OF THE PACKAGE UNKNOTTED EASILY AND THEY UNFOLDED THE DARKENED CANVAS. WITHIN THE CANVAS WAS ANOTHER LAYER OF HEAVILY OILED PAPER WRAPPED AROUND SOMETHING. IT'S SEAMS WERE SEALED WITH A DARK MAROON SEALING WAX THAT LOOKED LIKE THE COLOR OF RED WINE. THEY BROKE THE SEALS AND OPENED THE PAPER. "IT'S WRITING" LIBERTY WHISPERED TO JR. "PAGES AND PAGES OF WRITING LIBERTY SAID LIFTING ONE PAGE AFTER ANOTHER."

CHAPTER 20

THE RETURN OF THE VANISHING TWIN.

THE FRONT DOOR HAD OPENED AND MY TWIN BROTHER HAD DROPPED TO HIS KNEES WITH HIS FACE BLANCHED AND WITH HIS HANDS GROPING HIS THROAT AND IN A SUDDENLY SORE VOICE HE SAID "THE SPECKLED BAND! THE SPECKLED BAND!" J.R.SAID AS HIS SISTER LIBERTY WAS READING FROM THE PAGES THEY FOUND IN THE PACKAGE.

THE HANDWRITING WAS SMALL ALMOST FLAT ALONG THE LINE EVEN. IT WAS QUITE LEGIBLE SAID LIBERTY AS SHE READ ON. "I GLANCED AT MY OWN TWIN SHADRACH. HIS PALE PLUMP EYES NEVER LEFT THE FACE OF THE DEAD MAN HARRY STONER. AS HE LISTENED TO CHILLING TALE I COULD FEEL HIS HORROR FOR WE TOO KNEW THE SUBTLE LINKS THAT BIND TWO SOULS WHICH ARE SO CLOSELY ALLIED. WTIHIN THE NEXT FEW MINUTES MR. HENRY STONER WOULD TELL US OF THE LINKS THAT BOUND HIM TO HIS TWIN BROTHER BUT FOR NOW SHADRACH REMAINED FIXED AND HIS KEEN MIND HAD UNCANNY POWERS OF INDUCTION AT WORK AS HE OBSERVED THIS GENTLE BUT WEARY MAN WHOSE HAGGARD THE EXPRESSION THAT WAS WROUGHT BY FEAR AND SLEEPLESS NIGHTS.

THEY TOOK TURNS READING THE TALE AS IT WENT ON FOR SEVERAL PAGES. "I TOOK A STEP FORWARD AND IN AN INSTANT THE MAN'S CAP BEGAN TO MOVE AND FROM THE DEAD MAN'S HAIR REARED THE SQUAT DIAMOND SHAPE

HEAD AND PUFFED NECK OF A LOATHSOME SERPENT. IT WRITHED TOWARD THE DEAD MAN'S HAND AND A BOWL OF THE MOST LUSTROUS PEARLS EVER TO BE SEEN IN CHRISTENDOM."

NOW LIBERTY READ THE CONCLUSION OF THE STORY OUT LOUD FOR EVERYONE TO HEAR. "I HAD COME TO AN ENTIRELY ERRONEOUS OF A BIG CONCLUSION WHICH SHOWS MY DEAR SHERLOCK HOLMES HOW BADLY DANGEROUS IT MAY BE TO REASON WITH INSUFFICIENT DATA. I CAN ONLY CLAIM THE MERIT THAT I INSTANTLY RECONSIDERED MY POSITION AND HAD CORRECTED MYSELF IN MIDCOURSE. THE DANGER WHICH THREATENED MY BROTHER HENRY SOTNER AND KILLED HIS BROTHER HARRY CAME NOT FROM THE WINDOW OR THE DOOR BUT FROM THE BELL ROPE. A VENTILATOR THAT DOSE NOT VENTILATE AND A BELL ROPE WITH NO BELL BOTH CAN ONLY SERVE AS A BRIDGE FOR SOMETHING PASSING THROUGH THE HOLE TO THE BED AND OF COURSE THE VENTILATOR SERVED AS SAFE HIDING PLACE FOR THE JEWELS AS WELL.

"I SUPPOSE IN ONE SENSE THEN I AM INDIRECTLY RESPONSIBLE FOR THE DEATH OF HENRY STONER'S UNCLE BARTHOLOMEW SHOLTO BY DRIVING THE SNAKE BACK THROUGH THE VENTILATOR. I CAN'T SAY THAT THE DEATH OF A MURDERER HOWEVER A MAN OF SUCH MONUMENTAL GREED THAT HE WOULD KILL HIS OWN NEPHEW WEIGHS VERY HEAVILY ON MY CONSCIENCE SAID HARRY. LIBERTY THEN PAUSED FOR A MINUTE AND CONTUNED TO READ AND THEN SAID "THE END WRITTEN BY CONAN A. DOYLE 1887."

"THAT'S SO WEIRD!" J.R. SAID AS LIBERTY PUT DOWN THE LAST PAGE. "SHADRACH HOLMES!" PRECISELY! SAID LIBERTY. THERE WAS A DEEP SIGH FOR A MINUTE AND THEN J.R. AND LIBERTY STARED AT ONE ANOTHER. DID YOU SAY THAT? NO. DID YOU? OF COUSE NOT YOU FOOLS! I SPOKE ME SHADRACH HOLMES CREATION OF THE GREAT

SIR ARTHUR CONAN DOYLE AND YOU ARE THE FIRST ASIDE FROM DOYLE EVER TO SEE MY NAME WRITTEN IN WRITING BUT THE STORY IN WHICH I APPEARED WAS ALTERED BECAUSE DOYLE CUT ME OUT AFTER THE FIRST DRAFT. IN THE REWRITE THERE WAS NEVER A MENTION OF ME SO MY NANE SANK INTO OBLIVION AND NEVER TO BE SPOKEN OR READ OF AGAIN IT WAS GONE FOREVER UNTILL YOU TWO CAME ALONG.

I THOUGHT IT WOULD TAKE YOU FOREVER TO ACCUALLY SAY MY NAME. YOU SEE THE RULES OF THIS BUSINESS ARE SUCH THAT THE LITERARY GHOST'S NAMES MUST BE SPOKEN OUT LOUD BEFORE HE OR SHE CAN MATERIALIZE BUT BY SPEAKING THE NAMES YOU INVOKE THE LITERARY GHOST OR RATHER LITERARY STILLBORN I PREFER THAT TERM BECAUSE IT'S A MORE DESCRIPTION OF ARE SHADOWY EXISTENCE LANGUISHING IN UNPUBLISHED MANUSCRIPS AND FIRST DRAFTS.

IN ANY CASE AS I WAS SAYING ARE YOU TALKING TO US IN ARE HEADS? ASKED LIBERTY. YES MY DEAR. WOULD YOU PREFER ME TO TALK OUT LOUD? I CAN DO THAT TOO. THE VOICE SUDDENLY SHIFTED FROM INSIDE THEIR LITTLE HEADS AND COULD BE HEARD WITHIN THE ROOM. "PLEASE CHOOSE, EITHER WAY SUITS ME FINE. I CAN SPEAK OUT LOUD, WITHIN THE TELEPATHIC CHANNLES, I'M QUITE FLUENT IN BOTH WAYS. CHOOSE YOU MODE AND THEN I WE'LL GET ON WITH IT. HOW CAN I ENTER INTO YOU TELEPATHIC COMMUNICATION CHANNLES?

J.R. HAD BARELY THOUGHT THE QUESTION BEFORE SHADRACH WAS ANSWERING IT TELEPATHICALLY. I TOO WAS A TWIN ALTHOUGH BRIEFLY STILL IT COUNTS. YOU LEARN QUICKLY WHEN YOU LIVE IN A MANUSCRIPT EVEN IF IT'S ONLY A FIRST DRAFT AND AS YOU WELL KNOW FORM YOUR OWN EXPERIENCE TWINS HAVE AS MY CREATOR DOYLE WROTE IN HIS MANUSCRIPT YOU JUST READ MYSTICAL BONDS THAT DO YOU ALLOW SUCH COMMUNICATION BUT

THAT'S BETWEEN TWO TWINS OF ONE SET. HOW COME YOU GET INTO OUR TELEPATHIC PATTERNS?

WELL THAT COMES WITH THE TERRITORY OF BEING A GHOST WHO WAS ONCE A TWIN. IT'S THE GHOST PART THAT HELPS ME EAVESDROP. PARDON THE PUN BUT YOU OF COURSE REALIZE THAT IT IS WITHIN THESE EAVES THAT I MOSTLY HANG ABOUT. ONCE YOU HAVE BEEN A TWINS AND THEN BECOME A GHOST THE OPPPORTUNITIES FOR COMMUNICATING AND GATHERING INFORMATION IS ENDLESS. YOU AND YOUR OWN LITTLE SISTER WILL BE ABLE TO CROSS-COMMUNICATE BEAUTIFULLY WHEN YOU ALL BECOME GHOSTS.

YES I KNOW THEY HAVE SUCH DISORDELY LITTLE MINDS CHARLOTTE AND AMALIE. THE THOUGHT OF CROSS-COMMUNICATION WITH THEM IS RATHER DAUNTING TO SAY THE LEAST. ARE THEY STILL SO KEEN ABOUT THE PRESS ON NAILS?

"OH GEE YOU KNOW ABOUT THAT?" LIBERTY SAID WITH AN EMBARRASING LOOK ON HER FACE. OH YES MY DEAR WELL AS I WAS SAYING SHADRACH CONTINUED THE RULES OF THIS GAME ARE AS FOLLOWS. IF ONE IS A LITTLE LITERARY STILLBORN SUCH AS MYSELF AND THAT'S WHAT YOU CALL IT WHEN AS A CHARACTER YOU HAVE ONLY LIVED WITHIN THE PAGES OF A FIRST DRAFT ON OR UNPUBLISHED WORK YOUR NAME MUST BE READ OUT LOUD FROM THAT MANUSCRIPT AND THEN THE TWINS BOTH FELT AN INVISIBLE FINGER TO CALL ATTENTION TO A SPECIAL POINT BEING MADE AND THEN REPEATED SHADRACH THE NAME MUST ALSO BE MENTIONED OUT OF THE CONTEXT OF THE WORK ITSELF AND INSTEAD SPOKEN WITHIN THE FRAME WORK OF LITERARY CRITIQUE OR CRITICISM. SAMUEL JHONSON YOU'RE NOT BUT APPARENTLY JUST YOUR SAYING THAT IS SO WEIRD SHADRCH HOLMES WAS ENOUGH TO DO THE TRICK AND HELP ME TO MATERIALZE SO TO SPEAK. THE MORE I SPEAK

THE MORE PARTS OF ME APPEAR. FOR NOW YOU'LL HAVE TO BE CONTENT WITH JUST MY VOICE.

"WHO'S SAMUEL JOHNSON?" LIBERTY ASKED. DR. JOHNSON YOU'VE NEVER HEARD OF HIM? AGAIN THEY FELT A KIND OF GESTURE STIR THE AIR AN THIS TIME IT WAS NOT A FINGER BUT THE PALM OR MORE PRECISELY THE HEEL OF THE PALM OF THE HAND SLAPPING AN INVISIBLE FOREHEAD IN HIGH DISBELIEF. DON'T THEY TEACH YOU CHILDREN ANYTHING NOWADAYS? HE, SAMUEL JOHNSON OR DR. JOHNSON AS WAS KNOWN WAS THE GREAT ENGLISH LEXICOGRAPHER CRITIC AND AUTHOR OF THE LAST CENTURY OR RATHER TWO CENTURIES AGO IF WE COUNT BACK FROM YOUR TIME RATHER THEN MINE AND HE WOULD HAD HAVE A BIT MORE TO SAY ABOUT MY LITTLE EXISTENCE THAN "THAT IS SO WEIRD SHADRACH HOLMES." DO THEY DO NOTHING TO DEVELOP YOUR VOCABULARY A BIT MORE IN YOUR MIND AND SCHOOLING?

"WE HAVE WORDLY WISE" LIBERTY SAID. WORDLY WISE? SHADRACH HAD PAUSED FOR A SECOND. WHAT'S THAT? SHADRACH ASKED THE TWINS. "IT'S THIS KIND OF WORK BOOK THAT HAS A LOT OF VOCABULARY AND STUFF AND YOU WRITE SENTENCES AND FILL IN THE BLANKS WITH THE NEW WORDS AND LETTERS."

FILL IN THE BLANKS HE SAID THERE WAS A DEFINITE NOTE OF DISBELIEF IN HIS VOICE. THEY THINK CHILDREN CAN LEARN SYNTAX, NARRATIVE AND STORY FORM BY FILLING IN THE BLANKS? AS FAR AS I CAN ASCERTAIN MR. WORDLY WISE IS ONLY WISE TO A FEW WORDS SUCH AS "WEIRD, BORING, AND DANGEROUS." DO YOU HAVE ANY IDEA HOW MANY TIMES YOU CHILDREN SAY THOSE WORD EVERY DAY? YOU KNOW THEY WOULD DO MUCH BETTER GIVING YOU REAL BOOKS TO READ RATHER THAN THIS STUPID WORDLY WISE STUFF. WELL ENOUGH ABOUT THAT WE HAVE WORK TO DO.

"WE DO?" BOTH CHILDREN ASKED AT ONCE. OF COURSE WE DO SAID SHADRACH. YOU DON'T WANT ME TO HAVE REMAIN A LITERARY STILLBORN FOREVER DOOMED TO THIS PURGATORIAL EXISTENCE OF BEING DEAD BUT NEVER HAVING REALLY LIVED DO YOU? I MEAN WHEN YOU SEE ON A TOMBSTONE THE WORDS REST IN PEACE IT IS ASSUMED THAT THE PERSON HAS LAUGHED AND PLAYED AND WORKED AND LOVED IN LIFE AND IN SHORT HAS HAD A COMPLETE LIFE AND BECAUSE OF THIS THEY CAN REST IN PEACE. IT IS THE SAME FOR LITERARY GHOST OR STILLBORNS. THERE IS NO REST FOR US UNTILL WE'VE HAD OUR LIVES OR UNTILL OUR PLACE IN LITERARY HISTORY IS RECOGNIZED EVEN IF ONLY ON A CRUMPLED PIECE OF PAPER THROWN INTO A WASTEBASKET. TO BE RECOGNIZED THAT WE SERVED IN A HUMBLE WAY AS A TESTING GROUND. FOR THAT IS REALLY A FIRST DRAFT IS A SKETCH PAD FOR TRYING THINGS OUT. IT'S EXCITING TO SEE WHAT COULD HAVE BEEN AND IT HELPS READERS UNDERSTAND MORE ABOUT WHAT IT IS NOW. MY CASE OF COURSE IS PARTICULARLY POIGNANT IF I DO SAY SO MYSELF. "WHY IS THAT?" J.R. ASKED. IT'S A BIT OF A LONG STORY SAID SHADRACH.

"WE WANT TO HEAR" BOTH TWINS SAID. THEY WERE NOW STARING AT A SOFT ROSE COLORED GLOW THAT SEEMED TO BE LIGHTING THE SMALL CORNER OF THE EAVES THAT WAS THE SOURCE OF THE VOICE.

OH YOU'RE BEGINNING TO SEE MY CRAVAT AND WAIST COAT I BELIEVE NOT TOTALLY YOU UNDERSTAND. JUST A KIND OF COLORED FUZZY LITTLE OUTLINE. SOME OF MY GARMENTS COME THROUGH QUITE NICELY. THE BODY REMAINS RATHER ILLUSORY BUT THAT'S ALL RIGHT FOR DOYLE DESCRIBED ME AS BEING RATHER FLABBY AND AS FOR MY COMPLEXION WELL SWINE PINK WOULD BE THE BEST DESCRIPTION OF IT.

WE WERE NOT SHERLOCK AND I SUPPOSED TO BE IDENTICAL TWINS JUST FRATERNAL. IT WAS OKAY WITH ME

THAT HE WAS BETTER LOOKING BECAUSE AT THE START DOYLE DID GIVE ME ALL THE BRAINS. SO I WAS WILLING TO RELINQUISH THE DARK GOOD LOOKS AND SHARP FEATURES TO SHERLOCK BUT YOU CAN IMAGINE WHAT A LOW BLOW IT WAS WHEN I FOUND MYSELF BEING CUT TOTALLY OUT OF THE ACTION THEN LEFT IN THIS SORT OF BIG UNDISTINGUISHED PHYSICAL FORM WHILE SHERLOCK GETS ALONG WITH ALL THE GOOD LOOKS, BRAINS AND FAME. I WOULD HAVE SETTLED FOR WATSONISH ROLE. I DON'T HAVE BE THE MAIN CHARACTER AND I DON'T HAVE TO BE GOOD LOOKING AND SOLVE ALL THE CRIMES. I WOULD HAVE PLAYED SECOND FIDDLE AND BY THE WAY IN THAT FIRST DRAFT YOU READ YOU'LL NOTICE I WAS THE ONE WHO PLAYED THE VIOLIN NOT SHERLOCK BUT ALWAYS PLAYED IN THE OTHER STORIES THE ONES THAT FOLLOWED THERE'S OLD SHRELOCK PLUCKING OUT SOME DIRTY ON THAT DECREPIT LITTLE SMALL STRADIVARIUS VIOLIN. WELL AS YOU READ IN THE FIRST DRAFT HE WAS SUPPOSED TO BE TONE DEAF. I WAS THE TWIN WITH THE MUSCIAL TALENT AND AS FOR SHERLOCK'S FAMOUS "THE GAME IS A FOOT!" THAT WAS ORIGINALLY MY EXPRESSION AS YOU CAN SEE ON PAGE FIFTEEN BUT OF COURSE IT WAS SAID SOMEWHAT IN JEST. I WAS A BIT OF A PUNSTER AND WHEN I ACCIDENTALLY KNOCKED THE CHESS SET OVER AND IT FELL ON MY BROTHER'S FOOT I SAID "DRAT THE GAME IS A FOOT!" CONAN DOYLE SUBSEQUENTLY GAVE THE EXPRESSION TO SHERLOCK AND IT HAS BECOME ASSOCIATED WITH EVER SINCE. IT HAD THE INTENSITY OF BUILDING ACTION SUSPENSE. IF PEOPLE ONLY KNEW IT'S HUMBLE BEGINNINGS! OH BUT I'M JUMPING AHEAD IN MY STORY.

"BUT WAIT" LIBERTY SAID. "WERE YOU EVER A BABY?" "A BABY?" HIS VOICE ROLLED WITH INCREDULITY AND HIS DISBELIEF SEEMED TO POUR OUT OF THE VERY AIR. WHY IN HEAVEN'S NAME WOULD DOYLE WASTE TIME MAKING ME A BABY WHEN I COULD COME ALL GROWN UP? "BUT HOW DID YOU LEARN TO PLAY THE VIOLIN OR LEARN WHO THIS

SAMUEL GUY WAS AND ALL THE OTHER STUFF THAT YOU SAY WE DON'T KNOW?" WELL I JUST DID THAT PART OF BEING A CHARACTER EVEN ONE THAT NEVER MAKES IT OUT OF THE FIRST DRAFT. YOU ARIVE COMPLEATE IN ONE SENSE YOU DON'T HAVE TO DO ANY GROWING UP. YOU ARE THE AGE YOU ARE BUT YOU DO HAVE DO SOME GROWING IN.

"GROWING IN?" BOTH CHILDREN ASKED AT ONCE. YOU HAVE TO GROW INTO THE STORY AND THREAD YOUR WAY NIMBLY THROUGH THE PLOT AND BECOME BELIEVABLE IN TERMS OF HISTORICAL PERIOD IN WHICH THE STORY IS SET AND MOST IMPORTANT OF ALL YOU MUST ALWAYS BE CONVINCING.

THIS WAS NOT GRAFFITIC LIBERTY THOUGHT REMEMBERING WHAT SHE HAD SAID ABOUT SHERLOCK BEING JUST A CHARACTER IN A NOVEL WHEN THEY HAD FIRST ARRIVED IN LONDON AND HAD GONE TO BACKER STREEET. SHE HAD WONDERED THEN WHAT IT HAD REALLY MEANT TO BE A CHARACTER.

YOU CAN'T LOOK LIKE A PUPPET MANIPULATED AND CONTROLLED BY THE OTHER FORCES EVEN IF THAT IS THE CASE BUT OF COURSE THE IRONY OF THIS IS THAT YOU ARE CONTROLLED BY THE GREAT OTHER THE AUTHOR AND WHEN A WRITER'S WORDS BEGIN TO LIFT OFF A PAGE WHEN HIS BIG IMAGINATION BEGINS TO SPILL OVER INTO ANOTHER DIMENSION BECAUSE OF THE GRITTY REALITY OF THE WORD AND THE CHARACTERS HE HAS BEEN ABLE TO CONSTRUCT. HIS CHARACTERS START TO LIVE AND BREATHE AND I THINK IT'S A GREAT COMPLIMENT FOR A PERSON TO BE INTERESTING OR UNUSUAL ENOUGH TO BE CONSIDERED A "REAL CHARACTER" AND WHEN ONE IS REFERRED AS HAVING GREAT INTEGRITY AND MORE MORAL AND CONVICTION WE SAY HE IS A "CHARACTER."

"DID YOU EVER WANTED TO BE ANYTHING MORE THAN JUST A CHARACTER IN A FIRST DRAFT?" OH IT MIGHT BE

NICE BUT THE TRUTH IS I JUST WANT TO BE RECOGNIZED FOR WHAT I WAS IN THAT FIRST DRAFT THAT WOULD BE HONOR ENOUGH YOU SEE HOW ODD IT IS? HOW WHEN YOU WANT TO SAY THAT ANOTHER HUMAN BEING IS UNIQUE AND FULL OF LIFE IN THE BEST SENSE OF THE WORD BECAUSE THE UNIT OF COMPARISON IS TAKEN FROM THE WORLD OF BOOKS AND "A CHARACTER" MEANING A PERSON DRAWN IN THE IMAGINATION OF THE WRITER WHO THEN GOES ON TO LIVE IN THAT OF THE READER. IT HAS BEEN SAID THAT SHERLOCK HOLMES IS "A GENTLE MAN WHO NEVER LIVED AND WHO WILL NEVER DIE." THAT IS THE ULTIMATE IMMORTALITY FOR A LITERARY FIGURE BUT AT LEAST SHERLOCK CAN REST IN PIECE AND YOU WON'T SEE HIM KNOCKING ABOUT THE EAVES OF THIS OLD HOUSE ANY MORE.

"ARE THERE OTHER LITERARY STILLBORNS LIKE YOU?" OH YES ALL SCORES OF THEM. AUTHORS CREATE AND THROW OUT CHARACTERS WILLY-NILLY BEFORE THEY EVER FINALLY DEVELOP ONE THAT LASTS FOR THEM. "WHAT ABOUT THOSE OTHERS ARE THEY UNHAPPY TOO?" YES THERE'S PLENTY OF THEM RUNNING AROUND LONDON. "THAT MAN!" LIBERTY AND J.R. BOTH BLURTED OUT AT ONCE. WHAT MAN? SHADRACH ASKED WITH HIS VOICE SUDDENLY TENSE WITH SUSPICION.

"A MAN WE SAW IN PINCHIN LANE" AND HE SHOWED UP AT THE "TOWER OF LONDON" LIBERTY SAID. HER VOICE WAS TREMBLING AND HER EYES WERE BRIGHT WITH FEAR. "HE'S ONE OF THEM ISN'T HE?" LIBERTY SAID. YES AND A TROUBLESOME BLOKE AT THAT. HE'S ONE OF MANY AND HE DOSE THREATEN MY CASE. "YOUR CASE?" LIBERTY ASKED BUT SHADRACH HAD INGORED THE QUESTION. HE RUSHED HEAD LONG INTO A DISCUSSION OF LITERARY GHOSTS AROUNF THE WORLD. I UNDERSTAND THAT BETWEEN PUSHKIN AND TOLSTOY IN RUSSIA ONE CAN BARELY MOVE WITHOUT BUMPING INTO LITERARY STILLBORNS. ALL OF THEM RESTLESS LIKE MYSELF NEVER

HAVING LIVED AND UNABLE TO DIE UNLESS THEY MEET UP WITH SOMEONE LIKE YOURSELVES WHO CAN HELP. "US HELP YOU?" JR. ASKED. "WE WOULD HAVE TO GO TO RUSSIA TOO FOR PUSH AND THE OTHER GUY?" NO YOU WOULDN'T BE SUITABLE FOR THEM BUT FOR ME YOU ARE. "HOW?" BE PATIENT I DON'T WANT TO JUMP AHEAD IN MY STORY. IT IS ESSENTIAL THAT YOU UNDERSTAND AS MUCH AS POSSIBLE BEFORE YOU BEGIN YOU'RE MISSION. I MUST YOU A LOT MORE ABOUT THE MANUSCRIPTS AND THESE FIRST DRAFTS THAT YOU HAVE FINALLY FOUND.

CHAPTER 21

THE WORLD ACCORDING TO SHADRACH.

SO YOU SEE WHAT HE WAS TRYING TO DO IN THIS MANUSCRIPT? YOU DISCOVERED TWO COMBINED STORIES BUT AT THE TIME HE HADN'T REALIZE WHAT HE WAS WRITING IN THE YEAR 1887. IT WAS A FIRST DRAFT FOR BOTH "THE ADVENTURE OF THE SPECKLED BAND" AND "THE SIGN OF THE FOUR."

IT WAS MUCH TO AMBITIOUS BUT THIS IS A FAULT SHARED BY MANY BEGINNING WRITERS. THEY TRY TO TAKE ON THE WORLD AND TRY TO PACK IN TO MUCH ALL AT ONCE AND AS YOU CAN TELL MANY PARTS LIKE SNAKES, JEWELS, THE CASE OF THE THAMES, THE BELL ROPES AND VENTILATORS IT'S ALL TOO MUCH TO HANDLE AT ONCE AND THAT'S WHY YOU CAN TELL WERE OVER WRITTEN EXCESSIVES. WE LOSE ARE GRASP OF NOT ONLY THE PLOT BUT ALSO THE CHARACTERS AS WELL.

IF INDEED HE HAD LIMITED THE SCOPE OF HIS PLOT I COULD HAVE BEEN SAVED BUT HE HAD BECAME OVER WHELMED WHEN HE WENT BACK AND READ THE FIRST DRAFT. TWIN DETECTIVES AND TWIN VICTIMS COUNT LESS PLOTS AND SUBPLOTS SO HE THREW ME OUT ENTIRELY DESPITE THE FACT THAT HE HAD PLANNED FOR MONTHS EVEN OVER A YEAR IN FACT TO HAVE A GOOD DETECTIVE TEAM.

HE KEPT THE TWIN VICTIMS BUT CHANGED THEM TO WOMEN. THEY HAD WENT FROM HENRY AND HARRY

STONER TO JULIA AND HELEN STONER. IN THE SIGN OF FOUR HE REINTRODUCED TWIN MEN THADDEUS AND BIG BARTHOLOWMEW SHOLTO. BARTHOLOWMEW SHOLTO IF YOU RECALL IN THE FIRST DRAFT YOU READ OUT LOUD WAS THE WICKED UNCLE. YOU KNOW EVERYBODY GOT TO BE SOMEONE EXCEPT ME!

SHADRACH SAID THIS RATHER HUFFILY AND THE CHILDREN COULD SEE THE TASSELS ON HIS CAP SHAKE A BIT. THERE WAS NO HEAD BUT THE CAP HAD MATERIALIZED AS HE SPOKE. IT WAS A TASSELED MAROON VELVET SMOKING CAP FAVORED BY GENTELEMAN OF THE VICTORIAN PERIOD AND THERE WAS ALSO A WAISTCOAT THAT SEEMED TRANSPARENT DESPITE BEING HEAVILY BROCADED. THE CRAVAT SHIMMERED WITH A DESIGN OF MISTY ROSES.

WELL TO BE FAIR EVERYBODY DIDN'T GET TO BE SOMEONE EXCEPT ME AND THAT IS WHY YOU ARE HAVING TROUBLE NOW WITH THE BLOKE DOWN ON PINCHIN LANE. "WHAT DO YOU MEAN?" J.R. SAID. A BIG SHIVER STARTED UP BOTH TWINS SPINES.

WELL THAT FELLOW HAS INDEED BEEN A VILLAIN IN MORE FIRST DRAFTS THAN ANY CHARACTER IMAGINABLE BUT THE PROBLEM IS HE IS TOO DARN OBVIOUSLY EVIL SO NATURALLY DOYLE WOUND UP CUTTING HIM FROM THE STORY. THE BLOKE WAS FURIOUS WITH DOYLE. HE DESPERATELY WANTS TO BE A FULL FLEDGED LITERARY VILLAIN BUT HE HASN'T REALLY GOT THE STUFF LIKE PROFESSOR MORIARTY SHERLOCK'S ARCHENEMY AND WHAT HASN'T BEEN CROSSED OUT IN OLD MANUSCRIPTS IS SO ATROCIOUSLY WRITTEN THAT HE COMES OFF AS ALMOST COMIC. IF THERE IS ONE THING A VILLAIN DOESN'T LIKE IT'S TO BE LAUGHED AT. IF YOU GO BACK AND READ THE CROSSED OUT PARTS OF THE MANUSCRIPT YOU HAVE NOW SEE THAT THE BLOKE IS A COMPLETE IDIOT AND THE WRITING OF THAT MANUSCRIPT IS SO AWFUL DOYLE HAD TO RUN HIS PEN THROUGH IT. RIGHTFULLY

SO THIS LITTLE FELLOW IS ALWAYS CHANGING NAME AND DOYLE WAS THE ONE THAT WAS ALWAYS CHANGING IT TO SEE WHAT KIND OF ROTTEN VILLAIN HE WOULD MAKE. IT IS NOT IN HIS INTERESTS TO HAVE THIS PARTICULAR MANUSCRIPT SEEING THE LIGHT OF DAY. THAT IS WHY YOU ARE GOING TO HAVE TO OPERATE WITH EXTREME CAUTION WHEN THE TIME COMES.

"YOU MEAN HE MIGHT TRY TO INTERFERE OR DO SOMETHING TO US?" PRECISELY SAID SHADRACH. HE IS A MASTER OF DECEPTION ODDLY ENOUGH. HE'S PICKED UP A LOT FROM THE OTHER CHARACTERS AND HAVING TO RESIDE OFFTEN EVEN IF BRIEFLY IN SO MANY FIRST DRAFTS.

J.R. SQUIRMED UNCOMFORTABLY "WHAT ABOUT MYCROFT SHERLOCK'S OLDER BROTHER? DOYLE TALKS ABOUT HIM IN THE STORIES J.R. SAID. HIM? THE VOICE WAS DRENCHED IN DISDAIN. LISTEN BEING A LITERARY STILBORN IS BAD ENOUGH BUT BEING MYCORFT WOULD BE WORSE. I'D RATHER BE A VILLAIN IN LITERATURE THAN THAT STUFFY OLD MYCROFT SITTING AROUND ALL DAY IN HIS DARN CLUB OR THOSE LITTLE ROOMS HE RENTED OVER IN PALL MALL AND NEVER VENTURING FROM THIS ORBIT. OH YES AND ON OCCASION HE GO OVER TO HIS BROTHER SHERLOCK'S. IT WAS SO DULL AND SEDENTARY AND IT WAS ENOUGH TO PUT ANY READER TO SLEEP. NO THEY SAID BEING A LITERARY GHOST IS A FATE WORSE THAN DEATH BUT I DO BELIEVE I'D SETTLE FOR THIS RATHER THAN MYCROFT'S LOT.

THEY TALKED ON THOUGH THE NIGHT AND INTO THE COOL GRAY HOURS OF THE SUMMERS DAWN. SHADRACH WAS A GREAT TALKER AND BY TIME THE SUN HAD RISEN HIS WAISTCOAT CRAVAT TROUSERS AND DRESS PUMPS WERE FULLY VISIBLE TO SEE AND BOTH CHILDREN SENSED THAT SHADARCH COULD HAVE MADE MORE OF HIS PHYSICAL BODY PRESENT BUT HE HAD CHOSEN NOT TO DO SO.

WHAT SHADARCH HAD CHOSEN TO DO WAS TO GIVE THEM AS MUCH IFFORMATION AS POSSIBLE NOT JUST ABOUT HIMSELF AND HIS BRIEF LITTLE APPEARANCE IN THE PAGES OF A FIRST DRAFT EARLY IN THE CAREER OF SIR ARTHUR CONAN DOYLE BUT ABOUT HOW THE WHOLE COURSE OF WEITTEN ADVENTURES OF SHERLOCK HOLMES THE GREAT DETECTIVE IN LITERATURE COULD HAVE BEEN DRASTICALLY DIFFERENT.

"IT'S KIND OF LIKE TRYING TO IMAGINE WHAT MIGHT HAVE HAPPENED IF DINOSAURS HAD NOT DISAPPEARED. WOULD PEOPLE HAVE HAPPENED? LIBERTY ASKED. "EVOLVED" J.R. OFFERED.

OH DARWIN CHARLES DARWIN! SHADRACH EXCLIMED THE GREAT SCIENTIST! YOU REALIZE WE WERE BORN IN THE MIDST OF THAT MARVELOUS PERIOD. INDEED DOYLE WAS BORN IN THE VERY YEAR THAT DARWIN HAD PUBLISHED HIS GREAT WORK THE ORIGIN OF THE SPECIES. YOU MIGHT HAD IMAGINE THE APPEAL OF A BOOK LIKE THAT IN WHICH THROUGH THE BIG OBSERVATION AND DEDUCTION DARWIN PROPOSES THAT THE EARTH MUST BE A LOT OLDER THAN BIBLICAL TIME WOULD SUGGEST AND THAT SPECISE AND LIVING THINGS HAD NOT ALWAYS BEEN WHAT THEY APPEARED TO BE BUT HAD CHANGED OVER THE COURSE OF TIME.

YES LIBERTY AND J.R. I RATHER LIKE YOU COMPARISON OF MY EXISTENCE TO THAT OF THE DINOSAURS. WHAT MIGHT HAVE HAPPEN IF THEY HAD NOT DIED OFF? IT WOULD HAVE GIVEN US MAMMALS, LITERARY OR LIVING MUCH OF A CHANCE WOULD YOU NOW? "GUESS NOT" LIBERTY SAID.

SO WHAT MIGHT HAVE HAPPEN IF IT HAD BEEN ME IN STEAD OF SHERLOCK? YOU CHILDREN ARE THINKING IN SUCH SWEEPING HISTORICAL TERMS BECAUSE THAT IS THE KIND OF THINKING IT IS GOING TO TAKE TO GET

THESE DRAFTS TO THE PUBLIC AND FULLY APPRECIATED BECAUSE THIS IS A VERYSERIOUS PROBLEM AND UNLESS RESOLVED I SHALL SPEND MEY ETERNITY IN TERRIBLE KIND OF LIMBO SO YOU MUST FIRST HAVE YOUR DUCKS IN ORDER SO TO SPEAK AND BE TOTALLY PREPARED BUT STILL SHADRACH HAD AVOIDED THE QUESTION OF WHAT PRECISELY THE CHILDREN WOULD BE REQUIRED TO DO. THIS FIRST DRAFT THAT YOU READ WHICH LATER BECAME TWO SEPARATE STORIES "THE ADVENTURE OF THE SPEAKLED BAND" AND THE SIGN OF THE FOUR HE CONTINUED DESPITE BEING OVERLY AMBITIOUS WAS AS YOU CAN SEE QUITE LITERATE AND WELL PUNCTUATED NO MISS SPELLED WORDS EVEN. IT HAS SOME VERY NICE LANGUAGE ACTUALLY MUCH LESS STILED THAN SOME OF HIS OTHER ADVENTURES. THE DESCRIPTION OF THE SNAKE'S DESCENT THROUGH THE VENTILATOR AND DOWN THE BELL ROPE IS BRILLIANT.

SHADRACH WAS NOW EVIDENTLY PACING THE FLOOR FOR HIS LITTLE WAISTCOAT CRAVAT AND PUMPS SEEMED TO BE SWINGING BACK AND FORTH IN A SMALL ARC BETWEEN THE EAVES AND THE WINDOW. HE DID THIS IN MUCH OF THE SAME MANNER AS A LAWYER WOULD PACE BACK AND FORTH IN A COURTROOM WHEN TRYING TO CONVINCE A JUDGE AND JURY OF A CLIENT'S INNOCEENCE BUT HOW COME DOYLE CUT YOU OUT ENTIRELY? LIBERTY ASKED. "IT SEEMS KIND OF UNFAIR AND A RAW DEAL I SAY" J.R. ADDED. "I MEAN YOU DIDN'T . . . . LIBERTY'S THOUGHT DWINDLED OFF."

I KNOW WHAT YOU ARE THINKING MY DEAR WHAT COULD SHADRACH HOLMES FRATERNAL TWIN TO SHERLOCK HAVE DONE TO DESERVE SUCH A FATE? "DO YOU THINK SHERLOCK WAS JEALOUS?" J.R. OFFERED. "CHARLY AND MOLLY ARE ALWAYS JEALOUS OF US CONSTANTLY AND IT'S REALLY ANNOYING" LIBERTY ADDED. OH IT COULD BE THAT BUT I HAVE ALSO THOUGHT THAT PERHAPS DOYLE HIMSELF WAS SO VAIN THAT HE DID NOT WANT PEOPLE

TO THINK OF HIM AS THIS FLABBY RATHER UNATHLETIC LOOKING PINK BLUBBERBALL.

LIBERTY COULDN'T IMAGINE AN AUTHOR BECOMING THIS WRAPPED UP IN A CHARACTER AND SHADRACH READING HER MIND LIBERTY HAD REPLIED OUT LOUD.

YOU CAN'T PRY APART THE CREATOR FROM THE CHARACTER HE HAS CREATED AFTER A CERTAIN KIND OF BONDING TAKES PLACE ON THE PAGE. IT DOSEN'T MATTER THAT THEY MAY NOT BE IDENTICAL BUT IN THE AUTHOR'S MIND THEY SHARE A KIND OF SPIRIT DESPITE THEIR DIFFERENCES. YOU KNOW DOYLE WAS TERRIBLY PROUD OF HIS VERY PHYSICAL PROWESS. IT STOOD OVER SIX FEET TALL AND WEIGHED IN AT SEVENTEEN STONE AND THAT'S OVER TWO HUNDRED POUNDS IN YOUR MEASUREMENTS I BELIEVE. I ALSO BELIEVE HE WAS A GREAT CRICKET PLAYER TOO. TWICE HE TOOK ALL TEN WICKETS IN AN INNING AND HE ALSO PLAYED FOOTBALL BUT WHAT DO YOU CALL THAT SOCCER I DO BELIEVE AS HE GOT INTO HIS FORTIES AND HE WAS ALSO ONE OF THE FIRST PEOPLE EVER TO GO SKIING. HE WENT WHEN HE WAS IN THE BIG NICE CITY OF SWITZERLAND AND SOME SWISS MOUNTAINEER GUIDES HAD JUST INVENTED THE SPORT OF SLIDING DOWN MOUNTAINS ON BIG LONG BOARDS.

"ONE THING" LIBERTY HAD A SUDDEN THOUGHT "DO YOU MIND IF I ASK I MEAN SEEING AS YOU ARE HAVE ALREADY SAID YOU'RE SORT OF PLUMP?" OH GO RIGHT AHEAD DON'T BE AFRAID I'M THE FIRST TO ADMIT THAT I AM NOT A GRAND PHYSICAL SPECIMEN. "WELL ARE YOU THE ONE WHO'S BEEN EATING OUR JELLY BEANS?" AH YES I COULDN'T RESIST BECAUSE THEY BECOME QUITE A HIBIT WITH ME PARTICULARLY THE PINK ONES AND ADDICTION ONE MIGHT SAY ALTHOUGH I DON'T USE THAT TERM LIGHTLY FOR AS FAR YOU KNOW MY BROTHER SHERLOCK HAD A SERIOUS PROBLEM. "YES" J.R. SAID BUT ONE THING HOW DO YOU EAT IF YOU ARE A GHOST?" GASTROSPIRATION

SHADRACH SAID. "WHAT?" BOTH LIBERTY AND J.R. ASK AT THE SAME TIME.

GASTROSPIRATION HE REPEATED. YOU HEARD OF EXPIRATION? THE CHILDREN NODDED THEIR LITTLE HEADS. YOU ALSO KNOW ABOUT THE TRANSPIRATION, PERSPIRATION AND INSPIRATION TOO RIGHT? THE KIDS NODDED THEIR HEADS AGAIN. WELL GASTROSPIRATION IS HOW GHOSTS EAT. IT IS A VAPORIZATION AND DISTILLATION PROCESS BY WHICH THE FOOD IN THIS CASE JELLY BEANS DISAPPEARS OR IS CONSUMED BUT NOT BY THE NORMAL BIOLOGICAL PROCESS. WE CAN'T GASTROSPIRATE EVERYTHING AND NOTHING TO COMPLEX ONLY SIMPLEST SORT OF LIKE MOLECULAR STURCTURES AND WHAT ARE JELLY BEANS BUT A LOT OF SUGAR AND GLYCERIN AND COLOR. I CAN'T DIGEST THE COLOR THOUGH HENCE THE PASTEL PUDDLES LEFT BEHIND. WE CALL THIS BIOLUMINESCENCE AND THE COLORS OF MY CRAVAT AND WAISTCOAT ARE ANOTHER EXAMPLE OF BIOLUMINESCENCE. I THINK OF IT AS REMNANTS OF THE VISIBLE MAGNETIC ENEGRY THAT IS LEFT FROM A PRODUCT OR A LIVING THING FOR THAT LITTLE MATTER. I DABBLED SOMEWHAT IN PHYSICS YOU KNOW. SHERLOCK WAS MORE INTERESTED IN CHEMISTRY.

GETTING BACK TO ME AND MY LOVE OF CANDY YOU SEE THAT'S ONE BIG DIFFERENCE SMALL BUT NEVERTHELESS SIGNIFICANT BETWEEN ME AND MY BROTHER SHERLOCK. HE TENDED TOWARD A SHAPE AND I MIGHT SAY MONOTONOUS DIET. THE CHOP AND ALL OVER COOKED VEGETABLES FOR WHICH WE ENGLISH ARE FAMOUS WASHED DOWN WITH A GLASS OF CLARET AND RARELY DID HE TAKE THE PUDDING OR DESSERT AS YOU CALL IT WHILE I MYSELF COULD HAVE MADE ENTIRE MEALS OUT OF PUDDINGS AND SKIPPED THOSE HORRID LIMPVEGETABLES BUT HOWEVER I GAINED NO PLEASURE OUT OF COCAINES. THINK HOW DIFFERENT THE COURSE OF HOLMES'S BIG HUGE ADVENTURES MIGHT HAVE BEEN

IF INSTEAD OF COCAINE IF HE HAD BEEN ADDICTED TO THE CANDY?

"CANDY CAN MAKE YOU HYPERACTIVE" LIBERTY SAID OUT LOUD. AFTER CHARLY AND MOLLY EAT A LOT OF CANDY THEY'RE BOUNCING OFF THE WALLS." WELL THERE YOU GO SAID SHADRACH BUT I DON'T THINK I WOULD HAVE BOUNCED OFF THE WALLS IN SPITE OF BEING SO PORTLY. HE HAD CHORTLED BUT THINGS MIGHT HAVE CAME OUT MUCH DIFFERENTLY.

"SO DOYLE DIDN'T WANT TO BE LIKE YOU?" J.R. ASKED. NO I DON'T REALLY THINK HE WOULD HAVE WANTED TO BE A COCAINE ADDICT EITHER BUT THERE IS NO USE MINCING WORDS ABOUT IT. I JUST DON'T HAVE THE APPEAL FOR HIM THAT SHERLOCK DID BUT NOT ONLY THAT HE DIDN'T WANT TO HAVE TO SPREAD OUT THE GLORY OR HAVE A TWIN DETECTIVES SHARE IT NEITHER AND THERE WAS ALWAYS A COURSE THE SLIGHT DISDAIN FOR MY KIND OF THINKING. INDUCTIVE IS THE KIND OF THINKING THAT WAS GOING TO BE ASSOCIATED WITH INTUITION, EMOTION LEAPS OF FAITH IF YOU WILL AS OPPOSED TO THE DEDUCTIVE VARIETY WHICH WAS SHERLOCK'S BIG SPECIALTY WHICH IS THOUGHT OF IN TERMS OF COLD DISPASSIONATE BIG LOGIC BUT I NOTICE THAT YOU TWO INDUCE VERY NICELY AND I'LL WAGER THAT SOME OF THE BEST PROBLEM SOLVING IN THE WORLD IS DONE BY THE UTILIZING BOTH KINDS OF THINGS.

"YEA J.R. SAID. LIBERTY'S MUCH BETTER AT KEEPING WHOLE PICTURES IN HER HEAD. SHE CAN REMEMBER THE SHAPES OF THINGS AND SHE CAN ALSO HELP ME DRAW IN THE MAP OF THE GREAT LAKES IN A GEOGRAPHY TEST WE HAD IN SCHOOL LAST YEAR BUT MOLLY IS BETTER AT REMEMBERING LITTLE THINGS LIKE THE CAPITAL OF MINNESOTA."

"THE TWIN CITIES SHADRACH SAID YOU KNEW THAT?" BOTH TWINS SAID WITH SURPRISE. I TOLD YOU THAT I

ARRIVED ALL GROWN UP AND THAT MEANS A WORKING KNOWLEDGE OF GEOGRAPHY BUT GETTING BACK TO THOSE TWO THINGS WE WERE TALKING ABOUT BEFORE. "YES?" LIBERTY HAD SAID. WELL DOYLE WANTED ONE STYLE OF THINKING AND ONE TYPE OF DETECTIVE AND THAT DETECTIVE BECAME SHERLOCK HOLMES BUT THAT IS WHY IT IS SUCH LUCK THAT YOU HAVE MOVED IN HERE AND WITH YOU TWO WHO COMBINE THESE TWO WAYS OF THINKING IS WHY I HAVE BEEN GOING ON SO LONG ABOUT ALL THIS. FOR THE CHILDREN WILL NEED ALL THE INFORMATION AS POSSIBLE IF YOU ARE TO SUCCEED IN YOUR MISSION. I HAVE BEEN WAITING OVER A CENTURY FOR SOMETHING LIKE THIS TO BE HAPPENING TO ME.

"WHAT LUCK BUT IT WASN'T LUCK EXACTLY" J.R. SAID. HE REMEMBERED THE LONG COOL SHADOW THAT SHERLOCK'S HEAD CASTED ON THE WALL OF HIS BEDROOM BACK IN WASHINGTON AND LIBERTY REMEMBERED THE ECHOES PRESSING HER FROM SLEEP AT DAWN THAT MORNING WHICH NOW SEEMED SO LONG AGO.

"NO IT DIDN'T SEEMED THAT WAY TO US BECAUSE WE WERE SORT OF DRAWN HERE" LIBERTY SAID. BRIEFLY THE CHILDREN TOLD SHADRACH ABOUT WHAT HAD HAPPENED AFTER THEIR STRANGE JOURNEY TO PINCHIN LANE AND HOW THEY HAD FOUND THE HOUSE IN THE MEWS.

VERY INTERESTING SHADRACH SAID WHEN THE CHILDREN FINISHED THEIR STORY AND YOU KNOW THAT HORRID MAN IN PINCHIN LANE IS NOT ONLY A FAILED LITERARY VILLAIN BUT HE WAS CRUEL TO ANIMALS AS WELL. HE WAS MUCH MORE SUCCESSFUL AS AN ANIMAL ABUSER THAN AS A BIG TIME MURDERER IF THAT IS ANY COMFORT TO YOU.

"NOT REALLY" LIBERTY REPLIED. HOW COME WE COULD SEE HIM BUT WE COULDN'T SEE YOU?" J.R. ASKED. IT'S QUITE SIMPLE IF YOU DO HAVE THE GOOD LUCK TO MAKE IT INTO

A SECOND DRAFT YOU MAY BECOME VISIBLE ON OCCASION BUT BELIEVE ME I WOULD RATHER BE INVISIBLE AND REMAIN IN A FRIST DRAFT THEN EVER BE CRUEL TO ANIMALS. LIBERTY AND J.R. HAD NODDED IN SOLEMN APPROVAL.

YOU SEE TOBY THE DOG WAS SUPPOSED TO BE ANOTHER BREED BECAUSE OF THIS CASE WERE WORKING ON. SO THIS IS A CASE WHERE YOU HAVE BOTH A MAN AND A DOG RUNNING ABOUT EXILES FROM A SECOND DRAFT AND LITERARY STILLBORNS NONETHELESS BUT ONE CAN'T BE ALL THINGS TO ALL CHARACTERS AND IN THE CASE OF THE MAN ON PINCHIN LANE AND THAT OTHER HORRIBLE DOBERMAN PINCHER THERE IS NO EXISTING THE MANUSCRIPT SO UNLESS ONE IS WRITTEN IN WHICH THESE CHARACTERS ARE USED THESE LITERARY GHOSTS CAN'T BE PUT TO REST.

LIBERTY SHUDDERED HER SHOULDERS AS SHE REMEMBERED THE FOAM FROM THE DOG'S MOUTH SCALDING HER CHECK. SHADRACH NOTICED THIS AND ALMOST FELT SOMETHING LIKE A PAT ON HER HEAD. NO NEED TO FEAR MY DEAR IT'S ME THEY'RE REALLY INTERESTED IN NOT YOU. THAT FELLOW ON PINCHIN LANE COULD CAUSE ME SOME PROBLEMS BECAUSE HE WILL DO ANYTHING TO PREVENT THIS DRAFT FROM BEING PUBLISHED AND TO STOP IT BEFORE THE WHOLE WORLD SEES WHAT AN AWFUL CHARACTER HE IS. THEY MIGHT TRY TO USE YOU TO GET TO ME BUT IT'S NOT EXACTLY FATAL WHEN YOU'RE ALREADY A GHOST YOU KNOW BUT I'M NOT A GHOST LET LIBERTY SAID IN A SMALL WHISPER. "WHAT ABOUT THE LITTLE BOY WHO HAD LED ME TO THAT STOP CALLED THE BOW STREET RUNNERS?" J.R. ASKED.

AH HA! SAID SHADRACH NOW THAT'S ANOTHER STORY. THEY FELT THE PHANTOM FINGER PUNCTUATE THE AIR. "HE WAS A BAKER STREET IREGULAR WASN'T HE? LIKE ONE OF THE LITTLE STREET CHILDREN THAT WOULD HELP SHERLOCK GET INFORMATION" LIBERTY ASKED NOW.

HE WAS ALMOST A BAKER STREET IRREGULAR AGAIN CUT IN A FIRST DRAFT. I BELIEVE IT WAS FIRST DRAFT OF A SCANDAL IN BOHEMIA THE STORY WITH IRENE ADLER.

"IS THERE ANY EXISTING DRAFT OF MANUSCRIPT?" J.R. ASKED. NO I'M SORRY TO REPORT HE IS A LITTLE SPIRIT WHO DOSE DESERVE SOME REST THAT IS SAID SIMON. "SIMON IS THAT YOU'RE NAME?" YES THAT IS MY NANE BUT THAT'S ALL I KNOW ABOUT HIM RIGHT NOW. HE WAS JUST A FIGMENT OF DOYLE'S IMAGINATION BUT HE DID MAKE IT INTO SEVERAL SECOND DRAFTS OF VARIOUS SHERLOCK HOLMES TALES HE NEVER LASTED LONGER THAN A SPLIT SECOND HOWEVER AND THEN DOYLE WOULD JUST CUT HIM.

"OH J.R. SAID THERE WAS DEJECTION IN HIS VOICE. WELL THERE MIGHT BE A WAY YOU CAN HELP HIM IF YOU CAN HELP ME. THAT IS WHY YOU MUST PERFORM THIS MISSION SHADRACH OFFERED." WELL WHAT EXACTLY IS THE MISSION?" SHE COULDN'T STAND IT NO LONGER.

YOU MUST SIMPLY DO THIS BECAUSE YOU MUST BRING THIS MANUSCRIPT TO THE ATTENTION OF THE WORLD. IT WOULD BE EASY AND YOU WOULD HAVE TO HIRE SOLICITORS, LAWYERS AS YOU CALL THEM. YOU WILL ALSO HAVE TO FIND BIBLIO-DETECTIVES AND HANDWRITING EHPERTS. THE BIG PROCEDURES OF VERNIFICATION AND LEAGAL ENTITLEMENT WILL BE VERY COMPLICATED AND THEN OF COURSE YOU MUST NOTIFY THE VARIOUS SHERLOCK HOLMES SOCIETIES OF WHICH THERE ARE MANY ALL OVER THE WORLD. LONDON IS THE CENTER OF THEM AND I WOULD SUGGEST THAT YOU MIGHT CONTACT THE ONE KNOWN AS THE BLUE CARBUNCLES BUT HOWEVER I MUST WARN YOU THAT THERE SHALL BE DIFFICULTIES WITH THESE BLOKES ESPECIALLY IN TERMS OF LIBERTY AS A CO-DISCOVERER.

"WHAT?" WHY ME? LIBERTY ASKED. WELL THERE WAS A DEEP SIGH AND BOTH CHILDREN COULD SEE THE

WAISTCOAT EXPAND. "WHERE ARE THESE GUYS FROM?" THE VICTORIAN AGE DEAR STRAIGHT OUT OF IT I'M AFRAID THEY HAVE VERY STRICT RULES ABOUT THE PRESENCE OF WOMEN AT THEIR MEETINGS. IT IS STRICTLY FORBIDDEN. "I DON'T UNDERSTAND." LIBERTY WAS ABSOLUTELY BEWILDERED. IT WAS VERY DIFFICULT I ADMIT AND I AFTER ALL AM A VICTORIAN BUT I'VE LEARNED A LOT. HOWEVER IT WAS THE BELIEF BACK THEN THAT WOMEN WERE LESSER, WEAKER, NOT AS SMART AND NEEDFUL OF PROTECTION.

"THAT IS THE BIGGEST BUNCH OF MALARKEY I'VE EVER HEARD. THEY'RE GOING TO BE NEEDFUL OF PROTECTION IF THEY DON'T LET THEM IN" LIBERTY SAID. I DON'T DOUBT IT FOR A MINUTE MY DEAR AND WE SHALL FIGURE OUT A WAY TO WORK AROUND THIS PROBLEM. FOR YOU HAVE BOTH OF YOU DISCOVERED THE MANUSCRIPT THROUGH YOUR BRILLIANT COMBINATION OF DEDUCTIVE AND INDUCTIVE REASONING AND I FOR ONE SHALL NOT STAND PLACIDLY BY WHILE ONE TWIN GETS DELETED. I GIVE YOU MY SOLEMN WORD ON THAT LIBERTY. I DO THINK HOWEVER THAT YOU MIGHT NEED SOME OUTSIDE HELP WITH THIS. THIS IS A TALL ORDER FOR YOU BOTH CONSIDERING YOUR AGE.

"BUT WHO WOULD HELP?" ASKED LIBERTY. ZANNY THE NANNY SHE SAID THE WORDS SUCCINCTLY. HE MUST HAVE BEEN FINGERING HIS WATCH CHAIN NOW IT SEEMED TO JINGLE A BIT. I MUST BE ON MY WAY. THE SUN IS RISING AND I REALLY PERFER THE NIGHT TO THE DAY AND WITH THAT BEGAN TO MELT AWAY, FIRST THE DRESS PUMPS, NEXT THE TROUSERS THEN THE EMBROIDERED WAISTCOAT AND FINALLY THE CRAVAT WITH THE ROSES AND THE LITTLE VELVET SMOKING HAT WITH THE TASSELS. ONE TINY ROSE AND A TASSEL SEEMED TO LINGER FOR SEVERAL SECONDS THE BETTER PART OF A MINUTE IN A SHAFT OF THE EARLY MORNING SUNLIGHT AND THEN SHADRACH WAS GONE.

CHAPTER 22

THE COURT.

THE WORLD APPEARED RINSED AND LOVELY THAT MORNING AND NOT FOR ONE SECOND DID EITHER LIBERTY OR J.B. RAGOZZINO DOUBT THE STRANGE EVENTS THAT HAD TRANSPIRED IN THE ATTIC THE PREVIOUS NIGHT. BOTH HOWEVER HAD DOUBTS ABOUT LETTING ZANNY IN ON THEIR SECRET AT LEAST AT THIS POINT. AFTER ALL IT WAS ZANNY WHO HAD COME UP WITH THE NOTION THAT THE MAN FROM SLAUGHTER WAS A NATURALIST OR AT WORST JUST A RUN OF THE MILL PERVERT. WHAT WOULD SHE SAY ABOUT SHADRACH A SELFDESCRIBED LITERARY GHOST? SHE WOULD LISTEN TO THEM FOR THREE MINUTES TO GO TAKE A SHOWER RE-EMERGE AS A SUPER ADULT AND TELL THEM SOME PSYCHOLGICAL GOBBLEDYGOOK ABOUT THEIR OVERACTIVE IMAGINATIONS. PROBABLY TAKE THEM OFF CANDY AND PUT THEM ON A DITE OF WHOLE GRAINS AND CARROT JUICE.

THEY ATTRIBUTED SHADRACH'S ADVICE OF SEEKING HELP FROM A GROWN-UP TO THE TYPICAL KIND OF CAUTION AN ADULT WOULD THINK NECESSARY. SHSDRACH MIGHT BE A GHOST BUT HE WAS STILL A GROWN-UP EVEN IF HE HAD ONLY LIVED FOR A BREIEF TIME WITHIN THE PAGES OF A FIRST DRAFT. HE HAD BEEN CONCEIVED BY DOYLE AS A FULL FLEDGED ADULT IF NOT A FULL FLEDGED CHARACTER AND THERE WAS A DIFFERENCE. SO AS FAR AS LIBERTY AND J.R. WERE CONCERNED SHADRACH MIGHT BE A LITERARY STILLBORN AN UNREALIZED CHARACTER BUT HE WAS FULLY OPERATIONAL GROWN-UP IN TERMS OF HIS THINKING ESPECIALLY WHEN HE WAS THINKING ABOUT CHILDREN. MAYBE LIBERTY WAS RIGHT MAYBE

THEY WOULD NEED HELP BUT AS SOON AS YOU GOT GROWN-UPS INVOLVED THERE WAS ALWAYS THE CHANCE THEY MIGHT TAKE OVER THE WHOLE SHOW AND EVEN ZANNY. FOR NOW LIBERTY AND J.R. WANTED TO TRY IT ON THEIR OWN.

THAT AFTERNOON THEY WENT TO WERE THEY REMEMBERED THE BIG LONG SOLICITORS OR LAWYERS WHO HAD THEIR OFFICES TO THE PLUM COURT BEHIND FLEET STREET. THEY TOOK THE UNDERGROUND FROM BAKER STREET AND EMERGED AT THE HOLBORN STATION. THE TWINS MADE THEIR WAY PAST THE ROYAL COURTS OF JUSTICE AND SHOPS THAT SPECIALIZED IN THE WIGS AND JUDICIAL ROBES THAT ALL SOLICITORS WERE REQUIRED TO WEAR WHEN APPEARING IN COURT.

"IT'S ENOUGH TO MAKE YOU NOT WANT TO BE A LAWYER" J.R. SAID AS THEY STOPPED TO LOOK AT ON SUCH WIG ON THE HEAD OF A MANNEQUIN AND THE COARSE WHITE HAIR LOOKED MORE LIKE BRISTLES THAN ACTUAL HAIR AND HAD BEEN ROLLED INTO SAUSAGE SHAPES THAT LAY ACROSS THE BACK IN RIGID WIG AND THE BANGS WERE SHAPED INTO THE SAME LIKE SAUSAGE CURLS.

"CUTE!" SAID LIBERTY HER VOICE DRENCHED IN SARCASM. "REALLY CUTE." "WELL AS LONG AS WHOEVER WEARS ONE CAN THINK UNDER IT. THAT'S ALL WE CARE ABOUT RIGHT? RIGHT SAID LIBERTY. PUMP COURT WAS NOT A COURT OF LAW BUT A COURTYARD IN WHICH SOLICITORS HAD THEIR OFFICES. IT WAS TUCKED AWAY BEHIND AN ANCIENT CHURCH THAT ACCORDING TO A PLAQUE WAS BUILT BY THE KNIGHTS TEMPLAR OVER EIGHT HUNDRED YEARS BEFORE IN THE TWELFTH CENTURY. THAT MORNING A WEDDING IN THE CHURCH WAS ABOUT TO BEGIN AND CHORDS OF THE ORGAN MUSIC STREAMED OUT FROM THE CHURCH. LIBERTY AND J.R. HAD PAUSED TO WATCH. THE BRIDE STOOD BEFORE THE ARCHED DOORWAY OF THE CHURCH ABOUT TO ENTER. SHE CARRIED A HUGE

BOUQUET OF SMALL WHITE FLOWERS THAT ERUPTED IN A FROTHY CASCADE OF TINY BLOSSOMS.

LOOK YOU CAN SEE THE FLOWERS TREMBLE LIBERTY HAD TELAFLASHED TO MOLLY. THEY'RE SHIVERING MOLLY TELAFLASHED BACK. IT LOOKS LIKE MIST FROM A WATERFALL. THEY BOTH WISHED SUDDENLY THAT THEY WERE ANYWHERE BUT IN THIS QUIET ANCIENT PLACE. THE CHISELED STONE WAS ROUNDED WITH ARCHES AND CAREFULLY TRIMMED WITH SQUARES OF LITTLE GREEN GRASS WERE SO SERIOUS AND GROWN-UP. IT WAS A PLACE WHERE LAWS WERE STUDIED AND INTERPRETED AND PROMISES WERE MADE FOR LIFE.

MAYBE SHADRACH WAS RIGHT AND MAYBE WE NEED TO BRING ZANNY J.B. SAID. WELL WE'RE HERE SO WE MIGHT AS WELL FIND OURSELVES A SOLICITOR. EVERYONE OF THE BRICK BUILDINGS THAT ENCLOSED PUMP COURT HAD A LIST OF SOLICITORS POSTED AT THE DOOR AND FLOOR BY FLOOR.

HOW DO WE KNOW WHERE TO BEGIN? LIBERTY TELAFLASHED. DO YOU HEAR A CRACKLING? J.B. TELAFLASHED. WHY DO YOU? JUST FOR A SECOND THERE WAS A SIZZLE. NO IT'S BROAD DAYLIGHT LIBERTY WE'RE NOT IN DANGEROUS PLACE. THIS IS THE CENTER FOR ALL THE LAWYERS OF LONDON. PEOPLE ARE AT LEAST GOING TO BE LAW-ABIDING HERE.

TOO BAD THE LAWYERS DON'T LIST THEIR SPECIALTIES. I WONDER IF THERE IS SUCH A THING AS A LAWYER WHO SPECIALIZES IN OLD MANUSCRIPTS AND OLD STORIES.

AT THAT MOMENT A BEWHISKERED MAN SEEMED TO MATERIALIZE OUT OF A LITTLE TURNNLED ALLEY ALONGSIDE THE BUILDING. "CAN I HELP YOU?" HE ASKED CHEERILY. "ARE YOU LOOKING FOR SOMETHING IN PARTICULAR?" J.B. SAID. "WELL AS A MATTER OF FACT YES"

LIBERTY SAID QUICKLY. "WE'RE LOOKING FOR A SOLICITOR WHO SPECIALIZES IN OLD DOCUMENTS" AND ALMOST AS SOON AS SHE SAID IT SHE FELT SHE SHOULDN'T HAVE. SHE FELT SHE HAD LEFT THE CAT OUT OF THE BAG TOO SOON AND EXPOSED HERSELF BUT THEY HAD BEEN CAREFUL TO BRING ONLY TWO PAGES OF THE OLD MANUSCRIPT AND NOW ALREADY THIS MAN WAS ASKING AND ANSWERING QUESTIONS SO QUICKLY.

"WELL I MYSELF HAVE HAD SOME EXPERIENCE IN THIS FIELD. DO YOU HAVE THE MANUERUH DOCUMENT WITH YOU?" HE ALMOST SAID THE "MANUSCRIPT"! HOW DID HE KNOW? YOU AND YOUR BIG MOUTH LIBERTY! I'M SORRY!

NOW THE MAN WAS ACTUALLY TOUCHING LIBERTY'S ELBOW AND MOVING HER AWAY FROM THE BUILDING'S ENTRANCE WHERE THEY WERE STANDING AND THEN THE MAN SAID TO LIBERTY "I'M MR. SWEPSTONE" THE MAN SAID POINTING TO THE SIGN WHERE THE SOLICITORS WERE LISTED. "I'M AFRAID THAT MY OFFICES ARE UNDERGOING RENOVATIONS RIGHT NOW BECAUSE A WATERPIPE BURSTED LAST WINTER AND LEFT THE CEILING AND THE WALLS A MESS AND SO I'VE TAKEN TEMPORARY OFFICES JUST A FEW BLOCKS FROM HERE." HE HAD HIS HAND FIRMLY ON LIBERTY'S ELBOW AND SAID LET'S GO.

GOOD GRIEF IT'S HIM! AND I'M BEING ABDUCTED. DON'T TALK TO PEOPLE YOU DON'T KNOW. HOW MANY TIMES HAVE I HEARD MOM AND DAD SAY THAT? FORGET WHAT MOM AND DAD THINK AND REMEMBER WHAT ZANNY TOLD US! BY THIS TIME THE MAN HAD A HAND ON J.R.'S ARM.

"NOW YOU SAY BROUGHT THE DOCUMENTS WITH YOU." "NO! NO!" J.R.'S VOICE CAME OUT IN ABRUPT LITTLE BARK. "NO I SAID NOTHING LIKE THAT AND NO WE DON'T HAVE THE DOCUMENTS AT ALL. "WELL THEN WHAT'S THAT YOUR ARE CARRYING IN YOUR HAND?" THE MAN SAID.

HARSHNESS MIXED WITH IMPATIENCE HAD CREPT INTO SWEPSTONE'S VOICE. THE MAN WAS EYEING THE ENVELOPE AND IT WAS A VERY THIN ONE. WITHOUT EVEN THINKING J.R. BEGAN TO FOLD IT INTO A TRIANGLE AND THEN J.R. TURNED BACK TWO OF THE CORNERS TO FROM SMALLER TRIANGLES.

"NOW I THINK YOU SHOULD GET IT IN YOUR HEAD THAT IT WOULD BE VERY VALUABL . . ." A BLIZZARD OF W'S HAD HISSED THROUGH THE AIR LIKE WIPERS OR VIPERS ABOUT TO BE DROPPED ON TO THEIR HEADS OR SOMETHING BUT ABOVE ALL OF THOSE W'S SAILED THE ENVELOPE WITH TWO PAGES OF THE OLD MANUSCRIPT AND AS THE MAN REACHED OUT FOR THE ENVELOPE HE HAD LET GO OF J.R.'S ELBOW AND AT THAT MOMENT HE LET GO J.R. HAD RAISED HIS ARM AND LOFTED HIS PAPER AIRPLANE TOWARD THE ROOF.

SUDDENLY A SHRIEK PIERCED THE TRANQUIL COURTYARD AND SEEMED TO STRIP THE NOTES OF THE ORGAN MUSIC RIGHT FROM THE AIR. A RED TORNADO FULL OF FRECKLES AND SPITTING BLUE FIRE FROM HIS EYES HAD HURTLED TOWARD THEM WITH FLAIR. "STOP THAT INSTANTLY! STOP THAT BIG MAN! "HE'S KIDNAPPING THOSE CHILDREN STOP HIM." "ZANNY!" BOTH OF THE TWINS CRIED OUT AND THEN FROM THE OTHER CORNER OF THE BIG COURTYARD THERE WAS A GREAT FLAPPING OF BLACK LIKE SOME BIG ENORMOUS CROW ABOUT TO LAND. "UNHAND THOSE CHILDREN I SAY! UNHAND THEM RIGHT NOW!"

CHAPTER 23

THE SWAN SOLICITOR.

"MY GOODNESS! HE WAS A SLIPPERY LITTLE FELLOW AND HE JUST SEEMED TOO VANISHED INTO THIN AIR." THE YOUNG SOLICITOR'S WIG WAS ASKEW AND THE LITTLE PIGTAIL HUNG OVER ONE EAR. "I GUESS I DON'T NEED THIS ON NOW BECAUSE I'M NOT IN COURT." HE THEN HAD SNATCHED THE WIG OFF HIS HEAD AND PUT IT IN A POCKET OF HIS ROBES BEFORE HE WENT TO BED. "ARE YOU ALL RIGHT? HE DIDN'T HARM YOU DID HE?" THEY WERE SO COMPLETELY SHAKEN THAT IT TOOK THEM A MOMENT TO ANSWER.

"YES AND NO" LIBERTY AND J.R. BOTH ANSWERED. "I SAW YOU" THE YOUNG SOLICITOR SAID. "IF YOU'LL FORGIVE THE EXPRESSION YOU WERE LIKE A WOMEN POSSESSED." HIS EYES WERE RIVETED ON ZANNY AND OVERFLOWING WITH ADMIRATION AND THE CHILDREN HAD NOTICED SOMETHING ELES. IS THIS LOVE? LIBERTY WONDERED. IT COULD BE HE LOOKS LIKE A MOONY TO ME. IT CAN'T ALL BE JUST FROM RELIEF AT SAVING US.

WELL HE'S VERY CUTE J.R. SAID. ZANNY SHOULD LOOK AT HIM MORE. SHE SEEMS A LITTLE OUT OF IT. I GUESS THIS IS PART OF BEING A NANNY IS CHILDREN COMES FIRST HOW BORING!

"WHAT WAS HE DOING TO YOU?" "WHAT DID HE WANT?" ZANNY SAID. "THAT!" J.R. REPLIED LOOKING UP AT THE GUTTER WHERE THE ENVELOPE HAD FETCHED UP IT'S FLIGHT TO SAFETY. "WHAT WAS THAT?" BOTH ZANNY AND THE YOUNG SOLICITOR ASKED AND THEN BEFORE EITHER

ONE COULD HAVE ANSWERED ZANNY SAID, "DOES IT HAVE ANYTHING TO DO WITH SHERLOCK HOLMES AND SOMEONE NAMED SHADRACH?" THE TWINS ASKED AS THEY LOOKED DUMBFOUNDED.

"YES!" THEY BOTH SAID AT ONCE. "HOW DID YOU EVER KNOW?" LIBERTY ASKED. "IT'S A LONG STORY" ZANNY SAID. "NOT AS LONG AS OURS" J.R. SAID. "PERHAPS WE'D BETTER GO INTO MY OFFICE IT'S RIGHT HERE." THE SOLICITOR POINTED TO A NAME ON THE SIGN THAT SAID JONATHAN SWAN.

"FIRST I HAVE TO GET THAT ENVELOPE" J.R. SAID. "NO PROBLEM" SAID JONATHAN. "LET ME GIVE YOU A LEG UP AND THEN I THINK YOU CAN GET A PURCHASE ON THAT PILLAR AND REACH RIGHT INTO THE GUTTER." FIVE MINUTES LATER THE CHILDREN WERE SITTING JONATHAN SWAN'S OFFICE.

"WELL" HE WAS SAYING "THESE TWO PAGES CERTAINLY DO LOOK VERY AUTHENTIC TO ME AND YOU SAY THAT THE REST OF THE MANUSCRIPT IS BACK AT YOUR HOUSE IN DEVONSHIRE MEWS?" "YES SAID LIBERTY WE DIDN'T WANT TO RISK BRINGING ALL OF IT." "VERY JUDICIOUS" JONATHAN NODDED HIS HEAD AND THEN SMILED. "MY! YOU REALLY HAVE STUMBLED ONTO SOMETHING! SO IT COULD HAVE BEEN SHADRACH HOLMES INSTEAD OF SHERLOCK. GOODNESS! WHAT A DISCOVERY MY CONGRATULATIONS TO YOU BOTH."

THEY HAD PURPOSELY AVOIDED TELLING JONATHAN ABOUT THE GHOST OF SHADRACH AND THE WHOLE IDEA OF LITERARY STILLBORNS AND AS FAR AS JONATHAN KNEW THEY HAD MERELY FOUND THIS MANUSCRIPT STORY BY POKING AROUND IN AN OLD HIDDEN CLOSET AND THE HORRIBLE MAN WHO HAD NEARLY STOLEN IT FROM THEM WAS PROBABLY JUST SOMEBODY WHO HAD HEARD THEM ON THE UNDERGROUND AND FOLLOWED THEM. THE

TWINS HOWEVER WERE CONSUMED WITH CURIOSITY ABOUT HOW ZANNY KNEW TO FOLLOW THEM HERE. SHE MUST HAVE MET UP WITH SHADRACH IN SOME WAY BUT THEY DARED NOT TO ASK. LIBERTY HAD PUT HER FOOT DOWN TELEPHATICALLY SPEAKING.

WE CAN'T SAY A WORD ABOUT THESE GHOSTS IF ONLY FOR ZANNY'S SAKE OK. THIS GUY'S TOO CUTE AND WE DON'T WANT BLOW IT ROMANTICALLY FOR ZANNY. WE START TALKING ABOUT GHOSTS AND LIBERARY STILLBORNS AND HE'LL THINK WE'RE NUTS AND RUN OFF FASTER THEN YOU CAN SAY "SPECKLED BAND"! THE PROCEDURE WAS SIMPLE JONATHAN AGREED TO REPRESENT THE TWINS FOR A TOKEN SUM OF ONE POUND ABOUT TWO LITTLE DOLLARS. HE THEN TOOK AN AFFIDAVIT FROM THAT CONSTITUTED AN VERY GOOD OFFICIAL STATEMENT OF WHERE THEY HAD FOUND THE DOCUMENT WHAT THEY HAD BELIVED IT TO BE. THEY WERE THEN TO TAKE THESE TWO PAPERS AND COLLECT THE REST OF THE MANUSCRIPT FORM THE MEWS AND MEET JONATHAN IN ONE HOUR AT LEAPING LIZARDS BAR AND GRILL OF LONDON WHERE THE PRELIMINARY INSURANCE PLACE IS AND THEN WE CAN FIGURE OUT WHAT TO DO FROM THERE. THEN I COULD DRAW UP A DOCUMENT PAPER CALLED THE RIDER.

THE MANUSCRIPT WOULD THEN BE PUT INTO A LOCKED VAULT FOR VERY SAFEKEEPING. BY THE NEXT DAY JONATHAN WOULD HAVE CONTRACTED A SPECIALIST IN MANUSCRIPTS AND ANTIQUARIAN DOCUMENTS TO LOOK AT AND REVALUATE THE AUTHENTICITY OF THIS FIRST DRAFT. HE WOULD OF COURSE AT THE SAME TIME BRING IN A HOLMESIAN SCHOLAR.

"HOW DID YOU KNOW?" THE CAB BACK TO THE MEWS HAD HARDLY PULLED AWAY FROM THE CURB WHEN J.R. AND LIBERTY BLURTED OUT THEIR QUESTION. ZANNY SANK BACK AGAINST THE SEAT OF THE CAR AND THEN SAID "YOU KNOW ALL THOSE STORIES ABOUT PEOPLE CLAIMING

TO BE KIDNAPPED BY EXTRATERRESTRIALS? YOU KNOW THOSE THINGS YOUR KIDS LOVE TO READING IN THE SUPERMARKET CHECKOUT LINES THE TABLOIDS?"

"DON'T TELL ME SHADRACH KIDNAPPED YOU?" LIBERTY SAID. "WELL NOT EXACTLY BUT I GUARANTEE YOU IT WAS AS EXHAUSTING. HERE I THOUGHT I WAS GOING TO HAVE A NICE RESTFUL DAY OFF AND I GUESS YOU'RE MOTHER IS WAS PLANNING TO SPEND THE WHOLE DAY WITH CHARLY AND MOLLY AT THAT BIRTHDAY PARTY AT THE ZOO THAT ONE OF THE EMBASSY FAMILIES WAS GIVING. WELL I JUST COULDN'T RELAX BECAUSE SOMETHING WAS NUDGING ME MENTALLY BUT NOT PHYSICALLY BUT I JUST KNEW I HAD TO GO UPSTAIRS TO SEE HOW YOU GUYS WERE. I HAD THIS FEELING THAT SOMETHING WASN'T RIGHT SO I WENT UPSTAIRS AND I CAN'T DESCRIBE IT BUT ZANNY'S EYES HAD A FARAWAY LOOK. "I FELT THIS PRESENCE AN INESCAPABLE PRESENCE AND IT WAS PARTICUARLY STRONG IN ONE PART OF THE CORNER OF THE ROOM." "NEAR THE EAVES" J.R. SAID. "YES NEAR THE EAVES AND IT LOOKED AS A PANEL HAD BEEN REMOVED AND THEN PUT BACK INTO THE WALL." "I WAS AFAIRD TO GO NEAR THERE." "YOU WERE?" THEY BOTH ASKED. THEN LIBERTY SPOKE UP AND SAID "YOU MEAN THAT GHOST SHADOW OF SHADRACH CAME OUT WITHOUT YOU READING THE MANUSCRIPT OR SAYING HER NAME?"

"I'M AFAIRD SO AND I'M AFAIRD IT MIGHT HAVE CAUSED HER MORTAL DAMAGE IF YOU CAN SPEAK OF SUCH A THING IN REFERENCE TO A BIG LONG SHADOW GHOST." "MORTAL DAMAGE OH NO!" BOTH TWINS SAID OUT LOUD. "YES YOU SEE" AS ZANNY CONTINUED "HE MANIFESTED HIMSELF IN A WAY THAT WAS IN VIOLATION OF ALL THE RULES."

"OH NO!" J.R. WAILED OUT LOUD. "WHY DIDN'T YOU SAY HER NAME?" "WELL HOW WAS I SUPPOSED TO KNOW HER NAME? I MEAN SHADRACH IS NOT ONE OF THOSE NAMES THAT JUST POPS RIGHT INTO YOUR HEAD." "OH DEAR" SAID LIBERTY. "SO DID YOU ACTUALLY SEE HER?" "WELL

SORT OF THERE WERE THREE DIM ROSETTES HOVERING IN THE AIR."

"HER CRAVAT" THE TWINS SAID OUT LOUD. "THE MORE THE TWINS HAD TALKED THE MORE THE SHADOW OF SHADRACH'S GHOST HAD MOVED AROUND THE ROOM." LIBERTY HAD ASKED "THE MORE SHE HAD APPEARED RIGHT?" "WELL NOW THAT'S THE PROBLEM YOU SEE I THINK IT WEAKENED HER GREATLY TO HAVE COME FORTH AND MANIFEST HIMSELF IN THIS WAY BUT HE TOOK GREAT RISK BY APPEARING. HE TOLD ME THAT HE COULDN'T REALLY ASSESS THE DAMAGE IT HAD DONE."

"OH NO!" J.R. GROANED. "HOW DID IT HAPPEN?" HOW DID HE FINALLY APPEAR?" LIBERTY ASKED. "WELL I WAS JUST UP THERE AND TOO SCARED TO GO INTO THAT CORNER BUT ALSO TOO SCARED TO LEAVE AND WORRIED TO DEATH ABOUT THE TWO OF YOU. I THINK I MUST HAVE STARTED CRYING OR SOMETHING BECAUSE THIS VOICE JUST BLURTED OUT "I CAN'T STAND WHEN WOMEN CRY AND STOP SNIVELING." ZANNY PAUSED THEN SHE CONTINUED "SHE TOLD ME TO PULL MYSELF TOGETHER AND THEN SHE EXPLAINED THIS WHOLE THING AND WHAT YOU TWO WERE UP TO. YOU SEE SHE WAS VERY TERRIBLY FRIGHTENED THAT SOMETHING AWFUL MIGHT HAPPEN THOUGHT IT WAS WORTH THE RISK BUT SHOWING HIMSELF TO ME THE WAY HE DID EVEN RISKIER AND SEEMED VERY WEAK WHEN I LEFT HIM"

"OH NO!" BOTH LIBERTY AND J.R. CRIED OUT. "WHAT COULD HAPPEN TO HIM?" J.R. ASKED. "YEAH WELL HOW DO YOU DIE TWICE?" LIBERTY ASKED HER. "I'M NOT SURE BUT I FELT IT MIGHT BE SOMETHING WORSE THAN BEING A LITERARY STILLBORN. HE SEEMED TOO WEAK TO EXPLAIN BUT OBVIOUSLY IF HE WENT TO THIS GREAT RISK HE FELT THERE WAS SOMETHING TO BE GAINED BY IT AND IF WE WORK FAST ENOUGH AND GET THIS MANUSCRIPT OUT TO THE WORLD THERE'S HOPE HE MIGHT JUST SURVIVE IF YOU CAN USE THAT WORD FOR SOMEONE WHO IS ALREADY A GHOST."

CHAPTER 24

BACK INTO THE HONEY PIT.

LOOK! THERE ARE THOSE BIG SMOOCHY MARKS AGAIN MOLLY HAD TELAFLASHED. IT LOOKS LIKE A WORM GOING HEAD FIRST INTO A BIG HOT SMOKEY VOLCANO. OH GOOD GRIEF YOU LITTLE TWERPS AUNT HONEY'S GROSSED OUT ENOUGH WITHOUT YOUR LITTLE PLAY-BY-PLAY COMMENTARY J.R. SAID OUT LOUD.

SHUT UP I WANT TO HERE THIS GUYS LIBERTY SAID. EVER SINCE THE GHOST SHADOW OF SHADRACH HAD COME INTO THEIR LIVES THE CROSS COMMUNICATION HAD IMPROVED IN ALL FOUR OF THE TWINS. "WELL THIS IS ALL SO EXCITING" AUNT HONEY WAS SAYING. "WHO WOULD HAVE THOUGHT THAT THESE TWO WOULD EVER GET ALONG WITH EACH OTHER" SAID AUNT HONEY. JUST DON'T SAY IT HONEY BUCKETS PLEASE DON'T SAY IT TO THEM! I JUST KNOW SHE'S GOING TO SAY SOMETHING ABOUT HOW WE'RE UNDERACHEIVERS J.R. SAID LIBERTY. I JUST KNOW IT.! COOL IT SAID J.R. TO LIBERTY SHE HASN'T SAID ANYTHING YET. YEAH BUT YOU KNOW SHE WILL SAY SOMETHING SOONER OR LATER LIBERTY SAID BACK TO HER LITTLE BROTHER JR. "THIS SET ESPECIALLY" SAID AUNT HONEY. SEE WHAT DID I TELL YOU? YOU SAID IT BEFORE J.R. NO ASSEMBLY REQUIRED. "I MEAN I WAS TALKING ABOUT THE LITTLE TWINS NOT YOU OLDER TWINS" AUNT HONEY HAD SAID OUT LOUD.

DAD CLEARED HIS THROAT VIOLENTLY BEFORE HE SAID "HONEY MY DEAR." HE'S REALLY MAD AT AUNT HONEY HE ONLY CALLES HER "MY DEAR" WHEN HE WANTS TO CALL HER TURKEY.

"WELL PUTMAN LET'S BE REASNABLE AND HAVEN'T THEY CEEDED YOUR EXPECTATIONS?" "THEY'VE ONLY BEGUN HONEY YOU'RE STUCK DEAR." "WELL WHEN MADELINE CALLED ME AND TOLD ME THIS SPLENDID NEWS I THOUGHT I JUST HAD TO COME OVER. I MEAN YOU KNOW SHE ROLLED HER BIG EYES AROUND THE ROOM AND TOSSED HER SCARF DRAMATICALLY AROUND HER THROAT.

SHE SOULD JUST STRANGLE HERSELF WITH THAT SCARF NOW AND SAVE ME THE TROUBLE LIBERTY TELAFLASHED. THE TWINS ALMOST GIGGLED OUT LOUD ABOUT THAT. LISTEN CHARLY TELAFLASHED I THINK SHE'S JUST TRYING TO SAY THAT ME AND MOLLY ARE TEENY TINY BIT BETTER THAT'S ALL.

WITH THERAPISTS LIKE YOU WHO NEEDS CRAZY PEOPLE? J.R. TELAFLASHED SOFTLY. WE DON'T GET IT "WHAT'S A THERAPIST?" NEVER MIND YOU LITTLE SMART ASSES. LIBERTY DO YOU WANT THE SCARF NOW OR LATER? J.R. HAD SAID WE WERE THERAPISTS AND WE WANT TO KNOW WHAT IT MEANS. IS IT SOMETHING TO DO WITH PRESS ON NAILS? WAS LAURA INGALLS WILDER A THERAPIST TOO? ARE YOU GOING TO TELL US? SAID LIBERTY.

THERE WAS A VERITABLE TELEASHOUTING MATCH GOING ON BETWEEN CHARLY, MOLLY, J.R. AND LIBERTY. HEY EVERYBODY SHUT UP! HERE IT COMES AND HERE'S YOUR CHANCE LIBERTY LISTEN UP! "WELL IN MY CASE MADELINE I THOUGHT I'D WEAR THAT CREAMY CHIFFON IT SHOWS OFF MY COLORING DON'T YOU KNOW."

DON'T YOU JUST KNOW IT HONEY GUTS! "THEN I THOUGHT FOR A WRAP I WOULD WEAR THAT PINK FEATHERED BOA CONSTRICTOR." IF WE SHOULD BE SO LUCKY LIBERTY TELAFLASHED. SHE THEN TURNED TO AUNT HONEY WITH HER SWEETEST SMILE AND BIT HER LEFT CHEEK SO HER DIMPLE WOULD WINK. "WELL AUNT

HONEY I HATE TO TELL YOU BUT THEY DON'T ALLOW FEMALES TO BE PRESENT IN THE SAME ROOM WITH THE BLUE CARBUNCLES WHEN THEY ARE MEETING." "WHAT? I NEVER HEARD OF SUCH A THING!"

THEY ALL NODDED SOLEMNLY ALMOST MOURNFULLY AT AUNT HONEY. "THEN I GUESS I CAN'T BUT EVEN AUNT HONEY HAD THE GRACE NOT TO FINISH THAT THOUGHT SHE WAS THINKING." THE FOUR RAGOZZINO TWINS DID IT FOR HER. WEAR YOUR BOA CONSTRICTOR SCRAF THE TWINS SAID.

"AH!" SAID DAD. TRY TO HOLD YOURSELF TOGETHER DAD BECAUSE WE KNOW THIS IS TOUGH SAID ALL FOUR TWINS.

CHAPTER 25

THE BLUE CARBUNCLES.

"BEAUTIFUL!" "INCONTROVERTIBLE VERACITY AND A STUNNING REVELATION." BOGGLES YOU FEEL THIS WAS PROBABLY FINISHED SOMETIME AFTER HE AND LOUISE MOVED INTO THE MARYLEBONE HOUSE?

"BEAUTIFUL! BEAUTIFUL!" FIVE GENTELMEN, LIBERTY, J.R., THEIR FATHER PUTMAN, ZANNY AND JONATHAN SWAN WERE SEATED AT A LONG OVAL-SHAPED TABLE IN A PANELED CONFERENCE ROOM OF THE LEAPPING LIZARD BAR AND GRILL OF LONDON. IT WAS BECAUSE OF THE ABSOLUTE SECRECY REQUIRED AND NOT EVEN A SECRETARY FROM THE FIRM WAS IN THE ROOM TO TAKE NOTES.

"NOW WE ARE HERE TODAY PRESUMABLY TO DECIDE HOW WE SHALL PRESENT THIS LANDMARK DISCOVERY TO THE WORLD" MR. BOGGLES WAS INTONING IN A BRAVE VOICE. "IT WAS DUNPHY'S AND MY THOUGHT THAT INDEED IT WOULD BE MOST APPROPRIATE TO MAKE THE BIG ANNOUNCEMENT AT THE MONTHLY MEETING OF THE BIG BLUE CARBUNCLES WHICH WILL BE NEXT WEDNESDAY. WE WOULD OF COURSE HAVE A PRESS RELEASE PREPARED WITH ALL DUE CREDIT TO THE DISCOVERERS LIBERTY AND J.R. RAGOZZINO. NOW THERE IS THE GENDER PROBLEM."

LIBERTY BEGAN A SLOW SMOLDER THAT SHE HAD PREPARED FOR JUST THIS PROBLEM. SHADRACH HAD BEEN THE FIRST TO INFORM HER THAT THE FACT THAT SHE WAS A GIRL MIGHT PRESENT A MUCH BIGGER PROBLEM TO THE BIG BLUE CARBUNCLES BUT SOMEHOW NEITHER SHE NOR J.R. OR ZANNY HAD EVER BELIEVED THIS WOULD REALLY

BECOME A HURDLE AND NEITHER HAD JONATHAN OR PUTMAN BUT BOTH MEN WERE PREPARED TO PUT UP A GOOD FIGHT TO PROTECT LIBERTY'S RIGHT TO BE PRESENT AT THE MOMENTOUS OCCASION WHEN THE CHILDREN'S FIND WOULD BE REVEALED TO THE WORLD. "NOW WE ALL THINK MISS RAGOZZINO THAT IT WOULD BE A TERRIBLE SHAME FOR YOU NOT TO BE ABLE TO PARTICIPATE."

"WITH ALL DUE RESPECT MR. BOGGLES AS PUTMAN BARAGED INTO THE CONFERENCE ROOM SAYING "IT IS UNTHINKABLE FOR YOU NOT TO LET MISS RAGOZZINO PARTICIPATE IN THIS FINDING OF THE MANUSCRIPT THAT BOTH HER AND HER BROTHER J.R. FOUND. "MR. BOGGLES HAD COUGHED NERVOUSLY AFTER MR. PUTMAN SAID THAT. "YES OF COURSE MR. PUTMAN."

JONATHAN SHIFTED IN HIS SEAT AND HE WAS PREPARED TO ARGUE ON LEGAL GROUNDS FOR LIBERTY'S RIGHTS BUT HE DIDN'T WANT TO UNTIL IT WAS ABSOLUTELY NECESSARY. HE HAD HOPED TO BE ABLE TO GENTLY CONVINCE THEM OF LIBRTY'S INALIENABLE RIGHT BE PRESENT.

"THE BYLAWS OF THE ORGANIZATION LEAVE LITTLE DOUBT ABOUT SUCH ISSUES AS FEMALE PRESENCE AT MEETINGS. INDEED THE ONLY TIME THE WOMEN CAN ATTEND IS ON THE OCCASION OF SOME OF OUR SUMMER OUTINGS. THERE IS THE TEA IN HONOR OF THE QUEEN'S BIRTHDAY QUEEN VICTORIA THAT IS AND WOMEN ARE INVITED TO THAT BUT REALLY I DON'T THINK WE'D WANT TO WAIT UNTILL THEN TO ANNOUNCE THIS MARVELOUS DISCOVERY AND I'M SURE MISS RAGOZZINO WOULD NOT WANT US TO WAIT THAT LONG EITHER."

LIBERTY DIDN'T ANSWER BUT SHE DID GLARE AT MR. BOGGLEY. YOU REALLY TICK ME OFF YOU BUG-EYED OLD BOGGLEY BAT. COOL IT LIBERTY! J.R. TELAFLASHED. "MR. BOGGLES" SHE DIDN'T MEAN IT J.R. SAID. JUST THEN JONATHAN ROSE FROM HIS CHAIR. LIBERTY COULD

SENSE HE WAS PERTURBED. ZANNY LOOKED ON HER EYES BRIMMING WITH ADMIRATION AND BUY THEN LIBERTY FELL ASLEEP ON THE FLOOR. BY THE TIME LIBERTY WOKE UP SHE KNEW SOMETHING WAS GOING ON AND SHE WAS GOING TO FIND OUT WHAT IT WAS ONE WAY OR ANOTHER. LIBERTY THEN WENT INTO ZANNY'S ROOM AND STARTED TO SNOOP AROUND IN HER SISTER'S DRESSER DOOR AND THEN AFTER A FEW MINUTES OF SNOOPING AROUND SHE FOUND THIS LOVE LETTER WHICH SAID: "DEAR ZANNY I THINK I'AM STARTING TO FALL IN LOVE WITH YOU." DON'T LET ANYONE READ THIS LOVE LETTER. KISSES! JONATHAN. SO AFTER SHE READ THIS LOVE LETTER SHE PUT IT BACK AND WENT TO FIND J.R. SO SHE COULD TELL HER ABOUT ZANNY'S LOVE LETTER FROM JONATHAN. LIBERTY THEN FOUND J.R. AND TOLD HER ABOUT ZANNY'S LOVE LETTER FROM JONATHAN BUT J.R WAS SO MAD FROM THIS MORNING SHE DIDN'T GIVE A HOOT ABOUT THE LOVE LETTER ZANNY GOT FROM JONATHAN.

"YES?" MR. BOGGLES LOOKED UP. "IT IS MY UNDERSTANDING THAT THE MONTHLY MEETING OF THE BIG BLUE CARBUNCLES USUALLY OCCURS AT A PUB NOT FAR FROM HERE AND FURTHERMORE IT IS MY UNDERSTANDING OF ENGLISH JURISPRUDENCE THAT UNDER THE LAW CHILDREN AREN'T PERMITTED IN ROOMS WHERE WINE AND SPIRITS ARE SERVED. SO AS THE CASE NOW STANDS NEITHER ONE OF THE CHILDREN WOULD BE ABLE TO ATTEND THIS AUGUST GATHERING. IN MY CLIENTS BEST INTERESTS I COULD NOT AS THEIR SOLICITOR ALLOWED THEM TO ATTEND THIS MEETING IN THE FIRST PLACE."

WHAT IS HE GETTING AT? NEITHER ONE OF US GETS TO GO! "MY CLIENTS LIBERTY AND J.R. RAGOZZINO" JONATHAN CONTINUED "WOULD BE VERY PERFECTLY FREE TO ANNOUNCE THIS LANDMARK DISCOVERY ON THEIR VERY OWN AND THEIR FATHER PUTMAN RAGOZZINO SENIOR ATTACHE TO AMBASSADOR WHITMORE OF

THE COURT OF ST. JAMES HAS INFORMED ME THAT AMBASSADOR WHITMORE IS PREPARED TO OFFER THE AMERICAN EMBASSY AS THE SITE FOR THIS MARVELOUS ANNOUNCEMENT."

"THIS IS AN OUTRAGE!" MR. BOGGLES SAID AS HE JUMPED UP OUT OF HIS CHAIR. THE APPRAISER OF THE MANUSCRIPTS "THE HOLMESIAN LITTLE SCHOLAR" AND TWO GENTLEMEN FROM THE BIG BLUE CARBUNCHLES WERE AGHAST. "IMPOSSIBLE!" SPUTTERED MR. AMBERSLEY WITMORE. "WE ARE DEALING HERE WITH AN ENGLISH DOCUMENT THAT IS A PIECE OF THE ENGLAND'S LITERARY HISTORY. SIR. ARTHUR CONAN DOYLE WAS ENGLISH AND HIS CREATION THE CHARACTER OF SHERLOCK HOLMES IS ENGLISH TO THE CORE! IT WOULD BE A VIOLATION OF THE BRAVEST OLDER TO HAVE THIS ANNOUNCEMENT MADE IN THE EMBASSY OF FOREIGN POWER."

"RATHER REMINISCENT OF THE ENGLAND MARBLES" PUTMAN HAD SAID QUIETLY AND SMILED. ALL FIVE MEN TURNED AND HAD UNCOMFORTABLE SHADES OF PINK AT PUTMAN'S REFERENCE TO ENGLAND'S 1803 THEFT OF THE MARBLE FRIEZE FROM THE PARTHENON IN ATHENS GREECE. IT HAD BEEN A VERY TOUCHY SUBJECT FOR WELL OVER A CENTURY. THE BRITISH WERE SOMEWHAT USED TO BEING ATTACKED AND HAD STANDARD ANSWERS BUT PERHAPS THEY HAD NEVER HAD THE TABLES TURNED ON THEM SO DEFTLY AS PUTMAN WAS CONTINUING TO DO NOW.

I FORGIVE HIM FOR THE WAR ON FLUOROCARBONS LIBERTY TELAFLASHED TO HER SISTER MOLLY. THE GUY'S RELLY A PRO! "THE DIRECTOR OF THE BIG ACQUISITIONS OF SMITHSONIAN INSTITUTE IN WASHINGTON D.C. IS A VERY CLOSE PERSONAL FRIEND OF MINE." PUTMAN WAS SPEAKING ALMOST VERY CASUALLY NOW. "I AM SURE HE WOULD BE MOST INTERESTED IN THIS FIRST DRAFT DISCOVERED BY TWO YOUNG AMERICANS."

THE FIVE GENTLEMAN LOOKED ABSOLUTELY HORRIFIED AT THIS LITTLE SUGGESTION. ONE MIGHT AS WELL HAVE SAID THAT THE TOWER OF THE LONDON BUILDING WAS BACK IN BUSINESS AND THEIR OWN GRANDKIDS WOULD BE THE FIRST NEW INMATES. BOGGLES ACTUALLY REACHED INTO HIS BACK POCKET FOR A PILL BOX AND SLIPPED A TABLET INTO HIS MOUTH WITHOUT ANYONE REALIZEING IT. "I'M SURE THERE IS SOME WAY AROUND THIS" BOGGLES SAID OUT LOUD. "I'M SURE THERE IS" PUTMAN SAID RISING UP OUT OF HIS SEAT TO LEAVE. "I SHALL TELL AMBASSADOR WHITMORE TO HOLD OFF INFORMING THE PRESS UNTILL WE HEAR FROM YOU. THAT WILL BE TOMORROW AS I THINK WE'VE ALL AGREED THAT WE DO NOT WANT TO DELAY THINGS UNNECESSARILY SAID AMBASSADOR WHITMORE." "YES OF COURSE SAID PUTMAN." THEY'RE SCARED SAID LIBERTY. LOOK AT THAT GUY WITH THE OLD DOUBLE NAME AND THE STRAWBERRY SHAPED NOSE. HE'S QUAKING IN HIS BOOTS! SAID LIBERTY. YEAH SAID J.R. AND LOOK AT MR. BOGGLES HE'S GETTING MORE BUG-EYED BY THE SECOND J.R. SAID. "OF COURSE THERE WAS A CHORUS OF COUGHS AND LOW GROWLS THAT EMANATED FROM WAY BACK IN THE THROATS OF FIVE ENGLISH GENTLEMAN NAMED "THE JACKSON FIVE" SAID LIBERTY. "OF COURSE" J.R. SAID.

CHAPTER 26

THE BIG SOLUTION.

THE SOLUTION TO THE GENDER PROBLEM WAS NOT ALTOGETHER SATISFACTORY AT LEAST NOT FROM LIBERTY'S OF VIEW. NOR WAS WAS IT FROM PUTMAN'S POINT OF VIEW BECAUSE IT DID VIOLATE ALBEIT IN A LIMITED WAY MEANING THE RAGOZZINO'S FAMILY MOTTO "SUI VERITAS PRIMO" MEANING TO TELL THE TRUTH TO YOURSELF. HOWEVER JONATHAN SWAN ADVISED THEM TO GO ALONG WITH IT. AFTER AS HE POINTED OUT LIBERTY'S TRUE IDENTITY WOULD BE RECOGNIZED EVENTUALLY AND IT WAS ONLY FOR THE EVENING GATHERING AND DINNER OF THE BIG BLUE CARBUNCLES THAT LIBERTY WOULD HAVE TO DISGUISE HERSELF AND APPEAR IN THE CLOTHES OF A BOY.

WELL SHADRACH WAS SAYING, HE WAS STILL AILING ON ONLY HIS ROSETTES WITCH WERE HUNG DIMLY IN THE DYING LIGHT OF THE SUMMER EVENING AND LIBERTY DIDN'T WANT TO BURDEN HIM WITH HER TROUBLES BUT HE HAD APPEARED IN THIS RATHER WEAK ANEMIC FORM NEVERTHELESS. YOU SEE MY DEAR YOU ARE IN THE TRADITION OF A GREAT MANY LITERARY PARTICULARLY IN THE BIG SHAKESPEAREAN CHARACTER WHO DISGUISED THEIR SEX TO BE ABLE TO ACHIEVE THEIR GOALS. YOU HAVE HEARD OF THESE SO CALLED CHARACTERS HAVEN'T YOU?

YES NOW THAT'S A GOOD GIRL. SHE FELT SOMETHING LIGHTER THAN THE EARIEST MORNING BREEEZE BRUSH HER HAND. I REALLY THINK WE HAVE A CHANCE OF PULLING THIS OFF. "YES" LIBERTY SAID FIERCELY. SHE HAD

TO REMEMBER THE GOAL HERE LIBERATING SHADRACH FROM HIS UNHAPPY EXISTENCE. SHE HEARD HIM SIGH AND SHE KNEW WHAT HE WAS THINKING. THEY COULD PULL IT OFF IF HE COULD MAKE IT TO THE TIME OF THE ANNOUNCEMENT. HE HAD BEEN GROWING DIMMER EVERY DAY. YESTERDAY THERE HAD BEEN THREE ROSETTES VISIBLE THE DAY BEFORE THERE WERE FOUR AND NOW TODAY ONLY ONE. "YES SHADRACH I PROMISE I'LL DO MY BEST AT THE MEETING. ZANNY SAYS NO ONE WILL GUESS YOU'RE A GIRL. I'M GOING TO WEAR A DEERSTALKER HAT JUST LIKE J.R.'S AND SHERLOCK'S. I GUESS ALL THE MEMBERS OF THE BLUE CARBUNCLES WEAR THEM TO THEESE MONTHLY MEETINGS. SO I WON'T HAVE TO CUT MY HAIR JUST PUT IT UP." "GOOD THE WORD CAME LIKE THE WHISPER OF A WIND OVER DRY LEAVES. I'LL WEAR PANTS, SHOES, TIE, AND J.R. AND I WILL LOOK LIKE ABSOLUTELY IDENTICAL TWIN."

OH THANKS YOU LIBERTY. YOU KNOW I HEARD YOUR PARENTS TALKING THE OTHER NIGHT ABOUT A FRIEND THEY BACK IN WASHINGTON WHO WAS ADDICTED TO ALCOHOL.

"DON'T TALK SHADRACH BUT IT SEEMS WE WILL BE TIRING YOU OUT. IT'S NOT STRENGTHENING YOUR BIOLUMINESCENCE."

YES I KNOW BUT I MUST SAY THIS, "WITH THIS PERSON IT IS SAD THAT HE IS ADDICTED TO ALCHOHOL RATHER THEN LIFE AND LIKE MY BROTHER AND HIS COCAINE HABIT BUT THEN OF COURSE SHERLOCK ONLY LIVED IN A BOOK AND A CHARACTER IN A BOOK HAS NO CONTROL BUT THIS OTHER PERSON IS REAL DESPITE THE ILLNESS HE MUST CONTROL HIS OWN DESTINY AND HE CAN CONTROL IT BECAUSE HE IS REAL. I'M JUST FROM THE PAGES OF A DRAFT AN UNPUBLISHED MANUSCRIPT. IT IS MY LUCK TO BE WITHOUT CONTROL ALTHOUGH I HAVE TRIED AS HARD AS LITERARILY POSSIBLE TO JUMP THE BOUNDARIES OF THE PAGE.

IF THAT SEEMS GROSSLY UNFAIR BECAUSE OF MY POWERLESS STATE THEN PERHAPS IT IS OR PERHAPS IT ISN'T BUT ONE THE FEW JUST DESERTS IS THAT BECAUSE I HAVE NO POWER AND I CAN SEAK A NEW AUTHOR. IN A SENSE YOU AND YOUR BROTHER ARE AUTHORS WHO SHALL RE-CREATE ME FOR THE LITERARY WORLD. THE TWO OF YOU ARE MY CHOICE BECAUSE YOU, YOUR BROTHER AND YOUR ENTIRE FAMILY ARE ADDICTED TO LIFE AND YOU HAVE BROUGHT LIFE INTO THIS HOUSE AGAIN. YOU ALSO BROUGHT GOLDFISH, SQUABBLES AND CHINA VILLAGES THAT FLOAT ON LILYPADS AND YOU CAN PLAY EVER SINGLE MEMBER OF YOUR FAMILY'S CHARACTERS!

"DON'T TALK ANYMORE PLEASE SHADRACH!" LIBERTY'S EYES FOCUSED ON THE DIMLY PULSATING ROSETTE BUT LIBERTY YOU MUST NOW THINK AS A CHARACTER BECAUSE FOR THEY HAVE WRITTEN THE CHAPTER OF THIS LITTLE STUPIDITY ABOUT NO WOMEN AT THE METTING. IT IS AS IF YOU HAVE NO CONTROL LIKE A LITERARY CHARACTER BUT YOU DO HAVE THE POWER SO YOU MUST DO SOMETHING VERY SUBTLE HERE. REMEMBER WHEN I SAID THAT A CHARACTER MUST NEVER LOOK LIKE A PUPPET DESPITE THE FACT THAT HE OR SHE HAS NO CONTROL? YOU MUST DO THE SAME AND YOU MUST NOT LOOK LIKE A PUPPET BUT BE ABLE TO THREAD YOUR WAY NIMBLY THROUGH THE PLOT OF THIS MEETING. YOU MUST FIT BELIEVABLY INTO THE SETTING BUT IF YOU ARE REALLY CLEVER YOU CAN MANIPULATE THE PLOT AND REMEMBER YOU MAY LOOK LIKE A LITERARY CHARCTER BUT YOU'RE A FLESH-AND—BLOOD GIRL AND THERE ARE STILL THINGS THAT CAN BE DONE WHEN YOU ARE AT THE MEETING.

THEN THERE WAS A SLIGHT SIBILANT WHISPER LIKE A STREAM OF AIR THAT WAS TRYING TO FORM A WORD THAT BEGAN WITH A LETTER "S" BUT SHE COULD NOT HEAR WORD AND THE LAST ROSETTE HAD MELTED INTO THE LONG NIGHT. HAD SHADRACH GONE FOREVER? THERE WAS NO WAY OF KNOWING. LIBERTY HAD TEARS RUNNING

DOWN HER EYES BUT LET SHE HAD WONDERED WHAT DID HE MEAN? HOW COULD SHE BEHAVE LIKE A CHARACTER AND YET HAVE THE CONTROL OF A REAL PERSON? HOW WAS SHE SUPPOSED TO MANIPULATE THE POLT AND NIMBLY THREAD HER WAY THROUGH THAT MEETING IN HER BOY'S CLOTHES? WHAT WAS THE LAST WORD HE HAD STARTED TO SAY? "I DON'T REMEMBER" SHE SAID.

CHAPTER 27

JUST PLAIN OLD ME!

THE MONTHLY MEETING OF THE BLUE CARBUNCLES WAS TO BE HELD AT THE CARLTON CLUB LOCATED ON SAINT JAMES STREET AND FOUNDED IN 1832 BY THE DUKE OF WELLINGTON. BY HOLDING THE MOMENTOUS OCCASION IN A PRIVATE CLUB RATHER THAN A PUBLICAN HOUSE OR PUB THE STICKY ISSUE OF SERVING LIQUOR ON THE PREMISES WITH CHILDREN PRESENT HAD BEEN AVOIDED BUT THE WORLD LIBERTY AND J.R. ENTERED WHEN THEY WALKED THROUGH THE PORTALS OF THE CARLTON CLUB WAS MOST DEFINITELY A MASCULINE ONE FILLED WITH THE SCENT OF LEATHER AND HUNG WITH PAINTINGS OF BLOOD SPORTS.

DROOLING HOUNDS AND DEAD ANIMALS LIBERTY TELAFLASHED TO HER BROTHER. THEY THINK THAT'S REALLY MACHO DON'T THEY? SHE NODDED TOWARD A PORTRAIT OVER A HUGE FIREPLACE OF A DEAD RABBIT HELD IN THE MOUTH OF A HUNTING DOG. BLOOD WAS DRIPPING FROM GASH IN RABBIT'S NECK. I DON'T THINK BEATRIX POTTER WOULD HAVE LIKED IT J.R. REPLIED TELEPATHICALLY BUT MOST MEN ARE STUPID.

DON'T LOOK SO GROUCHY BECAUSE HERE COMES BOGGLES. "GOOD EVENING CHILDREN YOU LOOK VERY NICE." THE REMARK WAS MADE TO BOTH TWINS BUT MR. BOGGLES NODDED IN LIBERTY'S DIRECTION. THEN HE CAME UP CLOSE TO HER AND WHISPERED IN HER EAR "REMEMBER YOU ONLY HAVE TO KEEP THIS UP FOR THE DURATION OF THE METTING AND THEN AFTER THAT YOU CAN ANNOUNCE YOURSELF TO THE PRESS AND BE GIVEN

FULL CREDIT AS A YOUNG WOMEN WHO HAS DISCOVERED THIS WONDERFUL OLD BUT YET NEW MANUSCRIPT."

IT HAD BEEN ANNOUNCED THAT A NEW PIECE OF HOLMESIAN INFORMATION HAD BEEN DISCOVERED AND THAT TWO AMERICAN CHILDREN WERE IN SOME WAY INVOLVED. THOSE WERE THE ONLY DETAILS THAT WERE GIVEN OUT AND ONLY MR. BOGGLES AND THE GENTLEMEN WHO HAD COME WITH HIM TO LIZARD'S RESTAURANT OF LONDON KNEW THAT THE FIND WAS A LOST MANUSCRIPT THAT HAD OFFERED THE MOST IMPORTANT INSIGHTS EVER INTO THE CREATION OF SHERLOCK HOLMES. ALL THESE GENTLEMEN AS WELL AS PUTMAN, JONATHAN, LIBERTY, AND JULY WERE VERY NERVOUS AND COULD BARELY EAT A BIT OF THE ROAST-BEEF DINNER AS THE MEMBERS WERE FINISHING DESSERT MR. BOGGLES STEPPED UP TO THE PODIUM TO CALL THE MEETING TO ORDER. LIBERTY AND JULY WERE IN SUCH A FLURRY OF EXCITEMENT THAT THEY COULD HARDLY FOLLOW WHAT HE WAS SAYING. TELEPATHIC COMMUNICATION WAS VIRTUALLY AND VERY IMPOSSIBLE AND DISSOLVED INTO STATIC CRACKLINGS IN THEIR LITTLE HEADS.

LIBERTY WISHED THAT ZANNY AND THEIR MOTHER HAD BEEN THERE BUT AS WOMEN THEY WERE FORCED TO WAIT IN A SPECIAL ROOM ALONG WITH AUNT HONEY, MOLLY AND CHARLY. THE BIG OFFICIAL PRESS CONFERENCE WOULD BE HELD IN THIS ROOM FOLLOWING THE BIG ANNOUNCEMENT ALTHOUGH THERE WERE SOME MEMBERS OF THE PRESS IN ATTENDANCE AT THE DINNER.

NOW AFTER THE PRELIMINARIES OF CALLING THE MEETING TO ORDER MR. BOGGLES WAS GETTING TO THE HEART OF THE MATTER. "A DISCIVERY OF UNPARALLELED IMPORTANCE TO HOLMESIAN SCHOLARSHIP HAD RECENTLY COME TO LIGHT." A WAVE OF "AHHHS" ROLLED OVER THE ROOM AND MR. BOGGLES FLUSHED WITH

ANTICIPATION AND THE IMPORTANCE. HE WAS OBVIOUSLY RELISHING HIS MOMENT AS THE ANNOUNCER. "WHAT WOULD YOU SAY IF I WERE TO TELL YOU THAT BEFORE "THE ADVENTURE OF THE SPECKLED BAND" BEFORE EVEN THE SIGN OF THE FOUR THERE WAS THE DRAFT OF ANOTHER WORK THAT COMBINED THE CENTRAL THEMES OF BOTH THESE STORIES?"

"OOOOOHS NOW BEGAN TO HOVER IN THE AIR LIKE A FLOCK OF STARLINGS. THE TENSION IN THE ROOM MOUNTED VERY HIGH. PEOPLE STOPPED EATING THEIR DESSERTS AND SET DOWN THEIR FORKS AND FURTHERMORE MR. BOGGLES CONTINUED "WHAT WOULD YOU SAY IF I WERE TO TELL YOU THAT CONAN DOYLE THE MASTER OF DETECTIVE FICTION THE CREATOR OF PROFESSOR MORIARTY THE MOST PERFECT VILLAIN IN LITERARY TERMS?"

THERE WAS A GASP AND THEN A HUSH. "WE HAVE HEARD RUMORS OF HIM HAVEN'T WE?" HE NODDED KNOWINGLY AT HIS AUDIENCE. "A BRIEF APPEARANCE IN A BADLY DAMAGED SECOND DRAFT DISCOVERED IN A WET BASEMENT IN THE VILLAGE OF STOKES POACHES. THE NAME IN THE DRAFT WAS MOREBUTT NIGEL MOREBUTT."

MOREBUTT FLASHED LIBERTY AND JULY NEARLY GIGGLED OUT LOUD. WE CAN'T GIGGLE J.R. REMEMBER WHAT SHADRACH SAID ABOUT THE LITTLE VILAINS HATING TO BE LAUGHED AT BUT MOREBUTT SAID TO LIBERTY YOU KNOW HE DID SORT OF HAVE A FAT . . . ." DON'T SAY IT J.R. WE'LL BLOW EVERYTHING IF WE START LAUGHING. SHE WAS BITTING THE INSIDE OF HER LITTLE CHEEKS AND SHE WOULD BITE THEM ALL NIGHT IF SHE HAD TO BUT SHE WOULD NOT LAUGH.

BOGGLES WAS CONTINUING "AS THIS NEW FIND WILL DOUBTLESSLY PROVE HIS CHARACTERIZATION WAS SO ATROCIOUS THAT HE CAN'T BE CONSIDERED EVEN AS A

FORERUNNER TO THE INFAMOUS MORIARTY AND BE SECOND RATE ALL THE WAY WHEN BOGGLES SAID "SECOND-RATE" WAS NOT GOOD ENOUGH FOR HIM. LIBERTY AND JULY LOOKED AT ONE ANOTHER. THERE HAD BEEN A TINY CRACKLING OF STATIC IN THEIR HEADS AND THEN JUST THE DIM ECHO OF A SIGH AND THEY BOTH HAD FELT IT.

HE'S GONE I THINK LIBERTY FLASHED. HIS SECRET'S OUT SAID LIBERTY. NO EXACTLY HIS SECRET REALLY. YOU CAN'T BLAME THE CHARACTER FOR THE BAD WRITING AND THAT SEEMED TO BE WHAT BOGGLES WAS NOW SAYING AND "THIS OFFERS PROOF THAT DOYLE INDEED HAD HIS WEAKER MOMENTS AS A WRITER. NO ONE HOWEVER CAN DOUBT HIS PERSEVERANCE AND THE ABILITY TO LEARN FROM THE PAST MISTAKES AND DISASTER THE TRUE MARK OF A PRO BUT PERHAPS BEYOND ALL THIS AND THE MOST FASCINATING OF ALL WAS BOGGLES BUSHY SALT-AND—PEPPER EYEBROWS HIKED CLEAR UP TO HIS SHINY BALD HEAD AS HE WIDENED HIS EYES IN ANTICIPATION OF HIS NEXT ANNOUNCEMENT IS "THE REVELATION OF HIS NEXT MANUSCRIPT."

HE'S MILKING THIS FOR ALL HE CAN JULY TELAFLASHED. BOGGLES HAD INHALED DEEPLY AND THE PEOPLE WERE SITTING ON THE EDGES OF THEIR SEATS. "WELL WHAT WOULD YOU SAY IF I WERE TO TELL YOU THAT THERE WAS AT ONE TIME ANOTHER BROTHER TO SHERLOCK INDEED A OLDER TWIN BROTHER NAMED SHADRACH?"

A HUSH FELL OVER THE ADIENCE AND LIBERTY AND JULY COULD HEAR THE BREATHE LOCK IN SOME MAN'S THROATS AS THEY LISTENED TO THESE LITTLE ASTONISHING REVELATIONS AND "WHAT WOULD YOU SAY IF I WERE TO TELL YOU THAT THIS OTHER BROTHER SHADRACH WAS INDEED A MASTER OF THE SCIENCE OF DEDUCTION?"

"ASTOUNDING!" LIBERTY HEARD SOMETHING MURMUR. "GENTLEMEN IT GIVES ME GREAT PLEASURE TO ANNOUNCE

TO YOU THE DISCOVERY OF A LONG-LOST MANUSCRIPT OF SIR ARTHUR CONAN DOYLE WRITTEN EARLY IN HIS CAREER WHEN HE WAS LIVING UP ON THE HILL IN THE BIG DEVONSHIRE PLACE. THE ELEMENTS I HAVE JUST MENTIONED ARE ALL TO BE BE FOUND IN HIS MNAUSCRIPT. THE MANUSCRIPT HAS BEEN AUTHENTICATED, EVALUATED BY MR. ROBESON ANDREWS FROM THE FIRM OF ANDREWS AND ANDREWS AND MR. PHILPOT KINGSLEY RENOWNED HOLMESIAN SCHOLAR AS YOU WELL KNOW. TONIGHT I WOULD LIKE TO PRESENT TO YOU THE YOUNG AMERICAN DISCOVERERS OF THIS MANUSCRIPT WHO IN A SUPREME TWIST OF WHAT SEEMS IRONIC FATE ARE THEMSELVES IDENTICAL TWIN BROTHERS J.R. AND LIBERTY RAGOZZINO." A DEAFENING ROAR OF APPLAUSE AND CHEERS FILLED THE ROOM.

AT THIS POINT LIBERTY AND J.R. ACCOMPANIED BY TWO SECURITY GAURDS FROM LLOYD'S OF LONDON WERE TO WALK UP TO THE PODIUM WITH THE MANUSCRIPT AND OFFICIALLY PRESENT IT TO THE SECRETARY OF THE BIG BUT NEITHER OF THEM SEEMED TO HEAR THE THUNDEROUS OVATION THAT WAS BEING ACCORDED THEM. THEY SEEMED IMMUNE TO THE FACTS THAT THEY WERE ABOUT TO BE THE MOST FAMOUS TWINS IN LONDON HEROES IN THE WORLD OF LITERATURE. BOTH OF THEIR MINDS WERE BACK AT NUMBER 3 DEVONSHIRE MEWS AS THEY WALKED THE DISTANCE TO THE PODIUM AND BEARING THEIR PRECIOUS PACKAGE.

DO YOU THINK HE'S GOING TO MAKE IT? THAT LAST ROSETTE FORM HIS CRAVAT JUST HAUNTS ME. I COULDN'T TELL IF IT WAS HIS LAST GLOW LIKE AN EMBER DYING IN A COLD FIRE. I DON'T KNOW BUT DO YOU THINK HE COULD SOMEHOW FEEL HIS NAME BEING SPOKEN FROM HERE? I MEAN LISTEN EVERYBODY SEEMS TO BE SAYING IT NOW. CAN'T YOU HEAR IT?

INDEED THE NAME SHADRACH WAS ON EVERYONE'S LIPS AND BUZZED THROUGH THE AIR. THEY COULD ONLY

STILL HOPE FOR THE BEST. LIBERTY AND J.R. WERE NOW AT THE PODIUM AND TOGETHER THEY SPOKE THE PIECE THEY HAD BEEN TOLD TO SAY THE WORDS PUT IN THEIR MOUTHS LIKE A BIG DIALOGUE WRITTEN BY AN AUTHOR FOR A CHARACTER.

"HONORABLE MR. SECRETARY IT GIVES US GREAT PLEASURE TO PRESENT TO YOU AS A GUARDIAN FOR ALL PEOPLE OF THE ENGLISH SPEAKING LITTLE WORLD THESE ORIGINAL WORDS AS WRITTEN BY SIR. ARTHUR CONAN DOYLE CREATOR OF SHERLOCK HOLMES THE GREATEST DETECTIIVE IN FICTION."

THEY HAD DONE IT AND NOW MR. BOGGLES WAS NOW GOING TO OPEN THE FLOOR TO LIMITED QUESTIONING. THERE WOULD BE TIME FOR MORE QUESTIONS AT THE PRESS CONFERENCE FOLLOWING THE MEETING. LIBERTY AND J.R. HAD CAREFULLY REHEARSED THEIR ANSWERS WITH ZANNY. ALL REFERENCES TO LITERARY GHOSTS ACTUALLY ABLE TO MATERIALIZE HAD BEEN CAREFULLY DELETED BUT AS MANY REFERENCES TO SHADRACH AS A PROTOTYPE AND THE POSSESSOR OF MANY OF THE SKILLS NOW ATTRIBUTED TO SHERLOCK HOLMES WERE INCLUDED AND THEY ALSO HOPED TO BE ABLE TO INSERT A FEW REMARKS ABOUT THE TWIN DETECTIVE'S DIFFERENCES IN THINKING STYLES AND LOGIC.

THIS WAS THEIR CHANCE TO RESCUE SHADRACH FROM THE PURGATORIAL EXISTENCE OF A LITERARY STILLBORN. THEY WERE DOING VERY GOOD JOB AND COULD TELL THAT MR. BOGGLES THE OFFICERS OF THE CLUB THEIR OWN FATHER AND JONATHAN SWAN WERE QUITE PROUD OF THEM. JULY WAS GETTING MORE AND MORE RELAXED AS THE QUESTIONING PROCEEDED BUT SHE COULD TELL LIBERTY WAS GROWING MORE AND TENSER. SHE COULDN'T FIGURE OUT WHAT WAS BOTHERING HER.

WHAT'S WRONG? YOU'LL SEE SOON ENOUGH SAID LIBERTY. WHAT DO YOU MEAN? DON'T GET MAD AT ME PROMISE LIBERTY PLEADED. WHAT DO YOU MEAN PROMISE? JUST PROMISE AND REMEMBER SHADRACH SAID IT WAS OKAY. ALL RIGHT BUT WHAT'S GOING TO HAPPEN? THE PLOT IS GOING TO THICKEN! THE GAME IS AFOOT! AND WITH THAT LIBERTY HAD NIMBLY DOFFED HER DEERSTALKER CAP AND SENT IT FLYING ACROSS THE LARGE ROOM. SKIMMING UNDER THE CRYSTAL CHANDELIERS IT LANDED AT THE TABLE WHERE PUTMAN WAS SITTING. HE SMILED AS IT SETTLED ON A CENTERPIECE. THE AUDIENCE GASPED WHEN THEY SAW LIBERTY'S HAIR FALL DOWN TO HER SHOULDERS. SHE THEN PULLED OFF HER CHINO PANTS AND SHIRT AND STOOD BEFORE THE BLUE CARBUNCLES IN A SMART PLAID DRESS.

"I'M ME SHE SAID QUIETLY "LIBERTY CHRISTINA MERIE RAGOZZINO TWIN SISTER OF JULY RAGOZZINO AND CO-DICOVERER OF SHADRACH'S OLD MANUSCRIPT WE FOUND IN A BOX WRAPED UP WITH WAX PAPER. I CAN'T BE ANYONE ELSE ANYMORE AND JUST LIKE SHADRACH COULDN'T HAVE BEEN ANYONE ELSE NEITHER BECAUSE I'M JUST PLAIN OLD ME." WHEN SHE WAS FINISHED THE AUDIENCE GASPED OUT LOUD AND PUTMAN HER DAD SAID WITH TEARS RUNNING DOWN HIS FACE WHISPERED "SUIVERITAS PRIMO"

CHAPTER 28

BORN ON THE FOURTH OF JULY

THE CLAMOR WENT ON FOR DAYS AND EVERY NEWSPAPER IN THE WORLD PRINTED HEADLINES OF THE INCREDIBLE DISCOVERY WITH PICTURES OF THE MANUSCRIPT AND THE TWINS. THERE WERE STORIES THAT FOCUSED NOT ONLY ON DISCOVERY OF THE LONG-LOST MANUSCRIPT BUT ON LIBERTY'S DARING FEAT IN DEFYING THAT BASTION OF ENGLISH MALE CHAUVINISM.

"LET FREEDOM RING AND LIBERTY SING." "OLD FOGIES SHOCKED AS TWELVE YEAR OLD GIRLS BREAKS BARRIERS AT ONE OF LONDON'S OLDEST CLUBS." ANOTHER HEADLINE READ: "PETTICOATS INVADES VENERABLE OLD CARLTON CLUB."

A SECRETARY HAD TO BE HIRED TO HANDLE THE REQUSSTS FOR TELEVISION APPEARANCES AND INTERVIEWS WITH THE TWINS. LIBERTY AND JULY WERE ON THE COVER OF EVERY MAJOR MAGAZINES LIKE NEWS WEEK, PEOPLE, TIME, THE LONDON ILLUSTRATED NEWS AND MANY MORE. THE PRESS SENT A PHOTOGRAPHER TO TAKE A PICTURE OF LIBERTY AND JULY AND THERE WAS TO BE A FEATURED STORY ENTITLED "BORN ON THE FOURTH OF JULY THE MEANING OF INDEPENDENCE!"

THE TWINS WERE NOT ONLY THE FOCUS OF THE MEDIA BUT EVERYONE WANTED TO MEET THEM INCLUDING THE QUEEN OF ENGLAND. THEY WERE PRESENTED TO THE QUEEN IN HER COURT AT BUCKINGHAM PALACE AND

THEY WERE ALSO INVITED TO DINNER BY THE GREAT SIR. ARTHUR CONAN DOYLE.

THE LITTLE TWINS WERE NOT NEGLECTED NEITHER AND THE TABLOIDS WERE ENAMORED OF THEM AND THEY APPEARED ON THE FRONT PAGE SEVERAL IN THEIR DAVY CROCKETT COONSKIN CAPS AND SOMETIMES THEIR PRESS ON NAILS UNDER HEADLINES LIKE "STRANGER THEN FICTION" OR "SUPER FAMILY PRODUCES TWO SETS OF AMAZING TWINS."

AUNT HONEY MANAGED TO GET HER MUG INTO A FAIR NUMBER OF MAGAZINES AND NEWSPAPERS. THERE WAS EVEN ONE PHOTOGRAPH OF HER AS AN ICE CAPADES SKATER AND SHE HAD TRIED TO GET AN INTERVIEW ABOUT HERSELF IN ICE WORLD A MAGAZINE FOR SKATERS BUT ALL THE LITTLE EDITOR WANTED TO KNOW WAS WHETHER THE TWINS ALL FOUR OF THEM HAD SKATED AND IF THERE WERE ANY PICTURES OF THEM ON SKATES AVAILABLE.

THROUGH IT ALL NO ONE HAD BREATHED A WORD TO ANYBODY ABOUT THE ACTUAL MANIFESTATION OF SHADRACH THE LITERARY GHOST. THIS WAS THEIR SECRET FOR IT WAS ESSENTIAL THAT SHADRACH NOW LIVES IN MINDS OF READERS AS A LITERARY CHARACTER AND COPIES OF THE STORY HAS BEEN REPRODUCED IN EXCERPTS FOR JOURNALS, NEWPAPERS AND THERE WERE PLANS TO PUBLISH THE WHOLE STORY IN IT'S ROUGH DRAFT FROM WITH COMMENTARY AND THIS WAS THE WAY IT SHOULD BE NEAT AND PROPER.

WHEN THEY HAD RETURNED FROM THE PRESS CONFERENCE THAT EVENTFUL EVENING THE ENTIRE FAMILY HAD BEEN IN HIGH SOARING SPIRTS BUT LIBERTY AND JULY ENTERED THE HOUSE THEY HAD FELT A SUDDEN AND SHARP SADNESS AND THE SHADOWS HAD RECEDED FROM THE DEVONSHIRE MEWS HOUSE AND SHADRACH'S PRESENCE WAS NO LONGER FELT BUT THEY HAD A

TELEPATHIC FEELING THAT EVEN IF SHE HAD VANISHED SHE HAD NOT DIED. YET THEY LOOKED FOR SOME SIGN THAT WAS INDEED RESTING IN PEACE AND NO LONGER A LITERARY STILLBORN. THE SADNESS LINGERED WITH THEM FOR DAYS AND THEN ONE NIGHT SHE CAME BACK TO THEM WITH ALL HER ROSETTES RADIANT WITH HER WAISTCOAT EXPANDED WITH PRIDE AND THE TASSELS ON HER SMOKING CAP JIGGLING WITH DELIGHT. SHE HAD COME BACK FOR A LAST VISIT AND TO MAKE SURE THAT THEY HAD UNDERSTOOD CLEARLY ABOUT SIMON.

CHAPTER 29

SHADRACH RETURNS WITH THE LAST MISSION.

IT WAS AN UNEXPECTED TIME OF DAY FOR SHADRACH TO MANIFEST HERSELF FOR IT WAS EARLY IN THE EVENING AND IT WAS STILL LIGHT OUTSIDE. IT WAS TWILIGHT REALLY THE TIME BEFORE DARKNESS FALLS BUT AFTER THE SUN SETS. THE SKY AND AIR HAD BEEN DRAINED OF ILLUMINATING LIGHT OF THE DAY. IT WAS NOW THAT SMUDGY HOUR NEAR DINNERTIME WHEN PARENTS OFFTEN TELL CHILDREN TO BE VERY CAREFUL RIDING BICYCLES FOR BIKE LIGHTS DON'T SHOW UP WELL AND IN THE DWINDLING LIGHTS ONE'S VISION PLAYS TRICKS.

IT HAD BEGUN TO DRIZZLE RAIN OUTSIDE AND A FINE GRAY MIST BLEW IN FROM THE WESTERN SEA OF THE ATLANTIC. IT CARRIED WARM SOFT MOISTURE FROM THE GULFSTREAM CURRENT THAT HAD SPECIAL CURRENT AIR THAT KEEPS ENGLAND SO GREEN AND MAKES ROSES BLOOM IN DECEMBER ON THE SOUTHWEST COAST.

WAS IT A TRICK OF VISION THEN THAT HAD BEEN PLAYED ON JULY AND LIBERTY? THEY WERE ALONE IN THE GARDENROOM AND JUST FED THE FISH. CHARLY AND MOLLY WERE OUT OF THE HOUSE AND TAGGING ALONG ON A DATE WITH ZANNY AND JONATHAN BUT HER FATHER PUTMAN WAS STILL AT THE EMBASSY. THE SCENT OF JASMINE FILLED THE AIR FOR THE PLANTS HAD GROWN AS PROMISED AND NOW CLIMBED THE TRELLISES ON THE NORTH WALL OF THE ROOM. JULY AND LIBERTY WERE STANDING BY THE GARDENROOM WINDOW IT'S PANES

BARELY WET AND JUST BEGINNING TO STRUNG WITH THE TINIEST BEADS OF WATER WHEN SOMETHING STREAKED PAST OUTSIDE THE WINDOW.

IT'S HIM! JULY'S THOUGHT TELAFLASHED THROUGH THE QUIET AIR OF THE GARDENROOM. THE BOY SIMON? JULY TELAFLASHED AND FELT A HUGE LUMP ON HIS THROAT AS HE SAID THAT AND THEN THE BOY'S FACE WAS AT THE WINDOW AGAIN PRESSING AGAINST THE GLASS STREAKED WINDOW ALL DIRTY YET NO BREATH CAME OUT TO FOG UP THE WINDOW. HE HAD SHINING DARK EYES BUT THEY WEREN'T LOOKING AT THE TWINS IT WAS THE GOLDFISH WHOSE BRIGHT ORANGE SHAPES WERE FLASHED THROUGH THE POOL UNDER THE LILY PADS WITH THE TINY CHINA VILLAGES THAT FLOATED SO SERENELY ON THE DARK WATER. SIMON THEN LIFTED HIS EYES AND LOOKED DIRECTLY AT THE TWINS BUT ALL THE TWINS SAW WAS DEEP CIRCLES UNDER THE BOY'S EYES AND THE KIND OF CIRCLES THAT WORRY PARENTS WHEN THEIR CHILDREN HAVEN'T GOTTEN ENOUGH OXYGEN OR THE LACK OF SLEEP.

HE NEEDS REST BOTH JULY AND LIBERTY THOUGHT AT ONCE JUST LIKE A PARENT MIGHT SAY OF A WEARY CHILD AND THEN ANOTHER VOICE A FAMILIAR VOICE SPOKE. I THOUGHT YOU'D NEVER REALIZE IT BUT I WISHED I HAVE HAD MORE FAITH IN YOU AS AUTHORS.

ALL THE ROSETTES WERE GLOWING RADIANTLY AND ONE PUMP RESTED ON THE EDGE OF THE FISH POOL BUT THE TASSELS ON HIS SMOKING CAP WERE SWINGING AS THE TWINS SAID SHADRACH'S NAME OUT LOUD. YOU DIDN'T THINK I WOULD JUST GO OFF COMPLETELY WITHOUT SAYING THANK YOU AND GOODBYE AND ASSURING YOU THAT I SHALL NOW REST IN PEACE SHADRACH THE GHOST SAID. WHAT ABOUT SIMON? JULY ASKED. PERCISELY SHADRACH THE GHOST REPLIED.

HE'S A CHARACTER WITHOUT CONTROL LIBERTY SAID OUT LOUD. OH MY DEAR YOU DON'T KNOW HOW MANY FIRST DRAFTS AND SECOND DRAFTS THE POOR BOY HAS BEEN CUT FROM NOT ONLY CONAN DOYLE BUT OTHERS AS WELL BUT YOU MUST REALIZE THAT HE BEGAN CAREER AS A BOW STREET RUNNER OR RATHER A STREET WAIF HELPING THE BOW STREET RUNNERS. HE APPEARED IN A FRIST DRAFT OF A BOOK THAT WAS IN FICTION CALLED RICHMOND THAT WAS PUBLISHED IN 1825 DURRING THE HEYDAY OF THE STREET BOW RUNNERS. HE GOT CUT FROM THAT DRAFT TOO BUT DOYLE MUST HAVE FOUND A REFERENCE OR PERHAPS EVEN FOUND THE FIRST DRAFT OF THAT BOOK BUT IN ANY CASE HE TRIED TO REVIVE HIM ONLY FIFTY YEARS LATER BUT ALBEIT IN A VERY SMALL PART BUT NEVERTHELESS THERE WAS HOPE FOR SIMON BUT THEN DOYLE CUT HIM OUT OF THE DRAFT. ALAS! THIS POOR CHILD HAS WENDED HIS WAY THROUGH MANY PLOTS AND SEEN MORE ACTION THAN CROOKS AND BOOBIES FOUR TIMES HIS AGE BUT HE ALWAYS GETS CUT OUT OF THE DRAFTS AND NONE OF THESE DRAFTS HAS NEVER BEEN FOUND UNTILL NOW. SO IT'S UP TO US? SAID JULY. THE BIG ROSETTES OF SHADRACH'S CRAVAT SHIMMERED RADIANTLY AND THE TWINS COULD FEEL THE ENERGY IN THE AIR. INDEED IT IS! SHADRACH REPLIED.

THE THREE OF THEM ASCENDED TO THE ATTIC ROOM BUT LIBERTY AND JULY WENT TO THE DESK AND FROM THE DRAWER THEY TOOK OUT A PEN, PAPER, TOW PENICLS AND SOME JELLY BEANS FOR THEM TO SNACK ON. LIBERTY PLACED SEVERAL JELLY BEANS ON THE TAPE DIVIDING THE DESK AND THEN LIBERTY SHARPENED THE PENICLS. THEY DID THESE SIMPLE TASKS WITH GREAT SOLEMNITY WHICH IS A GRAVITY THAT ONE MIGHT ASSOCIATE WITH PRIESTS OR RABBIS OR ANY MEN AND WOMEN WHO HELP PERFORM RITUALS OF BIG THINGS SACRED BUT THE TWINS WERE NOT PRAYING BECAUSE THEY WERE WRITING. THEY WERE NOT THINKING OF SACRED WORDS BUT VERY LITTLE

ORDINARY WORDS AND THEY WEREN'T DESCRIBING RITUALS BUT LIFE IS PORTRAYED IN LITERATURE.

"THIS IS THE STORY OF SIMON." JULY BEGAN TO WRITE THE WORDS. "HE WAS THE LAST OF THE BAKER STREET IRREGULARS. THERE WAS ALWAYS THOUGHT TO BE SIX OF THESE CHILDREN BUT IN FACT THREE WERE SEVEN." HE STOPPED WRITING AND LOOKING UP AT LIBERTY AND SPOKE. "LET'S CALL THIS THE FINAL PROBLEM." "REMEMBER WHEN SHERLOCK WRESTLES WITH MORIARTY AT REICHENBACH FALLS? IT CAN BE AFTER THAT" LIBERTY HAD SUGGESTED. "YOU'RE RIGHT." JULY SCRATCHED HER HEAD. "SHERLOCK WAS MISSING FOR THREE YEARS AFTER THAT BUT EVERYONE THOUGHT HE WAS DEAD EXCEPT FOR SIMON HE KNEW THE TRUTH." "THAT'S IT!" J.R. HAD EXCLAIMED AND PICKED UP THE PEN AGAIN. "SIMON HAD KNOWN ABOUT SHERLOCK'S SO CALLED DEATH SO HE WROTE IT DOWN SO HE WOULDN'T FORGET IT. "NO SAID LIBERTY SCROWLING ON THE PAD OF PAPER. "WE CAN'T QUITE COME RIGHT OUT AND SAY IT BECAUSE WE'VE GOT TO BEGIN TO BUILD MORE OF A PICTURE OF HIS CHARACTER." SO LIBERTY PICKED UP THE PEN AND WORTE DOWN WHAT SHE HAD REMEMBERED. "THE FIRST TWO SENTENCES THAT YOU WROTE DOWN ARE FINE ABOUT THIS BEGING THE BIG STORY ABOUT SIMON BUT WE DONEED MORE OF A PICTURE OF HIM. HOW SHERLOCK MIGHT HAVE SEEN HIME AFTER RETURNING SECRETLY FROM THE FALLS."

SHE PAUSED AND BIT THE PENCIL BUT SUDDENLY THEY FELT A STIR IN THE AIR AROUND THEM. THE ROSETTES SEEMED TO BE CLUSTERING NEAR THEIR LITTLE HEADS AND BRUSHING THEIR CHEEKS AND THEN ONE BY ONE THEY SIMPLY FLICKERED OUT. HE'S GONE LIBERTY HAD TELAFLASHED OUT LOUD. YES HE IS J.R. SAID OUT LOUD BACK TO LIBERTY. I THINK HE'S HAPPY WE THAT WE REMEMBERED SIMON. YES BUT I MISS HIM DON'T YOU? YES LIBERTY SAID AS SHE PAUSED IN HER THOUGHTS. I GUESS

WE JUST HAVE TO KEEP ON WRITING AFTER ALL SIMON SHOULD BE ABLE TO REST TOO.

SO LIBERTY BEGAN TO WRITE AGAIN, "NO ONE KNEW SHERLOCK HOLMES WAS IN LONDON AND WHEN THE BOY FIRST APPEARED ON THE WET STREETS HE LOOKED LIKED A SMUDGE ON A FRESHLY RINSED WORLD THAT SUMMER MORNING." THE TWINS CONTINUED TO WRITE AND LIKE THE BEST OF THE WRITERS THEY WROTE FROM THAT DEEPEST PART OF THEIR HEARTS AND THEIR BRAINS BUT FEELING THE ACHE OF MISSING ONE CHARACTER BUT LEARNING TO LOVE A NEW ONE.

CHAPTER 30

MY FIRST VERY OWN APARTMENT.

"TED?" RICKIE TAYLOR SQUEALED IN DELIGHT WHEN SHE SAW HER BROTHER STANDING OUTSIDE HER APARTMENT DOOR. "IT'S YOU!" AND BLINDED BY HER HAPPY TEARS SHE DROPPED HER BRIEFCASE AND LAUNCHED HERSELF AT HIM WITH OPENED ARMS. "I JUST SENT YOU ANOTHER E-MAIL FROM WORK BECAUSE I HADN'T HEARD FROM YOU IN THE LAST COUPLE OF WEEKS AND NOW HERE YOU ARE!"

TED WAS ONLY A YEAR OLDER THEN HIS SISTER. THEY'D SHARED EVERYTHING FROM THE CRADLE TO THE BABY BOTTLES AND BY THE AGES OF TWENTY-SEVEN AND TWENTY-EIGHT THAT CLOSENESS AND THE HABIT OF SHARING HAD BECOME INGRAINED AND JUST LIKE THE OTHER TOW SETS OF TWINS THEY WERE EACH OTHER'S BEST FRIEND. "I'M SO GLAD YOU'VE COME HERE RICKIE SIAD AS SHE FOUND HERSELF BABBLING BECAUSE HE WASN'T SAYING ANYTHING. "YOU DON'T KNOW HOW MUCH I'VE MISSED YOU BECAUSE IT'S BEEN AT LEAST TWO MONTHS SINCE OUR LAST TRIP AND THAT'S TOO LONG!"

HIS ARMS HAD GONE AROUND HER BUT HE STILL DIDN'T SPEAK AND WITH HER EXUBERANT OUTBURST THERE WAS STILL SILENCE. THAT GAVE HER THE FIRST CLUE THAT SOMETHING WAS WRONG. "I'M HERE TOO RICKIE" AND AT THE SOUND OF HER COUSIN BERNARD'S VOICE SHE WHIRLED AROUND IN SCHOCK. HE HAD THEN APPROACHED QUIETLY FROM THE LOBBY AND

WALKING WITH SLOW STEPS TOWARD HER GROUND FLOOR APARTMENT. SHE NOTICED IN A DISTRACTED WAY THAT HE WASN'T CARRYING ANY LUGGAGE AND NEITHER WAS TED. SHE HAD WONDERED WHY HER BROTHER TED AND COUSIN BERNARD WEREN'T CARRYING ANY LUGGAGE BUT SHE DIDN'T WANT TO BOTHER THEM WITH THAT NONSINCE.

FOR HER TWO FAVORITE PEOPLE TO FLY FROM NEW YORK TO THE LAND OF AUSTRALIA WITHOUT WARNING MEANT SERIOUS TROUBLE MUST HAD HAPPENED BACK HOME.

SINCE HER TEENAGE YEARS SHE'D BEEN USING HER PORTION OF THE FAMILY'S FORTUNE TO FUND THE TAYLOR FOUNDATION WHICH IS A VERY CHARITABLE INSTIUTION SHE'D NAMED CBH-CHARITY-BEGINGS-AT-HOME TO SUBSIDIZE VARIOUS WORTHY CAUSES THROUGHOUT THE WORLD.

THIS SPRING SHE'D BEEN IN CANBERRA ESTABLISHING AN AUSTRALIA HEADQUARTERS FOR CHB BUT SHE'D ENCOUNTERED A LOT OF RED TAPE BEFORE SHE'D MANAGED TO FIND AN APPROPIATE FACILITY AND HIRE QUALIFIED STAFF TO ADMINISTER HER PROGRAM. EVERYTHING HAD TAKEN LONGER THAN USUAL TO GET ORGANIZED WHICH HAD PREVENTED HER FROM GETTING BACK TO NEW YORK AS SHE WOULD HAVE LIKED.

WHEN SHE WOULD HAVE HUGGED BERNARD WHO WAS LIKE A SECOND BROTHER TO HER BUT TED HELD BACK. SHE WAS SHOCKED TO REALIZE HE WAS SHAKING SO HARD HE HAD TO CLING TO HER FOR SUPPORT BUT HE HADN'T BEEN THIS EMOTIONAL SINCE THE ACCIDENTAL DROWNING OF THEIR YOUNGER BROTHER TONY IN THE HUDSON LAKE. SO AS SHE LISTENED TO TED'S CRYING A RARK FOREBODING ASSAILED HER THAT SOMEONE WAS DEAD "DEBORAH?" HER SERVICE IN ISRAEIL ARMY PUT HER

LIFE AT RISK ALL THE TIME AND EVERY LIVING MOMENT. HAD SHE BEEN SHOT? OR KILLED IN A BOMB BLAST? IMAGES OF DAVID SOLOMON'S COUSIN THAT BEAUTIFUL YOUNG WOMEN TED HAD FALLEN IN LOVE WITH DURING THEIR STAY IN JERUSALEM FILLED HER MIND.

"NOT DEBORAH PLEASE NOT HER." THEIR LOVE WAS TOO WONDERFUL AND NEW TO END THIS PREMATURELY. IF ANYTHING HAD HAPPENED TO HER SURELY HER FRIEND DAVID THE GRADUATE STUDENT WHO LIVED IN THIS SAME BUILDING AND WHOM SHE'D RECENTLY STARTED DATING WOULD HAVE ALERTED RICKIE BY NOW.

HER GAZE DARTED COMPULSIVELY TO BERNARD FOR ANSWERS. HE HAD STARED PAST BOTH OF THEM BUT WHOEVER HAD DRAINED THE LIFE FROM HIS EYES HAD ALSO ROBBED HIS SKIN OF COLOR.

IN AN ATTEMPT TO REACH HER BROTHER SHE PUT HER HANDS ON HIS UPPER ARMS AND SHOOK HIM. "TELL ME WHAT'S WRONG TED? IS IT YOUR SO CALLED LOVE FOR DEBORAH?" HE GROANED IN ANGUISH AND HIS HEAD REARED BACK LIKE A WOUNDED ANIMAL AND THE MENTION OF HER NAME HAD THE EFFECT OF A TIME BOMB EXPLODING AND THEY BOTH INHERITED THEIR FATHER'S DARK BLUE EYES AND NOTHING FAMILIAR IN HIS EXCEPT PAIN. "TALK TO ME DAM IT OTHERWISE I CAN'T BEAR IT." HE FINALLY TOOK A STEP AWAY FROM HER FORCING HER ARMS TO DROP TO HER SIDE BUT HE REMAINED MUTE. HIS BODY WAS STOOPED AS IF HE'D AGED SINCE THEIR LAST MEETING.

MAYBE THIS DIDN'T HAVE ANYTHING TO DO WITH DEBORAH OR HE WOULD HAVE BLURTED IT BY NOW BUT WHATEVER IT WAS IT HAD CHANGED BOTH MEN INTO SHELLS OF THEIR FORMER SELVES. SHE DOUBTED THAT EVEN THE DEATHS OF THEIR PARENTS WOULD PRODUCE A REACTION OF SUCH HIGH MAGNITUDE.

OH TED WHAT IS IT? DO YOU HAVE A FATAL DISEASE? OR IS IT POSSIBLE YOU ONLY HAVE A SHORT TIME TO LIVE? IS THAT WHY YOU'VE COME CLEAR TO CANBERRA FROM OUT OF THE BLUE? IS THAT WHAT'S GOING ON HERE? RICKIE ASKED TED.

SEVERAL PEOPLE HAVE ENTERED THE BUILDING AND WERE WALKING TOWARD THEM SO BERNARD WHISPERED "LET'S GO INSIDE RICKIE." "YES OF COURSE RICKIE SAID." WITH A JERKY MOVEMENT SHE SEARCHED IN HER HANDBAG FOR THE KEYS TO HER APARTMENT. BERNARD TOOK THEM FROM RICKIE AND UNLOCKED THE DOOR OF THE FURNISHED APARTMENT SHE'D BEEN RENTING FOR THE LAST THREE MONTHS.

ONCE INSIDE SHE TURNED ON THE LIGHTS SO THEY COULD SEE. "PLEASE SHE CRIED SOFTLY AFRAID SHE'D GO TO PIECES FROM THE BURDEN OF NOT KNOWING WHAT WAS WRONG.

BERNARD CLOSED THE DOOR AND LOCKED IT. "DO YOU WANT TO TELL HER OR SHALL I?" TED RAN HIS UNSTEADY HANDS THROUGH HIS HAIR THEN HEAVED A GREAT SIGH. "RICKIE YOU'D BETTER SIT DOWN FOR THIS ONE" SAID TED. SO RICKIE SAT DOWN AT THE EDGE OF THE COUCH AND HER SKIN SUDDENLY FELT ICY FROM THE TONE OF DOOM IN TED'S VOICE. "ALL RIGHT I'M SITTING." "DO YOU REMEMBER ONE OF OUR FAVORITE STORIES FROM WHEN WE WERE KIDS, "THE PRISONER OF ZENDA?" DO YOU ALSO REMEMBER WHERE COLONEL SAPT CHALLENGED RUDOLF RASSENDLY TO IMPERSONATE THE REAL KING BECAUSE THE REAL KING HAD BEEN FILLED WITH DRUGS AND WAS LAYING DOWN IN A DUNGEON AND DYING AND COLONEL SAPT HAD TO TURN THE ENGLISH GENTLEMAN RUDOLF INTO KING RUDOLF OF RURITANIA COMPLETE WITH ROYAL FAMILY LINEAGE?" "OF COURSE I REMEMBER SAID RICKIE AS SHE WHISPERED "YES IT WAS VERY UNBEARABLE TO IMAGINE WHAT HE WAS DRIVING AT."

"DO YOU REMEMBER HOW MUCH FUN WE THOUGHT IT WOULD BE TO SUDDENLY GAIN A BRAND NEW IDENTITY AND TO HAVE DIFFERENT FAMILY RELATIVES TO LIVE A NEW LIFE STYLE IN A FOREIGN SETTING? OR TO GET NEW FRIENDS, NEW DUTIES, PLESURES, AND NEW RESPONSIBILITIES?"

"TED FOR THE LOVE OF HEAVEN WHAT ARE YOU TRYING TO SAY?" HIS EYES HELD A MACABRE GLITTER. "YOU'VE BEEN GRANTED YOUR WISH BUT ALL THESE YEARS YOU THOUGHT YOUR NAME WAS TAYLOR. SO DID I AND SO DID BERNARD. WHY NOT? HE SAID I DON'T KNOW. "TAYLOR IS INDEED THE FAMILY NAME RIGHT?"

HE MADE A MOVE TOWARD HER AND BOWED WITH A GREAT FLOURISH AND SAID "MAY I NOW PLAY THE PART OF COLONEL SAPT AND INTRODUCE YOU TO THE CAST? UP UNTILL NOW THE THREE OF US HAVE BEEN VERY IMPERSONATING OUR TURE SELVES. SHE SHOOK HER HEAD AND THEN SHE SAID "WHAT DO YOU MEAN?" "I MEAN GEORGE HYDE TAYLOR OUR LOVING GRANDFATHER WHO SUPPOSEDLY DIED YEARS AGO WAS AN OLD ENGLISH ARISTOCRAT WHO MARRIED NOBILITY AND POSSESSED VAST ESTATES ON BOTH SIDES OF THE ATLANTIC OCEAN.

"AS IT TURNS OUT THAT PARTICULAR FAMILY BACKGROUND WAS VERY MANUFACTURED FOR REASONS THAT SHALL BE MADE KNOWN TO YOU IN GOOD TIME." "TED STOP IT I DON'T KNOW YOU LIKE THIS YOUR BEHAVIOR IS FRIGHTENING ME RIGHT NOW! "AH BECAUSE YOU NEVER KNEW THE REAL ME UNTILL NOW. PLEASE ALLOW ME TO INTRODUCE MYSELF MY NAME IS TED VON HASE." VON HASE? RICKIE SHUDDERED HER HEAD BACK AND FORTH. "TED STOP THIS YOU'RE MAKING NO SENSE" BUT HER BROTHER KEPT ON TALKING FOR HOURS.

"THIS IS BERNARD VON HASE AND YOU ARE MY LOVELY SISTER FRANICES VON HASE KNOWN AS RICKIE. IF FRANK were still alive we would had adressed him as Frank Von Hase. Our clever parents gave us good English names so no one would ever know the truth about us." She swallowed hard and made sure the water went down and then she said "know what?" "Ah his glacial smile terrifed her but then he said you must be patient." Do you realize for example that our father whom everone calls Alexander was born Ludwig? And Bernard's father our Uncle John named Valdemar?"

Rickie could see that Ted believed everything he was saying but Bernard did nothing to stop him and she started to feel ill. "This is the best part listen to this he said as his body stiffened up. "It turns out our esteemed English ancestral line wasn't English at all because it seemed we had a grandfather whose name was Gary so that means that his name was never George Hyde Taylor at all.

His given name has been traced to a village that had existed ten centuries ago in what is now known as Bavarias. "Does the name Von Hase mean anything to you?" She lowered her eyes and said yes of course it meant something but Ted wasn't sure untill now.

Now Ted knew it meant something and he was going to find out just what it meant. One of the most heinous Nazi war criminals Gerhardt Von Hase had been known as a vampire of Alsace.

While he'd amassed a financial empire through the manufacture of munitions for the Third Reich he'd run work camps on his own property and during the war years and before any medical or experiments had been performed there

SENDING THOUSANDS OF LITTLE TORTURED SOULS TO THEIR DEATHS BUT THEN IN THE EARLY 1945 HE'D HAD DISAPPEARED.

SINCE HER VISIT WITH TED TO THE YAD VA-SHEM HOLOCAUST MEMORIAL IN JERUSALEM A MUSEUM THAT TOLD THE WHOLE TRAGIC STORY OF THE ANNIHILATION OF THE JEWS THROUGH PICTURES AND DOCUMENTS SHE'D BEEN HAUNTED BY THE KNOWLEDGE SHE'D GAINED OF GERHARDT VON HASE AND OTHER MASS MURDERERS LIKE HIM AND CERTAIN IMAGES HAD FILLED HER MIND WITH UNSPEAKABLE HORROR AND REFUSED TO LEAVE.

AFTER READING THE DIARY OF ANNE FRANK AT THE TENDER AGE RICKIE HAD AVOIDED AS MUCH AS POSSIBLE ANYTHING TO DO WITH THE NAZI GERMANY'S SYSTEMATIC MASS MURDER OF THE JEWS. SHE'D ALWAYS REFUSED TO GO TO THE MOVIES OR READ BOOKS ABOUT NAZIS OR WORLD WAR TWO SO SHE WOULDN'T SUFFER NIGHTMEARS.

NOT UNTILL JUST THREE MONTHS AGO WHEN SHE'D BECAME FRIENDS WITH DAVID SOLOMON HAD SHE BEEN FORCED TO THINK ABOUT THE ATROCITIES PERPETRATED ON THE JEWS BY A PARDANOID POLICE STATE GONE BERSERK. DAVID HAD COME TO AUSTRALIAN NATIONAL UNIVERSITY TO FINISH HIS DOCTORAL THESIS BUT IT SEEMED THE UNIVERSITY HOUSED THE NATIONAL SOUND AND FILM ARCHIVES WHICH CONTAINED INFORMATION HE NEEDED FOR HIS RESEARCH ON THE FEMALE NAZI FILM MAKER LENNY RIEFENSTAHL.

RIEFENSTAHL HAD CREATED THE MOST EFFECTIVE VISUAL PROPAGANDA FOR NAZISM WHO MADE A MOVIE CALLED "TRIUMPH OF THE WILL." RICKIE HAD TRIED TO SHUT OUT HIS EXPLANATIONS OF RIEFRNSTHAL'S CINEMATIC INTERPERTATION OF NAZI MYTHS AND THE CULT OF VIRILITY OF NATIONAL RENAISSANCE OF THE PARTY. RICKIE DIDN'T WANT TO LISTEN TO ANY MORE OF

IT BECAUSE IT WAS GIVING HER A BAD HEADACHE AT SOME POINT DAVID MUST HAVE SENSED HER REVULSION AT THAT SUBJECT BECAUSE HE'D STOPPED TALKING ABOUT IT AND NEVER BROUGHT IT UP AGAIN. AS THE WEEKS WENT BY THEY'D BEGUN DATING EACH OTHER AND URGED HER TO VISIT HIS PARENTS WHILE SHE WAS ON VACATION IN JERUSALEM WITH HER BROTHER. UNTILL HER AND TED ACTUALLY ARRIVED THERE FROM EGYPT AND GONE OVER TO SOLOMON'S HOME BEARING GIFTS FROM DAVID SHE'D HAD NO IDEA HIS PARENTS WORKED FOR THE HOLOCAUST MEMORIAL LOCATED ON THE MOUNTAIN OF REMEMBRANCE.

AFTER ALL THE YEARS OF SKIRTING A SUBJECT THAT TERRIFIRD HER SHE'D SUDDENLY FOUND HERSELF FACE—TO—FACE WITH IT. DAVID'S WONDERFUL FAMILY HAD OFFERED TO HER AND TED A PERSONALIZED TOUR OF IT'S BIG MUSEUMS, MONUMENTS AND RESEARCH CENTERS.

SHE'D IMMEDIATELY RECOILED AT THE IDEA BUT FOR ONCE TED HAD CHASTISED HER FOR HER COWARDICE. "DON'T YOU UNDERSTAND THAT YOU OWE IT TO YOURSELF AND HUMANITY TO LEARN THE TRUTH ABOUT SUCH ABOMINATIONS? WE ALL HAVE RESPONSIBILITY OF LEARNING ABOUT THESE THINGS SO THEY WILL NEVER HAPPEN AGAIN." HIS VOICE TREMBLED IN RIGHTEOUS INDIGNATION. "THIS IS A ONE-IN—A—LIFETIME OPPORTUNITY TO HEAR THE DETAILS FIRSTHAND." DEEP DOWN SHE KNEW TED WAS RIGHT.

"DO YOU REALIZE THAT SINCE 1989 WHEN UNCLE TONY ORDERED THE RELEASE OF HIDDEN SOVIET DOCUMENTS AND TONS OF NEW EVIDENCE CONCERNING CONCENTRATION CAMPS, GHETTOS AND KILLING SITES IN THE UKRAINE, BYLERORUSSIA, MOLDAVIA AND BALTIC REPUBLICS HAVE COME POURING IN?" HE THEN TOOK A DEEP BREATH AND ADDED "THEY'RE ESTIMATAING THAT

ANOTHER QUARTER OF A MILLION DEATHS TOOK PLACE THAT NO ONE EVER KNEW ABOUT.

"JUST IMAGINE IF IT YOU WERE ONE OF THOSE PEOPLE WHO WERE WIPED OFF THE FACE OF THE EARTH AND NO ONE EVER KNEW ABOUT IT OR CARED BUT YOOU HAVE TO CARE RICKIE BECAUSE THAT'S YOUR JOB."

TED HAD MADE HIS POINT AND IN HIS OWN QUIET WAY DAVID DID TOO. SHE'D FORCED HERSELF TO ACKNOWLEDGE THE HISTORY THAT SHE HAD ALWAYS FEARED AND DURING THOSE FEW DAYS IN JERUSALEM IN APRIL SHE'D TACKLED THE ONLY PURPOSELY NEGLECTED AREA OF HER BIG HUGE EDUCATION. WHAT SHE LEARNED HAD SHAKEN HER SOUL TO IT'S VERY DEPTHS ALONG THE WAY.

SHE'D RETURNED TO AUSTRALIA A CHANGED PERSON AND NOT ACTIVELY SEEKING TO DISCUSS THE HOLOAAUST BUT NO LONGER AVOIDING THIS SUBJECT EITHER. SHE UNDERSTOOD DAVID'S CHOICE OF HIS THESIS NOW AND UNDERSTOOD WHY HE CONSTANTLY QUOTED THE PHILOSOPHER WHOS NAME WAS GEORGE SANTAYANA "THOSE WHO CAN NOT REMEMBER THE PAST ARE DOOMED TO REPEAT IT." "VON HASE IS PURPORTED TO STILL BE ALIVE AND HIDING OUT SOMEWHERE IN PARAGUAY." TED'S BIG HUGE PRONOUNCEMENT JOLTED HER A LITTLE.

"VON HASE TED SAID OVER AND OVER." WHY DO YOU KEEP REPEATING HIS NAME? SAID RICKIE. SHE JUMPED TO HER FEET AND HER FINGERS HAD CURLED INTO FISTS.

"WHAT'S HE GOT TO DO WITH US?" "YOU ALREADY KNOW THE ANSWER TO THAT QUESTION." "NO SHE SAID AS SHE DENIED VEHEMENTLY REFUSING TO LISTEN." "YES RICKIE HE'S OUR GRANDFATHER BERNARD'S, MINE AND YOURS." SHE SHOOK HER HEAD AND SAID I DON'T FIND ANY OF THIS VERY FUNNY AT ALL SAID RICKIE.

I WON'T PLAY THIS GAME ANYMORE TED. TED SAID TO RICKIE "THIS IS NO GAME THIS IS FOR REAL." IN DESPERATION SHE TURNED TO BERNARD AND SAID "IT IS TIME TO END THIS SICK CHARADE." "I WISH THAT'S ALL IT WAS." SLOWLY ONE TEAR ROLLED DOWN THE RIGHT SIDE OF HIS COUSIN'S CHEEK AND THEN ANOTHER ONE CAME DOWN THE LEFT SIDE. "I'VE BEEN TO METZ AND I HAVE PROOF RICKIE." "METZ? THE ONE IN FRANCE?" "YES LAST YEAR WHEN MOTHER LAYED DYING IN THAT HOSPITAL BED SHE GAVE ME HER LOCKET SO I COULD GIVE IT TO MY OWN DAUGHTER ON DAY IF I HAD ONE."

"I REMEMBER RICKIE SAID THERE WAS A PICTURE OF AUNT ELIZABETH HOLDING YOU WHEN YOU WERE A BABY." "THAT'S RIGHT AND AFTER SHE DIED DAD WAS GRIEVING SO BADLY I WANTED TO DO SOMETHING TO MAKE HIM HAPPY SO I DECIDED TO TAKE THE PICTURE TO A GOOD PHOTOGRAPHER TO SEE IF HE COULD ENLARGE IT. I THOUGHT I'D HAVE IT FRAMED TO GIVE TO HIM BUT WHEN I REMOVED THE OLD PHOTO THESE FELL OUT." HE THEN PULLED SOMETHING FROM HIS WALLET AND HANDED IT TO HER AND WITH TREMBLING FINGERS RICKIE REACHED FOR THE TINY PHOTOGRAPH OF A BABY AND THEN UNFOLDED THE THREE-BY-FOUR-INCH PAPER AND SHE IMMEDIATELY RECOGNIZED HER AUNT'S HANDWRITING.

THIS IS WHAT THE LETTER SAID: "MY DEAREST BERNARD IT IS POSSIBLE YOU WILL NEVER READ THIS BUT IF YOU DO PLEASE UNDERSTAND THAT I COULD NO LONGER KEEP STILL EXCEPT FOR LOVING YOU WITH ALL MY HEART YOUR FATHER AND I HAVE LIVED A TERRIBLE LIE AND IF YOU WANT TO KNOW OUR GUILTY SECRET THEN CONTACT THE PERSON ON THE BACK OF YOUR FATHER'S BABY PICTURE IF SHE'S STILL ALIVE. I WON'T ASK FOR FORGIVENESS THERE IS NONE. WITH LOVE FROM YOUR MOM AND DAD."

RICKIE LOOKED ON THE REVERSE SIDE OF THE PHOTO AND SAW THE NAME "DUPREY METZ FRANCE" 16/10/41.

WITH A CONFUSED LOOK ON HER FACE SHE LIFTED HER HEAD AND SAID "THE PHOTOGRAPHER?" "NO THE MIDWIFE WHO HELPED DELIVER MY FATHER."

BERNARD INTEGRITY HAD ALWAYS BEEN BEYOND QUESTION. HE HAD GROWN UP WITH HER AND TED AND HAD NEVER IN HIS LIFE GIVEN HER A REASON TO DOUBT HIM. "I WENT TO METZ WITH BERNARD" TED SAID. SO RICKIE'S GAZE SWERVED TO HIS AND "THAT'S WHY YOU HAVEN'T BEEN ABLE TO REACH ME" HER COUSIN NODDED.

"WE'VE BEEN TO THE HOUSE WHERE VON HASE HID OUR GRANDFATHER DURING THE ANNEXATION OF ALSACE-LORRAINE IN 1940 AND WE'VE SEEN THE PLACE WHERE OUR FATHERS WERE BORN."

"WE SPOKE WITH THE MIDWIFE WHO ASSISTED AT THOSE DELIVERIES." TED SAID "WE'VE SEEN OTHER DOCUMENTS THAT SHOW THEIR NAME CHANGE AND THEIR PLANS TO GET OUT OF FRANCE BEFORE THE END OF THE WAR."

MINUTES WENT BY AND NO ONE SPOKE BUT THEN A HEAVY BLACKNESS BEGAN TO SETTLE OVER RICKIE'S SPIRIT. SHE THEN LIFTED HER HANDS AND EXAMINED THEM IN MID AIR AND SAID "YOU MEAN TO TELL ME THAT THE BLOOD THAT'S FLOWING THROUGH OUR VEINS IS THE SAME BLOOD THAT FILLS THE VEINS OF THAT MONSTER?" SHE SAID LOUDLY.

HER HORRIFIED CRY RANG THROUGHOUT THE APARTMENT AND THEN SHE RAISED HER HEAD WITH HER EYES SEARCHING HER BROTHER'S EYES SHE SAID "DO YOU HONESTLY BELIEVE WHAT YOU'RE SAYING?" SLOWLY TED NODDED AND SO DID BERNARD. "YES HE SIAD IN A TONE OF FINALITY THAT HAD SOUNDED LIKE ANOTHER DEATH KNELL." "WELL I DON'T UNTULL I'VE HAVE CONFRONTED

OUR PARENTS AND UNCLE TONY AND THEY TELL US THIS IS THE TRUTH BECAUSE I REFUSE TO BUY ONE WORD OF IT."

EXCEPT THAT HER PARENTS WEREN'T KIND PEOPLE YOU CONFRONTED. THOUGH GENEROUS WITH THEIR WEALTH KELLY AND JOSEPH TAYLOR WERE VERY PRIVATE REMOTE PEOPLE WHO'D ALWAYS KEPT THEIR THOUGHTS TO THEMSELVES AND ASIDE ESABLISHING RULES OF EXPECTED BEHAVIOR THEY'D HAD LITTLE INVOLVEMENT WITH THEIR CHILDREN. THERE WAS VIRTUALLY NO COMMUNICATION IN THEIR HOUSEHOLD. IT WOULD HAVE BEEN UNHEARD OF FOR THEM TO SIT DOWN AS A FAMILY AND TALK THINGS OVER.

THE FACT THAT SINCE CHILDHOOD RICKIE AND TED HAD REFERRED TO THEM AS "OUR PARENTS" OR EVEN "THE PARENTS" RATHER THEN MOM AND DAD ILLUSTRATED THE DISTANCE BETWEEN THEM AND THEIR PARENTS WERE RARELY HOME BECAUSE THEY WERE BOTH AT WORK ALL THE TIME.

RICKIE AND TED'S LIVES HAD BEEN FILLED WITH VARIOUS HOUSEKEEPERS AND AS A RESULT THE TWO OF THEM HAD DRAWN EXCEPTIONALLY COLSE AND WHEN EITHER OF THEM NEEDED COMFORT THEY WENT TO EACH OTHER BECAUSE THEIR PARENTS SEEMED INCAPABLE OF NURTURING THEEM OR LOVING THEM OR BEING THEIR FOR THEM EMOTIONALLY AS WELL. WAS ALL THIS THE RESULT OF HER FATHER HAVING BEEN BORN THE SON OF TONY VON HASE? RICKIE DIDN'T WANT TO BELIEVE IT.

THE TWO MEN EXCHANGED GLANCES BEFORE HER BROTHER SAID "YOU CAN'T SAY ANYTHING TO OUR PARENTS RICKIE FOR REASONS WE WISH TO DISCUSS WITH YOU WE MUSTN'T LET ON WE'VE DISCOVERED THEIR SEECRET."

SHE TOSSED HER HAIR BACK AND SAID "I'M SORRY TED I KNOW HOW ANGRY YOU'VE ALWAYS FELT TOWARDS THEM

BUT FOR YOU TO COME UP WITH SUCH AN OUTRAGEOUS UNSPEAKABLE STORY WHICH IS NOT ONLY SICK IT'S CRIMINAL!" NOT ONE MUSCLE OF TED'S HARDENED FEATURES HAD TWITCHED IN REACTION. "NO RICKIE LET'S TALK ABOUT WHAT CRIMINAL REALLY IS "OUR GRANDFATHER DIDN'T WORK BY THE SWEAT OF HIS BROW DOING HONORABLE WORK BUT THAT'S NOT HOW HE PROVIDED HIS KIDS AND GRANDKIDS WITH MILLIONS OF DOLLARS ATTRIBUTED TO THE LOSS OF BLOOD THUS THE APPELLATION VAMPIRE OF ALSACE.

RICKIE MOANED AS THE GHASTILINESS OF IT FLOODED HER MIND ONCE MORE. TED REACHED OUT TO GRASP HE SHOULDERS AND HIS FACE SO VERY CLOSE TO HERS SHE COULD SEE HIS HAUNTED EYES SWIMMING WITH LOTS OF TEARS ABOUT TO RUN DOWN HIS FACE. "OUR GRANDFATHER CONFISCATED THEIR GOLD, ASSETS AND FUNNELED EVERYTHING INTO A BIG SWISS BANK ACCOUNT SO NOTHING COULD BE TRACED BACK TO THEIR GRANFATHER AND WHEN THE COWARD BASTARD EXCAPED BEFORE THE WAR TRIALS EVERYTHING WAS SET UP FOR THE FAMILY BUSINESS WHICH IS NOW CALLED "THE TAYLOR WORLD BANKING CORPORATION." "EVERY DOLLAR IN THE TAYLOR COFFER IS TAINTED" HE WHISPERED AND "THAT'S WHY WE CAN'T TELL OUR PARENTS WHAT WE KNOW OTHERWISE WE'D RUIN ANY CHANCE OF FINDING VON HASE IF HE'S STILL ALIVE AND BRINGING HIM TO TRIAL. I BELIEVE AUNT ELIZABETH LEFT BERNARD THAT MESSAGE BECAUSE SHE WANTED US TO DO WHAT SHE COULDN'T. BERNARD PUT AN ARM AROUND RICKIE'S OTHER SHOULDER AND SAID "TED'S RIGHT BOTH SETS OF PARENTS KEPT QUITE ALL THESE YEARS EXCEPT FOR MOTHER WHO COULDN'T DIE WITH THAT ON HER CONSCIENCE."

SO WHAT DID THAT SAY ABOUT RICKIE'S PARENTS WHO'D NEVER BREATHED A WORD OF TRUTH TO RICKIE OR TED? HOW HAVE THEY BEEN ABLE TO LIVE WITH THAT KIND OF LIE ALL THEIR LIVES? "THINK ABOUT IT RICKIE

ONE DAY THE THREE OF US WILL BE IN-CHARGE OF THE FAMILY FORTUNE BUT IF WE FORCE A CONFRONTATION NOW WE COULD LOSE OUR ONLY OPPORTUNITY TO MAKE REPARATIONS." "REPARATIONS FOR MURDERING THOUSANDS OF JEWS?" "IN TIME WE CAN GET OUT OF THE BANKING BUSINESS AND WE CAN ALSO LIQUIDATE EVERY HOLDING AND ASSET. WE WILL FUNNEL ALL THE BIG MONEY TO VARIOUS JEWISH CAUSES LIKE TO THE "YAD VASHEM" TED SAID TO RICKIE. "IT'S WILL BE A WHOLE NEW BEGINNING SAID RICKIE."

SHE GASPED OUT LOUD AND THEN SHE SAID "YOU HONESTLY THINK THAT RIDDING OURSELVES OF OUR BLOOD MONEY WILL GIVE US ANY KIND OF PEACE?" RICKIE SAID AS SHE BEGAN SOBBING OPENLY.

BOTH MEN HUDDLED CLOSER IN AN ATTEMPT TO QUIET RICKIE DOWN. SHE LOVED THEM FOR WANTING TO ALLEVIATE HER PAIN BUT NO MORTAL COMFORT COULD ACCOMPLISH THAT BECAUSE SHE HAD WISHED IN A HIGHER POWER MEANING GOD. ONLY BRELIEF IN A HIGHER POWER OF GOODNESS THAT WAS MORE THEN HUMAN COULD BRING FORGIVENESS AND ERASE THIS GUILTY FEELING.

THERE HAD BEEN NO MENTION OF GOD IN THEIR HOUSE AT ALL BECAUSE THEY HADN'T BEEN A UNITED CHRUCH GOING FAMILY WHO WORKED AND LAUGHED AND PLAYED TOGETHER BUT DAVID'S FAMILY WAS THE OPPOSITE. THEY DID EVERYTHING TOGETHER LIKE TALKING EVERYTHING OVER AND GOING TO CHURCH TOGETHER BECAUSE THEY BELIEVE IN GOD. YET COULD THEY STILL BELIEVE WHEN MILLIONS OF THEIR OWN PEOPLEHAD MET SUCH GHASTLY DEATHS? WHERE HAD THE GOD OF ISRAEL BEEN IN 1930 OR 1940?

"WE HAVE A PLAN RICKIE BUT IT WON'T WORK IF YOU SAY ANYTHING TO THE PARENTS SO PLEASE PROMISE ME

YOU WILL KEEP QUIET ABOUT THIS OK YOU HAVE TO SWEAR IT RICKIE" HER BROTHER BEGGED. "PLEASE RICKIE" BERNARD BEGGED TOO! "ONE WORD FROM YOU COULD RUIN EVERYTHING AND WE WANT YOU WITH US ALL THE WAY BUT WE'VE ONLY GOT A FEW DAYS TO WORKOUT THE . . . BUT JUST BEFORE BERNARD COULD FINISH THE SENTENCE THERE WAS A KNOCK ON HER APARTMENT DOOR WHICH HAD SILENCED THE CONVERSATION BUT BOTH MEN SENT RICKIE QUESTIONING GLANCES.

"THAT WILL BE DAVID" RICKIE WHISPERED. SHE COULDN'T THINK OF HIM WITHOUT SEEING THE GRAPHIC PICTURES OF NAKED PEOPLE MEANING DAVID'S OWN PEOPLE BEING HERDED FOR EXPERIMENTS ON VON HASE'S PROPERTY.

"I'T'S AFTER 9:00pm I WAS SUPPOSED TO CALL HIM AS SOON AS I GOT HOME FROM WORK BECAUSE WE WERE PLANNING TO GO OUT TONIGHT." "RICKIE?" HE KNOCKED AGAIN AND SAID "ARE YOU IN THERE?" TED'S EYES SOURHT HERS WITH FRESH COMPASSION AND LOVING DEBORAH AS HE DID GAVE HIM TOO MUCH UNDERSTANDING.

BERNARD HELD HER TREMBLING BODY CLOSE TO HIS. "DO YOU WANT ME TO ANSWER IT AND TELL HIM YOU'RE NOT FEELING WELL?" "NO SHE SAID SOFTLY AS SHE MADE AN INSTANT DECISION. "I HAVE TO TALK TO HIM RIGHT NOW." "WHAT ABOUT ME AND TED?" "YOU TWO GO INTO MY BEDROOM FOR A MINUTE SO DAVID WON'T SEE YOU GUYS. "I MAY NOT BE BACK FOR AWHILE SO MAKE YOURSELVES AT HOME HERE IN MY BEDROOM."

AS SHE STARTED TO PULL AWAY TED REACHED OUT TO CUP HER DRAWN FACE IN HIS HANDS. WITH HIS CHEST HEAVED UP HIGH HE SAID TO RICKIE "I'VE ALREADY BROKE IT OFF WITH DEBORAH BUT SHE WON'T HAVE GOTTEN MY LETTER YET BUT WHEN SHE DOES IT WILL

KILL ANY FEELINGS SHE MIGHT HAVE HAD FOR ME AND I'VE REJECTED HER IN NO UNCERTAIN TERMS."

RICKIE'S ANGUISHED HEART CRIED OUT NO BUT SHE REALIZED TED DIDN'T HAVE A CHOICE AND NEITHER DID SHE. TO HER SORROW HER BROTHER HAD THE MOST TO LOSE THOUGH SHE LOVED DAVID SOLOMON DEARLY TED WAS THE ONE IN LOVE WITH HER.

SECONDS LATER DAVID SAID "HI" AS SHE OPENED THE DOOR. "WHEN YOU DIDN'T CALL ME I DECIDED TO COME DOWN AND SEE IF EVERYTHING WAS OKAY WITH YOU I HOPE THAT'S ALL RIGHT." "OF COURSE IT IS SAID RICKIE." SHE KNEW HER WORDS SOUNDED STIFF BUT SHE COULDN'T GET ANY OTHER RESPONSE. SHE STEPPED INTO THE CORRIDOR CLOSING THE APARTMENT DOOR BEHIND HER AND THEN SHE STARTED TOWARD THE DARK PARKING LOT. SHE WAS AFRAID HE'D TRY TO HOLD ON TO HER ARM SO SHE HURRIED AHEAD OF HIM. THE PARKING LOT OUTSIDE THEIR BIG APARTMENT COMPLEX NEEDED MORE LIGHT BUT TONIGHT SHE FOUD HERSELF GRATEFUL FOR THE DARKNESS.

"DO YOU WANT TO GO TO PANDORA'S FOR DRINKS?" HE SAID AS HE WENT AROUND TO GET INTO THE CAR TO START THE ENGINE. "TO BE HONEST WITH YOU I'D RATHER STAY HERE WHERE IT'S PRIVATE BECAUSE I NEED TO TALK TO YOU." SO HE SWUNG HIS HEAD IN HER DIRECTION AND SAID "I KNEW SOMETHING WAS WRONG" BUT AFTER A FEW MINUTES WENT BY HE ASKED HER "WHY DIDN'T YOU JUST INVITE ME IN?" HE SPOKE WITH ASPERITY SHE'D NEVER HEARD IN HIS VOICE BEFORE.

"I DIDN'T INVITE YOU IN BECAUSE TED IS IN MY APARTMENT RIGHT NOW." "WAS HE BY HIMSELF OR WAS BERNARD WITH HIM?" SHE DIDN'T ANSWER RIGHT AWAY AND SINCE SHE DIDN'T ANSWER DAVID SAID "I GUESS I HAVE MY ANSWER." HE HIT THE HEEL OF HIS HAND

AGAINST THE STEERING WHEEL THEN TURNED OFF THE IGNITION.

SHE KNEW HE WAS SUFFERING BUT THE NEWS SHE'D JUST LEARNED HAD PLACED AN INVISIBLE BARRIER BETWEEN HER AND THE REST OF THE WORLD BUT WITH THE KNOWLEDGE OF HER TRUE LINEAGE OF WHO SHE WAS AND CATAPULTED INTO A PLACE WHERE NO ONE COULD FOLLOW.

PUT HIM OUT OF HIS MISERY RICKIE. YOU KNEW HE WAS STARTING TO HAVE FEELINGS FOR YOU AND FEELINGS YOU DIDN'T SHARE WITH HIM. I THOUGHT YOU SHOULD HAVE LEFT AUSTRALIA LAST WEEK BEFORE HIS EMOTIONS GOT MORE INVOLVED. YOU HAVE TO TELL HIM THERE'S NO HOPE FOR HIS RELATIONSHIP SO HE CAN MOVE ON WITH HIS LIFE. HE DESERVES AT LEAST THAT MUCH HONESTY.

"DAVID?" HER VOICE SOUNDED UNUSUALLY CALM EVEN TO HER. "I'VE TOLD YOU MANY TIMES I THINK YOU'RE THE BEST, THE FINEST . . ." "SPARE ME THE THE RHETORIC" HE INTERRUPTED IN A SHAKEN VOICE AND HAD REMOVED HIS SUNGLASSES. "THOSE ARE TWO WORDS EVERY MAN IN LOVE WANTS TO DREADS HEARING FROM THE WOMAN HE WANTS TO MARRY."

HE CLEANED THE LENSES WITH THE TAIL END OF OF HIS SHIRT. "YOU THINK I'M AFTER YOUR MONEY DON'T YOU?" "NO!" "THEN IS IT BECAUSE I'M JEWISH?" "YOU KNOW BETTER THAN TO SAY THAT TO ME!" SHE HAD REPLIED WITH ENOUGH CONVICTION TO SILENCE HIM. "I RESPECT AND LOVE YOUR HERITAGE BUT AS MUCH AS THIS PAINS ME TO SAY THIS AS SHE LOWERED HER HEAD "I JUST DON'T HAVE THE FEELINGS I SHOULD TO HAVE TO BE YOUR WIFE."

I'M NOT LIKE DEBORAH AND I CAN'T IMAGINE LOVING A MAN THE WAY SHE LOVES TED BODY AND SOUL. I'M NOT CAPABLE OF BEING IN LOVE LIKE THAT AND AFTER WHAT I'VE JUST LEARNED I'M NOT WORTHY OF A LOVE LIKE THAT.

THERE WILL NEVER BE A MAN IN MY LIFE BECAUSE I WILL MAKE CERTAIN OF IT.

HE SAT THERE MOTIONLESS. "HOW DO YOU KNOW THAT WHEN WE HAVEN'T SLEPT TOGETTHOER YET?" I'VE BEEN WAITING FOR THE RIGHT TIME TO ASK YOU TOMOVE IN WITH ME BUT IF THINGS HAD BEEN RIGHT WE WOULDN'T HAVE WANTED TO WAIT BECAUSE WE WOULD HAVE BEEN TALKING MARRIAGE. SHE RESPONDED "DON'T YOU SEE?" AFTER A TENSE SILENCE HE ASKED "HAVE YOU EVER WANTED TO GO TO BED WITH ME AT AT ALL?" "DON'T DO THIS RICKIE SAID." "ANSWER ME RICKIE." "OK THE ANSWER IS NO!" "THEN WHY HAVE YOU BEEN GOING OUT WITH ME?" HE SOUNDED SO ANGRY THAT IT MADE HER PAIN EVEN WORSE. I WENT OUT WITH YOU BECAUSE I THOUGHT IN TIM THOSE FEELINGS WOULD COME TO ME BUT THEY DIDN'T BUT I STILL CONSIDER YOU MY FRIEND AND MY LIFE IS RICHER FOR KNOWING YOU.

"IS THERE SOMEONE ELSE?" HE SOUNDED DEMANDED LIKE A YOUNGER MAN WHO NOT QUITE IN CONTROL OF HIS EMOTIONS. "NO I'VE NEVER BEEN IN LOVE DAVID." "HAVE YOU EVER BEEN TO BED WITH A GUY?" HE CRYED OUT IN EXASPERATION.

SHE STARED AHEAD INTO THE DARKNESS AND THEN AFTER A FEW MINUTES SHE SAID "NO BECAUSE MY FATHER WARNED ME EARLY IN LIFE ABOUT THAT BECAUSE OF OUR FAMILY FORTUNE I HAD TO BE VERY CAREFUL. I HAD TO MAKE SURE A MAN WANTED ME FOR MYSELF AND NOT MY MONEY. I'M AFRAID I GREW UP SO PARANOID I WAS TERRIFIED TO BECOME VULNERABLE TO A MAN WHO MIGHT NOT LOVE ME FOR ME. "SO AT THIS POINT I'M NOT SURE I KNOW HOW TO LOVE DAVID SO YOU'RE BETTER OFF WITHOUT ME" SHE SAID AS HER VOICE TRAILED OFF.

AFTER A LONG SILENCE HE HAD WHISPERED "A PART OF ME WHISHES WE'D NEVER MET." I WISH THE SAME

THING BUT NOT FOR THE REASONS YOU'RE THING OF. MY BROTHER AND I ARE VON HASES AND IT'S OUR LEGACY TO CONTINUE INFLICTING PAIN ON INNOCENTS LIKE YOU.

YOU'RE WELL RID OF ME AND YOU WILL EVENTUALLY MEET SOMEONE WHO ADORES YOU AND WANTS YOU AS HER HUSBAND BUT DEBORAH IS A DIFFERENT MATTER BECAUSE WHEN SHE READS TED'S LETTER I'M TERRIBLY AFRAID SHE WILL NEVER GET OVER IT.

"I'M SORRY SO SORRY FOR HURTING YOU I NEVER MEANT TO" RICKIE SAID OUT LOUD TO DAVID. "PLASE FORGIVE ME FOR HURTING YOU" SHE SAID AS SHE REACHED FOR THE DOOR HANDLE ON THE CAR DOOR.

"ARE YOU LEAVING CANBERRA?" HE ASKED WITH TEARS IN HIS EYES AND A SAD VOICE. HIS INSTINCTS RARELY FAILED HIM THIS WAY. "YES RICKIE SAID I'AM LEAVING CANBERRA" AND SOON. "YOU DON'T HAVE TO LEAVE ON MY ACCOUNT" SAID DAVID. "I'M NOT"! SAID RICKIE I'M FINISHING LAYING THE GROUNDWORK FOR CHB HERE AND I NEEND TO GET BACK TO MY OFFICE IN NEW YORK.

BEFORE SHE CLOSED THE CAR DOOR SHE SAID ONE FINAL THING "IF I KNEW HOW TO PRAY I'D ASK THE GOD YOUR WORSHIP TO SHOWER YOU WITH A LOT OF HAPPINESS IT'S NO MORE THEN YOU DESERVE GOODBYE DAVID.

CHAPTER 31

THREE STRUCTURES OF WORLD WAR TWO.

THIS MUST BE THE PLACE! THE THREE QUONSET STRUCTURES OF WORLD WAR TWO VINTAGE AND HANGAR SITTING ON THE EDGE OF A BIG GRASS-INFESTED RUNWAY OUTSIDE STANFORDVILLE JUST LIKE STONEY HAD SAID.

DECIDING TO ENTER THE BULIDING CLOSEST TO THE ACCESS ROAD JORDAN BROWNING STEPPED OUT OF THE SECONDHAND ECONOMY CAR HE'D BOUGHT AFTER BEING RELEASED FORM PRISON THREE DAYS AGO. AS HE APPROACHED THE FIRST STRUCTURE HE NOTICED A BATTERED FORD PICKUP TRUCK PARKED IN THE REAR. GOOD IT MEANT SOMEONE WAS AROUND HE FIGURED IT WASN'T STONEY THOUGH GESSNA WOULD BE VISIBLE.

TO HIS RELIEF THE DOOR OPENED EASILY AND HE FOUND HIMESELF INSIDE AN OFFICE OF SOME SORT. THE PLACE WAS INCREDIDLY UNTIDY WITH AN OLD CORKBOARD AND THE WALLS WERE COVERED WITH A DOZEN MESSAGES. A COUPLE OF IMITATION-LEATHER RIPPED CHAIRS SAT ON EITHER SIDE OF THE CARD TABLE.

THE CIGARETTE BUTS ALMOST HID THE ASHTRAY FROM VIEW AND HAD SEVERAL COPIES OF PLAYBOY AT LEAST TWENTY YEARS OLD HAD BEEN SCATTERED ALL OVER THE TABLE TOP AND THEIR WERE PAGES CURLED UP THAT LOOK LIKE THEY HAD THUMB PRINTS ON THEIR FROM YEARS AGO BUT STONEY HAD SAID THE PLACE NEEDED A MAJOR

FACE LIFT AND JORDAN FIGURED IT NEEDED TO BE TORN DOWN AND REBUILT.

"HEY ROGERS" A BELLOWING FEMALE VOICE REACHED HIS EARS AND HE BEGAN TO STRIDE TOWARD THE COMPUTER HOPING TO DISCOVER THE BIG OWNER OF SUCH AMAZING LUNG POWER. THE WOMEN WHOEVER SHE WAS SEEMED TO BE TALKING OR RATHER SHOUTING ON THE PHONE.

"STONEY SAYS TO GET THE HELL OVER HERE AND CHECK THE DC3'S LEFT ENGINE AGAIN" SHE SAID AS THE VOICE GREW STRIDENT. JORDAN'S EYES HAD WIDENED AS HE FINALLY SPIED THE WELL ADDED OLDER WOMEN LYING BACK IN HER CHAIR. SHE HAD THE TELEPHONE RECEIVER NESTLED BETWEEN HER CHEEK AND HER SHOULDER BLADE AND IN HER HANDS WAS A LARGE SANDWICH AND AN OPENED CAN OF POP ON THE DESK.

HE WATCHED HER TAKE ANOTHER BITE OUT OF THE SANDWICH. THEN AFTER SHE TOOK ANOTHER BITE OF THE SANDWICH SHE STARTED TO YELL ON THE PHONE AGAIN AND THIS IS WHAT SHE SAID "WHAT? THEN YOU BETTER GET SOMEBODY ON IT WHO KNOWS WHAT THEY'RE DOING OR ELSE!" THE MUNCHING ON THE SANDWICH CONTINUED FOLLOWED BY A SWIG OF BLACK-BERRY SODA. THE GUY ON THE OTHER END OF THE PHONE ASKED "HOW DO YOU KNOW ABOUT THAT STUFF? THE SHE REPLIED BACK "BECAUSE I WORK HERE!" SHE SAID.

HER LOUD BELCH WAS MET WITH A SPATE OF ABUSIVE LANGUAGE EVEN JORDAN COULD HERE UNTILL SHE PROMPTLY CUT IT OFF BY HANGING UP THE PHONE AND THEN SHE LAUGHED UNINHIBITEDLY UNTILL SHE SAW HIM.

THE WOMEN MAYBE IN HER LATE SIXTIES LOOKED SURPRISED TO HAVE A VISITOR. SHE STRETCHED HER

PINKISH-BLOND HEAD WAY BACK OVER THE SIDE OF THE CHAIR AS IF TO SATISFY HER CURIOSITY BUT HER AMBER EYES GAVE HIM THROUGH GOING-OVER.

"WHAT PART OF DUTCHESS COUNTY DID YOU COME FROM HONEY?" HER GLANCE TOOK IN HIS TAN WORK SHIRT AND JEANS. I WAS ABOUT TO ASK YOU THE SAME QUESTION BUT STONEY HADN'T TOLD HIM HE'D HAD HIRED SOMEONE TO HELP ME RUN THE PLACE UNTILL HIS PARTNER CLUED HIM IN HE'D BETTER STICK WITH THE PLAN AND FOLLOW THEIR STORY TO THE LETTER.

"I'M REVEREND BROWNING FROM THE INTERDENOMINATIONAL MINISTRY AND I'M DOING A LITTLE MISSIONARY WORK IN THIS NECK OF THE WOODS" MR. BROWNING SAID. SHE SWUNG HER LEVI CLAD LEGS TO THE FLOOR IN A SURPRISINGLY ANGILE MOTION. "A REVEREND HUH? THEN WHERE'S YOUR COLLAR?" THE REVEREND SAID "I FIND I MAKE FRIENDS EASIER IF I LEAVE IT AT HOME." SHE SQUINTED AT HIM AND SAID "WHAT DO YOU WANT TO SEE STONEY ABOUT?" DON'T WORRY I'M KIND OF A RELATIVE OF HIS BUT HE DOSEN'T LIKE THAT PASSED AROUND WHICH MIGHT BE THE TRUTH THEN AGAIN "I JUST WANTED TO DROP BY AND GET THE ACQUAINTED BUT I GUESS I WILL HAVE TO CATCH HIM WHEN HE'S BETWEEN FLIGHTS."

"SO SOMEBODY TOLD YOU STONEY COULD FLY DID THEY? I GUESS YOU CAN'T BELIEVE EVERYTHING YOU HEAR THESE DAYS." SHE BROKE INTO ANOTHER SPATE OF LAUGHTER AND THEN HER EYES STARTED TO WATER. "ARE YOU EXPECTING HIM SOON MAAM?" "RELAX HONEY" SHE SAID AS SHE TOOK ANOTHER SWIG OF POP. "DON'T BE IN SUCH AN FIRED HURRY THE END OF THE WORLD NOT GOING HAPPEN UNTILL JUNE THIRTEENTH AND THAT'S NOT FOR ANOTHER TWENTY-FOUR HOURS" SHE SAID AS SHE HAD CHUCKLED AGAIN AT HER OWN JOKE.

"HE WILL BE BACK IN A LITTLE WHILE BUT THERE'S NO TELL HOW LONG EXACTLY. HE HAD TO TAKE CARE OF A BIG ORDER SOMEWHERE IN THE BIG STATE OF MONTGOMERY COUNTY. SO SIT DOWN AND MAKE YOURSELF COMFORTABLE."

JORDAN COMPLIED SCHOOLING HIMSELF TO BE PATIENT EVEN THOUGH IT WENT AGAINST ALL HIS INSTINCTS. "TELL ME ABOUT YOURSELF WHAT CHURCH ARE YOU FROM? I'LL LET YOU IN ON A LITTLE SECRET I AIN'T BEEN INSIDE ONE IN TWENTY YEARS." "WHY IS THAT?" "I'M SCARED I'LL BE TOLD I'M GOING TO HELL!" YOU AND THE REST OF THE WORLD.

"I THINK WE'RE ALL A LITTLE SCARED OF THAT MS . . ." IT'S MRS. MOE NONE OFF THAT FEMALE LIBERATION STUFF FOR ME NO SIR EVEN IF MY HUBBY'S GONE TO HIS MAKER MY NAME IS STILL MRS. INGEVAR MOE BUT YOU CAN CALL ME MARY.

"SAY A HUGE SMILE BROKE OUT ON HER FACE MAKING IT ALMOST PRETTY. "YOU AND ME GONNA GET ALONG JUST FINE. SO WHAT DOSE A BIG MISSIONARY DO AROUND THESE PARTS?"

IN PRISON HE'D BEEN REHEARSING HIS NEW PERSONA UNTILL HE COULD GIVE THE DETAILS IN HIS SLEEP. "I HELP PEOPLE WHO'VE RECENTLY MOVED TO THE AREA HISPANICS MOSTLY. I INTERVENE IN CASE THEY'RE LOOKING FOR EMPLOYMENT, HOUSING, LEGAL SERVICES IF THEY NEED THEM THAT SORT OF THING."

"YOU SPEAK THEIR LINGO?" "ENOUGH." "WHERE DID YOU LEARN IT?" "TEXAS." "FESS UP NOW YOU CAME ALL THE WAY OVER HERE FOR FREE FLYING LESSONS RIGHT?" HE COULD HEAR THE SOUND OF THE 206 THAT WAS NOW APPROACHING.

"NO MA'AM." "THAT'S GOOD BECAUSE I CAN REMEMBER THE LAST MINISTER WHO SAUNTERED IN LOOKING FOR A FREE RIDE. STONEY TOOK HIM UP BUT THAT LOUDMOUTHED SON OF A REVIVALIST DIDN'T DO SO GOOD AND HAD TO BE CARTED OFF ON A STRETCHER.

"SINCE THEN STONEY DON'T TAKE JUST ANYBODY UP WITH HIM. I'M SORT OF HIS SCREENING COMMITTEE YOU UNDERSTAND. SOME ARE BORN TO FLYING BUT MOST AREN'T. "I WONDER WHICH YOU ARE?" IMMATURE BLADDERS HAVE THE WORST TIME OF IT.

AT THAT PRONOUNCEMENT JORDAN LAUGHED OUT LOUD SOMETHING HE HADN'T DONE FOR SO LONG HE THOUGHT HE'D FORGOTTEN HOW. "SEE? SHE SAID "I KNEW THAT FACE OF YOURS WOULDN'T CRACK IF YOU REALLY LET GO. FELT GOOD DIDN'T IT SON? YOU SHOULD TRY IT MORE OFTEN YOU HANDSOME DEVIL AND WITH A LITTLE BIT OF IMPROVEMENT YOU COULD ACTUALLY HAVE ME IN A CHURCH AS SOON AS NEXT SUNDAY.

SHE LEANED OVER AND SAID "COME CLEAN NOW IS THERE REALLY A HELL?" THERE WAS A HELL ALL RIGHT. HE'D BEGUN TO THINK IT WAS A PERMANET STATE OF BEING. MARY JO WAS LIKE A BREATH OF FRESH AIR BUT TOO DAM CURIOUS FOR HER OWN GOOD. "WHAT DO YOU THINK?" HE SAID OUT LOUD. "THAT'S YOU DEPARTMENT HONEY. SAY HAVE YOU EVER BEEN IN THE MOVIES?" "NO HE SAID."

"DIDN'T ANYONE EVER TELL YOU'RE A DEAD RINGER FOR THAT GUY WHO LOOKS LIKE STEVEN SEGAL AND WHO PLAYS IN THOSE ACTION FILMS?" "GOOD GRIEF I'M AFRAID NOT." "IF YOU'RE HERE FOR A DONATION STONEY DON'T HAVE ANY MONEY AND HE CAN'T PAY ANYONE A SALARY SO THAT'S WHY I WORK FOR HIM."

Jordan was glad to hear it since half their operating capital came from the life savings Jordan had accrued before the court-martial and he had turned everything over to Stoney.

Suddenly there was a banging on the door and in sprang Stoney known on his own birth certificate as Delbert Stonewall Leonard. He had the clean-cut appearance of a tennis pro and moved with the same effortless agility and no one would guess that in action his body turned into a powerful deadly machine.

They saw each other at the same time everyday. So intuned were they from six years of working together on a Navy SEAL team Jordan read Stoney's eye signal with ease and waited to be approached. "Hi I'm Stoney Leonard as he extended a frim hand in greeting. "What can I do for you?" Jordan stood up and said "I'm Jordan Browning as he gave his old friend a private hand squeeze in reciprocation. Stoney was loving this he could tell. It was good to see him again but in a way it wasn't. "He's a new reverend-missionary around these parts" Mary Jo had informed her boss "but don't he's not here for flying lessons or handouts."

Stoney's normally fierce gray eyes were smiling. "That's a big relief she said as she told the reverend to come on back." "Just call me Jordan if you need any help." "Say!" Mary said as she slapped her thigh and said "I like a man who don't take himeself so serious."

With a smothering grin Stoney vaulted over the counter and Jordan had followed him over the counter as well. "Any mail?" Stoney had asked

RIFLING THROUGH SOME PAPERS HE'D APPARENTLY HAD THROWN IN THE WASTEPAPER BASKET.

"YEAH I PUT ALL THE IMPORTANT STUFF ON YOUR DESK." THE MEN'S EYES CONNECTED IN SILENT LAUGHTER. "HOW MANY TIMES DO I HAVE TO TELL YOU TO PUT IT ALL ON MY DESK?" STONEY SAID OUT LOUD. MARY JO EYED JORDAN AND SAID "IF YOU WANT TO STAY ON HIS GOOD SIDE" SHE HAD WHISPERED OUT OF THE CORNER OF THE HER MOUTH "DON'T TALK ABOUT ME EVEN IF YOU'RE DYING TO." SHE SAID AS SHE WINKED AT HIM. "HE'D AS SOON SHOOT ME AS A FLY AND HE LIKES DOING THAT REALLY WELL."

"I CAN HEAR YOU MARY" STONEY CALLED OUT MOTIONING JORDAN TO INTO HIS OFFICE. HE WAS REWARDED WITH MORE OF HER BELLY LAUGHTER THIS REVERBERATED INSIDE THE HUT. TO JORDAN THE SOUND WAS LIKE LONG-FORGOTTEN MUSIC.

MARY JO WAS A HAPPY SOUL AND STONEY SAID "DEAR LORD WHAT WOULD THAT FEEL LIKE?" AFTER STONEY CLOSED THE DOOR THE TWO MEN GAVE EACH OTHER A BONE-CRUSHING BEAR HUG. JORDAN IMAGINED HIS FRIEND WAS DOING THE SAME THING HE WAS AND RELIVING CERTAIN MEMORIES KNOWN ONLY TO EACH OTHER AND THE SECRETS THAT WOULD BE LOST WHEN THEIR BODIES FINALLY TURN TO DUST BUT NOT YET BROWNING STONEY SAID. YOU'RE A FREE MAN AGAIN AND YOU'RE GOING TO STAY THAT WAY UNTILL IT ALL COMES TO A SCREECHING HALT.

AFTER ANOTHER HEARTFELT SLAP TO THE SHOULDERS THEY LET GO OF EACH OTHER AND SAT DOWN ON THE COUCH THAT'S IN HIS OFFICE SO JORDAN STRETCHED HIS LONG HARD MUSCLED LEGS IN FRONT OF HIM AND SAID "WHERE DID MARY JO COME FROM?"

Stoney's eyes widened in mirth as he said "She's my father's brother's wife's Aunt Mary Jo on her mother's side of the family untill my husband died a while back he had his own air-cargo business out of South Dakota. They couldn't have children so she helped him run the place.

"Through the family grapevine she found out I'd started up an air freight company and she asked for the job. She didn't want any pay just something to do." His eyebrows quirked as he said "Mary's an original and I decided she'd make a great front for our operation."

"I like her" Jordan said in a quiet voice. "I thought you would." As they stared at each other Stoney's smile slowly vanished. "I'am so gland you're out of the brig because I've been counting the long hours." "It wasn't so bad." "The hell it wasn't! I let you talk me into keeping silent when I should have spent those six months in there with you."

"Wrong!" Jordan told him forcefully. "You needed to be on the outside setting things up for us which you've done admirably I might add. Any regrets about leaving the Seals?" "None after a hesitation "How about you? You could reenlist. You'd be on probation but" But what? "Forget it Stoney" he interupted. "I killed a man against direct orders. I'm no good with a team and never could countenance blind obedience."

Stoney's jaw hadrened before he said "I helped you kill him so that makes two of us who do better work on are own." "Amen said the Reveren Browning "Except we don't have any money left" he said to Stoney. "I noticed Jordan's mouth was muttered dryl."

226

CHRISTINA RAGOZZINO

STONEY SAT FORWARD IN THE FOLDING CHAIR THINKING. THENE HE SAID "WHERE DID THE REST OF THE MONEY GO TO?" JORDAN SAID "I PUT THE REST OF THE MONEY INTO REMOLDELING THE OTHER HUTS BUT THE GOOD NEWS IS WE'RE PICKING UP NEW ORDERS EVERY DAY." HE SAID TO JORDAN "THAT SOUNDS GOOD HOW IS MICHELLE?" "I DON'T KEEP TABS ON HER SAID JORDAN." "IS SHE STILL REFUSING ALIMONY?" "YEP SHE SAYS SHE REGRETS EVER BEING MARRIED TO A GUY GOING NOWHERE AND SAYS SHE DOSEN'T NEED THE PITTANCE I CAN'T AFFORD TO SEND HER." "IS SHE STILL IN LOVE WITH YOU." "WHAT DOES THAT HAVE TO DO WITH ANYTHING?" SAID JORDAN. "QUITE A LOT SINCE YOU'RE STILL IN LOVE WITH HER." "I'LL GET OVER IT." SAID JORDAN. "I THOUGHT THAT'S WHAT YOU SAID LAST YEAR AND THE YEAR BEFORE THAT."

"YEAH BUT THIS YEAR SHE'S GETTING MARRIED TO A WALLSTREET BROKER WITH A NINE-TO-FIVE-JOB AND HE ALSO DRIVES A PORSCHE AND SITS AT THE COMPUTER ALL DAY WORKING ON RETIREMENT FUNDS AND INVESTMENTS IN THE WORKS."

"SHE'LL NEVER GO THROUGH WITH IT" JORDAN PREDICTED. "WATCH HER" SAID STONEY. "I DON'T NEED TO BECAUSE SHE WAS ONCE HAPPILY MARRIED TO YOU BUT YOU'RE TYPE COULD NEVER HOLD HER."

STONEY SMIRKED IN SLEF-DEPRECATION BECAUSE I WAS "RIGHT I RUINED HER FOR OTHER MEN." "YOU KNOW YOU DID BUT YOU'RE ONLY MISTAKE WAS SHUTING HER OUT." "I DID IT TO PROTECT HER BUT I DON'T WANT TO TALK ABOUT THAT ANYMORE."

WHAT DID YOU THINK OF REVEREND ROLON? I'T'S HARD TO TELL WHEN HE SOLD ME THE CAR AND GAVE MY PAPERS BUT HE DIDN'T HAVE VERY MUCH TO SAY. "THAT'S ROLON FOR YOU." HE'S BEEN DOING SO MANY SHALL WE SAY QUASI-LEGAL THING TO HELP REFUGEES AND RECENT

IMMIGRANTS THROUGHOUT THE YEARS WITHOUT HIS SUPERIORS KNOWING ANYTHING ABOUT IT BUT I THINK COVERT ACTIVITIES HAVE BECOME SECOND NATURE TO HIM. HE'S THE ONE WHO ARRANGED MY MEETING WITH FATHER DESILVA IN PARAGUAY.

"WHEN I TOLD ROLON OUR PLAN AND ASKED HIM TO HELP US AFTER YOU GOT OUT OF PRISON HE SUGGESTED MAKING YOU A MISSIONARY THAT WAY YOU'LL HAVE A LEGITIMATE REASON TO VISIT CHURCH MEMBERS THROUGHOUT THE AREA WITHOUT HAVING TO BE CONFINED TO ONE PLACE.

"ROLON'S ALREADY PASSED THE WORD THAT THE RECTORY WHERE HE'S LIVING WITH HIS FAMILY IS TOO SMALL TO ACCOMMODATE ANOTHER BOARDER SO HE ARRANGED FOR YOU TO LIVE HERE WITH ME. IN LIEU OF PAYING RENT YOU OCCASIONALLY LEND A HAND WITH THE CARGO BUSINESS. THAT'S OUR STORY OK?

"NO LAW-ENFORCEMENT OFFICERS ARE GOING TO QUESTION YOUR AGENDA OR ASK WHY YOU'RE NOT STAYING UNDER ROLON'S ROOF. HE'S GIVEN YOU THE PERFECT FRONT FOR OUR OPERATION."

"DO YOU TRUST HIM NOT TO CRACK UNDER PRESURE IF OUR PLAN IS BLOWS UP IN OUR FACES?" "AS MUCH AS I TRUST THE MAN WHO'S SITTING IN FRONT OF ME RIGHT NOW."

JORDAN NODDEN HIS HEAD AND SAID YES I AGREE WITH HIM. "OKAY SO I SHOULD ASSUME HE'S WILLING TO SEE OUR OPERATION THROUGH THE END." "THAT'S RIGHT OTHERWISE HE WOULDN'T HAVE GOTTEN YOU THAT FORGED ID SO I GUESS YOU CAN CONSIDER HIM AS OUR PARTNER IN THIS ENTERPRISE. FOR THE TIME BEING WE'RE SAFE BUT UNFORTUNATELY THERE'S SOME BAD NEWS. HE'S

BEEN TRYING TO GET FUNDING BUT NOTHING'S PANNED OUT."

"WHY NOT?" "EXCEPT FOR THE FRIENDS OF MERCY FOUNDATION WHO GAVE HIM A THOUSAND DOLLARS FOR THE FEW NEW AND OLD PHILANTHROPISTS AND HEADS OF CHARITIES HE'S TALKED TO WON'T UNDERWRITE AN ORGANIZATION."

"THEN WE NEED TO APPROCH IT A DIFFERENT WAY." "I FIGURED YOU'D SAY THAT. THERE'S ONLY ONE MORE CHARITY IN THE POUGHKEEPSIE AREA THE-BIG-ONE-BUT WHOEVER'S IN CHARGE WAS OUT OF THE COUNTRY UNTILL A FEW DAYS AGO. I HAD TOLD ROLON TO HOLD OFF TILL YOU GET HERE."

"I'LL RUN TO TOWN IN THE MORNING AND CHECK THINGS OUT FIRST OKAY. WHAT'S THE NAME?" "CHB." IT STANDS FOR CHARITY BEGINS AT HOME. IT'S A FOUNDATION RUN BY THE BIG TAYLOR CORPORATION." "THE WORLD BANKING DYNASTY?" "THAT'S THE ONE THAT FORBES LISTS THEIR ASSETS IN THE BILLIONS. CHB IS ONE OF THEIR TAX WRITE-OFFS. THEY'VE SET UP CHARITIES ALL OVER THE WROLD SINCE THEY HAVE HEARD OF BAKNING OFFICES IN NEW YORK AND THEY ALSO HAVE A CORPORATE BRANCH IN THE LAND OF POUGHKEEPSIE AND I FIGURED THEY JUST MIGHT BE RECEPTIVE TO THE RIGHT PITCH. YOU'RE A PERSUASIVE GUY AND I'M GOING TO COUNT ON YOU TO PULL THIS OFF. WE NEED A BUNDLE OF MONEY AND WE NEEDED IT YESTERDAY!

"I KNOW OUR AIR-CARGO BUSINESS MY BE GROWING BUT IT'LL BE YEARS BEFORE IT STARTS TO BRING IN THE KINK OF MONEY WE NEED TO FUND OUR OPERATION AND I'LL DO WHATEVER IT TAKES" JORDAN HAD VOWED.

They eyed each other with an understanding born of years of training and fighting side by side often under impossible odds.

"Walcome home" Stoney said simply. This is the only home you've got anymore Browning. Thank God for Stoney and thank God his crippled grandfather hadn't lived very long enough to see him go to prison. He'd been a Navy man through and through and the shock would have killed him along before he suffered that fatal heart attack.

He cleared his throat and then said "It's good to be here." "I think it's time to take you on a tour of the facilities your money helped remodel. You and I live in the far hut and it has a fridge, phone, shower and tub what else dose a man need?" I'd say Jordan Browning needs a good woman." "No woman is going to want a man with a prison record." "I'm talking way before that. You know there hasn't been anyone since the first year I knew you."

Jordan folded his arms across his chest and said "Lying to a women in order to protect her doesn't exactly constitute the basis for a lasting relationship. I learned a hard lesson from you." "Hush, but nevertheless I haven't lost hope for you yet and I know this cute little . . . . "Hold it right there that's not my job" said Jordan as he interrrupted Stoney. "Just the same way Michelle's not yours?" Jordan grunted. "I stand reproved now let's get off the subject."

"Good idea said Stoney." Now Mary is in the middle hut but we had a kitchen and sort of a dorm build in hers plus one room with desks and

COMPUTERS." "DOES SHE KNOW WHAT WE'RE DOING?" "I DON'T THINK SO SHE'S TOO BEHOLDEN TO ME TO ASK MANY QUESTIONS BUT I CAN TELL SHE'S DYING OF CURIOSITY."

THEY BOTH CHUCKLED OUT LOUD WHEN THEY HEARD THAT. "WE'LL TELL HER EVERYTHING TONIGHT BECAUSE I WANTED YOU TO BE HERE SO WE CAN FILL HER IN TOGETHER. IF SHE KNEW WAS GOOD FOR HER SHE'D BE OUT OF HERE LIKE A BAT OUT OF HELL BUT SOMETHING TELLS ME SHE"LL WANT TO STICK WITH US. WE'LL BRING IT UP TONIGHT AFTER OUR STEAK DINNER IT WILL BE MY TREAT SAID STONEY. "I'D THOUGHT YOU WOULD NEVER OFFER SAID REVEREND BROWNING."

THE SWELTERING HUMID JUNE DAY HAD MOST OF THE NEW YORKERS COMPLAINING. RICKIE HAD CAUGHT HER LONG GILT-BLOND HAIR BACK WITH A LARGE TORTOISESHELL COMB TO STAY COOLER BUT NOTHING HAD HELPED.

HER WHITE SLEEVELESS LINEN DRESS FELT DAMP AGAINST HER BODY AS SHE ENTERED THE TAYLOR CROPORATION BUILDING IN DOWN TOWN POUGKEEPSIE WHERE CHB WAS HOUSED.

AT LUNCH THE NEXT DAY TED AND BERNARD TALKED OVER FINAL PLANS WITH HER. THEY DETERMINED TO START LOOKING FOR A MAN A BOUNTY HUNTER WHO COULD GO TO PARAGUAY AND FIND THEIR GRANDFATHER IF HE WAS STILL ALIVE.

SHE FIGURED THE PRICE THEY'D AGREED ON OUGHT TO DRAW OUT THE BEST FROM AMONG THE WORST OF THEIR KIND. HOW ODD THAT WAS UNTILL SHE'D LEARNED SHE WAS A VON HASE SHE HAD CONSIDERED A BOUNTY HUNTER TO BE ABOUT THE LOWEST FORM OF LIFE THERE WAS.

When she entered her own air-conditioned suite of her offices she felt relief that an empty waiting room greeted her but on the hand her temporary receptionist didn't seem to be anywhere around but unfortunately Rickie's permanent secretary Peggy was out with appendicitis and won't be back untill next week.

"Susan?" "I'm right here." The girl suddenly made an appearance from behind the counter with a rag in her hand and looking very flushed around the face. "I had spilled my drink all over the floor and it got onto everything. I've spent the last ten minutes cleaning it up."

Once upon a time before the veils had been ripped from Rickie's eyes she would have been mildly amused rather than irritated by the younger women's explanations.

"I'll be in my office the rest of the afternoon and I don't want to be disturbed." "You do know you have an appointment at two!" That's an hour from now. "With whom?" "A Reverend Browning."

Rickie decided the receptionist sent over by the temporary services was too naïve and inexperienced for the job. She would have to call and ask them to send someone else tomorrow.

In the meantime Rickie had little choice but to keep Susan on for the rest of the day unless she wanted to answer the phones herself but she just didn't have the coping skills to deal with the public right now.

"You must have forgotten what I told you yesterday" she said more sharply then she'd

INTENDED. "WE DON'T FUND GOVERNMENT OR RELIGIOUS GROUPS." "I SPECIFICALLY TOLD HIM THAT THIS MORNING." HE SAID HE DIDN'T REPRESENT EITHER ONE. "THEY ALL SAY THAT UNTILL THEY'RE PINNED DOWN.

WOULD YOU PLEASE CALL THE CHURCH AND CANCEL THE APPOINTMENT? "I CAN'T HE'S DRIVING INTO THE CITY FROM SOMEWHERE." "THEN GET HIM ON HIS CELLPHONE." "I DON'T KNOW IF HE HAS ONE." RICKIE RUBBED HER FOREHEAD AND SHE COULD FEEL HER HEADACHE GETTING WORSE. "IT'S OKAY SHE SAID AND I'M SORRY FOR SNAPPING AT YOU." "THAT'S ALL RIGHT MS. TAYLOR IT'S BECAUSE OF THIS DAM HEAT!"

SUSAN RUSHED TO AMELIORATE THE SITUATION. "I'M SORRY I DIDN'T THINK TO ASK HIM FOR A NUMBER WHERE HE COULD BE REACHED." "IT'S UNFORTUNATE BECAUSE HE'LL HAVE MADE THE TRIP FOR NOTHING." "YOU MEAN I HAVE TO TELL HIM YOU CAN'T SEE HIM?" SHE SAID AS SHE SOUNDED HORRIFIED. "THAT'S RIGHT YOU HAVEN'T WORKED HERE LONG ENOUGH TO UNDERSTAND THAT WE'RE CONTENDING WITH LEGAL ISSUES AND COMPLICATED TAX LAWS THAT GET VERY STICKY. WHEN HE SHOWS UP SEND HIM TO THE FRIENDS OF MERCY FOUNDATION OVER ON CANAL STREET BECAUSE THEY'RE OPEN TO ALL DENOMINATIONS.

IF YOU DON'T THINK YOU CAN DO THAT THEN CALL ACCOUNTING AND ASK THEM TO DEAL WITH THE REVEREND." "IS THERE A SPECIAL PERSON I SHOULD TALK TO?" RICKIE'S EYES CLOSED IN DEFEAT. "BART KNOWS THE DRILL IS THERE ANYTHING ELSE YOU NEED TO TELL ME?" "OH! I ALMOST FORGOT YOU HAVE THREE PHONE CALLS FROM DAVID SOLOMON IN AUSTRALIA. I PUT THE NUMBER ON YOUR DESK. HE SYAS IT'S A BIG EMERGENCY."

A SHUDDER PASSED THROUGH RICKIE'S BODY BECAUSE IT WAS THE MIDDLE OF THE NIGHT IN AUSTRALIA AND

DAVID COULD ONLY BE CALLING THIS LATE FOR ONE REASON. DEBORAH WOULD HAVE RECEIVED TED'S LETTER BY NOW. WEIGHTED DOWN BY FRESH SORROW RICKIE HAD THANKED SUSAN THEN HEADED FOR HER OFFICE.

SHE DIDN'T WANT TO TALK TO DAVID NOT YET AND NOT WHEN THE PAIN IN TED'S EYES FILLED HER WITH DESPAIR. MAYBE TONIGHT SHE'D BE ABLE TO PHONE CANBERRA AFTER SHE'D WADED THROUGH THE HUGE BACKLOG OF WORK AND REACHED A POINT OF NUMBED EXHAUSTION.

THE SECOND SHE ENTERED HER OFFICE AND SHUT THE DOOR A SLIGHT GASP OF SURPRISE ESCAPED HER LIPS FOLLOWED BY A LITTLE THRILL OF ALARM. A MAN LIKE NONE SHE'D EVER SEEN STOOD GAZING AT THE BIG MAP OF THE WORLD ON THE FAR SIDE OF THE WALL AND HIS HANDS WERE JOINTED BEHIND HIS BACK. EVERYTHING ABOUT HIM WAS SO NOT RIGHT LIKE HIS SHEER MALE STANCE, HIS TALLNESS AND PROUD BEARING MADE HIM REMARKABLE. FORGETTING THAT SHE WAS STARING SHE LET HER GAZE DART TO HIS DARK BROWN HAIR TIED BACK AT THE NAPE OF HIS NECK WITH A THONG. OBEYING A COMPULSION TOTALLY FOREIGN TO HER SHE TOOK IN THE BROADNESS OF HIS SHOULDERS THAT RIPCORD STRENGTH OF HIS ARMS AND BODY REVEALED BENEATH THE THIN BROWN T-SHIRT TUCKED INTO A WELL WORN PAIR OF JEANS. JUST THEN HE TURNED AROUND IN HER DIRECTION AND A PAIR OF INTENSE BRIGHT GREEN EYES LOCKED WITH HERS SQUEEZING THE BREATH FROM HER LUNGS.

MORTIFIED THAT HE'D CAUGHT HER APPRAISING HIM IN SUCH A PERSONAL MANNER SHE LOOKED AWAY BUT HER REACTION HAD COME FAR TOO LATE BECAUSE A SLOW COIL OF HEAT WOUND IT'S WAY THROUGH HER BODY. "WHO ARE YOU AND WHAT DO YOU WANT?" SHE ASKED OUT LOUD FIGHTING FOR COMPOSURE BECAUSE

SHE DIDN'T WANT HIM TO KNOW HOW STRONGLY HIS PRESENCE HAD AFFECTED HER. HE MUST HAVE SLIPPED IN WHILE SUSAN WAS ON THE FLOOR CLEANING UP THE MESS SHE HAD MADE. TO HER RECOLLECTION NO STRANGER HAD EVER ENTERED HER PRIVATE OFFICE UNANNOUNCED OR UNINVITED.

HIS STRAIGHT NOSE AND HEAD-BONED FEATURES GAVE HIM THE RUGGED LOOK OF A MAN WHO'D LIVED VERY HARD LIFE AND A MAN IN HIS MID TO UPPER THIRTIES. THE TINY SCAR AT THE CORNER OF HIS MOUTH AND THE EDGE OF HIS RIGHT EYEBROW WHISPERED THAT HE WAS DANGEROUS.

SHOULD SHE BE AFRAID? IF SHE SCREAMED SUSAN WOULD GO TO PIECES AND AS FOR BART THE ONLY MAN WORKING FOR HER AT THE MOMENT HE WOULD BE NO MATCH FOR THIS STRANGER. IT APPEARED RICKIE WAS GOING TO HAVE TO USE HER WITS SINCE SHE WAS TOO FAR FROM HER PHONE TO BUZZ THE BUILDING'S SECURITY IF SHE HAD NEED PROTECTION.

"I GOT INTO TOWN EARLIER THEN I'D EXPECTED" HE EXPLAINED. HIS VOICE WAS DEEPAPPEALING AS A MALE. "WHEN I CALLED OUT NO ONE ANSWERED AND I THOUGHT THAT WAS STRANGE SINCE YOUR FRONT DOOR WAS UNLOCKED AND ANYONE COULD JUST WALK RIGHT ON INTO YOUR HOUSE WITHOUT YOU KNOWING ABOUT IT. SO I TOOK LIBERTY OF WANDERING AROUND TO MAKE SURE EVERYTHING WAS ALL RIGHT.

I HAVE TO ADMIT WHEN I COUGHT SIGHT OF THE WALL MAP THAT WAS DISPLAYING ALL YOUR CHARITIES I FOUND MYSELF FASCINATED. I HOPE YOU DON'T MIND THAT I CAME IN HERE TO WAIT. I'M REVEREND JORDAN BROWNING. INSTEAD OF EXTENDING HIS HAND HE HAD PRODUCED A WALLET WHICH HE OPENED TO DISPLAY HIS DOCTOR-OF—DIVINITY CREDENTIALS.

HE DIDN'T WEAR A COLLAR BUT HAD THE RIGHT DOCUMENTATION. HIS CHURCH WAS IN CLINTON NORTHWEST OF POUGHKEEPSIE. WAS HE MARRIED? RICKIE HAD SHOOK HER HEAD IN CONSTEMATION WONDERING WHY THAT PARTICULAR QUESTION HAD ENTERED HER THOUGHTS BUT KEEPING HER VOICE AS LEVELED AS POSSIBLE SHE COULDN'T ARGGUE WITH HIS REASONING. EVERYONE HAD GONE OUT FOR LUNCH EXCEPT SUSAN. EVEN RICKIE HAD THOUGHT THE PLACE WAS DESCRTED WHEN SHE FIRST RETURNED.

SHE COULDN'T QUITE FORGIVE AN UNDERSTATED AUDACITY ON HIS PART WHICH MIGHT OR MIGHT NOT BE UNCONSCIOUS. "YOU DON'T LOOK ANYTHING LIKE A MINISTER" SHE SAID. "ACTUALLY I'M A MINISTER WHO'S BEEN COMMISSIONED AS A MISSIONARY. I'M TO CONTINUE MY MINISTRY AMONG THE GROWING HISPANICS AND MINORITY POPULATIONS IN THE AREA.

"I SERVE UNDER REVEREND ROLON PASTOR OF THE INTER-CHURCH COUNCIL OF NEW YORK BUT I DO SO AS PART OF THE DENOMINATIONS NATIONAL HISPANIC PLAN A PROGRAM OF THE BOARD OF WORLD WIDE MINISTRIES.

"AN IMPORTANT PART OF MY ROLE IS TO FIT IN WITH THESE PEOPLE WHO OFTEN SUFFER PARANOIA AND A BASIC MISTRUST OF THE SO CALLED AMERICANS. THAT'S WHY I LEAVE MY COLLAR AT HOME AND WEAR MY HAIR LIKE MANY OF THEIR OWN PEOPLE TO MAKE MYSELF MORE APPROACHABLE ESPECIALLY TO THEIR YOUTH POPULATION." HIS EXPLANATION MADE PERFECT SENSE SO SHE SAID "PLEASE SIT DOWN REVEREND I'M RICKIE TAYLOR."

LET ME CORRECT MYSELF I MENT TO SAY RICKIE VON HASE. IF YOU KNOW WHO I REALLY WAS YOU WOULDN'T WANT TO BE THE RECIPIENT OF MY LARGESSE BUT UNFORTUNATELY BECAUSE OF YOUR AFFILIATION

WITH A CHURCH YOU'RE NOT GOING TO GET THE OPPORTUNITY.

HE WAITED UNTILL SHE'D GONE BEHIND HER DESK AND THEN SHE FELT HIS UNSETTLING DIRECT GAZE LIKE A BEACON OF LIGHT TOO STRONG TO LOOK INTO FOR MORE THAN A FEW SECONDS AT A TIME.

"MY RECEPTIONIST IS IN THE HOSPITAL" SHE TOLD HIM. "THE YOUNG WOMAN WHO ANSWERS THE PHONE AND TOLD YOU TO COME IN THIS AFTERNOON DIDN'T REALIZE THAT THE TAYLOR FOUNDATION DOSEN'T FUND RELIGIOUS CAUSES NO MATTER WORTHY. IT'S A QUESTION OF LEGALITY NOT TO MENTION OF CONFLICT OF INTEREST."

HE LOUNGED BACK IN THE CHAIR WITH ELOQUENT GRACE. WITH HIS PALMS TOGETHER HE PRESSED HIS INDEX FINGERS AGAINST HIS LIPS AS IF HE WAS WEIGHING A HEAVY DECISION. "I'M NOT REPRESENTING THE CHURCH" HE FINALLY SAID. "I'VE COME FOR THE EXPRESS PURPOSE OF OBTAINING SIX-DIGIT FUNDS FOR A HIGHLY ILLEGAL EXPENSIVE OPERATION THAT WILL ONLY BENEFIT A FEW AND COULD CONCEIVABLY COULD SEND EVERYONE INVOLVED TO PRISON ESPECIALLY YOU AND ME BECAUSE YOU REPRESENT THE ALMIGHTY CORPORATE DOLLAR AND I REPRESENT THE ALMIGHTY SO I'M TALKING ABOUT A SERIOUS RISK" HE SAID QUIETLY. "DO YOU WANT ME TO GO ON?"

CHAPTER 32

JORDAN'S HOMEWORK.

JORDAN HAD DONE HIS HOMEWORK ON THE TAYLOR FAMILY AND LEARNED THAT RICKIE TAYLOR WAS THE ONLY DAUGTHER OF THE BILLIONAIRE BANKER ALEXANDER TAYLOR WHO RAN THE SHOW AT THE CHB. JORDAN'S RESEACH HAD PROVIDED HIM WITH A MUCH NEEDED PICTURE OF THE WOMEN WHO COULD MAKE THE FINANCIAL MIRACLE HAPPEN.

THOUGH STILL UNMARRIED THE SPOILED PAMPERED WEALTHY YOUNG WOMEN OF TWENTY-SEVEN HAD MANAGED TO STAY AWAY FROM ALCOHOL AND DRUGS. SHE HAD DISTINGUISHED HERSELF BY GRADUATING MAGNA CUM LAUDE FROM WELLMAN COLLEGE AND HAD AVOIDED PUBLIC SCANDAL OF ANY KIND. SHE AND HER BIG BRTHER TED HAD TRAVELED THE WORLD EXTENSIVELY. SHE THEN HAD PROSSESSED AN ADMIRABLE COMMAND OF FRENCH AND SPANISH AND THUS FAR DEVOTED HER TIME, TALENT AND CONSIDERBALE ENERGY TO FOUNDING AND MANAGING THE TAYLOR INTERNATIONAL CHARITABLE FOUNDATION OF THE CHB AND IT WAS ALL DO TO HER CREDIT AND WEALTHYNESS.

SEEING HER IN THE FLESH HE'D DISCOVERED THAT SHE HAD A TOUCH ME-NOT BLOND BEAUTY THAT WOULD THWART A MAN LESS CONIDENT AND HER EYES A SHADE OF BLUE HE'D ONCE SEEN IN THE CORALS LAGOON OF TAHITI.

OBSERVING HER BEHAVIOR FIRSTHAND HE HAD LEARNRD SOMETHING ELSE ABOUT HIS SISTER RICKIE. THE fact that she hadn't immediately cried out for help or run away when she found a total stranger had invaded her office led Jordan to believe she had a lot more courage than her appearance suggested.

During his time in the SEALS Jordan had learned to navigate on his own intuition and something no amount of training could give him. Right now that gut instinct had him counting on her intellectual curiosity and moral fiber. He counted on her to think twice before she told him to get out of her office.

On some personal level he didn't understand quite apart from the despearate nature of his mission he found himself hoping she wouldn't show him the door just yet. The longer she waited to speak the better his chances were.

At last she flashed him a smile one that didn't reach her eyes. "Your approach wins hands down for originality. I assume you can make all this look good on paper." "You think I would approached you if I couldn't?" She then sat back in her chair which was at her desk. Through narrowed eyes she watched him speculatively. "I'm not sure what I think. So tell me what this highly illegal expensive operation is all about."

She's toying with you Browning so lets see if you can wipe that self-satisfide expression from her lovely face. "Briefly it's an effort to combat genocide in another part of the globe." He'd figured that would elicit a response of sorts but he'd never expected to see the blood literally drain from her face.

WHAT THE HELL? "MS. TAYLOR?" WHEN SHE DIDN'T ANSWER HIM HE HAD SPRANG FROM HIS CHAIR AND CAME AROUND TO HER SIDE CROUCHING DOWN BESIDE HER. HE THEN PUT A HAND ON HER FOREHEAD TO SEE IF SHE HAD A FEVER. SHE HAD FLET CLAMMY ALL OVER HER FOREHEAD. "YOU'RE ILL WHAT CAN I DO?" SHE TRIED TO MOISTEN HER LIPS BUT EVEN THAT LITTLE EFFORT SEEMED TOO DIFFICULT FOR HER. "I'LL BE ALL RIGHT IN A MINUTE." HE THEN ROSE TO HIS FULL HEIGHT. "LET ME BRING YOU SOME WATER." "NO!" SHE CRIED SOFTLY. "I'D ONLY THROW IT UP." SHE WHISPERED SOMETHING ABOUT IT NOT BEING HIS CONCERN. "IT IS NOW." HE SAID BACK TO HER. "IF YOU MUST KNOW I ALWAYS GOT THIS WAY WHEN I SUFFER FROM JET LAG. THE NAUSEA IS PASSING PLEASE SIT DOWN IN THE CHAIR REVEREND." HE DIDN'T BUY HER EXPLANATION BUT FINALLY DID AS SHE ASKED. "YOUR RECEPTIONIST SAID YOU'D JUST RETURNED FROM AUSTRALIA." "YES AND IT WAS A LONG FLIGHT." "THEN YOU OUGHT TO BE HOME IN BED." "BED WOULD BE EXACTLY THE WRONG PLACE FOR ME?" SHE MUTTERED SOUNDING FAR AWAY AT THAT INSTANT THAT JORDAN WANTED TO GET INSIDE HER MIND AND HE WANTED TO KNOW HER TO FIND OUT WHAT WAS GOING ON WITH HER. HE KNEW DAM WELL IT DIDN'T HAVE ANYTHING TO DO WITH JET LAG.

"I'D ONLY LAY THERE AND WORRY ABOUT THE WORK PILED ON UP ON MY DESK." SHE EXPLAINED QUIETLY. WITHOUT LOOKING AT HIM SHE SAID "YOU WERE TALKING ABOUT GENOCIDE IN ANOTHER PART OF THE WORLD REVEREND. IF YOU WERE REFERRING TO NORTHERN AFRICA OR BOSNIA I'VE BEEN INUNDATED WITH HUNDREDS MAYBE THOUSANDS OF PETITIONS BY WELL MEANING GROUPS BUT THESE AREAS ARE POLITICAL HOT SPOTS OUR FOUNDATION IS BARRED FROM ACCESSING."

"ANYTIME THERE'S AN ATTACK BY ONE FACTION AGAINST ANOTHER IT GETS POLITICAL MS. TAYLOR" HE interjected but that doesn't have to prevent us from finding ways to respond to the suffering of the innocent."

Her eyes flashed blue fire as her gaze lifted to his. "It does when the President of the United States himself asked me face-to—face for my cooperation when my father and I were invited to lunch at the White House months ago." He knew about the lunch because just this morning he'd seen the newsclippings in a file at the local newspaper archives. Of course the article centered on her father's talks with the President but the three of them had been photographed together. He had the impression she was telling the truth.

"So are you implying that if you weren't honorbound to accede to pressure put on by the President himself you'd be willing to cooperate?" At this point she'd propped her elbows on the desk so that her gently rounded chin rested on her clasped hands. He noticed she wasn't quite as pale as before this means the ice princess has thawed out a little bit.

He wondered what she'd be like if she thawed out all the way then chastised himself for not concentrating on what was important here. She didn't appear to be having the same trouble indeed but she didn't have any problem at all meeting his gaze with a level one of her own. "Judging by your question you're implying that whatever is you want would be in a blatant disregard of foreign policy."

She's no one's fool Browning. "That's right." Taking another calculated risk he got to his feet and reached into his back pocket for a paper.

"UNFORTUNATELY IF I STAY MUCH LONGER I'LL BE LATE TAKING CARE OF SOME IMPORTANT MISSIONARY BUSINESS BUT BEFORE I GO I'M GOING TO LEAVE YOU WITH THIS." HE THEN DROPPED THE PAPER ON HER DESK.

"I HOPE YOU'LL READ IT AND KEEP IT AS LONG AS YOU NEED. WHEN YOU'RE THROUGH THERE ARE MORE DOCUMENTS WHERE THAT ONE CAME FROM. YOU SHOULD UNDERSTAND THAT THIS IS A TRANSLATION. THE AUTHOR IS A PRIEST WHO'S BEEN AMASSING HIS OWN DATA FOR YEARS AND DON'T ASK HOW I CAME TO BE IN POSSESSION OF IT. I'M NOT AT THE LIBERTY TO DIVULGE THAT EVEN TO YOU. I'LL BE IN TOUCH."

IN A FEW SWIFT STRIDES HE WAS AT THE DOOR ANXIOUS TO BE FAR AWAY BEFORE SHE COULD CALL HIM BACK AND TELL HIM HE'D WASTED HIS TIME.

STONEY WAS RELYING ON HIM TO PULL THIS OFF. EVERYTHING ABOUT THEIR OPERATION DEPENDED ON MONEY BUT THOUGH HE COULD KEEP ASKING FOR SMALL DONATIONS HERE AND THERE NICKLE AND DIMMING PEOPLE TO DEATH OVER THE YEARS RICKIE TAYLOR HAD THE POWER AND THE MONEY TO GRANT THEIR WISH TODAY.

HE WOULDN'T HAD LEFT SUCH DAMMING EVIDENCE IN HER HANDS IF HE DIDN'T BELIEVE SHE HAD THE WISDOM TO ACT ON WHAT SHE HAD UNDERSTOOD.

HIS HANDS GRIPPED THE HANDLE OF HIS CAR DOOR TIGHTLY. I HAVE TO SEE HER AGAIN.

RICKIE WAS STILL ATTEMPTING TO GET OVER THE FEELING OF HAVING BEEN CAUGHT UP IN A TORNADO AND ABRUPTLY SET DOWN AGAIN IN A STRANGE LAND WHEN HER TEMP INTERRUPTED HER CHAOTIC THOUGHTS. "MS. TAYLOR?" "YES SUSAN?" "HOW DID THAT MAN GET

IN?" RICKIE DECIDED TO BE KIND. "I HAVE NO IDEA I THOUGHT YOU SENT HIM IN." "NO I DIDN'T BUT GUESS WHAT? THE REVERNED NEVER SHOWED UP." "THAT WAS THE REVEREND."

"OH SO I GUESS THAT MEANS I DON'T HAVE TO CALL BART DOWN IN ACCOUNTING AFTER ALL." "NO I GUESS YOU DON'T." "THANK GOODNESS." PEGGY PLEASE COME BACK SOON. "YOU'RE DOING FINE SUSAN. WHEN THE PHONE RINGS JUST KEEP TAKING MESSAGES. I'LL CALL EVERYONE BACK LATER." "SURE MS. TAYLOR NO PROBLEM."

AS SOON AS SHE'D SHUT THE DOOR RICKIE REACHED FOR THE PAPER THAT THE REVERNED PUT ON HER DESK AND SHE UNFOLDED IT. THE TEXT HAD BEEN WRITTEN LONGHAND IN SPANISH. SHE BLINKED HER EYES TWICE. HOW DID THE REVEREND KNOW SHE COULD READ IT? UNLESS HE ASSUMED SHE'D FIND SOMEONE TO TRANSLATE IT FOR HER.

NO HE MADE IT CLEAR THIS PAPER WAS FOR HER EYES ONLY AND COMPELLED BY AN UNKNOWN FORCE SHE TURNED ON HER DESK LIGHT AND BEGAN TO READ THE LETTER.

AT THE PRESENT WRITING I GATHERED CONCLUSIVE EVIDENCE THAT THE PEACEFUL FOREST TRIBES PARTICULARLY THE ACHE INDIANS AMONG WHOM I'VE WORKED MANY YEARS ARE BEING KILLED OFF EXTERMINATED IF YOU WILL IN A SYSTEMATIC MANNER THAT IS THE DIRECT RESULT OF GENOCIDAL POLICIES OF EXISTING GOVERNMENT.

THESE TRIBES ARE ON THE VARGE OF BECOMING EXTINCT BUT BY THE TURN OF THE CENTURY THEIR POPULATION WAS IN THE THOUSANDS AND NOW FEWER THEN FIVE HUNDRED.

ONNCE THEY WERE A GREAT RACE WHOSE FOREFATHERS CAME TO THIS LAND MANY CENTURIES AGO. NOW ANY SURVIVORS OF THESE MANHUNTS ARE FORCED ONTO CRUDE RESERVATIONS AND ABUSED. THE YOUNG GIRLS ARE SOLD INTO SLAVERY, RAPE AND MURDERED.

THIS IS WHOLESALE SLAUGHTER AND THE POWERS IN COMMAND CONSIDER THE ACHE AN OBSTACLE TO THE ECONOMIC DEVELOPMENT OF THE STATE IF YOU CAN IMAGINE. SUCH EVIL GOES AGAINST THE LAWS OF GOD NOT TO MENTION THE INALIENABLE RIGHTS OF HUMAN LIFE! I APPEAL TO YOU TO USE YOUR INFLUENCE TO HELP STOP THIS MASS MURDERERS.

AT LAST RICKIE PUT THE PAPER DOWN MID-SENTENCE TRYING TO SEPARTE THESE FACTS FROM THE HISTORY LESSON SHE'D BEEN FORCED TO LIVE AT THE COLLEGE OF THE WESTCHESTER YAD VANSHEM BUT THEY MIXED TOGETHER IN ONE HORRIFIC ETERNAL ROUND.

NEEDING ANSWERS SHE TURNED TO HER COMPUTER AND LOGGED ON TO THE INTERNET. SHE THEN TYPED IN "ACHE INDIANS" TO SEE WHAT WOULD COME UP. I WONDER WHERE DO YOU LIVE? SPAIN? MEXICO? OR SOUTH AMERICA? COME ON YOU DAM COMPUTER!

SOON SHE HAD READ "PROJECT FOR WORLD INDIGENOUS STUDIES. THE PROJECT RUNS ENTIRELY ON GRANTS AND PRIVATE DONATIONS." SO RICKIE SCROWLLED DOWN THE ARTICLE SOMEMORE AND FOUND MORE STUFF ABOUT THE ACHE INDIANS. "INDIGENOUS IS A TERM APPLIED TO PEOPLE WHO DESCEND FROM THE EARLIEST KNOW POPULATION OF SPECIFIED AREA AND THY GENERALLY HAVE LITTLE INFLUENCE WITHIN THE GOVERNMENT OF THE NATIONS IN WHICH THEY LIVE."

SHE KEPT UP HER SEARCH STAGGERED BY THE DOCUMENTATION OF GENOCIDE AGAINST THE INDIANS

OF SOUTH AMERICA. SHE THEN HAD SCANNED THE STATISTICS OF EIGHTY TRIBES OF BRAZIL SPECIFICALLY THE YANOMAMO AND SURUI WHICH HAD BEEN VIRTUALLY WIPED OUT OVER THE PAST FIFTY YEARS.

MORE WHOLESALE SLAUGHTER HAD OCCURRED IN GUATEMALA AND COLOMBIA AMONG THE CUIVA. FARTHER DOWN HER EYES CAUGHT SIGHT OF THE NAME ACHE. "THE INTERNATIONAL LEAGUE FOR HUMAN RIGHTS HAS A DETAILED REPORT OF PARAGUAYAN GOVERNMENT."

PARAGUAY? SHE SAID AS RICKIE'S HEARTBEAT ROSE UP INTO HER THROAT. "THE PARAGUAYAN GOVERNMENT'S INVOLVEMENT IN THE SYSTEMATIC EXTERMINATION OF THE ACHE INDIANS THROUGH TORTURE STARVATION AND SLAVERY OF THE 2,500 ACHE INDIANS ESTIMATED TO EXIST IN 1962 FEWER THEN 400 HUNDRED REMAIN TODAY."

ON A GROAN SHE LOGGED OFF THE INTERNET BURYING HER FACE INTO HER HANDS. PARAGUAY A LAND WHOSE GOVERNMENT CONDONED EVIL AND A KNOWN GRTHERING PLACE FOR POLITICAL CRIMINALS LIKE NAZIS.

IF THE RUMORS WERE REALLY TURE AND VON HASE HAD FLED THERE FOR ASYLUM WHAT BETTER PLACE FOR HIM TO TURN TO? HARDLY ABLE TO BREATHE FROM THE TUMULT OF EMOTIONS RACKING HER BODY SHE CALLED HER BROTHER ON HIS CELLPHONE AND WHEN HE DIDN'T ANSWER SHE THEN CALLED HIS OFFICE AND WAS FORCED TO RUN THE GAMUT OF SECRETARIES TO LOCATE HIM. FINALLY SHE HAD HEARD HIS VOICE ON THE OTHER END OF THE LINE.

"RICKIE?" "THANK HEAVENS YOU'RE STILL THERE! WHERE'S YOUR CELLPHONE? "I FORGOT IT IN THE MY CAR. WHAT'S WRONG YOU SOUND STRANGE?" "I FEEL STRANGE TOO BUT LISTEN TED, DAVID SOLOMON HAS LEFT SEVERAL

MESSAGES AT MY OFFICE AND AT MY APARTMENT BUT I HAVEN'T CALLED HIM BACK YET.

I'M PRETTY SURE IT MEANS SOMETHINGS WRONG. "I KNOW EXACTLY WHAT IT MEANS." TED'S VOICE WAS BLEAK. "DEBORAH GOT MY LITTLE LETTER. SHE ALSO LEFT A HALF DOZEN MESSAGES WITH MY SECRETARY ALREADY." SAID RICKIE.

RICKIE'S EYES FILLED WITH TEARS AS SHE SAID "I'M SO SORRY" SHE WHISPERED. HE MADE A MUFFLED SOUND THEN HE SAID "RICKIE I CAN TELL THERE'S SOMETHING ELSE ON YOUR MIND. WHAT IS IT?" SHE TOOK A DEEP BREATH AND THEN SHE SAID "I DON'T KNOW WHERE TO START."

"WHERE ARE YOU?" SAID TED. "AT MY OFFICE." SAID RICKIE. "STAY THERE I'M COMING OVER" TED SAID. "BRING BERNARD WITH YOU." SAID RICKIE. "OKAY SAID TED" I WILL BRING BERNARD WITH ME. SEE YOU IN A HALF HOUR RICKIE. OKAY SAID RICKIE AND BECAREFUL DRIVING. I WILL SAID TED.

AFTER TED AND BERNARD GOT TO RICKIE'S OFFICE THERE WAS A BRIEF SILENCE AND THEN TED ASKED "WHAT'S GOING ON?" SO AT LUNCH TED, BERNARD AND RICKIE MADE A DECISION TO HIRE A MAN WHO COULD GO TO PARAGUAY AND TRACK DOWN THEIR GRANDFATHER IF HE WAS THERE ALL THAT REMAINED WAS TO FIND THE RIGHT BOUNTY HUNTER.

IN ALL LIKELIHOOD THE MAN THEY NEEDED WOULD BE A MERCENARY WHO HAD FOUGHT IN SOUTH AMERICA AND WHO SPOKE THE NATIVE LANGUAGES AND WAS TRAINED IN GUERILLA-WARFARE TACTICS BUT THE LARGER-THEN-LIFE IMAGE OF REVEREND JORDAN BROWNING WHO HAD INVADED HER PRIVATE OFFICE WITHOUT PERMISSION SWAM BEFORE HER DOMINATING HER VISION. THE VERY NATURE OF HIS UNORTHODOX REQUEST PLUS THE FACT that he knew a great deal more about her than she knew about him had led her to believe there was more to this "missionary" than met the eye. "Ted I think I may have the perfect person to hunt down are grandfather Von Hase."

At a quarter after seven that evening Jordan turned onto the access road and saw the Cessna coming in at an angle. The timing couldn't have been more perfect because when the propellers stopped Stoney he had jumped down from the wing waving a piece of paper high in the air. A smile wreathed on his face. "Throckmorton's pulled through and got paid for that last shipment of copper wiring. One thousand nine hundred and seventy big ones and that's not bad for only three hours of work."

Jordan locked the car door and walked toward him. "That's the best news I've heard all day." "How come I don't like the sound of that?" Stoney stood at the end of the driveway in the enervating heat brushing the perspiration off his forehead. Jordan's comment had chased his smile away "Maybe because I had to play this one on a hunch and now I'm not sure I did the right thing."

"I'll take your hunch over another person's conviction any day of the week!" His friend said loyally.

"You're a fool Stoney." "I know my ex-wife used to inform me of that on a daily basis. Now tell me what happened and don't leave anything out. Weren't you able to meet the head honcho after all?"

Just recalling the image of Ms. Rickie Taylor and her heart—shaped mouth incongruously provocative in the icy beauty of the face Jordan briefly closed his eyes and then he said "I met her." "The head honcho is a her?" "That's right but the most important thing that it's Ms. Rickie Taylor herself who's going to be in charge." Stoney whistled.

"From what I learned at thenewspaper the morning she was the one responsible for setting up the foundation in the first place."

"I've seen pictures of her." Jordan flashed Stoney a frank little glance. "She looks like some babe." She has hot blue pools for eyes Stoney said. If you got to close you could get scorched by them.

"Jordan?" Stoney said out loud but Jordan didn't hear him and Jordan started for the office. "She's as cool as steel and just as hard" he said over his shoulder. "You didn't answer my question." "I didn't hear you ask it." "You know dam well what I meant." "Don't even think what you're thinking Stoney." Said Jordan.

"So you thinking what I though you were thinking" Stoney had baited him. Mary's head bobbed up when they entered the office. "Am I ever glad to see you boss! This phone's been ringing off the hook. There's a bunch of messages on your desk. At the rate of business is picking up I'm going to put in for a salary."

While he heard Stoney making sounds from his office Jordan leaned over the counter. "Anything for me Mary?" She was drinking another black-berry soda pop. "Yep" she said and she came out with the mail. "You're supposed to call Reverend Rolon on the double quickly. He said he'd be at the church

OR THE LITTLE RECTORY." SHE PLACED THE PHONE WHERE HE COULD REACH IT.

AFTER THANKING HER HE PUNCHED IN THE RECTORY NUMBER AND IT WAS A LUCKY GUESS BECAUSE AFTER ONE RING HE HEARD ROLON'S SOFT VOICE. JORDAN IDENTIFIED HIMSELF THEN ASKED ABOUT THE REASON FOR THE CALL.

"ABOUT AN HOUR AGO SOMEONE PHONED HERE ASKING FOR YOU." NOBODY IN THE SEALS KNOWS WHERE I AM OR HOW TO REACH ME. NOT YET AND NO ONE COULD TRACE ME TO THE CHURCH UNLESS . . . ."

HE STARTED TO GET A SUFFOCATING FEELING IN HIS CHEST. "DID THIS PERSON LEAVE A NAME?" "NO ONLY A NUMBER." "WAS IT A WOMEN OR A MAN?" "I'M NOT SURE. MY SECRETARY SAID YOU WERE OUT ON A MISSIONARY BUSINESS AND TOOK THE MESSAGE BEFORE SHE WENT TO HER CAR TO GO HOME. "DO YOU WANT ME TO GIVE YOU THE NUMBER NOW?" "YES HE SAID AS HE FORGOT TO KEEP THE EXCITEMENT OUT OF HIS VOICE.

AFTER GIVING THE NUMBER TO HIM ROLON SAID "ANY IDEA WHO IT IS?" "YES." "I ASSUME IT'S GOOD NEWS." "I HOPE SO YOU KEEP THE FAITH OK REVEREND." JORDAN PLACED THE RECEIVER ON THE HOOK AND CALLED TO STONEY WHO CAME RUNNING. "WHAT'S UP?" "MAYBE GOD'S ON ARE SIDE AFTER ALL."

STONEY'S GRAY QUICKENED. "WAS SHE SUPPOSED TO CALL YO IF SHE WAS INTERESTED?" "NO I TOLD HER SHE WOULD BE HEARING FROM ME." "THEN HOW DID SHE KNOW TO PHONE YOU AT THE CHURCH?"

"I HAD TO SHOW HER MY CREDETIALS. EVIDENTLY SHE SAW ENOUGH TO LOOK UP THE NUMBER IN THE DIRECTORY." "THAT MEANS SHE HAD SWALLOWED THE

BAIT." JORDAN FROWNED AS HE SAID "I'LL BE DAMED IF I KNOW WHY." "MAYBE SHE'S MORE INTERESTED IN YOU STONEY SAID TO THE REVEREND. "THAT'S INPOSSIBLE COME ON" SAID THE REVEREND AS HE POKED STONEY IN THE RIBS WITH HIS ELBOW.

"NO TRUST ME THAT'S NOT THE REASON" HE SAID AS HE SHOOK HIS HEAD. "ALL RIGHT I TRUST YOU" SAID STONEY. HE THEN SCRATCHED THE SIDE OF HIS HEAD. "HELL JORDAN WHO CARES WHY YOU'VE MADE HER CURIOUS?" STONEY SAID. "WE SHOULD BE GETTING DOWN ON OUR KNEES IN GRATITUDE THAT SOMEONE WITH HER KIND OF MONEY IS FINALLY WILLING TO LISTEN TO US. CALL HER BACK AS SOON AS WE LAND OK SAID STONEY. IF SHE WANTS TO MEET WITH US HAVE HER COME HERE SO WE CAN SHOW HER THE SETUP."

WHY THE HESITATION BROWNING? YOU'VE TAKEN RISKS BEFORE. SO WHY IS THIS DIFFERENT? WHAT ARE YOU REALLY AFRAID OF? JORDAN DIDN'T WANT TO KNOW THE ANSWER TO THAT LAST QUESTION.

"SHALL I PHONE AND ARRANGE A MEETING WITH HER?" STONEY'S QUESTION BROUGHT HIM UP SHORT. "NO NOT LET BECAUSE I'M GOING BACK TO THE HUT TO TAKE A SHOWER AND THEN I'LL MAKE THE CALL FROM THERE." "WHATEVER WORKS RIGHT? SAID STONEY. "RIGHT BOSS." JORDAN SAID OUT LOUD.

RICKIE STEPPED OUT OF THE SHOWER AND PUT ON HER BATHROBE. IT WAS ONLY EIGHT-THIRTY PM AND THAT WAS WAY TOO EARLY TO GO TO BED BUT ANYWAYS SHE WAS TOO KEYED UP FROM HER MEETING WITH TED AND BERNARD TO SETTLE DOWN TO ANYTHING AS IMPOSSIBLE AS A GOOD NIGHT'S SLEEP.

SHE SHOULD PHONE DAVID NOW BUT EVERYTIME SHE REACHED FOR THE RECEIVER SHE THOUGHT BETTER OF

IT FOR FEAR REVEREND BROWNING MIGHT PHONE BUT ON THE OTHER HAND SHE DID HAVE CALL WAITING BUT SHE COULDN'T PUT DAVID ON HOLD NOT WHEN IT WAS LONG DISTANCE. BE HONEST RECKIE YOU DIDN'T WANT TO DEAL WITH DAVID BECAUSE YOU CAN'T COMFORT HIM ESPECIALLY WHERE DEBORAH AND TED ARE CONCERNED AND YOU HAVE NO ANSWERS NOTHING AT ALL.

TED WANTED TO COME BACK TO THE APARTMENT WITH HER SO SHE WOULDN'T HAVE TO WAIT ALONE. RICKIE HAD BEEN TEMPTED TO TAKE HIM UP ON HIS OFFER BUT AT THE LAST SECOND SHE'D TOLD HIM SHE PREFERRED TO BE BY HERSELF.

SINCE THEY'D ALWAYS SHARED EVERYTHING ALL THEIR THOUGHTS AND FEELINGS HER DECISION HADN'T MADE SENSE TED AND IN ALL HONESTY IT DIDN'T MAKE SENSE TO HER EITHER.

BERNARD ATTRIBUTED HER BEHAVIOR TO THE FACT THAT SHE WAS STILL IN SHOCK AND STILL TRYING TO COPE WITH AN VERY OVERWHELMING BURDEN. MAYBE HE WAS RIGHT BUT THE MERE THOUGHT OF REVEREND BROWNING DISTURBED HER IN NEW DIFFERENT WAYS SHE DIDN'T UNDERSTAND AND COULDN'T TALK ABOUT NOT EVEN WITH TED.

JORDAN BROWNING WAS THE ANTITHESIS OF THE BOUNTY-HUNTER TYPE SHE HAD ALWAYS ENVISIONED. SHE HAD NO IDEA WHAT KIND OF DESPERATION HAD DRIVEN HIM TO COME TO HER OFFICE AHEAD OF TIME AND TAKE ADVANTAGE OF THE SITUATION TO PLEAD HIS CASE. SO WHY DID HE HAVE A PERSONAL STAKE IN THE LIVES OF A FEW HUNDRED TRAGIC SOULS WHOSE BONDAGE COULD ONLY END IN DEATH?

DID HE LOVE GOD SO MUCH THAT HE CARED NOTHING FOR HIS OWN LIFE? HOW DID A MAN WITH SO MUCH

PHYSICAL APPEAL FORGET THE FLESH IN PREFERENCE FOR THE SPIRITUAL LIFE?

EVEN MORE PUZZLING WAS HIS PROPITIOUS ARRIVAL AT A MOMENT WHEN SHE, TED AND BERNARD WERE DESPERATE TO FIND SOMEONE TO CARRY OUT A DANGEROUS MISSION FOR THEM.

DID THEY HAVE THE MORAL RIGHT TO ASK THAT OF ANY MAN EVEN IF THEY WERE OFFERING HIM A KING'S RANSOM? ESPECIALLY WHEN THEY WERE KEEPING THE SOURCE OF THAT TAINTED RANSOM AND THEIR GRANDFATHER'S TRUE IDENTITY A SECRET?

IF THE REVEREND KNEW IT WAS VON HASE HE WOULD REFUSED THEIR OFFER NO MATTER HOW MUCH MONEY THEY WERE WILLING TO GIVE TO HIM. RICKIE WASN'T AT ALL SURE IF SHE COULD GO THROUGH WITH THIS ANYMORE. MAYBE HE WOULDN'T CALL HER BACK AND MAYBE SHE DIDN'T WANT HIM TO. YES I DO WANT HIM TO CALL ME BACK BUT NOT DISCUSS BUSINESS.

YOU'VE LOST YOUR MIND RICKIE TAYLOR VON HASE. EVEN IF HE WANTED TO GET MARRY A MAN LIKE THAT COULD NEVER LOVE YOU. IN FACT HE WOULD HAVE EVERY RIGHT TO DAM YOUR SOUL TO HELL. MY SOUL IS ALREADY DAMED TO HELL BECAUSE OF WHO I AM.

SHE FELL DOWN ON HER BED CHOKING DOWN A SOB AT THAT PRECISE MOMENT THE PHONE RANG. RICKIE JERKED TO A SITTING POSITION ON HER BED. IT COULD BE ANYBODY SHE SAID TO HERSELF. SOME OF HER MARRIED GIRLFIRENDS KNEW SHE WAS BACK FROM AUSTRALIA. HER PARENTS COULD BE CALLING FROM THEIR NORWEGIAN CRUISE TRIP.

BY THE FOURTH RING SHE EXTENDED A TREMBLING HAND TO PICK UP THE RECEIVER. "HELLO?" SHE SAID.

Even to her own ears her voice sounded too emotional.

"Good evening Ms. Taylor." She shivered uncontrollably. "Good evening." There was a deafening pause. "You're not having another nausea spell are you?" No I'm something much worse but there's no name for it.

"I'm fine Reverend." "Then I'm assuming from your earlier phone call that you read the material I left you and are willing to hear my proposal." He said. "Yes she said." "When?" His mannr was too direct for her that's she couldn't think fast enough so she said the first thing that came to her mind "I'm free tomorrow afternoon."

"I thought you'd put me off for at least a week" he said dryly. She got to her feet absently torturing the phone cord. "When someone puts a worthy petition before me I try to attend to it straight away." "That's very admirable of you."

He was saying all the right words but she sensed a certain irony in his tone of voice. Warning bells prompted her to proceed with caution. "Can you come to my office at two?" She asked. "I have a better suggestion the Reverend said. Why don't I pick you up at two o'clock and drive you to the facility which is in dire need of financial help? You can meet the staff, look around and ask questions."

She blinked her eyes quickly because they were sore. "What does this facility have to do with the plight of the Ache Indians of Paraguay?" "Everything." Said the Reverend. The emotion in his voice robbed her legs of strength. Rickie sank down on her bed again.

"IT'S A FORTY-FIVE MINUTE DRIVE FROM YOUR OFFICE IF YOU'D PREFER TO MEET ME THERE INSTEAD I'LL BE HAPPY TO GIVE YOU THE ADRESS. THE ONLY REASON I DIDN'T SUGGEST IT IN THE FIRST PLACE IS BECAUSE IT'S EASY TO MISS."

DON'T LET HIM PICK YOU UP YOU GO MEET HIM THERE WHEREVER "THERE" IS OK. "FROM YOUR HESITATION I WONDER IF YOU'RE NOT NERVOUS AT THE THOUGHT OF BEING ALONE WITH HIM. LET ME ALLAY YOUR FEARS MS. TAYLOR THE REVEREND CELIBATE" SAID STONEY.

INEXPLICABLY HER GRAY WORLD DARKENED. "SO AM I REVEREND" SINCE I FOUNDING OUT I'M A VON HASE I WOLDN'T DREAM OF INFLICTING MY INHERITANCE OF MY FAMILY'S SINS ON ANYONE ELSE. SO FAR THERE'S BEEN NO GREAT LOVE IN MY LIFE AND I PLAN TO KEEK IT THAT WAY. "I WOULD APPRECIATE THE RIDE." "GOOD SAID THE REVEREND." I'LL BE AT YOUR OFFICE AT TWO O'CLOCK PM PROVIDED MY "72 FORD DOESN'T FAIL ME."

"SEVENTY-TWO WAS A GOOD YEAR FOR THE FORD COMPANY. I'LL BE WAITING OUT IN FRONT OF MY OFFICE." "HAVE YOU EVER RIDDEN IN A "72" FORD CAR BEFORE?" "LOTS OF TIMES." THE COOK AT OUR PLACE ON THE HUDSON WAS MORE MY MOTHER THEN MY OWN MOTHER. MY MOM WOULDN'T DRIVE ANYTHING BUT HER "72" FORD AND SHE TOOK ME AND MY BROTHER EVERYWHERE IN IT. SHE SAID TO THE REVEREND. "TELL ME REVEREND BEFORE YOU WERE A REVEREND AND GAVE UP ALL WORLDLY GOODS WHAT KIND OF CAR DRIVE?"

HIS LOW CHUCKLE WAS LIKE A BURST OF SUNSHINE PERMEATING HER WITH UNEXPECTED WARMTH. "A RESTORED CORVETTE" THE REVEREND SAID OUT LOUD.

"TED ALWAYS WANTED ON OF THOSE BUT HE HAD TO SETTLE FOR THE LAMBORGHINI UNCLE JOHN GAVE HIM FOR HIS EIGHTEENTH BIRTHDAY."

"TED WHO?" I DON'T THINK I KNOW HIM SAID THE REVEREND. "WHY PRETEND YOU DON'T KNOW HE'S MY BROTHER? IF YOUR SOURCES COULD TELL YOU I SPEAK SPANISH YOU WOULD CERTAINLY KNOW ABOUT MY BIG BROTHER."

"YOUR RIGHT I HAVE LEARNED WHAT I COULD ABOUT YOU BEFORE COMING TO YOUR OFFICE TODAY." "CORRECTION REVEREND YOU THOUGHT YOU'D LEARNED EVERYTHING ABOUT ME.

"I WOULD HAVE DONE THE SAME THING IF I'D BEEN IN YOUR SHOES BUT UNFORTUNATELY FOR ME I'M AT A COMPLETE DISAVANTAGE WHERE YOUR BACKGROUND IS CONCERNED BUT I'M ASSUMING YOUR LITTLE AFFILIATION WITH CHURCH HAS MORE THAN COMPENSATED FOR ANY PAST SINS." "DON'T COUNT ON IT I'LL SEE YOU TOMORROW MS. TAYLOR."

JORDAN HUNG UP THE RECEIVER WONDERING IF RICKIE TAYLOR HAD A HIDDEN AGENDA. HE SHOULD HAVE BEEN GLAD THAT SHE'D AGREED TO CONSIDER HIS PETITION FOR FUNDS AND VISIT THE SITE. HUMAN LIVES HUNG IN THE BALANCE. HELL HE WAS VERY GLAD THAT SHE DECIDED TO DO THIS FOR HIM BUT BENEATH THAT EUPHORIA LURKED A PUZZLING CONCERN OVER THE EASE WITH WHICH HE'D ELICITED HER WILLINGNESS TO LOOK INTO HIS CASE LET ALONE HER DECISION TO MEET WITH HIM AS EARLY AS TOMORROW.

SEVERAL THING SIMPLY DIDN'T ADD UP THE LUDICROUS ASSERTION THAT SHE LED A CELIBATE LIFE BEING ONE OF THE THINGS BUT JORDAN DIDN'T BUY THAT ANY MORE THAN HE BOUGHT HER REASON FOR CALLING HIM IMMEDIATELY. SHE'D TAKEN THE TROUBLE TO LOOK UP THE OFFICE NUMBER OF THE PARISH HE USED FOR A FRONT IN THE ATTEMPT TO REACH HIM THIS QUICKLY HAD TO REVEAL SOME KIND OF DESPERATION.

IT WAS MORE THEN LIKELY THAT SHE HID BEHIND A CLAIM OF CELIBACY TO WARD OFF THE INEVITABLE STRING OF FORTUNE HUNTERS THAT ARE ATTRACTED TO HER MONEY AND LOOKS. FOR THAT VERY REASON HE'D TOLD HER HE WAS CELIBATE.

HE REFUSED TO JEPOPARDIZE HIS AND STONEY'S OPERATION BY RAISING SUPICIONS THAT DOWN THE ROAD HE WANTED MORE FROM HER THAN A CHARITABLE DONATION.

RELUCTANT TO DISCUSS HIS RESERVATIONS ABOUT MS. TAYLOR WITH STONEY WHO HAD ENOUGH ON HIS MIND BUILDING THEIR AIR-CARGO BUSINESS JORDAN SLIPPED OVER TO THE OTHER HUT TO SEE IF PERHAPS THE INTERNET WOULD GIVE HIM MORE INFORMATION ABOUT CHB.

HE WAS CURIOUS TO DISCOVER THE FULL EXTENT OF HER PHILANTHROPY AND HE ALSO THOUGHT HE WOULD DIVINE A CLUE AS TO WHY HIS CASE HAD SUDDENLY TAKEN PRECEDENCE OVER A PLETHORA OF NEEDY CAUSES FAR REMOVED FROM GOVERNMENTAL OR ECUMENICAL ISSUES AND FRANKLY HE WAS BAFFLED ABOUT IT BUT JUST A FEW MINTUES LATER HE'D TURNED THE COMPUTER ON AND FOUND THE CBH'S WEB SITE PAGE.

CBH STANDS FOR CHARITY BEGINS AT HOME. CBH IS A BIG HUGE NONGOVERNMENTAL AND NONRELIGIOUS CHARITABLE INSTITUTION FOUNDED IN 1989 BY MS. TAYLOR OF THE TAYLOR WORLD BANKING CORPORATION LOCATED IN POUGHKEEPSIE NEW YORK. THE FOLLOWING IS THE INSTITUTION'S MISSION STATEMENT.

"CBH IS DEDICATED TO INDIVIDUALIZING THE CONCEPT OF CHARITY TO MEET THE NEEDS OF THE MANY OR FAMILY AND THE COMMUNITY TO TEACH HIM OR HER THE WORK EITHIC TO HELP HIME OR HER BECOME A

RESPONSIBLE, CONTRIBUTING CITIZEN AND TO PROMOTE HIS OR HER ECONOMIC FREEDOM."

JORDAN WAS IMPRESSED UNTILL HE READ THE LAST PART OF THE STATEMENT. "TO PERPETUSTE THE SPIRIT OF COMPASSION UNTILL NO MAN OR WOMEN IS IN NEED ANYMORE." THAT WILL BE THE DAY HE THOUGHT BEFORE HIS GAZE DROPPED LOWER. CBH FUNDS HUNDREDS OF PROJECTS THROUGHOUT THE WROLD AND THE FOLLOWING MAPS SHOWS THE SITES.

HE LET OUT A LOW WHISTLE AS HE STUDIED THE CBH OUTLETS LOCATED IN THE U.S., CANADA, MEXICO, EUROPE, ASIA, AFRICA AND SOUTH AMERICA. SINCE MS. TAYLOR HAD JUST COME BACK FROM A TRIP TO AUSTRALIA HE PRESUMED AUSTRALIA WOULD BE THE NEXT CONTINENT ADDED TO THE IMPRESSIVE LIST TO OBTAIN MORE INFORMATION, E-MAIL OF FAX CBH AT THE FOLLOWING ADDRESSES.

FOR THE NEXT COUPLE OF HOURS JORDAN VISITED EVERY SITE HE COULD CLICK ON TO. HER PROJECTS COVERED EVERYTHING FROM FLYING ONE CRITICALLY ILL LITTLE BOYS FROM CALCUTTA INDIA INTO JOHNS HOPKINS IN MARYLAND FOR SPECIAL MEDICAL TREATMENT TO PRAYING FOR TEXTBOOKS PUBLISHED IN BRAILLE TO ASSIST THE BLIND IN GRADUATING FROM COLLEGE AND FROM SUPPLYING LOANS TO PEOPLE WIPED OUT BY BY NATURAL DISASTERS TO PROVIDING MATERIALS FOR SEVERELY HANDICAPPED INVENTORS WHO NEED FUNDING TO DEVELOP THEIR PRODUCTS AND APPLY FOR PATENTS.

EVERY PROJECT WAS UNIQUE WORTHY AND FOR EACH PROBLEM SHE DEALT WITH THERE WERE A THOUSAND MORE JUST LIKE IT WAITING FOR HER KIND OF HELP.

ONE PATTERN HE DID NOTICE WAS THAT SHE HAD MEANT WHAT SHE'D TOLD HIM EARLIER. CBH SHIED

AWAY FROM ALL RELIGIOUS GOVERNMENT AND MILITARY ARENAS. MORE THEN EVER HE REALIZED THAT HER INTERST IN HIS PROBLEM WAS NOT ONLY UNPRECEDENTED BUT IT WAS ALSO IN BLATANT VIOLATION OF HER OWN HARD-LINE POLICIES AND THE PLIGHT OF THE ACHE INDIANS STOOD AT THE DEAD CENTER OF DANGEROUSLY CONFLICTING MILITARY GOVERNMENT AND RELIGIOUS BOUNDARIES. QUESTION OF IF SHE HAD AN UNDERLYING REASON TO MEET WITH HIM.

CHAPTER 33

BEING EARLY

"MS. TAYLOR?" "YES SUSAN?" "THE REVEREND IS HERE TO SEE YOU." RICKIE'S HEART RACED FOR NO GOOD REASON. SHE GLANCED AT HER WATCH TO SEE WHAT TIME IT WAS. IT WAS ONE FORTY-FIVE THAT MENT THE REVEREND WAS FIFTEEN MINUTES EARLY. IT SHOLDN'T HAVE SURPRISED HER NOT AFTER HIS UNORTHODOX ENTRY YESTERDAY.

"TELL HIM I'LL BE THERE IN A MINUTE." "HE'S ALREADY GONE HE SAID HE WOULD WAIT FOR YOU IN HIS CAR OUT FRONT."

PART OF HER WAS RELIEVED SHE WOULDN'T HAVE AN AUDIENCE WHEN SHE FACED HIM AGAIN BUT ANOTHER PART STIRRED WITH RESENTMENT BECAUSE HE'D TAKEN CONTROL OF THE SITUATION BUT HE HAD CHOSEN TO LEAVE BEFORE SHE COULD SHOW HIM THAT HIS BEING A MAN MADE NO INPACT ON HER WHATSOEVER ORDAINED MINISTER OR NOT.

"THATNK YOU SUSAN." "UM THERE'S SOMETHING ELSE I HAVE TO TELL YOU" THE REVEREND TOLD ME TO TELL YOU TO TAKE YOUR TIME BECAUSE A BEAUTIFUL WOMEN USUALLY REQUIRES MORE LEEWAY" AND HE WANTED TO MAKE SOME URGENT PHONE CALLS ON HIS CELLPHONE WHILE HE WAS WAITING FOR YOU."

RICKIE'S EYE BROWS MET IN A FROWN BECAUSE THE REVEREND WAS GOING OUT OF HIS WAS TO PROVOKE A NEGATIVE REACTION. PERHAPS HE HAD A HISTORY OF attracting unwanted female interest and had learned that an offensive attack dampened the hopes of the most ardent admirer.

She couldn't understand why he'd tried that approach with her. She'd given him no signals she was interested. Rickie Von Hase had no right to the normal expectations of life.

In any case a few hours in her company would convince the Reverend that he had nothing to worry about where she was concerned. Muttering something unintelligible to Susan Rickie pushed away from the desk and reached for he purse and left her office and she was glad she was wearing a pair of old jeans and a white t-shirt as she left today. Her sneakers made no noise as she left the suite and rolled down in the gold elevator to the ground floor.

Once she stepped out of the revolving front door a wave of heat envelpoed her and making her doubly thankful she'd had decided to put her hair back in a ponytail. She then slipped on her sunglasses to cut down on the glare of the sun.

In all probability the vintage blue Ford parked a few steps away had no air-conditioning which would explain why the windows were rolled down. Well the Reverend wouldn't get any grief from her. When she opened the passenger door and slid into the car he turned off his cellphone and casted her a covert glance in the process and she noticed his faceial muscles tauten. Good are you ready to go now Ms. Taylor? "Yes she said to the Reverend." "Then off we go he said."

HE HADN'T PLANNED ON HER SHOWING UP SO SOON AND SHE WAS HAPPY TO HAVE PUT HIM IN A DISADVANGED HOWEVER SLIGHT. SHE FELT ABSURDLY PLEASED THAT HE'D OPTED TO WEAR JEANS AND A T-SHIRT TOO. OBVIOUSLY HE HADN'T EXPECTED THEIR CLOTHING TO MATCH BUT SHE NEVER WORE DESIGNER OUTFITS TO THE OFFICE NO MATTER HOW MUCH MONEY SHE WAS FALSELY PURPORTED TO SPEND ON HER NEW WARDROBE.

HE MERELY NODDED THEN HE STARTED THE ENGINE NUDGING THE CAR INTO THE AFTERNOON TRAFFIC. "I'M SORRY ABOUT THE WINDOWS BECAUSE IF I CLOSE THEM THE HEAT WILL STIFLE US." "NO PROBLEM SHE SAID. THIS IS MILD COMPARED TO THE TEMPERATURES IN EGYPT" SHE SAID CONVERSATIONALLY. "I'M NOT THAT KEEN ON REFRIGERATED AIR ANYWAY SO THAT'S A GOOD THING."

A LONG SILENCE FOLLOWED AS SHE FOUGHT TO KEEP HER EYES STRAIGHT AHEAD INSTEAD OF ALLOWING THEM TO WONDER OVER AT THE MAN BESIDE HER.

"YOU'VE BEEN EVEYWHERE HAVEN'T YOU?" HE ASKED UNEXPECTEDLY. "WELL I HAVEN'T BEEN TO ANTARCTICA YET BUT I'VE SEEN ENOUGH DEPRIVATION WORLDWIDE TO MAKE ME DECIDE TO GIVE AWAY MY INHERITANCE WHILE I'M STILL ALIVE. I THOUGHT IT MIGHT HELP ME SLEEP BETTER AT NIGHT BUT I'VE ACTUALLY DISCOVERED THAT'S NOT TRUE."

ONCE UPON A TIME I USED TO BE ABLE TO SLEEP THOUGH. WHEN HE DIDN'T SAY ANYTHING SHE FILLED IN THE SILENCE. "NOW THAT YOU KNOW MY LIFE STORY TELL ME WHY YOU'RE INTERESTED IN A HANDFUL OF INDIANS IN PARAGUAY WHEN THERE ARE DOZENS OF INDIGENOUS TRIBES IN BRAZIL AND GUATEMALA EQUALLY THREATENED WITH EXTINCTION."

"YOU'VE BEEN TO THOSE PLACES TOO RIGHT?" "I'VE SET UP FOUNDATIONS IN LIMA AND BUENOS AIRES BUT IF YOU MEAN AM I ACQUAINTED FIRSTHAND WITH THOSE AREAS AND THEIR PARTICULAR HORROR STORIES THEN NO I HAVEN'T.

"HOWEVER I CAN FIND OUT WHATEVER I NEED TO KNOW ON THE INTERNET BY CLICKING ON MOUSE. THE PLIGHT OF MILLIONS FLASHED ON TO THE COMPUTER SCREN. PICK YOUR CONTINENT OR YOUR COUNTRY AND WE WILL FIND OUT WHAT WE NEED TO KNOW. IT'S ALL THERE LIKE SQUALOR, REPRESSION, TORTUNE, ELIMINATION." SHE DIDN'T GLANCE AT HIM AS SHE SPOKE STILL GAZING OUT THE WINDOW.

"YOU'RE RIGHT" THE REVEREND SAID. "IT'S OBSECENE." THE EMOTION IN HIS VOICE CONVINCED HER THAT HE WAS COMPLETELY SINCERE.

A FEW MORE MILES AND THEY WILL BE OUT OF THE CITY LIMITS BUT IT HAD APPEARED THEY WERE HEADED INTO THE DENSELY FOLIATED COUNTRYSIDE. SHE FINALLY LOOKED AT HIM AND ASKED "I GATHER YOU'VE SPENT TIME IN PARAGUAY?" SHE ASKED THE REVEREND. "I HAVE BUT NOT AS A TOURIST." "THEN AS WHAT?" SHE ASKED. "I WENT AS A ORDAINED MINISTER." "REALLY?" SHE SAID. "YES." SAID THE REVEREND.

THE MONOSYLLABLES FALLING FROM HIS LIPS DROVE HER TO ANOTHER QUESTION. "A KIDNAPPED JOURNALIST WHO BECAME A HOSTAGE AND UNDERWENT A SOUL-CHANGING EXPERIENCE DID THAT CAUSE YOU TO TURN TO GOD?" "HELL NO."

SHE COULD TELL SHE WASN'T GOING TO GET ANYTHING MORE OUT OF HIM. DECIDING TO TRY A DIFFERENT TACKTIC SHE PULLED THE PAPER HE'D LEFT HER FROM HER PURSE. "WAS THIS GIVEN TO YOU PERSONALLY BY

THE PRIEST YOU MENTIONED?" "NO I OBTAINED COPIES THROUGH A MEMBER OF THE CATHOLIC UNDERGROUND. ALL THE PRIEST'S DOCUMENTS WERE WRITEN IN HIS NATIVE LANGUAGE THEN TRANSLATED INTO SPANISH. THE ORIGINALS ENDED UP IN THE HANDS OF THE ARCHBISHOP OF BRAZIL WHO WAS TRAVELING THROUGH PARAGUAY SEVERAL MONTHS AGO. HE IN TURN GAVE THEM TO THE POPE BUT THE CHURCH CAN'T DO ANYTHING."

"BUT OF COURSE NOT OFFICAILLY THE CATHOLIC CHURCH'S HANDS HAVE ALWAYS BEEN TIED" SAID THE REVEREND. UNOFFICIALLY HOWEVER MANY PRIESTS AND NUNS HAVE SACRIFICED THEIR OWN LIVES TO HELP IN THOSE LITTLE TORTURED CORNERS OF HUMANITY." SHE TOOK A FORTIFYING BREATH THEN SAID "SO YOU TOO HAVE DECIDED TO TAKE ACTION IN YOUR OWN WAY."

HIS BRONZED RIGHT HAND GRIPPED THE WHEEL TIGHTLY. THE REVEREND SAID "WITH THE RIGHT FUNDING I CAN DO ANYTHING." THE FACT THAT HE KNEW SO MUCH ABOUT THE PLIGHT OF THE NATIVES IN PARAGUAY LED HER TO BELIEVE THAT HER INSTINCTS ABOUT HIM HAD BEEN RIGHT AND THE REVEREND WAS THE RIGHT MAN TO CHASE DOWN HER GRANDFATHER IN EVIL PLACE.

"YOU CAN'T DO ANYTHING FOR THEM WITHIN THEIR OWN BORDERS YOU KNOW." "I KNOW." "THE ONLY WAY TO HELP THEM WOULD BE TO SMUGGLE THEM OUT AND REPATRIATE THEM IN ANOTHER COUNTRY."

"YES." "YOU'D HAVE TO ORGANIZE A MASSIVE UNDERGROUND TO ASSIST YOU. EVEN IF THAT WAS POSSIBLE TAKING THEM OUT OF A LANDLOCKED COUNTRY LIKE PARAGUAY WITH EQUALLY HOSTILE GOVERNMENTS AT EVERY BORDER WOULD BE SUICIDAL."

"I REALIZE THAT." "THE ONLY FESAIBLE WAY TO PROVIDE AN EXCAPE WOULD BE BY AIR AND THAT WOULD

MEAN INVADING ENEMY AIR-SPACE AND THEN THERE ARE PROBLEMS OF GETTING ILLEGALS INTO ANOTHER COUNTRY AND FINDING HOUSING FOR THEM, FEEDING THEM AND HIDING THEM FORM THE AUTHORITIES.

"IN SOLVING THAT PROBLEM YOU'D CREATED A NEW ONE. A GROUP OF PITIFUL REFGEES WITHOUT A HOME, ROOTS, DOCUMENTATION OR THE ENGLISH LANGUAGE SKILLS. ALL YOU'VE DONE IS EXCHANGE ONE HELL FOR ANOTHER."

HE GRIMACED AND SAID "YOUR CORRECT ON ALL COUNTS." SHE HAD THE FEELING THAT SHE WAS RUNNING FROM SOMETHING UPHILL YET LOSING ALTITUDE. "WHAT HAPPENED TO YOU IN PARAGUAY?"

"MY EYES WERE OPENED" AS WE REACHED A WOODED AREA SHE DIDN'T RECOGNIZE. SUDDENLY HE TURNED ONTO A SIDE ROAD THAT HAD NO SIGN. HE HAD BEEN RIGHT ABOUT THE LOCATION AND ON HER OWN SHE PROBABLY WOULDN'T HAVE FOUND WHATEVER IT WAS HE WANTED ME TO SEE OUT HERE.

"HOW LONG WERE YOU THERE?" "LONG ENOUGH" HE SAID. "WHAT DOES THAT MEAN EXACTLY MONTHS? YEARS?" "DES IT MATTER?" IT MATTERS A GREAT DEAL TO ME IF YOU'RE GOING TO HUNT DOWN MY GRANDFATHER.

"DID THE EXPERIENCE TURN YOU INTO A RELIGIOUS MAN?" "LET'S JUST SAY THAT CERTAIN KNOWLEDGE REARRANGED MY PRIORITIES."

RICKIE SHIVERED RELATING TO THAT STATEMENT MORE THAN HE COULD EVER IMAGINED. SHE FELT HIS EYES ON HER AGAIN. "ARE YOU FEELING SICK AGAIN?" THE REVEREND'S INSTINCTS WERE UNCANNY. "NO WHY DO YOU ASK?" "YOU'VE GONE PALE." THE REVEREND SAID. "IT MUST BE A TRICK OF LIGHT." SAID RICKIE.

Ignoring her comment he said "It's a good thing that we have arrived because a cold drink ought to help you get your color back into your face."

As he spoke she saw a runway followed by three Quonset huts and a hangar unexpectedly emerge out of a clearing and no sign of a plane. The place looked deserted however she did see an old pickup truck parked near the first hut.

In a remote spot like this anything could happen. The outside world would never here about it and never find out where it is.

"Relax Ms. Taylor." The Reverend said huskily. "Whatever you're thinking you'd be wrong." "I've decided you must be a secret weapon of the military" he said trying for a note of levity. "Did they implant a bionic brain to give you psychic powers?" he said as he flashed her a quick smile. A devastating smile actually one she wished she had the right to return.

"Follow me." She walked a few steps behind him unconsciously admiring the lithe movement of his well-honed body as they entered the middle hut. The interior reminded her of a clubhouse with a lounge, small kitchen and the usual furnishings of a couch, table, and chairs.

Everything looked new and it was surprisingly nice considering the outside of the hut resembled the war time architecture of half a century ago.

"Mary we've got company!" She heard him say. Out came a voice from the rear structure saying "I'll be out in a minute!"

"SO MAKE YOURSELF COMFORTABLE! THERE'S SALAD AND SANDWICHES IN THE FRIDGE" HELP YOURSELF THE LADY SAID.

"WHERE'S STONEY?" "OVER IN CLOVERDALE ON A DELIVERY. HE SHOULD'VE BEEN BACK BY NOW."

THE REVEREND TURNED TO RICKIE AND SAID "FIRST DOOR ON THE LEFT DOWN THAT HALLWAY IS THE BATHROOM GO AHEAD AN FRESHEN UP WHILE I PUT THE FOOD ON THE TABLE. I DON'T KNOW ABOUT YOU BUT I'M STARVING.

SINCE THE DAY SHE'D LEARNED HER TRUE IDENTITY RICKIE HAD LOST HER PASSION FOR EVERYTHING ESPECIALLY FOOD BUT SHE KNEW HAD TO EAT TO KEEP UP HER STRENGTH. "IF YOU'LL EXCUSE ME I'LL BE RIGHT BACK." HIS EYES SWEPT OVER HER AS IF SHE WERE SOME KIND OF RIDDLE HE NEEDED TO SOLVE. THEN WITH A DISMISSIVE NOD OF HIS DARK HEAD HE TURNED TOWARD THE REFRIGERATOR ALLOWING HER TO ESCAPE.

INSIDE THE BATHROOM SHE SLUICED HER FACE WITH COLD WATER TRYING TO SORT OUT HER CHAOTIC THOUGHTS. SINCE THE ESTABLISHMENT OF CBH SHE'D HAD HUNDREDS OF MEETINGS WITH THOUSANDS OF WELL MEANING PEOPLE THROUGHOUT THE WORLD AND ALL OF THEM CHAMPIONING WORTHY CAUSES BUT SHE'D NEVER MET ANYONE AS INTENSELY PRIVATE AND ENIGMATIC AS REVEREND BROWNING. THERE WAS SOMETHING INTANGIBLE ABOUT HIM THAT WARNED HE WAS ONE OF A KIND UNTOUCHABLE, SHREWD, INTELLIGENT AND DANGEROUS WHEN PROVOKED.

SHE THOUGHT BACK TO YESTERDAY WHEN SHE'D FOUND HIM CASING HER OFFICE. THER WAS NO OTHER WORD FOR IT HE HAD BEEN LOOKING AROUND FOR

SOMETHING IN HER OFFICE YESTERDAY. I DON'T KNOW WHAT HE EXPECTED TO FIND?

STEALTHY AS A JUNGLE PREDATOR AND JUST AS BOLD. HE HAD THE KIND OF RUGGED GOOD LOOKS NOT GIVEN TO MOST MEN. NOTHING ABOUT HIM, HIS PHYSICAL APPEARANCE OR HIS MANNER ACTIONS WOULD EVER CAUSE ANYONE TO ASSOCITE HIM WITH A PROFESSION AS BENING AS THE CLERGY.

THE CONTRADICTION FASCINATED HER. SHE IMAGINED HE INTIMIDATED SUCH A MAN. IF HE TURNED DOWN HER PROPOSAL AND REFUSED TO SEARCH OUT VON HASE SHE KNEW IN HER GUT THAT NO FEMININE WILE WOULD CHANGE HIS MIND. SHE WOULDN'T BE GIVEN A SECOND CHANCE.

JORDAN HEARD THE DRONE OF THE PLANE ENGINE. HE WIPED HIS HANDS ON A DISHCLOTH BEFORE STEPPING OUTSIDE THE HUT TO ALERT HIS FRIEND THAT THE HEAD OF THE CBH WOULD BE EATING LUNCH WITH THEM.

"RIGHT ON TIME MY FRIEND" SIAD THE REVEREND AS STONEY JUMPED DOWN FROM THE WING OF THE PLANE GRINNING WIDELY. "WHERE'S MS. MONEYBAGS?" STONEY SAID OUT LOUD.

"INSIDE SUPPOSEDLY POWERING HER NOSE." "WHAT'S THAT SUPPOSED TO MEAN?" "I DON'T KNOW" JORDAN SAID AS HE RAKED A HAND THROUGH HIS HAIR. "I'M BEGINNING TO THINK SHE'S ILL."

"YOU MEAN SICK TO HER STOMACH OR SOMETHING?" "I MEAN I THINK SHE'S GOT A CONDITION OF SOME KIND. SOMETIMES SHE LOSES COLOR AND LOOKS FAINT."

"YOU'RE NOT TALKING ABOUT ANOREXIA?" "NO I'M NOT TALKING ABOUT THAT." MS. TAYLOR MIGHT BE SLENDER

BUT SHE WASN'T GAUNT OR EXCESSIVELY THIN. SHE WAS NICELY ROUNDED AS A MATTER OF FACT. "MAYBE IT'S SOME KIND OF VIRUS OR FEMALE TROUBLE."

STONEY'S COMMENT JERKED HIM FROM THE ERRANT PICTURES FLASHING THROUGH HIS HEAD. PICTURES OF RICKIE TAYLOR'S LOVELY FACE AND ALLURING BODY AND HE WAS ANGRY AT HIMSELF FOR HIS LACK OF CONTROL AS HE SUCKED IN HIS BREATH.

"YOU'RE PROBABLY RIGHT." "WHATEVER IT IS IT COULDN'T BE SERIOUS OR SHE WOULDN'T BE DRIVING AROUND THE COUNTRYSIDE WITH YOU."

JORDAN HAD HIS OWN THROUGHTS ON THAT PARTICULAR SUBJECT. RICKIE TAYLOR HAD WANTED TO DO BUSINESS WITH HIM SO BADLY THAT SHE HADN'T BEEN ABLE TO WAIT FOR A CALL FROM HIM AND HAD ACTUALLY GONE TO THE TROUBLE OF LOCATING HIM LAST NIGHT.

HE HAD A FELLING THAT MAKING CONTACT WITH HIM WAS VERY IMPORTANT ENOUGH TO HER THAT SHE WOULD PROBABLY HAVE LEFT A HOSPITAL BED TO ACCOMPLISH HER OBJECTIVE. MAYBE THAT WAS WHERE SHE SHOULD BE RIGHT NOW.

"OF COUSE" STONEY ADDED "IF YOU WERE RUNNING TRUE TO FROM AND GOT HER HERE IN QUARTER OF THE TIME IT TAKE A NORMAL PERSON THEN THAT'S ANOTHER STORY."

JORDAN LIFTED HIS HANDS SO HE CAN KEEP TO THE SPEED LIMIT. I SWEAR IT. "THEN HE STOP LOOKING FOR PROBLEMS."

I WISH I COULD BUT JORDAN DECIDE TO LET THE SUJECT DROP FOR MOMENT OF THE TWO MEN HE HAD ALWAYS BEEN THE MOST CAUTIOUS. "PARANOID" STONEY

CALLED IT. SOMETIMES HE DIDN'T KNOW HOW HIS FRIEND PUT UP WITH HIM.

BY TACIT AGREEMENT THEY STORLLED TOWARD THE HUT WITH THEIR HEADS INCLINED TOWARD EACH OTHER. "HOW MUCH HAVE YOU TOLD HER?" "I GAVE HER THE PAPER ON THE ACHE TO READ. SHE DID HER HOMEWORK AND KNOWS WHAT'S GOING ON DOWN THERE BUT I HAVEN'T EXPLAINED OUR INVOLVEMENT YET. IT MIGHT BE BETTER IF WE LET MARY MAKE THE INITIAL PRESENTATION. SHE'S NOT EMOTIONALLY INVOLVED IN THE SAME WAY AND SHE HAS A SIXTH SENSE ABOUT PEOPLE. SHE'LL BE ABLE TO SIZE UP OUR VISITOR AND SAY ALL THE RIGHT THINGS." "I AGREE AND BESIDES I'VE NEVER MET A ANYONE WHO DIDN'T LOVE CRAZY WOMEN RIGHT OFF THE BAT."

"GOOD THEN IT'S SETTLED WE'LL ONLY FILL HER IN AS WE HAVE TO." "THE LESS SAID THE BETTER." "AMEN TO THAT SAID THE REVEREND."

AS THEY ENTERED THE HUT MARY SAID "COME ON IN BOYS. WHAT TOOK YOU GUYS SO LONG? RICKIE AND I JUST ABOUT TO SEND OUT A SEARCH PARTY." IT WAS RICKIE ALREADY! JORDAN DIDN'T DARE LOOK AT STONEY ANYMORE BECAUSE HE TRIED TO SUPPRESS A SMILE OUT OF HIM BUT ONLY HALF SUCCEED.

IN THE TIME HE'D BEEN OUTSIDE TALKING TO STONEY AND MARY HAD MANAGED TO PUT ON A DELECTABLE SPREAD. HE HAD FAST LEARNED THAT AMONG HER MANY TALENTS AND SHE WAS A FABULOUS COOK. SHE HAD APPARENTLY ENTICED MS. TAYLOR INTO EATING ON OF HER TASTY SWISS-PASTRAMI SANDWICHES.

JORDAN SAT DOWN NEXT TO THEIR VISITOR WHILE STONEY PLACED HIMSELF BESIDE MARY WHO TAKE OVER THE INTRODUCTIONS.

"RICKIE TAYLOR? YOU'VE MET THE REVEREND BROWNING. NOW MEET STONEWALL LEONARD OWNER OF STONEWALL AIR-CARGO SERVICE. HIS FRIENDS CALL HIM STONEY FOR SHORT. I'M HIS RELATIVE SORT OF SO I'M ALLOWED TO CALL HIM THAT TOO."

JORDAN WATCHED HIM PUT OUT A HAND FOR HER TO SHAKE. THE MALE ADMIRATION IN HIS EYES SPOKE VOLUMES. "MS. TAYLOR." "PLEASE MY NAME IS RICKIE." "RICKIE IT IS THEN." "HOW DO YOU DO STONEY?"

A WARM SMILE BROKE OUT ON STONEY'S FACE. THIS WAS ONE TIME JORDAN WAS GLAD THAT MICHELLE STILL HAD STONEY'S HEART. "I'M FINE SHE SAID. WE'RE HONORED THAT SOMEONE AS FAMOUS AS YOU IS SITTING HERE HAVING LUNCH WITH US."

"WE ARE" JORDAN INTERJECTED. RICKIE TREW HIM A SEARCHING GLANCE BEFORE SHE LOOKED AWAY AGAIN AND MADE INROADS ON THE FRESH FRUIT SALAD. TO HIS RELIEF HER APPETITE HADN'T DESERTED HER AFTER ALL. WHY HE CARED WAS BYOND HIM.

MARY DRANK HALF OF HER FAVORITE BLACK-CHERRY POP BEFORE SHE SET THE BOTTLE DOWN ON THE TABLE AND EYED RICKIE SQUARELY.

"EVEN A MORON CAN SEE THAT WE'VE BEEN BUTTERING YOU UP FOR THE BIG MOMENT RICKIE. YOU JUST TELL US WHEN YOU'RE READY AND THE REVEREND WILL EXPLAIN WHY WE NEED THE KIND OF FINANCIAL HELP YOUR ORGANIZATION FUNDS."

"YOU'RE DOING FINE MARY" JORDAN SAID GIVING HER HIS APPROVAL TO CARRY ON. RICKIE THEN SAT HER FORK DOWN. "PLEASE BEGIN MARY. THAT'S WHY I'M HERE ACCORDING TO THE REVEREND THIS HAS TO DO WITH

SOMETHING CALLED THE ACHE INDIANS OF PARAGUAY." "THAT'S RIGHT SAID RICKIE. NOW I COULD TELL YOU A BUNCH OF MUMBO JUMBO GOBBLEDYGOOK OR I CAN JUST PUT IT TO PLAIN. WHICH WAY DO YOU WANT IT?"

THAT BROUGHT A FAINT SMILE TO RICKIE'S EXPRESSIVE MOUTH. "I THINK YOU KNOW THE ANSWER TO THAT."

MARY SLAPPED HER LEG AND SIAD "NOW WE'RE TALKING! ALL RIGHTY. YOU SEE THE GOVERNMENT OFFICIALS DOWN IN PARAGUAY ARE A BUNCH OF BAD HOMBERES. THEY GO OUT IN THE CHACO THAT'S KIND OF LIKE THE BUSH AND ROUND UP THE INDIANS WHO LIVE OUT THERE.

"THEY SLAUGHTER THE PARENTS AND THE BOY CHILDREN THEN SELL THE YOUNG GIRLS INTO SLAVERY OR KEEP THEM PENNED UP IN PRIVATE HOUSES TO USE AT WILL AS THEIR OWN AND WHEN THE GIRLS HAVE OUTGROWN THEIR USEFULNESS THEY'RE EITHER KILLED OR LIFT TO DIEOF DISEASE OR STARVATION."

THE WHOLE TIME MARY WAS TALKING JORDAN'S EYES FASTENED ON RICKIE TAYLOR'S FACE WHICH WAS GROWING WHITER AND WHITER. "TO MAKE A LONG STORY SHORT STONEY AND THE REVEREND HAVE DELIVERED CARGO TO SOUTH AMERICA AND THEY'VE SEEN SOME OF THIS.

"THEY'VE BEEN IN TOUCH WITH SEVERAL PRIESTS DOWN THERE MAINLY FATHER DESILVA WHO RUNS AN UNDERGROUND THAT GETS A FEW OF THOSE PEOPLE ACROSS THE BORDER INTO ARGENTINA BUT UNFORTUNATELY TOO MANY DIE IN THE PROCESS OR ARE HUNTED DOWN BY THE ARGENTINA POLICE. IT'S A BAD SITUATION BECAUSE THE UNDERGROUND CAN ONLY HELP ONE PERSON AT A TIME. IT BREAKS UP FAMILIES AND TEARS CHILDREN FROM THEIR PARENTS."

"THAT'S HORRIBLE" THE YOUNGER WOMEN MUTTERED IN A SHAKEN WHISPER. "STONEY'S IDEA IS TO BRING WHOLE SETS OF FAMILIES TO THE US STRAIGHT FROM CHACO. THE THREE OF US WILL ACT AS THEIR VERY OWN TEMPORARY SPONSORS SO THEY'RE LEGAL WHILE WE GET THE PAPERWORK DONE ON THEM.

"WE'LL LET THEM LIVE HERE AS FAMILIES, TRAIN THEM AND TEACH THEM ENGLISH TO PREPARE THEM TO ENTER SOCIETY AS A GROUP. AFTER A WHILE WE'LL FIND PERMANENT SPONSORS FOR THEM. FOR NOW WE'LL OFFER OUR PROTECTION UNTILL THEY CAN LIVE AND MANAGE ON THEIR OWN AND BECOME LEGAL IMMIGRANTS."

MARY THEN SAT BACK DOWN WHEN SHE WAS DONE TALKING. "BASICALLY THAT'S THE PLAN MARY SAID. WHILE STONEY CARRIES ON WITH HIS AIR-CARGO BUSINESS HE AND THE REVEREND WILL MAKE OCCASIONAL FLIGHTS TO PARAGUAY AND BRING FAMILIES HERE. I'LL LOOK AFTER THEM, CLOTH THEM AND FEED THEM. WE'VE REMOLDELED THESE FACILITIES TO ACCOMMODATE TWELVE PEOPLE AT A TIME. THE REVEREND WILL SPLIT HIS DUTIES BETWEEN THE PARISH AND HERE. HE WILL BE IN CHARGE OF THEIR EDUCATION."

MS. TAYLOR'S LOVELY BLOND HEAD SWERVED IN JORDAN'S DIRECTION AND HER PONYTAIL WAS SWISHING BACK AND FORTH. "YOU HONESTLY THINK YOU CAN DO THAT WITHOUT THE AUTHORITIES CATCHING ON?"

HE EYES NARROWED AS HE SAID "I GUESS WE WON'T KNOW UNTIL WE TRY." MANY IMMIGRANTS AND REFUGEES HAVE A NATURAL DISTRUST OF AUTHORITY BUT HOWEVER REVEREND ROLON IS ONE MAN WHO'S BUILT THEIR TRUST AND BECAUSE OF HIM THEY'RE MORE ACCEPTING OF ME AND MY MINISTRY EXPECILALY IN THE GROWING HISPANIC POPULATIONS. I SPEAK SPANISH AND GUARANI SO I'M

RESPONSIBLE FOR HELPING THEM GET JOBS, FILL OUT FORMS AND DEAL WITH THE LAW.

"I CAN FIND WORK FOR THESE PEOPLE IN THE VINEYARDS, ORCHARDS AND MANY OTHER PLACES. NO ONE IS GOING TO RAISE AN EYEBROW AT SEEING A FEW MORE MINORITY FAMILIES LIVING IN THE AREA."

"NATURALLY THIS IS GOING TO BE A PILOT PROGRAM TO BEGIN WITH" STONEY SAID AS HE BROKE IN ENTHUSIASTICALLY BUT IF IT'S SUCCESSFUL WE'LL TURN IT INTO AN ONGOING PROCESS. NOT ALL FAMILIES WILL WANT TO LEAVE THEIR COUNTRY NOT EVEN AT THE THREAT OF DEATH BUT THERE ARE MANY WHO TERRIFIED AND WILL DO ANYTHING TO GET OUT. IF NO ONE COMES TO THEIR RESCUE THE'LL CONTINUE TO BE HELPLESS VICTIMS OF A CORRUPT REGIME THAT WAS NEVER VALUED HUMAN LIFE."

JORDAN GOT TO HIS FEET AND SAID "WE HAVE A SPECIALLY OUTFITTED PLANE MS. TAYLOR AND A PILOT WHO CAN FLY IT." HE GESTURED AT STONEY AS HE SAID "WE HAVE FACILITIES TO HOUSE THESE PEOPLE, SOMEONE TO LOOK AFTER THEM, WE ALSO HAVE THE MEANS TO EDUCATE THEM, SET THEM FREE, AND WE HAVE A GROWING LIST OF SPONSORS FROM ALL OVER THE U.S. AND CANADA WHO CAN PUT THEM TO WORK.

"WHAT WE NEED IS MONEY FOR FUEL, PLANE PARTS, FOR PAYOFFS, BRIBES, FOOD, CLOTHING, THE BILLS AROUND HERE AND EDUCATIONAL SUPPLIES. WE'RE ESTIMATING ABOUT $50,000 THOUSAND PER PERSON PER YEAR. GIVEN THE POSSIBILITY OF AN UNFORESEEN EMERGENCY WE'LL PROBABLY NEED IN THE NEIGHBORHOOD OF $750,000 THOUSAND FOR THE NEXT FISCAL YEAR. WE'VE WORKED IT OUT ON PAPER AND WE'LL GIVE YOU A COMPLETE TOUR OF THE FACILITIES."

"HOW SOON WOULD YOU NEED THE MONEY?" SHE ASKED WITHOUT HESITATION. JORDAN LOOKED AT HER DUBIOUSLY. "WE NEEDED IT APPROXIMATELY A HUNDRED YEARS AGO WHEN THE ACHE HAD A POPULATION OF CLOSE TO 200,000 INDIANS BUT THE POINT IS YOU ARE INCLINED TO HELP US YOU COULD END UP IN SERIOUS TROUBLE."

STONEY WAS SHAKING HIS HEAD AS IF TO WARN JORDAN NOT TO SOUR THE DEAL BUT JORDAN HAD A PREMONITION SOMETHING WAS WRONG AND REFUSED TO TAKE THIS WOMEN AT FACE VALUE.

"IF WE'RE FOUND OUT" HE SAID "THE AUTHORITIES COULD TRACE THE MONEY TO YOU BUT WE WOULD TAKE THE BLAME OF COURSE AND SWEAR THAT WE'D LIED TO YOU AND THAT YOU HAD NO IDEA WHAT WAS GOING ON BUT NEVERTHELESS WE'RE NOT ABOUT TO MINIMIZE THE RISK AND IT'S POSSIBLE YOUR GOOD NAME COULD BE INVOLVED IN SOMETHING REALLY UGLY."

CHAPTER 34

THE SECRET LIFE OF THE UNDERGROUND PATH.

Rickie had to fight the hysteria inside her. My name had already been in involved in something so ugly that if you knew the truth you would shrink from me and my blood money.

You're such good people because what you want and what you're fighting for is so magnificent I have no right to be breathing the same air as you guys.

After sipping some cola as a way to give herself a moment to think she finally said "Because CBH is a charity I mustn't allow my legal entanglements with our government to be associated with it. Therefore CBH couldn't give you the money you're asking for."

Though no one move or made a sound she felt their long disappointment. It was like a thick black funnel cloud touching the ground and swallowing everything in it's path.

Taking a deep breath she then added "However if I were to instruct my attorney to use a private fund of mine to invest in a legitimate up-and coming-air-cargo business there would be no problems. No one other then my accountant and the IRS would have to know my money was spent."

TRAPPED BY THE REVEREND'S EYES WHOSE COLOR HAD CHANGED FROM A BLACK GRAY TO BLAZING GREEN IN A MATTER OF SECONDS SHE COULDN'T LOOK ANYWHERE ELSE.

OBVIOUSLY HER PROPOSAL HAD SHOCKED HIM. WHY WAS THIS SO IMPORTANT TO HIM? WHAT INTEREST DID THIS PARTICULAR GROUP ON INDIANS HAVE FOR HIM THAT HE IN FACT ALL THREE OF THEM WOULD RISK THEIR LIVES FOR A FEW HOPELESS HELPLES SCRAPS OF HUMANITY LIVING ON ANOTHER CONTINENT?

"I'M READY FOR THAT TOUR" SHE SAID TO NO ONE IN PARTICULAR. OBVIOUSLY THE REVEREND AND STONEY NEEDED TIME TO ABSORB THE NEWS THAT THEIR WISH WAS ABOUT TO BE GRANTED. THOUGH IT WAS TAINTED MONEY SHE WAS GIVING THEM A TINY PART OF HER REJOICED THAT SHE COULD MAKE THREE PEOPLE SO HAPPY. HAD SHE EVER MADE ANYONE THIS HAPPY IN HER WHOLE LIFE?

THEY CAN NEVER FIND OUT WHERE THE MONEY CAME FROM. GRINNING WIDELY MARY GOT UP FROM THE TABLE. "COME ON HONEY WE'LL START WITH THE BEDROOMS AND END UP IN THE SCHOOLROOM. WE INSTALLED A COUPLE OF COMPUTERS BUT WE'ER GOING TO NEED MORE!"

WHILE MARY KEPT UP HER STEADY CHATTER GOING JORDAN HAD STOOD THEIR IN PLACE AND HIS EYES NARROWED AS HE WATCHED THEIR PROGRESS UP THE STAIRS TO THE SECOND FLOOR. WHATEVER MS. TAYLOR WANTED IN RETURN FOR THE $750,000 THOUSAND DOLLARS EVIDENTLY IT WAS SO VITAL SHE WOULD TAKE MONEY FROM HER OWN PERSONAL ASSETS TO MAKE IT HAPPEN.

"JORDAN? HEY I'M TALKING TO YOU. WHAT'S GOING ON? WHY AREN'T YOU JUMPPING UP AND DOWN?"

HE TURNED TO STONEY WITH HIS EXPRESSION GUARDED. "BECAUSE THERE'S A PRICE TO PAY FOR THIS WINDFALL. I'M WAITING FOR HER TO NAME IT."

"WHAT PRICE? DAM IT JORDAN SOMETIME I JUST DON'T UNDERSTAND YOU." "THAT MAKES TWO OF US SAID STONEY. SO YOU TELL ME WHY MS. TAYLOR WOULD JUST GIVE YOU THAT KIND OF MONEY? YOU HEARD HER SHE CAN USE IT AS A CHARITY WRITE-OFF. THERE'S AN OLD ADAGE ABOUT GREEKS BRERING GIFTS THAT WE OUGHT TO KEEP IN MIND ABOUT NOW."

AFTER PACING THE FLOOR STONEY WHEELED AROUND AND SAID "HAS IT EVER OCCURRED TO YOU THAT SHE'S SIMPLY A VERY NICE PERSON WHO HAPPENS TO HAVE A TON OF MONEY SHE ENJOYS GIVING AWAY? THERE ARE PEOPLE IN THE WORLD LIKE THAT YOU KNOW. MAYBE SHE'S DEVOUT CHRISTIAN FOLLOWING HER RELIGION. "GIVE ALL YOU HAVE TO THE POOR AND COME FOLLOW ME" YOU KNOW THAT KIND OF THING.

STONEY YOU HAVE NO IDEA HOW MUCH I'D LIKE TO BELIEVE MS. TAYLOR IS THE ANGEL SHE APPEARS TO BE BUT I NEVER DID BELIEVE IN MIRACLES LET ALONE IMAGINE ONE COULD HAPPEN TO ME.

HE LET OUT THE BREATH HE'D BEEN HOLDING AND SAID "I'LL TELL YOU WHAT STONEY I STILL HAVE TO TAKE HER HOME AND IF NOTHING COMES UP DURING THE DRIVE BACK THEN I'LL CELEBRATE WITH YOU BUT NOT BEFORE."

"I'LL HAVE THE CHAMPAGNE WAITING." HIS PRONOUNCEMENT COINCIDED WITH THE SOUND OF FOOTSTEPS COMING DOWN THE LONG STAIRS. BLESS MARY FOR GIVING MS. TAYLOR THE GUIDED TOUR. THE TWO WOMEN CONVERSED LIKE OLD FRIENDS WHICH WAS AN EXCELLENT SIGN UNDER THE CIRCUMSTANCES JORDAN

ONLY WHISPERED. "REVEREND? "STONEY?" SHE CALLED OUT. "I HAVE TO ADMIT I'M VERY IMPRESSED WITH WHAT I'VE SEEN. THERE'S NO DOUBT IN MY MIND THAT THE THREE OF YOU WILL BE ABLE TO ACCOMPLISH WHAT YOU'VE SET OUT TO DO. IT PLEASES ME TO KNOW MY MONEY WILL PLAY A PART IN SOMETHING THIS HUMANITARIAN."

"JRODAN FELT STONEY'S NUDGE IN THE RIBS. "IF YOU WOULD BE SO KIND AS TO RUN ME BACK TO TOWN REVEREND WE'LL DISCUSS THE DETAILS WITH YOU IN MY OFFICE. TOMORROW I'LL INSTRUCT MY ATTORNEY TO GET IN TOUCH WITH YOU TO DRAW UP A CONTRACT AND WRITE YOU A BIG FAT CHECK."

HE NODDED HIS HEAD SOLWLY. "I'LL MEET YOU AT THE CAR." BEHIND HIM HE HEARD THE PROFUSION OF THANK YOUS PROFFERED BY STONEY AND MARY WHO HAD NO RESERVATIONS ABOUT ACCEPTING RICKIE TAYLOR'S OUTRIGHT GIFT TO THEM BUT NONE OF IT MADE SENSE TO JORDAN AND HIS APPREHENSION FORCED HIM FROM THE ROOM BECAUSE HE KNEW HE WAS RIGHT.

MORE CONVINCED THAN EVER OF A CATCH SOMEWHERE HE STRODE SWIFTLY TOWARD THE CAR NOT WAITING FOR HER TO FOLLOW. WHEN HE'D CLIMBED INTO THE DRIVER'S SEAT HE REACHED FOR HIS CELLPHONE IN THE GLOVE COMPARTMENT AND PHONED REVEREND ROLON TO UPDATE HIM ON THE LATEST TURN OF EVENTS.

THE REVEREND ACTED GUARDEDLY PLEASED THAT THEY'D COME UP WITH THE FUNDING BUT LIKE JORDAN SAID HE TENDED TOWARD CAUTION. THE POOR MAN DIDN'T HAVE THE SANCTION OF HIS OWN CHURCH FOR HALF THE COVERT THINGS HE DID.

IF ANYONE FOUND OUT THE KINDS OF ACTIVITIES HE WAS INVOLVED IN AND THEN INFORMED ON HIM NOT ONLY WOULD REVEREND ROLON BE IN TROUBLE WITH

THE GOVERNMENT HE'D BE EXCOMMUNICATED AND BE FORCED TO LEAVE THE COMMUNITY HE SERVED. JORDAN WOULD DO EVERYTHING IN HIS POWER TO PREVENT THAT FROM HAPPENING BUT SOMETIMES EVEN THE BEST LAID PLANS HAVE A WAY OF GOING AWRY.

"SORRY IF I KEPT YOU WAITING." MS. TAYLOR GOT INTO THE CAR AND SHUT THE DOOR JUST AS HE WAS PUTTING HIS CELLPHONE AWAY AND WHATEVER FRAGRANCE SHE'D USED THE LATE AFTENOON HEAT SEEMED TO RELEASE MORE OF HER SKIN'S FLOWERY SENT. HE FOUND HIMSELF VERY INTOXCATED BY IT.

ALREADY IRRITATED THAT SHE OCCUPIED TOO MUCH OF HIS THOUGHTS HE SAID TO HIMSELF. "NO PROBLEM I NEED ALL THE STOLEN MOMENTS I CAN FIND TO ATTEND TO PARISH BUSINESS."

SHE STARED STRAIGHT ADEAD FOR A WILE THEN SHE SAID "THEN IT'S A GOOD THING WE CAN TALK ABOUT OUR CONTRACT DURING THE DRIVE BACK TO TOWN SO I WON'T HAVE TO DETAIN YOU ONCE WE ARRIVE AT THE OFFICE."

HERE IT COMES BROWNING "I'LL GIVE THE ATTORNEY THE PARTICULARS AND MARY HAS AGREED TO SUPPLY ANY FIGURE WHEN HE CALLS. ALL THAT'S LEFT IS TO SETTLE ON THE AMOUNT OF MONEY YOU'LL NEED."

"AS I STATED EARLIER $750,000 THOUSAND DOLLARS WILL DO IT AND THEN SOME." "BUT THAT'S JUST FOR ONE YEAR." SHE ARGUED IN A CALM VOICE. "HOPEFULLY YOUR PROJECT WILL BE ABLE TO CONTINUE FOR AS LONG AS THERE ARE PEOPLE ANXIOUS TO LEAVE PARAGUAY TO START A NEW LIFE."

"WE DON'T KNOW HOW THIS THING IS GOING TO END BUT NO MATTER HOW WELL WE'VE PLANNED THE

DETAILS ON PAPER IS JUST A THEORY BECAUSE AS YOU KNOW REALITY HAS A WAY OF REARING IT'S UGLY LITTLE HEAD."

"I DO" SHE SAID IN A STRANGE VOICE SOUNDING VERY FAR AWAY BUT HOWEVER I THINK YOU'LL ALL FEEL A LOT BETTER ABOUT EVERYTHING IF YOU'RE NOT WORRIED THAT THE FUNDING WILL RUN OUT AFTER A TWELVE-MONTH PERIOD."

JORDAN CHANGED GEARS AS HE LEFT THE COUNTRY ROAD AND ENTERED THE MAIN HIGHWAY LEADING TO THE FREEWAY FARTHER ON DOWN THE ROAD. "YOU SEEM TO BRING AN UNUSUAL WEALTH OF EXPERIENCE TO YOUR JOB. FOR ONE SO YOUNG HOW HAVE YOU GLEANED THE KIND OF KNOWLEDGE THAT MANY PEOPLE THREE TIMES YOUR AGE HAVE NEVER LEARNED AND NEVER WILL?"

"HOW NICE IT IS TO BE CALLED YOUNG." HE DARTED HER AN VERY OBLIQUE GLANCE. SHE SOUNDED PERFECTLY SERIOUS BUT HE COULD BE FORGIVEN FOR THINKING HER COMMENT HAD BEEN SPOKEN BY AN EIGHTY-YEAR-OLD MATRIARCH. MORE AND MORE MS. TAYLOR WAS TURNING INTO AN ENIGMA.

"SOMEBODY MUST HAVE NOT LET YOU IN ON THE NEWS REVEREND. AGE IS A STATE OF MIND BUT TO ANSWER YOUR QUESTION MORE SPECIFICALLY I'VE SEEN ENOUGH OF THE WORLD'S PROBLEMS TO MAKE ME FEEL A HUNDRED YEARS OLD SOME DAYS AND SO THERE'S NO MYSTERY THERE.

"NOW LET'S GET BACK TO THE POINT. "I'VE DECIDED ON AN AMOUNT THAT SHOULD HELP MAKE YOUR OPERATION SELF-PERPETUATING. I'LL INSTRUCT MY ATTORNEY TO CUT TWO CHECKS FOR TEN MILLION DOLLARS TO STONEWALL AIR-CARGO AND ANOTHER TEN MILLION DOLLARS TO YOU PERSONALY."

JORDAN HAD BEEN WAITING FOR THE BOMB TO DROP BUT NOT TO THE TUNE OF TWENTY-MILLION DOLLARS.

HIS BODY WAS STIFENED AND WITHOUT SAYING A WORD HE SEARCHED FOR THE NEXT HOTEL BUT BY THEN HE PULLED OFF THE ROAD AND STOPPED THE CAR.

"THAT'S NINETEEN MILLION TWO HUNDRED AND FIFTY THOUSAND DOLLARS MORE THEN WE NEED MS TAYLOR. WHEN YOU PHONED YESTERDAY INSTEAD OF WAITING FOR ME TO GET IN TOUCH WITH YOU I KNEW YOU WANTED SOMETHING FROM ME PRETTY DESPERATELY."

HE JERKED HIS HEAD AROUND TO LOOK AT HER BUT SHE WAS STARING OUT THE SIDE OF THE WINDSHIELD STILL AS DEEP WATER. SHE SEEMED LIKE SHE WAS STARING AT A PICTURE OF INNOCENCE WITH THAT PONYTAIL HE LONGED TO RELEASE SIMPLY TO FIND OUT IF THE SILVERY GOLD STRANDS REALLY FELT THE WAY SHE LOOKED. LIKE SATIN HE SHOOK OFF HIS IMPULSE.

"CONSIDERING THE AMOUNT OF MONEY YOU'RE OFFERING I CAN ONLY CONCLUDE YOU WANT SOMEONE KILLED. "I'M NOT IN THAT BUSINESS BUT I AM IN THE BUSINESS OF SAVING LIVES."

LISTEN TO YOUSELF BROWNING, THE LIES JUST KEEP GETTING YOU IN DEEPER AND DEEPER. "DO YOU EVEN KNOW WHAT THE TRUTH IS ANYMORE?"

HER CHEST ROSE AND FELL BUT THEN SHE SAID TO THE REVEREND "I WANT SOMEONE FOUND" NOT KILLED SHE SAID. JORDAND HEARD THE UNMISTAKABLE SOUND OF GUT-WRENCHING RAGE AND ANGUISH IN HER VOICE ALL MIXED TOGETHER BUT HE ABSENTLY RUBBED A THUMB AGAINST HIS BOTTOM LIP WHEN HE HEARD WHAT SHE SAID.

WHO DO YOU WANT FOUND? AN ERRANT LOVER WITH A HIGH PROFILE? AN UNFAITHFUL HUSBAND SHE'D KEPT SECRET OVER THE YEARS?

NOT LIKING THE IDEA OF EITHER POSSIBILITY THOUGH FOR THE LIFE OF HIM JORDAN DIDN'T KNOW WHY IT MATTERED ONE WAY OR THE OTHER HE SAID AS HE SAT BACK DOWN WAITING FOR MORE OF AN EXPLANATION BUT DREADING IT.

TO HIS MIND ONLY A SECOND WOMEN OF GREAT WEALTH LIKE HERS WOULD OFFER SUCH A SUM TO SATISFY HER CURIOSITY OR HER PLAN HER REVENGE EXPECIALLY WHEN HER FAMILY HAD PROBABLY PAID MILLIONS TO KEEP THE SCANDAL HUSHED UP. IF IT WAS A SCANDAL AND JORDAN COULDN'T IMAGINE WHAT ELSE IT MIGHT BE.

SO FAR THE TAYLOR MONEY AND POWER WHICH REACHED RIGHT INTO THE WHITE HOUSE TO THE PRESIDENT HIMSELF HAD DONE THE JOB. NOTHING ABOUT HER LOVE LIFE HAD BEEN LEAKED OUT TO THE MEDIA OTHERWISE JORDAN WOULD HAVE COME ACROSSED IT WHILE HE WAS DOING HIS BACKGROUND CHECK.

"WHY ME MS. TAYLOR?" HE DEMANDED. HE HEARD HER SUDDEN INTAKE OF BREATH RAW AND SHARP. SHE WASN'T AS IN CONTROL AS SHE HAD APPEARED TO BE BUT ODDLY ENOUGH THE KNOWLEDGE MADE HIM FEEL BETTER THEN EVER.

"THE PERSON I'M LOOKING FOR COULD BE LIVING IN PARAGUAY." JORDAN FROWNED WHEN HE HEARD THAT NEWS. A PERSON WHO WANTED TO REMAIN LOST COULD GET SO LOST IN PARAGUAY THAT THERE'S VIRTUALLY NO HOPE OF PICKING UP HIS TRAIL. PARAGUAY IS WHERE CERTAIN ISOLATED AREAS HAD BECOME THE REPOSITORY OF THE WORLD'S MOST SLIME.

The idea that someone associated with Rickie Taylor or her privileged world could have any connections to that little corrupted hellhole was hard to fathom and particularly distasteful.

"There are parts of Paraguay that remain virtually unknown and no laws are in effect in those areas." "I know" she said. Her admission held a wisdom and an awareness beyond her years.

Who was this women? "What I'm asking is inpossible" she had added quietly. "That's why I've turned to you Lord." "I'm very convinced that if you aren't able to find him then it means it's not possible for him to be found."

"So it's a he I'm looking for. Without conscious thought Jordan started the car back up and pulled onto the highway once more. Driving usually helped clear his head and enjoying the sensation of speed he floored the accelerator.

Out of the corner of his eye he notice an agitated movement of her left hand and he couldn't help noticing that her fingers were ringless and cursed himself for it and then he said "I'm not asking you to do anything more than ascertain if he's living there that's all."

"Those lawless areas I was talking about are like convoluted riddles Ms. Taylor and they keep their secrets."

"The money will be yours whether you find him or not." She persisted as if he hadn't spoken. "Forget your millions" he said because not everyone can be bought for the proverbial thirty pieces of silver.

WHO IS THIS MAN YOU'RE LOOKING FOR? AND WHAT IS HE TO YOU?"

TO HIS CHAGRIN HE HEARD A SIREN BEHIND HIM AND IT WAS GETTING LOUDER BY THE SECOND PREVENTING HER RESPONSE. ONE GLANCE AT THE REARVIEW MIRROR AND HE SAW A POLICE CAR ON HIS TAIL AND THE LIGHTS WERE FLASHING.

WITH A LOW GROWN HE PULLED OVER TO THE SIDE OF THE ROAD AND DREW OUT HIS REGISTRATION FROM THE GLOVE COMPARTMENT AND REACHED FOR HIS WALLET. THIS WAS THE FIRST TIME HIS PHONY ID WOULD BE TESTED NOT COUNTING YESTERDAY WHEN SHOWED IT TO HER.

A YOUNG VERY OFFICAL LOOKING OFFICER WITH A THICK SPORTING MUSTACHE APPROACHED THE CAR. "MAY I SEE YOUR LICENSE AND REGISTRATION PLEASE?" JORDAN HANDED EVERYTHING OVER TO THE OFFICER. THE POLICE OFFICER THEN SCANNED THE LICENSE THEN SCRUTINIZED JORDAN. "THIS IS A FIFTY MILE AN HOUR SPEED ZONE AND I CLOCKED YOU AT SIXTY-EIGHT MILES AN HOUR YOU SHOULD KNOW BETTER REVEREND."

RELIEVED THAT THE POLICEMAN HADN'T TOLD HIM TO WAIT WHILE HE WENT BACK TO HIS CAR TO CHECK THE RECORDS JORDAN SAID TO THE POLICEMAN "I APOLOGIZE OFFICER I SHOULDN'T BE DISCUSSING PARISH BUSINESS WHEN I'M BEHIND THE WHEEL BECAUSE IT TENS TO MAKE ME LESS ATTENTIVE."

MS. TAYLOR LEANED CLOSER TO JORDAN'S SIDE. WITH THOSE SOULFUL BLUE EYES FASTENED ON THE OTHER MAN SHE SAID "IT WAS MY FAULT OFFICER NOT HIS I WAS TELLING THE REVEREND MY PROBLEM AND HAD DISTRACTED HIM. IF ANYONE SHOULD RECEIVE A TICKET I SHOLD." THE TINY TREMOR IN HER VOICE SOUNDED REAL EVEN TO JORDAN'S EARS.

WITH UNABASHED MALE INTEREST THE POLICEMAN TURNED HIS GAZE ONTO JORDAN'S PASSENGER.

"WELL NOW MA'AM" THE OFFICER SAID WITH A SMILE ON HIS FACE STRETCHING HIS MUSTACHE. "SINCE IT WAS PARISH BUSINESS AND YOU PUT IT LIKE THAT I'LL LET YOU GO WITH A WARNING THS TIME."

OH SURE JORDAN SAID UNDERNEITH HIS BREATH WITH THE URGE TO TEAR THE HAIR FROM THE OFFICER'S UPPER LIP WAS GROWING STRONGER.

"THANK YOU OFFICER." HE BARELY MANAGED TO HANG ON TO HIS CIVILITY TO ADD "I'M MUCH OBLIGED." THE POLICEMAN NODDED THEN TIPPED HIS HAT STILL GRINNING AT RICKIE TAYLOR LIKE AN IDIOT AND SAID "MA'AM YOU GUYS HAVE A GOOD DAY" AND WATCH YOUR SPEED AND THEN THE POLICEMAN WENT BACK TO HIS CAR AND TOOK OFF.

ONCE AGAIN JORDAN STARTED UP THE "72" FORD AND THEY WERE OFF AGAIN. WHEN HE ROUNDED THE CORNER HE COULD NO LONGER SEE THE POLICE CAR IN THE REARVIEW MIRROR HE THEN ASKED "DOSE THAT HAPPEN EVERY TIME?" "WHAT DO YOU MEAN?" "YOU KNOW EXACTLY WHAT I MEAN MS. TAYLOR I'M TALKING ABOUT A SECRET WEAPON." "FOR YOU INFORMATION I'VE NEVER BEEN PULLED OVER BY A POLICEMAN FOR ANY REASON." "NEVER?" "NO BUT IT DID SEEM UNFAIR FOR YOU TO BE BLAMED FOR SOMETHING THAT WAS MY FAULT."

HE TOOK A DEEP BREATH AND THEN HE SAID "I WAS THE ONE WITH MY FOOT TO THE FLOOR." "YES THAT'S TRUE BUT IT ISN'T EVERYDAY THAT A CLERGYMAN IS APPROACHED WITH WHAT YOU THOUGHT WAS A LARGE CONTRACT TO KILL SOMEONE EITHER. I SHOULDN'T HAVE HANDLED IT THE WAY I DID I'M SORRY."

LADY YOU'RE EITHER THE BEST CONARTIST I'VE EVER KNOWN OR ELSE YOU'RE THE LAST OF THE INNOCENTS AND I DON'T THINK THERE ANY LEFT. ANYWAYS BEFORE WE WERE RUDELY INTERRUPTED YOU WERE ABOUT TO ANSWER MY QUSETION. "WHAT MAN WOULD BE WORTH TWENTY MILLION DOLLARS TO YOU?"

THE QUESTION SEEMED TO REVERBERATE IN THE AIR. RICKIE HAD THOUGHT SHE COULD HANDLE THIS BUT NOW THAT THE MOMENT HAD COME SHE WAS FAST LOSING HER NERVE.

TED AND BERNARD HAD WARNED HER SHE SHOULDN'T TRY TO DO THIS ON HER OWN BUT SHE HAD INSISTED SHE COULD HANDLE IT. HOW MUCH COULD SHE TELL THE REVEREND AND STILL NOT GIVE THEIR SECRET AWAY?

"I HAVE A GRANDFATHER ON MY FATHER'S SIDE WHOM I'VE NEVER MET" SHE BEGAN TO SAY CAREFULLY, THEN SHE CONTINUED ON SAYING "AS A LITTLE GIRL I WAS TOLD HE'D DISAPPEARED FOR ENGLAND DURING WORLD WAR 2 AND WAS NEVER SEEN OR HEARD FROM AGAIN.

"JUST RECENTLY MY BROTHER TED AND MY COUSIN BERNARD CAME ACROSS SOME INFORMATION THAT SUGGESTED HE'D BEEN SEEN IN THE ALSACE-LORRAINE AREA BEFORE HIS DISAPPEARANCE AND MIGHT HAVE GONE TO PARAGUAY. WHETHER HE WENT THERE ON PURPOSE OR ACCIDENTALLY WE DON'T KNOW."

"WHAT DO YOU MEAN ACCIDENTALLY?" THE REVEREND HAD THE RIGHT TO ASK ANY QUESTION HE WANTED BUT RICKIE WAS TERRIFIED BECAUSE EVERYTIME HE FORCED HER TO GIVE HIM AN ANSWER HE WAS COMING CLOSER TO THE TRUTH.

"IF ANY INJURY HAD CAUSED AMNESIA OR SOMETHING LIKE THAT HE MIGHT HAVE ENDED UP THERE." THE SECOND

SHE SAID IT SHE COULD HEAR HIS MENTAL SCOFFING. EVEN HER TO HER OWN EARS IT SOUNDED INCREDIBLY LAME. SHE SHOULD HAVE KNOWN HE WOULDN'T GIVE CREDENCE TO SUCH AN ABSURD NOTION.

"I THINK YOU'D DO BETTER WITH YOUR FIRST THEORY. DID HE AND YOUR GRANDMOTHER HAVE A BAD MARRIAGE?" RICKIE HAD LOTS OF SHIVERS GOING UP HER SPINE WHEN HE ASKED THAT QUESTION BUT SHE WAS ABLE TO ANSWER IT. WHAT MARRIAGE COULD BE WORSE? BUT ANYWAYS HISTORY HAS SHOWN THAT THOSE BUTCHERS HAD OFTEN BRAINWASHED THEIR FAMILIES AND GONE TO GREAT LENGHTS TO PROTECT THEM FROM KNOWING THE WORST OF THEIR ATROCITIES. CERTAINLY IN THE CASE OF RICKIE'S FAMILY THE SECRET HAD BEEN HIDDEN UNTILL AUNT ELIZABETH'S DEATH.

"I HAVE NO IDEA" RICKIE SAID IN A QUIET VOICE. "ALL I KNOW IS THAT HE'D BE EIGHTY-NINE YEARS OLD BY NOW. MORE THEN LIKELY HE'S DEAD BUT IF HE'S STILL ALIVE WE'D LIKE TO LOCATE HIM."

"WHY?" RICKIE KNEW THAT QUESTION HAD BEEN LERKING IN HIS MIND BUT UNFORTUNATELY SHE HAD NO ANSWER FOR THAT QUESTION.

"IF HE'S BEEN LOST TO EVERYONE THIS LONG ON PURPOSE" THE REVEREND CONTINUED "WHY GO TO ALL THE TROUBLE NOW OF BRING UP THE PAST OR AS I PERFER TO CALL IT DERDGING UP THE PAST? EVEN FOR A FAMILY OF YOUR WELTH TWENTY MILLION DOLLARS IS A LOT OF MONEY."

YOU'RE RIGHT ON EVERY COUNT RICKIE SAID TO THE REVEREND AS SHE THEN BIT HER BOTTOM LIP BUT SURELY SHE COULD BE FORGIVEN FOR TWISTING A FEW FACTS. "BEFORE AUNT ELIZABETH DIED SHE URGED MY COUSIN BERNARD TO SOLVE THE MYSTERY OF HER FATHER-IN-LAW'S DISAPPEARANCE NO MATTER THE COST."

THE REVEREND FLASHED HER A PUZZLED GLANCE. "WHAT IF YOU FIND THE ANSWERS YOOU'RE LOOKING FOR AND IT'S TOO OFFENSIVE TO SHARE WITH THE REST OF YOUR FAMILY LET ALONE THE WORLD?

ANOTHER SHIVER RAN THROUGH HER BODY AFTER THE REVEREND ASKED THAT QUESTION! "THEN WE CAN DEPEND ON YOU DISCRETION CAN'T WE?" SHE HERD AN ODD SOUND FROM HIM AND THEN HE SAID OUT LOUD TO RICKIE "SO THE TWENTY MILLION DOLLARS IS REALLY HUSH MONEY?" "CALL IT WHAT YOU WANT" SHE BLURTED OUT TO THE REVEREND AS HER VOICE SHOOK. DAM! I HATE IT WHEN MY VOICE SHAKES SHE SAID OUT LOUD. "I'D PERFER TO LOOK AT THIS AS A MUTUALLY PROFITABLE BUSINESS ADVENTURE. WE SATISFY AUNT ELIZABETH'S WISHES AND ADD MISSING KNOWLEDGE TO YOUR FAMILY HISTORY. YOU RECEIVE THE MONEY TO CARRY OUT THE WORTHIEST OF COVERT ACTIVITIES NOT TO MENTION ADDING TO YOUR RETIREMENT FUND SO THAT MAKES EVERYONE A WINNER IN MY BOOK."

AN UNCOMFORTABLE SILENCE PERVADED THE HOT STICKY ATMOSPHERE INSIDE THE CAR. SHE STIRRED RESTLESSLY UNAWARE UNTILL THIS MOMENT THAT THEY WERE BACK IN THE CITY BATTLING THE FIVE O'CLOCK RUSH HOUR TRAFFIC.

"WE NEED YOUR HELP REVEREND BECAUSE YOU'VE BEEN TO PARAGUAY BEFORE AND YOU KNOW YOUR WAY AROUND THEIR. YOU'RE VERY WELL AQUAINTED WITH SOME OF IT'S UGLIER ASPECTS AND MAYBE SOMEONE IN PARAGUAY HAD SEEN HIM THEIR? YOU HAVE CONNECTIONS TO AN UNDERGROUND AS WELL RICKIE SAID TO THE REVEREND. YOU'RE OBVIOUSLY MET IMPORTANT PEOPLE THEIR WHO KNOW SECRETS AND MIGHT DIVULGE THEM IF GIVEN THE RIGHT INCENTIVE. MONEY IS THE ONLY INDUCEMENT THAT WORKS ONE

HUNDRED PERCENT OF THE TIME AND IT'S THE ONE COMMODITY WE TAYLORS HAVE IN QUANTITY.

"ALL WE ASK IS THAT YOU MAKE INQUIRIES WHILE YOU'RE DOWN IN PARAGUAY BECAUSE YOU SPEAK THE LANGUAGE AND YOU KNOW HOW TO INFILTRATE."

WHILE THEY WERE STOPPED AT A RED LIGHT HE EYED HER WITH SUSPICION. "THAT'S AN INTERESTING CHOICE OF WORDS" THE REVEREND SAID TO MS. TAYLOR. "THAT WAS AN INTERESTING INVASION OF MY PRIVATE SUITE OF OFFICES YESTERDAY" SHE SIAD RIGHT BACK TO THE REVEREND.

"INVASION?" HE QUERIED SOFTLY. "I DON'T THINK YOU CAN CALL IT ANYTHING ELSE BECAUSE MY TEMP SUSAN NEVER SAW YOU COMING IN AND HAD NO CLUE WHO YOU WERE WHEN YOU LEFT."

"I HAVE TO ADMIT I WAS SURPRISED YOU DIDN'T CALL THE SECURITY GARDS ON ME."

SHE'D BEEN SURPRISED TOO BUT HE HAD A PRESENCE OF CHARISMA THAT HAD MESMERIZED HER AND ON TOP OF THAT SHE'D LEARNED HE WAS A MEMBER OF THE CLERGY. THE COMBINATION OF SUSPECTED SINNER AND SAINT HAD CAUGHT HER OFFGUARD.

THE LIGHT FINALLY TURNED GREEN AND ONCE AGAIN THEY WERE MOVING TOWARD THE BLOCK WHERE HER OFFICE BUILDING STOOD.

"WHAT EXACTLY DID YOU HOPE TO ACCOMPLISH WHILE YOU HAD THE CHANCE REVEREND?" "ANYTHING THAT WOULD GIVE ME A CLUE AS TO HOW TO GET YOU TO PART WITH $750,000 THOUSAND DOLLARS."

"WELL IN THE END IT LOOKS LIKE YOU MANAGED TO GET ME TO PART WITH A GREAT DEAL MORE THEN THAT."

"NO MS. TAYLOR THAT'S WERE YOU'RE WRONG" SAID THE REVEREND.

RICKIE'S HEAD SWERVED IN HIS DIRECTION AS SHE ASKED "SO YOU'VE DECIDED YOU'RE NOT GOING TO HELP OUT OUR FAMILY AFTER ALL." FOR A NUMBER OF REASONS SHE SHOULDN'T EVEN BE CONTEMPLATING AND SHE ALSO FELT DISAPPOINTED AND THE DEPTH OF HER REACTION HAD FRIGHTENED HER MORE THEN A LITTLE.

A FULL MINUTE LAPSED BEFORE SHE HAD SAID "IF I DON'T HE BEGAN IN A GRAVELLY VOICE "DOSE THAT MEAN YOU'RE WITHDRAWING YOUR FINANCIAL SUPPORT OF OUR PROJECT?"

HE WAS GOOD AT DISGUISING HIS EMOTIONS BUT SHE DETECTED AN UNDERLYING NOTE OF ANXIETY. WHEN HE'D COME TO HER RICKIE KNEW THAT CBH HAD BEEN THE LAST UNTAPPED RESOURCE FOR THE KIND OF FUNDING HE AND STONEY NEEDED. WITHOUT THE MONEY SHE COULD GIVE THEM AND THEIR PLAN DIDN'T HAVE A PRAYER OF SUCCEEDING.

SHE TOOK A DEEP BREATH AND THEN SAID "NO THE PRESIDENT TIED MY HANDS ON THE BOSINAN AND AFRICAN ISSUES BUT HE NEVER SAID ANYTHING ABOUT SOUTH AMERICA AND I'D LIKE TO LIKE TO HELP YOU. MY OFFER OF TWENTY MILLION DOLLARS STILL STANS."

FOR ONCE HER ANSWER SEEMED TO HAVE SHAKEN HIM. THEY'D PULLED UP IN FRONT OF THE TAYLOR BUILDING BUT HE DIDN'T APPEAR TO NOTICE. "LET'S GET SOMETHING STRAIGHT STONEY AND I DON'T NEED TWENTY MILLION DOLLARS TO ACCOMPLISH OUR OBJECTIVE. THAT MONEY COULD BE USED TO SUPPORT A HUNDRED DESERVING CAUSES ALL KNOCKING ON YOUR DOOR AS WE SPEAK."

"YOU'RE RIGHT" SHE AGREED IMPATIENTLY. "YOU'VE MADE YOUR POINT REVEREND. I'LL HAVE MY ATTORNEY WRITE YOU UP A CHECK FOR THE $750,000 THOUSAND DOLLARS NO MORE NO LESS. YOU'LL RECEIVE IT BY COURIER THE DAY AFTER TOMORROW. NOW IF THAT'S EVERYTHING I'LL LEAVE YOU TO GET ON WITH YOUR PARISH BUSINESS."

"I'M NOT TROUGH" HE SAID WITH UNMISTAKABLE AUTHORITY. AFTER ONE LOOK AT HIS FIERCE EXPRESSION SHE DEEMED IT WISE TO STAY WERE SHE WAS. "EVEN IF I AGREED TO HELP YOU LOCATE YOUR GRANDFATHER I WOULD HAVE TO KNOW A LOT MORE ABOUT HIM THEN YOU'VE TOLD ME BEFORE I CAN HELP YOU FIND HIM. AS FOR YOUR PAYING ME TO FINE HIM WHEN I'M ALREADY GOING TO BE IN PARAGUAY THE IDEA IS LUDICROUS AND I WON'T ACCEPT THE MONEY."

HIS AVOWAL MADE RICKIE REALIZE SHE'D BEEN HANDLING THIS ALL WRONG. THE REVEREND WAS A GOOD MAN WITH STRONG PRINCIPLES AND AS FOR TELLING HIM MORE ABOUT HER GRANDFATHER UNDER NO CIRCUMSTANCES COULD SHE ALLOW HIM TO LEARN THE TRUTH.

HE WOULD CONSIDER YOU LESS THEN THE DUST OF THE EARTH RICKIE TAYLOR AND YOU COULDN'T TAKE THAT.

NO BUT THE BEST THING TO DO WAS TO GIVE HIM AND STONEY THE MONEY FOR THEIR PROJECT AND WISH THEM LUCK. AS SOON AS SHE RETURNED TO HER OFFICE SHE WOULD PHONE TED AND TELL HIM SHE'D BEEN MISTAKEN AND THAT THEY WOULD HAVE TO FIND SOMEONE ELSE.

"I UNDERSTAND REVEREND I REALLY DO AND JUST FORGET THAT I EVER MENTIONED MY GRANDFATHER. IN

ALL PROBABILITY HE DIED YEARS AGO IN SOME OTHER PLACE. IT WOULDN'T BE FAIR TO BURDEN YOU WITH THIS WHEN YOUR WORK IS ALREADY SO DIFFICULT BUT IT'S GOING TO MAKE A DIFFERENCE BETWEEN LIFE AND DEATH FOR SO MANY PEOPLE AND I TRULY HOPE YOU'RE SUCCESSFUL.

SHE GOT OUT OF THE CAR AND SHUT THE DOOR WITH MORE VIGOR THAN USUAL. "WE'LL KEEP IN TOUCH THROUGH MY ATTORNEY GOODBYE REVEREND."

"NOT SO FAST." IN THE NEXT INSTANT HE'D SPRUNG OUT OF THE CAR AND HAD PLACED HIS HARD MUSCLED BODY IN HER PATH. SHE DIDN'T FEAR HIM NOT PHYSICALLY ANYWAYS BUT YET SHE WAS SHORT OF BREATH AND HER HEART WAS RACING.

"AS I WAS SAYING MS. TAYLOR" HE SAID AS HIS EYES BURNED INTO HERS "TO BEGEN WITH I'D HAVE TO KNOW HIS FULL NAME AND BE GIVEN A PICTURE SO I COULD IMAGINE WHAT HE MIGHT LOOK LIKE AS AN OLD MAN."

RICKIE STARED AT HIM IN SHOCK BECAUSE HE WAS ACTUALLY CONSIDERING HER PROPOSITION WITHOUT TAKING ANY MONEY FOR IT BUT THROUGH HER WORK SHE'D OFTEN MET SELFLESS MEN AND WOMEN WHO WANTED TO AID THE WORLD'S SUFFERING. RICKIE HAD ALWAYS BEEN THANKFUL THAT THIS CAPACITY FOR GOODNESS EXISTED IN HUMANITY BUT NOW EXPECIALLY SHE WAS HUMBLED TO KNOW THAT THE REVEREND WAS ONE OF THOSE SPECIAL PEOPLE.

CAREFUL RICKIE YOU'RE ALREADY TO THE POINT OF HERO-WORSHIP WITH HIM AND ONE FALSE STEP YOU'LL BE IN LOVE WITH HIM.

"I REALIZE YOU HAVE CHURCH WORK YOU SHOULD BE DOING BUT PERHAPS ONE EVENING THIS WEEK YOU'D HAVE dinner with my brother Ted, my cousin Bernard and me? We'll give you what little information we have about my grandfather."

"I need my family around not only to make sure I don't give too much money away but also to provide a buffer against you. I'll be free tomorrow so I'll come by here at five-thirty tomorrow." "All right" Rickie answered shakily. "By then I'll know where we're meeting the others."

With a brief nod he got back into his car and drove off. She sensed his urgency to be elsewhere and to do whatever it was he needed to do. Swiftly she turned and entered the building feeling a pang of loss and not liking it.

CHAPTER 35

WORKING FOR THE MAN KNOWN AS THE REVEREND.

ONCE AGAIN RICKIE TAYLOR HAD DONE THE UNEXPECTED BY NOT INSISTING THAT HE TAKE ANY MORE THEN THE $750,000 THOUSAND DOLLARS HE'D ASKED FOR BUT SHE STILL WANTS YOU TO FIND HER GRANDFATHR REVEREND BROWNING.

WHAT GAME WAS SHE PLAYING NOW? HIS THOUGHTS IN TURMOIL JORDAN WAS GLAD HE HAD TO STOP AT BREEZY LANE HERB FARM THAT EVENING TO MAKE A DELIVERY FOR THE REVEREND ROLON BEFORE DRIVING BACK TO STONEY'S HOUSE.

HE HAD HOPED THIS LITTLE SIDE TRIP WOULD GIVE HIM TIME TO GAIN A NEW PERSPECTIVE ON HIS SITUATION BUT WHEN HE REACHED THE FARM OUTSIDE RHINEBECK HE REALIZED HE'D ONLY CONFUSED HIMSELF FURTHER.

RICKIE TAYLOR'S WILLINGNESS TO FUND THEIR DANGEROUS ILLEGAL PROJECT WITH ONE OF HER OWN INVESTMENTS DIDN'T ADD UP AT ALL. THE WAS MORE THAN A SIMPLE CASE OF LOCATING HER GRANDFATHER. SOMETHING ELSE WAS AT STAKE SOMETHING BIG.

DEEP IN THOUGHT HE ALMOST DROVE PAST THE TRAILER WHERE JOSE ORTIZ STOOD WAVING HIM DOWN. THE MAN CAME RUNNING UP TO THE "72" FORD BREAKING JORDAN'S CENTRATION.

THE ORTIZES ONE OF THE MIGRANT-WORKER FAMILIES LIVING ON THE FARM THANKS TO THE INTER-CHURCH COUNCIL OVER WHICH REVEREND ROLON PRESIDED HAD COME FROM GUATEMALA EARLIER IN THE YEAR. THEY WERE IN DESPERATE NEED OF FOOD FOR THEIR NEW BABY BECAUSE APPARENTLY THE MOTHER COULDN'T NURSE SO SEVERAL MEMBERS OF VARIOUS CONGREGATIONS HAS MAD A DONATION OF BABY FORMULA AND CEREAL.

ON THE ASSUMPTION THAT THEIR NEWBORN PROBABLY NEEDED LOTS OF THINGS JORDAN HAD SUPPLEMENTED THE CHURCH FOOD WITH HIS OWN FUNDS TO PICK UP A COUPLE OF BOXES OF DISPOSABLE DIAPERS, SOME STRETCHY SUITS AND A BLANKET.

HE DIDN'T WANT THEIR GRATITUDE AND WOULD HAVE IMMEDIATELY DRIVEN AWAY. TOO MANY NEEDY PEOPLE LIVED WITHIN THE PARISH BOUNDARIES OF THE OF THE CHURCH. JORDAN FELT HE WAS BETTER OFF NOT GETTING EMOTIONALLY INVOLVED WITH ANY ONE PERSON OR FAMILY BUT JOSE INSISTED HE STAY TO EAT SOME RICE AND BEANS AND SEE THE NEWEST DARK-HAIRED ADDITION TO THEIR SIX-MEMBER FAMILY.

THEY CRAVED JORDAN'S COMPANY AND HE KNEW HOW MUCH NEEDED TO TALK TO SOMEONE IN THEIR OWN LANGUAGE. HE DIDN'T HAVE THE HEART TO DISAPPOINT THEM. AS A RESULT HE ENDED UP STAYING MUCH LONGER THEN HE'D PLANNED.

FINALLY WHEN HE FELT A DECENT INTERVAL HE PASSED AND SAID HIS GOODBYES AND LEFT THE FARM BUT AT LEAST HE HAD THE SATISFACTION OF KNOWING THAT JOSE'S FAMILY WASN'T FACING IMMEDIATE DEATH BUT NOT LIKE THOSE POOR DEVILS IN THE CHACO.

THE CHACO THAT REMOTE PART OF PARAGUAY AND THE NAME CONJURED UP HORROR. NOW THE NAME

TAYLOR WAS LINKED WITH IT AND A HORROR STORY AS WELL!

ONCE AGAIN HIS THOUGHTS EXPLODED INTO CHAOS BUT TO HIS CONSTERNATION HE COULD FEEL THE PRESENCE OF THE WOMEN WHO HAD RIDDEN NEXT TO HIME EARLIER IN THE DAY. HER FRAGRANCE STILL LINGERED IN THE CAR AND HER EXQUISITE PROFILE WITCH WAS THE BLOOM IN HER CHEEK AND HER GOLDEN BLOND HAIR UP IN A A PONYTAIL AND EVERYTHING ELSE ABOUT HER FACE AND SOFTLY ROUNDED BODY HAUNTED HIM.

COULD ANYONE THAT LOVELY BE INVOLVED IN SOMETHING TRULY HORRIBLE? UNFORTUNATELY EXPERIENCE HAD TAUGHT HIM THAT THE ANSWER WAS YES. YES SHE COULD IT WAS CERTAINLY POSSIBLE.

BY THE TIME HE'D REACHED STONEY'S HOUSE HIS JAWS ACHED AND HE REALIZED HE'D BEEN GRINDING HIS TEETH ALL THE WAY HOME.

"HI" STONEY CALLED OUT. HE'D BEEN DOING SIT-UPS ON THE FLOOR BETWEEN THEIR TWO BEDS BUT NOW HE'S ON HIS FEET. JORDAN SAID SOMETHING NONDESCRIPT NOT WANTING TO GET INVOLVED IN THE KIND OF CONVERSATION STONEY HAD IN MIND AND HIS FRIEND LOOKED HAPPIER THAN HE'D SEEN HIM IN A LONG TIME AND JORDAN DIDN'T WANT TO BE THE ONE TO MAKE THAT HAPPINESS DISAPPEAR.

"YOU DO GOOD WORK JORDAN AND NO ONE CAN DO IT BETTER THAN YOU. DID WE GET THE WHOLE AMOUNT?" HIS EYES CLOSED TIGHTLY BUT THEN HE SAID "WE DID." THAT'S GOOD BUT BEWARE WHAT YOU ASK OF GOD LEST HE WILL GRANT IT.

STONEY WHISTLED AS HE SAID "SEVEN-HUNDRED-AND-FIFTY THOUSAND DOLLARS IN ARE

HANDS AND I KNEW I COULD COUNT ON YOU TO GET US WHAT WE WANTED." HE DROVE ONE FIST AGAINST HIS PALM NEEDING TO RELEASE THAT FAMOUS LEONARD ENERGY. IT COULD HAVE TURN VERY FEROCIOUS IN COMBAT SAID STONEY.

"WHILE I'M DOWN THERE IN PARAGUAY MS. TAYLOR WANTS ME TO LOOK FOR HER GRANDFATHER." STONEY'S HEAD HAD LIFTED ABRUPTLY AS HE SAID "RICKIE TAYLOR'S GRANDFATHER IS IN PARAGUAY?" STONEY SAID TO THE REVEREND.

"POSSIBLY I'M SUPPOSED TO LEARN WHAT I CAN." "WHY IN GOD'S NAME WOULD HE TRAVEL TO THAT BLACK HOE OF BEYOND?"

"ACCORDING TO HER HE MAY HAVE GONE THERE DURING THE WORLD WAR 2 BUT IN ANY EVENT NO ONE HAS SEEN HIM OR HEARD FORM HIM SINCE AND THE FAMILY IS CURIOUS"

AFTER A QUIET INTERVAL STONEY ASKED "HOW MUCH IS SHE PAYING YOU FOR TRACKING DOWN HER GRANDFATHER?"

JORDAN SHRUGGED OUT OF HIS SHIRT THEN SAID "NOT ONE DAM CENT." "HOW MUCH DID SHE OFFER?" STONEY PROMPTED KNOWING JORDAN TOO WELL FOR HIS OWN GOOD. "TWENTY-MILLION DOLLARS." TEN FOR THE AIR-CARGO BUSINESS AND TEN FOR ME PERSONALLY."

AT THAT PRONUOUNCEMENT STONEY'S EYES DARKENED IN ANGER. A STILLNESS TOOK OVER HIS BODY. "DID YOU TELL HER YOU WEREN'T A HIRED KILLER?"

"THOSE WERE THE FIRST WORDS THAT CAME OUT OF MY MOUTH." "AND?" "AND WHAT? SHE ONLY WANTED TO KNOW IF HE WAS THERE."

HIS FRIEND JUST SHOOK HIS HEAD. "FOR THE KIND OF MONEY SHE WANTS A LOT MORE THEN THAT." "I KNOW" SAID THE REVEREND.

"I KNOW YOU KNOW AND I'M SORRY FOR NOT TAKING YOUR EARLIER RESERVATIONS SERIOUSLY" SAID STONEY AS HE BEGAN PACING BETWEEN THE BEDS.

"FORGET IT I TOLD HER WE'D ACCEPT THE $750,000 THOUSAND DOLLARS FOR ARE PROJECT AND THAT WAS IT. AS FOR HER LONG LOST RELATIVE I EXPLAINED THAT I'D HAVE TO KNOW A LOT MORE ABOUT HIM CONSIDER LOOKING FOR HIM AND PAYMENT WAS OUT OF THE QUESTION."

"WHAT WAS HER REPLY TO THAT?" "SHE AGREED TO MY TERMS." "UH-OH THAT PUTS A WHOLE NEW TWIST ON THINGS." "YOU'RE RIGHT I GAVE HER AN OUT BUT SHE DIDN'T BACK DOWN BUT WAIT THERE'S MORE TOMORROW NIGHT SHE AND HER FAMILY WANTS TO MEET WITH ME AND GIVE ME WHATEVER CLUES THEY HAVE TO HELP TRACK DOWN THEIR LOST GRANDFATHER."

"SO WHAT YOU'RE SAYING IS HER FAMILY HAS HIRED YOU TO SEARCH FOR THIS UNKNOWN WHO MIGHT OR MIGHT NOT BE WHO THEY SAY HE IS." "EXACTLY" SAID THE REVEREND. STONEY CAME TO A ABRUPT STANDSTILL BEFORE HE SAID "IDON'T KNOW AND I DON'T LIKE IT EITHER." "THAT MAKES TWO OF US" SAID THE REVEREND. "HELL I WISH I KNEW WHAT WAS GOING ON WITH MS. TAYLOR BECAUSE SOMETHING TELLS ME SHE WANTED TO HIRE A CRIMINAL AND MANAGE TO FIND OUT I WAS JUST RELEASED FORM PRISON AND WHY I WAS THERE."

"NO! SHE COULDN'T HAVE LEAREND ABOUT THAT ITSN'T POSSIBLE." HE FROWNED. "REVEREND ROLON KNOWS THE TRUTH. WHAT HAPPENS IF HE SETS US UP?" STONEY JUST SHOOK HIS HEAD. "WHAT? NO WAY! FOR YEARS ROLON'S

BEEN FIGHTING FOR MINORITIES RIGHTS AND SO DID HIS FATHER BEFORE HIM. I'VE LIVED HERE MOST OF MY LIFE AND THEY WERE ALWAYS FIGURING OUT WAYS TO HELP AND MOST OF WHAT THEY'VE DONE IS VERY ILLEGAL SO BELIEVE ME THE REVEREND IS ON ARE SIDE."

JORDAN WASN'T CONVINCED. "WHOSE IDEA WAS IT TO GO TO CBH IN THE FIRST PLACE?" "IT WAS REVEREND ROLON'S IDEA BECAUSE HE CAN'T DO WHAT HE DOES FOR PEOPLE WITHOUT ALL THE CHARITABLE DONATIONS AND THE REVEREND KNOWS EVERY PERSON AND INSTITUTION IS WILLING TO GIVE MONEY WITHIN TWO HUNDRED SQUARE MILES OF THE PARISH."

"THEN IT FOLLOWS THAT HE WOULDN'T HAVE TO HAVE HIS ARM TWISTED VERY HARD TO CONDUCT BUSINESS WITH MS. TAYLOR NOT WHEN SHE'S OFFERING MILLIONS OF DOLLARS IN RETURN FOR A FAVOR."

"I DON'T THINK ROLON KNOWS ANYTHING ABOUT HER PROPOSITION." JORDAN RUBBED THE SIDE OF HIS JAW AND FOUND OUT THAT HE NEEDED A SHAVE. "YOU HAVE TO ADMIT HER PHONE CALL LAST NIGHT CAME AS A SHOCK."

STONEY LICKED HIS LIPS AS HE SAID "OR ELSE IT WAS PURE COINCIDENCE" AND A ANGRY LAUGH HAD ESCAPED JORDAN'S THROAT. "YOU MEAN LIKE OUR NEED FOR ALMOST A MILLION DOLLARS TO PULL OFF SOME ILL-FATE COUP IN PARAGUAY COMING AT THE PRECISE MOMENT SHE WAS LOOKING FOR SOME BOUNTY HUNTER TO DO GOD KNOW WHAT IN THAT HELLHOLE?"

"YEAH IT'S POSSIBLE. SHE GOT ONE GOOD LOOK AT YOU AND FIGURED SHE'D FOUND HERSELF A REAL WARRIOR."

"IF YOU CAN BELIEVE THAT THEN YOU'VE GOT MORE OF A IMAGINATION THAN I DO" JORDAN SAID AS HE THREW

HIS JACKET ON THE BED. "I HAVE HAD A BAD FEELING ABOUT THIS." "THEN CALL HER UP AND TELL HER THE DEAL IS OFF. "YOU KNOW VERY WELL YOU DON'T WANT ME TO DO THAT" JORDAN SAID AS HE SHOOK BECAUSE THEN "WE'D BE RIGHT BACK WHERE WE STARTED FORM WITH ALL DREAMS AND NO CASH."

"IF YOUR INSTINCTS ARE TELLING YOU TO LEAVE THE CBH ALONE THEN I'M NOT GOING TO ARGUE WITH THEM. HELL THEY SAVED MY LIFE ON MORE THEN ONE OCCASION AND BESIDES THERE ARE OTHER CHARITIES AND I GUESS WE'LL HAVE TO LOOK FARTHER AHEAD FOR HELP."

"FARTHER AHEAD?" JORDAN EXCLAIMED BITTERLY. "WE COULD SEARCH THESE ENTIRE UNITED STATES AND NEVER FIND ANYONE WHO'D GIVE US A TWENTIETH OF WHAT MS. TAYLOR IS WILLING TO GIVE OUT WITHIN THE NEXT COUPLE OF DAYS. LETS BE HONEST WE'LL NEVER SEE AN ANOTHER BIG OPPORTUNITY LIKE THIS AGAIN IN OUR LIFETIME."

THEY STARED AT EACH OTHER FOR A LONG WORDLESS MOMENT BEFORE THEY SAID ANYTHING AND THEN FINALLY JORDAN LET OUT A BIG HUGE BELCH AND THEN SAID "I'LL GO TO DINNER WITH THEM TOMORROW NIGHT BUT IT WILL BE DEPENDING ON WHAT THEY HAVE TO SAY." "AT THE FIRST SIGN OF TROUBLE" STONEY INTERRUPTED "PROMISE ME YOU'LL BAIL OUT BECAUSE I DIDN'T WAIT FOR YOU TO GET OUT OF PRISON ONLY TO SEE YOU GO ON SOME SUICIDE MISSION THAT MIGHT NOT EVEN WORK OUT IN ARE FAVOR."

I WASN'T PLANNING ON IT STONEY BUT LIFE ISN'T THAT SIMPLE BECAUSE THERE'S THAT LITTLE MATTER OF MS. TAYLOR AND THE WAY SHE MAKES ME FEEL I CAN'T EXPLAIN IT BUT I THINK I MIGHT BE IN LOVE WITH MS. TAYLOR. FOR THE FRONT PASSENGER SEAT OF BERNARD'S

BLACK MERCEDES RICKIE STRAINED TO CATCH SIGHT OF THE REVEREND BECAUSE THEY HAD AGREED TO MEET IN FRONT OF HER OFFICE BUILDING.

MY BROTHER TED WAS WEARING AN IMMACULATE THREE-PIECE GRAY SUIT AND WAS STANDING OUTSIDE. DEBORAH HAD ONCE CONFIDED IN RICKIE THAT HE WAS SO HANSOME IT HURT HER TO LOOK AT HIM AND DESPITE THE WEIGHT LOSS RICKIE COULD SEE WHAT OTHER WOMEN HAD MEANT ABOUT HIM.

INSIDE THOUGH TED WAS EVEN MORE WONDERFUL AND DEBORAH WAS SO BLESSED TO BE LOVED BY HIM BUT AT THE THOUGHT OF WHAT THE REJECTION MUST BE DOING TO HER HOT TEARS RAN DOWN RCKIE'S FACE.

AS A LITTLE GIRL RICKIE HAD PUT HER BROTHER ON A PEDESTAL AND ALL THESE YEARS UNTILL SHE'D HADN'T SPENT TIME IN REVEREND BROWNING'S COMPANY SHE HADN'T MET ANOTHER MAN WHO EQUALED HIM AND SPEAKING OF REVEREND BROWNING WHERE WAS HE?

IT HAD BEEN ARRANGED THAT WHEN THE REVEREND ARRIVED AN EMPLOYEE FORM THE UNDERGROUND GARAGE WOULD PARK HIS FORD AND HER BROTHER WOULD ESCORT THEIR GUEST TO THE CAR AND THEN THE FOR OF THEM WOULD DRIVE TO PINE PLAINS FOR DINNER. THE REVEREND WAS TEN MINUTES LATE BUT THAT WAS NO GREAT AMOUNT OF TIME THOUGH. CERTAINLY NOT ENOUGH TO PANIC OR TO WORRY THAT HE MIGHT MET WITH AN ACCIDENT OR MIGHT NOT BE COMING AT ALL.

ALTERNATE WAVES OF EXCITEMENT AND DREAD MADE RICKIE SICK TO HER STOMACH. WHAT DID RICKIE VON HASE GRANDFATHER OF ONE OF THE MOST DESPISED MEN EVER TO LIVE WERE TO DINNER WITH A MAN OF THE CLOTH?

FIRST OF ALL HOW WAS SHE GOING TO KEEP HER ATTRACTION TO HIM A SECRET? SHE WAS POSITIVE HE COULD TELL HOW OUTRAGEOUSLY HER HEART POUNDED WHENEVER HE CAME NEAR HER.

SHE'D CHANGED OUTFIT'S A DOZEN TIMES AND HAD ENDED UP WEARING A SILK PANTSUIT IN TWO SHADES OF BROWN WITH A CREAM COLORED SILK BLOUSE AND HER HAIR WAS SWEPT BACK WITH A PRINTED CHIFFON SCARF IN THE SAME COLORS AS HER PANTSUIT. IT WAS NOT TO DRESSY OR NOT TO CASUAL NOTHING THAT WOULD GIVE HER TRUE FEELINGS AWAY.

WHAT AN IRONY BECAUSE SHE HAD NEVER DRESSED TO PLEASE A HOT SEXY MAN BEFORE. YET NOW WHEN SHE WANTED TO DO EVERYTHING IN HER POWER TO BE ATTRACTIVE AND UNFORGETTABLE TO A MAN SHE DIDN'T HAVE THE RIGHT TO BE THAT WAY TOWARDS THE REVEREND EVEN THOUGH HE WAS SEXY. SHE HAD NO RIGHTS AT ALL NOT EVER AGAIN.

BERNARD'S HAND COVERED HERS AS HE SAID "YOU'RE COLD AS ICE" HE SAID TO RICKIE. "IT'LL BE ALL RIGHT RICKIE BECAUSE TED AND I WILL HANDLE EVERYTHING."

"I'VE FELT UNCLEAN EVER SINCE THAT NIGHT" SHE WHISPERED IN ANGUISH. "I DON'T KNOW IF I CAN GO THROUGH WITH THIS" SHE HAD SAID TO BERNARD. "HE WILL NEVER NEED TO HERE THE TRUTH SO STOP WORRYING SO MUCH."

"HE'S A GOOD MAN BERNARD AND I EVEN THINK HE MIGHT BE A GREAT MAN" RICKIE SAID AS SHE ALMOST CHOKED ON THE WORDS.

"IF YOU SAY SO THEN I BELIEVE YOU AND I'M THANKFUL HE'S THE ONE WHO'LL BE DOING MANDKIND A FAVOR."

"DO YOU REALLY THINK VON HASE IS DOWN THERE IN PARAGUAY?" SHE SAID AS HER VOICE SHOOK. "IT'S CERTAINLY POSSIBLE" BERNARD SAID TO RICKIE. "THEN THE REVEREND WILL BE IN GREAT DANGER" SAID RICKIE. "OF COURSE BUT HE ALREADY KNOWS THAT AND OBVIOUSLY HE ACCEPTS IT OR HE WOULDN'T BE ATTEMPTING TO FIGHT AN OPPRESSIVE REGIME ON THEIR OWN HOME GROUND AND THAT'S WHY WE'RE GIVING HIM WHAT HE WANTS TO FUND HIS PROJECT."

"HE MIGHT REFUSE TO HELP US" RICKIE SAID. BERNARD SQUEEZED HER HAND GENTLY AS HE SAID "TONIGHT WE'LL HAVE TO USE ARE COLLECTIVE TAYLOR CHARM TO PRESUADE HIM OTHERWISE." "THERE HE IS!" SHE CRIED OUT INTERRUPTING THEIR CONVERSATION.

RELIEVED THAT HE WAS ALL RIGHT SHE GAZED OPENLY AT HIM AS HE GOT OUT OF HIS CAR AND SHOOK HANDS WITH TED AND BERNARD. BOTH MEN STOOD TALL BUT ONLY ONE HAD LONG DARK HAIR LIKE A MOVIESTAR AND FOR THE OCCASION THE REVEREND HAD A BLACK CHARCOAL SUIT ON AND HE WAS WEARING HIS COLLAR AS WELL.

RICKIE KNEW WHAT IT REPRESENTED AND WHAT IT MENT TO REPRESENT. SHE LOOKED AWAY WHILE THE TWO MEN APPROACHED THE CAR AND GOT INTO THE BACK RICKIE FOCUSED HER ATTENTION ON SOME PEOPLE THAT WERE JAYWALKING FARTHER DOWN THE STREET AND THEN SHE HEARD TED INTRODUCE THE REVEREND TO BERNARD AS THEY DROVE OFF.

FOR THE FIRST TEN MILES OR SO RICKIE LISTENED TO THE REVEREND'S WORK AND BERNARD'S AND TED'S DUTIES AT THE TAYLOR WORLD BANKING HEADQUARTERS. NO ONE EAVESDROPPING WOULD HAVE RECOGNIZED THE GRAVITY OF THEIR SEPARATE MISSIONS.

Her cousin set the tone for the evening and everything was calm and low-key but the calm didn't go blow the surface because Rickie had feared she'd explode from the tension.

"Maybe you'd like to tell the Reverend where we're going" she heard Bernard say out loud. "Rickie?" he prompted. Heat had filled her cheeks as she realized he'd probably been talking to her for some time now and she hadn't been aware of it.

"Tonight t-the Millhaven Winery is putting on a wine-tasting celebration and dinner at the Ticino Gardens in Pine Plains and we've always wanted to go but never got a chance to go so we thought you might enjoy it."

"I'm sure I shall." Their guest's deep vibrant voice permeated her to the bone. For the lif of her Rickie couldn't find another word to say. She left it to Ted and Bernard to carry the big conversation untill they arrived at the Italian restaurant and outdoor garden with it's topiary trees and sparkling fountains.

This event was held one night a year and only the wealthy could afford to ensure a permanent reservation but of course a few tables were always held aside for the privileged few like the Taylor family who often made their arrangements at the last minute and never worried about being denied access to the food and pop or anything else in the restaurant.

All those beautifully dressed people smiling and nodding at the four of them and speculating how much they were really worth as they followed the waiter to their table and they would be horrified

IF THEY KNEW THE TRUTH ABOUT HER GRANDFATHER. VON HASE NOT TAYLOR WAS BORN IN BAVARIA NOT ENGLAND BUT RICKIE WAS HORRIFIED AND SICKENED BECAUSE THE THOUGHT OF WINE LET ALONE FOOD BROUGHT BILE TO HER THROAT. SHE HAD ENOUGH PRESENCE OF MIND TO MAKE SURE SHE WAS PLACED BESIDE TED AND DIRECTLY ACROSS FROM BERNARD AND AFTER THEY WERE SEATED SHE DRANK SOME WATER AND SUCKED ON A PIECE OF ICE ALWAYS KEEPING HER LIDS LOWERED SO SHE WOULDN'T LOOK AT JORDAN BROWNING.

THE SOFT SWEET AIR AND THE ITALIAN DÉCOR PLUS THE ENSEMBLE OF MUSICIANS PLAYING VIVALDI CREATED THE IMPRESSION OF DINING OUT ON HILLSIDE IN ITALY.

DURING AN UNGUARDED MOMENT SHE HAPPENED TO GLANCE UP AND DISCOVERED THE REVEREND'S ATTENTION ON HER AND HIS EXPRESSION WAS ENIGMATIC. AFRAID HER EYES WOULD GIVE AWAY THE INTENSE ATTRACTION SHE FELT FOR HIM AND THEN SHE TURNED HEAD TO ENGAGE TED IN CONVERSATION. HER BROTHER IS ALWAYS SENSITIVE TO HER MOOD AND OBLIGED HER READILY ENOUGH AND SAVING HER FROM TOTAL EMBARRASSMENT.

LOCAL WINES WERE INTRODUCED BETWEEN EACH COURSE OF THE DINNER AND THROUGHOUT THE LENGHTY DINNER ALL THREE MEN HAD APPEARED TO BE INTERESTED IN THEIR FOOD BUT RICKIE NOTICED THEY ATE AND DRANK SPARINGLY.

RICKIE WAS NO DIFFERENT BUT SHE'D WITH THE MANICOTTI AND SHE COULDN'T MANAGE MORE THAN A SIP OR TWO OF WINE WITH DINNER.

"THIS IS THE ONLY PICTURE WE HAVE OF OUR GRANDFATHER AS HE LOOKED PRIOR TO HIS DISAPPEARANCE." TED HAD SUDDENLY PLUNGED IN WITHOUT WARNING AND PULLED A SNAPSHOT FROM HIS

FRONT SHIRT POCKET AND HANDED IT TO THE REVEREND. "IT'S A COPY OF THE ORIGINAL AND HIS NAME IS GEORGE HYDE TAYLOR REPUTED TO BE AN ENGLISH ARISTOCRAT WHO FOUGHT DURING WORLD WAR 2."

RICKIE CLASPED HER HANDS BENEATH THE TABLE TO KEEP THEM FROM SHAKING. WE'RE LIARS ALL OF US ARE LIARS. "HE WILL BE FORTY YEARS OLD THERE" BERNARD ADDED. "ACCORDING TO MY LATE MOTHER WHO WAS GIVEN THIS BY HER MOTHER-IN-LAW IT WAS TAKEN ON THE DAY MY FATHER WAS BORN. HE'S HOLDING HIM IN HIS ARMS AND JUDGING BY WHAT AUNT ELIZABETH TOLD BERNARD" TED CONTINUED "THE BIRTH TOOK PLACE IN METZ FRANCE OBVIOUSLY AT THE TIME OF OCCUPATION OF ALSACE LORRAINE."

THEIR GUEST STARED AT THE SMALL PHOTOGRAPH WITHOUT SAYING ANYTHING. RICKIE FOUGHT TO SUPRESS A GROAN BECAUSE SHE WAS HAPPY THAT THE REVEREND WAS GOING TO TRY TO FIND HER SO CALLED GRANDFATHER.

"AUNT ELIZABETH RECALLED HER MOTHER-IN-LAW OUR GRANDMOTHER SAYING SHE'D GOTTEN SEPARATED FROM HER HUSBAND. THE DETAILS ARE SKETCHY BUT APPARENTLY HE MIGHT HAVE BEEN WOUNDED AND WAS ACCIDENTALLY SHIPPED OUT ON A BOAT LEAVING FOR SOUTH AMERICA WITH OTHER PEOPLE LIKE THE GERMANS MOSTLY AND ARE ANXIOUS TO ESCAPE THE WAR ALTOGETHER.

"WE DON'T THINK HER PRIDE WOULD HAVE ALLOWED HER TO ADMIT THAT HE WANTED TO GET LOST AND RICKIE TENDS TO BELIEVE HE HAD AMNESIA BECAUSE OF SOME INJURY AND DIDN'T KNOW WHAT WAS HAPPENING TO HIM AT ALL.

"BERNARD AND I ARE MORE INCLINED TO THINK HE MIGHT HAVE BEEN LOOKING FOR A WAY OUT OF HIS

MARRIAGE AND SEIZED THE BIGGEST OPPORTUNITY WHEN IT WAS PRESENTED. IF THAT WAS HIS PLAN THEN PARAGUAY WOULD HAVE BEEN THE IDEAL PLACE TO HIDE FROM HIS WIFE.

"THE CHAOS OF WAR WOULD HAVE BEEN THE PERFECT TIME TO ABDICATE ALL RESPONSIBILITY." RICKIE WAS ASTONISHED AT THE FACILITY WITH WHICH HER BROTHER LIED AND YET MUCH OF WHAT HE SAID WERE THE BELIEFS THEY'D GROWN UP WITH AND THE TRUTH AS THEY'D KNOWN IT UNTILL RECENTLY THAT IS.

"SO YOU SEE" TED FINISHED "WE DON'T HAVE MUCH INFORMATION." "WHAT WE DO KNOW IS THAT OUR GRANDMOTHER ENDED UP COMING TO AMERICA WITH HER TWO SONS WHICH WERE MY FATHER AND MY UNCLE. SHE ALSO HAD LIMITLESS FUNDS" BERNARD ADDED QUIETLY BUT AT THIS POINT WE'RE BEGINNING TO WONDER IF GEORGE TAYLOR WAS REALLY WHO HE SAID HE WAS BUT IT IS POSSIBLE HE WAS GOING TO START OPERATING UNDER A DIFFERENT IDENTITY."

"YOU MEAN HE WASN'T REALLY AN ENGLISH GENTLE MAN?" THE REVEREND SOPKE UP FOR THE FIRST TIME SOUNDING INTRIGUED. "WE DON'T KNOW BECAUSE OUR GRANDMOTHER NEVER TALKED ABOUT HIM AT ALL NOT EVEN ONCE. AS CHILDREN WE FIGURED OUT PRETTY QUICKLY THAT THE SUBJECT OF OUR GRANDFATHER WAS TABOO AND THAT THEIR WERE NO LETTERS, PICTURES AND NO CLUES OF ANY KIND BECAUSE HER SECRET DIED WITH HER."

RICKIE PRAYED TED WOULD STOP TALKING AND HE WAS ALSO DANCING TO CLOSE TO THE EDGE OF THE POOL AND THAT MADE HER START SHIVERING BECAUSE IT WAS COLD OUTSIDE TOO.

"IF WE DIDN'T HAVE THE MEANS AT OUR DISPOSAL WE'D BE FORCED TO LET THE MATTER DROP PARTICULARLY

SINCE WE'RE PLAYING SUCH A LONG SHOT" BERNARD INTERJECTED ONCE MORE BUT THE FACT IS DO HAVE THE MONEY AND MY MOTHER OPENED A PANDORA'S BOX WHEN SHE GAVE ME THAT PICTURE MINUTES BEFORE SHE DIED."

HER COUSIN'S FACE WAS PALED ADDING A POIGNANT CREDENCE TO HIS WORDS THAT THE REVEREND COULDN'T HELP BUT NOTICE BUT "OBVIOUSLY SHE HAD A REASON FOR SAYING AND DOING WHAT SHE DID AND SINCE HER PASSING I HAVEN'T BEEN ABLE TO LET IT GO."

"WE'VE BEEN CONSUMED BY IT" TED CONCURRED "BUT PARAGUAY IS OBVIOUSLY OUT OF OUR TERRITORY AND JUST IN CASE HE'S STILL ALIVE AND LIVING THERE WE'VE TALKED ABOUT HIRING SOMEONE TO GO THERE AND MAKE INQUIRIES WITOUT RAISING SUSPICION BUT IT WOULD HAVE TO BE A CERTAIN TYPE OF MAN WHO UNDERSTANDS THAT PLACE AND CAN TAKE CARE OF HIMSELF.

"UNTILL RICKIE MENTIONED THAT YOU'D PETITIONED HER FOR MONEY TO FUND A COVERT OPERATION OF YOU OWN DOWN THERE BUT WE DIDN'T FIND THE RIGHT PERSON TO APPROACH YET."

BERNARD LEANED TOWARD THEIR GUEST AND SAID "WE DON'T KNOW IF YOU ARE THAT PERSON OR IF YOU WOULD BE WILLING TO HELP US. "I SEE SAID THE REVEREND UNDERSTANDABLY YOU HAVE PROBLEMS OF YOUR OWN TO DEAL WITH AND WE WOULDN'T WANT TO COMPLICATE AN ALREADY DELICATE SITUATION."

RICKIE HAD TO GIVE HER FAMILY CREDIT FOR BEING SUCH CONSUMMATE ACTORS AND IF SHE HADN'T KNOWN THE TRUTH ABOUT GERHARDT VON HASE SHE WOULD HAVE BELIEVED EVERYTHING THE TWO OF THEM SAID THEY'D WOVEN JUST ENOUGH TRUTH AND HAD CONJECTURE INTO THEIR STORY TO SOUND TOTALLY CONVINCING.

THE FACT THAT THE REVEREND HADN'T RECOGNIZED A CONECTION BETWEEN THEIR GRANDFATHER AND VON HASE WAS THE FACT THAT HE HADN'T DISMISSED THEIR PROPOSITION. SHE DIDN'T KNOW WHETHER SHE WANTED IT TO BE RELIEVED OR IF SHE SHOULD BE FRIGHTENED.

TED FLASHED HER A SPARKLING GLANCE REMINDING HER THAT SHE NEEDED TO MAKE THE FINAL CONTRIBUTION. STILL TREMBLING SHE HAD REACHED HER HANDBAG AND PULLED OUT A PIECE OF PAPER. "WE GAVE THE PHOTOGRAPH TO POLICE SKETCH ARTIST AND ASKED HIM TO RENDER A DRAWING OF THE WAY ARE GRANDFATHER MIGHT LOOK TODAY."

BY THE QUICKENING OF THE REVEREND'S INTELLIGENT EYES RICKIE KNEW HE WAS AWARE OF HER FRAGILE STATE AND AS SOON AS SHE'D PASSED HIM THE DRAWING SHE AVERTED HIS GAZE AND DRANK THE REST OF HER ICE WATER.

"HE LOOKS FAIRLY TALL IN THIS PHOTO" THE REVEREND SAID QUIETLY BUT IF HE'S LIKE MOST ELDERLY PEOPLE THEN HE SHURNK SOMEWHAT." YEAH YOUR PROBABLY RIGHT TED SAID TO THE REVEREND. "NO DOUBT HE'S CHANGED BYOND RECOGNITION AND IT'S PROBABLY BECAUSE HE'S LIVING UNDER AN ASSUMED NAME TOO AND AS BERNARD SAID WE MIGHT HAVE SET OURSELVES AN IMPOSSIBLE TASK."

BENEATH THEIR CALM EXTERIORS RICKIE SENSED HER BROTHER AND COUSIN WERE HOLDING THEIR BREATH AND SO WAS SHE BUT NOT FOR THE SAME REASON. THROUGHOUT THE MEAL SHE'D COME TO THE REALIZATION THAT SHE WANTED REVEREND BROWNING TO TURN THEM DOWN AND SHE KNEW HER MOTIVATION WAS ENTIRELY SELFISH IF IT EVER CAME TO LIGHT THAT SHE WAS RICKIE VON HASE SHE COULDN'T BEAR TO SEE THE REVULSION AND HORROR IN HIS EYES BEFORE HE TURNED AWAY FROM THE UNSPEAKABLE.

"MS. TAYLOR?" HE'D SUDDENLY SINGLED HER OUT. "ARE YOU FEELING ILL AGAIN? IF YOU ARE THEN I THINK WE SHOULD GO." HE SEEMED TO NOTICE EVERYTHING SHE WAS DOING.

"NO I'M OKAY." "HE'S RIGHT RICKIE THAT FLU BUG YOU PICKED UP IN AUSTRALIA IS STILL GIVING YOU PROBLEMS. COME ON I'LL HELP YOU TO THE CAR." TED PUSHED AWAY FROM THE TABLE AND GOT TO HIS FEET TO ASSIST HER AND BERNARD WASN'T FAR BEHIND.

SHE COULD IMAGINE THEIR FRUSTRATION BECAUSE OF HER INABILITY TO HIDE HER FEELINGS AND THEY'D BEEN FORCED TO LEAVE THE NICE RESTAURANT BEFORE THE REVEREND COULD GIVE THEM THE ANSWER.

HE DIDN'T SAY ANYTHING UNTILL THEY'D RETURNED TO THE CAR AND HAD STARTED BACK FOR POUGHKEEPSIE.

"WHEN WE GO BACK TO PARAGUAY STONEY AND I WILL BE FLYING INTO THE CHACO BECAUSE THERE'S A JESUIT MISSION AND A COUPLE OF SMALL EUROPEAN SETTLEMENTS FARTHER DOWN STREAM FROM WHERE WE'LL BE PICKING UP ARE CARGO. WHILE WE'RE THERE I'M WILLING TO PUT OUT SOME FEELERS TO SEE IF ANYTHING TURNS UP."

HIS RESPONSE SENT RICKIE INTO A PANIC BUT IT HAD THE OPPOSITE EFFECT ON HER FAMILY. SHE HAD NO DOUBTS THAT IF THEY'D BEEN ALONE THAT BOTH BERNARD AND TED WOULD HAVE PICKED HER UP IN THEIR ARMS AND HUGGED HER BUT INSTEAD THEY THANKED THE SO CALLED REVEREND IN WELL MODULATED VOICES. THEN THEY ACTED IF AS WHAT HAD TAKEN PLACE WAS AN EVERYDAY OCCURRENCE AS IF THEY WERE MERELY BUSINESSMEN ENJOYING A FINE MEAL BEFORE DISCUSSING THEIR LATEST VENTURE.

THE REVEREND HAD NO IDEA HE HAD JUST AGREED TO SEARCH FOR ONE OF THE MOST HATED WAR CRIMINALS IN ALL THE HISTORY. IT'S ALREADY DONE NOW AND THERE'S NO GOING BACK.

ON THE RETURN TRIP TO POUGHKEEPSIE TED AND BERNARD PLIED THEIR GUEST WITH QUESTIONS ABOUT PARAGUAY. SHE HALF LISTENED TO HIS ANSWERS BUT IN TRUTH SHE FELT AS ILL AS IF SHE REALLY DID HAVE THE FLU. REVEREND BROWNING INSPIRED SUCH AMBIVALENT EMOTIONS THAT HE COULDN'T HAVE CONTRIBUTED TO THE CONVERSATION IF HE WANTED TO.

ARRIVING BACK AT HER OFFICE BUILDING BERNARD DROVE THE MERCEDES INTO THE UNDERGROUND PARKINGLOT DEPOSITING OF THE REVEREND AT THE GARAGE ATTENDANT'S CUBICLE. BEFORE HE GOT OUT OF THE CAR THEIR GUEST THANKED THEM FOR DINNER THEN TRAPPED RICKIE'S GAZE. "IF I WERE YOU MS. TAYLOR I'D GO SEE A DOCTOR ABOUT THAT FLU PROBLEM."

NO DOCTOR COULD FIX WHAT WAS WRONG WITH HER. "IF I THOUGHT ONE MIGHT HELP ME I WOULD BUT THIS IS VIRAL AND ANTIBIOTICS WON'T TOUCH IT" SHE HAD IMPROVISED. "THANKS FOR BEING SO CONCERNED ANYWAYS REVEREND. MY ATTORNEY WILL GET IN TOUCH WITH YOU TOMORROW AFTERNOON."

JUDGING FROM THE GUARDED EXPRESSION IN HIS EYES HE DIDN'T BELIEVE HER LIE ABOUT HAVING CAUGHT A VIRUS BUT NEVERTHELESS HE DIDN'T REFER TO IT AGAIN. "STONEY AND I WANT OUR MISSION TO SUCCEED AND THANKS TO OUR AMAZING GENEROSITY WE CAN ATTEMPT TO PULL IT OFF. WITH LUCK WE'LL BE ABLE TO LEARN SOMETHING ABOUT YOUR GRANDFATHER IN THE PROCESS BUT I DON'T THINK I HAVE TO REMIND ALL OF YOU THAT THIS IS IN GOD'S HANDS NOW."

AT THE MENTION OF GOD RICKIE'S EYES SLID AWAY AS SHE SAID "GOOD NIGHT TO THE REVEREND." THE OTHERS SAID THEIR GOODBYES BEFORE BERNARD DROVE OFF. AFTER THEY'D EMERGED FROM THE UNDERGROUND PARKINGLOT HE TURNED IN RICKIE'S DIRECTION AND SAID "SOMETHING TELLS ME THAT IF ANYONE CAN FIND VON HASE THE REVEREND CAN BERNARD SAID TO RICKIE BEFORE THEY WENT INTO HER OFFICE BUILDING."

"I GET THE SAME FEELING" TED AGREED WITH BERNARD. RICKIE DIDN'T KNOW WHAT TO BELIEVE AND AT THAT MOMENT SHE WAS STILL COMING TO GRIPS WITH THE REALIZATION THAT SHE'D FALLEN IN LOVE WITH THE REVEREND BROWNING.

CHAPTER 36

RICKIE'S IN LOVE WITH THE REVEREND.

THE REVEREND GRIMACED WHEN HE HAPPENED TO SEE HIMSELF IN THE BATHROOM MIRROR. WITH AN ANGRY JERK HE REMOVED THE COLLAR THAT HE WROE TO DINNER.

YOU'RE A FRAUD REVEREND BROWNING AND ALL ALONG YOU'VE ACCUSED THE TAYLOR FAMILY OF HAVING ULTERIOR MOTIVES WHEN THE REAL CULPRIT IS STANDING RIGHT HERE.

EVEN IF THEY HAVEN'T TOLD YOU EVERYTHING YOU CAN FEEL IN YOUR GUT THAT THEIR EXCEPTIONAL PEOPLE. TOO BAD YOU CAN'T SAY THE SAME THING ABOUT YOURSELF BECAUSE YOU'VE ACTUALLY LED THEM TO BELIEVE YOU'RE A SELFLESS HUMAN BEING DEDICATED TO SERVING GOD AND MANKIND BUT THE TRUTH IS YOU'RE AN EX-CON WHO'S BROKEN EVERY RULE IN THE BOOK AND ITENDS TO BREAK MORE AND EVEN WORSE YOUR SO CALLED FEELINGS HAS LED YOU TO WANT MS. TAYLOR IN ALL THE WAYS A MAN CAN WANT A WOMEN BUT THOSE WAYS ARE FORBIDDEN TO YOU.

SHE COULD VERY WELL BE YOUR DOWNFALL. "HELL SHE ALREADY IS" HE SAID VIOLENTLY BEFORE STRETCHING OUT ON TOP OF THE BED TO GET SOME SLEEP. PLAGUED BY VISIONS OF RICKIE TAYLOR AND TONIGHT'S MYSTERIOUS SICK SPELL THAT HAD STOLEN THE COLOR FROM HER

FACE AND BEADED HER HAIRLINE WITH PERSPIRATION HE WRESTLED WITH THE IDEA OF PHONEING HER.

STONEY HADN'T COME IN YET SO NOW WOULD BE THE TIME TO PHONE HER AND DRIVEN BY A COMPULSION THAT OVER RODE HIS COMMON SENCE HE THEN GOT UP OUT OF BED AND FOUND THE PAPER WITH HER NUMBER ON IT AND REACHED FOR THE PHONE.

WHAT EXCUSE WOULD HE GIVE? DOES IT MATTER? SHE'S IN YOUR BLOOD AND YOU KNOW YOU'RE GOING TO CALL HER SO GET IT OVER WITH ALREADY JORDAN SAID AS HE WALKED INTO THE BEDROOM.

ON THE SECOND RING SHE ANSWERED "HELLO?" HE DIDN'T KNOW IF THE TREMOR HE HEARD WAS A RESULT OF THE ILLNESS OR NERVOUSNESS OR BOTH SO HE GOT THE IMPRESION THAT SHE HADN'T GONE TO BED YET.

"I'VE BEEN WORRIED ABOUT THESE ATTACKS OF YOURS SO I THOUGHT I WOULD CALL TO MAKE SURE YOU'RE ALL RIGHT.

AFTER A STUNNED SILENCE HE HEARED "REVEREND?" RIGHT NOW SHE SOUNDED AS BREATHLESS AS HE FELT.

NO MY NAME IS JORDAN I WANT TO HEAR YOU SAY IT. I WANT TO HEAR YOU USE IT MORNING, NOON, AND NIGHT AND ALL THE TIMES IN BETWEEN.

"LORD SOMETHING TELLS ME YOU WORK TO HARD, AGONIZE TOO MUCH MS. TAYLOR. IS IT POSSIBLE YOU HAVE AN ULCER?" "IF I DON'T START TO FEEL BETTER SOON I'LL MENTION IT TO MY DOCTOR."

JORDAN'S HAND TINGHTENED ON THE RECEIVER AS HE SAID "DON'T WAIT TOO LONG. WHEN DID THE SYMPTOMS

START?" HE ASKED HER. HE FELT HER HESITATION BEFORE SHE SAID "A FEW DAYS PRIOR TO MY SO CALLED RETURN" SHE TOLD THE REVEREND.

"AS I TOLD YOU EARLIER THE ACHE WERE IN TROUBLE A HUNDRED YEARS AGO. ANOTHER WEEK WON'T MAKE THAT MUCH DIFFERENCE. DO YOU WANT TO PUT OFF MEETING WITH YOUR ATTORNEY UNTIL YOU'RE FEELING BETTER?" "I APPRECIATE YOUR SENSITIVITY BUT I THINK A BETTER PLAN MIGHT BE FOR ME TO TAKE A REAL VACATION ONCE WE HAVE FINISHED OUR BUINESS."

WHERE WOULD THAT BE? AND WITH WHOM? JORDAN DIDN'T LIKE THE SOUND OF THAT OR HIS OWN REACTIONS. "WHERE DO THE TAYLORS GO TO GET AWAY FROM THE STRESS OF THIS WORLD?"

"IF THERE IS SUCH A PLACE I'VE NEVER FOUND IT" SAID A SMALL VOICE AS IT CLUTCHED HIS GUT. "I WAS HOPING YOU COULD TELL ME" AND WITH THAT COMMENT SHE'D CAUGHT HIM OFF GUARD.

"STATE OF MIND IS EVERYTHING" HE SAID OUT LOUD AND SO IS THE SOLEMNLY IF ONLY TO REMIND HIMSELF. "HOW DOES ONE ACHIEVE ANY SORT OF TRANQUILLITY REVEREN?" THE SINCERITY OF HER QUESTION ASKED WITH SUCH EARNESTNESS DEFEATED HIM.

"SURELY YOU'VE EXPERIENCED SOME SUBLIME MOMENTS THROUGH YOUR PHILANTHROPY." "NOT REALLY I DIDN'T EARN THE MONEY I'VE BEEN GIVING AWAY. I'M A VICTIM OF BOTH LIKE EVERYONE ELSE. I JUST HAPPENED TO BE BORN WEALTHY."

THIS WOMEN MIGHT AS WELL HAVE BEEN GIVING HIM HER CONFESSION BECAUSE RICKIE HAD NEVER FELT SO INADEQUATE IN HER LIFE. "HAVE YOU EVER EARNED ANY MONEY OF YOUR OWN?" HE DIDN'T KNOW WHERE

THAT QUESTION HAD COME FROM CONSIDERING THE TOTAL QUIET ON HER END HE FEARED HE MIGHT HAVE OFFENDED HER THE LAST THING HE WANTED TO DO BEFORE HE LEFT FOR THAT BUSINESS TRIP.

"NO ONE'S EVER ASKED ME THAT BEFORE." HE HEARD WONDER IN THE TONE OF HER VOICE. "TO THINK THAT ALL THIS TIME I'VE BEEN LOOKING IN THE WRONG PLACE." JORDAN DIDN'T UNDERSTAND THAT CRYPTIC LITTLE COMMENT BUT HE RECGNIZED THAT SOMETHING PROFOUND WAS GOING ON INSIDE HER.

"THANK YO FOR YOUR WISDOM REVEREND AND YOUR CONCERN." WISDOM? IF I HAD ANY I WOULDN'T BE IN THIS SITUATION AND AS FOR CONCERN MS. TAYLOR IT'S TO BAD THAT PARTICULAR TRAIT ISN'T THE ONLY THING MOTIVATING ME SAID THE REVEREND.

I GUESS THERE GOES MY PEACE OF MIND HE SAID. "YOU'RE WELCOM NEEDLESS TO SAY STONEY AND I ARE INDEBTED TO YOUR ALTRUSIM AND THE FACT THAT YOU'RE WILLING TO SHARE YOUR UNEARNED ABUNDANCE MEANS LIFE IN PLACE OF CERTAIN DEATH AND SURELY THAT HAS TO BRING SOME COMFORT."

"SOME" SHE WHISPEARED BUT THERE WAS MUCH MORE TO THIS BECAUSE JORDAN FELT SURE OF IT AND HE HAD FOUND HIMSELF WANTING TO KNOW IT ALL BUT HE DIDN'T HAVE THE RIGHT BECAUSE RICKIE DIDN'T WANT HIM TO FIND OUT THE TRUTH."

"MAYBE YOU NEED TO FIND A CAUSE FUNDED BY SOMEONE ELSE AND SIMPLY GIVE THE SERVICE OF YOUR TIME AND TALENTS" HE TOLD HER. "AS I SAID REVEREND YOUR WORDS HAVE BEEN INSPIRATIONAL." "I'LL BELIEVE THAT WHEN I SEE YOU'VE RECOVERED FROM YOUR ILLNESS" THE REVEREND SAID TO RICKIE.

"HOW SOON WILL YOU LEAVE FOR PARAGUAY?" FRUSTRATED BY THE ABRUPT CHANGE IN CONVERSATION HE GAVE A TERSE RESPONSE. HE THEN SAID "TOMORROW IS MONDAY AND IF MY CONTACTS IN CHACO ARE READY WE'LL LEAVE ON THURSDAY" SAID THE REVEREND.

"THEN TOMORROW IS NOT TO SOON TO MEET WITH MY ATTORNEY" SAID RICKIE. "NO SAID THE REVEREND." HE WASN'T GOING TO LIE ABOUT THAT SAID JORDAN.

"HOW LONG DO YOU THINK YOU'LL BE GONE?" SAID RICKIE. IT IS ALL DEPENDING ON A VARIETY OF CRITICAL FACTORS SO ABOUT FOUR OR FIVE DAYS" SAID THE REVEREND.

"I DON'T THINK THE PARISH COULD SPARE YOU FOR MUCH LONGER THEN THAT EVEN WITH EVERYONE PITCHING IN SOMETHING ALWAYS NEEDS TO BE DONE AND SOMEONE IS ALWAYS IN NEED" SAID JORDAN. "I KNOW HE SAID AS HE SUCKED IN HIS BREATH." "YES YOU DO" RICKIE SAID.

THE WOMEN HAD ALREADY HELPED THOUSANDS AND SPENT MILLIONS AND IT WAS A PRIVILEGE TO KNOW HER THE REVEREND SAID TO JORDAN.

"PROMISE ME YOU WON'T LET THE ADDED BURDEN OF TRYING TO FIND MY GRANDFATHER DETAIN YOU. I WOULDN'T WANT TO HAVE THAT ON MY CONSCIENCE ALONG WITH EVERYTHING ELSE" RICKIE SAID OUT LOUD TO THE REVEREND.

"EVERYTHING ELSE?" HE HEARD HER INTAKE A BREATH. "GIVING YOU THE MONEY MEANS PLACING YOU IN DANGER FROM OUR GOVERNMENT AS WELL AS THE ENEMY'S. IF ON THE WAY DOWN SOMETHING WENT VERY WRONG AND YOU WERE HELD BY THE AUTHORITIES THAT WOULD

BE BAD ENOUGH BUT IF YOUR PLAN FAILED INSIDE OF PARAGUAY BOUTH YOU AND YOUR FRIEND COULD BE CAPTURED, TORTURED, IMPRISONED OR EVEN MURDERED IN HIDEOUS WAYS AND CERTAINLY NEVER BE SEEN OR HEARD FROM AGAIN. I'M NOT SURE I CAN BEAR THAT SAID RICKIE.

JORDAN WAS ASTOUNDED BY HER WORDS OF PASSION. "I'VE SPENT JUST ENOUGH TIME WITH MARY TO REALIZE THAT STONEY IS NOT ONLY THE CENTER OF HER LIFE BUT OF HIS EX-WIFE AS WELL AND WITHOUT HIM I WOULD IMAGINE THEY'D BOTH BE IN PERMANENT STATE OF MOURNING AND AS FOR PARISHIONERS I DON'T THINK I NEED TO TELL YOU HOW THE LOSS WOULD AFFECT THEM."

HE SHOOK HIS HEAD AND TO THINK HE'D NEVER THOUGHT OF HER AS COLD AND UNEMOTIONAL AND A ICE PRINCESS!

"I ENJOY A CHALLENGE" WAS ALL HE SAID. "THEN LET'S HOPE YOUR GOD PLANS TO ALLOW YOU A LONG AND HEALTHY LIFE IN SPITE OF THAT ENJOYMENT." HE BLINKED AND SAID "MY GOD?" "DID I SAY SOMETHING WRONG?" "ISN'T HE EVERYONE'S GOD?" "I DON'T KNOW" SAID RICKIE AS HER VOICE GOT TORTURED. "IF HE DOES EXIST HE HASN'T BEEN THERE FOR A LOT OF PEOPLE."

JORDAN HEARD SO MUCH GRIEF IN HER VOICE IT WEIGHTED HIM DOWN. "HE USES PEOPLE LIKE YOU TO HELP HIM DO HIS WORK."

AN UNMISTAKABLE GROAN EXCAPED HER THROAT AS SHE SAID "YOU DON'T KNOW ANYTHING ABOUT ME" SAID THE REVEREND BUT I'M AFRAID IT'S THE OTHER WAY AROUND SAID JORDAN BECAUSE HE WAS ON THE VERGE OF SUGGESTING THEY MEET SOME PLACE TO CONTINUE THIS

LITTLE CONVERSATION IN PERSON WHEN HE REALIZED HE COULDN'T DO THAT.

YOU'RE REALLY LOSING IT BROWNING EVEN IF YOU WEREN'T POSING AS A MINISTER-MISSIONARY DO YOU THINK SHE'D AGREE TO JOIN YOU SOMEWHERE AT THIS TIME OF NIGHT?

DID HE HONESTLY BELIEVE THAT JUST TALKING TO HER WOULD ASSUAGE THIS GROWING HUNGER INSIDE HIM? "WE ALL HAVE THING IN OUR PAST WE'D PERFER TO FORGET MS. TAYLOR BUT REST ASSURED YOU CAN BE VERY PROUD OF CBH. I LOOKED YOU UP ON THE INTERNET AND THE CAUSES YOU'VE CHAMPIONED HAVE BROUGHT MORE THEN ONE LUMP TO MY LITTLE SORE THROAT."

"THEN THAT MAKES TWO OF US WHO ARE IMPRESSED BECAUSE I THINK WHAT YOU'RE ABOUT TO DO FOR THE ACHE INDIANS IS MAGNIFICENT GOOD NIGHT REVEREND." "GOOD NIGHT RICKIE" THE REVEREND SAID BACK TO HER. THERE WAS A CLICK HE SHOULD HAVE BEEN TO ONE TO GET OFF THE PHONE FIRST THEN THE REVEREND HUNG UP THE RECEIVER AWARE THAT HE WAS IN SERIOUS TROUBLE.

"WELL WHAT DO YOU KNOW" A FAMILIAR MALE VOICE BROKE THE SILENCE. "AFTER ALL THESE YEARS IT FINALLY HAPPENED" THE REVEREND SAID TO STONEY.

THE REVEREND WHEELED AROUND AND SAID "STAY OUT OF THIS STONEY." "SURE SURE LIKE I'M GOING TO DO THAT" SAID STONEY. THE REVEREND HELD UP HIS HANDS AND SAID "YESTERDAY THE ELECTRICITY BETWEEN YOU TWO COULD HAVE LITE UP A CITY AND I COULDN'T BE HAPPIER FOR YOU SAID STONEY BUT WOMEN LIKE RICKIE TAYLOR DON'T COME ALONG TOO OFTEN NEITHER AND WOMEN LIKE HER DON'T GET INVOLVED WITH SO

CALLED EX-CONS AND LIARS STONEY ALSO SAID TO THE REVEREND."

"HEY SHE SPENDS ALL EVENING IN YOUR COMPANY THEN SHE'S ON THE PHONE WITH YOU WHEN YOU GET HOME. I'D SAY SHE'S ALREADY INVOLVED WITH YOU BIG TIME. WHEN SHE'S READY TO HEAR CHAPTER VERSE I'LL BE HAPPY TO EXPLAIN YOUR SINS TO HER."

"I'M NOT WORTH ON HAIR ON HER HEAD AND IF SHE BELIEVES I'M CELIBATE THEN MY WORK HERE IS DONE FOR NOW. SHE RELATES TO ME ON THAT LEVEL BECAUSE OF HER OWN PHILANTHROPIC BENT. I'M NOT A FLESH AND BLOOD MAN TO HER."

"THE WAY SHE REACTED AROUND YOU YESTERDAY BLOWS THAT THEORY ALL TO HELL." "I DON'T WANT TO TALK ABOUT IT." "THAT'S BECAUSE YOU KNOW IT'S TRUE AND YOUR'E FIGHTING IT." I WASN'T FIGHTING IT TONIGHT NOW WAS I. "WON'T BE SEEING HER BEFORE I LEAVE FOR PARAGUAY TONIGHT." "SO WE'RE GOING ON THURSDAY AS PLANNED?" JORDAN ASKED THE REVEREND. THE REVEREND NODDED HIS HEAD AND SAID "YES WE'RE GOING ON THURSDAY AS PLANNED."

"WHAT'S HER FAMILY LIKE?" "THEY'RE NICE" THE REVEREND ADMITTED GRUDGINGLY. "YOU MEAN THEY'RE LIKE HER" SAID STONEY. "YES SAID THE REVEREND." "OBVIOUSLY THEY HELPED YOU OVERCOME YOU RESERVATIONS" SAID THE REVEREND. "TO A POINT" SAID STONEY. "SO DO YOU THINK THEY COULD STILL BE LYING?" ASKED STONEY. "MAYBE" SAID THE REVEREND. "OKAY I'LL QUIT WITH THE QUESTIONS" SAID STONEY AS HE HEADED FOR THE BATHROOM BUT HE POKED HIS HEAD AROUND THE DOOR AND ABOUT FIVE IN THE MORNING WHEN YOU'RE GOING CRAZY BECAUSE YOU HAVEN'T SLEPT AND YOU NEED TO TALK ABOUT HER I'LL TRY TO LISTEN BUT

I'M NOT MAKING ANY PROMISES MIND YOU BECAUSE IT'S BEEN A LONG DAY."

"I DON'T DARE TALK ABOUT HER STONEY." "I KNOW TALKING HAS A TENDENCY TO MAKE YOU WANT THINGS." "I'M AFRAID ALREADY PAST THE TENDENCY PART" SAID THE REVEREND. "YEAH I KNOW THAT FEELING TOO" SAID STONEY.

"MS. TAYLOR?" "YES LINDA?" THE NEW TEMPORARY RECEPTIONIST WAS A VAST IMPROVEMENT OVER SUSAN.

"MR. CORBETT IS HERE." "GOOD SEND HIM IN AND BRING COFFEE WILL YOU?" "YES MS. TAYLOR DO YOU WANT SOME TOO?" "NO THANK YOU SUSAN." "I'LL GET RIGHT ON IT."

RICKIE THANKED HER THEN GOT UP FROM THE CHAIR ANXIOUS TO GREET HER ATTORNEY WHO WOULD HAVE HANDLED THE TRANSACTION WITH STONEWELL AIR CARGO YESTERDAY AFTERNOON.

JUST THINKING ABOUT REVEREND BROWNING QUICKENED HER PULSE AND GAVE HER A FLUTTERY FEELING IN THE PIT OF HER STOMACH. SINCE HER PHONE CONVERSATION WITH HIM TWO DAY AGO WHEN EVERYTHING HAD SPUN OUT OF CONTROL AND SHE HADN'T BEEN ABLE TO SLEEP.

TO HER SHAME SHE HAD WANTED IT TO BE MORE THAN COMPASSION THAT HAD DRIVEN HIM TO CALL HER. WHAT A FOOL SHE'D BEEN NOT TO HAVE ASSURED HIM SHE WAS FINE AND THEN HUNG UP THE PHONE BUT INSTEAD SHE'D TURNED IT INTO A MARATHON SESSION REVEALING TO MUCH RAW EMOTIONS BUT IT WASN'T UNTILL THEY'D STARTED DISCUSSING THE DANGER OF HIS IMPENDING MISSION AND SHE'D BEGUN SPEAKING HER FEARS OUT

LOUD THAT SHE REALIZED WHAT SHE WAS DOING AND HAD ENDED THE CALL.

SINCE THAT TIME HER EMOTIONS HAD BEEN SO CHAOTIC AND NOT EVEN HER BROTHER COULD ABIDE HER COMPANY BECAUSE SHE HAVE TO PRACTICE HER REPUTED TAYLOR SANGFROID TO GET THROUGH THIS BRIEFING WITHOUT GIVING HERSELF AWAY.

"RICKIE!" THE MID-FIFTIES ATTORNEYS WHO'D BEEN WITH THE TAYLOR CORPORATION FOR THE LAST EIGHTEEN YEARS KISSED HER CHEEK AND SAID "WALCOM BACKFROM THE LAND DOWN UNDER." "THANK YOU IT'S GOOD TO SEE YOU TOO LYLE COME SIT DOWN."

SHE FELT HIS SHREWD REGARD AS SHE RETURNED TO HER SEAT AND HE TOOK ONE OF THE CHAIRS OPPOSITE SIDE OF HER DESK.

"SINCE WE'VE ALWAYS BEEN FRANK WITH EACH OTHER I'M GOING TO TELL YOU SOMETHING STRAIGHT-OUT YOU'RE TOO YOUNG AND VERY ATTRACTIVE TO LOOK AS TIRED AS YOU DO. I WAS HOPING THAT WHEN YOU WENT TO AUSTRALIA TO ESTABLISH CBH YOU'D TAKE SOME TIME TO ENJOY YOURSELF BUT THAT OBVIOUSLY WASN'T THE CASE. DON'T YOU THINK A VACATION AWAY FROM THE WORLD'S WORRIES IS LONG PAST DO RIGHT NOW."

LYLE COBETT WAS ONE OF HER FAVORITE PEOPLE BUT RICKIE WASN'T OFFENDED BUT ON THE OTHER HAND SHE INTENDED TO KEEP THIS METTING SHORT SO HE WOULDN'T HAVE A CHANCE TO START PROBING.

"YOU'RE RIGHT LYLE I AM EXHUSTED I THINK I PICKED UP A BUG DOWN THERE AND I CAN'T SEEM TO SHAKE IT SO I'VE DECIDED TO TAKE A WEEK OFF FROM WORK RIGHT A WAY IN FACT."

HE WAS VISIBLY RELIEVED. "THAT'S GOOD SAID THE REVEREND. WHY DON'T WE TALK ABOUT THIS INVESTMENT OF YOURS AFTER YOU'RE BACK FROM YOUR VACATION?"

"NO I DON'T LIKE TO WALK AWAY FROM UNFINISHED BUSINESS AND BESIDES YOU'RE A VERY BUSY MAN AND SINCE YOU JUST MEET WITH THESE PEOPLE AND HAVE ALL THE PARTICULARS LEST'S GO OVER THEM RIGHT NOW WHILE IT'S FRESH THEN I CAN CLOSE UP SHOP KNOWING THERE AREN'T ANY LOOSE ENDS."

HE LOOKED AS THOUGH HE'D WANTED TO SAY SOMETHING ELSE THEN THOUGHT BETTER OF IT. "ALL RIGHT HE SAID AS HE OPENED HIS BRIEFCASE AND PULLED OUT A SHEAF OF PAPERS AND STARTED TO SPREAD THEM OUT ON HER DESK. PUTTING ON A PAIR OF STEEL RIMMED GLASSES HE EYED HER PENSIVELY. "STONEWALL AIR CARGO IS A NICE LITTLE OUTFIT WITH A SOLID BASE AND A PROMISING FUTURE. WHAT PROMPTED YOU TO INVEST THE STONEWALL AIR CARGO COMPANY?"

SHE'D BEEN WAITING FOR THAT QUESTION AND WITH A SMILE SHE SAID "YOU NEVER KNOW WHEN THERE MIGHT BE A RUN ON THE FAMILY BANK." "SURELY YOU JEST" LYLE DIDN'T SEEM TO FIND HER REMARK VERY FUNNY AT ALL. "I DON'T KNOW" SHE SAID QUIETLY BUT STRSNGER THINGS HAVE HAPPENED AND I DECIDED THAT IT'S A PRUDENT WOMEN WHO PLANS WISELY FOR AN UNCERTIAN FUTURE" AND LINDA CHOSE THAT MOMENT TO SERVE LYLE HIS COFFEE. HE STARED AT RICKIE OVER THE RIM OF HIS COFFEE CUP AFTER HE RECEPTIONIST HAD DEPARTED.

"YOU HAVEN'T CALLED ME IN HERE TO TELL ME SOME BAD NEWS HAVE YOU?" "NO MY KIND OF BAD NEWS ISN'T FIT FOR HUMAN EARS. "OF COURSE NOT" SHE LAUGHED GENTLY. "CALL IT A WHIM IF YOU WILL BUT SOMEONE AT FRIENDS OF MERCY TOLD ME ABOUT THE FINANCIAL

STRUGGLES OF THIS AIR CARGO COMPANY BUT DESPITE THEIR SO CALLED DIFFICULTIES THEY'VE GIVEN MANY HOURS OF FREE SERVICE TO OUR LOCAL AREA AND THEIR STORY TOUCHED MY HEART AND BECAUSE THE REVEREND IS INVOLVED WITH STONEWALL AIR CARGO I CAN'T TREAT IT AS CHARITY THAT'S WHY I'M INVESTING $750,000 THOUSAND OF DOLLARS IN THEIR BUSINESS AND LYLE I APPRECIATE YOUR HELP."

HE SHOOK HIS HEAD AND SAID "YOU'RE AN AMAZING WOMEN RICKIE." "PLEASE DON'T SAY THAT." PLEASE DON'T I'M NOT THE PERSON YOU THINK I AM. "IT'S TRUE AND THOSE PEOPLE ARE VERY GRATEFUL I'LL TELL YOU."

"ENOUGH!" SHE SAID AS SHE SIFTED THROUGH THE DOCUMENTS AND MAKING PERTINENT COMMENTS AND ASKING A COUPLE OF QUESTIONS. EVERYTHING ABOUT STONEWALL AIR CARGO LOOKED GOOD AND LYLE HAD DONE HIS USUAL SUPERB JOB BUT SHE WAS SEARCHING FOR A CERTAIN PIECE OF INFORMATION.

WHEN SHE FOUND THE INVENTORY SHEETS DESCRIBING THE TWO PLANES THEY OWNED AND THEIR SPECIFICATIONS SHE SAID "IF YOU YOU'LL EXCUSE ME I'D LIKE TO COPY WHAT'S IN THE FILE BEFORE YOU TAKE IT BACK TO YOUR OFFICE."

"OF COURSE IF YOU WANT MORE COFFEE I'LL TELL LINDA." "NO MORE FOR ME YOU CAN TAKE YOUR TIME WITH THE DOCUMENT" AND BEFORE LONG SHE AHD PHOTOCPIED THE INFORMATION AND ENDED HER CONFERENCE WITH LYLE AND AS SOON AS HE'D LFET HER OFFICE SHE LIFTED THE RECEIVER AND PUNCHED IN THE NUMBER OF THE HANGER AT NEW YORK AIRPORT WHERE HER FATHER KEPT A FELLT OF JETS WHICH THE FAMILY USED FOR BUSINESS AS WELL AS PLEASURE. "MACK HERE." HE WAS THE OLDEST MECHANIC EMPLOYED AT THE AIRPORT AND A FORMER PILOT AND HE HAPPENED TO BE ONE OF HER FAVORITE

PEOPLE TOO BECAUSE AFTER ALL THESE YEARS HE STILL KEPT HER AND TED ENTERTAINED WITH ACCOUNTS OF HIS HARROEING FLIGHT ADVENTURES.

"HI MACK IT'S RICKIE." "RICKIE TIKKIE?" HE CALLED HER THAT AS A CHILD AND THE NAME HAD STUCK. "I HAVE A BONE TO PICK WITH YOU. HOW COME YOU GOT HOME FROM AUSTRALIA ON MY DAY OFF? I HAVEN'T SEEN YOU AROUND IN AGES. "WHAT'S UP?" SHE COULD ALWAYS COUNT ON HIM. "DO YOU HAVE A SECOND?" "I HAVE AS LONG AS YOU NEED." "THIS'LL JUST TAKE A MINUTE I PROMISE." "SHOOT." HER HEART GAVE A LITTLE KICK AND THEN SHE BEGAN HER STORY HALF TRUTH AND HALF LIE. "ONE OF THE LOCAL GROUPS CBH FUNDS OWNS A DC-3. THEY'RE LEAVING TO TAKE EMERGENCY SUPPLIES TO FLORIDA. I'VE THOUGHT OF SOME THINGS TO ADD TO THE SHIPMENT INCLUDING A BIRTHDAY GIFT FOR THE PILOT BUT I WANT IT TO BE A BIG SURPRISE SO IS THERE A PLACE INSIDE THE PLAN WHERE I COULD STOW THESE ITEMS?"

"THAT SOUNDS LIKE MY RICKIE. SO YOU'RE GOING TO GET A MESSAGE TO THE PILOT WHEN HE LANDS RIGHT? AND THEN HE FINDS THE PRESENT RIGHT?" "RIGHT" SAID MACK AS HE CHUCKLED. "OKAY LET ME THINK WE'RE TALKING ABOUT A TWO-ENGINE TAIL-DRAGGER HERE. IT HAS A COUPLE OF CARGO HOLDS AND ONE IS BETWEEN THE CABIN AND THE COCKPIT AND THE OTHER AT THE REAR OF THE CABIN" BUT THOSE I KNOW HE INTERJECTED PATIENTLY. "YOU WANT A SECRET SPOT SO HERE'S WHAT YOU DO WHEN YOU ENTER THE PASSENGER DOOR AT THE REAR OF THE PLAN THERE'S A CARGO DOOR AND INSIDE THE CARGO HOLD THERE'S ANOTHER LITTLE DOOR LEADING TO A HOLLOW PLACE WHERE THE TOP OF THE TAIL-WHEEL EXTENSION COMES UP. IT'S FILLED WITH A BUNCH OF STUFF LIKE CABLES AND PAPERS. YOU COULD PUT THE STUFF IN THERE AND I'LL MAKES SURE HE FINDS IT AND NO ONE WOULD BE THE WISER."

A RUSH OF ADRENALINE HAD HER LEAPING OUT OF THE CHAIR. "THAT'S PERFECT! YOU'RE WONDERFUL MACK!" "IT'S THE OTHER WAY AROUND RICKIE AND YOU KNOW IT."

"THANKS FOR THE INFORMATION" SHE SAID QUIETLY WOUNDED BY TOO MUCH KINDNESS. "I'LL RETURN THE FAVOR ONE DAY SOON."

"IF I STARTED NAMING THE NICE THINGS YOU'VE DONE FOR ME YOU'D FIND OUT WHO'S BEHIND IN THE PAYBACK DEPARTMENT."

"TAKE CARE MACK I'LL TALK TO YOU SOON." TWO DOWN AND ONE MORE TO GO. SHE THEN DIALED ANOTHER PHONE NUMBER AND WAITED AND THEN "STONEY'S AIR CARGO THIS IS MARY MORE SPEAKING HOW CAN I HELP YOU." "MARY?" IT'S RICKIE TAYLOR."

"WELL IF THAT DON'T BEAT ALL! I WAS JUST GONNA CALL YOU TO THANK YOU ON BEHALF OF THE GROUP. I DON'T THINK YOU KNOW HOW GOOD IT FELT TO DEPOSIT THAT CHECK IN TH BANK TODAY. FOR ONCE I'M GOING TO LOOK FORWARD TO PAYING THE BILLS AROUND HERE."

HER WORDS ACTED LIKE A HEALING BALM. RICKIE WAS GRATEFUL SHE'D MET MARY AND PLANNED TO KEEP INTOUCH WITH HER EVEN IF ANYTHING SHOULD HAPPEN TO THE PROJECT. SHE ALREADY FELT A VERY STRONG ATTACHMENT TO THE OLDER WOMEN. "I WAS GLAD TO HELP OUT AND I ONLY HAVE ONE MORE QUESTION." "GO AHEAD." "WHEN WILL STONEY AND THE REVEREND BE TAKING OFF?" "ALL THINGS CONSIDERED AROUND 4:30AM THRUSDAY MORNING."

"I'D LIKE TO COME OUT TOMORROW WHEN THEY'RE NOT AROUND TO BRING A DONATION OF PILLOWS, BLANKETS AND SOME LITTLE CARE PACKAGES WITH

SNACKS FOR THEM AND FOR THE PASSENGERS THE'LL BE BRINGING BACK."

"YOU'VE DONE TOO MUCH ALREADY BUT I'LL HELP YOU ANYWAYS BECAUSE IT SOUNDS LIKE YOU WANT THIS TO BE A SURPRISE." "YES SAID RICKIE BUT YOU DO HAVE MY WORK AND HOME PHONE NUMBERS RIGHT?" WHEN THE COST IS CLEAR GIVE ME A CALL AND I'LL DRIVE OUT WITH THE THINGS I MEANTIONED."

"I CAN TELL YOU RIGHT NOW THEY'LL BOTH BE GONE FROM TEN UNTILL THREE SO YOU CAN COME ANYTIME BETWEEN THOSE HOURS." "I WILL THANKS MARY." "DON'T EAT HAVE LUNCH WITH ME HOPE YOU LIKE ROAST-BEEF SANDWICHES."

"I USED TO LIKE A LOT OF THINGS BUT NOT ANY MORE BUT ON THE OTHER HAND I DO LOVE ROAST-BEEF SANDWICHES SO I'LL SEE YOU TOMORROW" SAID RICKIE.

AFTER HANGING UP THE PHONE THE PHONE SHE REACHED FOR A SHEET OF PAPER TO WRITE TED A LETTER. FOR PRIVACY'S SHAKE SHE WOULD ASSRESS IT TO HIS CONDO AND POST IT ON HER WAY TO STONEY'S TOMORROW BUT THEN HE WOULDN'T GET IT UNTIL FRIDAYWHEN IT WAS TOO LATE FOR HIM TO TRY TO STOP HER.

HER PARENTS WERE STILL ABROAD SO THERE WAS NO NEED TO INFORM THEM OF ANYTHING. ALL THAT WAS LEFT TO DO WAS DEAL WITH LINDA HER TEMPORARY RECEPTIONIST.

TOMORROW RICKIE WOULD COME TO WORK AT 8:00AM AND LEAVE FOR THE AIRFIELD TWO HOURS LATER BUT ON HER WAY OUT THE DOOR SHE WOULD THANK LINDA FOR HER HELP, HAND HER A BONUS AND TELL HER SHE HAD THE REST OF THE DAY AND NEXT WEEK OFF.

PEGGY WOULD BE BACK THE FOLLOWING MONDAY AND RICKIE WOULD LEAVE DETAILED INSTRUCTIONS IN HER PRIVATE SECRETARY'S PLANNER. RICKIE HAD ONLY ONE MORE THING TO DO BEFORE SHE WENT SHOPPING FOR BLANKETS AND PILLOWS. SHE HAD TO PHONE DAVID SOLOMON.

IF NOTHING ELSE HE NEEDED TO HEAR SOMETHING RATIONAL FROM HER SO HE COULD TRY TO CONFORT HIS GRIEVING SISTER. HE NEEDED AN EXPLANATION OF WHY TED HAD BROKEN IT OFF WITH DEBORAH BUT RICKIE REACHED ONCE MORE FOR THE RECEIVER AND THE COWARD IN HER HAD SHRANK FROM THE TASK. SHE SIMPLY COULDN'T COME TO HIS RESCUE NOT YET.

"THAT'S THE BEST ROAST-BEEF SANDWICH I'VE EVER EATEN MARY. YOU REALLY DID YOUSELF PROUD TONIGHT."

"HE RIGHT" JORDAN AGREED. "YOUR HUSBAND MUST HAVE BEEN THE HAPPIEST MAN IN SOUTH DAKOTA." MARY BROKE INTO A BIG SMILE AND SAID "SINCE A MIRACLE HAPPENED TODAY I FIGURED WE OUGHT TO CELEBRATE. WE GOT THE MONEY! RICKIE TAYLOR'S ONE SPECIAL LADY.

"A FEW PEOPLE INHERIT A LOT OF MONEY AND DONATE SOME OF IT FOR A TAX WRITE-OFF BUT HOW MANY OF THEM GIVE IT AWAY OUT OF THE KINDNESS OF THEIR HEARTS? I TELL YOU NOT VERY MANY AND LIKE I SAID THAT WOMEN IS VERY SPECIAL."

"HERE HERE" STONEY SAID OUT LOUD. MARY HADN'T SAID ANYTHING JORDAN HADN'T ALREADY BEEN THINKING BEFORE HE MET RICKIE TAYLOR HIS ADMIRATION FOR HER WAS BASED ON WHAT HE'D READ IN THE LITTLE NEWSPAPER ARCHIVES AND ON THE INTERNET WHERE HE'D LEARNED OF HER ACTIVITIES AS A MODERN-DAY

PHILANTHROPIST BUT DURING THEIR LAST PHONE CONVERSATION HE'D BEEN GIVEN A LITTLE MORE INSIGHT INTO HER COMPLICATED NATURE. SHE WAS CARRING A BURDEN THAT SEEMED TO BE CAUSING HER GREAT PAIN.

WHEN HE GOT BACK FORM PARAGUAY HE'D INTRODUCE HER TO THE REVEREND ROLON WHO HAD MORE FAITH AND GUTS THEN ANY RELIGIOUS PERSON JORDAN HAD EVER MET. THE MAN DIDN'T JUST TALK ABOUT DOINGGOOD DEEDS HE DID THEM. MAYBE HE COULD HELP RELIEVE HER ANGUISH OF WHAT EVERE IT WAS THAT WAS MAKING HER FEEL THAT BURDEN OF PAIN.

DEEP INSIDE JORDAN WANTED TO BE THE MAN WHO COULD DO THAT FOR HER. HE ACHED TO BE ON WHOM SHE TURNED FOR COMFORT, JOY, AND LOVE.

DEAR GOD WHAT WOULD IT FEEL LIKE TO BE LOVED BY SUCH A WOMEN? AND TO KNOW THAT SHE WELCOMED HIS LOVE BUT THEN JORDAN HAD REALIZED HE DIDN'T HAVE THE RIGHT TO FANTASIZE LIKE THIS NOT WITH HIS PRISON RECORD. IT SEPARATED THEM AS DID HER PRIVILEGED AND HER BACKGROUND. WHAT CAME BETWEEN THEM MOST OF ALL WAS THE BIG INTENSE CONSUMING DANGEROUS NATURE OF THIS MISSION AND THE LIE HE HAD TO LIVE BECAUSE OF IT. THE MOST HE COULD DO WAS TRY TO LOCATE HER GRANDFATHER.

IF HE WAS STILL ALIVE SOMEWHERE IN PARAGUAY JORDAN DETERMINED TO FIND HIM AND PERHAPS HIS MYSTERIOUS DISAPPEARANCE HAD SOMETHING TO DO WITH HER UNHAPPINESS.

IN A DREAM LAST NIGHT HE'D HADN'T BEEN ABLE TO SURVIVE THE NEXT FIVE DAYS WITHOUT SEEING HER OR TALKING TO HER LORD HELP HIM.

CHAPTER 37

IT'S A MAN'S WORLD

EVEN IN THE SHADOWY HANGAR THE SILVER DC-3 WITH IT'S DARK RED TRIM STILL GLEAMED LIKE A BRAND NEW AIR-PLANE. METICULOUS CARE HAD BEEN TAKEN TO KEEP IT IN MINT CONDITION. RICKIE HAD TRAILED BEHIND MARY CARRYING SEVERAL BAGS OF THINGS SHE WAS DONATING FOR THE TRIP.

THEY ENTERED THE PLANE THROUGH THE REAR JUST AS MACK HAD DESCRIBED BUT THERE WERE SUPPOSED TO BE TEN SEATS ON EACH SIDE OF THE AISLE BUT MARY EXPLAINED THAT SOME OF THE SEATS HAD BEEN TAKEN OUT TO ACCOMMODATE A COUPLE OF ADDITIONAL FUEL TANKS AND BRINGING FUEL CAPACITY UP TO A THOUSAND GALLONS FOR THE LONG JOURNEY. THAT TRANSLATED INTO APPROXIMATELY EIGHTEEN HUNDRED MILES WITHOUT REFUELING.

RICKIE WAS NO STRANGER TO FLYING BECAUSE IN HER EARLY TEENS SHE'D FLOWN TO VARIOUS PARTS OF ASIA, SOUTH AMERICA AND EUROUP IN HER FAMILY'S FLEET AS WELL AS ON A LARGE LUXURY AIRPLANES LIKE THE CONCORDE. FOR TRIPS TO THE REMOTEST PARTS OF AFRICA AND THE YUKON SHE'D TRAVELED IN TWO SEATER BUSH PLANES BUT THIS WOULD BE THE FIRST TIME SHE'D TAKEN A FLIGHT WHERE SHE WAS UNINVITED, UNWANTED AND DEFINITELY FORBIDDEN DUE TO THE PHYSICAL AND POLIRICAL DANGER OF THEIR MISSION.

CARRYING THE BAGS SHE WORKED HER WAY TO THE FRONT OF THE CABIN. "SINCE I HAVE TO MAKE SEVERAL

MORE TRIPS TO THE CAR THIS IS GOING TO TAKE A WHILE MARY. WHY DON'T YOU GO BACK TO THE OFFICE? I'LL LOCK THE HANGAR DOOR AND BRING YOU THE KEY WHEN I'M THROUGH."

THE OLDER WOMEN NODDED HER HEAD AND SAID "MAYBE YOU'RE RIGHT STONEY'S ALWAYS LOOKING FOR A REASON TO FIND ME AND ALL IT WOULD TAKE IS ONE BIG MISTAKE."

RICKIE SMILED AT HER AND SAID "STONEY OBVIOUSLY LOVES YOU OR I DON'T THINK YOU'D BE WORKING FOR HIM BUT I AGREE HE'D BE UNHAPPY IF SOMETHING IMPORTANT CAME ALONG AND YOU WERE OUT HERE HELPING ME WHEN I'M NOT EVEN SUPPOSED TO BE AROUND."

"GOOD POINT I'LL SEE YOU WHEN YOU WHEN YOU FINISH UP. WORK FAST JUST INCASE THE BOYS GET BACK EARLIER THAN THEY'D PLANNED."

"I WILL" RICKIE SAID AS SHE STARTED TO PUT A PILLOW AND BLANKET ON THE SHELF ABOVE EACH WINDOW.

NOT LONG AFTER MARY HAD LEFT THE HANGAR RICKIE FINISHED EMPTYING THE BAGS AND CLIMBED OUT OF THE PLANE TO GET THE REST BUT FIRST SHE TOOK A LOOK AROUND THE BUILDING AND WAS PLEASED TO DISCOVER A BACK DOOR WHICH MIGHT NOT HAVE THE SAME LOCK AS THE FRONT.

MARY HAD LEFT THE KEY RING WITH RICKIE AND HER HANDS TREMBLED AS SHE TRIED TO UNLOCKING THE BACK DOOR WITH THE KEY THE OTHER WOMEN HAD USED TO LET THEM IN BUT SHE HAD NO SUCH LUCK.

RICKIE BROKE OUT IN A COLD SWEAT BECAUSE THE RING HAD A DOZEN KEYS ON IT AND METHODICALLY SHE

SET ABOUT TRYING TO FIND THE RIGHT ONE AND ON THE EIGHTH TRY SHE HEARD A CLICK.

    USING HER SHOULDER FOR LEVERAGE SHE PUSHED ON THE SLIDING METAL DOOR AND SHE WAS ABLE TO MANAGE IT ENOUGH TO SEE SOME DAYLIGHT OUTSIDE. EXCITED BY HER SUCCESS SHE EASED THE DOOR BACK IN PLACE AND LOCKED IT. SHE THEN PUT THE KEY IN HER POCKET AND MADE ANOTHER TRIP TO THE CAR ON THE RUN.

    ONCE EVERYTHING HAD BEEN PACKED ON THE PLANE INCLUDING FRUIT JUICE, BOTTLED WATER, GUM, AND GRANOLA BARS SHE MADE ONE FINAL TRIP FOR HER BACKPACK AND BESIDES FOOD IT CONTAINED ALL OF THE CLOTHES AND ESSENTIALS SHE'D NEED FOR THE NEXT FIVE DAYS OR SO.

    WHEN SHE BORADED THE PLANE FOR THE LAST TIME SHE FOUND THE LITTLE ROOM BEYOND THE CARGO HOLD THAT MACK HAD TOLD HER ABOUT AND THERE WAS ENOUGH SPACE FOR HER, A PILLOW, BLANKET AND NOTHING ELSE. SHE KNEW IT WOULDN'T BE COMFORTABLE. NO PADDED SEATS, NO WINDOWS JUST THE HARD FLOOR BUT SHE DIDN'T HAVE A CHOICE IF SHE INTENDED TO FLY WITH THEM UNNOTICED UNTILL THEY'D REACHED THE PARAGUAYAN AIRSPACE AND AT THAT POINT SHE WOULD MAKE HERSELF KNOWN AND THEY WOULD HAVE NO RECOURSE BUT TO ALLOW HER TO REMAIN WITH THEM.

    SHE REFUSED TO THINK OF REVEREND BROWNING'S REACTION BECAUSE ALL SHE KNEW WAS THAT SHE WANTED TO HELP HIM AND BE WITH HIM TOO BECAUSE SOMEHOW BEING NEAR HIM LIFTED THE UGLY BURDEN OF HER SECRET AND THE TRUTH ABOUT HER REAL BACKGROUND FOR A LITTLE WHILE.

SHE'D FALLEN IN LOVE WITH HIM AND THAT WAS ANOTHER SECRET SHE HAD TO KEEP. A FEW MINUTES LATER SHE RETURNED THE KEYS TO MARY AND THANKED HER FOR THE DELICIOUS LUNCH AND DROVE OFF AND WENT BACK TO THE PLANE TO SEE IF THE GUYS WERE THERE FORTUNATELY THE TWO MEN HADN'T COME BACK INTO THE OTHER PLANE YET SO FAR SO GOOD.

ON HER RETURN TO POUGHKEEPSIE SHE LOOKED UP HER APARTMENT AND CALLED FOR AN TAXI. IT WAS VITAL SHE REACH STONEY'S BEFORE DARK SO SHE COULD BE DROPPED OFF ON THE ACCESS ROAD WITHOUT ANYONE SEEING HER AND IN ROUTE SHE MAILED HER LETTER TO TED NOW SHE WAS READY.

"WHAT THE HELL?" JORDAN'S HEAD JERKED AROUND AS HE NOTICED THE NEATLY PLACED BUNDLES OF BLANKETS PILLOWS AND FOOD ABOVE EACH WINDOW EVIDENCE THAT SOMEONE HAD BEEN INSIDE THE CABIN DURING THE LAST TWELVE HOURS.

SINCE STONEY HADN'T MENTIONED IT JORDAN FIGURED MARY HAD GONE SHOPPING. IT WASN'T THAT HE DIDN'T APPRECIATE THE GESTURE BUT THE MONEY MS. TAYLOR HAD GIVEN THEM DIDN'T COVER THESE KINDS OF EXTRAS NO MATTER HOW WELCOME.

HOWEVER FOUR-TWENTY IN THE MORNING WAS NOT THE TIME TO HAVE A CHAT WITH MARY. SHE'D BEEN KIND ENOUGH TO MAKE BREAKFAST AND PACK THEM LUNCH THAT WOULD LAST SEVERAL MEALS.

AFTER GIVING HER A HEARTFELT HUG HE'D LEFT HER TO DEAL WITH THE HANGAR DOORS WHILE HE AND STONEY TOWED THE PLANE OUT TO THE RUNWAY AND WHEN THEY RETURNED FROM PARAGUAY STONEY WOULD HAVE TO PULL HIS AUNT ASIDE AND EXPLANE THEIR BUDGET IN DETAIL.

AS JORDAN MADE HIS WAY TO THE COCKPIT TO BEGIN THE PERFLIGHT CHECK HE FELT A FAMILIAR SURGE OF ADRENALINE. THIS WAS A RISKY OPERATION NOT A ROUTINE ONE AND THERE WAS ALWAYS THE POSSIBILITY THAT THEY WOULDN'T BE COMING BACK.

THE IDEA OF NOT SEEING RICKIE TAYLOR AGAIN HAD HIT HIM VERY SURPRISINGLY HARD BUT JORDAN PUT IT OUT OF HIS MIND.

HE'D LEARNED LONG AGO THAT NEGATIVE THINKING GOT YOU NOWHERE AT ALL AND IF YOU DIDN'T PLAN TO SUCCEED YOU PROBABLY WOLDN'T WITH STONEY AS CHIEF PILOT THE ODDS OF MAKING IT WERE SUBSTANTIALLY INCREASED.

THOUGH JORDAN HAD LEARNED TO FLY BEFORE HIS INDUCTION INTO THE SEALS AND KNEW ENOUGH TO PASS HIS 135 EVERY TWELVE MONTHS AND HE COULDN'T TOUCH STONEY'S TALENT OR TRACK RECORD. LONG BEFORE STONEY'S SIXTEENTH BIRTHDAY HIS FATHER WHO WAS A FORMER TEST PILOT FOR THE AIR FORCE HE HAD TAUGHT HIM THE KINDS OF THINGS YOU DIDN'T LEARN FROM TEXTBOOKS.

TO JORDAN STONEY WAS ONE OF THOSE PEOPLE WHO DID EVERYTHING A LITTLE BIT BETTER THAN ANONE ELSE AND ON SEVERAL BIG COVERT ASSIGNMENTS WITH THE SEALS JORDAN HAD PLACED HIS LIFE IN STONEY'S HANDS AND WAS STILL ALIVE TO TELL ABOUT IT SO THAT WAS GOOD ENOUGH FOR JORDAN.

HE STRAPPED HIMSELF INTO THE COPILOT'S SEAT THINKING OVER THEIR STRATEGY. THERE WOULD BE NO FLIGHT PLAN FILED SO THEY'D REFUEL IN MIAMI THEN FLY AROUND CUBAN AIRSPACE TO TANK UP ONCE AGAIN ON THE GRAND CAYMAN. FROM THERE THEY'D CRUISE AS LOW AS THEY COULD UNTILL LAND AT A SMALL AIRFIELD just inside the Brazilian border for refueling depending on the winds and various other factors their last stop would be the Paraugayan Chaco where they would pick up their human cargo.

Five minutes later Stoney entered the cockpit ready to go and whenever he chewed his gum that fast Jordan could tell that his so called partner's adrenaline had kicked in.

"When did you buy all that stuff for the cabin?" Jordan had almost forgotten to mention it. Apparently Mary had left both of them in the dark. "I didn't it's your aunt's doing obviously." After a slight hesitation Stoney broke into laughter. "That's are Mary oh well if we pull this thing off the passengers are going to be greatful." "You're right about that" said Jordan.

There plane stood poised on the runway while Jordan looked out the window for Mary but it was too dark to distinguish the shapes Jordan said out loud to Stoney. Still he waved in case she could see them.

"Too bad the'll never know this entire rescue is courtesy of Rickie Taylor" Stoney said. "She's incredible isn't she?"

I know Stoney said but since the moment she caught me trespassing in her office she's all I've been able to think about said the Reverend. This trip had better cure me or I don't know how I'm going stay away from her.

"Ready?" Stoney's question conveyed the same turmoil of emotions that was suffocating Jordan.

HE NODDED HIS HEAD AND SAID "LET'S GET OUT OF HERE."

"WHAT HAVE WE GOT?" "WE HAVE FLUID, PRESSURE IS UP RIGHT BOOST IS ON AND I'M CRANKING ON THE LEFT BOOSTER NOW SAID STONEY AND THE SIX BLADES AND IGNITION ARE ON SO WE ARE GOOD TO GO JORDAN SAID TO STONEY."

THE ENGINES COUGHED TO LIFE AND THE RPMS BEGAN TO BUILD AND BEFORE LONG THEY SETTLED DOWN TO A GALLOPING THROB AND WITH UNCONSCIOUS FINESSE STONEY ADJUSTED THE POWER AND EASED BACK ON THE YOKE AND THEY ACHIEVED LIFT-OFF.

THE LAST TIME JORDAN HAD EXPERIENCED SOMETHING LIKE THIS IT WAS HOMESICKNESS VAGUELY RESEMBLING IT HE'D BEEN AN EIGHT YEAR OLD BOY LEAVING HIS GRANDPA TO GO ON HIS FIRST OVERNIGHT CAMP-OUT WITH THE CUB SCOUTS.

ODD AFTER ALL THESE YEARS HE'D FEEL THAT SAME HOLLOW SENSATION LIKE HE WAS LEAVING SOMETHING FRAGILE AND PRECIOUS BEHIND BUT THIS MORNING IT WASN'T THE MEMORY OF HIS LONG-DEAD GRANDPA THAT TUGGED ON HIS EMOTIONS BUT INSTEAD HIS THOUGHTS WER ON A GOLDEN-HAIRED BLUE-EYED WOMEN. SHE'D MANAGED TO INFILTRATE HIS FIRST LINE OF DEFENSE AND NOW HAD A PAINFUL HOLD ON HIM. THERE PLANE HAD ALREADY REACHED SIX THOUSAND FEET AND RICKIE TAYLOR WAS A SPECK SOMEWHERE IN THE FAST DISSAPPEARING LANDSCAPE DOWN BELOW. THAT REALITY ONLY INCREASED HIS PAIN.

NO MATTER HOW HARD HE TRIED TO THINK ABOUT SOMETHING ELSE ANYTHING ELSE THEIR LAST CONVERSATION CONTINUED TO REVERBERATE IN HIS MIND. "IF YOUR PLAN FAILED INSIDE PARAGUAY YOU

AND YOUR FRIEND COULD BE CAPTURED, TORTURED, MURDERED, IMPRISONED AND NEVER HEARD OR SEEN FROME AGAIN AND I'M NOT SURE I COULD BEAR THAT" SAID RICKIE.

HAD SHE SAID THAT OUT OF CONCERN FOR THE SPIRITUAL WELFARE OF A CLEGYMAN SHE ADMIRED? OR HAD THOSE WORDS CAME STRAIGHT FROM HER HEART BECAUSE SHE'D SEEN BEYOND HIS COLLAR TO THE VERY HUMAN MAN BENEATH?

JORDAN COULDN'T ANSWER THOSE QUESTIONS BECAUSE HE DIDN'T KNOW HER WELL ENOUGH BUT YET HE FELT HE KNEW HER ESSENCE. AT THAT MOMENT NOTHING REALLY MADE SENSE OR SEEMED CLEAR. IT'S GOING TO BE A LONG TRIP.

IN HER CONFINED SPACE THERE WERE ONLY SO MANY POSITIONS RICKIE COULD MANAGE. AIR POCKETS AND SUDDEN TURBULENCE FORCED HER TO CURSHION THE WORST OF THE BLOWS WITH HER PILLOWS.

DURING THE PAST TWENTY HOURS THEY'D MADE THREE LANDINGS. SHE SURMISED THEY HAD REACHED SOUTH AMERICA AND WERE FLYING SOMEWHERE OVER BRAZIL NOW. ALL SHE HAD TO GO ON WERE THE BITS AND PIECES SHE'D GLEANED ABOUT THEIR FLIGHT PLAN FROM HER FRIEND MARY.

RICKIE'S ONLY PERIODS OF RELIEF CAME WHEN BOTH MEN TOOK TURNS USING THE BATHROOM THAT WAS THE ONLY TIME SHE FIGURED SHE'D BE SAFE FROM DETECTION.

IT FELT MARVELOUS TO STRETCH HER LEGS BECAUSE THEY WERE SO SORE FROM BEING CRAMPED IN A LITTLE SPACE FOR TWENTY HOURS OR UNTILL THE PLANE LANDS. SHE LONGED TO WALK UP AND DOWN THE AISLE FOR THE

EXERCISE BUT OF COURSE SHE COULDN'T DO THAT AND BESIDES THE FOOD SHE'D PACKED SHE'D THOUGHT IT WAS A VERY GOOD IDEA TO BRING ALONG A RECENTLY PUBLISHED PAPER BACK ON PARAUGAY. USING HER POCKET FLASHLIGHT SHE HAD PLANNED TO STUDY THE MAPS AND TRY TO ABSORB WHAT SHE COULD ABOUT THE CHACO AND IT'S FLORA AND FAUNA AS WELL AS IT'S HUMAN DWELLERS BUT SHE'D BEEN UNABLE TO CONCENTRATE ON READING AND HAS SLEPT PART OF THE WAY. SHE KNEW SHE'D BEEN DREAMING ABOUT REVEREND BROWNING BUT DID SHE THINK OF HIM AS "JORDAN?" HER DREAMS HAD LEFT HER WITH A SENSE OF JOYFULNESS THAT WAS ALMOST EUPHORIC BUT THEY ALLOWED HER TO BELIEVE BRIEFLY IN POSSIBILITIES.

RICKIE KNEW SHE HAD TO SHAKE OFF HER DROWSY CONTENTMENT BECAUSE THE PLANE WAS ALMOST AT IT'S DESTINATION AND AFTER THEY LANDED THERE WOULD BE NO TIME FOR EXPLANATIONS. SHE ALREADY DECIDED THAT THE LESSER OF TWO EVILS WOULD BE TO ANNOUNCE HER PRESENCE WHILE THEY WERE STILL IN THE AIR BUT OF COURSE THE MEN WEREN'T GOING TO LIKE LEARNING THEY HAD AN UNEXPECTED PERSON ON THE PLANE BUT IF SHE PROMISED TO FOLLOW THEIR ORDERS TO THE LETTER THEN SHE FELT SHE COULD BE AN ASSET BY ASSISTING THE BETTER OF THE FAMILIES BOTH BEFORE AND DURING THE FLIGHT.

SINCE THE PHONE CONVERSATION IN WHICH THE REVEREND HAD SUGGESTED SHE FIND WAYS TO GIVE THAT DIDN'T INVOLVE MONEY RICKIE HAD BEEN ON FIRE WITH THE IDEA OF GOING ALONG ON THIS TRIP. HER FEARS OF THE UNAVOIDABLE DANGERS HADN'T DAUNTED HER IN FACT THIS BURNING NEW CHALLENGE HER GIVEN HER A FELLING OF EXCITEMENT AND RIGHTNESS SHE HADN'T EXPERIENCED IN WEEKS BUT NOW THE MOMENT HAD COME TO REVEAL HERSELF AND SOME OF THE TAYLOR

CONFIDENCE SEEMED TO HAVE DESERTED HER. WITH HER LITTLE POCKET FLASHLIGHT TO GUIDE HER SHE UP ON STIFF LEGS AND LEFT HER SECRET HIDING PLACE FOR THE BATHROOM.

NO MATTER HOW SHE PLANNED IT HER PRESENCE WAS GOING TO SHOCK THEM BUT SHE FIGURED IT WOULD BE BEST IF THE FIRST MEETING HAPPENED AWAY FROM THE COCKPIT LEAVING ONE OF THE MEN IN CONTROL OF THE AIRPLANE.

SHE'D HAD ALL DAY AND NIGHT TO DETERMINE THAT HER BEST TACTIC WOULD BE TO SIT IN THE CABIN AND WAIT FOR ONE OF THEM TO MAKE AN APPEARANCE SINCE ON THERE LAST STOP NEITHER MAN HAD TAKEN A BATHROOM BREAK. IT COULDN'T BE MUCH LONGER NOW BECAUSE SHE HEARD THE COCKPIT DOOR CREAK OPEN.

USED TO THE ETERNAL BUMPS AND BUFFETINGS OF THE AIRCRAFT SHE FOUND IN NO DIFFICULT TASK TO MAKE HER WAY TO A SEAT IN THE CENTER OF THE CABIN. IT'S CUSHIONED COMFORT CAME AS A PLEASANT SURPRISE SHE THEN GAVE A DEEP SIGH AND SANK BACK CLOSED HER EYES IN FULL APPRECIATION OF THE MOMENT.

IN THE FAINT PREDAWN LIGHT THE ENDLESS SAVANNA SIX HUNDRED FEET BELOW THEM STRETCHED LIKE A MYSTICAL SEA. ANOTHER HOUR AND THEY WOULD SET DOWN IN A TINY CLEARING NO ONE BUT A HANDFUL OF PEOPLE KNEW ABOUT.

IN THE FULL LIGHT OF DAY IT WAS ALMOST IMPOSSIBLE TO LOCATE BECAUSE THE NEAR DARKNESS MADE FINDING IT ANOTHER MATTER ENTIRELY BUT ONLY A MAGICIAN LIKE STONEY KNEW WHEN AND WHERE TO LOOK FOR THE FLARES AND EVEN THEN THE CHACO WAS LIKE A LIVING THING SWALLOWING SIGHT AND SOUND.

EVER SINCE HIS FIRST MISSION TO PARAGUAY BFEORE HIS COURT MARTIAL AND RETIREMENT FROM THE SEALS JORDAN HAD CONSIDERED THIS REMOTE AREA OF THE CHACO WHICH WAS THE PERFECT TO HIDE THE DARKNESS IN MEN'S HEARTS AND THE PERFECT PLACE TO FIND IT.

"IT WON'T BE MUCH LONGER NOW" STONEY SAID TO JORDAN. JORDAN UNFASTENED HIS SEAT STRAP AND GOT UP TO HIS FEET. "SINCE WE'VE GOT SOME TIME I THINK I'LL VISIT THE BLUE ROOM NOW."

A FEW LONGS STRIDES CARRIED HIM FROM THE COCKPIT INTO THE CABIN AND ALMOST AT THE END OF THE AISLE HE FELT RATHER THAN SAW A PRESENCE THAT HADN'T BEEN THERE BEFORE HE THEN WHEELED HIS CHAIR AROUND THEN CAME TO A STANDSTILL.

IN THE SHADOWY INTERIOR HE COULD BARELY MAKE OUT A FORM HUDDLED IN ONE OF THE SEATS.

"REVEREND?" JORDAN WAS WONDERING IF HE WAS HALLUCINATING. "IT'S ME RICKIE TAYLOR." LORD HE WAS REALLY LOSING IT. THE HUSKY FEMININE VOICE CONTINUED TO SPEAK "I DIDN'T MEAN TO STARTLE YOU BUT I DIDN'T KNOW ANOTHER WAY TO LET YOU KNOW I WAS ON BOARD THE PLANE."

SHE'D FILLED HIS THOUGHTS FOR SO LONG HE'D ACTUALLY STARTED FANTASIZING THAT SHE WAH HERE WITH HIM. STONEY WOULD TELL HIM TO GO SEE A GOOD SHRINK WHEN THEY GOT BACK TO NEW YORK.

"I'M NOT A GHOST" SHE SAID STANDING AND TAKING A STEP TOWARD HIM. "PLEASE SAY SOMETHING, ANYTHING."

AS SHE GOT CLOSER A FAMILIAR PERFUME ASSAILED HIS SENSES CHARGING HIS BODY LIKE A CURRENT OF ELECTRICITY.

IT WAS FLOWERY FRAGRANCE HE IDENTIFIED WITH THE WOMEN HE'D OUT TO STONEY'S PLACE A FEW DAYS AGO.

"MS. TAYLOR?" HE SAID IN STUNNED DISBELIEF. SUDDENLY THE DONOR OF THOSE BLANKETS AND PILLOWS WAS NO LONGER A MYSTERY.

"YES" CAME HER BREATHLESS RESPONSE. "PLEASE DON'T BE MAD AT ME I HAD TO COME BECAUSE I NEEDED TO BE A PART OF YOUR SO CALLED OPERATION."

ALL THIS TIME HE'D THOUGHT OF HER THOUSANDS OF MILES AWAY SAFE AND UNREACHABLE. HE SHIFTED HIS WEIGHT AND HE COULDN'T BELIEVE SHE WAS STANDING THERE LESS THAN A YARD FROM HIM.

PRIOR TO HIS RELEASE FROM PRISON WOMEN HADN'T BEEN A PART OF THE DANGEROUS WORLD IN WHICH HE LIVED. THEY WERE FORBIDDEN NOT BECAUSE THEY WEREN'T CAPABLE OR EQUAL TO THE TASK BUT BECAUSE A MAN'S CHANCES OF SURVIVAL INCREASED SIGNIFICANTLY IF HE WASN'T DISTRACTED BY THE ALLURE OF A WOMEN'S SOFTNESS AND BEAUTY. AN ALLURE NO UNIFORM COULD CAMOUFLSGE.

AT THE TIME WHEN JORDAN NEEDED HIS FULL POWERS OF HIS SO CALLED CONCENTRATION RICKIE TAYLOR'S PRESENCE MADE HIM VULNERABLE AS HELL. THE GRAVITY OF THE SITUATION WAS ONLY BEGINNING TO DAWN ON HIM.

"WHERE HAVE YOU BEEN HIDING?" ANGER MASKED HIS CONCERN BUT HE COULDN'T HELP IT. "IN THAT LITTLE SPACE HOUSING THE TAIL EXTENSION." WHO WOULD HAVE THOUGHT? "WE MIGHT NOT MAKE IT BACK" HE SAID. "I KNOW SAID MS. TAYLOR."

HE SHOOK HIS HEAD BECAUSE HE NEVER MET ANYONE REMOTELY LIKE HER. "HUNDREDS OF PEOPLE IN

HUNDREDS OF PLACES WOULD MOURN THE DEATH OF THEIR GENEROUS BENEFACTOR."

"DON'T WORRY IF THAT SHOULD HAPPEN CBH WILL SURVIVE WITHOUT ME." "WOULD YOU FAMILY SURVIVE? LIKE YOUR BROTHER?" "NO DOUBT THEY'D BE AS DEVASTATED AS YOUR FAMILY."

SHE COUNTERED SWIFTLY "AND YOUR FLOCK." "I DON'T HAVE A FAMILY." THE ADMISSION WAS OUT BEFORE HE REALIZED WHAT HE'D SAID DAM. "I'M SORRY." "AS FOR WHAT I UNDERCOVER" HE CONTINUED NOT WANTING HER COMPASSION "MY FLOCK KNOWS NOTHING ABOUT IT BECAUSE I'M A MISSIONARY ALWAYS MOVING AROUND. IF I WERE TO DISAPPEAR THE REVEREND ROLON WOULD TELL PEOPLE I'D BEEN ASSIGNED TO ANOTHER PARISH."

"EVERYONE THINKS I'M ON VACATION AND TED WON'T KNOW THE TRUTH UNTILL HE RECEIVES MY LETTER TOMORROW OR THE DAY AFTER."

HIS HEART POUNDED LIKE A JACKHAMMER. "WHAT POSSESSED YOU TO COME WHEN YOU KNOW THE DANGER INVOLVED?" "YOUR WORDS SHE SAID TO THE REVEREND. DON'T YOU REMEMBER? YOU SUGGESTED I GIVE OF MY TIME AND TALENT."

JORDAN REELED AND THEN SAID "I SHOULD NEVER WASN'T REFERRING TO THIS PARTICULAR TRIP." "ON THE CONTRAY IT SEEMED THE PERFECT PLACE TO START."

"WHEN YOU'VE BEEN SO ILL?" "THAT WILL PASS. YOU HAVE NO IDEA HOW MUCH I WANT TO HELP WITH THE FAMILIES YOU'RE BRINGING BACK BECAUSE THEY'LL BE FRIGHTENED AND DISORIENTED ESPECIALLY THE LITTLE CHILDREN. IF MY PRESENCE WILL CAUSE COMPLICATIONS FOR YOU THEN I'LL SATY ON THE ENTIRE TIME. I'LL WAIT

IN MY HIDING PLACE AND I BROUGHT ENOUGH FOOD AND WATER TO LAST THE DURATION OF THE TRIP" SHE ADDED QUIETLY.

"THE PROBLEM IS WE WON'T KNOW WHAT WE'RE FACEING UNTILL WE MAKE CONTACT WITH THE UNDERGROUND. YOU MIGHT NOT BE SAFE STAYING IN THE PLANE ON YOUR OWN."

"I HAVE A GUN I KNOW HOW TO USE IT." "I'M SURE YOU DO BUT WERE FLYING OVER NO MAN'S LAND NOW AND THE NORMAL RULES SIMPLY DON'T APPLY. SWEAR THAT YOU'LL DO EXACTLY AS I SAY FROM HERE ON OUT OR THE WHOLE PROJECT COULD BE JEOPARDIZED."

SHE WAS CLOSE ENOUGH THAT HE FELT HER SHIVER. "I SWEAR SAID RICKIE." HER FERVENT AVOWAL SHOULD HAVE ASSURED HIM YET THE KNOWLEDGE THAT THEY'D BE LANDING WHININ THE HOUR ONLY INCREASED HIS FEARS FOR HER SAFETY. IF FATE DECREED THAT STONEY OVERSHOT THE CLEARING OR PUT DOWN TOO SOON THE PLANE COULD END UP SKIMMING THE TREEROPS AND RIPPING OPEN IT'S BELLY.

"WE'RE ALMOST AT OUR DESTINATION SO I SUGGEST YOU FIND A SEAT IN THE FRONT OF THE CABIN AND STRAP YOURSELF IN. "I'LL LEAVE THE COCKPIT DOOR OPEN SO WE CAN TALK ALL RIGHT."

A LITTLE MORE LIGHT COMING OVER THE HORIZON ILLUMINATED THE INTERIOR AND JORDAN'S EYES NARROWED AS HE WATCHED HER WALK THE SHORT DISTANCE TO THE FRONT SEAT ON HER LEFT.

AS FAR AS HE COULD TELL SHE WAS WEARING A SENSIBLE KHAKI SHIRT AND PANTS AND SHE HAD HER HAIR BACK WIITH A LARGE RED PONYTAIL HOLDER CLIP THAT LOOKED LIKE A SEASHELL AND HE FOUND HER UNDERSTATED elegance bizarrely at odds with the so called situation.

Apart from her temerity in stowing aboard Ms. Taylor had seemed quite perfect to Jordan. His jaw hardened and after thirty-six years he'd finally met the women who would always be unforgettable and the one women he could never have.

When he returned to the cockpit Stoney cast him a puzzled glance and said "what took you so long?" Jordan decided to come straight out with the truth. Stoney wouldn't like it but however Jordan wasn't sure how he felt. Not yet he couldn't tell Stoney because he was still reacting to the flesh and blood reality of her.

There was one thing he did know which was the strange hollow feeling that had tormented him since take off had dissapeared as if it had never been.

"We have a stowaway" said Jordan. Stoney's head jerked around toward him and said "a what?" "Ms. Taylor decided to come along" said Jordan.

His friend's face went slack and Jordan knew exactly what was running through his friend's head. "Tell me you're joking." Jordan shook his head and said "no I'm not joking he said to Stoney but I wish I was he said halfheartedly." A part of him rejoiced in the knowledge that she was as close as the next compartment.

"Damnation Jordan! She picked the wrong time and place. Take a look at that left engine gauge the temperature's up."

JORDAN'S GAZE AUTOMATICALLY FLEW TO THE DIALS AND NOT ONLY WAS THE ENGINE HEATING UP BUT THE OIL PRESSURE WAS DOWN TOO AND THE SIGNIFICANCE OF THOSE TWO PROBLEMS HIT HIM LIKE A LOW BLOW. "WE'RE LOSING OIL STONEY SAID TO JORDAN AND I HAD THOUGHT YOU SAID THAT ROB PUT ON A NEW SEAL BEFORE WE LEFT ON THURSDAY."

"HE DID BUT MAYBE THERE'S A LEAK IN THE HOSE." "IT DOSEN'T MATTER NOW" JORDAN SAID. "LET'S HEAD FOR THAT NEAR-EMPTY RIVERBED AT FOUR O'CLOCK. THERE MIGHT BE ENOUGH ROOM TO LAND AND THEN WE CAN TAKE A LOOK."

"BETTER GET PREPARE RICKIE" JORDAN SAID AS HE LEAPED FROM HIS SEAT IN THE COCKPIT. AS HE ENTERED THE CABIN HE SAID "IS YOUR SEATBELT FASTENED MS. TAYLOR?" WE GOT ENGINE PROBLEMS WHICH MEANS WE HAVE TO MAKE AN EMERGENCY LANDING."

HE CAUGHT A FLASH OF STARTLED INTENSELY BLUE EYES BEFORE SHE GLANCED DOWN TO TIGHTEN UP HER SEATBELT STRAP. ANYONE ELSE MAN OR WOMEN WOULD PROBABLY HAVE BECOME HYSTERICAL BY NOW BUT HIS ADMIRATION FOR HER INTENSIFIED.

"PUT YOUR HEAD DOWN AND USE THESE PILLOWS TO PROTECT YOUR BODY" JORDAN SAID TO MS. TAYLOR. HE GRABBED FOR THEM SILENTLY PRAISING THE ALTRUISTIC TRAIT THAT HAD PROMPTED HER TO BUY THEM IN THE FIRST PLACE. THE PILLOWS MUST JUST SAVE HER FROM SERIOUS INJURY AND WITHOUT CONSCIOUS THOUGHT HE GRIPPED HER UPPER ARM. SHE FELT WARM AND ALIVE. "LISTEN STONEY I'VE BEEN THROUGH MUCH WROSE AND I'M STILL ALIVE."

"DON'T WORRY ABOUT ME" SHE WHISPERED "PLEASE TAKE CARE OF YOURSELF AND THE REVEREND" MS. TAYLOR SAID TO STONEY.

He tried to swallow that thought that Ms. Taylor said but right now his strongest impulse was to take care of her in his arms and protect her from whatever might happen but he couldn't do that because he needed to be Stoney's navigator.

They needed to find a good place to land the plane. "I'll see you on the ground Ms. Taylor."

For the next little while time had no meaning. She found herself thinking I'm not worth saving but please let them die because they're such deserving men Ms. Taylor said to God.

At some point the plane started making it's descent and because of her cocooned position she couldn't see anything but it didn't prevent her from picturing the alien green canopy below waiting to swallow them alive. She then braced herself for the moment of inpact. It wasn't going to be long before the plane crashes down to the ground.

One second they were riding on a cushion of air and then the next she felt as if a giant hand had smashed the plane to the floor. Rickie waited for the explosion but instead she buried her wet face in on of the pillows and waited for the end to come but unbelievably nothing happened. The sound of splintering glass and crunching metal that she'd expected to hear never reached her ears because instead a couple of happy shouts rang out from the cockpit.

Too traumatized by the last few moments she could scarcely comprehend that the plane was still in one piece moving forward over bumpy ground but before it slowed to a full stop someone was lifting the pillows that were protecting her head and then she felt a pair of strong hands cradling the sides of her face.

"Are you all right Ms. Taylor?" said a achingly familiar voice full with concern. Solwly Rickie raised herself up and had discovered the Reverend crouched next to her and his eyes were searching her features while his thumbs smoothed the hair at her temples.

"We're not dead!" she cried in out loud. "No he whispered "we're all very much alive thank God" said the Reverend. Now that the shock was wearing off she didn't seem to have any control over her emotions because all she knew was that their lives had been spared and that this man who had become vital to her very existence was there before her.

Without conscious thought she reached for him needing to be held but the fastened seatbelt prevented her form making full contact. When she realized her hands could only stretch halfway around his neck she then gave out a little moan of desperation.

Whatever that sound signaled she saw an answering flicker in his eyes and some emotion that reduced her to a trembling supplicant.

When he undid her seatbelt the brush of his hands against her hips set her on fire. She couldn't catch her breath and in the next instant she found herself crushed in his arms.

Overriding her feeling of gratitude was an emotion of a completely different kind and a

COMPELLING OVERWHELMING EMOTION OF DESIRE TOOK OVER HER BODY.

DAVID SOLOMON HAD ONCE ASKED HER IF SHE'D EVER BEEN TO BED WITH A MAN. SHE'D TOLD HIM NO BUT LONG BEFORE SHE DATED HIM SHE WONDERED IF THERE WAS SOMETHING WRONG WITH HER.

BEING IN JORDAN BROWNING'S ARMS PUT THAT WORRY TO REST ONCE AND FOR ALL. THOUGH SHE KNEW IT WAS WRONG SHE CLUNG TO HIM AND WAS CRAVING HIS STRONG ARMS. TOO SOON HE WOULD RELEASE HER AND SHE WOULD HAVE TO ACCEPT THAT THIS MEMENTARY LAPSE OF HIS HAD BEEN PROMPTED BY THE NATURAL INSTINCT TO COMFORT HER BECAUSE OF THE DANGER THAT HAPPENED TO THE AIRPLANE AND THEY'D JUST LIVED THROUGH A HARROWING EXPERIENCE.

SHE WOULD HAVE TO FORGET THE HUNGER SHE'D SEEN IN HIS EYES MOMENTS AGO. MAYBE SHE HAD WANTED HIM SO BADLY SHE'D IMAGINED IT OTHERWISE WOULDN'T HE BE DOING A LOT MORE THEN HOLDING HER? LATER SHE WOULD FEEL SHAMED FOR THROWING HERSELF AT HIM. RIGHT NOW SHE WAS WHERE SHE WANTED TO BE SO SHE DREW CLOSER AND RECOGNIZING THAT THIS EXPERIENCE COULD NEVER BE REPEATED EVER AGAIN.

CHAPTER 38

THE PLANE CRASH.

THERE PLANE CRASHED DOWN IN SOME REMOTE PART OF BRAZILIAN SAVANNA AND THEY MIGHT NOT BE ABLE TO REPAIR THE ENGINE AND ALL JORDAN COULD DO WAS THINK ABOUT WAS RICKIE TAYLOR.

THE FEEL OF HER ARMS AROUND HIS NECK WITH THE WARMTH OF HER SOFT BODY AGAINST HIS HAD IGNITED NEEDS THAT WERE ABOUT TO START GROWING OUT OF CONTROL. YOU HAVEN'T EVEN KISSED HER YET STONEY SAID.

MAYBE SHE HAD NO IDEA WHAT SHE WAS DOING TO HIM OR MAYBE IT WASTHE WAY SHE WAS CLUNG TO HIM WAS SIMPLY A REACTION TO HER NARROW ECAPE FROM DEATH. WHATEVER THE REASON THERE WAS NO GETTING AROUND THE FACT THAT HE WANTED TO MAKE LOVE TO HER.

IF NOT FOR STONEY'S PRESENCE JORDAN WOULD HAVE TOLD HER EXACTLY HE FELT THEN HE WOULD HAVE PROCEEDED TO ACT ON THOSE FEELINGS. IN HIS GUT HE KNEW HE COULD HAVE PERSUADED HER. LORD SHE WAS MADE FOR ME! SAID THE REVEREND.

LET HER GO BROWNING BECAUSE IF YOU TAKE THIS SHE'LL FIND OUT YOU'RE NOT WHO SHE THINKS YOU ARE. HE'D BETTER KEEP UP THE LIE TO REMAIN HER ADMIRATION BECAUSE HE COULDN'T HANDLE HER REJECTION NOT WHEN THE SLIGHTEST TOUCH OF HER

HAND HAD BROUGHT HIM A HAPPINESS HE'D NEVER KNOWN BEFORE.

"HOW ARE YOU FEELING NOW?" HIS LIPS GRAZED HER FOREHEAD AS SHE SOPKE AND HER BODY SHOOK. SHE'S AS VULNERABLE AS YOU ARE BROWNING.

HE FOUGHT TO SUPPRESS A GROAN AS SHE REMOVED HER ARMS FROM ROUND HIS NECK AND SAT BACK. "I'M FINE REVEREND THANK YOU." SHE REFUSED TO LOOK AT HIM AND STARED AT SOME POINT BEYOND HIS SHOULDER. "FORGIVE ME FOR BREAKING DOWN LIKE THAT I FEEL LIKE SUCH A FOOL."

JORDAN'S BODY CLAMORED FOR ASSUAGEMENT BECAUSE HE WANTED TO KISS THAT TREMBLING LOWER LIP OF HERS. HE DESPERATELY WANTED TO FEEL HE MOUTH MOVING BENEATH HIS BUT THERE WAS FEAR OF REPUDIATION WHEN SHE LEARNED THE TRUTH ABOUT HIM HAD HELD HIM BACK. RATHER THEN TAKE WHAT HE DESIRED AND LIVE TO REGRET IT HE STOOD ENDEAVORING TO PUT SOME DISTANCE BETWEEN THEM.

AFTER A STEADYING BREATH HE SAID "NO APOLOGY IS NECESSARY BECAUSE IT ISN'T EVERY DAY YOU HAVE DITCH A PLANE UNDER THESE CONDITIONS AND FOR THE RECORD I'VE NEVER SEEN ANYONE HANDLE A CRISIS OF THIS KIND BETTER THAN YOU DID."

HER INCREDULOUS GAZE FLICKED TO HIS AND THE SUN CHOSE THAT MOMENT TO MAKE IT'S APPEARANCE OVER THE HORIZON BECAUSE STONEY HAD SET THEM DOWN IN AN ANCIENT RIVER-BED AND THE OPENING IN THE LUSH SHAVANNA ALLOWED THE FIRST SLANTING RAYS TO ILLUMINATE DETAILS OBSCURED IN THE PREDAWN LIGHT. HER IRISES SHONE A VIVID BLUE AND THEY MESMERIZED HIM.

"YOU'RE A VERY COURAGEOUS PERSON MS. TAYLOR." PAIN HAD CLOUDED HER EYES SHE SAID OUT LOUD. "IN THE FACE OF DEATH SOME PEOPLE ARE BRAVE BECAUSE THEY HAVE NOTHING ON THEIR CONSCIENCE BUT THE REVERSE CAN BE EQUALLY TRUE. FOR SOME DEATH IS PERFERABLE TO THE BURDEN OF THEIR EARTHLY HELL."

SHE SOUNDED TORMENTED BUT YET THE WOMEN WHO'D CLUNG TO HIM MOMENTS AGO WAS ANYTHING BUT SUICIDAL. ALREADY DAMED FOR IMPERSONATING A MINISTER HE DIDN'T FIGURE IT COULD MAKE MATTERS ANY WORSE IF HE ENCOURAGED HER TO UNLOAD ON HIM. HE KNEW ENOUGH ABOUT HUMAN NATURE TO SUSPECT A CONNECTION BETWEEN HER PAIN AND THE MYSTERIOUS ILLNESS BESETTING HER.

"I CAN'T ESTIMATE HOW LONG IT'S GOING TO TAKE STONEY AND ME TO REPAIR THE ENGINE BUT EVEN IF YOU'RE ASLEEP WHEN WE'VE FINISHED PLAN TO BE AWAKENED BECAUSE YOU NEED TO TALK AND IT'S MY JOB TO LISTEN."

NOT GIVING HER A CHANCE TO ARGUE HE HEADED FOR THE CARGO HOLD. I INTEND TO KNOW EVERYTHING THERE IS TO KNOW ABOUT YOU MS. TAYLOR AND I'LL DO WHATEVER IT TAKES TO FIND OUT THE REVEREND SAID OUT LOUD.

HOURS LATER NIGHT HAD FALLEN OVER SAVANNA CLOAKING AND MAKING EVERYTHING TURN INTO INKY BLAKNESS. EVERY SO OFTEN ALIEN SCREECHES AND EERIE CRISES RENT AIR. HUGE FANTASTIC BUGS RICKIE HAD NO IDEA EXISTED FLEW AGAINST THE WINDOWS AND CRAWLED AROUND DRAWN TO THE LIGHT FROM THE HER FLASHIGHT AS SHE TRIED TO READ IN HER SEAT.

AFTER DINNER SHE HAD BRUSHED HER TEETH CHANGED INTO A PAIR OF SHORTS AND A T-SHIRT AND WAS READY FOR BED. THE MEN WERE STILL OUTSIDE FIXING THE LEFT ENGINE ON THE PLANE AND THEY HAVE BEEN WORKING SINCE MORNING. IT TOOK SEVERAL TRIPS TO GET THE LADDER AND ALL THEIR TOOLS OUTSIDE AND ANOTHER COUPLE OF HOURS TO FINE WHAT HAD CAUSED THE FUEL LEAK.

AROUND ELEVEN THEY'D DISCOVERED THE SOURCE OF THE PROBLEM WHICH TURNED OUT TO BE A FAULTY HOSE FITTING. PLEASED WITH THEIR SUCCESS THEY BROKE FOR LUNCH. RICKIE HAD LAID IT OUT IN THE CABIN USING THE REST OF THE FOOD MARY HAD PACKED IN A COOLER PLUS A FEW CONTRIBUTIONS OF HER OWN. A SMALL CAMP STOVE PROVIDED HEAT FOR THEIR COFFEE. RICKIE CHOSE A BOTTLED CITRUS DRINK BECAUSE SHE SHE WANT'S TO STICK TO HER DIET.

STONEY HAD GREETED HER AS IF SHE'D BEEN EXPECTED AND NEVER SAID A WORD ABOUT HER STOWING ABOARD. HE AND REVEREND BROWNING HAD EVERY RIGHT TO BE FURIOUS WITH HER AND PROBABLY WERE BUT THEY'D LEFT THE SUBJECT OF HER SURPRISE APPEARANCE OUT OF THE CONVERSATION.

WHILE THEY'D DEVOURED HAM SANDWICHES AND SALAD THE TOPIC CENTERED MAINLY ON THEIR PREDICAMENT. THEY NEEDED TO FASHION A NEW HOSE FITTING AND IT HAD TO BE DONE BY DARK IF THEY HOPED TO TAKE OFF AT DAWN THE NEXT MORNING.

AS SOON AS THE MEN HAD EATEN THEY'D GONE BACK TO WORK SEEMINGLY UNAFFECTED BY THE DRERADFUL HEAT AND HUMIDITY. SINCE HER SERVICES WEREN'T NEEDED IN THAT DEPARTMENT RICKIE HAD STAYED ON BOARD.

For her own safety they'd discouraged her from exploring outside the aircraft. With time on her hands she'd reached for her book on Paraguay and read untill it was time to make dinner for the guys. The men had gone out again once they'd finished the simple meal and Rickie went back to her reading. To often however her eyes strayed out the window to them and she had marveled at their industry and teamwork.

They had to be exhausted but it didn't show as they discussed their progress and took turns climbing the ladder to make another adjustment to the engine.

More and more she yearned for the sight of Reverend Browning and to her he represented everything noble in a man if he had character flaws she hadn't noticed them. Physically she found him utterly male and desirable.

Though she was no longer free to love anyone why couldn't she have felt this way about David Solomon? He was handsome, brilliant, a wonderful human being and had loved her.

The chemistry that drove two people apart or forced them together baffled her. She closed her eyes wishing she could shut out the image of the man working in the oppressive tropical heat but it was making her so hot that she needed to be colled off. He and Stoney were determined to have the plane airworthy by the time darkness falls.

Any minute and they'd be coming back inside for the night. If she pretended to be asleep in her seat she didn't believe Reverend Browning would

WAKE HER UP EVEN THOUGH HE'D THREATENED TO DO SO WITH HIS LOUD VOICE.

HE SENSED SHE HAD SOMETHING TO CONFESS AND HAD BEEN KIND ENOUGH TO OFFER A LISTENING EAR. HE EMBODIED TRUSTWORTHINESS AND INSPIRED THE KIND OF CONFIDENCE SHE IMAGINED WAS RARE EVEN AMONG CLERGYMEN BUT THE BURDEN SHE BORE BY BEING THE SO CALLED GRANDDAUGHTER OF THE VAMPIRE OF ALSACE MADE CONFESSION VERY IMPOSSIBLE. IF THE SIN OF LIVING OFF THE MONEY HER GRANDFATHER HAD MADE AT THE EXPENSE OF THE JEWS HE'D ROBBED AND THEN HE HAD ALLOWED THEM TO BE TORTURED AND MURDERED ON HIS PROPERTY WERE AN ORDINARY SIN HAD HAPPEN AND SHE WOULDN'T HESITATE TO DISCUSS IT WITH THE REVEREND BUT IF HE EVER LEARNED THE TRUTH ABOUT THE SO CALLED ORIGINS OF THE MONEY SHE'D GIVEN THEM HE WOULD RECOIL IN HORROR.

SHE HAD AN UNCOMFORTABLE PREMONITION THAT HE WOULDN'T BE ABLE TO GET AN LEAD ON HRE GRANDFATHER WITH THE SPARSE AMOUNT OF INFORMATION HE HAD. THEN SHE WOULDN'T HAVE ANY CHOICE BUT TO TELL THE WHOLE TRUTH ABOUT VON HASE AND ACCEPT THE SO CALLED CONSEQUENCES BUT UNTILL THERE WAS NO OTHER WAY SHE REFUSED TO DESTORY THE RAPPORT THEY SHARED HOWEVER TENTATIVE. THIS TIME WITH HIM WAS SO PRECIOUS SHE WOULD TREASURE IT FOR AS LONG AS POSSIBLE.

TO CREATE THE IMPRESSION THAT SHE WAS A SLEEP SHE PUT HER HEAD BACK AS FAR AS IT WOULD GO GRABBED A PILLOW AND SETTLED IN FOR THE NIGHT WITH HER BODY TURNED TOWAD THE WINDOW.

PERHAPS SHE WAS MORE TIRED THAN SHE SUPPOSED BECAUSE SHE DIDN'T HEAR THE MEN COME IN. AROUND

TWO IN THE MORNING SHE WOKE UP SURPRISED TO DISCOVER SHE'D BEEN ASLEEP SINCE EIGHT O'CLOCK THE NIGHT BEFORE.

USING HER FLASHLIGHT SHE MADE A TRIP TO THE BATHROOM THEN DETOURTED TO THE CARGO SECTION IN THE REAR OF THE PLANE TO GET HER SLEEPING BAG BECAUSE AFTER THE CRAMPED SEAT SHE CRAVED THE CHANCE TO STRETCH OUT ON THE FLOOR FOR A COUPLE OF HOURS.

AS SOON AS SHE'D ARRANGED EVERYTHING INCLUDING HER PILLOW SHE SANK DOWN WITH THE INTENTION OF GOING BACK TO SLEEP. "MIND IF I JOIN YOU?" SHE HEARD HIS VOICE DARKNESS.

SHE GAVE A NERVOUS START AND SAT UP TO DISCOVER HE'D PLACED A BLANKET IN THE AISLE IN FRONT OF HER SLEEPING BAG AND SHE COULDN'T TELL IF HE WAS SITTING OR LAYING DOWN. ALL SHE KNEW WAS THAT HE WAS TOO CLOSE.

"I'M GLAD I DIDN'T HAVE TO WAKE YOU UP." HER HEART POUNDING SHE LOOPED HER ARMS AROUND HER RAISED KNEES. "AFTER SUCH A HARD LONG DAY IN THE HEAT I'M SURPRISED YOU'RE NOT ASLEEP."

"I SLEPT FOR A WHILE NOW I FEEL RESTED ENOUGH TO LISTEN TO WHATEVER IT IS HAVE TO TELL ME." "YOU'RE VERY KIND REVEREND BUT THIS ISN'T SOMETHING I CAN DISCUSS WITH YOU." DAM HE SAID TO HIMSELF HER VOIVE IS TREMBLING SHE MUST HAVE SOMETHING ON HER MIND SAID THE REVEREND.

"FORGET WHO I AM AND START AT THE BEGINNING. BY THE WAY MY NAME IS JORDAN AND I'D RATHER YOU USED IT AROUND ME AND STONEY FROM NOW ON."

I'VE ALREADY CALLED YOU JORDAN IN MY DREAMS! "I DON'T FELL WORTHY TO DISCUSS MY PROBLEMS WITH ANYONE." "I'M JUST A VOICE IN THE DARK AND YOU DON'T HAVE ANY SINS" SHE WHISPERED. "THE HELL I DON'T!" "I'M TALKING ABOUT MAJOR AWFUL SINS." THE VIOLENCE OF HIS REACTION SURPRISED HER.

"WHAT OTHER KIND IS THERE WHEN WE ACT AS OUR OWN JUDGE?" HE HAD COUNTERED ON SAYING AND IN PRINCIPLE SHE AGREED WITH HIM BUT THE SLAUGHTER OF THE JEWS WAS ANOTHER MATTER ENTIRELY. HER GRANDFATHER NEEDED TO PAY FOR HIS CRIMES NOW THAT SHE KNEW THE TRUTH SHE FELT CULPABLE FOR HAVING LIVED ALL HER LIFE OFF THE VON HASE'S BLOOD MONEY.

THE KNOWLEDGE BROUGHT A SOB TO HER THROAT AND SOON SHE WAS CONVULSED WITH TEARS. "RICKIE!" HE HAD NEVER ADDRESSED HER BY HER FIRST NAME BEFORE. THE KINDNESS AND CONCERN IN HIS TONE ESCALATED HER PAIN.

"NO!" SHE CRIED OUT WHNE HE REACHED OVER AND PULLED HER INTO HIS ARMS. "SOMETIMES THIS IS THE ONLY THING THAT HELPS." HIS LIPS MOVED AGAINST HER HAIR.

"THEIR CLOSENESS CONFUSED HER BUT SHE DOSEN'T KNOW WHY."

"HUSH" HE ADMONISHED GENTLY WITH ONE ARM AROUND HER SHOULDERS HE SMOOTHED THE DAMP HAIR AT HER TEMPLE WITH HIS FREE HAND.

HER FACE WAS BURIED AGAINST HIS SHOULDER AND SHE COULD FEEL THE WARMTH OF HIS SKIN THROUGH THE KHAKI SHIRT. "THIS ISN'T RIGHT." HER PANIC INCREASED

AS SHE INHAILED THE PLEASANT SENT OF THE SOAP HE USED.

"IT'S VERY RIGHT YOU NEED HUMAN COMFORT." "YOU'RE NOT A MAN?" "I ASSURE YOU I AM AND FURTHERMORE I COULD USE A LITTLE COMFORT MYSELF BECAUSE YOU WEREN'T THE ONLY ONE AFFECTED BY OUR CLOSE CALL."

THE SIGNIFICANCE OF HIS WORDS TORE AT HER CONSCIENCE. "I SHOULD NEVER HAVE COME HERE BECAUSE MYSELFSHNESS HAS MADE EVERYTHING MORE COMPLICATED FOR YOU."

AFTER A SLIGHT PAUSE HE SAID "SOMEHOW I HAVE THE IMPRESSION YOU WERE BORN FEELING GUILTY."

HOW DID HE UNDERSTAND SO MUCH ABOUT HER? SHE NEEDED TO GET AWAY FROM HIM BEFORE HE DIVINED HER SECRETS BUT THE SECOND SHE TRIED TO MOVE HIS HOLD SEEMED TO TIGHTEN.

"LET'S THIS BURDEN GO OR YOU'LL HAVE A BREAK DOWN RICKIE." "I'M ALREADY HAVING A BREAK DOWN" SHE SAID IN A DULL VOICE. "YOU WOULD DO BETTER TO SPEND YOUR TIME HELPING SOMEONE WORTH SAVING."

"THERE IS NO ONE ELSE AT THE MOMENT AND RICKIE YOUR ACTIONS HAVE GIVING ME NEW FAITH IN PEOPLE." "THEN YOU BEEN MISLED." "I PRIDE MYSELF ON BEING A GOOD JUDGE OF CHARACTER AND AS FAR AS I KNOW I'VE NEVER BEEN WRONG."

SHE GROANED IN FRESH ANGUISH AS SHE SAID "THAT'S BECAUSE YOU'VE NEVER MET ANYONE LIKE ME BEFORE." "YOU'RE RIGHT I HAVEN'T." UNABLE TO TAKE ANY MORE SHE SAID "I THINK I'M READY TO GO BACK TO SLEEP NOW."

"I'M AFRAID I'M NOT BECAUSE THERE'S A GREAT DEAL MORE I'D LIKE TO LEARN ABOUT RICKIE TAYLOR." HIS COMMENT LEFT HER AT A TOTAL LOSS FOR WORDS.

"WHO'S THE MAN IN YOUR LIFE BESIDES YOUR BROTHER AND COUSIN?" "THERE IS NO MAN." "THEN WHO'S DAVID SOLOMON?" HER HEAD LIFTED IN ALARM. "HOW DO YOU KNOW ABOUT HIM?"

"THE FIRST DAY I CAME TO YOUR I SAW HIS MESSAGE ON YOUR DESK." HER THOUGHTS FLASHED BACK TO THAT AFTERNOON AND SHE HAD REMEMBERED HOW HE'D CAUGHT HER APPRAISING HIM SO BOLDLY. JUST RECALLING THE INCIDENT BROUGHT HET TO HER CHEEKS AND DARKNESS CAN BE A BLESSING.

"THOSE MESSAGES HAD AN AUSTRALIAN COUNTRY CODE AND SINCE YOUR FIRST SICK SPELL I'VE BEEN ASKING MYSELF IF YOUR SYMPTOMS HAVE HAD MORE TO DO WITH HIM THEN THE LATEST FLU."

STOP SHE SAID I DON'T WANT TO HEAR THIS ANY MORE. "DID YOU BREAK HIS HEART?" PLEASE DON'T SAY ANY MORE. "IS THAT WHY YOU FEEL GUILTY?" "I WAS NEVER IN LOVE WITH HIM" SHE BLURTED OUT LOUD WITHOUT THINKING.

"ARE YOU IN THE HABIT OF BREAKING HEARTS?" "OF COURSE NOT!" SHE SAID TO THE REVEREND. "HAVE YOU EVER BEEN IN LOVE?"

THE LAST TIME A GUY ASKED HER THAT QUESTION SHE SAID NO BUT THAT BEFORE SHE'D MET JORDAN. HE CAN NEVER KNOW HOW I FEEL SHE SAID TO HERSELF SO SHE LIED AND SAID "NO I HVE NEVEN BEEN IN LOVE."

"THAT'S TOO BAD BECAUSE I'M CONVINCED THE LOVE OF A GOOD MAN COULD CHANGE YOUR WORLD."

"ALL THE GOOD ONES ARE TAKEN." "I SUPPOSE THAT'S AS CONVENIENT AN EXCUSE AS ANY TO AVOID THE FACT THAT FOR SOME REASON YOU FEEL TOO GUILTY TO ENTER INTO A RELATIONSHIP."

AT HIS ASTUTE OBSERVATION RICKIE STIRRED RESTLESSLY. I'REALLY AM TIRED." "I'LL HOLD YOU TILL YOU FALL ASLEEP." "THAT WON'T NECESSARY."

"ON THE CONTRARY I THINK YOU NEED TO BE HELD AND IN YOUR CASE THE TERM "POOR LITTLE RICH GIRL TRULY APPLIES." RICKIE BLINKED HER EYES IN SHOCK. "FOR A LONG TIME NOW YOU'VE BEEN TAKING CARE OF OTHER PEOPLE AND THEIR PROBLEMS BUT YOU HAVEN'T ALLOWED ANYONE TAKE CARE OF YOU AND PLEASE DON'T DENY ME THAT LITTLE PLEASURE."

THE SWELLING IN HER THROAT PREVENTED SPEECH. TIRED OF THE STRUGGLE SHE FINALLY RELAXED AGAINST HIS CHEST. MAYBE NOW HE WOULD ANSWER HER BURNING QUESTION. "WHY HAVEN'T YOU GOT MARRIED?" HE EXPELLED A DEEP SIGH WHEN HE SAID THAT. MARRIAGE INVOLVES DEVOTION TO ONE PERSON AND WITH THE LINE OF WORK I'M IN HAS PREVENTED ME FROM BEING ABLE TO MAKE THAT KIND OF VOW. I HAVE ENOUGH ON MY CONSCIENCE WITHOUT HURTING SOMEONE ELSE BECAUE I COULDN'T BE FULLY COMMITTED TO HER."

YOU WANT TO KNOW RICKIE. "DOSE YOUR FAITH FORBID YOU TO GET MARRIED?" "NO REVEREND ROLON HAS A WIFE AND FAMILY." SUDDENLY HER HEART BEGAN TO BEAT FASTER. "WHY DID YOU BECOME A MINISTER?" RICKIE ASKED HIM.

AFTER A BRIEF SILENCE HER TOLD HER "IT SEEMED THE ONLY WAY TO CARRY OUT THE THINGS I WANTED TO DO." AT LEAST HE WASN'T AVOIDING HER QUESTIONS LIKE HE'D DONE A FEW DAYS PREVIOUSLY.

"EARLIER YOU SAID YOU HAD NO FAMILY I ASSUMED YOU MEANT THAT NONE OF THEM ARE LIVING. WAS YOUR FATHER A CLERGYMAN?

THEN THERE WAS ANOTHER PAUSE BEFORE HE SAID "I NEVER KNEW MY FATHER BECAUSE HIM AND MY MOTHER WERE KILLED IN A BOATING ACCIDENT WHEN I WAS A CHILD. MY GRAND FATHER RAISED ME UNTILL HIS RETIREMENT HE'D BEEN IN THE MILITARY ALL HIS ADULT LIFE."

"WHAT BRANCH WAS HE WITH?" "THE NAVY." "REALLY THEN WHERE DID YOU LIVE?" "IN SOUTHERN CALIFORNIA."

AS FAR AWAY FROM NEW YORK AND IT'S LIFE-STYLE AS POSSIBLE. "WHERE EXACTLY?" "IMPERIAL BEACH." "ISN'T THAT NEAR TIJUANA?" "YES." "SO THAT'S WHERE YOU PICKED UP YOU SPANISH." "MORE PARTICULARLY FROM MY BEST FRIEND LUIS SALAZAR. THEIR FAMILY LIVED DOWN THE STREET FROM MY GRANDFATHER. LUIS AND I PLAYED TOGETHER AS CHILDREN AND GROWING UP WE WENT TO THE SAME SCHOOLS. I WAS OVER AT THE SALAZAR'S HOUSE MOST OF THE TIME AND PROBABLY SPOKE MORE SPANISH THAN ENGGLISH." THE AFFECTION IN HIS VOICE WAS UNMISTAKABLE.

"DO YOU STILL KEEP IN TOUCH WITH HIM?" "NO." "WHY NOT?" "BECAUSE HE'S DEAD" HE SAID.

HER BEREATH CAUGHT WHEN HE SAID THAT. "I'M SORRY." "SO AM I." SHE COULD HERE A DEEP BITTERNESS BEHIND HIS PAIN. SHE SUSPECTED HE HADN'T TALKED ABOUT THIS FOR A VERY LONG TIME.

"IF HE WAS YOUR AGE THEN HE WAS TOO YOUNG TO DIE. WAS HE ILL?" THERE WAS A PROLONGE SILENCE AS RICKIE GASPED.

"IT HAPPENED ON THE NIGHT WE GRADUATED FROM HIGH SCHOOL. WE'D GONE TO TIJUANA AND LUIS HAD A GRILFRIEND PERLA. THEY WERE PLANNING TO GET MARRIED AT THE END OF THE SUMMER.

AROUND TEN THAT NIGHT THE THREE OF US HAD DRIVEN UP THE HIGHSET HILL IN THE CORVETTE LUIS HAD HELPED ME RESTORE. WE WANTED TO SEE THE LIGHTSBEFORE WE HEADED BACK TO THE BORDER. WE DIDN'T REALIZE SOME GANG MEMBERS HAD BEEN FOLLOWING US. "AT GUNPOINT THEY FORCED ALL THREE OF US FROM THE CAR. AFTER THEY TOOK TUNS RAPING PERLA WHILE WE WERE HELD DOWN THEY SHOT HER THEN LUIS AND STILL HOLDING THE GUN ON ME THEY GOT IN THEIR CARS AND TOOK OFF. THEY WERE NEVER CAUGHT AND TO THIS DAY I DON'T KNOW WHY THEY DIDN'T KILL ME TOO."

THE SCENE HE DESCRIBED WAS SO APPALLING RICKIE MOANED AND HAD UNCONSCIOUSLY NESTLED CLOSER.

"THE FEELING OF UTTER HELPLESSNESS CHANGED MY LIFE. I CAME OUT OF THE TRAGEDY VOWING I WOULD NEVER ALLOW MYSELF TO BE SO VICTIMIZED BY THAT KIND OF VULNERABILITY AGAIN."

THE BARELY SUPPRESSED VIOLENCE OF HIS TONE SENT A SHUDDER THOUGH HER BODY. HER THOUGHTS DARTED BACK TO HER VERY FIRST IMPRESSION OF HIM IN HER OFFICE SHE THEN PUT THEM TOGETHER WITH WHAT HE'D JUST TOLD HER.

SUDDENLY THINGS THAT HAD SEEMED UNRELATED STARTED MAKING PERFECT SENSE. IN WONDER SHE CRIED "YOU TRAINED TO BECOME A GREEN BERET OR SOMETHING DIDN'T YOU? IS THAT HOW YOU MET SO CALLED STONEY?"

When he didn't answer she lifted her head from his shoulder sensing that she was getting closer to the truth. "There's a bond between the two of you that goes way back long before you became a minister."

He didn't conforim or deny he suspicions. "I can feel that rapport between you because I've felt it since I boarded the plane. Sometimes you and Stoney react in exactly the same way."

Slowly he released her arms and apparently she'd trespassed into forbidden territory and now he needed to distance himself physically and emotionally.

His revelations had meant so much to her and she couldn't let him stop here.

"Mary said you and Stoney delivered cargo to Paraguay but I think the two of you were in Paraguay for entirely different reasons and I think it had something to do with the Ache Indians and that's why you're so passionately involved."

He got to his feet and she felt the blanket brush her arms as he lifted it from the floor to flod. They'd been talking for a long time and the degree of darkness had changed it was no longer so absolute. She could make out his shadowy form and could sense the tautness of his posture.

He'd be joining Stoney any second because her prying had driven him away.

Disappointment swept over her and with her legs shaky she stood up placing her sleeping bag on one of the seats. "I didn't mean to offend you by

DELVING TO DEEP. YOU DON'T HAVE TO TELL ME ANYTHING IF YOU DON'T WANT TO BUT OBVIOUSLY SOMETHING HAD HAPPENED IN PARAGUAY SOMETHING THAT SET YOU ON THIS PARTICULAR COURSE. I THOUGHT MAYBE YOU NEEDED TO TALK TO ABOUT IT. IF I WAS WRONG I'M SORRY. HER APOLOGY HUNG IN THE AIR.

"YOU HAVE UNCANNY INSTINCTS MS. TAYLOR." SHE FOUND NO JOY IN BEING RIGHT BECAUSE HE'D GONE BACK TO ADDRESSING HER SO FORMALLY. THE LOSS OF INTIMACY WAS MORE PAINFUL THEN SHE WOULD HAVE EXPECTED.

"YOU'RE THE ONE FUNDING THIS OPERATION AND SINCE YOU'VE CHOSEN TO JOIN US YOU'RE INTITLED TO HEAR WHAT THIS IS ALL ABOUT" AND HE SOUNDED SO ANGRY BECAUSE THIS WAS THE LAST EMOTION SHE'D MEANT TO AROUSE IN HIM.

"A LITTLE MORE THAN EIGHT MOMENTS AGO STONEY AND I WITNESSED A SCENE SIMILAR TO ONE IN TIJUANA. SOME HIGH-PLACED PARAGUAYAN OFFICIALS WERE VISITING A REMOTE AREA OF THE CHACO WHERE THEY KEPT TEENAGE GIRLS STOLEN FROM THEIR VILLAGES.

"THE SCREAMS I HEARD COULD HAVE BEEN PERLA'S AND NO AMOUNT OF BEGGING OR PLEADING MAKD A DIFFERENCE BUT UNLIKE HER HOWEVER THESE YOUNG WOMEN WREN'T SHOT AND PPUT OUT OF THEIR MISERY. THE MEN RETURENED TO RAPE THEM NIGHT AFTER NIGHT."

AS HE RELATED ONE ATROCITY AFTER ANOTHER FLASHBACKS FROM HER TRIP TO JERUSALEM BEGAN TO INTERFERE. ALL THE DETAILS FLOWED TOGETHER LIKE PART OF ONE PERPETUAL EVIL ROUND AND JORDAN'S VOICE SEEMED TO BLEND WITH THE OTHER VOICES IN HER HEAD.

"THE EXPERIMENTS ON JEWISH TEENAGE TWINS WAS OF PARTICULAR INTEREST TO JOSEF MENGELE WHO FOUND A WILLING ACCOMPLICE IN GERHARDT VON HASE AT HIS HUGE FACTORY COMPLEX. VON HASE NEEDED MASSIVE QUANTITIES OF SLAVE LABOR TO HELP MANUFACTURE MUNITIONS FOR THE THIRD REICH."

"VON HASE HAD A FETISH FOR CLEANLINESS AND PRECISION WHICH CARRIED OVER INTO THE SELECTION PROCESS HE PERSONALLY SUPERVISED AND THOSE WITH SKIN BLEMISHES WERE SENT TO A SPECIAL HOLDING CELL BEFORE EXTERMINATION. EACH DAY HE DREW A LINE ON THE WALL. THOSE WHOSE HEADS COULD NOT REACHE THE LINE WERE MURDERED VERY IMMEDIATELY."

"FOR PLEASURE HE OFTEN CHANGED THE HIGHT OF THE LINE IN THIS WAY ENSURING THAT ALL WORLD EVENTUALLY DIE. WHILE HUMMING A TUNE FROM WAGNER OR STRAUSS HE DERIVED PLEASURE FROM WATCHING THEIR FACES AS THEY APPEOACHED THE LINE.

"OH DEAR GOD!" RICKIE SUDDENLY CRIED OUT "HOW COULD GOD IF THERE IS A GOD HAVE LET THAT HAPPEN? WHY DIDN'T HE STOP ALL OF IT?

CHAPTER 39

MAN ON THE RUN.

THE ANGUISH COMING FROM RICKIE TAYLOR RIPPED JORDAN'S HEART WIDE OPEN AND BROUGHT STONEY INTO THE CABIN FOR A RUN.

JORDAN SHOOK HIS HEAD AS HIS FRIEND SIGNALING THAT HE'D EXPLAIN LATER. STONEY HESITATED THEN WITH AN UNDERSTANDING NOD AND WENT BACK TO THE COCKPIT.

THE GREAT HEAVING SOBS THAT POURED FROM THE WOMEN THAT WAS ROCKING BACK AND FORTH IN FRONT OF JORDAN HAD BEEN TRIGGERED BY WHAT HE'D TOLD HER. HER SOUNDS OF DESPAIR AND HOPELESSNESS STRUCK A FAMILIAR CHORD INSIDE HIM AND FOR HE WISHED HE REALLY WAS AN ORDAINED MINISTER AND MAYBE THEN HE COULD OFFER SOME GENUINE SOLACE.

IF SHE'D FELT AS HELPLESS AS JORDAN DID IN PARAGUAY AND TIJUANA THEN HE WOULD UNDERSTAND WHY SHE WAS INCONSOLABLE AND UNDERSTAND IT ONLY TOO WELL.

CRAVING THE CONNECTION THEY'D SHARED EARLIER HE PUT A HAND ON HER ARM AND SAID "HOW CAN I HELP YOU RICKIE? WHAT DO YOU WANT ME TO DO?"

SHE TOOK A STEP BACKWARD SO HE WOULD RELINGUISH HIS HOLD ON HER ARM. ON A SUBLIMINAL LEVEL THE GESTURE WONDED. WHIT OBVIOUS EFFORT SHE PULLED

HERSELF TOGETHER AND IN THE SHADOWY LIGHT OF APPROACHING DAWN HE CAUGHT SIGHT OF HER FACE.

"YOU CAN LET HIM HELP THESE PEOPLE YOU'RE ABOUT TO RESCUE" SHE BEGAN TALKING AGAIN "AND YOU CAN LET ME COME WITH YOU ON THE SEARCH FOR MY GRANDFATHER."

HE HEARD TRACES OF RANGE IN HER VOICE AND THE RANGE WAS A POWERFUL EMOTION THAT JORDAN KNEW INTIMATELY. HE'D LIVED WITH IT FOR THE PAST EIGHTEEN YEARS.

APPARENTLY SHE'D BEEN PREPARED FOR AN ARGUMENT. HIS WORDS SEEMED TO TAKE FIGHT OUT OF HER. "THANK YOU" SHE SAID. "YOU'RE WALCOME" HE SAID RIGHT BACK TO HER. HE THEN WATCHED THE NERVOUS WAY SHE RUBBED HER PALMS AGAINST HER HIPS AS IF NOW SHE'D MADE A DEFIANT STAND AND SHE DIDN'T KNOW WHAT TO DO NEXT AND THEN THERE WAS THE COMBINATION OF DETERMINATION AND VALNERABILITY MOVED HIM DEEPLY.

HE CLEARED HIS THROAT AND THEN HE SAID "HOW GOOD ARE YOU WITH A GUN? SHE THEN SAID "I TOOK FIRST PLACE ALL FOUR YEARS IN TARGET SHOOTING AT THE INTERCOLLEGIATE GAMES AT ROSMORE."

INEXPLICABLY PLEASED BY THE INFORMATION JORDAN SMILED. "THAT WASN'T IN YOU PROFILE ON THE INTERNET." "THAT'S A SURPRISE" SHE RETORTED WITH A HINT OF HUMOR.

AFTER HER PAROXYSM OF TEARS HE HADN'T EXPECTED THIS SWIFT A RECOVERY BUT HE HAD TO REMEMBER SHE'D BEEN LIVING WITH HER PAIN FOR SOME TIME AND AT LEAST SINCE HER FLIGHT HOME FROM AUSTRALIA HAD THE TRAUMA OR WHATEVER HAD TAKEN PLACE THERE?

"I CAN SMELL COFFEE SHE SAID OUT LOUD. SHALL WE GO IN AND SEE STONEY NOW? HE'S NEVER BEEN A LONER AND HE'S MISSING HIS EX-WIFE MICHELLE LIKE CRAZY ALTHOUGH HE WON'T ADMIT IT."

SHE FLASHED HIM A MYSTERIOUS LITTLE SMILE AND IT FELT AS IF HE'D JUST BEEN CATAPULTED TOWARD THE SUN. "MARY SAYS MICHELLE HAS DECIDED NOT TO MARRY THE MAN SHE'S BEEN DATING."

JORDAN GRINNED AND HE COULDN'T WAIT TO TELL STONEY. "SHE COULD NEVER MARRY ANY ONE ELSE BECAUSE SHE'S STILL VERY MUCH IN LOVE WITH STONEY."

"WHAT'S KEEPING THEM APART?" THE SAME DAM THING SEPARATING YOU AND ME RICKIE TAYLOR. "THAT'S ALL RIGHT" SHE SAID. "I THINK I ALREADY KNOW THE ANSWER TO MY OWN QUESTION BUT IF MARY HAS ANYTHING TO DO WITH IT I HAVE A FEELING THERE'S HOPE FOR THEM."

"MARY'S A WOMEN WITH HIDDEN TALENTS AND SMUGGLING YOU ABOARD TOOK SOME INGENUITY." "YOU CAN'T BLAME HER FOR THAT BECAUSE I'M AFRAID ALL THE CREDIT GOES TO ME IN FACT I OWE HER A KEY TO THE BACK DOOR OF THE HANGAR THE ONE I TOOK OFF THE RING WHEN SHE WASN'T WATCHING."

"I SHOULD HAVE KNOWN AND YOU ACCUSED ME OF INFILTRATION!" FOR A BRIEF MOMENT THE HEAVY DESPONDENCY THAT HAD ENVELOPED THEM SEEMED TO HAVE DISSIPATED BECAUSE THEY BOTH SMILED AND AT THIS TIME IT REACHED HER INTENSELY BLUE EYES. RICKIE TAYLOR IF I HAD YOU ALON RIGHT NOW . . . "GOOD MORNING TWO YOU TOO" SHE SAID AS SHE BROK EYE CONTACT AND TURNED HE HEAD IN STONEY'S DIRECTION. "GOOD MORNING" SAID STONEY TO EVERYONE. "I'VE MADE YOU SOME ORANGE JUICE FROM THE POWERED STUFF."

"THANK YOU LET ME GET DRESSED AND I'LL BE BACK DOWN IN A MINUTE TO JOIN YOU.

I THINK I CAN CONTRIBUTE A PACK OF CINNAMON ROLLS AND SOME FRUIT ROLL-UPS." "YOU HEAR THAT JORDAN? CINNAMON ROLLS! I'LL BE DOWN SOON I'M STARVED."

JORDAN WAS STARVED BUT NOT FOR FOOD. HER SHORTS REVEALED A STUNNING PAIR OF LEGS THAT WERE LONG AND SLENDER AND AS SHE WALKED TO THE REAR OF THE PLANE STONEY APPEARED EVERY BIT AS FASCINATED.

WHEN SHE'D DISSAPEARED HE REGARDED JORDAN FRANKLY. "YOU TWO HAVE BEEN BACK HERE FOR HOURS. WHAT'S GOING ON?"

THERE WERE NO SECRETS BETWEEN STONEY AND HIM. "LET ME GRAB SOME COFFEE AND I'LL TELL YOU." THE PROCEEDED TO THE CARGO HOLD BEHIND THE COCKPIT AND JORDAN THEN REACHED FOR HIS MUG AND POURED SOME OF THE COFFEE STONEY HAD PREPARED ON THE HOT PLATE.

QUICKLY BEFORE SHE RETURNS JORDAN FILLED IN HIS PARTNER. STONEY TENDED TO BE TOO OVERPROTECTIVE WITH WOMEN AND JORDAN WAS READY FOR HIM WHEN STONEY QUESTIONED HIS JUDGMENT IN ALLOWING RICKIE TO GET INVOLVED.

"I PROMISED HER." "DAM IT JORDAN !" "I'LL TAKE FULL RESPONSIBILITY" HE SAID ADAMANTLY. "SHE'S MAKING YOU SOFT."

IN THE PAST A COMMENT LIKE THAT WOULD HAVE GOTTEN A RISE OUT OF JORDAN BUT SINCE RICKIE TAYLOR HAD COME INTO HIS LIFE EVERYTHING HAD CHANGED BECAUSE HE BARELY RECOGNIZED HIMSELF ANYMORE.

"MAYBE YOU SHOULD TRY IT." AT STONEY'S QUIZZICAL HE ADD "YOU KNOW WHAT I MEAN." "DON'T TALK TO ME ABOUT MICHELLE." "THEN I GUESS YOU DON'T WANT TO KNOW THAT SHE CALLED OFF THE WEDDING TO THE WALL STREET GUY."

WHEN JORDAN SAID THAT STONEY'S HEAD REARED BACK. "YOU MADE THAT UP." JORDAN SAID AS HE SHRUGGED HIS SHOULDERS. "MARY TOLD RICKIE AND IF YOU DON'T BELIEVE ME THEN ASK HER." HIS GLANCE SWUNG TO THE WOMEN WHOSE MERE PRESENCE QUICKENED HIS BODY.

"ASK ME WHAT?" SHE SAID AS SHE WAS WALKING TOWARD STONEY AND JORDAN.

AT THE SOUND OF HER VOICE STONEY WHEELED AROUND AND ASKED HER "DID MARY HONESTLY SAY MICHELLE BROKE IT OFF WITH THAT GUY?" "YES" SAID RICKIE AS HER EYES FILLED WITH COMPASSION AND STONEY'S EYES FILLED WITH UNCONCEALED RELIEF.

JORDAN STEPPED BACK LOOKING AT BOTH OF THEM FOR ONE LITTLE WHIMSICAL MOMENT HE THOUGHT SHE LOOKED EXACTLY LIKE A SMALL GOLDEN-HAIRED PRINCESS FROM A GRIMM BROTHERS FAIRY TALE TRYING TO COMOUFLAGE HIMSELF IN KHAKI PANTS AND LEATHER BOOTS AND THE DISGUISE WAS ACTUALLY A FOIL FOR THE PURITY OF HER PROFILE AND THE CLASSIC LINES OF HER BONE STRUCTURE AND YET RICKIE'S BEAUTY WAS SO MUCH MORE THAN THIS.

THE TIME HE'D SPENT WITH HER SINCE HE'D FOUND HER SITTING IN THE PLANE'S CABIN HAD ALTERED THINGS DRASTICALLY. LINES HAD BEEN CROSSED AND HE MIGHT NOT KNOW WHAT THE FUTURE HOLDS BUT THERE WAS NO POSSIBILITY OF RETREATING TO FORMALITY OF THEIR PREVIOUS RELATIONSHIP.

Jordan abandoned his reverie and turned his attention back to Rickie. She was still speaking to Stoney who was decribing the risks they might encounter on the trip. Stoney paused to accept a roll from the package she extended to them. "The problem is we don't even know what we're in for on this trip Rickie." "I realize that and I'll try to be an asset." He had stared down at her then flicked a glance to Jordan. "Well I guess there's no chance we can talk her out of it."

Jordan could tell that Stoney was becoming resigned to her presence but he couldn't know how dead-set this women was on being a part of the operation.

She'd only given Jordan glimpses into her so called complicated anguished thoughts but he'd learned enough to sense how vital this mission had become to her.

"It's easy to write a check for a project Stoney" Rickie said. "I've only been on the money giving end and money that's not even my own" she said as her voice was trembleing noticeably. Jordan realized that whenever she talked about her unearned fortune she grew nervous or averted her eyes and that unusual behavior peaked his curiosity.

She put the food she'd pulled from her pack on the little TV tray Stoney had set up. "I'm convinced there must be a tremendous satisfaction from jumping into the trenches where the real work's going on. I've never known what that felt like so this is a opportunity for me to find out."

"THIS ISN'T ORDINARY WORK RICKIE AND IT'S POSSIBLE NONE OF US WILL MAKE IT OUT ALIVE." "I REFUSE TO BELIEVE THAT."

THE LOOK STONEY SHOT JORDAN SAID IT ALL AND THAT HE'D JUST GIVEN UP. HER UNDAUNTED DETERMINATION HAD DEFEATED HIM.

"STONEY THANK FOR TRYING TO PROTECT ME BUT IT'S JUST THAT FOR SOME WOMEN THE DANGER DOSEN'T REPRESENT AS GREAT A THREAT AS THE SECRETS AND LIES EMPLOYED TO COVER IT UP. WHAT'S THAT SAYING ABOUT THE TRUTH THAT IT WILL SET YOU FREE?"

"WOMEN ARE SOFT AND SWEET" STONEY MUTTERED STUBBORNLY. "IT IS AN UGLY WORLD OUT THERE" SHE SIAD AS SHE SMILED BUT HER TONE SERIOUS RESOLUTE. "I AGREE BUT STILL MANY WOMEN AREN'T AS SOFT AS YOU THINK AND WANT THE CHOICE BECAUSE THEY WANT TO DECIDE FOR THEMSELVES. IS THAT SO HARD TO UNDERSTAND?"

STONEY STARTED TO NOD HIS HEAD TO AGREE WITH JORDAN. "YEAH IT'S HARD FOR ME I GUESS I HAVE A PROBLEM WITH THAT AND I GUESS IT'S SOMETHING I'M GOING TO HAVE TO WORK ON."

"THANK YOU FOR WORKING ON THIS TRIP ANYWAY" SHE SAID. "YOU'RE WELCOME" HE ANSWERED GRUFFLY BUT IN HIS EYES JORDAN SAW REAL AFECTION FOR HER AND HE WONDERED IF STONEY REALIZED THAT SHE'D HIT ON THE CRUX OF HIS DIFFICULTY WITH MICHELLE.

"HEY JORDAN?" STONEY MUST HAVE BEEN NUDGING HIM IN THE RIBS FOR THE LAST FEW SECONDS BUT A CERTAIN FEMALE STOWAWAY HAD DRIVEN EVERY OTHER THOUGHT FROM HIS MIND. "IF YOU'VE FINISHED EATING LET'S CLEAN UP AND TAKE OFF."

"HOW ABOUT YOU RICKIE ARE YOU READY TO GO?" SHE LIFTED HER GAZE TO HIS STARING AT HIM WITH AN INTENSITY THAT TOOK HIS BREATH AWAY. "WHENEVER YOU ARE." "THEN SIT DOWN AND STRAP YOURSELF IN BECAUSE THIS IS GOING TO BE AN INTERESTING TAKE OFF."

"SPEAK FOR YOURSELF" STONEY INTERJECTED IN THE CONVERSATION WITH THE BRIGHTEST SPIRITS JORDAN HAD SEEN IN OVER A YEAR. JORDAN FELT SURE IT WAS BECAUSE OF THE NEWS ABOUT MICHELLE AND HOW HE AND RICKIE'S COMMENTS WERE TO PROFOUND TO PONDER FOR THE REST OF THE TRIP. HER OBSERVATION AND HER EXAMPLE MIGHT MAKE THE DIFFERENCE AND IT MIGHT HELP STONEY RECOGNIZE THAT HIS EX-WIFE WANTED HIS TRUST AND RESPECT NOT HIS PROTECTION. AMONG RICKIE'S ACCOMPLISHED ROLES HE COULD ADD MARRIAGE COUNSELOR HE HAD THOUGHT WRYLY.

IT BEWILDERED HIH THAT A WOMEN SO COMPASSIONATE AND PERCEPTIVE LACKED THE ABILITY TO SEE HERSELF AS CLEARLY OR THE ABILITY TO FORGIVE HERSELF FOR WHATEVER TERRIBLE THING SHE IMAGINED SHE'D DONE OR HADN'T DONE.

ONE DAY WHEN SHE WAS READY TO CONFIDE IN HIM HE'D LEARNED THE TRUTH AND THEN WHAT BROWING? IS THAT WHEN YOU'LL COME CLEAN AND TELL HER YOU'RE NOT A MINISTER? OR THAT YOU'VE SPENT TIME IN PRISON FOR MURDER?

IN AN INSTANT HIS HAPPINESS EVAPORATED LEAVING EVERYTHING BLEAKER THAN BEFORE. "I'M GOING OUTSIDE TO MAKE A FINAL CHECK." STONEY SHOT HIM A PUZZLED GLANCE BUT JORDAN IGNORED IT AND STRODE SWIFTLY PAST BOTH OF THEM.

RICKIE HADN'T FLOWN TO SOUTH AMRICA IN ANYTHING BUT A 747 AND AS A RESULT SHE'D NEVER BEFORE SEEN THE vast green expanse of the continent from a few hundred feet above.

At any other time she would been awed by sight especially this soon after sunrise. The swampland and scattered forests appeared so close to the plane she felt she could reach down and brush the foliage with her hands but Jordan's sudden change in demeanor had hurt a lot and she could no longer took pleasure in the morningm because after he'd come back on board she'd wanted to ask him how long they'd be in the air but his implacable expression had discouraged her from speaking.

She reviewed all their conversations but no matter how many times she went over it she couldn't come up with a reason for the abrupt change in his mood and judging by Stoney's questioning glance she didn't think he knew what was bothering Jordan either.

Wearily she rested her head against the seat and took in the ever-changing landscape of grassland and savanna below and flying under these conditions probably constituted one of the greatest thrills for an experienced pilot.

Rickie had no fear for her safety but Stoney and Jordan had made an emergeny landing and repaired the plane and then taken off from a riverbed as if it were and everyday occurrence. She had the utmost confidence in them. What troubled her was the co-pilot's state of mind.

Obviously he didn't realize how much his mood affected those around him but perhaps when he'd spent more time with her and he would before

THIS MISSION WAS OVER HE'D BE WILLING TO SHARE HIS TROUBLES.

FOR NOW SHE'D HAVE TO WAIT UNTILL JORDAN CHOSE TO CONFIDE IN HER AGAIN BECAUSE AFTER ALL HE'D TOLD HER ABOUT THE MURDER OF HIS BRST FRIEND BUT SHE DIDN'T IMAGINE VERY MANY PEOPLE WERE PRIVY TO THAT PART OF HIS PAST AND IF HE REGRETTED TELLING HER IT WAS TO LATE AND HE CALLED HER RICKIE AND TOLD HER TO CALL HIM JORDAN IF FRONT OF STONEY. THEIR RELATIONSHIP HAD CHANGED BECAUSE THEY WERE SO MORE THEN MINISTER AND ACQUAINTANCE NOW AND MORE THEN THE MISSIONARY AND BENEFACTOR AND OF COURSE THEY WERE MORE THEN FRIENDS BUT WHEN HE FINDS OUT WHO YOU REALLY ARE RICKIE VON HASE YOU'LL NEVER BE LOVERS.

THE REALIZATION BROUGHT A SHARP PAIN TO HER HEART SO SHE HAD SQUEEZED HER EYES SHUT TO FIGHT THE TEARS AND LATER WHEN SHE HAD OPENED THEM AGAIN SHE DISCOVERED THAT THE PLANE HAD BEGUN IT'S DESCENT AND BEFORE LONG THE GROUND CAME RUSHING UP FASTER AND FASTER SO SHE GRIPPED THE ARMRESTS AND PREPARING FOR A JOLT BUT UNLIKE THEIR EMERGENCY LANDING THIS TOUCHDOWN WAS GENTLE. THE PLANE COASTED OVER BUMPY GROUND AND GRADUALLY CAME TO A STOP SHE THEN UFASTENED HER SEATBELT AND HURRIED TO THE REAR OFF THE CARGO LOOKING FOR HER BACKPACK.

WHILE SHE MADE A LAST STOP IN THE BATHROOM SHE'D STRAPED HER HOLSTER AROUND HER WAIST. IT CARRIED HER RUGER SEMIAUTOMATIC PISTOL AND SOME CARTRIDGES AND WITH HER WEAPON CONCEALED UNDER HER LOOSE KHAKI SHIRT SHE FELT READY TO FACE ANYTHING. BY THE TIME SHE EMERGED THE MEN WERE COMING DOWN THE AISLE AND IF SHE HADN'T KNOWN WHO THEY WERE SHE MIGHT NOT HAVE RECOGNIZED

THEM AND THOUGH THEY WERE BOTH WEARING KHAKI TROUSERS THEY CHANGED INTO SHORT-SLEEVED BLACK COTTON SHIRTS WITH WHITE CLERICAL COLLARS, WIDE-BRIMMED STRAW HATS ON THEIR HEADS AND PLAIN SUNGLASSES COMPLETED THEIR OUTFITS. NO PAIR OF MISSIONARIES HAD EVER APPEARED MORE HARMLESS FROM THE START. STONEY STRUCK A POSE IN FRONT OF HER AND SAID "HOW DO I LOOK?" RIKIE COULDN'T HELP SMILING. "LIKE YOUR WELL DRESSED CLERGYMAN ON A HOLIDAY" RICKIE SAID.

"GOOD" JORDAN SPOKE UP BEHIND HIM "THAT'S EXACTLY THE IMPRESSION WE WANT TO GIVE AND THE NATIVES AND THE CHACO DON'T SEE MANY PEOPLE FROM OUTSIDE BUT WHEN THEY DO THEIR VISITORS ARE USUALLY MEMBERS OF A CHRISTIAN-BASED CHURCH."

SHE REALIZED HE'D ONLY SAID THAT BY WAY OF EXPLANATION BUT HER GUILT INCREAED BECAUSE SHE'D FORCED THEM TO TAKE HER ALONG WITHOUT ANY CONSIDERATION FOR THEIR METICULOUSLY LAID PLANS AND THEY HAD EVERY RIGHT TO ACCUSE HER OF BEING AS HEADSTRONG AND SPOILED AS SOME TABLOIDS MADE HER OUT TO BE.

AVOIDING JORDAN'S EYES SHE ASKED "HOW ARE YOU GOING TO EXPLAIN MY PRESENCE?" "I'M SURE OUR CONTACTS CAN RUSTLE UP SOMETHING THAT WILL IMPLY YOU'RE ATTACHED TO THE RED CROSS OR OTHER RELIEF ORGANIZATIONS SO DON'T WORRY ABOUT IT RIGHT NOW LET'S GO."

PUTTING ON HER SUNGLASSES SHE FOLLOWED THEM OUT OF THE PLANE JORDAN ASSISTED HER TO THE GRASS AND ONE TOUCH OF HIS HAND ON HER ARM AN AWARENESS SHOT THROUGH HER BODY BUT FORTUNATELY STONEY'S SHOUT DISTRACTED BOTH OF THEM.

"THERE'S FATHER DESILVA RIGHT ON CUE!" HE WAVED TO THE SHORT WIRY FIGURE COMING OUT OF THE TREES. RICKIE SAW NO OTHER SIGN OF HUMAN LIFE.

DESPITE HIS DARK CLOTHING THE SIXTYISH-LOOKING PRIEST WITH SHORT—CROPPED GRAY HAIR RUSHED FORWARD LIKE A MAN TWENTY YEARS YOUNGER AND HIS KEEN BROWN EYES PASSED OVER THEM RESTING BRIEFLY ON RICKIE BUT SHE COULDN'T TELL WHAT HE WAS THINKING. "FATHER DESILVA? MEET RICKIE TAYLOR THE WOMEN WHO HEADS THE CBH AND HAS FUNDED OUR OPERATION AND SHE IS GOING WITH US. SHE CONSIDERED THIS SITUATION IMPORTANT ENOUGH TO COME WITH US AND SHE SPEAKS SPANISH SO WE FELT SHE COULD BE OF HELP" JORDAN SAID.

"YOU ARE WELCOM" THE PRIEST RESPONDED GRACIOUSLY IN ENGLISH. "I THANK YOU FOR YOUR MONEY AND THE TALENTS YOU BRING.

"NOW FOLLOW ME AND WE'LL TALK LATER." "LET'S GO RICKIE" SHE FELT JORDAN'S HAND THE BACK OF HER WAIST. AS IMPERSONAL GESTURE YET SHE DELIGHTED IN HIS TOUCH.

THEY HURRRIED THROUGH THE LONG GRASS INTO A SPARSELY WOODED SCRUB FROEST. SHE HARDLY HAD TIME TO ORIENT HERSELF BEFORE THEY CAME UPON AN OLD PICKUP HALFHIDDEN IN THE FOLIAGE.

FATHER DESILVA POINTED TO RICKIE AND THEN SAID "YOU WILL SIT NEXT TO ME AND THE REVEREND WILL SIT ON THE OTHER SIDE OF YOU." STONEY ALREADY KNEW HIS ASSIGNMENT SO HE CLIMBED INTO THE BACK OF THE TRUCK AND SEATED HIMSELF AMONG SOME CRATES WHILE THEIR HOST GOT INTO THE DRIVER'S SIDE.

JORDAN HELPED RICKIE INTO THE CAB THEN HE JOINED HER. HIS THIGHS PRESSED AGAINST HERS IGNITING

Her body breathtakingly aware of his presence she tried in vain to create some space between them.

After a couple of false starts the engine turned over and the cab finaly started up. With no road or tire tracks to guide him so the prirst drove through an obstacle path of coarse tropical shrubs and tangled plant life. He appeared to be following some invisible path to their destination.

As she began to take in her surroundings she noticed that the temperature seemed to be in the mideighties and the air was fairly dry and a pleasant surprise after the humidity of the day before.

Jordan had said the Chaco kept it's secrets and Rickie could understand what he meant. She felt as if they were completely alone in this isolated world and yet she knew it was still home to several obscure Indian tribes. The tribes whose numbers had dwindled because of a dictatorship's genocidal policies.

The truck lurched frequently on the uneven ground cover and despite her efforts not to think about Jordan all too often she was thrown against him and everytime this happened she allowed herself to take a few seconds of pleasure in warmth and strong arms. He represented a haven to her a haven she'd had clung to during the night.

A few mintues later they came to a clearing surrounded by red quebracho that for secrecy's shake they hadn't used this clearing to land before. A rectangular bungalow built of plank

BOARDS WITH PALM THATCH FOR A ROOF STOOD OFF TO ONE SIDE AND SCREENING COVERED THE WINDOWS BUT WHAT MADE THE BUILDING STRANGE WERE IT'S THREE FRONT DOORS. ABOVE THE FRIST ONE ON THE LEFT HUNG A SMALL SIMPLE HAND-CARVED CROSS, TACKED TO THE SECOND DOOR THE ONE IN THE MIDDLE WAS A FIRST AID SYMBOL AND ON THE THIRD DOOR THE ON RIGHT HAD NO SIGN.

THE PRIEST ALIGHTED FROM THE TRUCK FIRST AND THEN HE BECKONED THEM TO FOLLOW HIM THROUGH THE RIGHT-HAND DOOR. JORDAN TOOK HER ARM TO HELP HER DOWN AND SHE FELT THE SAME BRIEF SURGE OF EXCITEMENT AND REASSURANCE AT HIS TOUCH.

THEY THEN ENTERED A MULTIPURPOSE ROOM WHICH APPARENTLY SERVED AS A COMBINED LIVINGROOM, BEDROOM, DININGROOM AND KITCHEN. FATHER DESILVA INDICATED THERE WAS AN OUTHOUSE THAT WAS ATTACHED TO THE BACK.

"THE TWO OF YOU WILL SLEEP IN HERE AND MS. TAYLOR WILL SLEEP IN THE SURGERY. COME I WILL SHOW YOU WHERE TO YOUR THINGS."

SHE SHOULDN'T HAVE BEEN DISAPPOINTED ABOUT THE SLEEPING ARRANGEMENTS BUT SHE WAS. INAPPROPRIATE AS HER REACTION WAS UNDER THE CIRCUMSTANCES SHE SEEMED TO HAVE NO CONTROL OVER HER EMOTIONS. OBEYING AN UNCONTROLLABLE IMPULSE SHE DARTED A GLANCE AT JORDAN AND SHE WAS SURPRISED TO SEE A STRANGE LOOK IN HIS EYES.

HER HEART BEGAN TO BEAT FURIOUSLY AND SHE FELT STRANGELY LIGHT-HEADED. SHE TURNED AWAY AND HURRIED AFTER THE PRIEST. THE SURGERY WAS NO MORE THEN A SMALL CLEAN EXAMINATION ROOM WITH TWO cots and various medical supplies placed neatly in the cupboards.

"The sink doesn't have a faucet because we have no running water" he explained. "There's a cistern around the back of the building and you may draw water in this bowl to wash your hands. Do you not think to use if for drinking or brushing your teeth. I keep a supply of treated water in the other room for that purpose. Please join us when you're ready."

Once he'd left she stood in the middle of the plank floor for a minute attempting to understand the feelings that had come to life and were churining inside her.

It seemed incomprehensible that a little over a week ago she'd never heard of Reverend Jordan Browning or the Ache tribe and never in all the her travels had she visited a land as strange and remote as the Chaco but yet given the choice she wouldn't be anywhere else or with any other person.

She didn't want to think about the fact that all of this would come to an end when they returned to the States but far worse was the thought of never being this close to Jordan again as she'd stowed away for this flight to Chaco but after the close call they'd had with the engine breaking down she feared he might refuse to let her accompany them on future missions because she was in love with him and she knew the essence of this man like his goodness, his courage and strength. How would she goodbye to him? How could she bear to let him go? You'd

BETTER START SEPARATING YOURSELF FROM HIM RIGHT NOW BECAUSE IF YOU SPEND ANOTHER NIGHT LIKE LAST NIGHT IT MIGHT JUST BE TO LATE FOR YOU TO LET HIM GO RICKIE SO IT'S BETTER IF YOU DO RIGHT NOW BEFORE IT'S TO LATE.

JORDAN KNOCKED ON THE SURGEY DOOR. WHEN RICKIE HADN'T COME BACK TO THE LOUNGE AFTER AN HOUR HE'D DECIDED TO FIND OUT WHY. MAYBE SHE WAS TIRED BUT HE DOUBTED SHE'D BE ABLE TO SLEEP WHEN IT WASN'T EVEN NOON.

NO MATTER HOW INDEPENDENT AND RESOURCFUL SHE WAS THIS HAD TO BE A STRANGE NEW EXPERIENCE FOR HER. CARRYING THAT UNNAMED BURDEN OF HERS SHE BROODED TOO MUCH AND KEPT HER SECRETS TO HERSELF. WHETHER SHE KNEW IT OR NOT SHE NEEDED PEOPLE AND HE WANTED HER TO WANT HIM.

FOR HIS OWN SELFISH REASONS HE RESENTED ANY TIME SPENT APART FROM HER. SINCE THEIR FIRST MEETING HE'D DEVELOPED A CRAVING FOR HER COMPANY THAT WASN'T ABOUT TO GO AWAY. SHE OCCUPIED HIS THOUGHTS CONTINUALLY BECAUSE IT WAS SOMETHING NO OTHER WOMEN HAD COME CLOSE TO DOING AND BECAUSE OF HER HE HADN'T A DECENT NIGHT'S SLEEPIN MORE THEN A WEEK.

ON THIS TRIP HE'D ALREADY GLIMPSED DIFFEERENT FACETS OF HER COMPLEX PERSONALITY LIKE HER, SORROW, PERCEPTIVENESS AND COURAGE AND JUST KNOWING SHE WAS ON THE OTHER SIDE OF THE DOOR BROUGHT AN ELATION HE COULDN'T CONTAIN.

WHEN SHE DIDN'T ANSWER HE GREW BOLDER AND KNOCKED AGAIN. "RICKIE ARE YOU ALL RIGHT? IF YOU'RE TRYING TO SLLEP JUST TELL ME TO GO AWAY." STILL THERE WAS NO ANSWER.

WITHOUT WAITING FOR PERMISSION HE OPENED THE DOOR A CRACK. HE COULD ONLY SEE ONE EMPTY COT AND HER BACKPACK AND HE WAS NOT SATISFIED WITH THAT SO HE OPENED THE DOOR ALL THE WAY AND STEPPED INSIDE TO LOOK AROUND AND THEN HE FOUND OUT SHE WASN'T THERE.

IN THE NEXT SECOND HE LUNGED BACK FOR THE DOOR BUT SHE WAS STANDING IN FRONT OF HIM BLOCKING HIS EXIT. SHE LOOKED COOL AND ELEGANT AND IN FACT SHE SEEMED TO BE IN TOTAL POSSESSION OF HERSELF WHILE HE DREW IN SOME MUCH NEEDED AIR AND THEN SAID "I COULDN'T FIND YOU."

SHE MOVED INSIDE AND CLOSED THE DOOR AND THEN SAID "I MADE A TRIP AROUND BACK TO USE THE OUTHOUSE." IT WAS THE SIMPLEST OF REASONS BUT A DOZEN UNSPEAKABLE SCENARIOS TO EXPLAIN HER DISAPPEARANCE HAD SPRUNG INTO HIS MIND AND HE STILL HADN'T RECOVERED FROM HIS FLIGHT.

IF HE'D HAD AND DOUBTS ABOUT THE DEPTH OF HIS FEELINGS FOR HER THIS INCIDENT HAD CLEARED THEM OF THEM UP FOR GOOD.

"FATHER DESILVEA HAD ICE-COLD LEMONADE WAITING FOR US." "OUT HERE?" SHE SOUNDED INCREDULOUS. "HIS FRIDGE RUNS ON POWER FROM AN INVERTER CABLE THAT'S HOOKED UP TO A HIGH-VOLTAGE BATTERY.

"WHATEVER YOU SAY." HER MOUTH LIFTED AT ONE CORNER AND HERE I THOUGHT WE WERE GOING TO ROUGH IT." "THAT'LL CAOME LATER SAID JORDAN. HER EXPRESSION SOBERED WHEN SHE SAID "HOW SOON WILL WE WMMET THE FAMILIES WE'RE TAKING BACK WITH US?"

"THAT'S WHAT WE'RE GOING TO FIND OUT OVER LUNCH BECAUSE FATHER DESILVA IS ONE OF THE GO-BETWEENS."

AFTER A SLIGHT PAUSE SHE ASKED "IS HE A MEMBER OF THE UNDERGROUND?"

"HE'S THE HEAD OF IT IN THIS SECTOR OF CHACO." "IF HE GET'S CAUGHT" "HE HAS BEEN CAUGHT AND SPENT EIGHT YEARS IN EMBOSCADA PRISON."

"EIGHT YEARS?" SAID RICKIE. "YES JORDAN NODDED HIS HEAD. "FOR INTERFERING WITH THE ARREST OF AN ACHE WHO HAD THE AUDACITY TO GO LOOKING FOR HIS KIDNAPPED DAUGTHER IN ASUNCION AND THE TORTURE THEY INFLICTED ON FATHER DESLIVA LEFT HIM DEAF IN ONE EAR BECAUSE HE SUFFERS FROM CHRONIC DIZZINESS."

THE SORROW HE HAD HATED TO SEE COME BACK INTO HIS EYES. "WHAT MADE THEM RELEASE HIM?" "HE WASN'T RELEASED SOMEONE BREAK INTO THE PRISON AND GOT HIM OUT. HE'S A VERY IMPORTANT PRIEST ONE WHO WAS HIGHLY EDUCATED AND FOUND GREAT FAVOR WITH THE CHURCH BUT THEY CAN'T DO ANYTHING FOR HIM NOW."

"NO" NOW HE'S HERE RISKING HIS LIFE AGAIN !" SHE WHISPERED. "THAT'S RIGHT HE'S ARRANGED THE ESCAPE OF MANY POLITICAL PRISONERS TO AGRENTINA AND BOLIVIA. THE AUTHORITIES ARE IN A RAGE BECAUSE THE UNDERGROUND'S WORKING TOO WELL AND THEY'RE LOOKING FOR HIM."

HER BODY SHUDDERED WITH THE KNOWLEDGE AND JORDAN WANTED TO TELL HER SO BADLY HIS HANDS WERE SHAKING. "WE COULDN'T TAKE HIM BACK TO THE STATES WITH US BECAUSE HE WOULDN'T GO." THIS LITTLE HUT IN THE MIDDLE OF NOWHERE IS EXACTLY WHERE HE WANTS TO CONTINUE HIS MINISTRY. HIS GREATEST WISH IS TO STAY ALIVE SO HE CAN HELP THE HELPLESS. LIVING OUT HERE ALONE INCREASES HIS LIFE EXPECTANCY. THERE ARE FEWER EYES AND EARS TO BETARY HIM.

UNSPOKEN THOUGHTS FLOWED BETWEEN THEM AND HE COULD HAVE SWORN HE PICKED UP ON THE ONE FOREMOST IN HER MIND. "THERE ARE HUNDREDS OF MEN AND WOMEN LIKE FATHER DESILVA WORKING FOR THE LIBERATIONS OF PARAGUAY." "SO ARE YOU AND STONEY SAVIORS LIKE THEY ARE?" SHE SAID WITH TEARS RUNNING DOWN HER FACE AND FEAR IN HER VOICE.

"DON'T SET US ON ANY PEDESTAL BECAUSE WITHOUT YOUR MONEY WE WOULDN'T BE HERE." "IT'S NOT MY MONEY." HE'D BEEN WAITING FOR THAT OPENING AND SHE HAD JUST PROVIDED IT.

"FOR THE SAKE OF ARGUMENT I'LL AGREE THAT IT'S YOUR FAMILY'S MONEY. WHY DO YOU SEEM UPSET WHENEVER THE TAYLOR FORTUNE IS MENTIONED?" HE WATCHED IN SHOCK AS HER LOVELY FACE BECAME PALE AND DISTORTED.

"RICKIE ! FOR THE LOVE OF GOD HE SAID OUT LOUD, FORGETTING THE ROLE HE'D BEEN FORCED TO PLAY HE THRUST OUT HIS HANDS AND HAD GRIPPED HER SHOULDERS AND SAID "LET ME HELP YOU."

"YOU CAN'T !" SHE CRIED OUT LOUD IN BITTER ANGUISH AS HER FACE WAS ALL STICKY AND WHITE. "I'M NOT WORTHY OF YOUR HELP."

"THERE'S THAT WORD AGAIN. ARE YOU TRYING TO TELL ME YOUR FAMILY BELONGS TO THE MAFIA OR SOMETHING LIKE THAT?" HE THEN SHOOK HER AND SAID "IS THAT WHY YOUR GUILT IS SO HORRIFIC? HE HAD SAID AGAIN BUT SHE DIDN'T ANSWER HIM.

WHEN HE THOUGHT IT WAS UNELESS TO PROD HER ANY FURTHER SHE BLURTED OUT "I WISH THAT WAS ALL! IS THAT ENOUGH OF AN ANSWER FOR YOU?" SAID RICKIE.

SHE JERKED AWAY FROM HIS AND FLEW OUT OF THE ROOM AND JORDAN STOOD THERE IN PLACE PONDERING HER WORDS. HE TRIED TO IMAGINE WHAT MIGHT BE WORSE THEN BELONGING TO A FAMILY OF MOBSTERS.

"I WISH THAT WAS ALL." I WONDER WHAT COULD RICKIE HAVE POSSIBLY MEANT BY THAT? EXCEPT FOR THE MYSTERY SURROUNDING HER MISSING GRANDFATHER JORDAN KNEW OF NO SCANDAL IN THE TAYLOR DYNASTY AND NO FAMILY SKELETON S AND OF COURSE NO HINT OF ANY CRIMES ASSOCIATED WITH ORGANIZED CRIME LIKE PUTTING OUT CONTRACTS ON PEOPLE WHO WERE BAD.

SHE OFFERED YOU TWENTY MILLION DOLLARS DIDN'T SHE? IN YOUR GUT YOU BELIEVED SHE WAS BYING YOU OFF BECAUSE SHE WANTED SOMEONE TAKEN DOWN AND STONEY THOUGHT SO TOO BUT IN THE END SHE DIDN'T PRESS IT.

IN THE END YOU SAID YOU COULD HAVE THE $750,000 AND FORGET THE SEARCH FOR HER GRANDFATHER. HAD IT ALL BEEN A LIE? WAS IT A FANTASTIC CON ONLY SOMEONE LIKE RICKIE TAYLOR COULD PULL OFF? COULD SHE POSSIBLY BE INVOLVED IN SOME KIND OF CRIME RING?

WAS CBH A FRONT FOR HER OWN SUBVERSIVE ACTIVITIES? DID SHE OWN HIGH PLACED OFFICIALS LIKE SOMEONE IN THE NAVY SEALS WHO KNEW OF JORDAN'S IMPRISONMENT? DID SHE OWN REVEREND ROLON? IS THAT WHY SHE CONTACTED YOU FRIST BROWNING? DID SHE NEED AN EXPENDABLE HIT MAN TO GUN DOWN ANOTHER MOB BOSS RUNNING THE LUCRATIVE DRUG CARTELS IN PARAGUAY?

ALL THIS TIME HAS SHE BEEN SETTING YOU UP BY GETTING YOU TO FALL IN LOVE WITH HER? IF SO WHAT WAS HER DRAMATIC DISPLAY OF GUILT ALL ABOUT? WAS EVERYTHING AN ACT?

COULD SHE FAKE THE WAY SHE TREMBLED WHEN YOU PULLED HER INTO YOUR ARMS? COULD SHE HAD FACKED THE FRANTIC BEATING OF HER LETTLE HEART? WAS SHE ABLE TO SUMMON AT WILL THE LOOK OF DESIRE THAT DARKENED THOSE EYES TO MIDNIGHT BLUE? JORDAN REELED FROM THE POSSIBILITY THAT ANY OF THOSE QUESTIONS COULD BE ANSWERED WITH A YES.

CHAPTER 40

WORST CASE SCENARIO

STONEY HAD BEEN TALKING TO FATHER DESILVA WHEN RICKIE HAD ENTERED THE LOUNGE OUT OF BREATH. AS SOON AS THEY SAW HER THE PRIEST GOT TO HIS FEET AND HANDED HER A DRINK. "WHERE IS REVEREND BROWNING?"

THAT WAS A GOOD QUESTION BUT SHE COULDN'T BELIEVE WHAT SHE'D JUST DONE BUT SHE STAYED IN THE SURGERY ONE MORE MINUTE JORDAN WOULD HAVE FOUND A WAY TO GET THE TRUTH OUT OF HER.

BEING IN LOVE WITH HIM HAD MADE HER TOO VULNERABLE BECAUSE SHE WAS AFRAID HER PARTING REMARKS HAD ONLY SUCCEEDED IN REINFORCING HIS SUSPICION THAT SHE HAD ANOTHER AGENDA.

"HE'LL BE ALONG SHORTLY" SAID FATHER DESILVA. SO SHE FOUND THE NEAREST CHAIR AND SAT DOWN BEFORE HER LEGS BUCKLED UP ON HER. "THANK YOU FOR THE LAMONADE IT'S DELICIOUS" SAID RICKIE.

"OVER THE YEARS I HAVE DISCOVERED THAT AMERICANS PREFER IT TO OUR NATIVE YERBA MATE." THE TEA HE REFERRED TO WAS AN ACQUIRED TASTE. "I TRIED THAT ONCE IN CHILE" HE SAID.

WITH HER KNOWLEDGE OF THE HEROIC SERVICE HE RENDERED THE PEOPLE OF HIS COUNTRY RICKIE FELT NOTHING BUT ADMIRATION FOR THIS MAN. IT IMPRESSED

HER THAT HE'D RETAINED A CHARMING SENSE OF HUMOR DESPITE EVERYTHING HE'D SUFFERED.

"YOUR ENGLISH IS EXCELLENT FATHER." "LONG AGO I HAD THE OPPORTUNITY TO STUDY AT OXFORD ENGLAND FOR SOME TIME. I'M SORRY TO SAY I HAVE NOT YET VISITED THE UNITED STATES."

"MAYBE ONE DAY IT WILL BE POSSIBLE." "THE REVEREND HAS TOLD ME OF THE IMPORTANT WORK YOU'VE BEEN DOING HERE" SHE AMITTED WITH A GASP IN HER THROAT. "I'M IN AWE OF YOU FATHER."

"WE ALL AREA" A THIRD VOICE SUDDENLY INTERJECTED STARTLING RICKIE SO MUCH AHE ALMOST DROPPED HER GLASS OF LEMONADE. SHE HADN'T HEARD JORDAN COME IN.

"THEN THE FEELING IS MUTUAL" FATHER DESILVA SAID. "THE THREE OF YOU ARE ANGELS OF MERCY FOR PUTTING YOUR LIVES IN DANGER TO RESCUE SOME OF OUR POOR DEFENSELESS ACHE INDIANS WHO AREN'T EVEN YOUR OWN COUNTRYMAN.

"FOR YEARS THEIR RACE HAD BEEN SYSTEMATICALLY DESTROYED BY MEN WHOM GOD WILL HAVE TO PUNISH BECAUSE THE OUTSIDE WORLD KNOWS NOTHING OF THEIR CRIMES. LITTLE BY LITTLE THE REGIME IN POWER HAS ENCROACHED ON ACHE LAND TO RAISE CATTLE AND ONE DAY THEY WILL HAVE DESPOILED THESE PEOPLE'S BIRTHRIGHT UNTILL THERE IS NOT ONE CHACO LEFT AS WE KNOW IT."

MOVED BY HIS WORDS SHE SAID "I WISH WE COULD SEND AN ARMY TO PROTECT THEM! TAKING A HANDFUL OF PEOPLE TO A NEW LIFE DOSEN'T SEEM VERY MUCH."

"HE NODDED HIS HEAD IN UNDERSTANDING AND WITHOUT YOUR HELP THAT LITTLE HANDFUL WOULD BE MURDERED WITHIN THE YEAR. THOSE SOULS WILL BE ETERNALLY GRATEFUL TO YOU. PUT YOURSELF IN THEIR SO CALLED PLACE AND YOU WON'T THINK THAT WHAT YOU'RE ABOUT TO DO IS INSIGNFICANT."

HIS WORDS HAD SHOOKEN HER INTO A COLD SHIVER. "RMEMBER THE SCRIPTURE "IF YOU HAVE DONE IT UNTO THE LEAST OF THESE YOU HAVE DON IT UNTO ME." THE FACT THAT YOU ARE HERE AND ARE WILLING TO DO ANYTHING AT ALL IS A MIRACLE."

"THE REAL MIRACLE IS MS. TAYLOR'S MONETARY CONTRIBUTION FATHER." JORDAN'S REMARK SOUNDED INNOCENT ENOUGH ON THE SURFACE BUT RICKIE KNEW THERE WAS A LOT MORE TO IT THEN JUST A MEANING THAT WAS INTENDED FOR HER EARS ALONE.

AFTER THE SLIP SHE'D MADE IN FRONT OF HIM HE WAS NOW INFORMING HER THAT HE WOULDN'T LET THE MATTER DROP. "AS YOU WELL KNOW FATHER ALL THE MONEY IN THE WORLD CAN'T HELP UNLESS THERE'S A PLAN IN PLACE" RICKIE HASTENED TO EMPHASIZE. "THE REAL CREDIT GOES TO MR. LEONARD AND REVEREND BROWNING FOR CONCEIVING THIS PROJECT AND KNOWING HOW TO CARRY IT OUT."

STONEY POURED HIMSELF ANOTHER DRINK. "AS YOU'RE DISCOVERING FATHER MS. TAYLOR HAS A HARD TIME ACCEPTING COMPLIMENTS LET ALONE RECEIVING THEM GRACIOUSLY. FOR EXAMPLE SHE WOULD NEVER LET YOU KNOW THAT THROUGH CBH A CORPORATION SHE CREATED AND HER MONEY HAS GONE FOR GOOD WORKS ALL OVER THE GLOBE BUT UNFORTUNATELY THIS IS ONE TIME NO ONE WILL BE ABLE TO KNOW WHERE THE FUNDS CAME FROM." THE PRIEST EYED RICKIE KINDLY AS HE LEFT THE BAR TO GO TO HIS CAR.

"GOD KNOWS AND APPROVES MS. TAYLOR YOU CAN REST ASSURED OF THAT" SAID THE REVEREND. THOUGH HE AND STONEY WERE GENEROUS IN THEIR PRAISE RICKIE WAS IN TOO MUCH PAIN TO RESPOND AND HAD LOOKED AWAY.

"NOW WE WILL HAVE WHAT YOU AMERICANS CALL "LUNCH." FROM MY OBSERVATIONS YOU PREFER BUTTER ON YOUR BREAD A SINGULAR HABIT SAID FATHER DESILVA. HE SMILED AS HE CONCEEDED TO SERVE THEM LOTS OF BOWLS OF HOT THICK SOUP CONSISTING OF BEEF, RICE AND LOTS OF VEGETABLES WITH LARGE CHUNKS OF BROWN BREAD.

RICKIE MIGHT HAVE ENJOYED THE MEAL IF IT NOT BEEN FOR JORDAN WHO SAT ON THE COUCH ACROSS FOR HER STUDYING HER THROUGH HIS NORROWED EYES.

WHEN THE PRIEST HAD FILLED A BOWL FOR HIMSELF HE SAT ON A CHAIR FACING RICKIE. "THERE ARE MANY ACHE FAMILIES WHO WISH TO GO TO THE UNITED STATES AND BEGIN A NEW LIFE. WE HAVE SELECTED THOSE WITH DAUGTHERS FIRST BECAUSE YOUNG WOMEN ARE THE MOST SOUGHT OUT FOR EXPLOITATION." HE SHOOK HIS HEAD SADLY AS HE SAID "GIRLS ARE AT RISK IN MANY PARTS OF THE WORLD AS YOU ARE AWARE OF. WE WILL SAVE AS MANY FROM THE CHACO AS WE CAN."

RICKIE FELT HER BLOOD CHILL AND TEARS CAME INTO EYES. "FOR SEVERAL REASONS IT IS PROVIDENTIAL THAT YOU ARE HERE MS. TAYLOR BECAUSE THESE PEOPLE SPEAK GUARANI AND A SMATTERING OF SPANISH AND THE FACT THAT YOU ARE A WOMEN AND SPEAK SOMETHING OF THEIR LANGUAGE WILL GIVE THE WOMEN MORE CONFIDENCE DURING THIS SO CALLED AIRLIFT." "THEY MUST BE TRRIFIED." "THEY ARE" HE COCURRED BUT THERE FACED WITH IMMINENT DEATH AND ANYTHING ELSE IS NOT PREFERABLE."

WITHOUT KNOWING HOW IT HAPPENED SHE GLANCED AT JORDAN WHO HADN'T TAKEN ACCUSING EYES OFF HER SINCE THEY'D STARTED TO EAT LUNCH. WHAT A FOOL SHE'D BEEN TO LET HIM GOAD HER INTO SAYING SOMETHING THAT HAD CREATTED NEW QUESTIONS IN HER MIND.

"YOU WERE PLAGUED BY ENGINE TROUBLE AND ARRIVED A DAY LATE SO THE PEOPLE HELPING WITH THE ESCAPE PLANS HAD TO COME UP WITH A DIFFERENT STRATEGY. THE AIRLIFT HAS BEEN RESCHEDULED FOR THE DAY AFTER TOMORROW. IN THE MEANTIME YOU WILL STAY HERE AS MY GUESTS BECAUSE I WANT YOU TOO. I'M SORRY I HAVE SO LITTLE TO ENTERTAIN YOU WITH. THERE ARE A FEW PUZZLES AND GAMES ON THE SHELF OVER THERE HE SIAD."

"WE DIDN'T COME FOR THAT FATHER" RICKIE PROTESTED. HE SMILED AND SAID "THIS AFTERNOON THE LOCAL DOCTOR WILL BE BY TO SEE PATIENTS IN SURGERY FOR A FEW HOURS. WHILE HE'S HERE YOU'RE WELCOME TO STAY IN THE LOUNGE MS. TAYLOR." "THANK YOU FATHER" SAID RICKIE. "NOT AT ALL AND AFTERWARD I'LL CONDUCT MASS FOR MY FLOCK WHO WILL WONDER IN AND DINNER WILL BE AT SUNDOWN."

"THAT'S VERY KIND OF YOU FATHER." JORDAN HAD SPOKE BEFORE RICKIE COULD SAY ANYTHING ELSE. "SINCE WE HAVE THIS UNEXPECTED FREE TIME ON ARE HANDS IT MIGHT BE INTERESTING FOR MS. TAYLOR TO VISIT SOME OF THE COMMUNITIES FARTHER DOWNSTREAM."

WITHOUT WARNING JORDAN HAD ANNOUNCED THAT THE SEARCH FOR HER GRANDFATHER WAS ABOUT TO BEGIN. IT WAS WHAT SHE'D WANTED YET THE PROSPECT LEFT HER WEAK WITH TREPIDATION.

STONEY FRONEW AS HE SAID "THAT'S SEVERAL DAYS WALK." "NOT IF WE NEGOTIATE FOR SOME MULES." THE

PRIEST SHOOK HIS HEAD AND SAID "WITH TIME OF THE ESSENCE IT WOULD BE BEST IF YOU BORROWED THE REVEREND'S TRUCK."

"WE DON'T WANT TO TAKE ADVANTAGE." "I HAVE NO NEED FOR IT TODAY SAID THE REVEREND. TAKE IT IF YOU LIKE YOU COULD STOP AT THE JESUIT MISSION FOR THE NIGHT. THEY RUN HOSPICE AND WILL SUPPLY YOU WITH EXTRA PETROL FOR YOUR RETURN TOMORROW."

DIRECTING HIS REMARKS TO RICKIE HE ADDED "IT WOULD BE WISE IF YOU BORROWED A LABCOAT FROM THE SURGERY ROOM. YOU'LL FIND A FRESH ONE IN THE MIDDLE CUPBOARD. THAT WAY YOU'LL LOOK LIKE A MEDIC OUT ACCOMPANYING A GROUP OF CLERGYMEN AND THAT'S NOT SUCH AN UNUSUAL SIGHT HER IN CHACO."

"I'LL DO THAT FATHER THANK YOU FOR THE GENEROSITY." "WE ALL THANK YOU" STONEY SAID SINCERELY AS HE AND JORDAN STOOD UP. "SINCE THERE'S A LOT TO SEE I PROPOSE WE LEAVE NOW TO MAKE THE MOST OUT OF THE DAY."

"IF YOU'LL EXCUSE ME I'LL GET MY THINGS." RICKIE HEADED FOR THE DOOR IGNORING JORDAN'S STARE. WHEN SHE REACHED THE PRIVACY OF THE SURGERY ROOM SHE HID HER FACE IN HER HANDS.

IF STONEY WASN'T COMING TOO SHE'D NEVER SURVIVE THE NEXT TWENTY-FOUR HOURS IN JORDAN'S PRESENCE. THE NEGATIVE TENSION HAD BEEN BUILDING UNTILL SHE WAS POSITIVE FATHER DESILVA COULD FEEL IT.

THE ONLY OTHER RECOURSE WOULD BE TO STAY BEHIND BUT THE THOUGHT OF THAT WAS EVEN MORE INSUPPORTABLE BECAUSE SHE COULDN'T STAND BEING SEPARATED FROM JORDAN AND THEY'D BE LOOKING FOR GERHARDT VON HASE HER GRANDFATHER.

THAT IS IT RICKIE! JORDAN SAID AS HE TOSSED A DUFFEL BAG INTO THE TRUCK CONTAINING A BEDROLL AND A FEW PERSONAL THINGS. STONEY WASN'T FAR BEHIND AND HE THREW HIS STUFF INTO THE BACK OF THE BACK OF THE TRUCK AS WELL THEN VAULTED OVER THE TAILGATE WITH HIS HAT IN HAND.

"WHAT THE HELL ARE YOU DOING?" STONEY'S MOUTH QUIRKED AS HE SAID "I'M GOING TO TAKE A SIESTA." "SINCE WHEN?" HE SAID. "SINCE YOU AND RICKIE NEED TIME ALONE. IF EVER TWO PEOPLE WERE CRAZY IN LOVE WITH EACH OTHER IT'S YOU TWO. GOOD GRIEF JORDAN IT'S GETTING TO THE POINT THAT EVERY TIME YOU TWO OCCUPY THE SAME SPACE I THINK THERE'S GOING TO AN EXPLOSION ! YOU'D BETTER DO SOMETHING ABOUT IT AND THIS OUTING'S A GOOD TIME AS ANY."

JORDAN DIDN'T BOTHER TO DENY IT BUT KNOWING THE TRUTH AND DOING SOMETHING ABOUT IT WERE TWO DIFFERENT MATTERS. AFTER REVIEWING EVERYTHING HE KNEW ABOUT HER AND HE DIDN'T HONESTLY BELIEVE RICKIE WAS INVOLVED IN ANYTHING CRIMINAL BUT SHE WAS EXPERIENCING SOME KIND OF CRISIS. UNTILL SHE COULD TRUST HIM ENOUGH TO DIVULGE THE SOURCE OF HER PAIN THERE COULD BE NO HOPE OF A RELATIONSHIP.

THERE'S NO HOPE ANYWAYS BROWNING NOT EVEN WITH YOUR PAST. "I'VE LIED TO HER FROM DAY ONE AND I'M STILL LYING." "SO YOU LAY IT ALL OUT IN FRONT OF HER. WHAT'S THE WORST THAT COULD HAPPEN?"

"YOU KNOW THE ANSWER AS WELL AS I DO." "I ADMIT IT'S POSSIBEL SHE COULD HATE YOUR GUTS AND REFUSE TO NEVER SEE YOU AGAIN."

JORDAN INHALED SHARPLY AS HE SAID "THAT'S EXACTLY WHAT WILL HAPPEN." "THEN AGAIN IF SHE IS THE WOMEN

I KNOW SHE IS SHE'LL UNDERSTAND AND SHE'LL LOVE YOU EVEN MORE FOR DEFENDING A HELPLESS YOUNG INDIAN WHO'D BE DEAD IF YOU AND I HADN'T KILLED THAT BASTARD FIRST.

"DO YOU HONESTLY THINK RICKIE WILL CARE THAT YOU WENT TO PRISON WHEN SHE FINDS OUT YOU DEFIED ORDERS RATHER THAN SEE A GIRL GET MURDERED? COME ON JORDAN ALL SHE HAS TO DO IS PUT HERSELF IN THAT YOUNG WOMEN'S PLACE. NO RICKIE TAYLOR WON'T HAVE A PROBLEM WITH WHAT YOU DID."

STOP TALKING STONEY BECAUSE YOU MAKE IT SOUND POSSIBLE HELL YOU EVEN MAKE IT SOUND EASY. "HERE'S THE PLAN" STONEY CONTINUED "IF WE SPLIT UP WE CAN COVER TWICE THE TERRITORY SO YOU DROP ME OFF AT THE JESUIT MISSION AND I'LL SPEND THE NIGHT THERE AND START ASKING QUESTIONS ABOUT RICKIE'S GRANDFATHER. WITH THIS COLLAR ON THERE'S A GOOD CHANCE SOMEONE WILL CONFIDE IN ME. I MIGHT LEARN SOMETHING IMPORTANT.

"YOU TAKE RICKIE SIGHT-SEEING AND MAKE INQUIRIES AS YOU GO. WHEN IT'S TIME FOR BED FIND A ISOLATED SPOT LIKE THIS ONE WHICH SHOULDN'T BE TO HARD AND TALK TO HER AND BARE YOUR SOUL AS THEY SAY. I CAN GUARANTEE YOU'LL BE A NEW MAN SOMETIME TOMORROW MORNING."

STONEY WASN'T COMING UP WITH ANY IDEAS AND JORDAN HADN'T ALREADY CONTEMPLATED SINCE THE MOMENT FATHER DESILVA TOLD THEM THERE BE A TWENTY-FOUR HOUR DELAY.

IT WAS ONE THE REASONS HE AND STONEY HAD MADE SUCH A GOOD TEAM IN THE SEALS AND THEIR MINDS ARE FUNCTIONED ALIKE TOO BUT SOMETIMES IT WAS SCARY TO REALIZE HIS PARTNER COULD BE SO ATTUNED TO HIS THOUGHTS AND HIS FEELINGS.

"JUST BE SURE YOU DON'T DRIVE OFF INTO THE SUNRISE AND LEAVE ME STRANDED TOMORROW" STONEY SAID WITH A GRIN. JORDAN EYED HIS FRIEND CANDIDLY AND SAID "IF EVERYTHING TURNED OUT THE WAY YOU'RE SUGGESTING I MIGHT BE TEMPTED TO GO OFF SOMEPLACE WITH HER BUT . . . ." NO BUTS IF I HAVEN'T TOLD YOU THIS BEFORE I . . . . WHEN HE STOPPED MID-SENTENCE JORDAN TUREND IN THE DIRECTION OF STONEY'S GAZE. RICKIE HAD STEPPED OUT OF THE SURGERY ROOM AND STARTED WALKING TOWARD THEM CARRYING HER BAG FOR THE TRIP. EVERY TIME HE SAW HER WAS LIKE THE FIRST TIME. HIS PAULSE HAD RACED OUT OF CONTROL AND HE COULD HARDLY BREATHE AND THEN AFTER HE GOT SETTLED DOWN HE PUT HIS HAT ON HIS HEAD.

AS SHE DREW UP TO HIM HE REACHED FOR HER BAG AND HANDED IT TO STONEY. JORDAN WANTED HER TO LOOK AT HIM BUT SHE REFUSED TO. "READY TO GO?" "YES AND WAKE ME UP WHEN WE GET THERE" STONEY CALLED OUT TO NO ONE IN PARTICULAR.

IN THE NEXT INSTANT HER EYES OPENED WIDE AND HER ANXIOUS GAZE MET JORDAN'S. OBVIOUSLY SHE WASN'T AS COMPOSED AS SHE'D TIRED TO MAKE HIM BELIEVE. HE DERIVED A GRATE DEAL OF SATISFACTION FROM THAT.

"STONEY'S TIRED DO YOU MIND ACTING AS MY NAVIGATOR?" SHE HAD LOOKED DAZED WHEN SHE SAID THAT. "FATHER DESILVA GAVE ME A MAP."

A PAUSE ENSUEDA "I'LL TRY" FATHER DESILVA SAID TO RICKIE. HER LACK OF ENTHUSIASM WOULD HAVE BEEN DEVASTATING IF HE HADN'T SEEN THE THROBBING OF TINY NERVE IN HER THROAT WHERE THE LAPELS OF HER KHAKI BLOUSE LAYED OPEN.

"GOOD LET'S GO." HE SENSED SHE DIDN'T WANT HIM TO TOUCH HER. NO ONE UNDERSTOOD THAT BETTER

Then he did. All the more reason to grip her elbow firmly and help her onto the passenger side of the red pickup truck.

Once behind the wheel he pulled the hand-drawn map out of his front pocket and unfolded it. When he leaned toward her to point out their location and all he could see was her demure profile.

He longed to put his lips to the flushed skin of her throat where the sent of her perfume lingered. She'd never worn her hair down in front of him before and with one sweep of his hand he could undo the tortoiseshell clip and let the silky strands of her long hair spill over his fingers.

"Where are we exactly?" Her stammer gave tangible proff of the highly aroused state of her emotions. It seemed he wasn't alone in his desire.

We're here" he pointed to a spot in the northwestern part of the Chaco. "We'll follow this stream as it meanders south to the Jesuit mission about ten miles from here. There's no road so we'll just travel over the grass and after we drop off Stoney we'll keep going."

"Why aren't we staying together?" She said as she sounded panicked. "So we can make twice the inquiries about your grandfatherin the same amount of time and that is what you wanted."

Another tense minute passed by before she finaly said "yes" in a ragged voice. The more upset she sounded the more reassured he felt it proved she wasn't indifferent to him.

He waited a discreet interval then continued "You'll note a Mennoite community Father Desilva's marked here. We'll visit it too so let me know the approximate distance so I can watch for signs on the road."

He purposely studied her reaction as he added "There's another community about thirty miles from here. It's a isolated settlement made up of Europeans and South Americans. There might even be a few English still around.

"It's the most remote of all the Chaco communities miles from the Trans-Chaco Highway and any form of civilization. The priest told me that not even the Indians live nearby because they say it has an evil spirit and according to the Ache the ground is infertile."

Her expression underwent another sobering change. Mystified he added "Father Desilva said there's been a government ban on all religious proselyting in that vivinity for decades. He feels that if someone was going to hide out in Paraguay that particular settlement would be the place."

She looked haunted again but this time he wouldn't let her hide behind that wall of guilt and pain.

"When we get close to the settlement I'll remove my collar. You can leave the labcoat in the truck and we can walk in their pretending to be a newlywed couple out exploring new sites."

Her hands fluttered in her lap as she said "Surely that wouldn"t be necessary." The more she

PROTESTED THE MORE DETERMINED HE WAS BECAUSE "WE COULD PRETEND TO BE ANY NUMBER OF THINGS SO IN THAT CASE WE PROBABLY WOULDN'T BE ALLOWED TO STAY BUT IF YOU ARE A COUPLE OF HONEYMOONERS THEN THAT ARE UNIVERSALLY RECOGNIZED AS HARMLESS EVEN BY CRIMINALS."

"ACCORDING TO FATHER DESILVA WHO IS A PERSONA NON GRATA IN THIS COMMUNITY SOME OF THE PEOPLE HERE ARE IN HIDING FOR CRIMES AGAINST HUMANITY. THERE ARE RUMORS THAT IT WAS ONCE A NAZI STRONGHOLD AND OUSTED DICTATORS FROM THIRD WORLD COUNTRIES APPARENTLY SETTLED THERE TOO.

"IF YOU GRANDFATHER INTENDED TO STAY LOST FOR PERSONAL REASONS OR IF FOR EXAMPLE IF HE'D DESERTED HIS PEOPLE THEN IT STANDS TO REASON HE MIGHT HAVE BEEN TOLD ABOUT THIS PLACE AND HEADED FOR IT.

"WE CAN AT LEAST ASK A FEW QUESTIONS WITHOUT AROUSING SUSPICION AND IN THE PROCEES WE'LL KEEP ARE EYES OPEN AND SEE IF ANYONE MATCHES THE POLICE SKETCH YOU GAVE ME."

JORDAN STARTED THE TRUCK AND DROVE THROUGH THE GRASS WEAVING AROUND THE OCCASIONAL TREE OR SHRUB. HE STAYED AS FAR AWAY FROM THE STREAM AS POSSIBLE TO ADVOID THE DENSER VEGETATION NEAR IT'S BANKS BUT THEN FIVE MINUTES HAVE PASSED AND SHE STILL HADN'T SAID A WORD.

"DON'T BE FRIGHTENED RICKIE I WON'T LET YOU GET HURT I SWEAR IT" HE VOWED SAVAGELY. IF ANYTHING HAPPENED TO HER . . . . "I'M NOT AFRAID" SAID RICKIE. "YOU COULD HAVE FOOLED ME" SAID JORDAN.

FEAR ISN'T WHAT I'M FEELING RIGHT NOW RICKIE SAID TO JORDAN. I CAN'T BEGIN TO DISCRIBE WHAT'S

GOING ON INSIDE OF ME." THE KNOWLEDGE THAT NAZI WAR CRIMINALS GERHARDT VON HASE MIGHT ACTUALLY BE ALIVE AND LIVING A FEW MILES FROM HERE WAS SO OVERWHELMING. INCAPABLE OF MAKING SMALL TALK SHE STUDIED THE MAP FATHER DESILVA HAD DRAWN UP. WHILE THE OUTSIDE WORLD HAD REMAINED IGNOANT OF THIS DEDICATED PRIEST HE QUIETLY WENT ABOUT AIDING HIS FELLOW MAN WITH NO REGARD FOR HIS OWN SAFETY.

TRULY GOOD AND EVIL EXISTED SIDE BY SIDE IN THE PARAGUAYAN CHACO. A TAP ON THE WINDOW BEHIND THE SEAT BROUGHT RICKIE OUT OF HER DEEP CONCENTRATION. HER HEAD WHIPPED AROUND AND FOR A LITTLE WHILE SHE'D FORGOTTEN ABOUT STONEY.

HE'D RISEN TO HIS FEET POINTING AT SOMETHING IN THE DISTANCE SO SHE SQUINTED TO SEE THEN CAUGHT SIGHT OF A SIGHT OF A WEATHERED MAKER MAYBE THIRTY FEET FROM THEIR TRUCK. "WE'VE REACHED SAN RAFAEL DE FLORES JORDAN SAID. WITHOUT ANY ROADS I DON'T KNOW HOW YOU FOUND IT" SAID RICKIE.

HE MERELY SHRUGGED HIS SHOULDERS AND SAID "I WAS GIVEN GOOD DIRECTIONS." SOON THE TOP OF THE BELL TOWER CAME IN SIGHT IT'S BASE WAS HIDDEN BY VEGETATION. A FEW MORE FEET AND RICKIE SAW A HIGH WALL LEADING TO A SPANISH-STYLE CHURCH PERHAPS FROM THE EIGHTEENTH CENTURY IT'S COLOR WHICH WAS A BROWNISH YELLOW FROM YEARS OF BAKING IN THE SUN.

THE TRUCK PULLED TO A STOP AND STONEY JUMPED DOWN WITH HIS BAG AND STILL WEARING HIS CLERICAL OUTFIT AND HAT. JORDAN THEN LEVERED HIMSELF FROM THE DRIVER'S SEAT.

THEIR LOW VOICES DRIFTET IN THE OPEN WINDOW BUT RICKIE COULDN'T HERE WHAT THEY WERE SAYING. FROM

THEIR GESTURES AND FACIAL EXPRESSION SHE COULD TELL THEY HAD DONE THIS SORT OF THING BEFORE AND WERE IN PERFECT ACCORD.

IT GAVE HER A SENSE OF SAFETY AND SHE HAD FATITH THAT THEY KNEW WHAT THEY WERE DOING AND COULD TAKE CARE OF THEMSELVES SO FINALLY STONEY TOOK HIS LEAVE AND AMBLED OVER TO THE TRUCK AND SAID "SEE YOU IN THE MORNING." "MAYBE SOMEONE HERE CAN GIVE ME A LEAD ON YOUR GRANDFATHER."

THOUGH HE WOULD DENY IT STONEY WAS DOING HER THIS FAVOR OUT OF AFFECTION FOR HIM MADE RICKIE'S VOICE TREMBLE.

"THANK YOU STONEY" SHE MANAGE BUT PLEASE DON'T PUT YOURSELF AT RISK ON MY ACCOUNT." HE FLASHED HER A QUICK SMILE AND SAID "THERE'S NOTHING I LOVE MORE THAN A MYSTERY THAT WANT'S SOLVING."

SHE COULD BELIEVE IT SHE ALSO IMAGINED THAT CHARACTERISTIC OF HIS PROBLEMS WITH MICHELLE. THAT AND HIS IMPULSE TO SHIELD WOMEN FROM DANGER AND UGLINESS AND IF HIS EX-WIFE KNEW THE KIND OF STAKES THAT WERE INVOLVED IN THIS MANHUNT.

RICKIE SHIVERED WHEN SHE SAID "YOU CAN'T THINK ABOUT THAT RIGHT NOW." "WHAT IS ARE NEXT DESTINATION?" JORDAN HAD JUST RETURNED TO THE TRUCK AND THEY WERE ON THEIR WAY ONCE MORE.

SHE BLINKED WHEN SHE SAID "IT LOOK'S LIKE RUPERT HEINZ." THERE ARE SO MANY GERMANS IN SOUTH AMERICA. "THAT WILL BE THE MENNONITE CHURCH ACCORDING TO FATHER DESILVA HEINZ WAS ONE OF THE FIRST MEMBERS OF THE GERMEN MENNONITE GROUP TO SERVE ON THE SIDE OF THE PARAGUAYAN GOVERNMENT COUNCIL FOR SOCIAL REFORMS. THE ATTACHED SCHOOL IS RUN BY A

BRITISH COUPLE AT THE MONENT AND THEY MIGHT JUST BE ARE BEST SOURCE OF INFORMATION."

AFTER A HALF HOUR LATER THEY WENT TO VISIT THE OFFICE OF HENLEYS BUT THE PRODUCED NO NEW LEDS ON AN OCTOGENARIAN NAMED GEORGE HYDE TAYLOR WHO MIGHT HAVE LIVED HERE SINCE WORLD WAR 2 AND MIGHT HAVE CHANGED HIS NAME.

JORDAN PRODUCED A COPY OF THE SKETCH WHICH WAS SHOWN TO NUMEROUS PEOPLE WORKING AT COLONY BUT NO ONE RECOGNIZED THE OLD MAN.

RICKIE HONESTLY HADN'T EXPECTED RESULTS BECAUSE SHE FELT SHAME TO BE LEADING JORDAN ON THIS WILD-GOOSE CHASE WHEN SHE KNEW HER GRANDFATHER WAS GERMAN NOT ENGLISH.

WOULD A MONSTER WITH NO CONSCIENCE AND NO RECOGNIZABLE REDEEMING TRAITS HAD BOTHERED TO CHANGE HIS NAME IF HE HAD COME TO THIS DREADFUL PLACE? A HELLHOLE NO ONE BUT A FEW INDIANS HAD EVER SEEN OR HEARD OF?

SHE DIDN'T THINK SO BUT FOR SOME REASON SHE HAD CHILLS TRAVELE OVER HER BODY AND WITH EACH PASSING MILE THEY GOT WORSE. SHE HAD A PREMONITION AND THE ANSWER HAD LAYED AT THEIR NEXT DESTINATION WITCH WAS THE FORMER NAZI HIDING PLACE AND THE OLDEST INDIAN COMMUNITY OF EVIL. RELUCTANTLY SHE LOOKED DOWN AT THE MAP BUT IT WAS JORDAN WHO NAMED THE PLACE AFTER RICKIE'S GRANDFATHER AND HE CALL IT "STROESSNERPLATZ."

CHAPTER 41

THE INDIAN COLONY.

"HOW DO YOU KNOW THIS IS IT? RICKIE FINALLY SPOKEN SINCE THEY'D LEFT MONNONIE COLONY BUT SOMETHING PROFOUND HAD BEEN GOING ON INSIDE HER. IT WAS SOMETHING CHANGE OR RESOLUTION. DID IT HAVE TO DO WITH HER GRANDFATHER AND THE PROSPECT OF FINDING HIM? WAS HER GRANDFATHER THE REASON FOR HER SADNESS AND GUILT? HE'D DECIDED TO LEAVE HER ALONE SENSING THAT THEY WERE ON THE BRINK OF DISCOVERY AND SHE SENSED IT TOO SO WORDS WERE VERY UNNECESSARY.

"I'DON'T" JORDAN ANSWERED HER. "THERE'S NO SIGN POST OF ANY KIND BUT I'VE BEEN WATCHING THE ODOMETER AND WE CAME TO THE EXACT NUMBER OF MILES. "WE'LL WALK FROM HERE SAID JORDAN."

HE PARKED THE TRUCK NEXT TO A COPSE OF STUNTED TREES THE GOT OUT AND CLIMBED IN THE BACK. THROUGH THE RE ARVIEW MIRROR SHE SAW HIM TOSS HIS HAT ASIDE THEN HE TOOK OFF THE SHIRT AND COLLAR.

HELPLESS TO DO OTHERWISE SHE STARED AT HIS POWERFUL ARMS AND WELL-DEFINED CHEST WITH IT'S DUSTING OF DARK HAIR. IT WAS THE FIRST TIME SHE SEEN HIM LIKE THIS AND THE SIGHT OF IT MADE HER MOUTH GO DRY.

FEARING HE MIGHT CATCH HER STARING SHE OPENED THE PASSENGER SIDE DOOR AND JUMPED TO THE GROUND WITH SHAKY LEGS THAT WERE ALL BLACK AND BLUE FROM

THAT PLANE CRASH THAT HAPPENED A COUPLE DAYS AGO.

THE NEXT TIME SHE LOOKED HE HAD PUT ON A HAWAIIAN SHIRT LEAVING IT HALF WAY OPEN AND HE HAD LOOPED A INSTAMATIC CAMERA AROUND HIS NECK.

HE HAD DONE ONE MORE THING AND THE THONG HE USED TO TIE BACK HIS HAIR HAD BEEN REMOVED SO HIS LONG HAIR LOOKED HEALTHY DARK BROWN AND IN THE SUNLIGHT HE LOOKED VERY SEXY, TOURISTY AND AMERICAN WITH THE PERSONIFICATION OF THE ATTRACTIVE GROOM WITHOUT A CARE IN THE WORLD AND A WOMEN AT HIS SIDE.

SUDDENTLY HE LOOKED DOWN AT HER AND HER LASHES WERE SO LONG THAT HIS EYES GLOWED AN INCANDESCENT GREEN. "I TOOK THE LIBERTY OF GOING THROUGH YOUR PACK I THINK YOU SHOULD WEAR THIS INSTEAD OF THAT KHAKI SHIRT I'LL TURN AROUND SO YOU CAN CHANGE."

HE THREW HER ONE OF THE PLAIN OVERSIZE WHITE T-SHIRTS SHE'D BROUGHT TO SLEEP IN. WITH HER PULSE RACING SHE TURNED HER BACK TO HIM UNBUTTONED HER SHIRT AND TRIED TO PULL THE T-SHIRT ON BUT HER HAIR CLIP GOT IN THE WAY AND IN FRUSTRATION SHE MADE A NOISE.

"HERE LET ME HELP YOU SAID JORDAN. HE THEN PULLED THE CLIP OUT OF HER HAIR AND HELPED DRAW THE SHIRT DOWN OVER HER HIPS. IF HE HAD NOTICE HER GUN HE DIDN'T SAY BUT THE INTIMATE TOUCH OF HIS FINGERS AGAINST HER SPINE BROUGHT A HEAT THAT SWEPT THROUGHOUT HER LITTLE THIN BODY.

NOW HER HAIR WAS AS FREE FLOWING AS HIS AND THE MERE ACT OF RELEASING IT SEEMED TO RELEASE AN

EARTHY RESPONSE INSIDE HER. SHE FELT RECKLESS AND OUT OF CONTROL AND SHE'D HEARD OTHER WOMEN DESCRIBE THAT FEELING BUT THIS WAS THE FIRST TIME IT HAD HAPPENED TO HER AND THIS MEANT THAT ONLY HE COULD SATISFY HER.

"LET'S GO" HE SAID IN A LOW VOICE. "FOLLOW MY LEAD AND DO EXACTLY AS I SAY." "ALL RIGHT" SHE SAID BUT SHE COULDN'T SPEAK ABOVE A WHISPER BECAUSE HE'D SLUNG HIS ARM AROUND HER SHOULDER AND NOW THEIR HIPS BRUSHED AGAINST EACH OTHER AS THEY MOVED TOWARD THE HEAVIER FOLIAGE NEAR THE STREAM.

BEFORE LONG THEY PICKED UP A WINDING PATH AND SLOWLY BUT SURELY RICKIE BEGAN TO SEE FLATTENED CIGARETTE BUTTS AND BITS OF PAPER SCATTERED HERE AND THERE AND THE LESS ATTRACTIVE SIGNS OF HUMAN HABITATION.

THEY HADN'T BEEN WALKING MORE THEN A FEW MINUTES WHEN HE SAID "SOMEONE'S WATCHING US SO LET'S GIVE THEM SOMETHING TO LOOK AT" SAID JORDAN.

RICKIE WASN'T NAÏVE AND SHE KNOWN THAT AT SOME POINT DURING THIS CHARADE JORDAN WAS GOING TO KISS HER BECAUSE SHE HAD ANTICIPATED IT.

WHEN THE MOMENT CAME HOWEVER THERE WAS NOTHING FEIGNED ABOUT THE WAY HIS MOUTH CLOSED POSSESSIVELY OVER HERES. HE WAS SUPPOSED TO BE HER HUSBAND WHO IS FAMILIAR WITH HER MOUTH AND BODY THAT HE HUNGRY FOR BOTH.

DEAR GOD RICKIE REELED FROM THE SENSATIONS THAT HIS MOUTH AROUSED BUT CRAVING IT'S TASTE AND INTENSITY SHE GAVE HIM FULL ACCESS DENYING HIM NOTHING. ONE OF THEM HAD GROANED NOT AWARE OF

THE TIME OR HER SURROUNDINGS SHE CLUNG TO HIS HARD MUSCLED BODY REVELING IN THE DIFFERENCES BETWEEN THEM.

AS THEY STOOD WRAPPED TOGETHER WITH THEIR ARMS LOCKED AROUND EACH OTHER'S WAISTS RICKIE KNEW A FULLNESS OF JOY.

IN THIS MAN'S EMBRACE SHE'D FOUND ALL SHE COULD ASK FOR IN LIFE. NO OTHER EXPERIENCE WOULD EVER COMPARE TO IT BUT RICKIE'S ONLY PROBLEM WAS THAT SHE COULDN'T GET ENOUGH OF HIM.

APPARENTLY THEIR DESIRE WAS A MUTUAL THING BECAUSE ONE IMPASSIONED KISS FOLLOWED ANOTHER AND AS THE MINUTES PASSED AND THEIR KISSING CONTINUED PROLONGED AROUSING THAT SHE HAD STOPPED THINKING AND RAN ON PURE FEELING.

"RICKIE" SHE HEARD JORDAN'S VOICE. THIS MIGHT HAVE STARTED OUT AS A PERFORMANCE FOR THE BENEFIT OF ANYONE WATCHING BUT ALL SHE KNEW WAS THAT SHE NEVER WANTED IT TO STOP. OBEYING A DRIVING NEED SHE MOLDED HERSELF AGAINST HIM TRYING TO GET AS CLOSE AS ONE PERSON COULD TO ANOTHER.

WHEN HE ALLOWED HER LIPS THE FREEDOM SHE EXULTED IN A LOUD EXPLORATION OF HIS FEATURES SINCE THAT FIRST DAY IN HER OFFICE SHE'D BEEN DESPERATE TO KNOW THE HARDNESS OF HIS JAW AND THE SOFTNESS OF HIS LASHES BUT IN HIS CORDED THROAT WAS A PULSE THAT THROBBED AS FAST AS RICKIE'S HEARTBEAT DID.

NOW THAT SHE'D BEEN GRANTED PREMISSION SHE FELT NO SO CALLED COMPUNCTION ABOUT TAKING THE KINDS OF LIBERTIES OF A WIFE WOULD TAKE WITH HER HUSBAND WHICH SHE HAD ADORED.

RICKIE HAD NEVER DATED A MAN WITH LONG HAIR AND THE SENSUOUS EXPERIENCE OF RUNNING HER HANDS THROUGH IT FILLED HER WITH LOTS OF INEXPLICABLE DELIGHT SO SHE DREW CLOSER TO KISS HIS SWEET LIPS ONE MORE TIME.

"DON'T REACT" HE WHISPERED AGAINST HER LIPS "BUT SOMEONE'S COMING OUR WAY SO PLAY ALONG WITH ME." SUDDENLY HE BROKE THEIR KISS THOUGH SHE KNEW THEY HAD AN AUDIENCE RICKIE ALMOST CRIED OUT AT THE SHOCK OF DEPRIVATION. DISORIENTED SHE STARTED TO SWAY SO JORDAN CAUGHT HER AROUND THE SHOULDERS SO HE COULD PROTECT HER FROM FALLING OVER.

"YOU MUST BE AMERICANS" THE SMALL DARK SIXTYISH MAN WHO HAD SOPKEN ENGLISH WITH AN HEAVY SPANISH ACCENT REVOLTED HER IN SOMEWAY. HE'D BEEN STANDING IN THE SHELTER OF THE TREES ALL THE TIME WATCHING WHAT HAD BEEN THE MOST EXCITING AND SACRED MOMENT OF HER LIFE.

"THAT'S RIGHT" JORDAN RESPONDED. SHE MARVELED THAT HE COULD RECOVER SO QUICKLY AFTER WHAT THEY'D JUST EXPERIENCED. "MY WIFE AND I WERE RECENTLY MARRIED IN ASUCION AND DECIDED TO GO EXPLORING." HE KISSED HER TEMPLE THEN LIFTED HER HAND TO HIS LIPS AND CARESSED THE PALM WITH A KISS.

THE SENSATION FLOWED UP HER ARM SPREADING IT'S HEAT THROOUGH HER BODY. "I'M JIM AND THIS IS MY WIFE ANDREA WE PARKED IN THE BACK THERE." HE GESTURED VAGUELY AS HE SAID "WE'RE HUNGRY AND WE NEED A PLACE TO SPEND TH NIGHT SO CAN YOU RECOMMEND A GOOD HOTEL IN TOWN?"

THE MAN WHO HAD A SPACE BETWEEN HIS FRONT TEETH LAUGHED AS HE SAID "STROESSNERPLATZ HAS NO

HOTELS AND SERVICES FOR THE PUBLIC BUT IF YOU TRAVEL NORTH YOU WILL COME TO THE MENNONITE AND JESUIT MISSIONS THEY WELCOME VISITORS."

"WE WERE LOOKING FOR THE GERMAN-RUN MENNONITE COMPOUND AND I THOUGHT BECAUSE OF THE NAME THIS WAS THE PLACE." "THEN YOU THOUGHT WRONG" SAID THE GUY WITH THE FUNNY LOOKING TEETH.

IT WAS OBVIOUS TO RICKIE THEY WERE BEING TOLD TO GET OUT. SHE WANTED TO LEAVE BECAUSE JORDAN HAD SENSED HER IMPATIENCE TO GO BECAUSE HIS ARM TIGHTENED AROUND HIS SHOULDERS.

"SO WHAT IS THIS PLACE?" THE STRANGER'S EYES FLASHED SUSPICIOUSLY AS JORDAN SAID WHAT HE HAD SAID. "IN THE UNTIED STATES YOU HAVE TO KNOW HOW TO SAY IT RETIREMENT CENTERS?"

"THAT'S EXACTLY WHAT THEY ARE" JORDAN ACKNOWLEDGED WITH A SMILE. "YOUR VOCABULARY IS EXCELLENT THERE MUST BE A LOT OF WEALTHY ENGLISH LIVING HERE. NO WONDER YOU WERE HIRED AS A SECURITY GUARD. "YOU MUST GO NOW" HE SAID BUT HIS VOICE HAD SOUNDED PEEVED. "THIS PLACE IS PRIVATE." "OH COME ON JORDAN CAJOLED HIM AS HE SAID "WE JUST WANT TAKE A LOOK AROUND AND MAYBE BUY A DRINK. DO YOU KNOW IF THEY HAVE COKE HERE?"

THE MAN'S ANGER HAD GRWON TANGIBLE AND RICKIE HAD TO HOLD HER BREATH. "NO I DON'T KNOW NOW IT'S GETTING DARK YOU WOULD BE WISE TO LEAVE NOW WHILE IT'S STILL LIGHT OUTSIDE."

"I GET IT YOU LET THE DOGS LOOSE AT NIGHT. AM I RIGHT?" "YOU ARE RIGHT." "MY WIFE LOVES TAKING PICTURES FOR HER SCRAPBOOK. COULD WE AT LEAST GET A PHOTP OF YOU BY THE SIGN BEFORE WE HEAD

OUT? A SOUVENIR OF OUR HONEYMOON?" "THERE'S NO TIME." "I'LL PAY YOU." AS JORDAN STARTED TO REACH FOR THE WALLET IN HIS BACK POCKET THE MAN PULLED A GUN ON THEM AND RICKIE FROZE ON THE SPOT.

"KEEP YOU MONEY AND GO" HE ORDERED. "HEY SENOR THAT'S MY BEAUTIFUL BRIDE YOU'RE POINTING THAT THAT AT."! I WAS ONLY TRYING TO BE FRIENDLY. THEY MUST PAY YOU PERTTY WELL TO TURN DOWN A HUNDRED DOLLARS."

THE MAN SPAT SAYING "YOU AMERICANS THINK YOU CAN BUY ALMOST ANYTHING IF YOU HAVE ENOUGH MONEY." "IT'S WORKED SO FAR BUT I CAN SEE YOU'RE TOO WELL PAID BY YOUR EMPLOYER TO NEED IT SO WE'LL LEAVE. NO HARM DONE RIGHT? "HASTA LA VISTA" AS THEY SAY IN THE MOVIES.

IN THE NEXT BREATH HIS HEAD DESCENDED AND GAVE RICKIE A HARD SWIFT KISS ON THE MOUTH AND SAID "LET'S GO FIND A PLACE TO BED DOWN FOR THE NIGHT SWEETHEART."

THEY RETRACED THEIR FOOTSTEEPS ALONG THE PATH ACTING LIKE A NEWLY MARRIED COUPLE MADLY IN LOVE AND OUT FOR A LEISURELY STROLL. FROM THE TIME JORDAN PAUSED TO KISS HER CHEEK BEFORE MOVING ON.

"WE'LL KEEP WALKING FOR ANOTHER FIVE MINUTES" HE SAID AS HE TWISTED HER HAIR ON HIS FINGER. "HE DOSEN'T KNOW WHERE THE TRUCK IS AND WE DON'T WANT HIM TO FOLLOW US AND FIND OUT."

RICKIE NOODED HER HEAD WITHOUT SAYING ANYTHING BECAUSE SHE HAD TOO MANY THOUGHTS AND EMOTIONS RUNNING INSIDE HER. WHEN THAT GUN WAS BRANDISHED IN THEIR FACES THE SEARCH FOR VON HASE HAD TAKEN ON A DIFFERENT REALITY.

SHE'D INSISTED THAT STONEY AND JORDAN ALLOW HER TO COME ON THIS MISSION NO MATTER WHAT BUT SHE HADN'T COUNTINED ON THE SUDDEN APPEARANCE OF HER OWN PROTECTIVE INSTINCTS.

THIS WAS NO GAME AND IF PROVOKED ANY FURTHER THAT SECURITY GAUARD WOULD HAVE PULLED THE TRIGGER ON BOTH OF THEM WITHOUT COMPUNCTION.

EVEN THOUGH JORDAN HAD BEEN TEN STEPS AHEAD OF THE SECURITY GUARD AND HAD A COUNTERMOVE IN MIND BEFORE ANYTHING COULD HAPPEN SHE WAS STILL AT FAULT FOR PUTTING THEM IN THIS POSITION.

NOT ONLY THAT SHE'D LIDE ABOUT VON HASE BEING ENGLISH BUT AT THE TIME OF THE FAMILY DINNER IN PINE PLAINS IT HAD SEEMED VERY NECESSARY TO GIVE JORDAN THE WRONG INFORMATION BUT IN LIGHT OF WHAT HAD JUST OCCURRED SHE REALIZED THE DELIBERATE MISINFORMATION HAD PLACED HIM IN DANGER BECAUSE HE SHOULD HAVE BEEN WARNED ABOUT WHAT KIND OF MAN HE WAS LOOKING FOR BECAUSE OF HER FAMILY'S OBSESSION WITH HUNTING DOWN VON HASE THEY'D HAD FORGOTTEN THE HUMAN ELEMENT IN ALL THIS.

EVEN THE ODIOUS SECURITY GUARD HAD PRICKED HER CONSCIENCE WHEN HE'D SAID THE AMERICANS THOUGHT THEY COULD BUY ANYTHING WITH ENOUGH MONEY.

THAT WAS EXACTLY WHAT SHE'D BELIEVED WHEN SHE MADE THE TWENTY-MILLION DOLLAR OFFER TO JORDAN AND HE TURNED IT DOWN FLAT.

TALK ABOUT PLAYING GOD WITH PEOPLE'S LIVES! TONIGHT TWO VERY REMARKABLE MEN WERE OUT IN THIS CORRUPT BACKWATER RISKING THEIR LIVES BECAUSE OF RICKIE TAYLOR HAD BEEN PULLING ALL THE PUPPET STRINGS AS THEY SAY IN SHOW BIZ.

It was wrong because she'd been compounding evil with evil and nothing in the world could erase the atrocities of her grandfather but she did have the power to put an end to this insane suicide mission. Ted and Bernard wouldn't like it very much but they weren't the ones out here eyeing death from the wrong end of a gun.

Jordan's primary reason for being in Paraguay had already put him in mortal jeopardy and would continue to do so as long as the government suppressed people's freedoms and she couldn't let him take it any further risks and she also had to call a hult to this far-fetched plan of her family's doomed to fail from the outset because of her family's blood money.

It felt longer then five minutes before they'd circled back to the spot where they had left the truck and to her relief nothing looked tampered with or out of place. After helping her into the passenger side of the truck Jordan went around and slid behind the wheel. "We'll head back toward the Jesuit mission untill it's gets dark to without turning on the headlights then we'll make camp."

Rickie nodded her assent anxious to get as far away as possible to call off the search but night fell fast in the silent Chaco and the land came alive after dark and the sounds of wild and exotic instruments but their foreign noices sent chills whispering over her skin.

Too soon for her liking they had to stop so Jordan parked next to an outcropping of vegetation. "You haven't said a word since we got in the truck." "He shut off the engine and there

WAS NEVER ANY QUESTION OF YOUR BEING IN DANGER FROM THAT FOOL." "I KNOW SHE SAID QUIETLY BUT MY FEAR FOR YOU IS GREATER THEN MY FEELINGS." "I WARNED YOU WE'D HAVE TO PLAY THE SO CALLED HONEYMOONERS TO BE CONVINCING."

HEAT ROSE IN HER CHEEKS, "I KNOW THAT TOO." IF ONLY WE RELLY WERE NEWLYWEDS WITH A BRIGHT FUTURE BEFORE US AND NO TRACE OF SHADOWS.

SHE HEARD HIM TAKE A LABORED BREATH BUT "YOU MUST BE HUNGRY I WON'T BE LONG." HE TURNED ON A FLASHLIGHT AND GOT OUT OF THE TRUCK AND SHE COULD ALSO HEAR HIM MOVING THINGS AROUND IN THE BACK BUT WHEN HE RETURNED HE BROUGHT SOME CANNED GOODS AND SPOONS.

"THERE'S NOTHING LIKE COLD CHILI AND PEACHES WHEN THERE'S NO RESTAURANT AROUND" SAID JORDAN. WITH A DEFT MOVEMENT OF HIS SWISS ARMY KNIFE HE OPENED THE LIDS AND HANDED HER TWO SMALL CANS BUT THE FOOD WAS AMERICAN AND REASSURINGLY FAMILIAR AND IT TASTED GOOD.

HE ATE TWO SERVINGS TO HER ONE SERVING AND AFTER THEY FINISHED HE PROPPED THEIR EMPTY TINS ON TOP OF THE DASHBOARD. "ON OUR NEXT TRIP STONEY AND I WILL INFILTRATE THE SETTLEMENT TO FIND OUT WHO'S THERE BUT BEFORE WE DO THAT I NEED TO SCOUT THE PERIMETER TONIGHT BUT I ALSO WANT TO KNOW IF OUR FRIEND THE SENOR IS THE GOING TO BE THE ONLY WATCHDOG ON DUTY AND SINCE I WORK BETTER ALONE YOU'LL HAVE TO STAY IN THE TRUCK."

"DON'T GO!" HER CRY REVERBERATHED IN THE CAB SO SHE DIDN'T CARE IF SHE SHE'D INTERRUPTED HIM BUT NOTHING WAS WORTH THE DANGER HE'D BE EXPOSED TO.

"IT WON'T BE LONG" HE SAID REASONABLY. "YOU'LL BE SAFE HERE AND DON'T FOR GET YOU GOT YOUR GUN FOR PROTECTION." "YOU DON'T UNDERSTAND JORDAN "THERE'S NO REASON FOR YOU TO GO OUT THERE BECAUSE I HAVE CHANGED MY MIND."

TENSION SUFFIUSED THE AIR AS HE SAID "CHANGED YOUR MIND ABOUT WHAT?" "YOU MEAN ABOUT LOOKING FOR YOUR GRANDFATHER" SAID JORDAN. YOU WERE RIGHT WHEN YOU SAID THERE WAS NOTHING TO BE GAINED FROM DREDGING UP THE PAST BECAUSE AFTER FORTY-NINE YEARS AND NOT ONE WORD FROM HIM OR ONE PIECE OF EVIDENCE TO PROVE THAT HE'S STILL ALIVE AND I DON'T SEE THE POINT. THIS HAS ALL BEEN A RIDICULOUS EXERCISE IN FUTILITY.

"IF MY BROTHER AND COUSIN WANT TO CONDUCT A SEARCH OF THEIR OWN THEN THAT'S UP TO THEM BECAUSE THE MONEY THAT BROUGHT US DOWN HERE FOR YOUR PROJECT IS MY MONEY NOT THEIRS. YOU HAD VOLUNTEERED TO TRY TO FIND OUR GRANDFATHER IN YOUR SPARE TIME AND YOU'VE DONE THAT AND NOW I AM RELEASING YOU FROM YOUR OBLIGATION AND I'LL TELL STONEY THE SAME THING WHEN WE PICK HIM UP IN THE MORNING.

JORDAN'S HANDS MOVED SO FAST RICKIE DIDN'T HAVE TIME TO GASP. HE CLASSPED HER UPPER ARM AND TURNED HER TO FACE HIM. SHE HAD PANICKED KNOWING HE WOULDN'T FREE HER UNTILL HE'D HAD HEARD THE TRUTH FROM HER.

"EARLIER TODAY YOU WENT COMPLETELY PALE WHEN I MENTIONED WHAT FATHER DESILVA HAD SAID ABOUT THE SETTLEMENT AT STROESSNERPLATZ. UP TO THAT POINT YOU WERE ALL RIGHT WITH LETTING STONEY AND ME MAKE INQUIRIES.

"HOW COME IT ISN'T ALL RIGHT NOW?" SHE SAID OUT LOUD. "ANSWER ME RICKIE !" HIS FINGERS TIGHTENED UP WHEN HE SAID "ARE YOU AFRAID GEORGE TAYLOR IS A CRIMINAL? SO WHAT IF HE IS? IT HAS NOTHING TO DO WITH YOU!" OR DOES IT! WHEN YOU LEARN WHO I REALLY AM AND I HOPE I HAVE ENOUGH STRENGTH TO HANDLE YOUR LOATHING.

I'M SO FRIGHTENED I WISH A MOUNTAIN WOULD BURY ME TO DROWN OUT THE CRIES OF THOSE TORTURED SOULS. SHE TOOK A RAGGED BREATH BEFORE SHE SAID "HIS NAME ISN'T GEORGE TAYLOR AND HE'S NOT AN ENGLISHMAN."

SHE COULD SENSE THE UNEVENNESS OF HIS BREATHING. "I KNEW YOU WERE HOLDING SOMETHING BACK" HE SAID. "GO ON" HE SAID TO RICKIE AS HE SAW HER HUNG HER HEAD. "MY GRANDFATHER WAS A NAZI AND NOT YOUR COMMON GARDEN-VARIETY NAZI BECAUSE WE TAYLORS COME FROM ARISTOCRATIC STOCK." THE TEARS STARTED DRIPPING FASTER AND FASTER. "HIS NAME IS GERHARDT VON HASE."

THERE WAS AN OMINOUS SILENCE BEFORE HE SAID "GOOD LORD RICKIE" SAID JORDAN. "LIKE EVERYONE ELSE IN THE WORLD I CAN SEE YOU'RE FULL ACQUAINTED WITH THE HEINOUS ACTS OF THE NOTORIOUS VAMPIRE OF ALSACE. YOU KNOW HE ESCAPED BEFORE THE WAR ENDED AND WAS NEVER BROUGHT TO TRIAL.

"BY DAY HIS PLANTS TURNED OUT AMMUNITION AND WAR MATERIALS FOR THE THIRD REICH GARNERING HIM WEALTH BEYOND IMAGINING. "BY NIGHT HE INVITED DOCTORS TO EXPERIMENT ON HIS HUGE SLAVE-LABOR FORCE TURNING THOSE SAME PLANTS INTO LABORATORIES OF TORTURE AND DEATH FOR THOUSANDS OF HUMAN BEINGS.

"ACCORDING TO THE NAZI WAR-CRIMES TRIBUNAL VON HASE HE TOOK PARTICULAR DELIGHT IN EXPERIMENTS HAVING TO DO WITH STUDIES OF BLOOD. HE WAS CITED FOR PARTICULAR CRUELTY TO NURSING MOTHERS AND BABIES BY DRAWING OFF THEIR BLOOD LEAVING THEM TO DIE BY THE HUNDREDS.

"THE DITCHES OF HIS LAND RAN WITH BLOOD" BUT SHE PAUSED THE SOBBING HELPLESSLY BEFORE SHE SAID "THAT'S MY BELOVED GRANDPA" RICKIE SAID.

"ALREADY IT MUST BE SINKING IN THAT YOU'VE KISSED RICKIE VON HASE AND SOON NOW YOU'RE GOING TO FEEL VERY SICK I KNOW HE SAID AS HIS VOICE TREMBLED BECAUSE I'VE BEEN VERY SICK SINCE MY BROTHER HAD FLEW TO AUSTRALIA AND INFORMED ME THAT WE'RE VON HASE'S GRANDCHILDREN.

"DID YOU KNOW TED WAS GOING TO MARY DEBORAH SOLOMON DAVID'S COUSIN? HE MET HER IN JERUSALEM AND THEY FELL IN LOVE. IT WAS DEBORAH'S PARENTS WHO TOOK TED AND ME AROUND THE YARD OF VASHEM MEMORIAL. IT WAS THERE THAT I WHO COULDN'T EVEN FINISH THE DIARYOF ANNE FRANK IN JUNIOR HIGH SCHOOL OR LEARNED ALL ABOUT THE LEGACY OF MY GRANDFATHER LEFT TO MANKIND."

SHE STOPPED LONG ENOUGH TO BRUSH THE WETNESS FROM HER FACE AND CHIN. "TED AND BERNARD AND I THOUGHT WE COULD DO WHAT THE WORLD HASN'T BEEN ABLE TO TRACK DOWN VON HASE AND FORCE HIM TO FACE HIS ACCUSERS WHO'VE BEEN WAITING FORTY-NINE YEARS FOR THE SATISFACTION AND YOU REVEREND BROWNING WERE THE LUCKY ONE CHOSEN TO HELP US ACCOMPLISH THIS IMPOSSIBLE TASK SO AT LEAST I HAD THOUGHT IT WAS IMPOSSIBLE UNTILL WE TRESPASSED BACK THERE A LITTLE WHILE AGO.

STROESSNERPLATZ MIGHT JUST BE WHERE THAT FRIEND'S BEEN HIDING ALL THESE YEARS.

"IF THAT'S THE CASE I DON'T WANT YOU OR STONEY GOING ANYWHERE NEAR IT AND I DON'T WANT YOU INVOLVED SAID JORDAN. YOU'RE GOOD AND DECENT AND UNTAINTED AND YOU ALSO HAVE GREAT WORK TO PERFORM FOR THE POOR SOULS DOWN HERE WHO NEED HELP.

"MY GRANDFATHER'S EVIL RESTS WITH OUR FAMILY AND HE'S OUR PROBLEM JORDAN. I THINK THE ONLY REASON I HAVEN'T COMMITTED SUICIDE IS BECAUSE I'M TERRIFIED TO ADD ONE MORE PERSON TO THE DEATH TOLL EVEN IT'S ONLY ME.

"PLEASE DON'T LET ME HAVE YOU BLOOD ON MY HANDS AS WELL BECAUSE THAT'S THE ONE THING I COULDN'T BEAR AND ON THAT SO CALLED AGONIZED NOTE SHE FLED FROM THE TRUCK.

STUNNED BY THE DEPTH OF HER SORROW AND THE GUILT SHE WAS FEELING JORDAN DIDN'T REALIZE SHE WAS GOING ANYWHERE UNTILL HE HEARD THE PASSENGER DOOR CLOSE.

SHE COULDN'T GET VERY FAR IN THE DARK SO HE CLIMBED OUT OF THE CAB AND FOLLOWED THE SOUND OF HER MUFFLED SOBS. AFRAID TO TOUCH HER WHILE HIS EMOTIONS WERE SPILLING OUT HE PLANTED HIMSELF A COUPLE OF FEET AWAY AND WAITED UNTILL SHE'D SHED ALL HER TEARS.

"RICKIE?" JUDGING BY HER STARTLED CRY SHE HADN'T BEEN AWARE OF HIS PRESENCE. "YOUR GILTY COMES FROM MERE ASSOCIATION RICKIE AN ACCTDENT OF BIRTH AS YOU ONCE PUT IT YOURSELF. YOU OUGHT O TRY LIVING

WITH THE KNOWLEDGE THAT YOU MURDERED A MAN WITH YOUR BEAR HANDS."

"WHAT?" AT LAST HE'D GAINED HER ATTENTION WHEN HE SAID "YOU HEARD ME I'M A EX-CONVICT. "YOU'RE A EX—WHAT SHE SAID AS SHE HAD SOUNDED AGHASTED.

IT RANG A DEATH KNELL IN HIS HEART AS HE SAID "SO MUCH FOR TELLING HER THE TRUTH." "THAT'S RIGHT REVEREND BROWNING HAS DONE TIME" SAID JORDAN. SHE WAS SO QUIET AND HIS PAIN WAS JUST BEGINNING. "I COULDN'T ALLOW YOU TO PUT ME ON A PAR WITH FATHER DESILVA OR REVEREND ROLON. THERE ISN'T ANY COMPARISON" SIAD JORDAN.

IT SEEMED LIKE MINUTES INSTEAD OF SECONDS BEFORE SHE HAD ASKED "WAS IT IN SELF-DEFRNSE?" HIS EYES CLOSED TIGHTLY WHEN HE HAD SAID BACK TO HE "NO." "DO YOU WANT TO TALK ABOUT IT?" HER QUSTION SOCKED HIM.

"AS YOU ONCE REMINDED ME" SHE CONTIUNED "YOU'RE A MAN AS WELL AS A MINISTER. IF YOU NEED SOMEONE TO LISTEN TO YOU I'M THE LAST PERSON QUALIFIED FOR THE JOB BUT I AM HERE AND WE'RE QUITE ALONE."

"WE ARE SHE SAID TO FATHER DESILVA. "YOU'RE NOT AFRAID OF ME?" "SINCE I'M THE MOST FRIGHTENING PERSON I KNOW I DON'T THINK SO."

HE'D READ ENOUGH ABOUT THE GUILT SUFFERED BY RELATIVES OF NAZI CRIMINALS TO LET THAT COMMENT SLIDE FOR NOW.

"I NEED YOU TO LISTEN TO ME RICKIE SAID FATHER DESILVA BUT THEN RICKIE SAID "WE'D BE SAFER IN THE TRUCK THEN OUT HERE." "I'M NOT SURE WHERE THE

TRUCK IS AND MY EYES ARE SWOLLEN AND IT'S STILL DARK OUTSIDE."

WHETHER OR NOT THAT WAS AN INVITATION HE TOOK IT AS ONE AND REACHED FOR HER HAND AND AT LEAST SHE DIDN'T PULL AWAY WHEN HE LED HER TO THE TRUCK AND HELPED HER INSIDE BUT THE SITUATION WAS A FRY CRY FROM THE HONEYMOON SCENARIO OF A FEW HOURS AGO.

EARLIER TONIGHT HE'D PLANNED TO MAKE UP THEIR BEDS IN THE BACK OF THE TRUCK AND LET WHATEVER HAPPENED BETWEEN THEM HAPPEN BUT CERTAIN DEVELOPMENTS HAD CHANGED ALL THAT. HE WOULD HAVE TO FEEL HIS WAY FOR A WHILE.

"ARE YOU THIRSTY?" "YES." HE HANDED HER CANTEEN AND SHE DRANK HER FILL AND THEN HE PUT HIS MOUTH TO THE OPENING AND DRANK THE REST AND DESPITE THE PRECARIOUSNESS OF THEIR RELATIONSHIP BEING WITH RICKIE IN THE INTIMACY OF THE CAB BROUGHT HIM MORE JOY THAN ENYTHING HE'D EVER EXPERIENCED IN HIS LIFE.

SHE SAT TO FAR AWAY FROM HIM HUDDLED AGAINST THE DOOR. HE WANTED TO COMFORT HER BUT FIRST THEY HAD TO GET PAST THE OBSTACLE OF HIS PRISON RECORD BEFORE SHE'D TRUST HIM AGAIN. SHE DIDN'T KNOW IF SHE WOULD EVER TRUST HIM AGAIN.

"YOU TOLD ME YOU KILLED A MAN" SHE SAID HOARSELY BUT THE SO CALLED REVEREND BROWNING I KNOW COULD NEVER HAVE DONE THAT WITHOUT A COMPELLING REASON."

"WHEN IT HAPPENED I WAS'T A REVEREND RICKIE I WAS A NAVY SEAL." "I KNEW IT HAD TO BE SOMETHING LIKE THAT. WAS STONEY A NAVY SEAL TOO?" "YES TECHNICALLY

WE WERE TOO OLD TO BE ON ACTIVE DUTY BUT WE WERE ASKED TO TAKE PART IN A SPECIAL OPERATION THAT WAS NOT NORMALLY ASSIGNED TO THE NAVY SEALS. FOR ONE THING THE MEN WHO WERE CHOSEN HAD TO BE FLUENT IN SPANISH AND THEN WE WERE PUT THROUGH INTENSIVE LANGUAGE IMMERSION CLASSES IN THE COUNTRY OF GUARANI."

"WAS STONEY MARRIED THEN?" "YES BUT IT WAS SO HARD ON HIS POUR WIFE." "IT WASN'T EXACTLY EASY ON STONEY EITHER." "NO I DON'T IMAGINE IT WAS." "OUR PLATOON HAD BEEN SENT TO PARAGUAY TO ENSURE THAT THE NEW LEADERSHIP WOULDN'T SUFFER A MILLITARY COUP AT THE HANDS OF THE OLD REGIME OR RIVAL FACTIONS. THE U.S. WANTED THAT PARTICULAR PARTY TO GET IN POWER AND STAY THERE. PERSONALLY I COULD NEVER SEE THE DIFFERENCE BETWEEN ANY OF THEM BECAUSE I THINK THEY'RE ALL CORRUPT.

"ANYWAY OUR ASSIGNMENT WAS IN THE CHACO NEAR A NIVER WHERE THE NEW PARTY WAS MEETING IN SECRET TO PLAN IT'S STRATEGIES BECAUSE IT'S KIND OF LIKE A CAMP DAVID PARAGUAYAN STYLE. WE HAD ORDERS TO STAY HIDDEN AND MAKE SURE THEY WERE LEFT UNDISTURBED BECAUSE THE PLAN WAS TOP-SECRET NATURE AND NO ONE WAS TO KNOW WE WERE THERE AND UNDER NO CIRCUMSTANCES WERE WE TO SHOW OUR HAND UNLESS IT WAS TO DEFEND THE PERIMETER SO IN OTHER WORDS WE WERE TO REMAIN INVISIBLE YET PROVIDE BACKUP FORCE IF NECESSARY."

"WAS THAT THE TIME YOU SAW THOSE MEN RAPING THE INDIAN GIRLS?" SHE SAID AS HER VOICE SOUNDED LIKE IT WAS SHAKING. "YES BUT THE GIRLS WERE KEPT IN OUT DOOR PENS AND NIGHT AFTER NIGHT HE HAD TO STAND BY WATCHING AND LISTENING AND NOT LIFTING A FINGER. EVERY MAN IN THE PLATOON WAS THINKING ABOUT HIS WIFE OR GIRLFRIEND AT HOME AND HOW IT

WOULD FEEL IF THE SAME THING WAS HAPPENING TO HER AND NO ONE CAME TO HELP.

"MAYBE IT WAS BECAUSE STONEY AND I WERE OLDER AND LESS AFRAID OF AUTHORITY BUT WHATEVER THE REASON WENE WE WERE SAW THE NEW CHIEF OF POLICE GOING AFTER THE SAME TERRIFIED GIRL NIGHT AFTER NIGHT SOMETHING JUST SNAPPED INSIDE MY HEAD.

"I LEFT MY DESIGNATED SPOT AND CREPT UP BEHIND THAT MONSTER AND STRANGLED HIM." "I'M SO GLAD YOU DID!" RICKIE CRIED OUT AND THOSE WORDS GAVE JORDAN HOPE.

"I DECIDED TO KILL HIM IN THAT MANNER RATHER THAN INFLICT A WOUND THAT COULD BE TRACED BACK TO A WEAPON. HE WAS A HUGE MAN WELL OVER THREE HUNDRED POUNDS AND BECAUSE IT WAS DARK I DIDN'T SEE HIS KNIFE. HE COULD HAVE DONE SOME DAMAGE IF STONEY HADN'T TURNED IT ON HIM AND USED IT TO FINISH HIM OFF.

"THE GIRL WAS CROUCHED IN THE A CORNER. WE MOTIONED FOR HER TO RUN SHE THEN TOOK OFF LIKE THE WIND ON A COLD DAY. STONEY AND I WENT BACK TO OUR POST AND PRETENDED NOTHING HAD HAPPENED BUT BEFORE MORNING THE MAN'S BODY WAS FOUND.

"NO ONE COULD PROVE WHO KILLED HIM BUT OUR GOVERNMENT CATEGORICALLY DENIED ANY RESPONSIBILITY FOR IT. THE PLATOON HAD STOOD SOLIDLY BEHIND ME AND STONEY BUT WHEN THE POWERS THAT BE GRILLED EVERYONE TO DISCOVER THE TRUTH I MADE THE CONFESSION TO MY COMMANDING OFFICER AND WAS BROUGHT UP ON LOTS OF FORMAL CHARGES.

"THEY COURT-MARTIALED ME FOR INSTIGATING AN INCIDENT THAT HAD RESULTED IN THE DEATH OF

A HIGH-RANKING GOVERNMENT OFFICIAL AND FOR CREATING DISTRUST BETWEEN TWO GOVERNMENTS BECAUSE I HAD GONE AGAINST DIRECT ORDERS AND I WAS PUT IN PRISON FOR SIX LONG MONTHS. IT WAS A LIGHT SENTENCE UNDER THE CIRCUMSTANCES AND IT WAS A BIG WARNING TO THE OTHERS."

"WHAT HAPPENED TO STONEY?" SHE ASKED QUIETLY. "THERE WAS NO POINT IN INVOLVING HIM BECAUSE I DIND'N HAVE A WIFE AT HOME BUT HE DID."

CHAPTER 42

THE PERFECT MIX.

"He still does apparently only they've got a lot to work out." The same can't be said of you though can it Jordan? You don't want a wife said Rickie and the truth cut to the bone.

"I'm sorry you had you had to go to prison" she continued. "I can't possibly know what that experience was like but I do think what you and Stoney did for that girl was heroic.

"It's another reason I don't want either of you involved in the Taylor-family business so as of now the case on my missing grandfather is closed." "If that's what you've decided." "It is she said." "You sound tired Rickie so I'm going to let you stretch out in here while I bed down in the back."

"Please don't leave me" she blurted out before she realized how revealing those words sounded. "You said it could be really dangerous outside and I don't want to have to worry about you" "Then I won't go outside because I don't want you to start worrying about anything tonight." "Was that just his kindness talking? "Jordan?" "Yes?" he called back to her.

"Do you despise me very much?" As soon as the question was out she feared his answer. "I could ask you the same thing "How much do you despise me?" "I'm being serious please don't mock

ME." "I WOULDN'T DREAM OF IT" BECAUSE I'VE ALREADY EXPLAINED THAT I THINK WHAT YOU DID FOR THAT GIRL WAS HEROIC."

"I TOLD YOU AT THE BEGINNING OF THIS CONVERSATION THAT WHETHER IT WAS GEORGE TAYLOR OR GERHARDT VON HASE THAN HITLER'S MOTHER COULD BE BLAMED FOR GIVING BRITH TO A MONSTER. DO YOU BLAME HER RICKIE? "OF COURSE NOT SAID RICKIE."

"THEN YOU'VE ANSWERED YOUR OWN QUESTION. NO DOUBT YOUR PARENTS KEPT SILENT ALL THESE YEARS TO SPARE YOU. IT'S TOO BAD YOUR AUNT COULDN'T HAVE HANDLED THE BURDEN ALONE. THE THREE OF YOU WOULD HAVE BEEN SAVED POINTLESS AND NEEDLESS GRIEF.

"SO AS I SEE IT OUR COLLECTIVE DUTY AS HUMAN BEINGS LIES IN HELPING OUR FELLOW MAN BECAUSE PREVENTING GENOCIDE IS PART OF THAT SO CALLED DUTY.

"LONG BEFORE YOU LEARNED ABOUT YOU GRANDFATHER YOU CREATED CBH SO YOU SHOULD TAKE COMFORT IN THE KNOWLEDGE THAT YOU'VE BEEN PERFORMING ACTS OF COMPASSION AND RESCUE SINCE YOUR SO CALLED TENN YEARS. YOU CONSIDER YOUR MONEY TAINTED AND THERE'S ONLY ONE WAY TO CLEANSE IT AND THAT'S BY DOING WHAT YOU ARE DOING HELP OTHERS. YOU'RE A VERY RARE INDIVIDUAL FATHER DESILVA SAID TO RICKIE BECAUSE YOU CHOSE TO HELP STONEY AND ME WHICH IS TESTIMONY TO THE FACT THAT YOU'VE BEEN ON THE RIGHT TRACK ALL THIS TIME AND YOU DIDN'T EVEN KNOW IT.

"THE ONLY REAL SIN I SEE YOU COMMITTING IS THE INABILITY TO FORGIVE YOURSELF FOR SOMETHING THAT HAPPENED LONG BEFORE YOU WERE BORN AND COULDN'T POSSIBLY HAVE BEEN YOUR FAULT.

"NOT FORGIVING YOURSELF WILL THWART YOUR OWN PROGRESS AND CREATING SIN WHERE THERE WAS NONE." JORDAN WAS MAKING PERFECT SENSE AND HE ALWAYS DID. AS A MINISTER HE MUST BE A SOURCE OF COMFORT AND WISDOM TO SO MANY PEOPLE.

SHE COULD TELL THAT A HEALING HAD STARTED AND HER LOVE FOR THIS MAN WAS GROWING UNTILL SHE FELT READY TO BURST WITH IT. CLEARING HER THROAT SHE SAID "YOU ALWAYS KNOW THE RIGHT THING TO SAY. DO YOU HAVE ANY MORE WORDS TO MAKE THE HORRIBLE PICTURES IN MY MIND GO AWAY?"

"NO I'M AFRAID WE ALL LIVE WITH THOSE TWISTED THOUGHTS AND I SHOULD KNOW BECAUSE I'VE GOT MY OWN SET OF TWISTED THOUGHTS AND THEY HAUNT ME FROM TIME TO TIME."

"I KNOW" SHE WHISPERED. "MAYBE THOSE PICTURES AREN'T SUCH A BAD THING RICKIE. CERTAINLY THEY REMIND US EVERY SO OFFEN THAT WE MUSN'T WEAKEN IN THIS FIGHT FOR HUMAN RIGHTS."

SHE NODDED IN HER HEAD IN THE DARKNESS. "I'M SURE THE YAD VASHEM WAS CREATED FOR THAT VERY REASON." HER THOUGHTS HAD TURNED TO BERNARD AND TED AND AFTER THE EXPERIENCE WITH JORDAN SHE WAS CONVINCED THEY'D BEEN HEADED DOWN THE WRONG PATH WHERE THEIR GRANDFATHER WAS CONCERNED AND RICKIE WANTED TO SHARE WITH THEM EVERYTHING SHE'D LEARNED FROM JORDAN.

SHE EXPECIALLY WANTED TO REACH HER BROTHER WHO'D HAD BEEN SUFFERING UNTOLD GRIEF BECAUSE OF THAT GRIEF HE WAS HURTING DEBORAH.

JORDAN HAD SPOKEN THE TRUTH "NOT FORGIVING YOURSELF WILL THWART YOUR OWN PROGRESS AND

CREATING SIN WHERE THERE WAS NONE." RICKIE LONGED TO MAKE TED SEE WHAT JORDAN HAD HELPED HER SEE BUT UNTILL SHE COULD DO THAT BUT SHE WOULD CONCENTRATE ALL HER ENERGIES ON THE MAN SITTING NEXT TO HER AND THE ONE WHO HAD TRANSFORMED HER LIFE.

"JORDAN?" CAN I ASK YOU ONE MORE QUESTION BEFORE WE GO TO SLEEP?" "ASK AS MANY AS YOU LIKE" SAID JORDAN. "IS GUARANI LANGUAGE DIFFICULT TO LEARN?"

HE SHIFIED HIS WEIGHT AND IN THE PROCESS HE HAD TURNED MORE FULLY TOWARDS HER. "REPEAT AFTER ME 'MBA EICHAPA NEDEPYHARE?" SHE IMITATED HIM AS BEST SHE COULD. "EXCELLENT YOU JUST SAID GOOD EVENING HOW ARE YOU?" A SMILE BROKE OUT ON HER FACE. SO HOW DO I ANSWER "I'M FINE HOW ARE YOU?"

MAYBE IT WAS HER IMAGINATION BUT SHE THOUGHT HE MIGHT BE SMILING TOO. "CHEKO'E PORA HA NADE?" SHE REPEATED THE LINE SEVERAL TIMES THEN ASKED HIM TO PRACTICE BOTH PHRASES WITH HER UNTILL HE DECREED HER ACCENT AND INTONATION WAS PERFECT.

"THANK YOU NOW I'LL FEEL BETTER WHEN I GREET THE FAMILIES ON BORAD THE PLANE." "THEY'LL FEEL BETTER TOO KNOWNING YOU'VE MADE AN EFFORT TO COMMUNICATE IN THEIR LANGUAGE."

EVERYTHING HE SAID WARMED HER A LITTLE MORE. "JORDAN? FORGIVE ME I KNOW I WAS ONLY GOING TO ASK YOU ONE QUESTION BUT "WHAT ELSE HAVE I GOT TO DO?" "THE THING IS I KNOW YOU'RE HORRIBLY BUSY DOING PARISH WORK AND HELPING STONEY RUN THE AIR-CARGO BUSINESS AND OF COURSE THE RESCUE MISSIONS BUT I WAS WONDERING IF YOU COULD TEACH ME GUARANI? ONLY IN YOUR SPEAR TIME."

SHE FELT HIS CHEST RISE AND FALL AS HE HERD HER SAY THAT. "I'LL NEVER BE AS BUSY AS THE HEAD OF THE CBH." "YES WELL HER MIND WAS TEEMING WITH NEW IDEAS AND POSSIBILITIES AND I'M PLANNING TO DO SOMETHING ABOUT THAT SO I CAN HELP MARYJO NURTURE THESE FAMILIES BUT THAT'S IS ONLY IF NONE OF YOU MIND."

PLEASE DON'T MIND AND PLEASE SAY YES. "WE'D BE FOOLS TO TURN DOWN AN OFFER LIKE THAT. IF YOU CAN FIND THE TIME IN YOUR HECTIC SCHEDULE TO HELP OUT I'M SURE I CAN FIT YOU IN SOME LANGUAGE LESSONS TO ACCOMMODATE YOU."

THANK YOU MY DEAREST DARLING. I PLAN TO BE UNDERFOOT ALMOST EVERYDAY AND EVERYWHERE YOU TURN I'M GOING TO BE THERE AND MAYBE ONE DAY YOU'LL DECIDE YOU NEED A WIFE AFTER ALL BUT UNTILL THEN I'M GOING TO ENJOY THE NEXT BEST THING AND THAT'S YOUR COMPANY FOR AS LONG AS YOU'LL ALLOW IT.

"SINCE YOU'RE SO BUSY I ASSUME EVENINGS WILL PROBABLY BE BETTER FOR YOU AND MAYBE I CAN ARRANGE IT WITH MARY TO HELP IN THE AFTERNOONS AND THEN I COULD STAY ON AND STUDY WITH YOU AFTER WE EAT DINNER." "YOU'RE PUSHING IT RICKIE BUT ONLY IF IT'S CONVENIENT FOR YOU OF COURSE" HE SAID.

JUST SO HE DIDN'T THINK SHE WAS TRYING TO KEEP HIM ALL TO HERSELF SHE ADDED "MAYBE MARY COULD JOIN US SOMETIMES IF SHE WANTS TO UNLESS SHE ALREADY KNOWS THE BASICS."

RICKIE COULD HAVE SWORN HE WAS SMILING AGAIN. "MARY KNOWS A LOT OF THINGS BUT THE ONLY LANGUAGE SHE'S MASTERED IS SOUTH DAKOTAN."

"WELL I GUESS IT'S DIALECT ANYWAY" RICKIE SAID AS SHE REDLECTED BACK ON SOME HUMOROUS COMMENTS OF MARY'S AND STARTED TO LAUGH OUT LOUD.

"YOU SHOULD DO THAT MORE OFTEN" HE SAID WHEN THE LAUGHTER HAD SUBSIDED. I WANT TO DO IT MORE OFTEN BECAUSE IT MAKES ME MORE HAPPY AND YOU MAKE ME WANT TO SHOUT MY HAPPINESS TO THE WORLD.

"I HAVE ANOTHER IDEA" SHE BEGAN TO SAY. "I THOUGHT AS MUCH" HE SAID. "IT'S ABOUT STONEY ISN'T HE WONDERFUL." "HE IS" JORDAN SAID AND THE EMOTION IN JORDAN'S VOICE SPOKE CLEARLY ABOUT HIS SO CALLED FRIENDSHIP WITH THE OTHER MAN. "I GATHER HE'S BEEN A LITTLE TOO PROTECTIVE WHERE HIS EX-WIFE IS CONCERNED."

"THAT'S FOR SURE" SAID RICKIE AS SHE BIT HER LIP. "ACTUALLY MY IDEA HAS MORE TO DO WITH HIS EX-WIFE." "I'VE BEEN WORRIED ABOUT THEM FOR A LONG TIME BUT JUST MAYBE IF SHE DIDN'T FEEL SO LEFT OUT AND MAYBE IF SHE KIND OF INSINUATED HERSELF BACK INTO HIS LIFE AND WAS ALLOWED TO MAKE A CONTRIBUTION WHETHER HE LIKED IT OR NOT I WAS THINKING SHE COULD TAKE LESSONS TOO?" SAID JORDAN. "YOU MUST HAVE BEEN READING MY MIND RICKIE."

"I'M GLAD" SHE SAID AND SMILED UNABLE TO QUELL THE EXHILARATION SHE WAS FEELING. "IT WOULD FILL HER EVENINGS AND STONEY HANGING AROUND HERE WOULDN'T BE ABLE TO HELP HIMSELF."

"YOU'RE RIGHT ABOUT THAT" SHE SAID. "I WAS THINKING SOMETHING ELSE HE SAID "HAS SHE EVER TAKEN FLYING LESSONS?" "NOT THAT I KNOW OF BUT SOMETHING TELLS ME YOU'LL HAVE HER SIGNED UP WITH A FLIGHT INSTRUCTOR BEFORE STONEY KNOWS WHAT

HAD HIT HIM. I'D OFFER MY SERVICES BUT I WOULDN'T BE ABLE TO KEEP IT A SECRET."

FIRE SCORCHED HER CHEEKS WHEN SHE SAID "I KNOW I SOUND LIKE I'M GETTING CARRIED AWAY BUT IF THEY COULD SHARE SOMETHING THAT IMPORTANT HIS FEARS WOULD LESSEN BUT OF COURSE WHAT DO I KNOW? I COULD BE TOTALLY WRONG. DON'T MIND ME I'M FAMOUS AROUND THE OFFICE FOR GOING IN TEN DIRECTIONS AT ONCE."

"DON'T EVER APOLOGIZE" HE SCOLDED BUT SHE HEARD THE AFFECTION BEHIND IT. "THERE MUST BE THOUSANDS OF LUCKY SOULS WHO THANK GOD FOR THAT EVERYDAY AND IT'S NO LONGER A MYSTERY TO ME WHY CBH IS ALREADY A GOLBAL FORCE AND IT'S HEAD ISN'T EVEN IN HER THIRTIES YET."

"I'M ALMOST THERE JORDAN" SHE SAID WITH AN EXAGGERSTED SIGH. "WHEN I LEARN ENOUGH GUARNI I'LL FIND OUT IF THEY HAVE AN BIG EXPRESSION TO DESCRIBE A MAIDEN WHO'S LONG IN THE TOOTH."

HE BROKE INTO LAGUHTER AND IT MADE HIM SOUND LIKE A DIFFERENT PERSON. "WHERE DID YOU LEARN THAT?" FROM SOME ANCIENT APACHE WESTERN STARRING JIMMY STEWART?"

"I'M SURE I DON'T KNOW" SHE CHUCKLED BECAUSE HIS LAUGHTER WAS SO CONTAGIOUS. RICKIE COULDN'T BELIEVE SHE WAS SITTING IN A VERY SMALL VINTAGE TRUCK DEEP IN THE HEART OF CHACO SHARING ALMOST EVERYTHING TWO HUMANS COULD SHARE EVEN LAUGHTER AND THE SO CALLED HAPPINESS IRRADINTING HER SPIRIT FRIGHTENED HER AND SHE DIDN'T HAVE FAITH IT COULD LAST.

NOT WHEN SHE KNEW SHE HAD TO FACE TED AND BERNARD WHO WERE EXPECTING JORDAN TO RETURN

WITH NEWS OF THEIR GREAT GRANDFATHER. THE CAPTURE AND PUNISHMENT OF DERSTAND JORDAN'S REASONING TO BE WILLING TO LET IT GO?

"YOU'VE GONE ALL QUIET ON ME RRICKIE" HE SAID AS PATTED HIS THIGH AND THEN TURNED OFF THE FLASHLIGHT. "LIE DOWN HERE AND REST I'LL SLEEP AFTER I PICK UP STONEY WHICH ACCORDING TO MY WATCH HE SAID AS HE GLANCED AT IT WILL BE ABOUT FIVE HOURS FROM NOW." THEY'D BEEN TALKING THAT LONG? SHE HAD NO IDEA SO MUCH TIME HAD PASSED. IF SHE NEEDED PROOF THAT HIS EARLIER KISSES HAD ONLY BEEN PART OF AN ACT TO FLOOL THE SECURITY GUARD. THE INVITATION TO LAY HER HAND ON HIS LAP MIGHT HAVE BEEN EXTENDED TO A CHILD WHILE SHE KEPT VIGIL SHE WOULD PE PERFECTLY SAFE BUT SHE'D NEVER FELT LESS CHILDLIKE IN HER LIFE AS SHE MOVER A LITTLE CLOSER TO HIM AND RESTED HER HEAD ON HIS UPPER LEG. THE FIRM MUSCLED FLESH DROVE THAT POINT HOME AS NOTHING ELSE COULD BECAUSE JORDAN WAS SO BREATHTAKINGLY MALE.

SHE'S HAD HER SHARE OF BOYFRIENDS SOME MORE SERIOUS THAN OTHER BUT SHE'D NEVER KNOWN THIS KIND OF INTIMACY WITH A MAN AND IT MADE HER LONG TO TOUCH AND BE TOUCHED. WHAT THEY'D STARTED EARLIER HAD TURNED INTO AN ACHE AND JORDAN COULD RELIEVE IT.

HE'S NOT GOING TO DO ANYTHING RICKIE BECAUSE HE WAS PLAYING A ROLE EARLIER TO FOOL THAT HORRABLE MAN SO YOU BETTER MOVE BEFORE YOU MAKE A SERIOUS MISSTAKE.

"CAN'T YOU SLEEP?" "NO SHE SAID AS SHE SAT ALL THE WAY UP AND TURNED AWAY FROM HIM AND THEN SHE SAID TO HIM "WHY DON'T I KEEP A LOOKOUT WHILE YOU NAP FOR A LITTLE WHILE?"

"SHALL I GET IN THE BACK OF THE TRUCK?" "NO! I MEANT WOULD YOU LIKE TO JOIN ME IN THE BACK?" HE ASKED QUIETLY. "I DON'T THINK THAT WOULD BE A GOOD IDEA." "I'D PROTECT YOU" HE SAID. "I KNOW THAT BUT YOU'RE AFRAID I MIGHT START KISSING YOU AGAIN IS THAT IT?"

I'M NOT AFRAID I WANT YOU JORDAN AND AS WE DISCUSSED EARLIER I MAY BE A MINISTER BUT I'M A MAN FIRST AND I THOROUGHLY ENJOYED KISSING YOU FOR THE BENEFIT OF THAT LOWLIFE GUARDING THE SO CALLED SETTLEMENT I THOUGHT YOU ENJOYED IT TOO."

SHE STRUGGLED FOR HER BREATH AS SHE SAID "I DID AND AS LONG AS WE'RE BEING HONEST I'LL ADMIT TO WANTING TO KISS YOU AGAIN" SAID RICKIE.

THE AIR ELECTRIFIED AROUND THEM AND SHE COULDN'T MOVE OR SPEAK AND SO HE SAID TO RICKIE "DOSE IT SHOCK YOU THAT I WOULD HAVE BEEN THINKING ABOUT IT?" HIS VOICE SOUNDED SILKY. "IT SHOULDN'T HE SAID TO RICKIE AS SHE STIRRED RESTLESSLY.

"THE PROBLEM NOW IS THAT A FIRE'S BEEN LIT AND IT'S THE KIND THAT ISN'T GOING TO BURN OUT." HE HAD TOUCHED HER FACE AND RICKIE TREMBLED. "THAT MEANS ONLY ONE THING EITHER I GET IN THE BACK OF THE TRUCK ALONE OR I STAY UP HERE AND LET NATURE TAKE IT'S COURSE SO THE DECISION IS YOURS."

THOUGH JORDAN'S METHODS WERE EFFECTIVE HE DIDN'T ALWAYS OPERATE IN A CONVENTIONAL MANNER AND IN OFFERING HER A CHOICE WHETHER THEY WERE GOING TO SPEND THE REST OF THE NIGHT TOGETHER OR NOT HE'D JUST ERASED EVERY PRECONCEIVED NATION SHE'S HAD ABOUT CLERGYMEN AND HE DIDN'T PLAY FAIR.

YOU KNOW YOU WANT HIM TO STAY RICKIE BUT IF YOU TELL HIM THAT YOU'VE OPENED YOURSELF UP FOR HEARTACHE BECAUSE HE'S ALREADY INFORMED YOU HE'S NOT WILLING TO GET MARRIED.

RICKIE KNEW HERSELF TOO WELL BECAUSE OTHER WOMEN MIGHT BE WILLING TO ENJOY A NIGHT OF LOVEMAKING DESPITE THE LACK OF ANY PROMISES BUT SHE REFUSED TO DELUDE HERSELF.

FOR HER MAKING LOVE WOULD SET THE SEAL ON THE VOWS SHE'D ALREADY MADE IN HER HEART AND SHE WANTED HIM FOR HER HUSBAND NOTHING LESS THAN A LIFETIME COMMITMENT WOULD DO AND HE WOULD BE SHOCKED BY THE DEPTH OF HER FEELINGS.

MEN WERE DIFFERENT BECAUSE THEY COULD DESIRE A WOMEN WITHOUT ANY THOUGHT OF MARRIAGE AND JORDAN HAD ADMITTED THAT THAT HE DESIRED HER AND KNOWING THE KIND OF MAN HE WAS SHE WAS FAIRLY CERTAIN HE DIDN'T MAKE A HABIT OF THIS BUT SHE ALSO REALIZED THAT WHERE HE WAS CONCERNED PHYSICAL WANTING TO STOP SHORT OF A MARRIAGE AT LEAST IT HAD IN THE PAST.

MAYBE IF SHE KEPT INSINUATING HERSELF INTO HIS LIFE HE WOULD CHANGE HIS MIND AND REALIZED HE COULDN'T LIVE WITHOUT HER EITHER. THE NEXT THING SHE KNEW HE'D GOTTEN OUT OF THE TRUCK BUT BEFORE HE MOVE AROUND TO THE BACK HE SAID "YOU WERE WISE TO MAKE THE DECISION YOU DID BUT WHAT TROUBLES ME IS WHY I'M HAVING SUCH A DIFFICULT TIME ACCEPTING IT SO GOOD NIGHT RICKIE."

THE CLICK OF THE DRIVER'S SIDE DOOR HAD TO BE THE LONELIEST SOUND ON EARTH AND RICKIE HAD THE SINKING FEELING SHE'D MADE ANOTHER MISTAKE DO TO HER FEELINGS TOWARD JORDAN.

"THERE'S STONEY!" JORDAN GRIMACED BECAUSE THE SECOND RICKIE SAW HER PARTNER WALK INTO THE MIDDLE OF THE ROAD SHE LEANED OUT THE WINDOW AND STARTED WAVING HER HANDS. SHE DIDN'T HAVE TO ACT SO DAM HAPPY TO SEE HIM.

ONLY THOUGHT THE GREASTEST WILLPOWER HAD JORDAN MANAGED TO STAY AWAY FROM HER LAST NIGHT AND AS A RESULT HE'D SAT UP FOR THE REMAINING HOURS BATTLING THE NEEDS OF A BODY THAT CLAMORED FOR FULFILMENT.

TO HIS CHAGRIN RICKIE HAD FALLEN ASLEEP ON THE CAB SEAT WITHIN MINUTES OF HIS LEAVING HER AND THIS MORNING HE'D BEEN FORCED TO WAKE HER UP SO HE COULD DRIVE AND SHE'D STILL BEEN IN A DEEP SLEEP WHEN HE TRIED TO WAKE HER UP. SHE'D APPARENTLY HAD MANAGED TO FORGET WHATEVER FRUSTRATION SHE'D SUFFEERED.

"WELL LOOK WHO DECIDED TO DROP IN FOR BREAKFAST SORRY JORDAN IT'S ALL GONE. GOOD MORNING RICKIE." "GOOD MORNING WE DIDN'T MEAN TO BE LATE BUT WE WERE DATAINED BY A FLAT TIRE."

"IS THAT SO?" STONEY SENT JORDAN ONE OF THEIR PRIVATE EYE SIGNALS BUT FOR ONCE HE HAD ABSOLUTELY NOTHING TO ANSWER BACK. IT WAS RICKIE'S FAULT AS SOON AS SHE'D COME FULLY AWAKE THIS MORNING SHE'D STARTED CHATTERING AWAY AS IF LAST NIGHT'S EVENTS HAD NEVER TAKEN PLACE AND TO MAKE MATTERS WORSE SHE'D PREPARED THEIR CANNED BREAKFAST WITH A CHEERINESS THAT HAD PUT HIM IN THE FOULEST MOOD THAT MORNING.

"RICKIE'S TELLING THE TRUTH STONEY, WE WOULD HAVE BEEN HERE A LOT SOONER BUT ALONG THE WAY the left rear tire went bad and I had to put on the spare."

Stoney flashed him another look that questioned the veracity of his words. Jordan's hand curled into a fist because just about everything was getting to him this morning.

Before he exploded he needed to channel his energy in another direction because Stoney was jumping down from the cab and walking over to his partner. Stoney took one look at Jordan and his expression sobered. "You look like hell." "You don't look so dam chipper yourself." So at this point they were both speaking in whispers. "I have a good reason it's because no one's ever seen or heard of a George Hyde Taylor and the old priest who's been here at least froty years said he would have know if an Englishman was living here.

"He's not English" Jordan interrrupted. Stoney squinted at him and asked "Did Rickie say that?" Jordan nodded his head back and forth and said "I'll tell you about it later just so you know the search for her grandfather has been officially called off."

"Was that her idea?" "Yes it was her idea." "What the hell is going on around here?" "Like I said I'll explain everything to you later when we're alone."

He slapped Stoney on the shoulder and said "How did you sleep last night?" "Like a baby said Stoney." "Well aren't you the luckiest ace in the squadron" he retorted testily. "Now I won't have to suffer from a guilty conscience when I sleep

ALL THE WAY BACK TO FATHER DESILVA'S AND LEAVE THE DRIVING TO YOU."

STONEY STUDIED HIM CRITICALLY AS HE SAID "YOU KNOW WHAT YOUR PROBLEM IS? YOU HAVEN'T TOLD HER THE TRUTH YET AND IT'S EATING YOU ALIVE JORDAN."

"YOU'RE WRONG I TOLD HER EXACTLY HOW I SPENT TIME IN PRISON." WITH THAT HE WENT TO THE BACK OF THE TRUCK AND CLIMBED INSIDE TO UNTIE HIS BEDROLL.

STONEY FOLLOWED HIM AND THEY TALKED IN LOW VOICES THOUGH THE SLATS. GOOD FOR YOU YOU'RE MAKING PROGRESS BUT SHE STILL THINKS YOU'RE A MINISTER."

JORAN FIGURED THAT HER RESPECT FOR HIS SUPPOSED RELIGIOUS OFFICE WAS THE REASON SHE HADN'T STOPPED HIM FROM GETTING OUT OF THE TRUCK LAST NIGHT. IT WOULD HAVE BEEN A PERFECT OPPORTUNITY FOR HIM TO COME CLEAN BUT AFTER THE TRAUMA OF HER OWN LITTLE REVELATIONS AND THEN HIS AND HE DIDN'T WANT TO BURDEN HER WITH ANY MORE PAINFUL TRUTHS. THIS WAS ENOUGH FOR ONE NIGHT BECAUSE HE DIDN'T SHE COULD ABSORB ANY MORE.

"UNTILL YOU SPILL ALL YOUR GUTS THAT CONSCIENCE OF YOURS WON'T LET YOU HAVE A DECENT NIGHT'S SLEEP." DON'T YOU THINK I KNOW THAT STONEY? IT HAD BEEN BAD ENOUGH WORRYING THAT SHE WOULDN'T BE ABLE TO HANDLE THE REASON FOR HIS PRISON SENTENCE THOUGH SHE'D MADE HIM OUT TO BE SOME KIND OF HERO BECAUSE OF IT. WHICH HE RECALLED STONEY HAD ACTUALLY PREDICTED BUT WHEN SHE LEARNED THAT HE'D LET HER POUR OUT HER SOUL TO HIM AS IF HE HAD THE RIGHT TO LISTEN AND PROVIDE COUNSEL SHE WOULD WALK AWAY FROM HIM AND NEVER LOOK BACK.

"WAKE ME UP WHEN WE GET THERE." "RICKIE'S NOT GOING TO LIKE THIS ARRANGEMENT" AND SHE'S NOT THE ONLY ONE. AT THE MENTION OF HER NAME JORDAN MAND THE MISTAKE OF GLANCING THOUGH THE REAR WINDOW. HER HOT BLUE GAZE LOCKED WITH HIS FOR A HEART STOPPING MOMENT BEFORE SHE LOOKED AWAY. THERE GOES ANY CHANCE FOR SLEEP NOW. JORDAN FLUNG HIMSELF ON HIS BACK AND LET THE SUN'S RAYS BEAT DOWN ON HIM. IF THE GOAL OF THE CHACO WERE KIND MAYBE THE HEAT WOULD BAKE HER IMAGE FROM HIS CONSCIOUSNESS FOR A WHILE.

"RICKIE? WE NEED TO TALK BECAUSE THERE'S BEEN A CHANGE IN PLANS AND IT AFFECTS YOU." FROM THE WAY JORDAN'S VOICE SOUNDED SHE KNEW HE MEANT BUSINESS.

SHE WAS STARTLED BECAUSE OF HOW JORDAN'S VOICE HAD SOUNDED. SHE'D JUST SHUT HER DOOR AFTER VISITING FATHER DESILVA'S CHARMING LITTLE CHAPLE AND HADN'T SEEN JORDAN COMING.

THEY'D ONLY BEEN BACK A FEW HOURS AND UPON THEIR RETURN THE PRIEST HAD PREPARED LUNCH. WHILE THEY ATE HE'D GONE OVER THE DETAILS OF THE AIRLIFT WITH THEM. IT WAS SCHEDULED TO TAKE PLACE THE NEXT MORNING AT DAWN.

ONCE FATHER DESILVA HAD COVERED THE SALIENT POINTS RICKIE HAD ESCAPED TO THE SURGERY ROOM AND EXCEPT FOR A DESULTORY CONVERSATION IN FRONT OF OTHERS JORDAN HAD AVOIDED HER NICE COMPANY SINCE REMOVING HIMSELF FROM THE BACK OF THE TRUCK THIS MORNING. WITH TENSION THICKENING BETWEEN THEM SHE DIDN'T THINK IT WAS A GOOD IDEA TO BE IN THE SAME ROOM WITH HIM.

POOR STONEY SHE SAID TO HERSELF BECAUSE SHE REALIZED HE DIDN'T KNOW WHAT TO THINK OF THE situation let alone about her calling off the search but the gentleman that he was he hadn't pried into her business or asked uncomfortable questions.

In time she would tell him everything but not while they were still in Paraguay. She was the one who'd barged in uninvited on this rescue mission and because of her they'd been gone all of last night hunting for some trace of her grandfather with the false information she'd given them.

Full of remorse since she'd put their lives at unnecessary risk when their main reason for being here was to help the Ache Indians and she vowed to take a back seat for the rest of the trip.

At least Jordan was seeking her out right now and not the other way around but when she reached the door and opened it his questing green eyes made such an intimate sweep of her body she had to cling to the door handle for support.

At first glance she noticed his hair once again been tied back and he was wearing a clean navy t-shirt and jeans. The scent of soap was strong and there was no doubt he and Stoney had gone to the river for a bath and he looked so wonderful to her and then she lowered her eyes. "What's wrong?" he had asked Rickie and then she said "Can I come in?"

He nodded his head and stood aside. He entered mudging the door shut with his boot and with his hands on the side of his hips he said "One of Father DeSilva's contacts reached him over the raido as they said "There's been a problem at the other

END WHICH MEANS WERE MOVING UP THE TIME OF THE AIRLIFT SO WE'RE GOING TO FLY THEM OUT TONIGHT AND WE'LL BE TAKING THE TRUCK TO PICK THEM UP IN ABOUT TEN MINUTES"

HER ADRENALINE INSTANTLY STARTED TO KICK IN AS HE SAID "I'LL BE READY WHENEVER YOU SAY." HE RUBBED HIS CHEST ABSENTLY AND TOLD RICKIE "YOU'RE NOT GOING WITH US." SHE STARED AT HIM AND ASKED HIM "WHY NOT?" HE SAID BACK TO HER "THERE'S ONLY ROOM FOR THREE IN THE CAB AND WE NEED THE BACK OF THE TRUCK FOR THE FAMILIES." SHE SAID "BUT SURELY THERE'S ENOUGH SPACE FOR ONE MORE!" "YOU DON'T UNDERSTAND" HE SAID AS HIS EXPRESSION HAD HARDENED GIVING HIM A DANGEROUS FORBIDDING LOOK. "EACH FAMILY MEMBER WILL BE HERE SOON BUT THEY WILL BE ARRIVING IN A BARREL WHICH WE'LL PLACE IN THE BACK OF THE TRUCK AND WE WON'T BE ABLE TO OPEN THEM UNTILL WE'RE ON BOARD THE PLANE."

"A BARREL?" "YES HE SAID THERE CALLED PETITGRAIN OIL BARRELS LARGE ENOUGH TO HOLD A SMALL MAN. WE'RE DRIVING TO A POINT UPSTREAM WHERE WE'LL WAIT WHILE THE BARRELS ARE FLOATED ACROSS THEN WE'LL LOAD THEM ON TO THE BACK OF THE TRUCK."

HER HANDS FLEW TO HER MOUTH JUST BEFORE SHE SAID "YOU MEAN THE CHILDREN AND BABIES ARE IN THEM TOO?" HIS EYES HAD DARKENED AS HE SAID "YES THEY'VE BEEN TRAVELING LIKE THAT FOR MORE THEN A DAY AND ONE OF THE CHILDREN IS VERY ILL SO THAT'S WHY WE ARE SPEEDING THINGS UP." TEARS STUNG HER EYES AS SHE SAID "DEAR GOD."

"YOUR SERVICES ARE GOING TO BE SORELY NEEDED ONCE EVERYONE'S ON BORAD SO GO GET PACKED AND I'LL DRIVE YOU TO THE PLANE. YOU WILL BE SAFE INSIDE AND I DON'T ANTICIPATE ANY PROBLEMS BUT I DO IMAGINE YOU'LL FEEL BETTER IF YOUR GUN IS HANDY."

"I COULDN'T SIT ON ONE OF YOUR LAPS IN THE TRUCK?" SHE HEARD A SHARP INTAKE OF BREATH AND THEN SHE HEARD THE WORD "NO."

HE'D WARNED HER THIS MERCY FLIGHT WOULD BE DANGEROUS AND THAT MIGHT NOT MAKE IT BACK. SHE'D TOLD HIM SHE DIDN'T CARE AND WANT TO BE PART OF THIS MISSION. I'LL DO WHATEVER YOU ASK SAID RICKIE.

IT APPEARED THE TIME HAD COME FOR HER TO PROVE THOSE WORDS. "I'LL BE READY IN FIVE MINUTES" SAID RICKIE. HER PACK STOOD IN THE CORNER SO SHE RAN AND GOT IT. "RICKIE?" HE SAID URGENTLY. SHE WHIRLED AROUND AND HE HEART WAS POUNDING. "YOU'LL BE SAFER ON THE PLANE." HE'D ALREADY SAID THAT ONCE IT WAS A WARNING.

SOMETHING HAD GONE WRONG AND SHE COULD FEEL IT. DIDN'T HE REALIZE IT WAS HIS SAFETY SHE WORRIED ABOUT? WHAT IF SHE NEVER SAW HIM AGAIN? OR WHAT IF THIS WAS THE END OF EVERYTHING?

"I WISH I'D ASKED YOU TO STAY WITH ME LAST NIGHT." THERE WAS A LONG SILENCE BEFORE HE WHISPERED "WHY DIDN'T YOU?" TAKING HER COURAGE INTO HER OWN HANDS SHE SAID "BECAUSE ONE NIGHT IN YOUR ARMS WOULDN'T HAD BEEN ENOUGH FOR ME BECAUSE I'M IN LOVE WITH YOU" SAID RICKIE. HER VOICE THROBBED WITH EMOTION. "I KNEW I WOULDN'T BE ABLE TO HOLD BACK THE TRUTH."

"RICKIE PLEASE DON'T BE EMBARRASSED BECAUSE YOU CAN THINK OF THIS AS A CONFESSION FROM YOUR PARISHONERS. JORDAN YOU MAD IT CLEAR FROM THE BEGINNING THAT YOU HAVE NO PLANS TO GET MARRIED SAID RICKIE.

"MY PROBLEM IS I WANT TO BE YOUR WIFE SAID RICKIE" AND ANYTHING LESS WOULDN'T BE ENOUGH FOR ME BECAUSE AS YOU SAID EARLIER WE MAY NOT MAKE IT OUT OF THIS ALIVE. IF WE DON'T I JUST WANT YOU TO KNOW THAT THE TIME I'VE SPENT WITH YOU HAS BROUGHT ME MORE HAPPINESS THAN I EVER THOUGHT POSSIBLE."

NOW THAT SHE'D TOLD HIM THE TRUTH SHE COULDN'T SEEM TO STOP. "THERE'VE BEEN A NUMBER OF PROFOUND CHANGES IN MY LIFE RECENTLY AND THE IMPORTANT ONE BEGAN THE DAY I DISCOVERED YOU PROWLING AROUND MY OFFICE AND THEN I REALIZED NOW THAT ALTHOUGH I'VE EXISTED FOR TWENT'Y-SEVEN YEARS AND I NEVER REALLY LIVED UNTILL I MET YOU. "THANK YOU FOR THAT JORDAN. "SHE THEN BLURTED OUT SOMETHING WHEN SHE STARTED TO SAY SOMETHING IN RESPONSE TO WHAT JORDAN HAD SAID. "I DON'T WANT YOUR COMPASSION OR PITY I WANT YOU TO GO SO I CAN CHANGE AND GET PACKED AND I'LL MEET YOU AT THE TRUCK IN A FEW MINUTES."

CHAPTER 43

LOTS OF THINGS TO DO.

JORDAN STOOD OUTSIDE THE CLOSED OF THE SURGERY ROOM.

HE'D JUST HEARD THE WORDS HE'D NEVER THOUGHT TO HEAR FROM THE ONE WOMEN WHO MEANT EVERYTHING TO HIM BUT SHE'D SAID THOSE WORDS TO THE MAN SHE KNEW AS THE REVERND BROWNING.

IF YOU TELL HER THE TRUTH DO YOU THINK SHE WILL FEEL THE SAME WAY ABOUT YOU? A TREMOR OF FEAR SHOOK HIS POWERFUL FRAME AND HIS HAPPINESS STOOD BEFORE HIM. ALL HE HAD TO DO WAS REACH OUT AND TAKE IT BUT NOW THAT HE'D HEARD ALL OF HER TRUTH SHE DESERVED ALL OF HIS IN RETURN.

IT WOULD BE SO EASY TO STAY SILENT AND JUST TAKE HER IN HIS ARMS BUT SHE WOULD HAVE COME TO HIM WITH THE SAME PASSION SHE'D SHOWN HIM LAST NIGHT.

THE LIE WILL DESTROY YOU BROWNING AND THE ONLY WAY YOU'LL EVER EXPERIENCE JOY WITH THIS WOMEN IS TO END THE CHARADE AND SEE IF SHE ACCEPTS YOU WITH ALL YOUR FLAWS.

AS THE BATTLE RAGED INSIDE HIM HE MADE A VOW THAT IF THEIR MISSION WAS SUCCESFUL AND THEY GOT BACK TO NEW YORK IN SAFETY HE WOULD TELL RICKE EVERYTHING AND SUFFER THE SO CALLED CONSEQUENCES.

"JORDAN?" STONEY CALLED OUT JERKING HIM FROM HIS THOUGHTS. "IS RICKIE COMING? WE BETTER MAKE SOME TRACKS TO THE PLANE." "SHE'LL BE OUT IN A MINUTE."

"HOW DID SHE HANDLE THE NEWS THAT'S SHE'S NOT GOING WITH US?" "LIKE SHE HANDLES EVERYTHING ELSE." "HAVE YOU CONFESSED LET?" "NO NOT LET BUT SOON." "YOU'RE A FOOL TO WAIT." I DON'T HAVE RICKIE'S COURAGE. FATHER DESILVA STEPPED OUT OF THE CHAPEL AND THEN THE THREE OF THEM MADE THEIR WAY TO THE TRUCK.

RICKIE EMERGED FROM THE SURGERY ROOM A FEW MINUTES LATER HURRYING TOWARDS THE TRUCK WEARING A CLEAN PAIR OF KHAKI PANTS AND A SHIRT.

FATHER DESILVA AND JORDAN WERE IN THE BACK AVOIDING JORDAN'S PROBING EYES SHE HANDED HIM HER BACKPACK THEN WALKED TO THE FRONT AND GO IN THE PASSENGER SIDE OF THE TRUCK. STONEY HAD ALREADY STARTED THE ENGINE AND THEY WERE OFF. THE AFTERNOON NOW HAD THE AIR OF A FANTASTIC DREAM.

"AS SOON AS WE'RE ON BOARD I WANT TO SHOW YOU HOW TO WORK THE RAIDO" STONEY SAID. "IF THE WORST HAPPENED AND WE DIDN'T GET BACK YOU'D NEED TO KNOW OUR COORDINATES SO SOMEONE COULD COME RESCUE YOU."

HER HEAD WAS BOWED WHEN SHE SAID "FIRST JORDAN AND NOW YOU. I REFUSE TO BELIEVE THAT ANYTHING BAD'S GOING TO HAPPEN."

"YOU KEEP THINKING THAT WAY AND WE'RE ALL HOME FREE." "IF IT ALL GOSE WELL HOW LONG DO YOU THINK IT'LL BE BEFORE YOU'RE BACK?"

"FOR HOURS MORE OR LESS." THE NORMALLY GREGARIOUS STONEY REMAINED UNNATURALLY QUIET AS THEY DROVE BACK TO THE PLANE. IT LOOKED EXACTLY THE WAY THEY'D LEFT IT GLEAMING SILVER IN THE LATE AFTERNOON SUN AND THE REASSURING SIGHT LIFTED RICKIE'S SPIRITS.

EVERYONE WENT ON BOARD AND RICKIE FOLLOWED STONEY TO THE COCKPIT WHERE HE GAVE HER A QUICK RAIDO LESSON AND WROTE DOWN THE PLANE'S COORDINATES WHILE JORDAN DID A COUNTDOWN CHECK IN PREPARATION FOR THEIR DEPARTURE SHE TRIED HARD TO CONCENTRATE ON STONEY'S INSTRUCTIONS.

FINALLY SATISFILED THAT SHE'D REMEMBERED THEM SHE LEFT THE TWO MEN IN THE COCKPIT AND WENT TO THE CABIN TO SAY GOODBYE TO FATHER DESILVA.

WHEN SHE COULDN'T SEE HIM SHE CLIMBED OUT OF THE PLANE AND FOUND HIM BEHIND THE STEERING WHEEL OF THE TRUCK. "THANK YOU FATHER FOR EVERYTHING AND GOOD LUCK."

THE PRIEST SMILED WARMLY AND SAID "YOU ARE VERY BRAVE AND A VERY GOOD WOMEN AND GOD WILL KEEP YOU SAFE AND TELL THE OTHERS WE MUST LEAVE NOW."

SWALLOWING THE LUMP IN HER THROAT RICKIE NODDED HER HEAD THEN HURRIED TO BOARD THE PLANE. THE TWO MEN WERE WALKING DOWN THE AISLE TOWARD HER IN ORDER TO LET THEM PASS SHE BACKED INTO THE CARGO HOLD.

STONEY WENT BY FIRST AND HER HEART THUBBED PAINFULLY AS SHE WAITED FOR JORDAN HE WAS PAUSED THE THRESHOLD.

"WHEN WE COME BACK I'LL TURN THE FLASHLIGHT ON AND OFF FIVE TIMES TO SIGNAL YOU AND DON'T FORGET TO LOCK THE DOOR BEHIND US WHEN WE GO I'LL SHOW YOU HOW."

"THIS REMINDS ME OF PLAYING COPS AND ROBBERS WHEN WE WERE LITTLE." SHE INTERJECTED A LIGHT NOTE TO COUNTER HER FEAR AS THEY REACHED THE AIR PLANE DOOR AND GAVE THE FINAL INSTRUCTIONS.

"RICKIE?" HE TURNED TOWARD HER UNEXPECTEDLY HIS EXPRESSION SOLEMN. "I WOULDN'T LEAVE YOU IF THERE WAS ANY OTHER WAY." "I KNOW" SHE SAID AS HER VOICE QUAVERED DESPITE HERSELF. WITH A MUFFLED SOUND HE LOWERED HIS HEAD AND COVERED HER MOUTH WITH A SWIFT HARD KISS BEFORE HE DISAPPEARED FROM THE PLANE.

SHAKEN BY HIS PASSION AND THE FEEL OF HIS LIPS ON HERS SHE DAZEDLY LOCKED THE DOOR HE HAD CLOSED THEN RAN TO THE NEAREST WINDOW TO WATCH THEM DRIVE OFF AND IT WASN'T LOG BEFORE THEY WERE OUT OF SIGHT.

SHE THOUGHT THE NEXT FOUR HOURS OF WAITING WAS THE HARDEST THING SHE'D EVER DONE IN HER LIFE. THE POTENT MEMORY OF JORDAN'S KISS STILL CLUNG TO HER LIPS AND IT WAS THE ONLY THING THAT HELPED HER GET THROUGH THE WORST OF IT.

THE TIME STRETCHED TO FIVE HOURS THEN SIX AND THE OUTSIDE WORLD HAD GONE COMPLETELY BLACK AND THAT WAS WHEN SHE BEGAN TO BE REALLY AFRAID FOR THEM AND ULTIMATELY FOR HERSELF AS WELL AND IT WASN'T THE ANIMAL NOISES PIERCING THE NIGHT THAT FRIGHTENED HER AS MUCH AS THE IDEA OF HUMAN EVIL SKULKING ABOUT IN THE DARKNESS.

SHE PRESSED HER FOREHEAD TO THE WINDOW AND WATCHED FOR ANY SIGN OF THEM BUT BY NOW HER HEART WAS POUNDING SO LOUDLY IN HER EARS SHE COULD HEAR NOTHING ELSE.

ANOTHER TEN MINUTES WENT BY AND SUDDENLY SHE SAW SOMETHING OUT THERE IN THE DISTANCE THAT MADE LITTLE STREAKS OF LIGHT AND THEY LOOKED ALMOST LIKE FIREFLIES AND IT HAPPENED AGAIN AND AGAIN SOMETHING WAS COMING.

HER MOUTH WENT DRY AND SHE THEN REACHED FOR A GUN.! THE SO CALLED STREAKS CAME CLOSER AND CLOSER UNTILL SHE RECOGNIZED THEM AS THE HEADLIGHTS OF STONEY'S TRUCK AND SHE SAID "PLEASE LET IT BE THEM."

THE PERSPIRATION BROKE OUT ON HER FOREHEAD WHILE SHE WAITED FOR JORDAN'S SIGNAL AND WHEN SHE THE FIVE FLASHES APPEARED SHE CRIED OUT FOR JOY WHILE SHE WAS PUTTING HER GUN BACK IN HOLSTER ABOVE THE SEAT AND REACHED TO THE REAR DOOR OF THE PLANE WITH HER OWN FLASHLIGHT AND SO SHE OPEN IT AND STEPPED INSIDE.

"RICKIE?" JORDAN'S REASSURINGLY STRONG VOICE CALLED TO HER FROM THE TRUCK "I'M HERE." "THAT'S ALL I NEEDED TO KNOW." HIS VOICE SOUNDED GRUFF WITH EMOTION AND IT FILLED HER BODY WITH WARMTH.

"WE'VE GOT PRECIOUS CARGO COMING ABOARD" STONEY SAID. "HOW CAN I HELP?" "BE READY TO TAKE CARE OF THE BABY BECAUSE HIS MOTHER'S MILK STOPPED. THE IFANT'S EIGHT MONTHS OLD AND GETS DEHYDRATED SO TRY TO FIGURE OUT A WAY TO FEED HIM THAT JUICE YOU BROUGHT."

"IF I HAD A RUBBER GLOVE FROM SURGERY I COULD PUT A HOLE IN ONE FINGER AND LET HIM DRINK THAT WAY." "GREAT IDEA RICKIE" STONEY PRAISED HER. "I'LL BRING SOME WITH ME AFTER I RUN FATHER DESILVA BACK." THE NEXT FIVE MINUTES PASSED IN A BLUR AS THE YOUNGER MEN CAREFULLY LIFTED THE HUGE YELLOW-ORANGE BARRELS FROM THE TRUCK INTO THE CARGO HOLD AND THERE ARE EIGHT IN ALL.

IT WAS A PAINSTAKING PROCESS BECAUSE AS SOON AS ONE WAS BROUGHT IN THEY WENT FOR ANOTHER WHILE THE PRIEST USED A TOOL TO PRY OPEN THE LIDS AND RICKIE COULD ONLY MARVEL AS THE BROWN FACES OF TWO ACHE FAMILIES WERE EVENTUALLY REVEALED. THEY STOOD ALMOST AHEAD SHORTER THEN THEIR CAUCASIAN COUNTERPARTS AND WERE DRESSED IN MODERN CLOTHES NO DOUBT GIVEN THEM BY THE UNDERGROUND.

ALTOGETHER THEY FORMED A GROUP OF NINE SO THAT'S TWO SETS OF PARENTS FOUR GIRLS AND THE BABY BOY EXCEPT FOR THE EIGHT-MONTH OLD WHOSE SICK WHIMPERS SPOKE VOLUMES AND NO ONE SAID A WORD.

DOCILE WITH STOICAL EXPRESSIONS THAT SHOWED NOTHING OF THEIR FEELINGS THEY ALLOWED STONEY AND JORDAN TO LIFT THEM FROM THEIR CLAUSTROPHOBIC PRISONS AND HELP THEM TO VARIOUS SEATS WHERE THEY WERE STRAPPED IN AND THROUGHOUT THE EXHUSTING LITTLE PROCESS THE THREE MEN SPOKE GUARANI IN TONES REASSURING THEM AND AS RICKIE DREW DOWN A BLANKET FOR EACH OF THEM AND SPREAD IT OVER HIM OR HER SHE ALSO TRIED TO FIGHT BACK HER TEARS AND IMAGINING THEIR FRIGHT AND THE SITUATION MUST SEEM BOTH SO TERRIFYING AND BIZARRE TO THEM AND THEY'D ALSO HAD NO EXPERIENCE ABOUT MODERN TECHNOLOGY.

THEY'D NEVEN BEEN ON A AIRPLANE AND THEY WERE LEAVING THEIR FRIENDS AND THE ONLY HOME THEY'D EVER KNOWN BEHIND BECAUSE THEY WOULD NEVER COME BACK BUT YET THEY WERE WILLING TO DO ALL THIS TO SURVIVE AND TO ENSURE THE SURVIVAL OF THEIR CHILDREN.

RICKIE WAS VERY SURPRISED BY THEIR FAITH AND COURAGE THAT SHE WENT TO HELP THE ADORABLE LITTLE DARK-HEADED CHILD WHO DIDN'T LOOK OLDER THEN SIX MONTHS BUT THE MOTHER CLUNG TO HER INFANT OBVIOUSLY AFRAID TO GIVE HIM UP.

REMEMBERING WHAT JORDAN HAD TAUGHT HER RICKIE GREETED THE WOMAN IN GUARANI AND IT WAS FAR FROM PERFECT BUT RICKIE SAW A GIMMER OF SOMETHING STIR IN THE WOMAN'S BROWN-BLACK EYES BEFORE SHE ANSWERED.

ENCOURAGED RICKIE REACHED FOR A BOTTLE OF JUICE OPENED IT AND URGED THE MOTHER TO DRINK THE JUICE THEN SHE MOTIONED TO THE BABY AND AT THIS POINT JORDAN DREW UP ALONGSIDE HER AND SPOKE TO THE WOMAN IN GUARANI.

IN ASIDE TO RICKIE HE SAID "I EXPLAINED WE'D GET HER SOMETHING SO SHE COULD FEED HER BABY AND I ALSO TOLD HER TO DRINK THE JUICE YOU'VE GIVEN HER IT'S ALL YOU CAN DO FOR HER RIGHT NOW."

RICKIE NODDED HER HEAD AND MOVED ON TO THE THREE OLDER GIRLS WHO'D BEEN PLACED ACROSS THE AISLE FROM EACH OTHER AND THEY COULD BE ANYWHERE FROM EIGHT TO THIRTEEN YEARS OLD. THEY STARED AT HER AS IF SHE WERE AN APPARITION SO JORDAN OPENED A BOTTLE OF JUICE AND GRANOLA BARS FOR EACH OF THEM TO EAT AND DRINK.

"THEY DON'T SEE MANY PEOPLE WITH BLUE EYES AND BLOND HAIR LIKE THE COLOR OF THE SUN" HE WHISPERED IN HER EAR. "YOU WON'T SEEM REAL TO THEM UNTILL THEY'VE BEEN AROUND OTHER BLONDES AND EVEN SO I'VE NEVER SEEN A MANE LIKE YOURS IT'S MORE WHITE-GOLD THAN BLOND SO THEY CAN BE FOREGIVEN FOR STARING."

EVERYTHING HE SAID REDUCED HER TO TREMBLING AND SHE HAD CROUCHED DOWN AND GREETED EACH OF THE GIRLS IN GUARANI AND THEY GREETED HER BACK WITH TENSE STARES AND BRIEF NODS AND MORE THEN SHE WOULD HAVE EXPECTED WHILE THEY CHEWED THE STRANGED FOOD THAT HAD.

SHE MOVED ON TO THE OTHER WOMEN WHO SAT ACROSS FROM HER HUSBAND AND THEY BOTH DRINKING JUICE. THE MAN NODDED TO HER AND GREETED HER IN GUARANI BEFORE SHE COULD GOT THE CHANCE TO SAY ANYTHING. CHARMED BY THE GESTURE SHE ANSWERED HIM AND THEN HE SAID SOMETHING SHE DIDN'T RECOGNIZE JORDAN TRANSLATED.

"HE THANKED YOU FOR TAKING CARE OF THEM AND THE OTHER COUPLE WITH THEIR CHILDREN ARE HIS BROTHER AND SISTER-IN-LAW SO TELL HIM IT'S A PRIVILEGE."

RICKIE'S EYES MET JORDAN'S IN A LON UNSMILING LOOK AND SHE WOULD HAVE LOVED TO KNOW HIS THOUGHTS BEFORE HE FINALLY TRANSLATED HER REMARK.

"MS. TAYLOR?" THE PRIEST SPOKE UP BEHIND HER SO RICKIE WHIRLED AROUND TO LISTEN TO WHAT THE PRIEST HAD TO SAY. "I TRUST WE WILL MEET AGAIN AND IT'S AN HONOR TO HAVE MET YOU." "THE HONOR IS ALL MINE SAID RICKIE AND TAKE CARE FATHER DESILVA."

HE MADE THE SIGN OF THE CROSS BLESSING EVERYONE THEN HAD FOLLOWED STONEY FROM THE CABIN. "COME WITH ME RICKIE" SAID JORDAN YOU NEED NO URGING TO ACCOMPANY HIM TO THE COCKPIT WHERE HE STRAPPED HIMSELF IN BECAUSE WE NEED TO PREPARE THEM FOR TAKEOFF BUT YOU'RE THE ONLY ONE THEY'LL LOOK TO FOR THE REASSURANCE ONCE WE LEAVE THE GROUND."

"I'LL DO EVERYTHING I CAN." "YOU THINK I DON'T KNOW THAT?" HIS VOICE WAS HUSKY SOUNDING WHEN HE SAID THAT. "I THINK WHAT YOU'RE DOING FOR THESE PEOPLE IS GREAT BUT SHE COULDN'T GET THE REST OF THE WORDS OUT OF HER MOUTH."

"I DON'T KNOW" HE SAID AS HIS VOICE SIGHED DEEPLY. "I HOPE IT'S THE RIGHT THING BECAUSE I'M NOT SO SURE THAT TAKING THEM AWAY ISN'T GOING TO DO A DIFFERENT KIND OF HARM."

WITHOUT CONSCIOUS THOUGHT SHE PUT HER HAND ON HIS BROAD SHOULDER ABSORBING HIS STRENGTH. "YOU GAVE THEM A CHOICE DIDN'T YOU?" "YOU THINK I DON'T KNOW THAT?" HE SAID AS HIS VOICE SOUNDED HUSKY.

"MAYBE YOU'RE FEELING DOUBTFUL BECAUSE YOU'RE NOT A PARENT. THOSE COUPLES BACK THERE DON'T WANT WHAT YOU SAW WITH THAT YOUNG WOMEN TO HAPPEN TO THEIR DAUGHTERS. I NEVER BEEN A MOTHER BUT I'VE HEARD STORIES OF WOMEN WHO ENTER BURNING BUILDINGS AND ICY RIVERS TO SAVE THEIR CHILDREN SO A RIDE ON AN AIRPLAINE COULDN'T BE ANY WORSE COULD IT? OR STARING A STRANGE NEW LIFE WHEN YOU'RE DOOING IT FOR THE CHILDREN?"

SHE FELT A STRONG WARM HAND SLIDE ON TOP OF HERS AS SHE HEARD JORDAN SAY "THANK YOU FOR REMINDING ME WHAT THIS IS ALL ABOUT BECAUSE YOU

HAVE AN UNCANNY ABILITY TO BE IN THE RIGHT PLACE AT THE RIGHT TIME AND YOU KNOW EXACTLY WHAT TO SAY."

RICKIE HAD RECEIVED MANY ACCOLADES FROM HUNDREDS OF PEOPLE BUT NONE HAD EVER TOUCHED HER AS MUCH AS IT DID JORDAN SO BEFORE SHE MADE A TOTAL FOOL OF HERSELF AND EMBARRASSED HIM AGAIN SHE RELUCTANTLY PULLED HER HAND AWAY FROM HIS AND HAD HURRIED BACK TO THE CABIN AND STONEY WOULD MET HER THERE IN THE AISLE BACK AT THE CABIN AS SOON AS HE GOT DONE ON THE PLANE.

"I'VE SHOWN THEM WHERE TO FIND THE BATHROOM BECAUSE THEY KNOW WE WILL BE MAKING THREE STOPS FOR FUEL AND BYOND THAT POINT THEY'RE IN YOUR CARE RICKIE." HE HANDED HER THE RUBBER GLOVES AND SAID "WE'LL BE LEAVEING IN A COUPLE OF MINUTES."

"I'LL GO AND FIX THESE UP." SHE RACED TO THE HOLD AND RUMMAGED IN HER BACKPACK FOR HER COSMETIC BAG AND WHEN SHE FOUND THE CUTICLE SCISSORS SHE RETURNED TO THE CABIN AND GOT ANOTHER LITTL BOTTLE OF JUICE.

WITH UNCOMPREHENDING EYES THE MOTHER HOLDING THE BABY WATCHED RICKIE AS SHE POURED A LITTLE OF THE LIQUID INTO ONE OF OF THE FINGERS THEN CUT A TINY HOLE IN THE TIP AND DURING THIS PROCEDURE THE WOMEN'S HUSBAND GAVE RICKIE A BLANK STARE AS WELL AS THE OTHER MOTHERS AND FATHERS DID.

ON A BURST OF INSPIRATION SHE HELD THE GLOVE ABOVE HER AND SQUEEZED A LITTLE OF THE FLUID INTO HER OWN MOUTH. UNDERSTANDING DAWNED THE WOMEN OFFERED HER A TIMID SMILE AND LIFTED HER HAND TO TAKE THE GLOVE.

IT TOOK SEVERAL TRIES AND MISHAPS WHICH RESULTED IN JUICE RUNNING ONTO THE BABY'S FACE BUT EVENTUALLY THE MOTHER FIGURED OUT HOW TO GIVE HER CHILD THE MUCH-NEEDED FLUID.

PLEASED THAT THIS WOMEN COULD FINALLY DO SOMETHING TO NOURISH HER FEVERISH BABY RICKIE FLICKED ON THE LIGHT SWITCHES OVER EACH SEAT THEN HURRIED TO SIT DOWN AND STRAP HERSELF IN WITH THE SEATBELT BECAUSE THE FIRST ENGINE BEEN FIRED UP AND THEN THE SECOND WAS TURNING OVER AND THE VIBRATIONS ROCKED THE BODY OF THE PLANE.

THOUGH THE RIDE OVER THE GRASS PROVED FOR A BUMPY LIFTOFF WHICH HAD GOTTEN SMOOTHER AS WE WENT ALONG. STILL RICKIE HAD REALIZED AGAIN THIS HAD TO BE A FRIGHTENING EXPERIENCE FOR THESE ACHE FAMILIES.

SHE LISTENED OVER THE NOISE OF THE PLANE AS IT CLIMBED HIGHER BUT TO HER SURPRISE NONE OF THEM MADE A SOUND NOT EVEN THE GIRLS. SHE HAD NOTHING BUT ADMIRATION FOR THEIR COURAGE.

AS SOON AS THEY REACHED CRUISING ALTITUDE RICKIE GOT OUT OF HER SEAT AND WALKED AROUND TO SEE IF EVERYONE WAS ALL RIGHT. "DAZED" MIGHT BE THE WORD TO DESCRIBE THEIR REACTIONS AND IN A EFFORT TO DIVERT THEIR ATTENTION SHE GRABBED SOME FRUIT ROLL-UPS FROM THE RACKS AND HANDED THEM AROUND BUT THE PARENTS REFUSED BUT THE GRILS HESITANTLY ACCEPTED THEM BECAUSE THEY WERE HUNGRY.

RICKIE SHOWED THEM HOW TO UNWRAP THE CELLOPHANE AND THE FRUITY ODOR ENTICED THEM ENOUGH TO TAKE A BITE OF THE STRAWBERRY LEATHER AND IN A FEW SECONDS THEY REWARDED RICKIE WITH

HUGE SMILES THAT TRANSFORMED THEIR PRETTY FACES. THEIR THIN BROWN LEGS SWUNG BACK AND FORTH DRAWING HER ATTENTION TO THE CHILDREN'S FEET WHICH THEY HAD NO SHOES ON. IMMEDIATELY RICKIE BEGAN MAKING A LIST OF CLOTHES THEY WOULD REQUIRE TRYING TO GUESS THEIR SIZES. SHE HAD ORGANIZED SUB FOR SANTA PROJECTS EVERY CHRISTMAS BUT THIS WOULD BE THE FIRST ONE SHE'D DONE IN THE MIDDLE OF JUNE. THEY NEEDED EVERYTHING AND SHE WAS GOING TO GIVE IT TO THEM!

ONE OF THE THINGS SHE'D DO WHEN THEY REACHED NEW YORK CITY WAS CALL HER PEOPLE AT THE CBH IN BUENOS AIRES AND LIMA THROUGH THEIR SOURCES WAS WANTED THEM TO PUT OUT A SEARCH FOR ANYONE WHO SPOKE BOTH GUARANI AND ENGLISH.

JORDAN AND STONEY COULDN'T BE ON THE PREMISES DAY AND NIGHT TO TRANSLATE BECAUSE NOT ONLY DID STONEY HAVE A AIR-CARGO BUSINESS TO RUN BUT THE REVEREND'S PARISH DUTIES PROBABLY KEPT HIM AWAY UNTILL EVENING. THE SOLUTION WAS TO HIRE SOME NATIVE TEACHERS MAYBE A HUSBAND AND WHIF TEAM WHO COULD STEP IN TO HELP AND SHE WOULD PAY THEM TOP SALARY.

THE POWER OF MONEY SHE SAID "WHEN SHE REFLECTED ON THE ORIGINS OF THE TAYLOR FORTUNE NOW SHE FELT NO ATTENDANT GUILT ONLY LOTS OF GRATITUDE THAT SHE'D BEEN GIVEN THE OPPORTUNITY TO USE HER MONEY IN WAYS LIKE THIS.

THE VERY FIRST THING SHE PLANNED TO DO WHEN SHE GOT BACK TO POUGHKEEPSIE WAS TELL TED AND BERNARD HOW THIS TRIP AND JORDAN'S WISDOM HAD CHANGED HER LIFE AND LIFTED HER BURDEN. SHE WANTED HER FAMILY TO UNDERGO THE SAME TRANSFORMING EXPERIENCE.

TED PARTICULARY OWED IT TO HIMSELF AND GOT ON WITH LIVING. IN FACT THE THREE OF THEM NEEDED TO SHED HIS GUILT AND GET ON WITH THE DECICION TO FIND THEIR GRANDFATHER AND EXPOSE HIM. RICKIE WAS NO LONGER SURE IT WAS THE RIGHT THING TO DO NOT WHEN IT MEANT HAVING TO INVOLVE OTHER PEOPLE LIKE JORDAN AND STONEY AND AFTER THE EXPERIENCE AT STROESSNERPLATZ SHE REALIZED THE FAMILY QUEST HAD REQUIRED PUTTING INNOCENT PEOPLE'S LIVES AT RISK AND IT HAD SEEMED WRONG THEN AND EVEN MORE WRONG NOW.

AS FAR AS SHE WAS CONCERNED THIS DESIRE FOR REVENGE WOULD BECOME A TWO-EDGED SWORD ESPECIALLY IF VON HASE COULDN'T BE FOUND. RICKIE HAD FEARED IN TIME THAT IT COULD END UP CONSUMING THEIR LIVES BECAUSE IF YOU LOOK WHAT IT DONE TO TED ALREADY! HE'D CUT OFF DEBORAH WITHOUT A EXPLANANTION AND SABATISEING THE HAPPINESS OF TWO PEOPLE WHO WERE TERRIBLY IN LOVE AND FOR WHAT?

RICKIE HAD BEEN ASKING HERSELF THAT QUESTION OVER AND OVER AGAIN BUT SHE COULDN'T COME UP WITH ANY SATISFACTORY ANSWERS AND IF VON HASE WAS STILL ALIVE THEN HE WAS AN OLD MAN WHO COULDN'T BE EXPECTED TO LIVE MUCH LONGER AND EVEN IF THEY DID FIND HIM AND HAD HIM BROUGHT BEFORE A TRIBUNAL THERE WAS A GOOD CHANCE HE HAD SOME DEBILITATING PHYSICAL AND MENTAL ILLNESSES ASSOCIATED WITH OLD AGE.

SHE COULD UNDERSTAND HOW JEWS WHO'D SURVIVED THE HOLOCAUST WANTED TO SEE THEIR TORMENTORS IN A COURTROOM ONE LAST TIME AND LOOK APON THESE INSTRUMENTS OF EVIL WHILE THEIR SENTENCES AND PUNISHMENTS WER READ OUT LOUD FOR THE WORLD TO HEAR BUT HOW MUCH SATISFACTION COULD THERE BUT IN HAULING SUCH A MONSTER INTO A COURTROOM

FIFTY YEARS LATER IF HE DIDN'T POSSESS HIS FORMER FACULTIES? AND IF IT DIDN'T CHANGE ONE THING ABOUT THE ATROCITES HE'D BE COMMITTED?

MAYBE IT WOULD BRING CLOSURE TO SIMPLY LOOK AT HIM TO KNOW HE HADN'T ELUDED THE JUSTICE AFTER ALL. EVEN IF HE WAS NOTHING NOW BUT A PASSIVE EMPTY SHELL AND RICKIE HAD NO IDEA SHE HADN'T BEEN A VICTIM BUT SHE'D COME TO BELIEVE THAT JORDAN'S IDEA WAS THE BETTER ONE BUT TO LET GO OF THE GUILT AND LOOK FORWARD NOT BACK AND TO LEAVE VON HASE'S FATE TO GOD AND USE THE TAYLOR MONEY TO HELP STOP THE SAME KIND OF EVIL IN TODAY'S WORLD AND TO MITIGATE THE SUFFERING WHEREVER AND WHENEVER THEY COULD.

HER GAZE WANDERED OVER THE BRAVE LITTLE GROUP OF INDIANS JORDAN AND STONEY HAD LITERALLY PLUCKED FROM THE JAWS OF CERTAIN PARAGUYAN AUTHORITIES WHOSE POLITICAL AGENDA WAS SIMPLY TO KILL OFF THE ACHE RACE.

NEITHER TED NOR BERNARD OR RICKIE COULD DO ANYTHING ABOUT THE MILLIONS OF JEWS WHO WENT TO THEIR DEATHS DURRING THE 1940'S AND AS FOR FINDING THEIR GRANDFATHER AND FORCING HIM TO FACE WHAT HE'D DONE WOULDN'T GIVE BACK EVEN ONE LIFE BUT THESE PRECIOUS SOULS HAD A CHANCE FOR A FULL LIFE AND THE TAYLOR MONEY WAS GOING TO HELP MAKE IT HAPPEN OVER AND OVER AGAIN.

DOZENS OF NEW IDEAS EXPLODED IN RICKIE'S MIND AND SHE COULDN'T WAIT TO START PUTTING THOSE IDEAS INTO ACTION ESPECIALLY ONE SECRET PLAN THAT WOULD KEEP HER CLOSE TO JORDAN BUT THAT'S IF HE WOULD LET HER STAY CLOSE NOW THAT HE KNEW SHE WAS IN LOVE WITH HIM AND SHE MIGHT HAVE RUINED HER CHANCE AT THAT PRIVILEGE.

RICKIE ENTERED HER APARTMENT DESPERATE FOR A HOT STEAMING BUBBLE BATH AND A CHANGE OF CLOTHES. SO AFTER ARRIVING AT THE AIRFIELD LATE THE NIGHT BEFORE EVERYONE INCLUDING MARY SHE HAD SPENT THE REST OF IT HELPING THE FAMILIES GET SETTLED IN THEIR SO CALLED TEMPORARY HOUSE QUARTERS.

THIS MORNING STONEY HAD KINDLY LENT RICKIE HIS TRUCK SO SHE COULD DRIVE INTO POUGHKEEPSIE AND SHE SAID SHE'D INTENDED TO RETURN THE TRUCK IN THE LATE AFTERNOON LOADED WITH THE RESULTS OF HER FIRST SHOPPING EXPEDITION.

IF ALL WENT AS SHE HOPED SHE WOULD ASK JORDAN TO DRIVE HER BACK TO TOWN AFTER DINNER BUT SINCE THEIR RETURN SHE'D CAUGHT HIM STARING AT HER MORE THEN ONCE AND SHE LONGED TO KNOW WHAT HE WAS THINKING BECAUSE SHE CRAVED SOME TIME ALONE WITH JORDAN.

WHILE SHE RAN HER BATH AND WATERED HER PLANTS SHE LISTENED TO HER ANSWERING MANCHINE BECAUSE THERE WERE AT LEAST TWENTY MESSAGES BUT ONLY ONE VOICE STOPPED HER IN HER TRACKS.

"RICKIE IT'S DEBORAH SOLOMON." RICKIE'S EYES CLOSED TIGHTLY WHEN SHE HEARD THAT VOICE. "I'M IN POUGHKEEPSIE AND I'M NOT LEAVING UNTILL I TALKED TO YOU." RICKIE COULD HERE THE OTHER WOMEN'S VOICE SHAKING. "TED REFUSES TO SEE ME OR ANSWER ANY OF MY CALLS." THERE WAS A LONG SILENCE INTERSPERSED WITH MUFFLED SOBS OF CRYING.

"YOU'RE MY ONLY HOPE TO GET THROUGH TO HIM AND I'VE BEEN AT YOUR OFFICE BUT YOUR SECRETARY SAYS YOU'RE ON VACTION FOR THE NEXT WEEK. WHEN I HEARD THAT I WIRED MY PARENTS FOR MORE MONEY AND

I'M STAYING AT THE HUDSON ARMS HOTEL UNTILL YOU GET BACK AND I'M IN ROOM #503.

"IF THIS WAS A MATTER THAT AFFECTED ONLY TED AND ME I WOULD HAVE ACCEPTED HIS DECISION TO END OUR RELATIONSHIP BUT IT ISN'T." RICKIE COULD READ BETWEEN THE LINES AND GROANED BECAUSE SHE KNEW DEBORAH WAS PREGNANT WITH TED'S CHILD.

IT DIDN'T TAKE ANY STRETCH OF IMAGINATION TO KNOW HOW TED WOULD REACT TO THIS NEWS AND INSTEAD OF BEING THEILLED BY THE KNOWLEDGE THAT HE WAS GOING TO BE A FATHER HIS NIGHTMARE WOULD INTENSIFY BECAUSE IN HIS MIND THEIR CHILD WOULD BE ANOTHER VON HASE.

SHE KNEW HER BROTHER TO WELL AND HE WOULD BE SO HORRIFIED TO THINK THAT THE BLOOD OF NAZI WAR CRIMINAL HAD DEFILED DEBORAH AND RICKIE DIDN'T DARE CONSIDER THE CONSEQUENCES.

AFTER DASHING TO THE BATHROOM TO SHUT OFF THE WATER SHE HAD LOOKED UP At THE HUDSON ARMS HOTEL PHONE NUMBER AND RANG THROUGH TO DEBORAH'S ROOM. THE OTHER WOMEN PICKED UP THE PHONE ON THE SECOND RING AND SAID "HELLO?" "DEBORAH? IT'S RICKIE." "AT LAST!" SHE CRIED BEFORE THE SOUND OF GREAT HEAVING SOBS COME OVER THE PHONE.

"I'LL BE THERE WITHIN THE HOUR DEBORAH SO DON'T GO ANYWHERE." "OH RICKIE THANK YOU SAID DEBORAH."

CHAPTER 44

THE MORNING AFTER THE BIG NEWS FORM DEBORAH.

Jordan wielded the ax one more time while Stoney burned the petitgrain barrels. They couldn't afford to leave any evidence of the covert air lift for prying eyes to see.

While they worked he watched for Stoney's truck and dinner had come and gone and it would be dark before long and still no Rickie.

"What the hell do you soppose is keeping her?" "Relax Jordan you ought to know Rickie's style by now. She's probably been buying up a storm and dosen't know when to quit. I mean it isn't like you're going to tell her the truth about yourself tonight."

I don't know about that Stoney because the longer I keep silent the harder it's going to be to level with her but if I decide to tell her everything I risk losing something so precious I will never recover. "Stop brooding and help me checkout the so called Cessna.

"Mary has me scheduled to pick-up some cargo at Niagara Falls in the morning." Stoney was right it's better to stay busy otherwise he'd be jumping out of his skin with anxiety over Rickie's nonappearance.

EARLIER IN THE DAY JORDAN HAD DRIVEN TO REVEREND ROLON'S AND BROUGHT BACK A DOCTOR AND TO EVERYONE'S RELIEF THE BABY DIDN'T REQUIRE HOSPITALIZATION ONLY FLUIDS WHICH WOULD HAVE TO BE FORCED FOR A LITTLE WHILE.

WHEN THE DOCTOR HAD FINISHED JORDAN TOOK HIM TO THE RECTORY THEN STOPPED AT THE STORE FOR THE BABY'S FORMULA AND BOTTLES AND AS HE RETURNED TO STONEY'S HOUSE HE WORKED NON-STOP GETTING RID OF THE REST OF THE BARRELS.

IT WASN'T UNTILL THEY'D LOCKED EVERYTHING UP AND GONE BACK TO THE LOUNGE THAT THEY HEARD THE SOUND OF THE TRUCK PULLING UP INTO THE DRIVEWAY. JORDAN'S HEART RACED AND DURING THE LAST TWELVE HOURS HE'D DISCOVERED THAT HE DIDN'T LIKE BEING SEPARATED FROM RICKIE FOR ANY REASON AND THE TIME APART HAD FELT MORE LIKE TWELVE YEARS AND HE HAD CALLED SEVERAL TIMES DURING THE LATE AFTERNOON BUT THERE WAS NO ANSWER AND HE'D GONE A LITTLE CRAZY NOT KNOWING WHERE SHE WAS.

BY TACIT AGREEMENT HE AND STONEY HEADED OUT THE DOOR OF THE HUT AS RICKIE WAS JUST WALKING AROUND THE FRONT OF THE TRUCK AND HIS BREATH CAUGHT AS HIS EYES MADE AN IMMEDIATE ASSESSMENT OF HER FACE AND FIGURE BUT HE COULDN'T HELP STARING.

SHE HAD DRESSED IN SPOTLESS WHITE COTTON PANTS AND A SHORT SLEEVED BEIGE LINEN BLOUSE WITH HER FRESHLY SHAMPOOED HAIR BACK IN A PONYTAIL AT THE BACK OF HER NECK WITH A BEIGE & WHITE SCARF FORM A DISTANCE SHE EXUDED ELEGANCE SOPHISTICATION BUT AND WHEN HE DREW CLOSE TO HER HE SAW THAT HER EYES WERE SHADOWEDHER EXPRESSION HELD A GRIMNESS THAT HADN'T BEEN THERE WHEN SHE'D LEFT THIS MORNING.

"WHAT'S WRONG RICKIE?" HE ASKED IN A LOW A VERY LOW VOICE.

SHE SHOOK HER HEAD DESPAIRINGLY AND SAID "I JUST CAME FROM VISITING MY BROTHER AND I NEED TO TALK TO YOU BUT WE HAVE TO YOU BUT WE HAVE TO EMPTY THE TRUCK FIRST. "MAYBE I'LL RUN YOU BACK TO THE CITY WHEN WE'RE THROUGH HERE." "THANK YOU" SHE MURMURED.

AN HOUR LATER THEY WERE ON THE ROAD HEADED FOR POUGHKEEPSIE JORAND HAD SAID TO RICKIE AS HE GLANCED AT HIS PASSENGER SEVERAL TIMES BUT NO EXPLANATION WAS FORTHCOMING.

"I CAN IMAGINE HOW UPSET YOUR BROTHER WAS WHEN HE FOUND OUT YOU'D FLOWN TO PARAGUAY WITH STONEY AND ME." HE FINALLY HAD BROACHED THE SUBJECT SHE SEEMED RETICENT TO DISCUSS. "IF I HAD A SISTER LIKE YOU I'D REACT THE SAME WAY BUT YOU DON'T REALLY UNDERSTAND SHE INTERRUPTED "IT HAS NOTHING TO DO WITH THAT AND DEBORAH SOLOMON WAS WAITING FOR ME WHEN I GOT BACK TO THE CITY BECAUSE SHE'S EXPECTING TED'S BABY AND SHE REFUSES TO SHE HIM OR TLAK TO HIM SIAD RICKIE."

AT THE SURPRISING REVELATION HIS EYE BROWS MET IN A FROWN. "YOU DIDN'T TELL HIM THAT HE'S GOING TO BE A FATHER LET DID YOU?" "I CAN'T DEBORAH SWORE ME TO SECRECY BECAUSE SHE INSISTS ON TELLING HIM HERSELF FACE-TO-FACE WHICH IS HER RIGHT AFTER ALL BUT TED IS GOING TO BE IMMOVABLE ON THAT SUBJECT OF EVER TALKING TO HER AGAIN.

"WHEN HE FOUND OUT HE WAS A VON HASE HE WROTE HER A VERY CUREL LETTER SEVERING THEIR RELATIONSHIP IN THE HOPE OF KILLING ANY FEELINGS SHE MIGHT HAVE

HAD FOR HIM BUT DEBORAH'S IN LOVE WITH HIM AND SHE DIDN'T BUY HIS REASON FOR BREAKING UP WITH HER SO SHE PHONED HIM INCESSANTLY AND SENT HIM LETTERES BUT HE REFUSES TO RESPOND AND SHE CAN'T GET ANYWHERE NEAR HIM SO SHE TURNED TO ME AS HER ONLY HOPE OF MAKING CONTACT WITH HIM."

"WHAT DID YOU TELL HER?" "THAT I'D FIND A WAY TO MAKE TED FACE HER." "HOW WILL YOU ACCOMPLISH THAT RICKIE?" "SHE ASKED ME SOME QUESTIONS BUT I TOLD HER I DIND'T KNOW YET. I GUESS IT WILL BE BETTER FOR AND THE BABY TO GO BACK TO JERUSALEM TO BE WITH HER FAMILY AND IN THE MEANTIME I'LL WORK ON TED TO GET HIM TO TALK TO HER.

"WILL SHE DO THAT?" RICKIE NODDED HER HEAD AND SAID YES I THINK SHE WILL BECAUSE I MADE HER A SOLEMN PROMISE BUT NOW I'M TERRIFIED I MAY NOT BE ABLE TO KEEP MY WORD BECAUSE MY BROTHER MAY HAVE HARDENED HIS HEART EVEN AGAINST ME FOR SOME REASON BUT HE'S NEVER DONE THAT BEFORE AND HIS VOICE SHOOK WHEN HE SAID IT."

"HE'S IN HELL RIGHT NOW BECAUSE OF THE WAY YOU WERE." SHE BURIED HER FACE IN HER HANDS. "I KNOW HE'S IN HELL RIGHT NOW BUT I COULDN'T MAKE HIM SEE THE REASON AND HIS GUILT HAD DESTORYED OUR PARENTS LIVES AND THAT'S BECAUSE THEY'D FELT SO UNWORTHY THAT THEY'D HIDDEN THE TRUTH FROM US CHILDREN AND HAD DISTANCED THEMSELVES AND CUTTING OFF ALL DIALOGUE AFFECTION TOWARDS US.

"I TRIED TO MAKE HIM UNDERSTAND THAT HE WAS REPEATING HISTORY BY DOING THE SAME THING TO DEBORAH AND BY SHUTTING HER OUT NOT ONLY THAT I TOLD HIM HE WAS COMPOUNDING THE PROBLEM AND HE'S PUNISHING HER BUT SHE'S AN INNOCENT VICTIM."

"WHAT DID HE SAY TO THAT?" "ABSOLUTELY NOTHING BECAUSE HE'S CONSUMED BY THE POSSIBILITY THAT VON HASE IS ALIVE AND HIDING AT STROESSNERPLATZ BUT I DID TELL HIM ABOUT OUR EXPERIENCE BUT HE'S MORE DETERMINED THEN EVER TO AFTER HIM."

"HE CAN FLY DOWN TO PARAGUAY WITH STONEY AND ME ON ARE NEXT RUN RICKIE AND MAYBE LETTING HIM LOOK FOR YOUR GRANDFATHER WILL APPEASE SOMETHING INSIDE HIM SO HE CAN GET ON WITH LIFE EXPECILALLY NOW THERE'S A BABY ON THE WAY."

HER HEAD REARED BACK VIOLENTLY AS SHE CRIED OUT "NO!" "THAT'S THE ONE THING I DON'T WANT YOU TO DO SO PLEASE PROMISE ME YOU'LL REFUSE HIM WHEN HE ASKS BECAUSE IT'S TO DANGEROUS! AND I DON'T WANT ANYTHING TO HAPPEN TO YOU OR HIM."

IF HE WANTS TO GO AFTER OUR GRANDFATHER THEN HE'LL HAVE TO FIND SOMEONE ELSE TO HELP HIM AND PLEASE PROMISE ME YOU'LL REFUSE HIM JORDAN!" HE SUCKED IN HIS BREATH AND SAID "YOU HAVE MY WORD RICKIE." "THANK YOU" SHE SAID AS HER VOICE WOBBLED A LITTLE. "TED ISN'T HIMSELF RIGHT NOW BECAUSE HE DOSEN'T CARE THAT STONEY'S RUNNING A BUSINESS OR THAT YOU HAVE RESPONSIBILITIES TO THESE FAMILIES YOU'VE BROUGHT HERE. HE'S FORGOTTEN THAT YOU OWE YOUR ALLEGIANCE TO THE PARISH."

THE PARISH? HE SAID NOW IT'S TIME FOR THAT PARTICULAR LIE TO END BECAUSE HE COULDN'T KEEP UP THE PRETENSE ANY LONGER AND THE GUILT WAS TEARING HIM APART.

"WE'RE BACK INSIDE THE CITY LIMITS RICKIE. WHAT ROAD DO I TAKE TO YOUR APARTMENT?" "STAY ON THIS STREET FOR FOUR BLOCKS THEN TURN RIGHT AND THEN GO ONE

MORE MILE ON DEERBORN AND IT WILL BE THE BUILDING ON THE RIGHT WITH THE GREEN CANOPY ACROSS THE LONG SIDEWALK."

HE FOLLOWED HER DIRECTIONS AND BEFORE LONG THEY'D PULLED UP IN FRONT OF AN UNPETENTIOUS SIX-STORY APARTMENT BUILDING AND NO DOUBT A FAR CRY FROM HER FAMILY'S MANSION.

"WOULD YOU CARE TO COME IN FOR SOMETHING TO EAT OR DRINK BEFORE YOU GO BACK?" SHE ADDED. WOULD I CARE TO COME IN? AND WOULD I CARE TO CLOSE THE DOOR ON THE WORLD AND SHUT MYSELF INSIDE WITH YOU FOREVER? IF YOU ONLY KNEW.

"I DON'T THINK IT WOULD BE A VERY GOOD IDEA." HE SAID AS HE TOOK A DEEP BREATH TO GIVE HIMSELF THE COURAGE TO SAY WHAT HE HAD TO BE SAID. THIS COULD VERY WELL BE THE END OF RICKIE TAYLOR IN HIS LIFE OF HAPPINESS AS HE'D KNOW IT.

"FORGIVE ME" SHE SAID FORMALLY "I FORGOTTEN THAT IT'S FROWNED UPON FOR A CLERGYMAN TO BE SEEN ENTERING A SINGLE WOMEN'S APARTMENT PARTICULARLY THIS LAT AT NIGHT."

HIS JAW HAD HARDENED AS HE SIAD "I'LL JUST WALK YOU TO THE DOOR SO I KNOW YOUR SAFE." BEFORE HE COULD GET AROUND TO HER SIDE OF THE CAR DOOR SHE'D ALREADY BOUNDED OUT AND HE CAUGHT UP WITH HER NEAR THE FOYER DOORS AND FORTUNATELY NO ONE WAS ABOUT AND STREET TRAFFIC WAS LIGHT.

SHE SHOOK OFF THE HAND HE PUT OUT TO DETAIN HER. "GOOD NIGHT" SHE SAID. "I'VE BEEN COMING AND GOING ALONE FOR YEARS YOUR PROTECTION ISN'T NECESSARY REVEREND." FINALLY HE AHD SAID "I'M NOT

A REVEREND." SHE'D BEEN FACING THE BUILDING BUT AT HIS SO CALLED DECLARATION SHE TURNED HER HEAD AND STARED UP AT HIM BLANKLY.

"WHAT DO YOU MEAN?" "I MEAN HE MUTTERED GRIMLY "WHEN I GOT OUT OF PRISON I DELIBERATELY TOOK ON THE PERSONA OF A BIG HUGE MINISTER-MISSSIONARY AS A FRONT FOR OUR CONVENT OPERATIONS HERE IN NEW YORK. THE IDENTIFICATION I FLASHED AT YOU THAT DAY IN YOUR OFFICE WAS FORGED BY REVEREND ROLON BECAUSE HE'S THE ONLY CLERGYMAN NOT ME."

"LET ME EXPLAIN I HAD NO ECCLESIASTICAL AUTHORITY, NO PARISH AND NO PARISHONERS. I HAD MADE IT ALL UP TO DO THE KINDS OF ILLEGAL THINGS I NEEDED TO DO IF I'M GOING TO GET THE ACHE OUT OF PARAGUAY AND BEING A MINISTER I MEAN PRETENDING TO BE ONE LETS ME WALK INTO ALL KINDS OF SITUATIONS WITH RELATIVE SAFETY AND IT GIVES ME CERTAIN AUTHORITY HERE AND IN SOUTH AMERICA AND IT LETS ME GET THE JOB DONE.

"RICKIE I ALSO KILLED A MAN AGAINST DIRECT ORDERS AND I WAS KICKED OUT OF THE SEALS AND I'M AN EX-CONVICT RENEGADE AND I WILL ALWAYS BE INVOLVED IN DANGEROUS PURSUITS. I LIED TO YOU AND I LED YOU TO BELIEVE I WAS A MINISTER OF THE CHURCH BUT THE TRUTH IS I'M THE FURTHEST THING FROM ONE. "I'M NO GOOD FOR ANY WOMEN AND EXPECIALLY NOT FOR YOU.

"REST ASSURED I'LL HONOR YOUR REQUEST TO TELL YOUR BROTHER NO IF AND WHEN HE COMES LOOKING FOR ME AND NOW I'LL MAKE ONE LAST REQUEST OF YOU. "FORGET ANY FURTHER PLANS TO HELP OUR CAUSE BUT ONLY GOD COULD HAVE DONE MORE THEN YOU'VE DONE ALREADY. ENOUGH'S ENOUGH DON'T COME BACK TO STONEY'S AGAIN AND I WOULD LIKE YOUR WORD ON THAT."

She looked as if he'd just kicked her down a steep flight of stairs and that looked crucified him but he had to like an very anguished warith she hovered there for a for a moment then vanished the next so he had his answer. This is what you wanted Browning a clean break and no ragged edges to blur the lines. "Stoney's Air Cargo "This is Mary More speaking." "Mary? It's me Rickie." Her heart had started pounding so hard she felt almost sick. "Please don't let anyone know I'm calling and if you can't talk now just hang up." "Relax honey nobody's here but me. That Argentinean couple you flew here from South America to help out has been a godsend. This morning they picked up everyone in the van and both families are out sight seeing in their tennis shoes and shorts and those girls are the cutest things you ever saw.

"I can't believe the change in them over the last six weeks! The baby must have tripled in size and I've kind of adopted him. They're all learning English faster than I'm learning Gauarani."

Mary's words came tripping out at double speed and they had warmed Rickie's heart. "A child picks up everything ten times as quickly as the rest of us. No problems with the authorities so far?" said Rickie. "None thank haven" said Mary.

"We've been mighty lucky but just when in tarnation did you disappear to?" Mary suddenly demanded in a very stern voice "Everyone's been asking about you because things aren't the same around here anymore their in mourning.

"Jordan gave Stoney and me some gobbledygook story that you had emergency CBH business out of

UNTIL THERE WAS YOU MY SWEET HEART

THE COUNTRY BUT I DON'T BUY IT THEN AND I SURE AS HELL DON'T BUY IT NOW.

"HE'S BEEN DOWNRIGHT IMPOSSIBLE TO BE AROUND SINCE HE TOOK YOU HOME THAT NIGHT AND HE BITES EVERYONE'S HEAD OFF IF HE EVEN THINKS YOU'RE LOOKING AT HIM OR PLANNING TO ASK HIM A QUESTION HE DOSEN'T WANT TO ANSWER. "HE AND STONEY WALK WIDE CIRCLES AROUND EACH OTHER THESE DAYS AND IT'S ACTUALLY DRIVEN STONEY TO SPEND SOME TIME WITH MICHELLE. "I'M KEEPING MY FINGERS CROSSED ON THAT ONE SAID JORDAN." EMOTIONS WERE HITTING RICKIE TOO HARD AND FAST. "THAT'S THE BEST ANSWER I'VE HEARD IN A LONG TIME" SHE FINALLY MANAGED IN A BARELY AUDIBLE VOICE.

"YOU AND ME BOTH AND NOW I WANT TO KNOW WHAT'S GOING ON. "YOU'VE GOT TO UNDERSTAND I PROMISED JORDAN I WOULDN'T CALL YOU OR INTERFERE BUT I NEVER PROMISED I WOULDN'T TALK TO YOU IF YOU CALLED ME. SO START TALKING HONEY OK BUT NOT HERE LET'S FIND SOME PLACE QUITE. "I'VE MISSED YOU AND THAT'S THE TRUTH" MARY SAID. "IV'E MISSED YOU SO MUCH TOO MARY."

"I KNOW YOU'RE IN LOVE WITH JORDAN AND I KNOW HE'S IN LOVE WITH YOU SO LET'S START THERE." AT THAT POINT RICKIE BROKE DOWN COMPLETELY AND STARTED TO CRY. "WHAT DID HE DO TO YOU?" IT TOOK DAYS BEFORE RICKIE COULD GET HER VOICE BACK AGAIN.

"HE ADMITTED THAT HE WASN'T A MINISTER AND THAT HE'D BEEN LYING TO ME ALONG." "YOU DIDN'T FOGIVE HIM DID YOU MARY?" HE ASKED AS HE SOUNDED SCANDALIZED. "HELL HE DUPED ME TOO AND I FORGAVE HIM BUT FIRST I CHEWED HIM OUT." MARY GIGGLED LIKE A TEENAGER SHE LOVED JORDAN TOO AND RICKIE LOVED HER FOR OFFERING HER SUPPORT AND LOYALTY.

"THERE WASN'T ANYTHING TO FORGIVE MARY BUT HE WOULDN'T LET ME SPEAK AND AFTER HE SAID HE WAS NO GOOD FOR ANY WOMEN AND HE MADE ME PROMISE TO STAY AWAY." "DID YOU PROMISE HIM RICKIE?" "NO! I DIDN'T SAY A WORD BECAUSE I KNEW I WOULDN'T BE ABLE TO KEEP A PROMISE LIKE THAT. HE WASN'T IN ANY FRAM OF MIND TO TALK THAT NIGHT SO I DID THE ONLY THING I COULD AND WENT INSIDE TO MY APARTMENT."

"YOU SHOULD HAVE SEEN THE SHAP HE WAS IN WHEN HE HAD CAME BACK! ALL HELL BROKE LOOSE! HE STILL ISN'T TALKING TO ANYBODY AND NOW YOU KNOW WHAT IT'S BEEN LIKE AROUND HERE FOR US." "I'VE TRIED TO STAY AWAY MARY BUT TODAY SHE COULDN'T FINISH.

"WELL HALLELUJAH ! AT LAST YOU HAVE THE GOOD SENSE TO END THIS NIGHTMARE. TELL YOU WHAT LAST WEEK HE GO SO IMPOSSIBLE STONEY AND I THREW HIM OUT AND WE TOLD HIM TOGET LOST UNTILL HE CAME TO HIS SENSES."

HE WASN'T THERE? RICKIE'S HEART PLUNGED TO HER FEET. "WHERE DID HE GO MARY?" "I'LL ONLY TELL YOU ON ONE CONDITION." "I ALREADY KNOW WHAT IT IS. I KNEW I COULD COUNT ON YOU I LOVE YOU MARY." "I LOVE YOU TOO HONEY. ALL RIGHTY I FIGURE YOU CAN BE THERE ABOUT FOUR HOURS IF YOU TAKE YOUR FAMILY'S COMPANY JET NONSTOP TO SAN DIEGO."

"HE WENT HOME." "THAT'S RIGHT, IMPERIAL BEACH OF COURSE WHY DIDN'T I THINK OF THAT. HIS GRANDFATHER'S PLACE IS SOLD SO NOW HE'S LIVING ON THE BEACH."

"DID HE TELL YOU THAT?" "NO BUT WHEN HE LEFT HERE ALL HE TOOK WITH HIM WAS HIS CAMPING GEAR. I BET YOU'LL FIND HIM OUT IN THAT WATER SOMEWHERE BECAUSE HE LIKES TO SWIM LIKE A FISH YOU KNOW OR SHOULD I LIKE A SEAL?" SHE CHORTLED. "THAT WAS HIS

EXPERTISE AS A NAVY SEAL. UNDERWATER DEMOLITION AND ALL THAT STUFF."

"WISH ME LUCK MARY." "HONEY YOU TWO WERE MENT FOR EACH OTHER IF ANYONE EVER WAS. I'VE GOT ALL THE FAITH IN THE WORLD BUT DON'T COME BACK WITHOUT HIM." "I WON'T RICKIE VOWED BUT AS SHE DROVE HER RENTAL CAR ALONG CALIFORNIA'S PACIFIC COAST HIGHWAY THAT SAME DAY IN FIVE O'CLOCK TRAFFIC.

SHE FEARD IT WAS A VOW SHE MIGHT NOT BE ABLE TO KEEP. EVERYWHERE SHE LOOKED IMPERIAL BEACH A CITY TWENTY-EIGHT THOUSAND ACCORDING TO THE SIGN WAS OVERRUN WITH SUNBURNED TOURISTS AND EVEN THE TRAFFIC WAS WORSE THERE BECAUSE CARS WERE POURING OVER THE BORDER INTO TIJUANA.

SHE SAW A SERVICE SATATION WITH A MINI MART AND TURNED OFF TO ASK FOR WHERE THE PUBLIC CAMPGROUND WAS LOCATED BUT TO HER DISMAY THE WOMAN AT THE COUNTER TOLD HER THERE WASN'T ONE BUT SHE COULD DRIVE THREE MILES NORTH TO SILVER STRAND BEACH. THEY HAD CAMPING GROUNDS THERE.

BACKTACKING THE SHORT DISTANCE THROUGH I HAD TO WAIT IN THE TRAFFIC THEN WAIT IN LINE TO ENTER THE CAMPING GROUNDS TOOK ANOTHER HALF HOUR AT LEAST AND BY THE TIME SHE'D FOUND HER OWN LITTLE SOPT OF SAND AND ERECTED HER TENT THE SUN HAD ALREADY BEGUN TO GO DOWN.

SHE CHANGED QUICKLY INTO HER ONE-PIECE SHOCKING PINCK SWIMSUIT WHICH HAD NO BACK TO SPEAK OF AND UNFORTUNATELY THE FRONT AND THE LEGS WERE MODESTLY CUT. AFTER BRAIDING HER HAIR AND PINNING IT TO THE TOP OF HER HEAD SHE LOCKED EVERYTHING IN HER CAR ZIPPED UP HER TENT AND HEADED FOR THE WATER.

SHE LOVED THE SMELL OF BRINE BECAUSE IT'S BEEN A LONG TIME SINCE SHE'D BEEN TO A BEACH AND SHE'D ALWAYS FELT THIS KIND OF SETTING PROVIDED THE MOST ROMANTIC BACKDROP FOR LOVERS AND TO KNOW THAT THE MAN SHE LOVED COULD BE HERE SOMEWHERE-ANYWHERE SET HER PULSE FLUTTERING.

TO AID HER IN HER SEARCH SHE BROUGHT HER OPERA GLASSES WITH HER AND TRYING TO BE UNOBTRUSIVE SHE STUDIED THE LANDSCAPE FOR SIGNS OF JORDAN. HE MIGHT NOT EVEN BE HERE OR MAYBE HE HAD ALREADY CAME AND GONE.

SOLWLY SHE MADE HER WAY SOUTH ALONG THE SAND PAST OTHER SWIMMERS BUT THE WATER FOAMED AND CURLED LAYING IT'S DEPOSIT OF KELP AT HER FEET BEFORE FLOWING BACK OUT AGAIN. THEY HAD COOLED HER SKIN BUT IT WAS STILL WARMED BY THE INTENSE HEAT OF THE AFTERNOON SUN.

FROM TIME TO TIME SHE SCANNED THE CARS AND VEHICLES CHECKING TO SEE WHICH ONE'S WERE RENTALS. HE COULD HAVE SET UP HIS CAMP THERE CLOSER TO THE PARKING AREA THEN HEADED TOWARD IMPERIAL BEACH. GOING ON A HUNCH SHE PLODDED FORWARD CONSTANTLY LOOKING TO SEE IF ONE OF THE HEADS BOBBING IN THE WATER HAD BELONGED TO HIM.

THE LOWER RIM OF THE HUGE ORANGE SUN SKIMMED ON TOP OF THE BLUE WATERS AND IN A FEW MINUTES IT WOULD SLIP BELOW THE BIG HORIZON OF THE ROCKY MOUNTAINS.

WHERE ARE YOU JORDAN? LITTLE BY LITTLE SHE NOTED MOST PEOPLE HAD GATHERED UP THEIR BLANKETS AND CHAIRS TO LEAVE AND THE BEACH WAS ALMOST EMPTY BUT SHE KEPT WALKING DOWN THE BEACH ANYWAYS TO SEE IF SHE COULD FIND JORDAN.

Something told her Jordan didn't like crowds so I guess he'd probably be one of the last swimmers to come out of the water soon. Once again she scanned the wave farther out to see if she could see Jordan in the water. Several teens lying on surfboards paddling into the shore with their arms obviously they are through for the day.

Feeling increasingly desolate because Jordan didn't seem to be anywhere around and she started back towards the Silver Strand Beach but at the halfway point between Imperial Beach the campgrounds she came to a standstill and her attention drawn to a lone swimmer out bodysurfing. For an infinitesimal moment she saw that the man's dark hair appeared to be tied at the nape of the back of his neck.

Galvanized into action by even the tiniest hope she hooked her keyring to her suit strap and put her glasses under a log far away from the foam and then she ran into the water which had big waves running through it.

He didn't seem to be to far out in the water so she swam beneath the water not eager to let him know she was there untill she was able to identify him one way or the other. The closer she drew the more she realized that this swimmer was a powerful man who moved with fluid grace yet had the swiftness of a shark.

In fairy tales he would have been a "Merman" but in real life who could he be but someone like a Navy Seal? She got closer to him as she lifted her head out of the water for a peek. The tanned harden-muscled body she saw suspended in the air before it turned back into the swell body it use to

BE. HOW COULD THAT BODY BELONG TO ONLY ONE PERSON? I'VE FOUND YOU JORDAN AND YOUR'RE NOT GETTING AWAY FROM ME AGAIN.

EVERY DAY FOR THE LAST PAST WEEK JORDAN HAD PUT HIMSELF THROUGH THE FAMILIAR PRACTICE MANEUVERS BUT OVER AND OVER AGAIN HE'D PUSHED HIS ABILITIES TO THE LIMIT AND HE WOULD WEAR HIMSELF OUT TO THE POINT OF EXHAUSTION SO HE COULD SLEEP TONIGHT.

HE'D LOST RICKIE TAYLOR BECAUSE OF HIS LIES AND NOT ONCE IN THE SIX WEEKS THEY'D BEEN APART HAD SHE EVEN TRIED TO CALL HIM LET ALONE SEEK HIM OUT.

RICKIE WAS A FIGHTER AND HE KNEW HER BETTER THEN ANYONE. SHE'D CONFESSED HER INNERMOST THOUGHTS TO HIM BUT HE KNEW HER FEARS, STRENGHTS, WEAKNESSES AND HER MOTIVES. IF SHE REALLY WANTED HIM SHE WOULD HAVE FOUND A WAY BY NOW.

LIKE A NAÏVE CHILD HE'D BEEN PRAYING THAT SHE'D COME AFTER HIM AND TELL HIM SHE'D FORGIVEN HIM FOR LIEING ABOUT SOMETHING THAT WAS SACRED TO HER AND TO HIM.

IT HADN'T HAPPENED YET HE SAID TO HIMSELF AND THE PAIN OF LOSS WAS UNBEARABLE AND IT WOULDN'T LEAV HIM ALONE AND NEITHER WOULD THE GUILT.

IT SURPRISED HIM THAT HE HADN'T EXPERIENCED ANYTHING THAT HAD BAD AND APPROACHING ALL THAT GUILT WHEN HE'D FIRST DONNED THAT CLERICAL COLLAR AND NOW HE COULDN'T FORGIVE HIMSELF FOR TRYING TO IMPERSONATE A MINISTER.

THIS TRIP BACK TO THE PLACE HE'D ONCE CALLED HOME WAS SUPPOSED TO HAVE BROUGHT HIM SOLACE BUT HE'D LEARNED A HARD LESSON. YOU CAN'T GO BACK

BECAUSE NOTHING IS THE SAME IT'S ALL DIFFERENT AND BESIDES YOUR HEART IS BURNING TO GET BACK WITH RICKIE. WHEREVER SHE IS THAT'S WHERE YOUR HOUSE IS ONLY SHE'S LOST TO YOU NOW.

ABRUPTLY HE DECIDED HE WOULD MAKE ONE MORE DIVE THROUGH THE NEXT SET OF WAVES AND THEN GO BACK TO THE SALAZARS AND PICK UP HIS THINGS AND FLY BACK TO NEW YORK CITY TO GET RICKIE BACK.

HE'D LEFT STONEY AND MARY IN THE MIDDLE OF LUNCH AT THE TIME WHEN THEY NEEDED HIM THE MOST. THOSE FAMILIES DEPENDED ON HIM EVEN THOUGH RICKIE HAD ARRANGED FOR THE HUSBAND AND WIFE TEAM FROM ARGENTINA TO HELP OUT DURING THIS CRITICAL PERIOD BECAUSE HE AND STONEY HAD MASTERMINDED THE PROJECT AND HE SHOULD BE THERE DOING HIS PART.

MORE GUILT CONSUMED HIM BECAUSE OF ALL THE PEOPLE HE WAS LETTING DOWN AND MORE HEARTACHE ASSAILED HIM WHEN HE HAD COSIDERED GOING BACK TO A PLACE ONLY FORTY-FIVE MINUTES AWAY FROM RICKIE'S APARTMENT. SO NEAR BUT YET SO PERMANENTLY OFF LIMITS TO HIM. HOW WAS HE GOING TO GET THROUGH THE REST OF HIS LIFE WITHOUT HER?

IN HIS PERIPHERAL VISION HE COULD SEE THE WAVES MOUNTING INTO A SWELL OF BIGGER WAVES AND LUNGING BLINDLY FOR THEM HE HAD UNEXPECTEDLY FELT HIS LEG SNARED BY SOMETHING THAT HAD FELT LIKE IT WAS HUMAN.

WHAT THE HELL? MAYBE IT WAS A SWIMMER WHO'D BEEN CAUGHT IN THE UNDERTOW AND NEEDED HELP. YEARS OF TRAINING TRIGGERED AN AUTOMATIC RESPONSE.

He brought her up against his chest and shielded her from the waves crashing over them and lifted them right out of the water.

That wonderous glint of blue eyes and white-gold hair could only belong to one person and he knew who it was but he had to be hallucinating but he'd thought that once before and she'd turned out to be real.

Treading water he continued to hold her so he could feel the shap of her breathtaking body in the pink swimsuit along with curve of her waist and the womanly flare of her hips.

"Rickie?" he cried out in disbelief. "It is you." "Yes darling." Jordan groaned as he said "Say that again." "Darling." "You really mean it?" He couldn't stop his voice from shaking.

Her eyes glowed blue fire against the twilight and Jordan knew in his bones that only a woman in love could look like that meaning everything was revealed and was open to being vulnerable.

She loved him the way he loved her and she had come for him but she didn't forgive him yet. Was it true? Could this really be happening to him?

"I've been calling you "my darling" since you first drove me out to Stoney's place. I'm surprised you didn't hear me but I felt so guilty because of the lies I told you." "Hush" he whispered covering her mouth and every sound was muffled except the pounding of their hearts and the lapping of the water against their bodyies.

"DON'T EVER SAY THAT WORD AGAIN YOU HAVE TO PROMISE ME RICKIE." "I PROMISE SHE SAID TO JORDAN. IT'S THE ONE WORD THAT SHOULD BE STRICKEN FROM THE VOCABULARY OF LIFE." "AGREED" HE SAID AS HE KISSED HER AGAIN BUT THIS TIME IT WAS LONG AND VERY PASSIONATELY. "WHERE DID YOU COME FROM?" HE ASKED AS HE WAS STILL HOLDING THE BACK OF HER NECK AND STILL IN A EUPHORIC DAZE.

"SILVER STRAND BEACH." HE HAD TO BE DREAMING BUT THEN HE ASKED "DID YOU BRING A TENT?" "YES IT'S ALREADY SET UP. I COULDN'T FIND YOU SO I HAD CALLED MARY THIS MORNING OUT OF DESPERATION AND SHE TOLD ME YOU WERE HERE. I HAD PLANNED TO CAMP OUT TILL I HAD FOUND YOU AND I DIDN'T KNOW HOW LONG THAT WOULD TAKE."

HE COVERED HER FACE WITH KISES ENTICED BY THE SALT WATER. "YOU DIDN'T ARRIVE A MOMENT TOO SOON BECAUSE I WAS GOING TO LEAVE IN THE MORNING TO FLY BACK TO NEW YORK CITY."

"IF I HADN'T BEEN ABLE TO FIND YOU I WOULD HAVE FOLLOWED YOU HOME." SHE WOULD HAVE BUT RICKIE HAD TO DO EVERYTHING SINGLEHANDEDLY AND WITH DETERMINATION. "COME WITH ME MY DARLING." HER BODY EXPERIENCED A THRILL OF SENSATION AS HE PROPELLED THEM THROUGH THE WATER WITH TREMENDOUS SPEED. "WHERE ARE WE GOING?" SHE CRIED IN WONDER. "TO GET MARRIED JORDAN SAID." "JORDAN !" WAIT A MINUTE SAID RICKIE.

HE KNEW THAT HE HAD TO SHOW HER HOW HE FELT SOON BUT FOR HIM UNFORTUNATELY THE CAMPSITE HAD COME INTO VIEW. "WHERE'S YOUR TENT RICKIE?" "IT'S THE GREEN THREE MAN NEXT TO THE WHITE CAR WAY DOWN AT THE END OF THE BEACH. I GOT THE LAST SOPTS SAID RICKIE."

As soon as his feet could touch bottom he walked out of the water carring her in his arms. "Jordan?" she whispered pink-cheeked everyone's looking at us please put me down."

"Not on your life because the threshold of a tent is still a threshold and besides we're not even married yet." said Rickie.

"I'm a renegade remember?" I make my own rules and it's too late for you to back out now." "I don't want to back out because I'm in it for the duration." she murmured before she kissed him with an ardor that matched his own.

His heart was going crazy beyond normal and he was so happy that it terrified him. He then reached for her tent that was all neatly pegged in place and everything she did had her own inimitable signature and she also made things happen and did things right. She is a renaissance women that is unafraid, giving and exceptional which he had adored her for.

"Open the tent darling." He allowed her just enough latitude to pull down the tent's zipper so they could shut out the world for a little while. Once inside the tent she zipped it up again without him having to say a word.

She wants this as badly as you do Jordan. They stood in the middle of the tent and then he slowly lowered her to the floor and feeling the miracle of her legs intertwined with his.

"Rickie, Rickie" he whispered pressing his hot sexy body against hers as he kissed her with his eyes closed. She had tasted of like the sunshine

Until There Was You My Sweet Heart ~471~

AND SALT WATER FROM THE OCEAN BUT SHE HAD ALSO TASTED LIKE SOME EXOTIC FRUIT HE'D BEEN SEARCHING FOR ALL HIS LIFE BUT IT WAS ALWAYS OUT OF REACH UNTILL NOW."

"WHAT HAVE I DONE TO DESERVE YOU?" HER HOT SMOLDERING BLUE EYES ROSE TO HIS AS SHE SAID "I'M THE ONE WHO FEELS PRIVILEGED SAID RICKIE BECAUSE YOU'VE HELD MY HEART AND MY SOUL IN YOUR HANDS SINCE WE FIRST MET AND YOU BROUGHT ME OUT OF THE DARKEST DEPTHS INTO THE LIGHT.

"WHETHER YOU KNOW IT OR NOT A PART OF YOU WILL ALWAYS BE THE REVEREND TO ME SHE SAID AS HIS VOICE CLAMED UP. YOU'RE MY ROCK JORDAN BROWNING." HER VOICE CHOKED AND SHE COULDN'T GO ON SO SHE WRAPPED HER ARMS AROUND HIS NECK INSTEAD AND SHE HAD TO STAND ON HER TOES TO KISS HIM.

HE RAISED HER FROM THE GROUND AS THEY KIEESED EACH OTHER AND HE WANTED TO MAKE LOVE TO HER RIGHT THERE IN THE TENT AND NOW THEY WERE FINALLY ALONE AT LAST WITH NOTHING TO STOP THEM FROM SATISFYING THE LONGINGS THEY'D KEPT IN ABEYANCE FROM THE VERY BEGINNING BUT IT WAS PRECISELY BECAUSE HE HONORED HER FOR THE MAGNIFICENT WOMEN SHE WAS THAT HE WANTED THEIR FIRST TIME TOGETHER TO BE UNDER PERFECT CIRCUMSTANCES. HE WANTED TO BE HER HUSBAND WHEN THEY CAME TOGETHER FOR THE FIRST TIME.

HE WANTED A PROPER SETTING FOR HER AS WELL BUT NOT THIS SANDY TENT SURROUNDED BY HUNDREDS OF TOURISTS BECAUSE RICKIE HAD DESERVED MORE.

SHE'D CONFIDED THAT SHE'D HAD OTHER BOYFRIENDS BUT SHE'D NEVER BEEN TO BED WITH JUST ONE MAN BEFORE AND SHE TRUSTED HIM. HE KNEW IN HIS GUT

THAT SHE'D FOLLOW HIS LEAD ANYWHERE HE HAD TAKEN HER. SUCH RESPONSIBILITY HUMBLED HIM AS HE LIFTED HIS HEAD.

HE WANTED THEM TO START OUT THE WAY HE INTENDED THEIR LIVES TO GO AND HAVING DECIDED THIS HE BROKE THEIR KISS AND SAID "I CAN'T DO THIS I CAN'T MAKE LOVE TO YOU WITHOUT BEING YOUR HUSBAND FIRST. "WHERE DO YOU WANT TO GET MARRIED?" "I DON'T CARE AS LONG AS IT'S SOON" SAID RICKIE. "YOUR PARENTS WILL CARE BECAUSE YOU'RE THEIR DAUGHTER. Now THAT MY GRANDFATHER'S GONE THEY'RE GOING TO BECOME MY FAMILY AND I'M SURE THE'LL WANT TO GIVE YOU THE WEDDING OF YOUR DREAMS."

HER EXPRESSION SOBERED AS SHE SAID "I LOVE YOU FOR CONSIDERING THEIR FEELINGS AND I'M SUSPECT THAT BECAUSE OF THEIR GUILT ABOUT MY GRANDFATHER THEY'VE NEVER KNOWN REAL HAPPINESS BUT MAYBE SEEING ME HAPPILY MARRIED MIGHT BRING THEM A LITTLE JOY AND IN FACT "HER EYES LIT UP" AS SHE SAID "IT BE THE MEANS OF BRINGING TED AND DEBORAH TOGETHER!" "WHAT DO YOU MEAN?" HE MURMURED BURROWING HIS FACE INTO THE SIDE OF HER NECK.

"THE NEWS ABOUT THE TRUE IDENTITY OF OUR GRANDFATHER HAS CHANGED TED BEYOND RECOGNITION BUT I DO KNOW ONE THING HE WOULD NEVER REFUSE TO BE APART OF MY WEDDING AND HE COULDN'T VERY WELL IGNORE DEBODAH IF WAS TO SHOW UP AND CONGRATULATE THE BRIDE AND GROOM.

"TED WOULD TAKE ONE LOOK AT HER AND SEE SHE'S OBVIOUSLY VERY PREGNAT AND HE'D BE FORCED TO DEAL WITH THE SITUATION." THE DEPTH OF HER LOVE FOR HER BROTHER WAS NEVER MORE APPARENT THEN RIGHT NOW. JORDAN CUPPED HER HANDS AND KISSED HER FINGERTIPS. "THAT JUST MIGHT WORK NOW BACK TO MY

EARLIER QUESTION "WHERE WOULD YOU LIKE TO GO TO GET MARRIED DARLING?"

SHE DIDN'T HESITATE TO ANSWER "IN MY HEART OF HEARTS I'D LOVE TO BE MARRIED IN CHURCH BECAUSE MY FAMILY HAS NEVER BELONGED TO ONE AND MY PARENTS WEREN'T INTERESTED. THEY LIVED LIFE LIKE THEY WERE DETACHED FROM EACH OTHER PEOPLE EVEN FROM TED AND ME."

SHE KNEADED HIS SHOULDERS WITH HER HANDS. "BECAUSE OF YOU MY LIFE HAS BEEN TRANSFORMED AND IT HAPPENED WHEN WE WENT TO THE CHACO AND IF YOU WANT TO KNOW THE TRUTH I'D LIKE FATHER DESILVA TO MARRY US IN HIS LITTLE CHAPEL."

JORDAN NODDED HIS HEAD THRILLED BY WHAT HE'D JUST HEARD. "THAT WOULDN'T BE FAIR TO MY PARENTS WHO IN THEIR WAY HAVE BEEN VERY GOOD TO ME ALL MY LIFE AND HAVE BEEN INCREDIBLY GENEROUS WITH THEIR MONEY BUT SHE DIDN'T CARE.

"JORDAN?" SHE SAID WITH HER BLUE EYES BESSECHED HIM. "DO YOU SUPPOSE FATHER DESILVA WOULD FLY TO NEW YORK CITY? I WAS THINKING THAT SINCE HE AND REVEREND ROLON WILL ALWAYS BE A BIG PART OF OUR LIVES THAT MAYBE THEY COULD BOTH PERFORM THE CEREMONY? I'D LIKE THEIR BLESSINGS."

HIS THROAT SWELLED UP AS HE SAID "THEY'D BE HONORED DARLING." HER SMILE LIT UP HIS UNIVERSE. STONEY AND MICHELLE CAN BE OUR WITNESSES AND IT MIGHT EVEN GIVE THEM THE IDEA TO GET MARRIED BECAUSE MARY SAID THEY'VE BEEN SEEING EACH OTHER AGAIN AND SPEAKING OF MARY WE CAN PUT HER IN THE GUESS BOOK AND AFTERWARDS WE'LL LEAVE FOR ARE HONEYMOON.

DON'T ASK ME WHERE WE ARE GOING BECAUSE IT'S A SECRET. I'VE BEEN PLANNING IT SINCE THE MOMENT WE FIRST MET IN YOUR OFFICE AND BY THE TIME I GAVE YOU THAT DOCUMENT TO READ I KNEW I HAD WANTED YOU IN MY LIFE. SHE KISSED HIS MOUTH FERVENTLY AS SHE SAID "I WANT THE SAME THING."

"OUR MARRIAGE WILL NEVER BE A CONVENTIONAL ONE" HE HAD WHISPERED. "THAT'S WHY I LOVE YOU SO MUCH" SHE SAID AS HER VOICE SHOOK. "BEING THE WIFE OF JORDAN BROWNING WILL BE A CONSTANT ADVENTURE. OUR CHILDREN WILL HAVE AN EXCEPTIONAL FATHER. "DO YOU WANT CHILD?" SHE CRIED OUT. THEN SHE ASKED HIM WHAT DO YOU THINK?"

"I THINK LOVE YOU JORDAN AND I'M SO HAPPY!" JORDAN NEVER THOUGHT A LOVE LIKE THIS COULD HAPPEN TO HIM AND HE HAD NO WORDS FOR IT. THERE WAS SO MUCH HE WANTED TO SHARE WITH HER AND HE HAD FIGURED IT WOULD TAKE THE REST OF THEIR LIVES AND BEYOND FOR EVERYTHING TO GET SAID BUT RIGHT NOW THE ONLY HE COULD DO WAS SHOW HER HOW HE FELT WHILE HE ABSORBED THE WONDER OF IT ALL AND THEY LIVED HAPPY EVER AFTER WITH TWO LOVELY KIDS.

THE END.

Get Published, Inc!
Thorofare, NJ 08086
03 February, 2010
BA2010034